SHARM

BEST
WISHES!

2012.

"… Book two is an absolutely must read!!!!!! It's the waiting for the next one!!..... Oh my…"   JUDY

"….Thank you for writing the Angelic Letters series. I have to say I have thoroughly enjoyed reading Pewter Angel and Another Angel of Love and patiently waiting for the next one to arrive. "Once you start reading, you can't put the book down."   VERONA

"… I just wanted to let you know how much I thoroughly enjoyed the two books of your Angelic Letters Series! You autographed my books and I will treasure them forever. I passed them on to my mom and dad to read and they loved them…as did my daughter…I do have one complaint….the next book just can't come out soon enough."TAMMY

"…I can't wait for book three both me and my 13 year old daughter have read the first two books and they are amazing."   TAMARA

"… Truly enjoyed the first two books. Rereading the books again. Thank you for two beautiful books! Waiting for the third!" LAURA

"… Ohhhhh can't wait. Amazing story line…love the Christian flavour, blessing!"   DIANE

"… Wondering when the Angel of Thanksgiving is coming out? Cannot wait to read it. Just finished Pewter Angels and Another Angel of Love and they are amazing books!!! Could not put them down!!!! Really excited for the part 3."   JENNY

"… I just finished the second book… I love how you again weaved faith and sound counseling strategies into the book to give people good advice on how to live out a faith based life with integrity, to feel better and cope with the troubles of this life.   MARLA

"… My 85 year old mother is absolutely enthralled with your angel books. She can't wait for the next…"   BEV

"… I have read both books and loved them both! Truly inspirational! Really looking forward to book 3.   SHERYL

"… Thank you for your God inspired creation of the "Angelic Letters" series. I am in the middle of the second book, Another Angel of Love. I must admit that I haven't been able to put down the books once I start. Once you open the first page, the characters draw you in. You cannot help but fall in love with them.

 It is so refreshing in this day and age to find a book that speaks from the heart of God's love for us. Lessons of Faith and Trust are sewn into the pages. When Mr. Engelmann shares his wisdom to Henry behind the store, I find myself taking in his grace as well. Imagining myself sitting next to Henry...   CHERYL

"....It is this book that has brought a renewal of faith to me. A light through the darkness. The biblical verses throughout the books are so very uplifting, and I find myself grabbing my bible and reading the next few lines of the verses found in the books...."

It was my mother who first introduced me to your books. She had met you at one of your book signings. An avid reader herself, she poured over the first two books within a week, and knew she had to share them...

Thank you for sharing with us your love of Christ and his heavenly angels. These books are so filled with love and inspiration. We are anxiously awaiting book three in the series.   CHERYL

"... Pewter Angels and Another Angel of Love were both fantastic! I could picture the story happening in my head. When is book 3 coming out? I can't wait much longer.   TRISHA

"... Just finished the first two books, read them in four days, can't wait for the next one to be done. Thanks for the great books."   ESTHER

"... I have read both books and wondering when the third one is going to be released. These books are really hard to put down. They are great and have told many people they need to read them." ANDREA.

"... I really love your captivating writing style. I picked the first two books up around Christmas, couldn't put them down...Its wonderful to find books such as yours with moral "fiber." Anxiously waiting book 3!   CLAUDIA

Please e-mail Henry at: **henry@henryripplinger.com** or visit **www.henryripplinger.com** for more information about Henry's work and art. He would love to hear from you!

ANGEL
OF
THANKSGIVING

ANGEL OF THANKSGIVING   H.kRIPPLINGER/2012t

Also by **Henry K. Ripplinger**

THE ANGELIC LETTERS SERIES
Book One....Pewter Angels
Book Two....Another Angel of Love

OTHER WORKS
If You're Not From the Prairie...
(Story by David Bouchard, Images by Henry K. Ripplinger)

Coming soon from Pio-Seelos Books:

BOOK FOUR OF THE ANGELIC LETTERS SERIES
The Angelic Occurrence

THE ANGELIC LETTERS SERIES,

Book Three

———— ✳ ————

ANGEL OF

THANKSGIVING

1962 -1983

HENRY K. RIPPLINGER

Best Selling Author of Pewter Angels

Angel of Thanksgiving is a work of fiction. Names, characters, places and
incidents are either the product of the author's imagination or are used
fictitiously. Any resemblance to actual events, locales, business
establishments or persons, living or dead, is entirely coincidental.

Library and Archives Canada Cataloguing in Publication
Ripplinger, Henry
Angel of Thanksgiving/ Henry Ripplinger.

(The angelic letters series ; bk. 3)
ISBN 978-0-9865424-7-3 (pbk)

I. Title. II. Series: Ripplinger, Henry. Angelic letters series ; bk 3.

PS8585.I565A54 2012   C813'.6   C2012-901213-0

Author photo: Bruce Vasselin, Designer Photo
Cover concept by Henry K. Ripplinger
Cover design and production by Brian Danchuk Design
Page layout by Human Powered Design

PIO-SEELOS BOOKS
Ph: (306) 731-3087, Fax: (306) 731-3852.
E-mail: henry@henryripplinger.com

Printed and bound in Canada by Friesens Printers
April 2012

This novel is dedicated to the memory of Michael, our first born son.

A Note of Appreciation
to the Readers of my Books

Since the release of the first two books in the "Angelic Letters Series," something quite out of the ordinary has occurred. In fact I consider it a miracle.

Within months of the release of book one, Pewter Angels on May 9, Mother's Day, 2010 it sold over 5000 copies, becoming a Canadian Bestseller. What also surprised me, as well as others in the publishing industry, was how almost immediately the book was carried by Chapters and other big chain stores. This is almost next to impossible for a self published author, especially for one not yet established in the literary field.

From the start, the sales at all of my book signings were also out of the ordinary; at times selling upwards of over 200 books in a day. No doubt this played a significant part in having accounts opened so quickly in big chain stores but this is part of the miracle. It was not that I was doing anything out of the ordinary in letting others know of my book, people just seem to be attracted by the books. In fact, many customers initially just walked by or declined, only to return within a few minutes and buy the book.

Adding to the success of Pewter Angels, it tied for a Gold Medal IPPY Award (Independent Publishers Book Award, an annual competition drawing submissions from all over the world) in 2011 for Best Fiction in the Religious Fiction category.

When the second book of the series, Another Angel of Love, was released exactly one year later, May 8, 2011 on Mother's Day, the same pattern continued. Within two months of its release, it too was a Canadian Bestseller.

To date, March, 2012, Pewter Angels is now in its fourth printing and Another Angel of Love in its second printing. Combined sales of both books is well over 26,000 books.

But perhaps the best thing of all is that all of this happened because of you, the reader! I have long known in business that the best advertising is the kind you can't buy: the personal recommendations of one reader to another. To a large degree, that is what is now selling the books: word of mouth. The emails and calls and internet notifications on the "Angelic Letters Series" so far has been overwhelming; many readers claiming that the books' contents have helped them personally.

To this I would add that it is not my writing that is touching the hearts of readers, but rather the Lord. And further, simply because the books share so many life lessons and spiritual values, does not mean that I am blessed with any particular wisdom. Should we fall into such folly, 1 Corinthians 1:26-29 quickly reminds us that 'God's wisdom is revealed to the foolish, weak, and common... lest no one can boast that he achieved salvation by his intellect.'

I am simply relating what I learned in the journey of life that prepared me for the gift of this story from the Lord to pass onto you. I am still in the process of growing and developing in my relationship with the Lord and if we can help each other along the way by sharing our gifts, we are then doing what Jesus wants us to do.

I would like to take this opportunity to thank you, the reader, for making time in your busy lives to read my books and for telling your friends about them. It is my sincere hope that the rest of the "Angelic Letters Series" continues to enrich your lives and gives you many hours of reading enjoyment.

I am very grateful and appreciative of your support!

Henry K. Ripplinger
March, 2012

ACKNOWLEDGEMENTS

As ALWAYS, I have to thank my wonderful wife, Joan, for 50 years of marriage. Don't know what I would do without your support, friendship and love. Thank you for reading, assisting with the editing and being a sounding board. The theme of this novel, *Angel of Thanksgiving*, in part has to do with acknowledging our daily blessings. Perhaps it was you that was the inspiration for book three!'

Thank you to my daughter, Tracy, for finding the time in her busy schedule to proof read *Angel of Thanksgiving* and for your helpful suggestions. And to my sister Darlene, thank you for also proof reading the manuscript and giving it your critical eye!

Every author will admit the importance of having their book edited before publication. It's too difficult if not impossible for the author to see his writing objectively after spending months writing the story. It's imperative to have a fresh mind and set of eyes take over the important task of editing: correcting grammar, re-phrasing sentences, adding and chopping until all the wrinkles are taken out of the prose, all the while being ever cognizant of the author's writing style and voice is a challenging task indeed!

Well, I always knew that there was a special reason why my wife and I brought our daughter Jody into the world. Bedsides being a lovely daughter, Jody, you have done an excellent job in editing this book and it was a pleasure working with you! I am very grateful to you for carrying out the tasks that a good editor does and more!

The ideas and changes you suggested all helped to make the story the best it can be! Thank You!

Lastly, the *Angelic Letters Series* is a gift that the good Lord gave to me to pass on to you. I claim no credit for any of it. Without His inspiration and the constant guidance of the Holy Spirit and the guardian angel He sent to *my* side, this series simply would not exist. It is my constant and sincere prayer that these books give praise and glory to Him!

PREFACE

I T IS SAID that within each of us is a story to tell. For years, I must admit, it was my heart's desire to write a novel. For the longest time I thought it was just wishful thinking, an illusion or fantasy I was nurturing. Over the years, I started several stories that never went anywhere except into my drawer and then fizzled away in the recesses of my mind. And yet, I have long known that if one has a dream, a burning passion in his heart, that someday it will come to pass. Never would I have envisioned, however, the wonderfully creative way it would come about. How, one day, an unbelievable occurrence would eventually transform a fantasy into reality.

The "occurrence" tugged away at me for days, months, and then years, begging my attention. Seeking understanding, I spoke of it to family and friends but I was too focused on the event itself that I missed the underlying significance of it all. It wasn't until I found myself in the sunroom of our farmhouse one sleepless morning in June 2005, watching the sun near the edge of the earth that the deeper meaning of the occurrence came to me. As the rising sun brightened the room in which I sat, it also seemed to illuminate my mind. Insight, previously obscured in the shadows of my psyche, bloomed and intensified as dawn spread out across the prairie sky. As I traced the occurrence back to its beginning, I finally realized how it was a testament to the enduring miracle of love. Immediately, an overwhelming, almost feverish rush to write my story welled up inside me, and I began.

Without any outline or any knowledge of how to write a novel, I picked up a pen and scribbler on the end table and simply began to write. For two weeks, I wrote almost non-stop until my wrist and hand gave out. Then I purchased a laptop computer—the best investment of my life—and continued to write as fast as my fingers could type. Corrections could be made in an instant. Paragraphs moved here and there with incredible ease. The thoughts began to flow. It was as if during all the years I had been thinking about the occurrence, ideas had been incubating in my mind, stored, packed, imprisoned inside, until the writing process released them like a gusher, exploding and spilling onto the pages.

Sentence followed after sentence almost effortlessly as the scenes unfolded in my mind's eye. I relied not so much on my intellect as I wrote but rather on my imagination, ablaze as it was with imagery and thoughts. I began to write an outline, a list of chapters that would take me from beginning to end. It was like going on a journey, and I was tracing out the map where I wanted and needed to go to reach my destination.

Characters came alive and I followed them and their lives; we talked and laughed and cried together. They took me in directions I never would have thought of on my own … they led and I followed. This resulted in more chapters. My map expanded as twists and turns in the road came from nowhere and everywhere and from deep within. As the weeks of writing progressed, the vision before me became clearer and richer. It was like watching a movie. All I had to do was write down what I saw before me on the screen of my mind.

Incredibly, two years to the date I started writing, when all was said and done, a huge book of over 1000 pages was in my hands. Once the editing process began, even more pages were added, strengthening the story and dividing it into five parts and time-frames. The result is a chronicle of love and adventure in the lives of two people whose story shows us how angels and the heavens are intricately involved in our lives and that miracles happen when we follow our hearts.

As I look back on this experience, I am still amazed by the effortlessness with which the story emerged, as if the chapters, their order and all the key elements were guided, predetermined—or perhaps more accurately—inspired.

The writing of this book also answered another prayer long held in my heart. As a teacher and then a high school guidance counsellor, it was always my aspiration to write a self-development book. From an early age, insights and understanding of human behaviour came naturally to me, and my study of psychology and counselling in university further added to my empathetic abilities.

Writing this novel utilized those aptitudes. Through the lives of the characters, I could infuse values and principles to live by and show how the choices we make determine our happiness. I wanted to demonstrate the importance of living our lives in the now so as to carry out our life mission to love and serve our Lord and others. These teaching and counselling skills were indirectly at work while I also re-examined my own life and the direction I was going. Ultimately, I realized that lessons are more effectively absorbed intellectually and emotionally when revealed through a story; my novel had simultaneously become my self-development book.

The story begins in Regina, Saskatchewan in the 1950s—the place and time of my own coming of age—though I have taken liberties with the details of its places and events. But though this book is a work of fiction, the occurrence that motivated it was something I experienced personally. My initial intention was to simply write about the occurrence; what resulted was a work of fiction that took on a life of its own. As I'm sure must be the case for many writers, my own life experiences provided the ideal backdrop for the story and moulded the development of the main character to the extent that it was inextricably woven into the fictional narrative.

I firmly believe that God has a plan for each one of us. The desire to write was planted in my heart long before the Lord had me experience the occurrence. Fortunately, I finally listened to His calling to do so, to carry out His plan. I think the Lord knew that as I began to realize the underlying love associated with that event, the power of that love would draw me into the wonderful world of writing and give witness to love's beauty and ever-enduring wonder. And, just like the warm prairie summer sun eventually ripens a crop of golden wheat for the harvest, so too, as the seed of this story took root, warmed and nourished by the timeless love of two people, "The *Angelic Letters Series* grew and blossomed. You and I are its reapers.

Henry K. Ripplinger

"You must love the Lord your God with all your heart, and with all your soul, and with all your mind, and with all your strength. The second most important commandment is this: You must love your neighbour as yourself. There is no other commandment more important than these two."

MARK 12:30-31

"I am the real vine, and my Father is the gardener. He breaks off every branch in me that does not bear fruit, and prunes every branch that does bear fruit, so that it will be clean and bear more fruit. You have been made clean already by the message I have spoken to you. Remain in union with me, and I will remain in union with you. Unless you remain in me you cannot bear fruit, just as a branch cannot bear fruit unless it remains in the vine."

JOHN 15:1-4

"Whoever believes in Me, streams of living water will pour out from his heart."

JOHN 7:38

Since you have been chosen by God who has given you this new kind of Life and because of his deep love and concern for you, you should practice tenderhearted mercy and kindness to others.

COLOSSIANS 3:12

Love suffers long and is kind; love does not envy; love does not parade itself, is not puffed up does not behave rudely, does not seek its own, is not provoked, thinks no evil; does not rejoice in iniquity, but rejoices in the truth; bears all things, believes all things, hopes all things, endures all things. Love never fails.

CORINTHIANS 13:4-8

Prologue

A THOUGHTFUL MAN ONCE said that what is lacking most in the world is unconditional love; the kind of love that comes straight from the heart. The kind of love out of which God created the world and everything in it, including you and me. The all encompassing love of the Holy Spirit that gives mankind strength and transforms lives. The selfless love that Jesus demonstrated over and over when he walked the earth.

Unlike the restrictive and conditional love that is so prevalent in the world today, this love is freely given, heals the broken-hearted and accepts others just the way they are. It does not abuse or manipulate others through reward or power. It does not seek retaliation or keep score of wrongs. It is not resentful. It doesn't harbour grudges or love only when love is returned. There is no spirit of unforgiveness in this heart… only compassion.

Perhaps most important, it is this kind of love that simultaneously brings us inner peace and freedom. When we are full of unconditional love, we escape the endless replaying of past hurts and injuries that crowd out our present existence. Similarly, we no longer dwell in apprehension or worry about the future since we are fully experiencing each moment in love, and the future simply unfolds as a continuation of the peace we keep creating in the present!

And yet, as easy as it is to see the immense benefits from loving unconditionally, why is it that so few of us have been able to practice loving straight from the heart?

My heart grows heavy at the thought. I would even venture to say that many of us have not even experienced unconditional love in our lives. We don't even know what it feels like to give or receive this kind of love. How can this be? Were we not made by God, whose very essence is love? Is God's love not already within us all? Planted at the very core of our being like a kernel of hope so that we might nourish the seed of His love and reap peace and joy in our hearts and those of our neighbours?

Yes! The answer came swiftly.

Yes, the love is there, inside of us all, but it is up to each one of us to choose to nourish that love, to choose to love unconditionally. We must come to it of our own free will, and that is our gift from God. He gave us free will, the freedom to accept or reject Him in a world filled with forces of good and evil, pulling us either toward or away from loving unconditionally. God could have eliminated our free will to have us do His wishes unwittingly. But what kind of love would that have been, even love at all? We would have been no more than puppets under His control and direction created simply to do His bidding.

For years, I thought I was living such a love. Perhaps like you, I read the Bible and tried to live by His Word daily. But it wasn't until I went for a brief time to the other side that I was granted a magnificent vision which instantly revealed how it is possible for mankind to love with God's love in all its glory and power.

As I've shared with you before, when I arrived on the doorstep of heaven I was greeted by my lifelong guardian angel, Zachariah. Within the precious few minutes I was there, the learning and knowledge I acquired of both our earthly life and the celestial heavens was breathtaking. Just as the Lord sees and knows the past, present and future simultaneously, so within a single moment I saw, in vivid detail, my life from conception until the present. And it was there, in that realm of radiant peace, that I saw so clearly how far short I fell of the love that matters. How often I had turned my back on the Lord and did not show kindness, forgiveness, patience, compassion or tenderheartedness toward my fellow man. My sorrow sank even further when Zachariah showed me into the hearts of my friends and neighbours, so many wounded souls, emotionally crippled, lonely and starving for love. I could no longer bear the weight of it all. I fell to my knees in tears. As I cried out on behalf of myself and all humanity for forgiveness, for mercy, for absolution, I felt the tender touch of my protector's hand upon my shoulder.

"Look," he said with eyes full of compassion.

And there before me was a glimpse of the unseen. It was as if ten thousand suns had suddenly washed over the previous vision I had just witnessed. My spirits soared at the wonder of it all. Hundreds of glowing angels were flitting about like butterflies, darting from here to there, soul to soul, helping, comforting, protecting and guiding those in their charge. I could see the ardent prayers and solicitudes they were sending to God on behalf of their earthly assignees, pleading for their mercy and healing. And all the while the angels were ministering to mankind in their resplendent, unacknowledged glory; they were praising and adoring our Father and theirs, the Creator of heaven and earth.

My tears of sorrow turned into tears of gratitude. "Thank you, thank you!" I cried, rising up from my knees. I could see so vividly what our lives would have been like without the assistance of our heavenly protectors! The beauty of this apparition not only lifted my spirits, it instantly revealed to me what it was that gave the angels such unimaginable joy and power to transform lives: they trusted completely in God's sovereignty to turn all situations into good. They possessed the true, pure love of their Creator in their hearts. They had given their free will to the Lord and in turn, received the power of His love.

"Just imagine, Zachariah, the healing that would sweep throughout the universe if all of mankind loved like the angels do! Our hearts would be constantly overflowing with song and praise as well!"

Zachariah nodded and patted my shoulder, aware of my understanding.

"It is possible for mankind to love like this. In many ways

angels and humans are different but there is one thing we have in common: we both possess free will. We are both free to choose to love the Lord our God or reject Him. With angels, it is a one time decision that is firm, final and irrevocable. Once an angel decides to love God, that bond is immediate, everlasting and will never lessen. It is true that in the beginning some angels chose not to love the Lord and were cast out of heaven. Their decision was also irrevocable. Those angels became demons and were forever banned to hell.

"With humans, the decision to turn their will over to the Lord is a lifelong process and one that must be made repeatedly. Unlike the angels, human beings must choose God's love time and again, and at any time can change their mind, their will, the course of their life, their destiny."

"Yes, yes, Zachariah, your overflowing joy is proof enough of your choice for the Lord. But, alas, it is all too clear that we humans so often start with a commitment to the Lord, and then fail. All too often, we turn our backs on the Lord and pursue our own selfish, limited interests. We are surrounded by temptations. And not only that, there are just so many broken-hearted souls who only know of conditional love, who simply can't choose God's love because they cannot see the light, they don't even know it is there..."

"Don't despair." The face of my protector was bright, his eyes filled with hope. "Nothing is impossible for the Lord, my dear friend. We in God's heavenly kingdom know of mankind's condition. The first huge step for man is to accept Jesus into his heart. That is why God sent His son into the world to die for the sins of us all. For it was through walking the earth as a man that Jesus taught mankind how to live in love. It is through His example that humans can overcome their limitations. Jesus experienced earthly life. He experienced the human condition, all the pain and all the shortcomings. And yet, Jesus lived in love. He chose to live God's love even at the depth of his suffering. Apart from Him, the human struggle is too great if not impossible."

I nodded in full agreement. Jesus' words in the fifth verse of the fifteenth chapter of the Gospel of John glared before me in my mind's eye as I quoted aloud:

"'I am the vine, you are the branches. If a man remains in Me, and I, in him, he will bear much fruit: apart from Me, you can do nothing.'"

I nodded again and Zachariah continued.

"You, my friend, are one of the few who acknowledge this. I have seen so many times how humbly you have come before the Lord asking for forgiveness and yielding your will. You have been a faithful servant of the Lord and as a result, your burdens have been light and you have achieved much joy and inner peace. Your ability to love unconditionally, to live by Jesus' example, has in turn set an example for all in your neighbourhood to see. And those times in which you fell short only signify your humanness and gave you opportunity to choose God's love again and again."

"But there are so many who don't know the Lord, or don't believe, or are so distracted by life."

"That is the reason why the Lord sent a guardian angel to the side of every human soul at the moment of conception. We angels are here to pray to the Lord on your behalf, to help and guide you, to give you the grace and strength to make a firm choice to yield to His will and receive the power of His love and the Holy Spirit in your heart."

Zachariah's words were soothing and hopeful. The despair I had felt earlier had vanished and was replaced by an overwhelming excitement and optimism. This was all part of God's divine providence for the salvation of mankind. He did not leave us alone to fend for ourselves. He did not place the seed for this kind of love in our hearts and then abandon us, knowing that we would never be able to love in such a manner on our own.

No!

My excitement spilled over with words of unimaginable promise: "Lives would be healed and transformed! Such a love would give us all a peace that surpasses all understanding. In such an atmosphere, mankind would grow in leaps and bounds. If we all were able to feel, see and know God's love, to carry the power of the Holy Spirit, to live by His word and to spread His word, the ripple affect would be enormous! Soon the entire world would be on fire with the Lord! If humans loved like this, the world as we know it would be no more!"

Zachariah smiled tenderly as he gave me a warm hug, my mission written clearly in his equally warm brown eyes. As much as I wished to stay in this haven of bliss and peace, I knew I had to return to tell others what I had seen and heard.

"Yes," I whispered, "*if a man remains in the vine, it is possible to have the heart of an angel!*"

CHAPTER ONE

THE NEWLYWEDS HAD just settled into their third year of university in Saskatoon when Julean suspected something she could no longer keep to herself.

As she lay awake in bed one night, Henry's breathing having long since grown deep and rhythmic, Julean turned over and surveyed the back of his shoulders under the light of the moon shining through their bedroom window. She ran her fingers up and down his back. He moaned and groaned a bit, but kept sleeping. She pushed a little harder.

"Come on, honey, go to sleep." Henry lifted the blankets over his shoulder and rolled slightly away from his playful wife.

She moved closer, and knowing how ticklish her husband was, slowly moved her hand to his side and dug in with her fingers.

The blankets flew as Henry jumped in the air and rolled over at the same time. "What's *with* you?"

"What's with *you*, you mean? You never turn down my advances."

Henry opened one eye. There was just enough light to see his wife's face in front of his. Her eyes and white teeth glistened in the light. "Well, I could be persuaded with a little more encouragement, I guess."

"Since when do you need persuasion?"

Henry grabbed Julean and drew her in, hard. "I guess I'm persuaded enough." He moved to kiss her.

She quickly brought her hands up and pushed him away.

"What's going on? First you want me and now you chuck me away?"

"Honey, I've got something to tell you! I haven't had my period for over two months and I think I may be—"

"Are you pregnant?" Henry sat up and looked at her. He couldn't read her expression in the darkness. He felt more than saw her nod.

"I'm pretty sure. I made an appointment to see the doctor on Friday for confirmation."

"Oh, honey, that's wonderful! I can't believe it! We've only been married a couple of months."

"It only takes once, you know."

"Well, I guess we *have* done it a couple of times," Henry chuckled as he settled back down into the bed. He looked into his wife's eyes and murmured, "I love you, Momma."

"I love you too, Daddy."

Henry gently drew Julean in and caressed her. Within moments their lips found each other in the moonlit room. They made love, falling asleep in each other's arms.

Around three in the morning, Julean felt Henry's fingers run up and down her back. She turned over to face him.

"Why am I not surprised?"

"Oh, Mommy, you're just *toooo* irresistible."

WITH EACH PASSING day Henry and Julean got more excited about their baby. They had called home and told each of their parents. Henry's mom and dad welcomed the news with joy, but Julean's had reservations. Would this affect their daughter's education? Julean assured them that she would definitely complete her degree but wouldn't be able to work in her father's office next summer.

Henry and Julean loved their basement suite apartment. It was only four blocks south of the university and they walked back and forth to classes every day. They even came home for lunch. Some days they skipped lunch altogether and made love. That often happened when Julean slipped Henry a note just before they separated for their respective morning classes. The notes were always filled with much love and seductive luring. It seemed a little out of character for Julean, but Henry loved it and some days couldn't get back to their apartment fast enough.

What they also liked about their suite was that it was only four steps below ground level so it didn't even seem to be in a basement. The windows were large and let a lot of light into the small kitchen and spacious living room. The landlady had fixed it up real nice with frilly curtains and every room painted a pale yellow so it seemed like the sun was shining all the time. It had two bedrooms; one of which they slept in, of course, and the other Henry and Julean used as their study room. There was just enough space for two desks and a bookshelf.

Their landlords, who had four children of their own, welcomed Henry and Julean's news, too. Their youngest was a boy, four years old, who often came down to visit Henry and Julean on the weekends. Sammy and Julean hit it off immediately. But then, Henry had already known that Julean was going to be a wonderful mother.

Helen, the landlady, said it would be okay if Henry and Julean wanted to repaint the second bedroom of the basement suite and turn it into a nursery. She also quite kindly offered to lower the rent a bit the following year when they returned to complete their last year of university.

Although Henry was thrilled about their impending arrival, ever since Julean had told Henry they were expecting, he had felt a sort of roiling anxiety in the pit of his stomach. It was a familiar feeling, one he'd felt a long time ago. At first he couldn't recall when or why he had experienced such unease before until one day, while walking to university with Julean, he remembered it was the same feeling from ninth grade when he'd had the ridiculous notion that Jenny might be pregnant. The feeling had stayed with him for days and then months, gnawing ever more persistently as time went on. And now, even though he tried to keep it hidden, Henry knew Julean sensed his nervousness by the way she looked at him at times.

It sort of came to a head one night. Julean lay on the bed in her nightgown, reading a book. Henry had finished studying for a midterm exam and came to the edge of the bed to sit beside her. He placed a hand over Julean's still flat belly.

"I can't wait for our little one to be born, Julean."

She put down her book and looked at Henry lovingly.

"I can't wait, either. I wonder what it is. I have a feeling it's a girl."

Henry put his head to her stomach and listened for the heartbeat. "I still can't hear anything. Well, it's only three months old, right?"

Julean nodded. "Yes, I think I became pregnant while we were on our honeymoon and November is just about over."

Henry did some quick calculations. "So we should expect our first addition in June sometime."

Henry lay back on his side with his head resting on Julean's belly and stared dreamily at his lovely wife. His anxiety ebbed away as it usually did in moments like this.

Julean reached out and touched Henry's face and gently stroked his cheek. Her eyes misted as she spoke in a very soft but deliberate voice. "Hank...?"

"Hmm?" Henry had closed his eyes, reveling in the warmth and tenderness of his wife's touch.

"Do you love me? I mean really, *really* love me?"

Henry opened an eye and took Julean in to see if she was serious, then quickly sat up and met her gaze head on. When he read Julean's earnestness, his brow wrinkled, his jaw dropped and his eyes focused even more intently on his dear, sweet wife.

He was stunned and momentarily speechless. Although a day didn't go by when he didn't think, even for the briefest of moments, of Jenny, he was deeply in love and happy with Julean.

"Of *course* I do, Julean, what a silly question." Henry shook his head in disbelief. "Why would you ask such a thing... Are you serious?"

Julean felt somewhat embarrassed. Yes, it was foolish. It's just that her instincts played upon her feelings every now and then... And there was *something*, a part of Henry that she couldn't explain. She'd felt it occasionally when they were dating, but even more so now. He seemed nervous... Julean felt that his heart was divided.

Divided between her and...?

Oh, I'm being ridiculous. Julean's concern softened into a warm smile. "I'm sorry, Hank, it's just that I love you so much. I never want to lose you."

Henry came to Julean's side and put his arm around her.

"Julean, I love you with all my heart. Please don't let any more silly thoughts enter that pretty mind of yours." And placing his hand upon her tummy, he added, "and I love our baby too. I can hardly wait until he or she is born!"

AROUND THE FIRST week of December, while sitting in class listening to a lecture on classroom discipline, the nervousness that Henry had been feeling of late suddenly skyrocketed, sending him into a panic. He shuffled in his chair as his stomach churned and then a rush unlike anything he'd ever experience before swept from the pit of his stomach to the top of his head. His heart began to palpitate uncontrollably. He thought he was having a heart attack. He could feel the heat overtake his face and the sweat running down his armpits. He could no longer sit still as the threat of some sort of impending doom overtook him. He was embarrassed to get up and leave, but he had no choice, the fear gripping him was overwhelming.

He hurried outside, his heart still pounding wildly, nausea threatening. *How much longer can my heart beat this fast without giving out?* He slowed his pace, trying to control his racing heart. Finally, he inched his way to a bench and collapsed on the seat. He took in deep breaths of cool air, hoping to calm down but his heart continued to gallop. He wished Julean was there so he could tell her how much he loved her just in case he didn't make it. He was supposed to meet her at the Faculty of Agriculture building, halfway between their respective colleges.

Henry checked his watch. They were scheduled to meet in another thirty-five minutes. Would he last that long?

Please dear Jesus, don't let me die.

Suddenly the palpitations stopped and relief swept over him. Even though it was cold and there was snow all around him, he felt like a furnace inside. The perspiration covering his face gave testimony to the internal combustion he felt. Slowly Henry regained control and his worry subsided somewhat. What on earth had just happened? Was his heart starting to give out?

With another fifteen minutes until he was to meet Julean, he decided to make his way slowly there. Although his heart rate was now under control, his anxiety wasn't; he could still feel the steady churning of his stomach.

Henry was relieved to see Julean waiting for him at the corner. Her warm, welcoming smile relaxed him and the anxiety fell away from him in a rush. As they walked home, Henry shared with her what had happened.

"I don't think it's your heart, Hank. Maybe it has to do with the pressure of university and the added responsibility of being a father and all." Julean was going to add another possible explanation but decided not to—it had to do more with her feminine intuition that Hank was clinging to something in his past, something that could come between them... *Oh it's too foolish to discuss,* Julean said to herself, *and he's already feeling the pressure.*

"Yeah, that might be it," Henry agreed. "But it sure felt like I was having a heart attack, Julean. It scared the hell out of me."

Julean took his hand and they walked back to their apartment.

That evening, right after dinner, Henry had another attack. Julean came to his side and felt his chest.

"My gosh, Hank, your heart is just racing. Do you want me to phone my dad and get his advice?"

Henry wasn't sure what to do or whether he should bother his father-in-law with it. He already felt his in-laws didn't like him much and he certainly didn't want to make matters worse.

"No, that's okay, hon. I'll make an appointment to see a doctor first thing in the morning."

HENRY WAS RELIEVED when the doctor told him his heart was fine. The doctor repeated much of what Julean had suggested, but he did add that the attacks could also be a culmination of past concerns adding to present ones. It reminded Henry of his worries over Jenny and what had happened to her—and the guilt he sometimes felt when his thoughts drifted to his first love.

The doctor prescribed sedatives, which Henry was reluctant to take. But once he did, the medication quickly alleviated his apprehensions and seemed to stop what the doctor had referred to as anxiety attacks. But Henry felt that the medicine was only treating the symptoms. There was something at the core of it all that he didn't totally understand... Yet.

The young married couple could hardly wait to get home for the Christmas holidays. Julean's expanding belly was visual proof to family and friends that she was having a baby. She was looking more and more radiant with each passing day.

Since the Carters had extra room, Henry and Julean stayed with them instead of trying to squeeze into Henry's old bedroom at his parents' place. Although Mr. and Mrs. Carter were friendly, Henry continually felt an undercurrent of not being accepted. Julean told him not to worry himself over it, that he was married to her and not to them. She further stressed that time would make everything right. Henry wasn't so sure; he'd thought the same would happen with Jenny's parents but it never had.

It was great to see Mr. Engelmann, though. Neither Henry nor his parents could believe how much younger Henry's mentor looked each time they saw him. It was as if he were taking some sort of youth pill. Wrinkles that had covered his face and circled his eyes had diminished—some even seemed to have disappeared. The slight paunch that prevented him from closing his vest all the way had all but vanished; the vest hung so loosely now it didn't even seem to fit him anymore. It seemed his new vocation had given him a new lease on life.

"Boy do you ever look good Mr. Engelmann!" Henry said after giving his mentor a huge hug. "What happened to the other half of you?!"

"Yes, I have lost considerable weight. It's the early morning walks I take down the country road at Gravelbourg. Rain, snow or shine, I walk with the Lord and chat about the day ahead and what He wants of me."

"Well, by the looks of it He sure is preparing you to serve in your new capacity as a parish priest!"

"Yes, I can hardly wait to be an official shepherd for the Lord."

"Will we see you at Mom's for Sunday dinner?"

"Of course, that is something else I always look forward to, Mary's cooking!"

"That's great, Mr. Engelmann, Julean is sure looking forward to seeing you as well. I think the weight you lost, Julean has put on."

"Ah yes, the baby. So it's growing and shows already?"

"Yeah, it's amazing how skin can stretch and she's not even half way there."

"Not to worry Henry, the Lord has looked after everything."

Just then Father Connelly walked out of the rectory study.

"Hello Henry. How is the young Pederson keeping?" Father said as he extended his hand.

"Just great, Father. I'm looking forward to the new addition to our family. And you must be looking forward to your addition, too," Henry added, clapping a hand on Mr. Engelmann's shoulder.

"I can hardly wait, and so many of the parishioners are also impatiently expressing the same sentiments. This is a large parish and it will be a welcome sight to see David walk through the door with his priestly clothes on."

"With his weight loss and youthful look I hope he still wears his checkered vest under his black jacket otherwise we may not recognize him!"

They all chuckled and then Father Connelly turned to Mr. Engelmann. "The Miller's called and want to see me. They said it was urgent so perhaps tell Millie I may be late for dinner."

"Yes, yes I will, and give all my best to Peter and Maggie."

Father Connelly nodded.

"It was nice seeing you, Henry. Say hello to Julean and con-gratulations to you both. When is the little one due, by the way?"

"Around May or June sometime."

"That is wonderful! Well, I must be off."

"Yeah, see you Father," and turning to Mr. Engelmann, Henry said parting words to him as well. "Guess I better be going too, Mr. Engelmann. See you at my folk's on Sunday."

"Yes, and I just might see you and Julean at church in the morning as well."

"Oh yeah, for sure. See you at Mass… Father!"

Mr. Engelmann smiled and modestly nodded.

IN THE SEVENTH month of Julean's pregnancy the doctor noticed that the baby was in the breech position.

"The head is supposed to be down, not up," said Dr. McCall.

"I guess he wants to come out running," quipped Julean.

The doctor, however, didn't see it as a joking matter; breech deliveries were highly risky. He decided to try and turn the baby even though the procedure could cause the umbilical cord to become entangled around the baby's throat. For over twenty minutes Dr. McCall pushed painfully on Julean's swollen belly, maneuvering as much as willing the baby to turn around. Finally, much to Julean's relief, the doctor relented.

"Well, now that we've got this little guy or gal in the right spot, I hope he or she stays there," Dr. McCall smiled kindly at Julean, her eyes still moist with tears from the unpleasantness of his handiwork. "See you next month."

"Yes," Julean replied, "that'll probably be the last time; we're going back to Regina for the summer."

"That's right. Have you decided on a doctor there?"

"My father, Dr. Carter, is making arrangements for that and either he'll notify you or I can tell you when I see you next month."

HENRY COULDN'T GET over how huge Julean was.

"My God, Julean, I'm amazed how much skin can stretch!

And it's only seven and a half months; you still have nearly two months to go. How on earth will that baby keep growing? And how are you going to deliver something that big?"

Julean laughed, "Well, nature has looked after it all so far, Hank. The cervix does dilate quite a bit once labour starts."

Henry was always amazed how easily Julean spoke of sex and anything else that might cause others to blush. Clearly it was a part of her upbringing, something Henry hadn't experienced in his own family, and would definitely serve her well as a nurse. He was getting used to it, though, and was glad their children would be raised with that kind of openness.

With the landlady's permission, Henry and Julean started to plan the nursery. They moved their desks out into the living room, and instead of painting they decided to wallpaper the room in a nursery theme that would welcome either a boy or a girl. The landlady also gave them a crib, a change table and baby carriage that her children had outgrown. The time was getting closer and the two of them could hardly focus on their final exams. And although Henry rarely mentioned it anymore, permeating his joy and anticipation was an almost constant undercurrent of anxiety that he simply tried to ignore.

When Julean went to see Dr. McCall for her eight-month checkup, he was dismayed to note the baby had turned breech again.

"This is my last appointment with you, Dr. McCall. I wish we were staying in Saskatoon so that you could deliver the baby."

"Well, I'll forward your files to your new doctor in Regina after today's examination. Now, let's see if we can turn this little bundle of joy."

Julean smiled bravely at the doctor's words and then began to squirm as the doctor pushed and pulled on the hard wall of her womb.

"EVERYTHING'S PACKED AND ready to go, Julean. I'm not sure you'll fit in the car, though!"

"Henry!" Julean smacked him playfully and then said, "yes, I can feel the strain on my back. Oh well, the baby will soon be here."

"And I'll be one very proud father!" Henry came over and kissed Julean tenderly. She held onto him for a few moments longer and gazed into her husband's eyes.

Yes, she thought, *our baby will truly unite us. And it will take away all my foolish thoughts.*

Henry kissed his wife once more and then led her into the nursery. "The room sure looks nice the way you've decorated it, Julean."

Julean cradled her belly in her hands. "Yes, I just love it too, Hank. It was so nice of Helen to give us all her baby things. We're ready to bring our beautiful little angel home!"

Chapter Two

FEAR GRIPPED JENNY as she stared into James' eyes. Her thumb worked the engagement ring he had just placed on her finger round and round. The large diamond irritated the adjoining fingers, fuelling the burning in her stomach.

"Well?" asked James, as he squirmed behind the steering wheel of his Jaguar. "Aren't you going to say yes?"

Jenny remained silent, desperately seeking a moment of clarity.

"Remember, we were going to get married last spring and you convinced me to wait another year? Well, I waited and—"

"You were so busy with the family business, you almost didn't have time to get married, and it seems like you still don't."

"We were involved in a merger—"

"There always seems to be another takeover, another acquisition, James. I'm afraid there won't be any time for us."

"I promise, Marj… Jenny, I'll make time. I'll fit it into my schedule."

"The way you put it, it seems like our wedding will just be another appointment to attend to."

Silence fell in the interior of the lush vehicle. The cold leather seats helped cool Jenny's flushed body. Even though she knew this day was coming, she still felt completely unprepared and put on the spot; she needed more time and didn't want to rush into it.

She knew James wanted a son. He had spoken so many times about making sure he had an heir to his business, but Jenny was still unsure of whether she even wanted to have another child after the guilt of having given Camilla away. She still hadn't told him about Camilla. She wanted to, but she wondered if he would still accept her if he knew? She even wondered if she would be able to conceive again… James would be devastated if she were unable to produce an heir. Or, God forbid, what if they had a child born with some defect or requiring special needs? Could James handle that? Jenny shifted in her seat, frantically trying to come up with some excuse to give her a little more time.

"James, there are a couple of things I'm concerned about. Marriage is a big commitment and I want to give it my all. Next fall, I'll be starting my librarian position at the new high school and that will be a big adjustment and take up so much of my—"

"For God's sake, Jen, people get married and start new jobs all the time. That doesn't interfere with their private lives that much."

"Well, look at your job and how much it already interferes with us, and we're not even married yet!"

James didn't reply, and Jenny knew he knew she had a point. Before he could come up with a counter argument, Jenny posed another reason to hold off on the wedding.

"Mom and I met with the president that took over my dad's position at the firm and he is allowing us to continue to live on the company's estate. He would prefer a condo residence and made Mom an offer that she couldn't refuse."

"What on earth has that got to do with us?" James' face twisted.

"Well, now that we don't have to leave the estate, Mom will need some company and companionship for a while. I should stay with her."

"Well, Marjorie, we can't keep putting off the wedding forever. We've been talking about this for years now."

"I know, James, and please *don't* call me Marjorie. You know I don't like it. Anyway, everything seems to be happening at once and there is so much planning to do for a wedding. Even though it's been almost a year since Dad's passing, Mom still isn't over it and I want to help her adjust to living alone."

"Well, I need a wife! You can't baby-sit your mother forever. And, and... this waiting until we are married to make love is just all too much, Jen! I, I just don't know what to think anymore..."

Jenny stared at James, her heart softening. She knew he had a right to put a date on it all and it wasn't fair to keep stalling like this, either. He had shown great restraint and respect for her wishes to remain chaste, and there were some very admirable qualities about James that she loved. But... if she searched deep in her heart she would very quickly realize that there still remained a tiny lingering bit of hope that her first love, Henry, would somehow swoop out of the heavens and scoop her up into his embrace. Off they would fly together and live happily ever after.

It had all come down to this... this living in a fairy tale, a dream relationship in which reality no longer existed! Jenny knew it was ridiculous, but she just couldn't put finality on a dream. The hope she held so firmly and deeply in her heart that one day her prince charming would return simply could not be uprooted. *Oh guardian angel, my guardian so dear, please help me...*

Jenny turned from James to gaze out onto the snow covered grounds of the estate. It, too, was like wonderland, so picturesque and beautiful. The moon shone brightly in the clear sky, its rays sparkling off the snow crystals. Jenny had to admit she lived much of the time in a fairyland where everything seemed right and all dreams came true. She knew she had to put an end to it.

James was growing antsy and impatient with Jenny's silence. "Well?..."

"Why don't we settle for the spring of 1965 or '66? We both agree that we want a big wedding. That will give us lots of time to plan and organize it well."

"Surely we don't need to wait two or three more years! Let's do it next spring... in May." Noticing the concern in Jenny's eyes, James added, "If I have to, I'll wait till May of 1965, but that's it, Jen."

Jenny knew she couldn't keep putting it off forever. She felt she loved James, in a way, but there were things about him that concerned her and at times, even alarmed her. For one thing, James was so possessive, Jenny wondered if he really wanted her as a wife or if he just wanted to claim ownership over her? He worried excessively over other men who kept calling on her, despite the fact that she always declined any invitation from anyone other than James. Still, James was so fiercely jealous, his temper was not only embarrassing, but frightening... And then there was his fetish over cleanliness and his need to have everything around him shiny and new... That would be so difficult to take... But then, everyone has their issues.

Jenny turned back to James and gazed into his pleading eyes. As her heart went out to him once again, her father's words pushed in front of her relenting spirit: *It is a hard life, Jenny. You saw how the company consumed mine. Go out with other boys.* Something about James had concerned her father, perhaps the same things that concerned Jenny herself about him. But she had never heeded her father's advice, despite the nagging doubts that had plagued her for years.

James took hold of Jenny's hands. "Please. Say yes. Let's get married next spring."

Jenny knew life with James would not be easy and yet there was something that drew her to him that she just couldn't understand... Maybe he needed her to show him the way out? It confused Jenny as to exactly what it was, but Jenny felt certain there was a hidden purpose underlying their relationship. Whatever it was, it drew out the accepting part of Jenny's nature to look on the bright side of life, to rely on her faith in others and the promise of hope... and made her understand that somehow, James needed her. The thought was sufficient to weaken her resolve.

"Okay, James, this will be a big wedding, so let's get married in May of 1965. But you'll have to promise to make time for me and the wedding. This has to assume some priority on your list."

"Jenny, I promise. But are you sure we can't do it next year? Two years seems like forever. It's been on my mind for so long. I can't wait for the day you will be mine."

The word "mine" made Jenny cringe.

"James, the time will fly by... And besides, you're so busy with the company, we're hardly together lately as it is. This way I can finish university and be able to concentrate completely on the wedding plans after I graduate."

Reluctantly, James shrugged his shoulders and nodded in a half-hearted agreement.

Jenny gazed deeply into James' eyes as she took in a deep breath and exhaled slowly. The proposal had felt more like a negotiation than a romantic gesture of love and commitment. Feelings of ambivalence swept over her. Had she done the right thing?

Jenny walked into the living room still reeling emotionally from the decision she had made moments ago. She knew she should be happy, jumping out of her skin, exhilarated, but instead her world seemed to be closing in on her.

"How was your night out with James?" her mother asked cautiously.

Jenny didn't know how to answer. Her mom liked James, especially his family background and wealth, and Jenny knew she would be ecstatic at the news. But when she opened her mouth to speak, she could no longer hold back the tears.

Her mother rose and put her arms around her. "Did you and James have a fight?"

Jenny shook her head, still unable to speak.

"Come, sit down and tell me all about it."

They sat on the sofa, the fire in the fireplace dispelling the chill clenched around Jenny's heart. She slouched deep into the back of the soft chesterfield while her mother sat on the edge, facing her. Jenny hadn't felt this kind of despair since the day they had left Regina.

"Did you and James break up?"

"No… we didn't," Jenny answered between sobs. But in a way, Jenny wished they had. She just felt so unsure.

"Well, what then? Did you have a fight?"

Jenny slipped her right hand from under her mother's and wiped away the tears coursing down her cheeks.

"No, Mom, we didn't have a fight… We got engaged!" Jenny could barely get the words out before bursting into tears again.

"Is this what you are so upset about?" Her mother's eyes brightened with relief.

Jenny nodded. "He wants us to get married in the spring of 1965. And I said yes."

Her mother took both of Jenny's hands and waved them up and down, trying to instill the excitement she knew her daughter should be feeling.

"Oh, Jenny! This is wonderful news! You're just feeling pre-marriage jitters. It's common, Jenny."

"But I should be feeling happy—"

"I'm certain you are. We all have concerns about the one we are going to marry. Well, at least at times. And this has been such a trying time for both of us with your father passing. Oh, Jenny, James is such a fine catch and he's been so loyal and patient with you. He will be able to look after you and give you the life you deserve." Her mother looked at her. "Come on, smile. This is a great day! I am excited already!"

Jenny looked at her mom, shook her head, and managed a slight smile.

"There, that's better. I know, let's celebrate."

Edith jumped up and headed to the liquor cabinet, "Let's have a glass of wine."

Minutes later, Jenny took a glass of chilled white wine from her mother who rejoined her on the sofa.

"Here's to you and James. May you have a long, happy, success-ful life together!"

Jenny tried to reciprocate her mother's enthusiasm. "I do so hope we will be happy together, Mom."

"Of course you will be. Come now, let's toast." Her mother pushed her glass towards Jenny's until they clinked together.

Yet, for Jenny, the clink lacked brightness. It sounded muted and dull, reflecting her insecurity. Edith, for her part, kept up the patter, trying to overshadow Jenny's concerns with her excitement.

"You know what? I've already started a list of friends and some relatives in Kelowna that I would like to have attend the wedding. I just knew you and James were meant for each other. Oh! and maybe we can fly to Toronto and look at some of the wedding gown shops there. Make a weekend of it... stay at the Four Seasons!"

Jenny had to admit that her mother's energy was starting to work.

"Now, Mom, I'm sure Ottawa has enough wedding stores."

"Oh, Jenny, I'm so excited. You're our only child. I want this to be the best wedding ever."

"Who will give me away?"

"I'm sure we'll come up with someone. Perhaps your Uncle John from BC."

"Uncle John? Goodness, Mom, I don't know anything about him. We haven't seen them in years."

"Well, let's not complicate things now. There's plenty of time for that… Or, what about that faculty advisor you're so fond of?"

"Hardly, Mom. He's too young and sometimes I think he wants more than to advise me."

"Well, let's decide on that later. I wonder where we should start looking for shoes and a gown. And what about the invitations? And where are we going to have it? Oh my, Jenny, I have to get the phone book and make a list."

Her mother downed the rest of her wine as she headed into the kitchen. "Would you like some more wine?"

"No thanks, Mom, I'm fine. And there's no need to hurry! We still have two years before the wedding."

"That may be true, but time moves swiftly. You'll thank me for being ready for this wonderful celebration!"

Mom's more excited about this than I am. I hope I've made the right decision.

Jenny wished her father were alive so she could talk this all out with him. Somehow she had always found it easier to talk with him than with her mom. She just knew he wouldn't be as elated as her mother was about the news. *Oh, Dad, am I doing the right thing? Should I marry James?* A sudden chill swept through her entire body.

Jenny stood and hovering over the fireplace, turned her backside to the dying fire. The fear that had gripped her earlier in the car with James returned.

"We must invite the McKenzies," shouted her mother from the kitchen. "And what about the Rileys?"

BUT JENNY WAS already on her way to her room. She tossed herself onto the bed and sobbed into her pillow. If only James didn't have those same, certain traits that had reminded her so strongly of Henry… Maybe she wouldn't be so transfixed by him and more willing to see or consider the multitude of other suitors knocking at her door.

But it was more than that. There was something about James that needed healing, almost saving. Jenny didn't quite understand her purpose in it all, but it drew her to him. And despite all her confusion over their relationship and the rocky road ahead, she had overcome her resistance and yielded to his proposal. The saddest part wasn't imagining the difficult, perhaps even lonely, marriage she would likely have with James. No, the saddest part was the realization that once she married James, the chance that she would ever reunite with Henry would be gone forever.

Jenny turned over and curled up on top of the bed. She gazed out through her window into the star studded sky. *How many wishes are made upon those stars? How many are ever answered?* Jenny recalled the wish she had made to that shooting star last fall: that Henry return to her so that she could once again gaze into his warm green eyes and kiss his tender lips. She had felt so certain at the time that her guardian angel had heard her heart's desire, that ever since she had been filled with an irrepressible, burgeoning hope.

And yet, why haven't you answered my wish like you did Tammy's?

Trying desperately to accept her fate at long last, tears surfaced again, *Oh guardian angel, my guardian so dear, is it truly over? Cannot even you bring Henry back to me?* The thought broke her heart and Jenny finally … let go.

After a long while, Jenny once again whispered into the darkness, "*Please help me to accept that it's really over and get on with my life…with James.*"

Chapter Three

Y OU'LL HAVE TO hurry Julean or we'll be late and won't get a seat."

"I'm doing the best I can with this big tummy in the way of buttoning up my top."

Finally, Julean appeared at the front door ready to go. Henry couldn't get over how radiantly beautiful his wife looked. The luminosity of her skin, the overall vitality of her being, everything about her expressed the inner joy of impending motherhood.

"Wow, do you ever look beautiful, honey. I hope I won't smudge your lipstick, but I just have to give you a kiss."

They approached one another, leaning forward in order to circumvent Julean's protruding belly, until finally their warm lips touched.

"I love you, Julean," Henry said as they parted. He offered his arm as they made their way down the front four steps to the side parking lot where the car was situated.

"I'm sure glad we found this place on Broadway Avenue so quickly."

"It's nice, but I think it would have worked out at my parents' place, too. They have the extra two rooms now that my sister is gone to Saskatoon. Her room would have been good for the baby and it's only for the summer..."

"Yeah I know, but I keep feeling your parents don't want me there and don't accept me."

"Well, we can't keep running away from it. One of these days you and dad will have to sit down and talk it out."

"Maybe so, but I still think it's best for married people to be on their own. In any case, let's not worry about it now. I don't want that pretty little head of yours to be concerned about anything else but bringing our new baby into the world." Henry reached over to Julean and she put her warm tender hand in his, squeezing it lovingly.

"Holy cow, look at all the cars," Henry noted as they pulled up to the church. "This is our third week home from Saskatoon and you can see how the church gets more packed each Sunday. I knew this would happen once Father Engelmann joined the parish as a priest! I just wish we could have been here last month when he was ordained. Mom said she couldn't stop crying, that it was the most beautiful ceremony she had ever witnessed."

"Well, it is unfortunate that our final exams coincided with Father's entering into the priesthood, but we better get inside or we won't get a seat."

"Yeah, for sure. I told Mom yesterday to save a place for us up near the front."

SURE ENOUGH, HENRY's parents were sitting in the third pew from the front with two empty spaces next to them for Henry and his wife. Henry and Julean whispered hi to Mary and Bill as they slid into the pew. Henry knelt down and crossed himself. Julean's tummy was way too big, so she just slid her buttocks to the edge of the seat and leaned forward with her hands resting in a prayerful position on the back of the pew in front of her. She bowed her head and began to pray, as well. She usually said the rosary before Mass began, but they had come too late and there was no time for that today.

Henry knew what his dear wife would be praying for since it would be the same prayer he was lifting up to the Lord. Julean's last visit to the doctor showed that the baby had turned into the breech position yet again. It was getting more difficult each time to rotate the baby to put its head in the down position. The doctor was concerned about it and was considering a cesarean delivery, but Julean wanted a natural birth if at all possible.

Just as Henry's thoughts were pleading with God to keep the baby in the right position and take away the ever present nervousness in the pit of his stomach, the door to the sacristy opened and four altar boys dressed in white tops over black gowns approached the altar in a single line. Behind them, Father Engelmann appeared wearing a white chasuble with a gold coloured stole around his neck that hung down almost the full length of his garment. He was carrying a chalice concealed under the chalice veil that was the same colour as the chasuble.

Henry still wasn't used to seeing Mr. Engelmann as a priest, donning anything other than his worn checkered vest, let alone the impressive vestments he was now wearing. But even though his old, habitual "uniform" had been replaced by such distinguished priestly garb, Mr. Engelmann's familiar, warm smile and sparkling eyes hadn't changed a bit.

Father greeted everyone and then he approached the altar and began the Mass. He said the Mass in Latin while the parishioners followed the English translation in the Sunday missal. Henry was surprised how well Father said the Mass in the foreign language. Even though Henry didn't understand any of it, there was something holy and mysterious about the Latin language. He whispered the only sentence he knew in Latin: the sign of the cross. "*In nominee Patris, et Filii, et Spiriyus Sancti.* Amen." He liked the sound of it out of his mouth, as well.

After the Epistles were read by two different parishioners, Father approached the pulpit and read a part of the twelfth chapter of the Gospel of Mark. The reading described two of the commandments Jesus had instructed his disciples at the time to follow: to love God with their whole heart and to love their neighbour as themselves. Henry wondered how Father was going to approach this subject and relate it to their lives.

Father slowly closed the Holy Bible before him, giving the congregation a little time to digest the reading, and in his usual way, surveyed the large church with compassionate eyes and a benevolent smile. Suddenly Henry couldn't help but feel exactly as he did when he and Mr. Engelmann would sit out back on the old grey crate behind the store. Only instead of just Henry reaping the rewards of his mentor's wisdom, it was now the entire parish who was about to benefit from Father Engelmann's teachings. Henry felt so happy Mr. Engelmann had decided to become a priest; there couldn't be a job more perfect for him.

"In the name of the Father and the Son and the Holy Spirit. My dear brothers and sisters in Christ, as I wondered what I was going to say when preparing for this week's homily, the Lord, in His perfect timing, sent a stranger to our rectory door. He introduced himself as Steve and asked if he could have a few minutes of my time to talk about something he felt was very important. Of course, I invited Steve in and together we walked to the study. No sooner had we sat down than he nervously pulled out a letter and began to explain how it had come into his possession. What he shared fits in perfectly with today's reading as you shall soon understand.

"'Father,' he said, 'I'm a married man with a good and loving wife and two boys that are a year apart. George is entering into his eleventh grade and my oldest, Gregory, is going into Grade 12. Two nights ago when I came home, my wife, Doreen, and the boys were just leaving. Doreen said that she and the boys were going out for dinner and then off to a movie. Naturally, I was very puzzled and a bit annoyed that she would do this without asking me to come along or even let me know in advance. She just told me I had been working very hard lately and she thought I needed a little time to myself.

"'I have prepared your favourite meatloaf for you,' she went on. 'It's in the oven, and the potatoes and corn are on top of the stove. By the way, there's a letter for you on your dinner plate on the kitchen table.' And without another word she came over to me, kissed me on the cheek and left with the boys.

"'Suddenly I felt very alone, Father. The house was too quiet. Usually a radio is blaring or the television is on, but tonight there was nothing but silence. I made my way into the kitchen. My hunger left me when I noticed the sealed letter on my dinner plate, just as my wife had told me.

"'I began to feel worried. Although I am a good provider, I can be hard to live with at times and I know I haven't always been the best husband and father in the world. As I sat down and opened the letter, my heart was pounding. Were my wife and family about to leave me? Was this what the letter would be about?'

"Steve started to tell me the contents of the letter, but tears flowed so hard and strong from his eyes, he couldn't go on. He handed the letter to me and motioned with his hand for me to go ahead and read it. And that's what I am simply going to do now. This was Steve's purpose for coming to me that I would share with parents in the parish about loving their children."

Father paused for a minute and surveyed the parishioners. There wasn't a sound in the large church, not even the usual coughing. Henry swore everyone leaned a little closer towards the pulpit just like he always had on the old grey crate, not wanting to miss a word the teacher was about to say. The letter crackled through the microphone as Father unfolded it. He smoothed it onto the surface of the pulpit, looked the paper up and down and began to read:

"Dear Steve,

The other night Gregory and I had a heart to heart talk; he said he was leaving. He plans to quit school and find a job. It's not what he really wants to do at this time, but he feels he should support himself and not be a burden on anyone. He's already asked your parents if he can stay with them temporarily until he gets a job and finds a place to stay.

I was shocked to hear how lonely Gregory felt living in our family and dismayed that he feels he is a burden to us. You and I have talked many times about raising our children differently than how we were raised, but in the busyness of life nothing really has changed. We learned about parenting from our parents, who learned from their parents before them and so on. You, too, have shared with me your own struggles with your father's lack of affection and understanding, and I must tell you that your dad recently told me how he sees so much of himself in you and the way you relate to the boys. So imagine how Gregory must feel – not unlike you yourself felt growing up with your dad: misunderstood, disconnected, a burden.

Actually, your dad told me that now that he is older and wiser, he realizes that his ways were not the best for you. He wishes he had developed a better relationship with you when you were growing up and accepted you for who you were. You can see how your dad is so much more open with our boys now than he ever was with you. He's trying to change and he's trying to set an example. I sense that Gregory feels closer to and safer with his grandfather at this point than he does with you.

My purpose for writing this letter is to make us more aware of how we are doing as parents. I am going to pretend I am Gregory writing to you. I hope in writing this on his behalf I am totally true to his feelings and where our son is at in his life. I don't mean to be critical in any way. Please accept this in all sincerity as food for thought.

Dear Dad,

It's late Wednesday evening and I keep thinking about our relationship. I know I don't measure up to your expectations of what you want me to be. I feel your disappointment in me, it's all I think about and I'm sorry to say it makes me feel so hateful and resentful towards you. I want you to like me, to love me. That's why I keep coming back to you, asking for your advice, so I can make decisions that you will approve of.

But then I think, *do you really want a son that you have made to your liking, or do you want me to be me*? If only you would believe in me, or express confidence in me, then I could begin to accept myself and realize the aptitudes and abilities that are within me. Right now I dwell so much on your criticisms and expectations that I feel restricted, confused, insecure and so afraid that I will make a fool of myself, that I never just let myself be me.

I know that it will be hard for you to accept me. I know how much you admire a competitive and aggressive nature, like George has, but that's just not who I am. And from talking to Grandpa, I think you know how I feel. Grandpa said he regrets now making you feel like a weakling and trying to toughen you up instead of letting you be you and accepting you unconditionally.

Do you understand what I am saying? I'm always going to want your advice and support and encouragement. I just want you to support and encourage me as I am, not as you want me to be. I know I will make mistakes, but I think you would feel proud of me in this way too, Dad.

The way things are now, we are only fooling each other. I really don't want to move out, Dad, it's not the solution. All that will happen is the wall between us will grow even bigger. We will just go through life mad at each other, and that would make me really sad. I really love you, Dad and so deeply want your friendship, understanding, love and acceptance of me just the way I am. I hope you're not mad at me over the comments I have made and that you accept what I have written with an open spirit and heart.

Can we try one more time Dad? Can we?

Love Gregory

Father looked up at everyone, then folded the letter back up again. He was silent for a long time, allowing the parishioner's heads to catch up to what their hearts had just learned. At last, he spoke.

"My dear friends, there is so much we can learn from this letter and how Steve's wife approached the matter at hand. By leaving her husband alone with words of love and compassion, she removed any need on his part to be defensive or critical or argumentative. His pride intact, Steve was there alone, open to the moment and profoundly moved by his wife's honesty.

"*This is the secret to change my friends.*

"It is when we are alone in silence that we lose ourselves and hear the whispers of God. That is when we are open to change. In that silence we grow and begin to become the person that God wants us to be.

"This is why I am going to say over and over to you today and in the months and years to come: if you want to grow and have more happiness and inner peace in your lives, then you must get up early every morning to read the Bible, meditate, pray and examine your life. If you don't, you will simply go about living the same way, day in and day out, doing the same thing, thinking the same thoughts and reacting the same way. Is it any wonder that we complain how hard life is and how unhappy we are, lacking in inner peace?

"More often than not, we don't understand that we alone – with God's good guidance, of course – are responsible for our happiness. Instead of turning inward towards God for help with changing ourselves, we mistakenly and misguidedly believe that changing *others* to suit our needs is the answer. We turn away from ourselves; we turn away from Jesus' teachings, in search for fulfillment. And in the process, we profoundly limit ourselves and hurt our loved ones.

"I ask you: no matter how good our intentions may be, when we set out to try and change another to be the way we want them to be and justify that it's for their own good, *is this love?* When we are critical, judgmental or fault finding in the hope we can change someone for the better, *is this love? Is it love* when we force others to meet our approval to the exclusion of discussion or independent thought? *Is it love* when we force ourselves to live up to someone's expectations so as to feel worthy of their love? If you answer 'yes', I ask you: what *kind* of love is this?

"*As we can see, my brothers and sisters, love wears many different mantles and in most cases we are only relating to ourselves and others under the guise of love!*

"Loving *unconditionally* is the key. *Meine lieben Freunde suchen sie nicht weiter, als Jesus, wie man auf diese weise Liebe.* My dear friends, look no further than to Jesus as to how to love this way."

Father turned and pointed to the large cross hanging behind the altar.

"When we turn to Jesus and live by his example of unconditional love, we pave the way for good relationships both between parents themselves and their children. Most of you know it is the little things we do daily that add up to big things over a lifetime. The home should overflow with acts of kindness, compassion, acceptance, understanding and most of all, forgiveness.

"We learn by identification and imitation. *Affe sehen, zu tun Affe!* Monkey see, monkey do. When children grow up they repeat what they learned in the home. Some become guilty of the very thing they are blaming their parents for, as you saw in Steve's case! Children should leave the home filled with love and respect for their parents and themselves. Their upbringing should be such that they in turn become good husbands and wives and parents.

"The purpose of my homily today was to share with you one family's journey. We all have our own story. I am not here to judge or criticize but to point out the way we should strive to be in a family. It is never too late to change, to make amends, to reconcile and forgive, no matter where we are in our journey with our spouses or children. We are only human and both parents and children must be understanding and forgiving. We should never be too proud to make a new beginning. If the Lord can get down on his knees to wash our feet, can we not do the same for others, especially those within our family?

"So, let us all pray together daily as a family and bring Jesus into every situation of our lives! Through this communion with our Lord and each other, the more we will make Godly decisions and the more we will be at peace. Happiness will fill your home!

"In closing, I would like to share with you my grandmother's favourite recipe for a double loaf of homemade bread."

At this, the silence in the church turned to peels of laughter. After such a moving and profound sermon, most of the congregation appreciated a break in the tension. After it quieted down again, Father Engelmann continued.

"Just like flour is to a loaf of bread, the main ingredient in a marriage is our Lord; putting Jesus into the marriage first keeps it sticking together, while prayer and faith leavens it.

To this we should add:

1cup caring,
1cup kind acts,
1cup understanding,
2 cups sacrifices,
5 cups forgiveness
and a whole lot of acceptance!

"Thoroughly mix the above ingredients. Add tears of joy, sorrow, and compassion and a pinch of spice.

"Now roll it and hug it all over. And after it rises a bit, beat down all the fault finding, resentment, and especially the anger.

"Never let the sun set on anger and carry over to the next day's baking. It will lose its freshness and quickly spoil for sure.

"Once well formed, place it into a home with walls made of loving arms and bake in an oven of human kindness.

"Never take making good bread for granted, as it quickly becomes stale and hard, even overnight.

"Start each day with a new double loaf so when you pull it apart, it is always warm and fresh inside, ready to be spread with the butter of love and served with a smile."

Again, the church filled with chuckles and murmurs of appreciation at Father Engelmann's lighthearted message.

"*Meine lieben Freunde,*" the joyous priest boomed, bringing the sermon home, "Please make it a point to get up early each morning this week. Go on your knees and pray to God and invite His son into your heart. Remember always: He is the way, the truth and the life! Then read His word and mediate on it and how it applies in your life. Pray for the Lord's grace and strength to carry it out. Then you are ready to love your family and go out to love your fellow man as Jesus did and commands us to do. In this way we can make a difference in our lives and help God bring all His children to Him in heaven. Do this in the name of the Father, the Son, and the Holy Spirit. Amen!"

As the parishioners began singing the final hymn, Father and the altar boys made their way down the centre aisle to the foyer of the church where Father waited for the congregation to exit. The mood was almost festive as people poured into the lobby of the church. No one seemed in any particular hurry to leave and most stood as close to Father Engelmann as they could, eager to shake his hand. One by one, he made a point of greeting everyone.

"Henry and Julean, it was so good to see you in the church. And I see you are still with child, Julean. The day must be coming soon, no?"

"Yes, Father, it could be any day, although the actual due date is in mid-June. So another couple of weeks or so."

"Well, it better be soon or she won't fit into the car." Henry winked at Father while Julean rolled her eyes.

"So, are you coming for supper tonight?"

"Yes, I accepted Mary's invitation earlier this week. The parish cook has family in from out of town and is taking the night off. Fortunately, both Father Connelly and I have been invited out to dinner this evening. I would hate to think what a disaster of a meal we would inflict upon each other had we been left to our own devices."

"Well, you know you're always welcome at my mom and dad's place and our place, too, for that matter!"

Noticing the line of people still waiting to greet Father Engelmann, Julean gently pulled Henry toward the front door and chimed,

"Anyways, it was a lovely sermon, Father. We'll see you tonight."

Just then, all three of them noticed Eddy Zeigler coming out of the church, approaching them wearing a big smile.

"Hey Hank, Julean. How ya doing?" Turning to shake Father's hand, Eddy continued, "Hi Padre, another cool sermon."

"As long as they keep you coming back, that's the main thing," replied Father as he placed his left hand on top of Eddy's right, giving him a firm, warm handshake.

"Second time this spring! I may be your first convert!"

"I'd sure like to see that, Eddy," replied Father earnestly.

"Great to see you Eddy," Henry broke in. "You still making millions in the stock market?" Throwing his right arm around Eddy's shoulder and holding Julean's hand, Henry maneuvered their way out of the church.

"I've got the Midas touch, Hank. Every buy and sell order I place, I make money. Boys at the office can't believe it."

As the three of them stepped into the bright, late morning sunshine, Eddy put on a pair of sunglasses and turned to Julean.

"So, Julean, I can see the tummy is blossoming and the bambino is just about ready to make its big debut."

"Yes," replied Julean, shielding her eyes from the sun. "Anytime now. I can't wait… Within two weeks for sure."

"Well, I hope it looks like you and not the old man here. Give the kid a chance." Eddy winked at Henry and poked him at the same time.

"That's no joke, Eddy. I hope the baby *does* take after Julean!"

"Oh Hank, it will take after both of us."

As they made their way to the parking lot, Henry had a thought.

"So, how about a game of pool at the Royal this week sometime Eddy? I'm still looking for a summer job and not tied down yet.

"Yeah, better do it before the little one comes along," Eddy added as he took out a pack of smokes from his shirt pocket. "Wednesday might work. I'll give you a dingle mid-week, ok?"

"That would be great, Eddy."

After Eddy finished lighting his cigarette, he took a deep drag, grabbed it between his thumb and second finger, held it in mid-air and jabbed his straight forefinger first at Henry, then Julean.

"Adios, folks." Eddy turned and swaggered along the sidewalk, leaving a trail of smoke behind him.

"Bye Eddy," Henry and Julean replied almost in unison as they gazed after the young millionaire who didn't seem to be affected one iota by the fortune he had accumulated. Eddy was Eddy, clean through.

"That Eddy always impresses me," Henry remarked as they made their way home from the church. "The way he accepts life as it is. Always positive, never complains, always fun to be around. And I know his upbringing wasn't the best, his dad being an alcoholic and all. Yet he never speaks badly of his folks, shows respect and takes them the way they are. Sometimes I wish I were more like him... you know? Being more true to myself, not worrying so much about what other people think or spending so much time seeking others' approval. Eddy really accepts himself and doesn't try to fit into any mold of expectation. Did you see the way he walked away after church, so confident and sure of himself? I would say Eddy has a very healthy self esteem."

"He does seem very self assured."

"I bet if Eddy were in my shoes he would handle this thing that I have with your dad very differently..."

"Now there's a perfect example of what Father was just talking about in his sermon! I've told you many times Hank, if Dad wants to be cold towards you that's his problem. Whereas Eddy wouldn't let it bother him, you are forever allowing Dad's faulty thinking to control your life. It's just the way Dad sees things now and hopefully he will change for the better, but in the meantime, do what Eddy would do."

"Yeah, I can just see Eddy going up to your dad and saying, 'So Pop, is there something I'm doing you don't like? Maybe I can change it and maybe I can't. But let's lay it out so we can move on. What d'ya say, Pop?'"

Julean chuckled. "He wouldn't be as concerned about it as you are, that's for certain. In a way we create our own reality, don't we? How we think of ourselves and situations might be completely different for someone else. And it just came to me that in a way, you are as guilty as Dad is for not accepting him, either. I know you may feel justified, but maybe Dad does, too. It reminds me of what

Father said in his sermon two weeks ago... 'the blind cannot lead the blind or else they both fall in the ditch.'"

"That's right exactly!" Henry blurted out. "Geez, here I am all uptight, feeling rejected, hurt, and blaming your dad for not liking me, when that may well not be the case at all. I have a choice, just like Father said in his sermon. I can rise above, forgive and move on like Eddy would for sure, or I can continue on the way I am and stay stuck by blaming others."

Henry shook his head as he waited for a red light to turn green. "How foolish... We sure can be our own worst enemy at times. If only we could see things clearly, we could straighten out our thinking."

"Yes, that's right Hank..." Julean's words trailed off ...

Then almost in a whisper she added, "Sometimes keeping our thoughts straight, though, is easier said then done."

CHAPTER FOUR

S O, WHAT'S YOUR medicine Hank, snooker or eight ball?"

"Geez Eddy, this is my first game since last summer. Let's play a few games of eight ball first."

Eddy took the basket of balls resting on the bench, dumped them on the table and racked them up. After exchanging a few spots with stripes and vice versa, he finally put the black eight ball in the centre of the rack and rolled the cue ball down the table.

"Okay Hank, bust 'em up."

Henry took a stick off the cue rack, rolled it on the table to check for straightness and chalked the tip. He moved the cue ball slightly to the right behind the line, leaned over, lined up the stick and slammed the cue ball into the triangular-arranged rack of balls. The balls dispersed in all directions but not one found a pocket.

"Nice break, Hank! You might as well hang up your stick, though, 'cause that's your last shot, buddy," Eddy quipped.

"Okay, hot shot, a buck says I'll clean your clock."

"Forget it Hank, I hate to take your money. You're expecting an increase in the family soon. Better hang onto your cash, if you know what I'm saying."

"Cut the crap and shoot Eddy. A buck's riding on this one."

"Don't say I didn't warn you, man."

HENRY K. RIPPLINGER

Eddy chalked his stick and lined it up with the cue ball. "Ten in the corner."

Wham. In she went.

"Lucky shot, Ed. So I'm spots."

"That's all you're going to see on the table in a few minutes, man."

The cue ball came to rest almost in a perfect position for the thirteen ball in the side. Eddy didn't bother calling the shot as it was obvious where it was going to go. Eddy chalked his stick and aimed it low on the cue ball, moved the stick back and forth, making a minor adjustment, and hit the ball smartly. The thirteen ran into the pocket while the cue ball sucked back all the way to the rail in perfect alignment with the twelve and the corner pocket.

"Nice stuff, Eddy. I can see you've been practicing."

"You ain't seen nothing yet, kid." Eddy surveyed the table to see where he wanted the cue ball after his next shot. As he walked around the table he pulled out his smokes and lit one up.

"I see you've changed brands."

"Yeah, the Export's have a little more kick."

Henry chuckled as Eddy leaned over the table for his next shot with the smoke dangling from the corner of his mouth. He squinted his left eye to keep the rising smoke from getting into his eye and hit the cue ball firmly on the top. It hit the twelve and followed it down the rail. The twelve went into the corner pocket but the cue ball's direction was slightly to the left. It hit the end rail and rebounded back to near the centre of the table.

Henry couldn't believe it. The cue ball was in great shape to bank the nine into the corner. Still, it was a tough shot and Henry anticipated his turn was finally coming up.

"Did you hear Red moved to Alberta to work for an oil company out of Edmonton?" Eddy chalked his cue.

"So, that's where he went. I've been calling Travis' place but his mom said that he's away. She mentioned something about him leaving town, but I find it hard to understand her heavy European accent. Come to think of it, I remember him telling me he was taking a course in seismology."

"Ya never know Hank, he might strike it rich like Jimmy Dean and find oil in his backyard."

62

"That'll be the day. So when did he leave?"

"Last March. I talked to him at the Roxy theatre the day before he left. That was quite the damsel he had with him. He said he might be back for his parent's 50th anniversary this August."

"Hope he does, it would be good to see him again. So, he still playing the field?"

"Yeah, every time I see him he's with a different chick."

Henry chuckled. "A lot of fire under that red roof of his."

"Okay Hank, corner bank. I'll probably hook myself for the next shot but I'll give you a chance."

"Yeah, yeah. Just shoot, hot shot."

Eddy chalked his stick, took a deep drag of his smoke then rested the cigarette on the edge of the railing and bent over the table to line up his shot. Henry hoped he'd miss.

Eddy hit the cue ball slightly off centre of the nine ball that rested against the railing. The nine banked off the rail and Henry couldn't believe his eyes as it sped directly into the corner pocket. The only consolation was that the cue ball ended up at the far end of the table and Eddy's three remaining striped balls were hidden behind a sea of spots and the eight ball. As Eddy had predicted, he was hooked. Eddy picked up his smoke and took a deep drag.

"Figured that would happen." He took another drag and dropped his smoke on the floor. He stepped on it and snuffed it out with a twist of his foot and picked up the cube of chalk. As he walked around the table chalking his stick, he said something that immediately grabbed Henry's attention.

"I've got a touchy thing to ask you, Hank."

"Oh, what's that?"

"Do you remember my pals back in Grade 9? Pete and John and…?"

Eddy's words trailed off. How could Henry ever forget that night when Eddy's buddies took Jenny to the park and… Henry never was quite sure exactly what had happened. Although he'd forgiven Eddy for that night, he knew his heart had never forgotten nor forgiven Eddy's friends. Hot anger churned in Henry's gut and Eddy recognized the rising heat seething from Henry's face. He remembered that day in the gym when they had had a fight over the same issue he was about to bring up again.

"If this bothers you too much, Hank, we can skip it."

Henry looked hard into Eddy's eyes. "What's this all about, Eddy?"

"Well, Pete was in town last month and he wanted to know what ever happened to that blonde chick? You know... Jenny."

Eddy could see Henry's eyes widen and his neck turn red.

"What the hell does Pete want to know that for?"

"He still figures he did it to her that night they took her out to the park."

"I thought you told me they didn't have enough time to do anything. We were right behind them!"

"That's what John and Bud thought, but Pete still thinks he did it to Jenny. The thing is Hank, Pete says he keeps dreaming about that night..."

Eddy could see Henry's face turning redder and redder. "You okay Hank? If you want me to stop..."

"No, keep going. Pete isn't the only one who's been dreaming of that night for years. To this day, I still am not sure what happened."

"Well, Pete doesn't either and it's bothering him so much he wanted me to ask you if you knew where he could get a hold of Jenny. He wants to look her up and apologize."

"Apologize! Geez Eddy, that's a bunch of crap."

"Pete's sincere, Hank. He's gone into the ministry. He's studying at some Bible college in Calgary. He's not the same guy we knew back in ninth grade, that's for sure."

Henry just stood there, dumbfounded. After all these years he couldn't believe the subject of that night with Jenny would come up again. Just when he thought he'd laid the matter to rest, it rears its ugly head.

When Henry didn't answer, Eddy continued. "Pete feels so guilty and sorry over that night, he says the only way he is ever going to stop the recurring dreams is to talk it out with Jenny."

"What does he dream about?"

"Apparently, he dreams about what happened that night, but in the end of the dream, she's giving birth to a little girl with blonde hair."

"No way...?" Henry recalled the time when he and Jenny were walking in the neighbourhood and she said that if she ever had a daughter, she would call her Camilla. *I wonder...*

Henry held his breath as he asked the next question, "Does Pete know what the little girl's name is in the dream?"

"The topic came up, Hank, and Pete said he recalls Jenny calling the little girl by name, but after all these years he still can't remember what it is after he wakes up."

"Do you think it might be Camilla?" Henry wanted to know.

"He didn't say, Hank, but I'll mention the name to him... See if that stimulates the man's mind, know what I mean?"

"Yeah, I know what you mean. But to answer your question, I don't know where Jenny is now. Last I heard, she was in Ottawa somewhere."

Suddenly, Henry remembered that he did have Jenny's phone number. Geez, it was still in the secret compartment of his wallet. He suddenly remembered the last time he had called and that guy... James Hamilton, answered the phone. *Man, that was some crazy guy.*

"No Eddy, I don't know how to get a hold of her," Henry said again, looking straight into Eddy's questioning eyes, hoping to mask his lie.

After several seconds, Eddy broke the gaze between them and chalked his cue again.

"By the way, whatever happened to those other two guys that were with Pete that night?"

"Ya mean Bud and John McBryne?"

"Yeah, I remember that John guy was pretty big."

"I don't know what happened to Bud after high school, but John went in the total opposite direction than Pete. He was into drugs in high school and since then things just got worse. He's been in the can a couple of times for possession of drugs and petty theft. I saw him about two months ago and he looked pretty haggard. And yeah, he was big back in Grade 10, but since then he sure shot up. He's almost twice the height I am."

Henry stared at Eddy. *At least Pete seemed to turn out okay.*

"Well, I better put this game to rest." Eddy took out another

weed and lit it up. He went down to the end of the table and surveyed the balls and then called a shot that Henry knew would be
next to impossible. *So he hoped!*

"Okay Hank, since I'm hooked my only shot is to come off the
cushion and do a combination play. Hit the eleven then the fifteen
into the corner."

"Dream on, Eddy."

Henry had a hard time returning to the game. He shook his
head, trying to clear it of memories of the past as he watched Eddy
about to make the shot. If Eddy misjudged the cue ball's bank off
the cushion even slightly he could hit the eight ball next to the
eleven, automatically forfeiting the game. Henry didn't like to win
a game that way, but those were the rules.

Henry's mind oscillated between Eddy's almost impossible
shot and Jenny. Eddy took a drag of his smoke and rested it on
the rail and leaned over to line up his shot. He slowly aimed the
tip of his stick behind the cue ball. Just as he was about to shoot,
he straightened up and walked to the other side of the table where
the cue ball would strike the cushion first. He licked his finger and
dabbed it on the rail, leaving a wet spot as a guide to where he
might shoot the cue ball. He slowly returned to the other side of
the table. He picked up his smoke, took a drag and with the smoke
dangling out of his mouth, he leaned over, took aim at the sheen
of the wet spot he left on the rail, and struck the ball. In the split
second it took the cue ball to travel to the cushion and bounce
off in the direction of both the eight ball and the eleven, Henry's
mind escaped the preoccupation of Jenny. He was present to the
moment.

The cue ball, narrowly missing the eight ball, struck the eleven
which then hit the fifteen. Henry held his breath as the ball traveled to the corner pocket, wobbled side to side at the entrance of
the hole and then... dropped in.

"No way!" was all Henry could utter. It was an amazing shot.
Since the remaining two balls Eddy had to sink were both in that
area, he easily won the game. Henry hadn't even taken a shot.

"Gotta hand it to you buddy, that was some game. Are you sure
you're selling stocks and not spending your days at the pool hall?"

"Just got lucky, man. Rack 'em up and weep," Eddy added with a confident chuckle.

They played nine more games and Henry ended up loosing ten bucks; he didn't win one game. Not only was he out of practice, but after Eddy had told him about Pete's dilemma, Henry couldn't concentrate on the games that followed. Even worse, Henry feared that the anxiety churning in his stomach might escalate into another anxiety attack as the evening progressed. Why was he worrying about Jenny and the possibility that she had given birth to a child, when his own wife was at home ready to give birth herself? That part of his life with Jenny was over.

Wasn't it?

After they played their last game, Eddy said, "So, the missus just about ready to deliver?"

"Yeah, it almost happened yesterday. It turned out to be false labour, though. Doctor says if she doesn't come on by next week he's going to induce the labour."

Eddy stuck his hand out towards Henry. "Best of luck, buddy... Hope you didn't mind me bringing up the topic of Pete and that girl, Jenny."

"Nah, that's okay. I think I understand what Pete is going through. Tell him... tell him I have no hard feelings..."

Lying for a second time that evening, Henry just hoped that eventually, his last statement would be true.

Chapter Five

JENNY WOKE JUST before eleven. She had wanted to get up sooner and attend a church service, but she had fallen asleep too late last night, or rather, too early this morning, to get up in time. Jenny rolled onto her back and stretched as she squinted out her bedroom window into the blue sky above. How many hours had she spent the night before gazing into the starry heavens, searching for that connection she had felt with Henry? It had been so strong early last evening when she saw the first star of the east, but then the feeling had quickly faded as the evening progressed. After that, she had been unable to recapture the feeling, no matter how long she sat there wishing.

One thought after another had tumbled over in her mind throughout the night. Just over a week ago, on May 24, Jenny had celebrated her little girl's sixth birthday. Camilla would be entering Grade 1 this fall. Jenny imagined her daughter full of life and curiosity. What joy must be filling the minds and hearts of Camilla's adoptive parents? Jenny would give anything to step into their shoes, even for just a day, an hour, a minute. She would burn the image of her daughter so deeply into her heart, she would never forget a single detail. The colour of her eyes, her hair, who she looked like.

Would she resemble me or… or her father?

For the first time in ages, images and memories of that awful night back in Regina filled Jenny's mind as she had gazed upon the stars well into the morning hours. Amazingly, Jenny's anger toward the man who had raped her in the park had long passed. Yes, it was a terrible wrong, but he was drunk and not in control of his normal self. But perhaps most of all, Jenny did not want to have hatred in her heart toward Camilla's father, no matter how heinous his deed. During her pregnancy, Jenny had so wished that Henry was the real father, she almost convinced herself it was true. Since then, however, Jenny had come to accept the reality of life that had affronted her when she was fifteen years old.

What was he really like? She wondered. *Who was this person who fathered her child?* In all of the commotion of that eventful night back in 1956, Jenny was so terrified and the confrontation so swift, she never really got a look at any of those three boys. The only thing she could vividly remember was looking into the glazed, frenzied eyes of the boy who forced her to the ground and thrust himself upon her. Then she had passed out.

Jenny realized her eyes were clamped shut as she relived the moment. Snapping herself back to reality, she took a deep breath and again fixed her eyes to the pale blue sky outside her window. Jenny was glad and fortunate her guardian angel had saved her from the awful memory of what had happened next. Yet, if she had only gotten a better look at her attacker, perhaps she would have a clue as to what Camilla might look like.

Will I ever meet Camilla's father some day?

Jenny finally got out of bed and made her way outside to her favourite spot. It was a gorgeous Sunday afternoon. The sky was clear and not a breath of wind stirred the garden. The sun was directly overhead, flickering through the lattice gazebo, lighting in spurts Jenny's golden hair. Gently nestled in the swing that hung from the roof rafters of her haven, she removed a small key from her pocket and used it to open her diary to the back section, the part that housed her innermost thoughts and secrets. Still deeply immersed in her thoughts of Henry from the night before, she entered the date, June 2, 1963, and realized that their upcoming anniversary was just over a month away.

Just as she was just about to continue with her entry, she heard footsteps coming down the winding stone pathway. She turned to see Carlos' smiling face.

"Good afternoon, Miss Jenny. Enjoying a beautiful Sunday in your favourite gazebo, I see."

"Yes, I am. What brings you here on a Sunday, Carlos? Isn't this your day off?"

"*Si*, Miss Jenny. I told my good wife, Maria, that right after church I have to go and water the plants in front of the patio. I remembered we had forgotten to water them and I don't like the flowers to thirst for too long. They are just like us when we are thirsty on a hot day. They desire a drink as much as we do, no?"

"Yes, I suppose so. My, you sure have a love for your plants."

"*Si*. As much as you love your wildflowers."

"That's for sure. Just look at how beautifully so many have awoken from their winter nap and flowered."

"*Si*, Miss Jenny. It gives my heart joy as well. Well, I see you are writing in your diary. I do not wish to disturb you further, so I'll be on my way. Enjoy this God-given day, *Señorita*." Carlos turned to go, but Jenny's voice stopped him.

"Oh, not at all, Carlos! I enjoy your company. You don't have to hurry off. Do you remember me telling you about my friend Henry back in Saskatchewan? Well, I was just thinking about our upcoming anniversary on July 6 and was about to tell my diary, but I might as well share it with you, instead!"

"July 6! Of course I remember, Miss Jenny. It falls on the same day I celebrate the parting of my mother and her entry into heaven to be with the Lord. In just another month and four days, I look forward to seeing a big yellow butterfly land on that rose bush over there. It happens every year since her departure. I believe with all my heart it is my mother sending her love."

"I just love what you said, Carlos. That is such a beautiful way to remember your mother's passing. Isn't it something that we should both celebrate the parting of our loved ones on the same day?" And then Jenny quickly added, "Of course my loved one is still in the land of the living. At least, I think he still is." Jenny chuckled.

Still looking in the direction of the rose bushes, Carlos suddenly realized he had something to share with Jenny, too.

"Oh, Miss Jenny, did you notice the new shrubs I planted in several different locations?"

"Yes, Carlos, I noticed several of the milkweed plants you added throughout the garden. I can hardly wait for the return of the Monarch butterflies. Do you recall two summers ago when they returned a month early? They filled my spirit to such overflowing I thought for certain I would take on wings and flit about the sky with them."

"*Si*, I remember only too well, Miss Jenny. When I told my cousin Fernando about it, he said it was a miracle, impossible for the butterflies to have arrived all that way in such a short amount of time. But, Miss Jenny, the shrubs I am referring to are the ones I planted at your request. Remember? You asked me last summer for one of your favourite flowers."

Jenny's suntanned face took on a puzzled look.

"See? There is one just on the other side of the wildflower garden." Jenny followed his arm pointing to the medium sized lilac shrub covered in buds, ready to open. How had she missed it?

"Oh Carlos, that is so thoughtful and kind of you. I can smell them already just thinking on it. Lilac is my favourite scent." Jenny's heart and eyes brightened so much; the very air surrounding her seemed to brighten, too.

"And yes, Miss Jenny, you are correct. I planted more milkweed plants all over, as well. There should be even more butterflies coming this year than last!"

"Oh Carlos, I can hardly wait for their return."

"*Si*, it should be any day now."

"Really Carlos, you should be home with your family today. I remember you telling me you have three children and they are all married?"

"*Si*, that is correct. Two are in the city but the third resides on the West Coast, in Vancouver. Why just this morning, our son Freddy and his family joined us at Mass. It is so good to play with the grandchildren."

"Tell me about your grand-kids, Carlos. How old are they and are they boys or girls?" Jenny was eager to know.

"The oldest is a girl, she is six and..."

Jenny just had to interrupt. "Oh, please tell me about your six year old granddaughter! What is she like? What grade is she in? Is her hair long? What colour is it? What is her name? Please tell me all about her."

Carlos was surprised at the intensity of Jenny's interest.

"Well, Teresa is such a lovely girl with long brown hair and dark brown eyes to match. She is very intelligent and curious. She asks so many questions all the time; Maria has no time to prepare the meals when she is around. Next fall she is going into grade two... You seem so interested...?" Carlos' words trailed off as he waited for Jenny to respond. He sensed something deeper behind her eager interest in his little granddaughter.

Jenny could feel the pride and love Carlos carried for his granddaughter. Jenny was envious and wanted to share about her little girl, as well. But there was nothing to share, only a brief memory of Camilla being born. Everything else Jenny imagined about her had simply been conjured in her mind, a mental invention of what her little girl might be like. But still, it would be so good to just be able to talk freely about it. Tammy, her best friend, was the only person Jenny could confide in about her daughter; her mom always avoided talking about Camilla, afraid that it might stir up painful memories for Jenny.

Jenny wondered if she should share her little girl with Carlos. He seemed so understanding... Jenny decided to make up a little story.

"Well, Carlos, I am so interested in your six year old granddaughter because in Grade 9 my cousin had a child that she had to give up for adoption and I've often wondered what her daughter would be like now, six years later. I think about how she might look, what it would be like to brush and smell her hair, feel her youthful skin, or take her shopping to buy her different outfits..."

Carlos' eyes saddened as he studied the girl before him. He didn't want to make Jenny uncomfortable, or cross a boundary, but something in his heart told him to trust his instinct that Miss Jenny was yearning to reveal to him the truth.

"You speak of your own little girl… No, Miss Jenny?"

Tears came to Jenny's eyes. The gardener before her was too perceptive and sensitive to fool; it was impossible to hide the truth from him. He was just like Tammy.

"Yes," Jenny whispered, "it happened to me. I speak of my little girl."

"Is the father the boy you celebrate with on the sixth of July?" Jenny simply shook her head and softly whispered, "I wish he were." Carlos took a brief step towards Jenny and then stopped. Jenny knew he wanted to comfort her. Reconsidering, he spoke his understanding from a distance and comforted her with his compassionate words.

"I feel your sorrow and your deep love for your child, Miss Jenny. It hurts me to feel your loss." And then like a seasoned counsellor, he attempted to draw out her repressed feelings.

"You say she would be six now?"

Jenny nodded, unable to speak.

"Do you have any pictures of her or know who the adoptive parents are?"

"No, Carlos." Jenny wiped a tear rolling down her cheek. "As soon as she was born they wrapped her in a white blanket and took her away from me. I just saw her dangling for a brief moment from the doctor's hands when she cried after delivery. I still hear her first tiny squeals… the only sound I ever heard her make."

"How you must wish to hold your daughter and hear her speak."

"All the time, Carlos. You remember my friend, Tammy? She had a little girl two years ago and remember, she stayed with us…"

"*Si*, I remember. She spent the summer on the estate. What a lovely girl and her baby, so beautiful."

"Well, that was the closest I ever came to reliving what it would be like to have had Camilla. But they moved to Florida… or rather, they are now in Texas. Her husband is a basketball player and he was traded just a month or so ago. I miss Tammy and her daughter very much."

"Someday you will see your little flower, Miss Jenny. I feel it in my heart."

"I feel the same, Carlos." Jenny's spirits lifted. "I know Camilla is bringing great joy to someone, but I have always felt that there is some beautiful plan for her life that will bring her back to me."

"*Si*, the Lord will make good out of everything. Your little girl, your Camilla, has her own guardian angel, watching over her. You have no need to worry about her."

Jenny's eyes brightened over Carlos' comforting words.

"My Maria and I will pray a Novena for you and for Camilla's return to you. It never fails, Miss Jenny. We will put in a request to the blessed Mary, our Holy Mother; she understands the heart of a mother."

Jenny gazed at the gardener, not knowing what to think, but his words did stir her faith. "Thank you, Carlos, I would appreciate your prayers."

"I am so honoured that you shared your treasure with me, Miss Jenny. It is good to talk of things in our heart, especially of our loved ones."

"Yes, it is so good to share this with you. So often it feels like Camilla was never even born, just a fantasy, a dream. Speaking about her brings her back to my mind and heart, and makes her real and alive."

"*Si*, that is exactly what sharing does: it heals the heart and the hurts. Together we now carry this secret, no?" Carlos eyes were filled with compassion and tenderness.

Jenny smiled, "Yes, Carlos, together we share this secret. Thank you for listening."

"It is my greatest pleasure. Well, I best be off and give the plants a drink, I hear them calling and can already see the poor petals drooping."

Jenny smiled at the image. Just before Carlos turned to leave, Jenny blurted out, "I should also tell you, Carlos, that I have accepted the proposal of the man I am seeing, James Hamilton. In two years we will be married."

Carlos looked puzzled, "Is it not the boy from…?"

Jenny knew Carlos was thinking of Henry. He could see the love she held for him when she spoke about him. Jenny didn't know how to respond. She just stared blankly at her insightful friend, making every effort to conceal her sadness.

"Ah, yes!" Carlos recovered buoyantly, "the young man who comes to see you occasionally. Yes, a fine young man. See, Miss Jenny? A family may soon be in the offering for you. Besides your lost little angel, you will have many other children, as well."

Jenny forced a smile. Yes, she thought, that might be a possibility. But deep down Jenny feared she might never be able to have children for giving up her little girl.

Would the trauma of that night and the ensuing decision she made be with her forever?

Carlos was no more than ten steps down the path when Jenny suddenly shouted after him. "Look Carlos, look behind you!"

He turned to see a large, beautiful, black and orange butterfly flitting about just above his head.

"Praise the Lord, Miss Jenny, the Monarchs have returned for the summer! By tomorrow the garden will be full of angels."

Jenny's heart soared with the gardener's. She raced out of her gazebo and ran after the butterfly, raising her hand as if to greet it. "Oh Carlos, just the sight of them makes me want to sing and fly!"

"*Si*, it is a happy sight. *The Lord gives us so much beauty to be thankful for!*"

CHAPTER SIX

"PUT OUT A call to all the interns and residents to come to the delivery room. This baby may be a tough one to deliver," Dr. Richter told the presiding nurse.

He had just finished examining Julean and was alarmed to see that in the last week, the baby had somehow turned again into the breech position. Dr. Richter had taken Julean on as a patient when she and her husband had returned to Regina for the summer university recess. Julean's doctor in Saskatoon had indicated in his report that Julean's baby liked to turn a lot. Twice Dr. McCall had had to turn the infant from the breech position.

"I guess this baby is determined to enter the world feet first," Dr. Richter muttered to himself.

When the contractions were two minutes apart, Henry kissed his wife tenderly before they wheeled her into the delivery room, tears bedding their eyes as their hands parted. Dr. Richter and his team were waiting for her.

"She is dilating rapidly," said the doctor after examining Julean. The contractions were very close together and Julean was in constant pain. The nurse gave her gas to ease the stabs of the contractions.

"I can see the baby's feet, Julean. Push a bit, if you can."

Julean didn't hear the doctor over her cries. The rest of the body was emerging. The interns gathered around. One shoulder slipped out and then the other, but the head was stuck behind the cervix. Dr. Richter gently pulled on the baby but it wouldn't budge. He knew time was of the essence.

"Forceps!"

He pushed the metal instruments in and gently closed them around the baby's head. He slowly pulled. He pulled harder. The baby began to move. "Come on," he whispered. Then, much louder, "Push, Mrs. Pederson push!"

This time Julean heard him and bore down as best she could. The doctor pulled one last time and to everyone's relief, the baby was born.

"It's a boy, Julean!" The doctor held the baby high enough for her to see. Julean let her head fall back against the bed and cried tears of joy and relief as a nurse began to sponge her.

"Can I hold him?"

"They'll have him ready for you in a minute, Mrs. Pederson," replied the nurse.

Henry was in the waiting room unable to sit or stand for any given period of time. He had just sat down for the umpteenth time when the doctor emerged from the delivery room and removed his surgical cap. When he was a few feet from the anxious father, the doctor broke into a broad grin.

"Congratulations, Mr. Pederson, it's a boy."

Henry could barely get the words out he was so emotionally distraught, "How are Julean… and the baby?"

"Well, we had trouble getting the baby out. The head was caught, but finally he came through. Everything seems to be fine now. Julean will be in her room in about fifteen minutes." Dr. Richter extended his hand. "Congratulations, again."

"Thank you, doctor."

Henry turned and walked toward the window of the waiting area. Leaning against the cool glass for support and turning his face to the sky, completely oblivious of the tears streaming down his cheeks, Henry whispered, "Thank you, Jesus. Thank you for protecting Julean and our baby." He instinctively brought his hands to his eyes and wiped away the tears, but they just kept coming.

Henry had almost convinced himself that something bad was going to happen, he just felt so relieved that everything was okay. For months now his stomach had been cramping with the anxiety that plagued him, despite the medication his doctor had prescribed and the prayer and meditation Father Engelmann had recommended.

Henry shook his head and tried not to think of how awful he had felt these past several months and how similar the experience was to when he had suspected Jenny was pregnant.

What if Jenny really did have a baby back then?

Thinking back to his conversation with Eddy at the pool hall where he had learned about Pete and his recollections of that night, and his dreams… Henry shuddered at the thought and abruptly turned his attention back to the moment at hand.

Henry was so glad his baby had arrived safe and sound and just hoped the pervasive, foreboding feeling in the pit of his stomach would finally go away. Taking out a handkerchief, Henry blew his nose and dried his eyes. He tried to see his reflection in the window, but his image was too dark to assess how he looked. Slightly embarrassed by his red and still teary eyes, but too proud and happy to care, Henry strode by the nurse's station into the maternity ward to meet his son.

When Henry entered the room, Julean was wearing a surgical mask and nursing their baby. The sight of his son nursing on his mother's breast… His wife, a mother… and he, the father… The image overwhelmed Henry and at once a joy flowed through him. All the earlier pain, anxiety, worry and concern vanished as new tears of joy began to flow. Julean gazed in her husband's eyes momentarily before looking back down at her son. She looked radiant. Henry neared the bed, bent over and kissed her forehead.

"I love you, honey." He looked down at his son. "And I love you, too, little guy." Henry bent further and kissed his son's tiny cheek. The infant didn't stop suckling for a minute, but his eyes fluttered open briefly at the feel of his father's lips brushing his soft, new skin.

Julean, ever thoughtful, remarked, "You look tired, Hank. Perhaps you should go home and have a good night's sleep."

"I will in a few minutes. How are you feeling?"

"Tired and exhausted, too. A little sore."

"Are we still going to name him Benjamin?"

"Yes, Benjamin Jack. I just love those names together."

"Your dad will be happy to see we've given his grandson his name."

Suddenly, Benjamin started to cry. Julean tried to get him to latch onto her breast again, but he refused and kept crying.

"A mind of his own already," said Henry.

A nurse walked in. "Well, how are we all doing? You must be the proud papa. Congratulations. That's a big boy your wife delivered, eight pounds, four and half ounces. So, you think he's done feeding?"

"I'm not sure. I hope he's getting enough milk," Julean fretted.

"Oh, I'm sure he is. If not, we'll know soon enough," the nurse consoled. Then turning to Henry and handing him a hospital gown and mask from the cupboard next to the bed, she instructed, "By the way, when you visit your son in the nursery, or if he is in the room, please put on this mask and gown."

"Yes, for sure. Sorry about that." Henry quickly placed the mask over his mouth and nose, securing the elastic behind his head.

"Well, let me take the little guy back to the nursery. Try to get some rest. The next feeding will come all too soon."

As soon as the nurse left with Benjamin, Henry removed the mask and returned his gaze to Julean. They looked at each other for a long moment. "I love you, Mom. I'm so proud of you."

Julean smiled, "I love you, too, Daddy."

Henry bent over and kissed his wife tenderly.

"Make sure you phone everybody and tell them it's a boy and what he weighed!"

"For sure, I'll call everyone as soon as I get home. I better go so you can get some sleep. I'll be back in the morning around eleven. Do I need to bring anything up?"

"No, I packed everything in my case. You better go before you fall over."

Henry kissed Julean again, "Good night, honey. See you, tomorrow."

"Good night." Julean smiled and threw him a kiss before he walked out the door.

Julean nursed Benjamin that evening at eleven-thirty, and then again at three-forty-five and six-thirty in the morning. Shortly after the nurse brought Benjamin in three hours later for his nine-thirty feeding, she returned almost immediately.

"Oh, I'm sorry, Mrs. Pederson, I wasn't supposed to bring the baby in to you. He had a convulsion an hour ago and threw up his last feeding. The doctor wants to check him over."

"Is anything wrong?"

"I'm sure it's nothing to worry about. The doctor will come in as soon as he examines the baby."

As the nurse rushed out of the room with infant, panic claimed Julean's heart and mind. She wished Henry were there. She phoned him, but there was no answer. He said he would come at eleven, less than an hour away.

Shortly before eleven, Dr. Richter entered Julean's room. She studied him as he walked over to her bed. His eyes looked grim and foreboding.

"I hope you're made of strong stuff, Mrs. Pederson."

"What do you mean? Is Benjamin okay?"

The doctor tightened his lips and laid his hand on Julean's shoulder, "I'm afraid he passed away a few minutes ago."

Julean looked at him in disbelief. "Are you serious?"

Dr. Richter nodded and almost in a whisper said, "Yes."

"Oh no!" Julean yelled, followed by a haunting scream that the nurses on duty that morning would remember for a long time.

Henry was just down the hall when he heard the scream. It could have been anyone on the ward, but Henry instantly knew it was Julean. He sprinted down the hall and burst into the room to see Dr. Richter lay his hand on Julean's shoulder.

"What's wrong?" Henry looked at Julean and back to Dr. Richter.

"Benjamin's… Benjamin… Oh Henry, he died!" Julean cried.

Henry turned to the doctor, his eyes ablaze. "How can this be? What happened?"

"It seems a blood vessel ruptured during the delivery, causing his brain to hemorrhage. It was too deep to get at it. I had a pediatrician look at him, too. There was nothing we could do. I am so sorry—"

Henry came towards the doctor with an outstretched arm. It initially appeared as if Henry was going to strike him, but it was more for support.

This wasn't real. It couldn't be real.

It was like the time Jenny told him she was leaving or when Father Connelly had told him his dad had run off with another woman. How could such things be possible? Yet they all turned out to be true. Henry looked at Julean. She was in a state of shock as well. Devastation and anguish filled her eyes. Somehow, Henry made it to her, sat on the edge of the bed, put his arms around her and drew her in.

"It will be all right," Henry whispered, as he rocked her back and forth.

Dr. Richter patted Henry's shoulder, then turned and left the couple who had experienced the joy of parenthood for less than a day.

Father Engelmann arrived at the hospital just after lunch and learned that they had already moved Julean to another floor. He found Henry sitting on a chair next to Julean's bed holding her hand, his eyes reflecting their anguish.

"I am so sorry to hear of your loss," Father said as he put one arm around Henry and reached for Julean with the other.

"Just this morning I held my baby in my arms and now he is no more. I just can't believe he was taken away from us. Why?"

Father looked into Julean's grief-stricken eyes, "Things happen in this life that defy all reason."

"But why would God want to take away our son? For what possible reason? You always preach that good comes out of all things. What good? Tell me, what good?"

Anger and sorrow raged in Henry's red swollen eyes.

"We had so many plans, Mr. Engelmann … I mean Father, and I couldn't wait to see and hold him…." Julean's thoughts trailed off into sobs.

"Life is so cruel," Henry continued. "There are over fifteen babies in the nursery. Why ours, Father? Why should any of them have to...?"

Henry and Julean vented their heartache and disappointments for over an hour. Had the doctor done enough? Should the baby have been turned? Should the doctor have delivered the baby by caesarian section? Why didn't God do more? Father simply nodded to acknowledge their grief or softly said "yes" to encourage them to speak and get it out. And after all was said, after Father allowed himself to be a victim, a target towards which they lashed out their innermost hurts, at once he became their healer. Eventually a peace and calm pervaded the room. A reluctant acceptance of one of the tragedies of life began to take hold.

Father could have said words of healing and comfort but decided to leave it for now. His presence and silent support along with the peace and quiet filling the room was sufficient. Now was the time for them to become aware of the good Lord and his angels ministering to their sorrowful hearts.

After a long while, Father got up and blessed the couple. Before leaving, Father ever so gently brought up the unpleasant subject of the burial. "Would you like me to go with you to the funeral home to select a casket?"

They looked at one another and then Julean burst into tears. In all the planning for bringing a baby into the world, the thought of having to bury their son had never occurred to them. Henry looked at his troubled wife for a moment and then at Father.

"No, that's fine Father, I would like to do this myself."

"Very well. Call me, this evening, and we can discuss the arrangements."

CHAPTER SEVEN

J ENNY STARED AT the phone for over fifteen minutes, trying to muster up the enthusiasm to phone her friend Tammy. Over the past two years they had made it a habit of phoning each other every Sunday night. They had missed last Sunday due to a basketball game Robbie was playing in Chicago that Tammy and Chloe had attended. Jenny thought Tammy would be thrilled over the news of her engagement to James and it would be difficult to not share with her friend all of her doubts about him. But the real reason for Jenny's hesitancy was the heavy feeling of dread she had felt throughout the day.

Something had happened to Henry, she was sure of it. She had been praying to her guardian angel all day to watch over him. The feeling she had was so foreboding and she felt completely helpless. The only thing she could think of to do was to pray and plead that her unseen helpers do what she was not able to.

If only she and Henry had kept up communication she wouldn't be in this predicament. Nor would she have to face the other issue weighing on her heart … *Her decision to marry James.*

Jenny got up off the bed, walked to the desk where the phone was situated and picked up the receiver. She just had to let Tammy know about the wedding news.

"Hello?"

"Hi Tammy, it's Jenny. I could hardly wait for Sunday night to call you."

"Yes, me too! I really missed talking to you last week, but we had fun at the game. They won 88 to 68. So how've you been, Jenny?"

Jenny hesitated for a minute and then dug deep to be as excited as she could and blurted out, "James and I set a date to get married! In two years, the spring of '65."

"My God, Jen, you didn't need to wait all this time to phone me with that news! And you're waiting another two years? And James agreed to that!?"

"Well, I still have another year of university left and then I'll be starting a new job..."

"Jenny, people get married all the time while they are still in school, just look at Robbie and me. And what has starting a new career got to do with it?"

"That's just what James said, but... I don't know, Tammy, I just don't want to rush into it."

"Jenny, you have been dating the guy since Grade 11 and you're still not having sex with him, are you?"

"My gosh, you're blunt, Tammy. No we still aren't. You and I both made the vow to remain chaste until we married, remember?"

"Yes, I remember. But do you remember that was after I got pregnant and Robbie and I started dating again?"

"Well, after that you remained true to our pack, right?"

"You know I did, Jenny, but still... knowing James, that's a long time for him to wait. But then, look what the guy's prize is after the wait... Every guy who lays his eyes on you wants to marry you, Jenny. James is no fool."

"Really, Tammy..." Becoming uncomfortable, Jenny wanted to steer the conversation away from herself. "So, how's your little angel, Chloe?"

"Chloe's fine, but not so fast Jen. What's eating you? There's more than going to school and starting your job that's holding you back from marrying James right away. If your dream guy from Regina asked you to marry him, would you put him off for two years, too?"

"Tammy, you're awful. Don't put me on the spot like that."

"I'm not. It's just that I want to talk this out so you're sure of what you're doing. Your heart just doesn't seem to be in this engagement."

That Tammy sees right through me. She knows me better than I know myself. She is such a good friend; I don't know what I would do without her.

"Well, it sure has made my mom happy. When I told her, she jumped for joy and began making up an invitation list that very night."

"Jenny! Your mom isn't marrying James, you are. Is this what you really want?"

"Oh Tammy, some days I think it is and then some days I'm just not sure. I know if Dad were alive he wouldn't be as enthused about it as Mom. He always encouraged me to go out with other boys…"

"I've always thought that, too. There are so many guys out there that would just love to date you, and for years you've seemed pretty lukewarm towards James. You never know Jen, if you freed yourself up, Mr. Right might just come along and leave both Henry and James in the dust."

Jenny chuckled and made another attempt to change the subject. "Oh, did I ever have a nice conversation with the gardener last Sunday. You remember Carlos, don't you?"

"For sure, he was the Mexican with the brilliant white teeth and the friendly smile. I don't recall one morning when he didn't greet Chloe and me when we stayed with you on the estate for those two months. He is a very kind and wonderful man."

"I think so, too. I find him a lot like you, Tammy, in so many ways."

"Ah, that's sweet of you, Jen."

"Anyway, he was telling me that day about his granddaughter who is six years old."

"Exactly the same age as Camilla, of course."

"Well, he talked so lovingly about his granddaughter, Teresa, it made me want to tell him about Camilla, as well. Once I started, he seemed to know exactly what had happened. Before I knew it, I had shared the whole thing with him. We both agreed on one thing for sure: that someday, Camilla is going to come back to me. I just know there is some wonderful plan unfolding."

"Oh Jen, you're such an angel. And I completely agree. I know your little girl will come back to you someday."

"You know Tammy, it was so wonderfully uplifting to talk about my baby without fear or feeling guilty or worried. It felt so freeing to be able to talk and express my love for my child openly with someone, other than you of course. It was one of the most beautiful and easy conversations I have ever had with anyone other than you and my dad at times when he was alive."

"Well Jen, that's how it should feel when you and *James* talk. Have you told him yet about Camilla?" Tammy brought the conversation right back to the point.

Jenny was silent for a long moment. Tammy's words hit her hard as she realized where her relationship with her fiancée really stood.

"No, Tammy. I still haven't shared that with James."

"It doesn't sound good to me, Jenny. In a truly healthy relationship, a husband and wife are open to each other. There is nothing to fear; openness is the basis for trust."

"I know you're right, Tammy. Someday I will tell him. In so many ways he's a nice guy and he does have his good days and… I do seem to be drawn to him, Tammy. I mostly feel he *needs* me, like there's a bigger purpose to our relationship. Like I've been placed in his life to help him somehow… And, of course, I still see traits in him that I so loved in Hen…"

Tammy interrupted, "In Henry, right! Why do we always keep coming back to him?"

"Yes, you're right again, but James can change, Tammy. Look how concerned you were about Robbie before you got married. Well, he changed and look how happy you are now."

"That was a miracle Jen, plain and simple. Going to Florida and getting involved with that Campus Crusade for Jesus, turned Robbie's life around. I was trying to change Robbie through my feeble efforts and wham, God comes along and zaps him so fast and hard, he changed miraculously almost overnight. I just don't see that happening to James. But, who knows? I've been wrong before. All I know, Jen, is I completely trust Robbie. He's so loving and considerate and… well, I could just go on and on."

"Oh Tammy, that is so wonderful! I'm so happy for you both. And your marriage is such an awesome role model for me and especially little Chloe."

"And you know Jen, I have to thank you for getting this all started. You got me praying to my guardian angel which led me to pray more to God. It helped me make the decision not have an abortion and later to keep Chloe and raise her… Anyway, it's all so perfect, Jen… Angels are our unseen link to God."

"I believe that too, Tammy. My angel is my very best friend and has protected and guided me in so many ways over the years."

"You want to know something else, Jen? Robbie and I read the Bible together all the time now. I think that's the secret of our success! It's drawn us closer together than I ever thought possible and it's so good for Chloe to see us so much in love with Jesus at the centre of our lives. I believe it instills faith into our little girl."

"Wow! That's amazing Tammy! I've never heard anyone speak with such commitment to Jesus, let alone you."

"You should hear Robbie, he'd give you an earful instantly."

"I have to admit, I don't read the Bible very often, but I do meditate and pray all the time when I go into the garden. Being around nature and all the beautiful flowers draws me so close to my guardian angel, especially when the Monarch butterflies return in the spring. They're like little angels filling my heart and bringing beauty to the world. I thank God for his helpers all the time. And nature itself, it was all created by God… I think more than anything it is this oneness we share with each other and everything in the world that unites us."

"That's why you're so accepting of everything, Jen. I've always felt that God gave you the heart of an angel the moment you were conceived."

A brief moment of silence filled the line as Jenny was choked up by her friend's kind words, and then she blurted, "My gosh, Tammy, this has been one heavy duty session. If I don't get down on my knees and repent after we hang up, I don't know what will happen!"

The girls laughed. Jenny felt so much better just talking so freely with her friend.

"Well Jen, I better go, we'll talk more next Sunday. I have to get Chloe to bed and Mom is calling at nine. You know, we've become so much closer, lately, and she just loves Chloe. A month ago she was actually in tears begging for my forgiveness for even suggesting that I abort Chloe. The thought of her missing out on the joy she gets from that little girl had become unbearable for her."

"You know, that reminds me, I read in the paper the other day that more and more women are protesting that it is their right to have an abortion and many doctors are agreeing with them."

"It just makes my blood boil to hear that. To imagine that I almost did that to Chloe is unthinkable now. I know it would have devastated my life. I've been thinking of getting involved, perhaps as a counsellor to pregnant girls. I think maybe I can help girls in that position to make the right decision and show them how wrong it is to murder their child."

"Yes, if you have the time Tammy, you would be a wonderful example. And knowing you, when you get motivated about something, there's no stopping you."

"Well, that's one thing I'm starting to pray for… I'll see what Jesus wants me to do."

"Women have to be pretty desperate to abort their child. It must be unbearable for women who go ahead with it only to realize that what they did was wrong. How on earth do they handle their regret, Tammy?" Jenny wanted to know.

"Well, that's exactly what I'm interested in. One thing is for sure, Jen, Jesus will heal and forgive all hearts who come to Him."

"Well, thanks for the talk, as always, Tammy. I miss you and Chloe so much! Oh, and tell Chloe that the Monarch butterflies are back. A few arrived last Sunday when Carlos and I were talking and by nightfall literally hundreds arrived on the scene. They are so beautiful to watch, Tammy. I wish Chloe were here to see them."

"Well, perhaps we might ship her down your way this summer so Robbie and I can have a romantic getaway, just the two of us."

"Tammy, that would be wonderful! Just set a date, any date. I'll take your little angel anytime for as long as you want!

"Actually, come to think of it, my Mom keeps asking to see Chloe all the time too. I'll talk to Robbie and see if Chloe and I can come to Ottawa for a few days this summer. I can spend some quality time with Mom and you can watch Chloe for two or three days."

"That would be wonderful, Tammy, I am so excited already, I can't wait! I'll ask Carlos if his granddaughter can sleep over at that time as well and we can have a girl's pajama party and play games and chase butterflies!"

"Oh Jenny, sometimes you're just too much. Talk to you next Sunday. And please, think very seriously about that marriage you're about to get into."

"For sure, Tammy. Love you!"

"Love you, too."

CHAPTER EIGHT

F OR THE FIRST time in his life, Henry found himself shopping for a casket. The funeral director led Henry to a room full of infant and young child-sized coffins, and then left him alone. As Henry studied each one, the thought came to him that this was utterly wrong. A mistake.

I should be out celebrating the birth of my son and making plans. I didn't even hold him in my arms or see the colour of his eyes or examine his tiny body. I should be out buying him new outfits and toys, not here purchasing... a coffin.

Tears welled up in his eyes as he looked at the tiniest of coffins, so unfathomably small. It was sad enough to picture one's parents passing on, resting in a casket, but simply unimaginable to picture his infant – *any* baby, for that matter – lying lifeless in one.

The casket directly in front of him was made of oak and lined with white satin that billowed out all around. The one beside it was similar, only darker in colour and with more brass on the sides and corners. Henry felt in a daze, not knowing how he could possibly choose, when he turned and saw a white casket to his left with a decal of an angel on the side. He instantly knew that was the casket he wanted.

When the director returned to check on his progress, Henry showed him the white casket and they went back to the office to make the funeral arrangements. Henry gave the man Father Engelmann's name and phone number so he could coordinate things. Then Henry handed the man a cheque to pay for the burial of his son.

Although it pained him to see his wife in such misery over their loss, Henry promptly returned to the hospital to be with Julean. He sat on the bed next to her, put his arm around her and told her of the casket he had selected. They cried and held each other and remained silent. Nurses came in and went. Julean's dinner was wheeled in and wheeled out. The nurse encouraged Julean to eat and offered to get Henry something, but both declined.

Around seven o'clock that evening, Father Engelmann arrived. Julean had fallen asleep, but Henry was still awake, still holding his wife. Sensing the solemnity of their vigil, he quietly entered the room, settled into the chair in the corner of the room, pulled out his Rosary beads and began praying in silence. Julean stirred and Henry gently laid her head on the pillow. Finally, Father Engelmann spoke.

"How did you make out at the funeral home, Henry?"

"I bought a white casket with a picture of an angel on the side."

At hearing the men's voices, Julean awoke in a much calmer state than she had been in for the last two days.

As Julean blinked back and forth between Henry and Father, trying to orient herself to where she was, Father calmly leaned towards her.

"Hello Julean," said Father gently. "How are you feeling tonight?"

She didn't answer for the longest time. When she finally did, she spoke slowly and softly.

"For so long Benjamin and I lived together, our hearts beating in unison as he grew and developed. I always felt him squirming and kicking whether I was asleep or awake. We were one while he was inside of me and after he was born and he nursed from my breasts, we were one. And even now that he is gone, he is still not apart from me. There was no time for him to grow apart. To become a separate little boy with his own identity."

Tears streamed down Julean's face, her chest heaved as she spoke. Henry, still at her side, squeezed her hand as tears filled his eyes, as well.

"I... I still feel him inside my womb, his mouth on my nipples, his heart in mine. I feel like I've lost a limb or a hand or an eye. You will be burying a part of me in that little coffin. How will I ever separate him from me?"

Silence fell over the room as the sun dipped behind the horizon, stealing the last ray of light from the room.

After a time, Father spoke. "You cannot separate him from you. He will always be a part of you and Henry. You two came together in love and created a new life. And though Benjamin's physical body will no longer be here, his spirit and memory will live and be a part of you, forever. His spirit is here, right now. You both have another angel in your midst to look after you and the rest of the family you will bring into this world."

In the twilight of the room, Father's gentle words painted a soothing picture filled with promise.

"It is important to remember, my children, that life on earth is bright and sunny even though some days may be cloudy and stormy. Right behind the heavy dark clouds the sun still shines. It's there waiting for us, bursting with life and renewed hope."

And with that, Father bowed his head and prayed. "Oh Lord, we ask you to come amongst us with your healing power. Grant us wisdom and courage to accept the early calling of our beloved Benjamin. Help us to recognize that every day has strength and potential for great things, yet it is also fragile. Sorrow and death can come at any time. Grant us strength, oh Lord, not to become an ally of death by getting stuck and overwhelmed by our grief, to never lose sight of the counterpart of sorrow. Give us the courage to rise up each day and move along with it."

Father rose and placed his hands on the heads of Henry and Julean, "I now bless you both with God's peace, in the name of the Father and the Son and the Holy Spirit."

And slowly, as it had happened so many times before, Henry, and now his dear sweet wife, received not only some of Father's wisdom, but his peace, strength and spiritual healing as well.

Only Henry and Julean's parents and a few relatives attended the funeral – far from the celebration they'd had for Anna years before. Julean's doctor had tried to convince her to stay in the hospital, but Julean couldn't fathom not attending her son's funeral. Father Engelmann said a Mass before they all headed to the cemetery for the internment.

At the end of the prayers, everyone dispersed slowly. Julean's parents took their daughter back to the hospital to continue her recuperation. Father Engelmann waited in the car for Henry while he stood at the foot of the casket for a long time, wanting to prolong his fatherhood for just a little longer.

The only vision he had held in his heart for months was that of Father Engelmann baptizing their baby, not burying him. For so long, he had imagined how happy everyone would be, the whole family together, welcoming their new baby. Henry had even fantasized many times that the arrival of Benjamin Jack would finally heal the strained relationship between him and his father-in-law.

As Henry gazed at the white casket, he recalled what Father had said at the Mass:

"One of the greatest tragedies one can suffer is the death of a child, but someday we will be together again."

Henry clung to that hope. There was another life beyond the one he knew. His son was just called a little earlier. For now, Benjamin's job would be to watch over his mom and dad. But someday they would play ball or hockey or have tickle fights and roll around in the snow. Yes, someday they would walk hand-in-hand and go fishing in one of the many streams in heaven and bask under a warm, sun-filled celestial sky.

Just as Henry was about to turn and head back to the car, a swarm of brightly coloured butterflies began to circle the tiny white casket. One of them separated from the group and landed on its closed lid. Golden yellow and orange shimmered in the sunlight like a tiny angel as the butterfly perched and slowly opened and closed its wings. It then took flight and flitted about Henry as if sending out a message of love. A gentle peace permeated the air. Finally, Henry turned to go.

As he made his way back to the car Henry saw his friend Eddy

Ziegler standing in the distance leaning against a tree. An ever present smoke was dangling from his mouth. He took a drag of the cigarette and with his usual flair, flipped it off to the side. Slowly he and Henry made their way to each other.

"Tough break, buddy. That's the way the chips fall at times."

"Yeah..."

"How's the wife doin?"

"As good as can be expected, Eddy..."

Eddy just nodded, not knowing what to say. They stood in an awkward silence for a few moments and then, trying in vain to distract his friend from his grief, Eddy said, "Look maybe next week sometime we can shoot a game of pool at the Royal again. Take your mind off things. What do ya say?"

"I don't know, Eddy. Give me a call when you have a free night and we'll see."

"Sure thing."

Eddy gazed hard into Henry's eyes, gave him a light punch on the shoulder, turned and walked away. Not more than ten feet away, Eddy pulled out his smokes and lit one up.

AFTER HENRY DROPPED Father off at the parish, he drove to the hospital to see Julean. As he walked down the corridor, Henry ran into her parents who were just leaving after seeing her back to her room. Even under such a horrible circumstance as the death of their son, Henry felt a lack of compassion from his father-in-law. Somehow, Henry felt that they blamed him for the loss...

Henry quietly entered Julean's room. She was propped up in her bed and the room was filled to overflowing with flowers. Without a word, Henry climbed onto the bed next to his wife and again, they lay together holding each other and weeping silently until Julean finally drifted off to sleep. Henry watched his beautiful wife as she slept; her face blotched with redness from days of mourning. After a while, he quietly left the room and headed to his parents' place.

When Bill answered the door he threw his arms around his son.

"Come in, Henry. Come in and sit down."

His mother emerged from the kitchen and rushed towards

Henry. They embraced and his mother held him for a long time.

"Come, sit down, Henry. I'll get some tea on."

Henry followed his mom to the kitchen and sat down at the table. His father sat across from him. Henry noticed his dad's rosary lying beside the sugar bowl. The black wooden beads sparkled under the kitchen light. His parents must have just finished saying the rosary.

His mom filled the kettle then set it on the stove. "How is Julean doing?"

"She's sleeping now. It was probably too much for her to attend the funeral, but she insisted. I know she was in much more pain than she let on. Her milk really came in today and her breasts were hurting quite a bit, not to mention the soreness she has from the birth."

"She is a strong woman, Henry. She'll heal, but she needs time. It's such a devastating loss."

His mom put her hand on his shoulder and the kitchen fell quiet until the kettle whistled. His mother prepared the tea then brought a cup over to Henry.

"Care for some, Bill?"

"Maybe coffee, if it's on."

"It'll just take a minute. I baked a pie this morning, would either of you care for a piece?"

Both men declined so Mary sat down next to Bill.

"So, how are Julean's parents taking this? We didn't get a chance to talk after the funeral as Bill had to go back to work."

"As well as can be expected Mom, I guess. I haven't seen them for a few days, either, except briefly at the funeral. I ran into them at the hospital earlier, but we didn't exchange words. Think I'll drop over tomorrow and pay them a visit."

His mother placed a cup of coffee in front of his dad then sat down again. Being in the familiar, love-filled room soothed Henry's heart. He reached for the rosary and held it with the finger tips of both his hands. He started to work the beads through his fingers but he uttered no prayers. A tear fell from his bowed head and fell on the rosary. Bill and Mary reached out to Henry, covering their son's hands with theirs.

In a low, trembling voice, barely audible, Bill began to recite the rosary, "I believe in God, the Father almighty, creator of heaven and earth. And in Jesus Christ, His only Son…"

AFTER TEN DAYS in the hospital, Julean was discharged. Her spirits had improved over the last few days, but going home without the baby was almost too much to bear. They had had such high hopes and dreams for their son and their life together. Tears sat on the edge of their eyelids as Julean and Henry, empty handedly walked out of the hospital toward their car. Henry was a little disappointed Father wasn't at the hospital to escort them home. He had said he would try to make it, but something must have come up.

They didn't speak on the drive to their apartment as they were both absorbed in their own thoughts. Henry knew it was best to talk about it, but he just didn't seem to have the energy or spirit to do so. All he could do was hold Julean's hand. When they arrived at the apartment, there, sitting on the step was Father Engelmann, wearing the broadest, happiest smile Henry had ever seen upon his mentor's face. As Henry and Julean got out of the car, he got up and opened his arms wide.

"Welcome home!"

They felt wonderful to see Father. The peace and inner joy he always exuded seemed to flow into them, lifting them out of the cobweb of anguish.

They invited Father in and made their way to the kitchen where they sat talking and praying for most of the day. What would have otherwise turned into an evening of silence and sorrow became one of solemn joy. Father's words of comfort and hope that they would soon have other children soothed their grief-stricken hearts.

Whereas they had anticipated arriving home to an empty house, Father Engelmann had turned it into a home filled with renewed faith, and one that glowed with love and the promise of a bright future. His insightful, caring friendship was truly angelic; he knew what was needed in the heart of every moment!

JULEAN STOOD ON the front step, watching as Henry walked Father Engelmann down the sidewalk to the car. It was a Godsend that

Father was there to greet them when they came home from the hospital. His ability to soothe and comfort, provide hope and strength was truly a God-given gift. *And yet, Julean felt troubled.*

Tears slid down her luminous cheeks as thoughts of their loss flooded her mind and how it might affect their marriage. Hank had looked so forward to being a father and Julean had hoped the child would draw them closer together, unite them in their marriage and remove the uneasy feeling that Henry was holding a secret in his heart. And now with the death of their son, she felt more uncertain than ever of their future.

Julean wiped the moisture from her eyes. The love she held for Henry was deeper than his love for his teacher. She prayed that someday Henry would return that love to her in equal strength, but somewhere inside of herself, she knew that her husband had given away a part of his heart to another that he could never relinquish.

"I love you, Hank, more than you will ever know or understand," she whispered in a soft tone that was gently carried away by the warm, evening summer breeze. But the bright shining moon hanging directly overhead in the heavens caught a look in Julean's eyes that she could no longer hide. A look that Julean herself had seen in the eyes of those women on the Colony.

That unmistakable look of sharing their loved one with another.

CHAPTER NINE

IT WAS SATURDAY, July 6, 1963, and both Julean and Henry had had a restless sleep. The week after Benjamin's death, Henry had gotten a summer job as a draftsman for the Department of Defense, drawing the elevations and floor plans for the war time houses in the west end of the city and keeping a record of each of the properties on file. A couple of weeks later, Julean, having healed physically and wanting to busy herself, decided to return to work at her father's office for the summer and was scheduled to begin that Monday. Although they were both coming to terms with Benjamin's death and the summer weather was glorious, Henry and Julean were both inwardly full of discontent.

When Julean woke up that Saturday morning, she was surprised to find Henry already out of bed. Usually he got up later than she did on the weekends. As she lay there with the sheets a bit tangled around her, Julean thought about Henry's dream that had awakened her in the middle of the night. He was tossing and turning and kept shouting the name, "Jenny!" over and over. Julean had tried to rouse him, but he wouldn't wake up. He finally settled down and although he was no longer shouting, he kept murmuring something about a letter. Julean had been unable to fall back to sleep until well after Henry had quieted down.

Although she could have stayed in bed all day, Julean's growling stomach forced her to get up. She made her way to the kitchen to find Henry sitting at the table, reading what appeared to be a letter. Julean's heart skipped a beat at the sight.

"Henry?"

Her husband, startled, looked up at her, then broke into a huge grin. "Good morning, honey! Look, I finally got a letter from Gary. It must have taken about two months to get here."

"Gary?" echoed Julean, still mired in her thoughts from the night before.

"Yes," replied Henry, taking a sip of his orange juice. "He and Jane wanted to congratulate us on our wedding and Gary apologized again that he couldn't be my best man." Looking back down to the page, Henry continued. "He says Jane was very ill. She contracted some disease or parasite that was carried by the Ucayali River when it flooded the village they were working at in the Amazon rainforest. He writes that part of their job is to educate the tribes about the role water purification plays in their very survival and Jane does a lot of work teaching young mothers about hygiene and nutrition and the spread of disease."

Julean set a glass of orange juice next to Henry and sat opposite of him at the table. She looked at her dear husband as he read the letter from his friend. She loved him so much. Tears filled her eyes.

Henry didn't look up at Julean as he read aloud excerpts he wanted to share with his wife.

"'I never thought I'd see the day Jane and me would grab a hammer and help to build a church. I've learned that the biggest skill one needs here is to have a willing heart and you'll learn all you need to know...'

"And listen to this honey, they are going to the Philippines next for a year and then on to India to work with Mother Teresa. Wow... what an experience they're having!"

Henry looked up at Julean. "What's wrong, honey?"

Julean was sure Henry had no recollection of his dream and was completely unaware of what his wife had witnessed. Contemplating whether or not she should bring it up with Henry, Julean turned away and her eyes settled on the calendar hanging on the wall next to the cupboard above the sink. She picked up a pen lying on the table, walked over to the calendar, and proceeded to draw a circle around the day's date.

"July 6. Does this date have a special meaning to you, Hank?"

Henry quickly looked down and began eating his cereal, simply shaking his head from side to side.

"Are you sure?"

Not daring to look up at his wife, Henry took another mouthful of cereal and got up.

"Nope, it doesn't honey." Trying to act as casual as possible, Henry put his empty bowl and spoon into the sink and turned to face Julean. "Do you know where the can of 3-in-One Oil is? The front door is squeaking; I thought I'd give it a quick squirt before going to Dad's place. He wants some help with a new water heater he's installing in the basement. I told him I would be over around nine and it's already eight-forty-five."

Julean, looking steadily at Henry, was about to press her previous question but then said, "I think the oil can is on a shelf in the furnace room."

"Oh yeah, I remember putting it there the last time I oiled the furnace fan."

Wondering what had gotten into Julean, but anxious to get away, Henry leaned over and gave her a kiss on the cheek. "On second thought, I think I better get going, sweetie. I'll oil the door when I get back." Julean turned and leaned her back against the counter as she watched Henry rush toward the front door.

Henry was all flushed and relieved to hit the outside fresh air. He wondered if Julean sensed his nervousness. Contrary to what she thought, Henry recalled vividly his dream from the night before. It was the same recurring dream he had every year to the day since he had met Jenny in Mr. Engelmann's store.

July 6, 1956. Seven years ago! Why can't I get that day out of my head?

Henry was angry at himself. It wasn't fair to his wife to keep thinking about Jenny, and the recurring dreams were beginning to torment him. The discussion he had with Eddy a few weeks ago at the pool hall didn't help matters, either. It had just stirred up so many memories of premonitions he had about what had happened to Jenny.

Did she really have a baby? Did she really have a baby girl with blonde hair?

JULEAN SAT AT the kitchen table for almost an hour after Henry left the house. After thinking about it for some time, she decided to call her Auntie Netta in Alberta. Auntie Netta was her dad's sister and still lived on the Mormon colony just outside of Cardston with Uncle Jacob. Julean took a deep breath and dialed the long distance number.

"Hi Uncle Jacob," Julean's voice quavered.

"Is this Julean?'

"Yes, Uncle, it's me. How are things on the colony?"

"Everything is good, Julean. And how are you and that good man of yours doing?"

"We're okay, Uncle… still adjusting to our loss."

"It takes time."

"Yes, it takes time."

"How is the weather there, Julean? It's been raining here for four days. We are all praying for the sun to shine."

"It's beautiful here, Uncle. The sun is shining nonstop and everything is starting to dry up. Maybe we need to ask God to send that rain of yours our way and you can have our sun."

"Indeed, Julean! A good idea."

"Uncle, I'm wondering if Auntie Netta is free to talk for a while?"

"She is just gathering the eggs in the chicken coop. She should be along soon, but I can go get her if you want to hold on?"

"Yes, thank you, I'll wait."

Julean hung onto the receiver and reached over to the stove to turn on a burner. The telephone cord uncoiled just long enough to fill the kettle with fresh water and set it on the burner.

"Julean? Is that you?"

"Oh, hello Auntie!"

"How are you, Julean? What a nice surprise to hear from you."

"I'm fine. I'm back to work for father at his office on Monday."

"That is good, Julean. You need to get out of the house."

"Yes, I think it's best, too. Hank is working full time and the house is too quiet… Too much time for idle thoughts."

"You have healed from the delivery and every…"

"Yes, Auntie. Physically I am fine, but of course Hank and I are both still adjusting to the loss."

"It takes time, Julean. Trust in the Lord …"

"Yes, the Lord heals everything. Is Uncle Jacob still there?"

"No, he went to the barn to feed the cows."

"Good… Then you are alone?"

"There is no one here…"

"Good. I have something I need to talk to you about. It's… it's difficult for me to say this, Auntie. I don't know how to start… It has to do with Hank and me."

"Go on Julean. I am a good listener. What is it?"

"Well… I think Hank still loves another woman…"

"Are you sure of this, my child?"

"No, I am not sure…"

"Then how do you know, Julean?"

"A woman knows these things, Auntie Netta…"

"But Julean, there must be proof. What is it that you know? Has he been going out and coming home late? Have you found some love letters from another woman?"

"No, no none of that…"

"Well then…"

Julean took a deep breath and exhaled slowly. It was all so foolish and yet she needed to get it out. "Oh Auntie, he loves me and assures me of it all of the time! I know this might sound foolish Auntie, but it's when he is asleep that he reveals himself…"

There was a long silence, as if the phone had gone dead. Julean's soft sobbing became audible.

"Now Julean, my dear child, how can a man be unfaithful in his sleep?"

"It is when he is dreaming, Aunt Netta," Julean replied with a tear-filled, quavering voice. "He dreams of this girl and he talks in his sleep with such passion. He calls her Jenny. It happened on the very night of our wedding day. After we went to sleep I awoke to hear him. He was making love to this lady…"

Auntie Netta remained silent.

Julean went on. "And yet, during his waking hours he is so loving, considerate and affectionate. He is the most devoted husband in the world towards me. I feel so foolish thinking this way. I thought..." Julean's voice caught, then she continued haltingly. "I thought when we had our child this would all go away and bring us closer together... But now with the death of our son, I just don't know... Just last night he dreamt of their anniversary, the day he met her. It was as if he was reliving the moment."

"Have you spoken of this to him?"

"Not directly... This morning I asked him if the date July 6, had special meaning for him and he said no. It is all so foolish, Auntie. He assures me of his love every day by his words and actions. To ask him if he loves another would inflict such pain on him. He would think of me as a jealous woman filled with suspicion and mistrust. He's already suffering so much over the death of our son, I would only be adding to the grief the man already bears."

Once again silence ran through the lines.

"Tell me Auntie," Julean continued, "what was it like on the colony before it split up? I mean, back when most of the men had two or more wives? I know that it didn't last and there was all the controversy, but before all that? What was it like for those women who shared a husband? Why could they not all live in harmony?"

"Oh Julean, the division was so great. The church was divided, the community was divided. Sisters against sisters, children against parents, wives against husbands. The anger ran so deep. Suspicion and jealousy and all kinds of ugly emotions we humans are capable of were on display. In the end, those who wished to love several wives went to British Columbia and the rest stayed on here. And some, like your parents, decided to leave altogether and begin anew, on their own."

"But Auntie, what was it like for the women who shared one man? I know they shared their duties and work. I know there must have been the usual squabbles and differences from daily living. But, what I want to know, Auntie Netta, is whether it's possible for the women in such a marriage to be loved the same – equally – by one man?"

"Well, I suppose it is possible, Julean. Certain husbands did have their favourites, just as a parent might have a favourite child, or niece or nephew. That is how humans are, we cannot love perfectly. But it is possible for a woman to share her man with another, or even more, as we have seen. These women are willing to make that sacrifice to have at least a part of their husband for their own rather than have no husband at all."

"That is what I wanted to know. I love Hank so much that if I had to, I think I could share him if it meant I would otherwise lose him. Oh, Auntie Netta, if only I could meet this other woman, this Jenny. I suspect she's very different than me, more spontaneous, more beautiful. But of course, the less I know of her the more I make up in my mind. Hank's dreams are so vivid, it seems so clear that there is something she fulfilled in him that I'm unable to."

"Oh my dear child, you are making too much of all this. Perhaps it is just a recurring dream from some past moment, or a mere fantasy of some kind and there's nothing more to it than that!"

"Auntie Netta, when you lie beside a man and he goes on and on with such depth of feeling, with such passion... Believe me Auntie, it is more than just a fantasy."

"I say this Julean: a dream is no match for the real love of a woman. You are so sincere and loving, Julean. You are also beautiful and outgoing. He knows and recognizes it and confuses things when he's asleep. It could be a woman who was in his life long before he even knew you, but I am sure when he is dreaming he is just confusing you for this other woman. I am certain, Julean, that the passion is directed to you.

"Dreams are dreams, Julean, everything gets distorted. It's nothing more than a harmless dream that has mixed things up. And I will dare to tell you a secret that may even confirm what I am saying. At times, Julean, even when I am making love to Jacob, I fantasize about other men. We are all frail and have weaknesses. The mind can play many tricks on us. We are human Julean, our weaknesses are many."

"Yes, I know, Auntie Netta. But at times I feel certain the connection he has with this woman Jenny is not earthly at all, but spiritual. It goes beyond the real life we know."

Once again the phone went silent and neither spoke again.

CHAPTER TEN

B Y THE END of August, Jenny and her mother had looked at all the shoes and wedding gowns in Ottawa. They had put a hold on one of the gowns, but her mother still wasn't convinced it was the one and bought two airline tickets to Toronto for the Christmas holidays. Jenny tried to convince her mother that it wasn't necessary; there was still a lot of time to find a wedding dress in Ottawa, but her mother would have none of it.

"Jenny, it's better to be prepared and not leave anything to the last minute. As the day approaches, there will be a million and one things to do. The sooner we attend to the basics like the dress, shoes and… what about the hotel and band?"

"The Hamiltons have looked after that, Mom. James told me last night that his parents booked the Chateau Laurier to hold the reception and wedding. It all sounds very hoity-toity, if you ask me. I'd hate to tell you what it costs for two hundred and fifty people."

"Money should be no object for this wedding. I'm sure they want this to be the best for the both of you, just like I do."

"In hindsight, it was a good thing I talked James into waiting two years before the big day. I really hadn't anticipated such elaborate preparations."

"Yes, we're definitely going to need all that time to get everything in order for such a big wedding. Anyway, let's get the dress matter out of the way and see what Toronto has to offer. Besides, it will be fun to go shopping in another city."

Jenny looked at her mom and smiled. How could she refuse? This was the happiest her mom had been for as long as she could remember.

"Yes, it will be fun. Thanks, Mom." Jenny kissed her mother's cheek.

"Oh, by the way, Print One called and they have two samples of invitations to choose from. The one that gives a little story about how you and James met sounds so lovely, I can hardly wait to see it. I've never seen a card like that; it's almost like a fairy tale."

"Hardly, Mom."

"Well, I'll pick up the samples before your university classes start and then we can make a decision. I think we should show them to Mrs. Hamilton as well so she can put in her two cents."

"I suppose so," said Jenny as she headed for the stairs. "I have a book I want to finish reading so I think I'll head up now. Thanks again for all your help, Mom."

Jenny trudged up the stairs, longing to lose herself in the novel she had started the night before, but as soon as she entered her bedroom Jenny decided to call her friend, Tammy. She quickly changed into her pajamas and pulled the phone from the desk to her bed, settling comfortably against her pillows for a nice, long chat.

"Hi Tammy, it's Jen."

"Well, of course it's you! My, what a pleasant surprise," Tammy said, coating her words in a Texan drawl.

"Oh Tammy, you're starting to pick up the accent of the locals down there!"

"Isn't it something Jenny? I can't help myself. The more time I spend with the people here, just hearing the southern accent all the time, does it to me. I must admit I love it."

"I know what you mean, Tammy. Whenever I'm around people from England I end up picking up their accent in no time. I love it, too… 'ta, ta my dear, I prefer the Tetley tea of course!'" Jenny finished off with a perfect British accent. The girls laughed.

"So are you getting out more, Tammy, and making some new acquaintances?"

"Actually, I've been spending a lot of time volunteering at the local health clinic, trying to offer pregnant girls some guidance away from choosing to end their pregnancies, and I've also been joining some pro-life rallies down here. Remember me telling you I wanted to do that? Well, I'm just loving it. It makes me feel so involved in an important cause and like I'm really helping others with something that I struggled with so much."

"That's awesome, Tammy! I'm so proud of you for following through with that."

"So, what's up with you, Jen? Why are you calling sooner than our usual Sunday night jam session? Is everything okay or do you just miss me that much?"

"To be honest Tammy, it's Chloe that I miss terribly. I can't live without her."

"And what about me? I'm her mother, you know."

"Oh Tammy, I miss you too, but little angelic Chloe just steals my heart. Sorry!" Jenny laughed. "So where is my little darling?"

"She's outside playing on the swing set. So, what's up Jen? I know you better than that; what's troubling you?"

"It's just my mom. She is so excited about the wedding and I can't seem to share her enthusiasm. She's not happy with any of the wedding dresses in Ottawa even though I like one that I tried on and now she's determined to take me to Toronto to check the gowns out there."

"Really Jenny? I don't think this is about the gown... What's really troubling you?"

"Can't hide anything from you, can I? Tammy, I know this sounds crazy, but I'm still uncertain about the wedding... the marriage to James. I care for him and yet deep down, the love I *should* be feeling for him just doesn't seem to be there..."

"... Like it is for Henry back in Regina, right?" Tammy finished Jenny's thought.

"See, there is nothing I can hide from you."

"And that's how it should be with true friends, Jenny. But it sounds like what you and Henry had was more than friendship. Every time you mention him I get goosebumps all over."

"It's really something, Tammy. It was in 1956 when we met

– seven years ago! And the feelings I have for him today are as strong as they were back then."

Jenny was surprised to hear herself say that.

"Jenny, it really tears at my heart to hear you express such strong feelings for this guy and not *do* anything about it. And here you are, about to marry someone else you're not even sure about while still holding onto this dream for Henry! It's crazy. Why don't you phone him and find out what happened to him? Perhaps he's still available and wanting you as much as you're desiring him."

"Oh Tammy, I wrote so many letters to him and he never answered even one of them. And do you remember that pewter angel Christmas ornament you traded with me for…"

"Yeah, I'll never forget the look in your eyes when I showed you that angel. I still think I got the better deal. The hand painted ball of Santa streaking through a midnight sky with his reindeers was a real treasure."

"Well, then we both lucked out, Tammy. That pewter angel was too beautiful for words. Anyway, I sent it to Henry as a Christmas gift, thinking for *sure* he would respond!"

"And…?"

"And, nothing! It's almost as if he disappeared off the face of the earth. If only he would have returned at least one of my letters… I'm sure by now he has found another girl and is probably married, maybe even a father."

"Well, you'll never know, Jenny, unless you find out for certain."

"But how? I just can't simply call him up out of the blue and ask. He may not even remember who I am—"

"But Jen, you're just assuming that. You don't know anything for sure! I think that's what's bothering you and why you can't make a decision about James. You never had any closure with Henry and until you do, you're never going to have peace in your heart over this. I remember reading about a family whose daughter went missing and three years later they found the girl's body. The mother said she had always suspected that her daughter was dead but once she knew for certain, she was able to find peace in her heart. I'll never forget that, and that's exactly what you need, Jenny."

"I know, Tammy. I feel that way too, but there's more to it

than that. It's not just that I didn't get closure, which is terribly unsettling, but our connection was simply heaven sent. I think it started out like a normal attraction between a boy and a girl, but then something happened… Something magical that changed me forever…"

"What!? Tell me what happened, Jen? I'm getting goosebumps again!"

"Well, it's hard to explain Tammy. Maybe I'll start from the beginning."

"I'm all ears… Hurry! Get it out."

"Well, it was July 6, 1956, only the second or third day after we had moved to Regina. Mom needed some baking supplies and asked me to go to the corner grocery store. As I walked past the house on the corner, just three doors down from ours, I suddenly had this feeling someone was watching me. I looked back over my shoulder and there, behind the screen door, was this cute guy staring at me. I smiled and walked further but something compelled me to look back again. It was the strangest feeling, Tammy."

"What happened, Jen?"

"Well, when I turned back again I saw that he had opened the door and it looked like he was about to come over to me. But as soon as he saw that I had turned around again, he jumped back inside and slammed the door. I stood there for a minute, but he didn't come back out, so I just continued on my way. I have to tell you, though, I was just filled with the strangest feeling; it almost felt like I floated the rest of the way to the store…"

"My God," whispered Tammy.

"Anyway, when I got to the store I started to look on the shelves for the items my mom needed, when suddenly the door opens and in walks this guy. At the time I couldn't tell for sure if he was the same boy I saw earlier, but the strange feeling in me strengthened. I could feel heat going through my entire body and for the first time ever I didn't know how to react so I hid behind one of the shelves!"

"Did he see you?"

"Well, the way he was peering up and down the aisles, I knew he was looking for me. The thought sent my heart racing. I'm not sure, but it seemed like we were the only two customers in the store. Time seemed to stand still as I peeked past the cans of peas, straining to spy him. Then the store owner suddenly hollers out to the boy, 'Henry! Are you looking for the young girl who came in a few minutes ago?'"

"Really, Jen? Sounds like he was in on it. This is getting eerie..."

"It gets even better, Tammy. I guess Henry must have been so startled at hearing the store owner call his name, he swung around so fast his arm accidentally hit a pyramid of salmon tins, sending them flying in all directions! Oh, I felt sorry for him, yet it was so funny all at the same time. He scrambled to the floor and started picking up the tins to stack them again. I was so drawn to him Tammy; I stepped out from behind the shelf, bent down in front of him and started to help. Our eyes met briefly before we both turned away, and then... well, here's the thing..."

"What Jenny? What happened?"

"I turned back to look at him and he was just staring at me. I could see the heat in his face colour his cheeks and then I started to feel a rush that began at my heart and rose so quickly up into my face and eyes and... well, to this day I don't know what happened. It was like science fiction... like we were both lifted up and transported into another time and space where nothing else existed... *where we were as one...*"

"Whoa, Jenny, this is too weird..." whispered Tammy.

"We seemed to almost hover there for I don't know how long and then a voice in the distance drew us back. It was the store owner. Just like that, I felt my chest pound and my eyes twitch as my feet seemed to hit the floor with a jolt like I had just jumped from a tall ledge and landed in the middle of that store. I don't know Tammy, but something supernatural happened there that morning. I can't explain it, but it was the beginning of a connection between us that only grew stronger by the day over the next two months..."

"I feel goosebumps running up and down my spine, Jen. No wonder you can't get over this guy. You just have to find out what happened to him!" Tammy paused...

"Why didn't you ever just pick up the phone and call him, Jen? You can't sit around waiting for a man to call. Look at how I hounded Robbie when I was carrying his child. I called him oodles of times before he ever picked up the phone and called me. Boys sometimes haven't got the courage like us girls to take charge, Jen. You know what I mean?"

"Yes, I do Tammy. I just can't give you an answer. I actually did call Henry once when I was pregnant, but I didn't speak to him… He answered the phone and I just couldn't say a word. I think I just wanted to hear the sound of his voice. And then, you know, my mom was constantly discouraging me from calling him and yet… There's something else, Tammy. Like, despite it all, I think maybe I'm just meant to be with James, you know? He came along and sort of took away that strong urge I had to call Henry. The problem is, the closer I get to marrying James, the urge to contact Henry is returning stronger than ever."

"This is all very strange, Jenny. You'd think that as more time passes and the closer you get to marrying James, you'd become less and less invested in what ever happened to Henry. Well, one thing is for sure: you have to find out before you marry James. You just have to know, Jen."

"But how? I'm too afraid to call him up now. What if he is married and his wife answers…? My God Tammy, I would just die."

"His last name is Pederson right?"

"Tammy, you have such a good memory."

"Not really, Jen. It's just that I listen closely to you when you share your heart with me."

Jenny's heart filled with such love at her friend just then. Not many people were able to see so clearly into her heart and mind or took the time to listen so closely and carefully to her.

"Jen? Are you there? I asked you if you know his phone number?"

"Well, I still remember what it was back in ninth grade, but I have no idea if he or his parents still live in the same house… I guess we could find out, right? He lived on Broder Street."

"In Regina, right?"

"Yes, but what are you going to do? What are you thinking of? Oh Tammy …"

"Don't get so worried, Jen. Why don't you get his number and call me back with it and I will think of some way to find out what has happened to him. Just trust me, Jen. I won't involve you in the least. Leave it up to me."

The thought of getting in touch with Henry sent shivers up and down Jenny's spine. Her eyes brightened. Her heart jumped. Her feelings soared!

"Oh Tammy, do you really think you can find out what happened to Henry?"

"Absolutely Jen. I'm like a hound dog. Give me the scent and I'll track him down in no time."

The girls laughed again but this time their laughter carried an indescribable hope.

"Okay, Tammy, I'll get his number. He may not be living at home anymore but it will give you a start. And Tammy, please don't involve me."

"Don't worry, Jen, leave it up to detective Charlie Chan." Tammy's voice suddenly took on a Chinese accent and the girls laughed once again.

Just before they hung up a door slammed loudly and Jenny heard Chloe yell, "Mommy!"

"Is that Chloe, Tammy?"

Tammy didn't answer as she was talking to her daughter and then suddenly, Jenny heard Chloe's tiny voice.

"Hi Auntie Jen. When are you coming here? I miss you so much!"

"Hi angel. I miss you too. I can't wait to give you a hug. Maybe next summer we can get together. How does that sound?"

"I want to see you now, Auntie Jen."

"I want to see you too, Chloe, soooooo much. I'll tickle that little tummy of yours."

Chloe laughed at the thought.

"Were you out playing?"

"I was on the swing and I know how to pump. I can go so high. Mommy tells me to stop."

"Well don't go too high sweetie, I know you are an angel but you can't fly for long." Jenny laughed.

Once again, Jenny heard Tammy talking to Chloe and then she came back on the phone.

"Okay Jen, we have to go. Get that number for me right away and let's see if we can't track down that secret man of yours!"

Jenny tingled throughout her being. *Was it possible that Henry was still at home? That he still wasn't attached? That he still cared for her?* The thought sent Jenny's heart into space before she was instantly overwhelmed by guilt for not having the same rush of feelings toward the man she was going to marry. *I better get Henry's number before I chicken out.* Jenny picked up the receiver and dialed zero.

"Yes Operator, could you please look up the phone number for a Pederson... that's right, with a "d"... Henry Pederson on Broder Street in Regina, Saskatchewan."

"One moment please ... I have a number for a Bill Pederson on Broder Street."

"Yes, that's his father..."

"The number is..."

As Jenny wrote down the number she immediately recognized it as the same number she had committed to memory so long ago.

But something else jarred her memory!

Jenny had never written down Henry's number before, but seeing it now on paper reminded her of one other time she had seen that number...

"Oh my God," Jenny whispered. She was certain this was the very same number she had seen written on a pad in front of the phone in the kitchen one day after her father had died. Her mother had said she was just doodling while talking to a friend, but she *must* have written down that number.

Why didn't I make the connection back then? What is going on? Could Mom have dialed Henry's number that day? Who would she have been talking to? To Henry...?

"Impossible!" Jenny blurted out.

Why on earth would Mom have phoned the Pederson residence? It just doesn't make any sense. I must be mistaken.

CHAPTER ELEVEN

THE SUMMER HAD passed quickly for Julean and Henry. Within two weeks of starting his job at the Department of Defense, Henry impressed his superiors with his excellent mechanical drawing skills and how quickly he grasped all the technical information. The head draftsman had encouraged Henry to consider going into engineering or architecture since he seemed to have an uncanny ability to perceive two dimensional plans of a project as already built in his mind, but Henry felt strongly about pursuing a teaching career.

On their last Saturday evening in Regina before heading back to Saskatoon for their final year of university, Henry and Julean were invited to her parents' place for supper. Over a meal of roasted chicken, the subject of Henry's summer work came up.

"Oh my, are you now thinking of changing your career plans?" Mrs. Carter asked after Julean had gushed to her parents of Henry's success.

"No, although I like drawing and the challenge of engineering I still think being a teacher is the way I want to go."

Dr. Carter looked up from his plate and addressed Henry directly for the first time that evening. "You will make a lot more money in engineering than teaching, you know."

"Maybe so, Jack, but I prefer teaching. I think it's a very

important job to educate young people."

"Well, you could be an engineering professor... Think of the prestige and the pay," Dr. Carter said, gazing directly at his son-in-law in what seemed to Henry like a challenge.

"Money isn't everything," replied Henry, unflinchingly. "And like I said, teaching in a high school is what I want to do now."

"I think Hank could go into anything and be good at it," Julean chimed in. And turning to her husband, she looked confidently into his eyes and said, "you will be a wonderful teacher, the students will just love you!"

Dr. Carter let out a bit of snort at the end of the table while Mrs. Carter surveyed somewhat longingly the loving scene between her daughter and the man she obviously adored.

On their way home, Julean was the first to speak. "I can see what you mean about my dad. I can't for the life of me see why he is so cold towards you. Maybe I'll talk to him about it on my last day of work at his office on Wednesday."

"Just forget it Julean, I'd sooner have your dad come around on his own and accept me for who I am without you getting involved. It's not worth anything if someone has to be told to love someone; it has to come freely from their heart."

Henry knew that was the only way the nervous feelings of rejection swirling in the pit of his stomach would go away.

"Hank, your mind's not on your driving! You should have turned left on Broadway."

"You're right as always Julean. But actually, I'm not heading home just yet." He reached out and took Julean's hand in his. "Let's end this evening on a memorable note, shall we?" Henry drove west on 25th Avenue and then turned left onto Albert Street.

"Oh, now I know where you are going." Julean smiled, her white teeth gleaming under the city lights. She squeezed Henry's hand. At the Legislative buildings, Henry turned left and then left again to enter Wascana Park.

As soon as they entered the park driveway along the lake side, the discussion Henry had had with Eddy at the pool hall a few weeks ago surfaced. It was here where Eddy's friends took Jenny that night and where they may have actually raped her. Henry shuddered at the thought and tried his best not to show what was crossing the screen of his mind, but Julean was too sensitive to his feelings and immediately turned to him.

"Is something wrong, Hank?"

"No. I was just thinking of the conversation I had with your dad earlier," he lied. "But that's going to change as soon as I park! And besides, how could anything be wrong when I have the most beautiful and adorable wife in the world sitting next to me?"

Henry parked the car facing the water. The hint of fall weather was unmistakable. The strong, prairie breeze was agitating the water, obscuring any romantic moon reflections in the lake. The couple snuggled together in the front seat, comfortable silence enveloping them as they both reflected on the summer past. After some time, Julean quietly spoke.

"Do you think a lot about Benjamin?"

"Yeah… I like to think of him more as another angel beside us, looking after us and…" Familiar by now with his wife's ways and concerns he quickly added, "And if you're thinking that I'm disappointed in you for not giving me a son, please don't, honey." Turning now to face Julean straight on and taking both of her hands in his, Henry continued in earnest.

"Please, Julean. It always bothers me so much when you think I'm disappointed in you or think less of you for what happened. It's so unfortunate Benjamin died so soon after birth but these things happen and there is no one to blame, especially not yourself. I'm learning more and more to accept it as one of life's misfortunes and I hope you are coming to accept it too, sweetheart."

Julean just nodded, placed Henry's right arm back around her shoulder and buried her head deep into Henry's chest. Julean knew it was good to keep talking about Benjamin, but she was also aching to bring up Henry's dreams of Jenny, as well. There hadn't been another dream incident since the morning of July 6 and there hadn't been a good opportunity for her to raise the subject since then. Julean also knew that bringing it up would put Henry on the spot. He would just deny it and get upset at her for bringing up such a foolish thing. It would create a problem when there might not even be one.

No, perhaps her Auntie Netta was right and Henry was just mixing up some past girlfriend with her in his dreams. He was always so reassuring… Yet, it would be good to know more about this woman from his past.

As odd as it seemed, Julean was curious to know what Henry had been like when he was with her. Was he different? Did she bring out another side of him that Julean didn't know? Would Julean finally feel like she was getting all of Henry, his whole self, if she were somehow able to experience Henry while he was also with Jenny?

Could she share Hank with another…? Would she dare…?

Julean snuggled closer to Henry and he tenderly squeezed his wife.

"I love you so much, honey," Henry said, gazing down at Julean and leaning down to kiss her soft lips.

"I love you too, Hank," Julean murmured between kisses, "more than you know…"

On Wednesday, just as she was returning to the Medical and Dental building after lunch on her last day of work for the summer, she heard someone call her name.

"Hey, Julean."

She turned to see Eddy Zeigler walking down 11th Avenue.

"Hi Eddy, are you going to work?"

"Yeah, I just shot a game of pool at the Royal and was heading back when I spotted this good looking brunette in a nurse's dress." Eddy winked good naturedly. "You're looking great, Julean. I see your figure has returned."

"Thanks Eddy. Yes, I'm finally getting back in shape."

"I thought you and Hank would be in Saskatoon by now. You haven't dropped out, have you?"

Julean chuckled, "Oh no, classes start next Thursday. We're heading back first thing Monday morning."

Julean studied Eddy for a long moment while he fished for a smoke from his shirt pocket and lit up. She decided to take a chance.

"Can I ask you something in secret, Eddy?"

"If it has anything to do with my height, forget it. What you see is what you get."

Julean chuckled nervously again, "Well, I hope I don't get into trouble asking you this, promise me you won't breathe a word of this to anyone..."

Eddy studied her quizzically, "Okay, my interest is peaked. What's it that I'm promising to guard with my life?"

"Eddy... Did Hank have a girlfriend named Jenny?"

Eddy gave Julean a quick once over. "Yeah, seems to me he checked her out a few times. But that was way back in Grade 9."

"What did she look like?"

"She was a blue eyed blonde... But if you're worried about the competition, don't be. Hank's one lucky guy to have latched onto you. And besides, she moved to Ottawa at the start of Grade 9 and no one ever heard of her since. As far as I know, Hank hasn't either."

Eddy found it strange that he had just talked to Hank about Jenny a few weeks ago and now his wife brings up the topic. He wondered what was up. He knew it was better to be quiet about Pete and the boys and all that business with Jenny in the park. Just as Eddy was about to say adios and head back to work, Julean launched in again.

"Well, what was she like, Eddy?"

"Don't know, Julean. I saw her a few times at school but never met the girl. The Padre might know, you could ask him..."

"You mean Father Engelmann?"

"Yeah... But the best person to ask is Hank and he probably can't remember much anyway. That was a long time ago, Julean and... Why would he want to remember Jenny when he's got a chick like you!?"

Julean smiled, her cheeks blushing just a tinge.

"I gotta go, Julean, lots to do before the markets close for the day. Have a good year at school. And say hello to the worse half for me!"

"Yes, thanks Eddy, I will," Julean laughed. "And please forget what we talked about. It was foolish of me to ask."

Eddy waved it off as if nothing, as he tossed his cigarette and swaggered off down the street.

Julean hoped Eddy would keep their conversation to himself. Hank would be upset with her if he knew, but Eddy seemed trustworthy.

When Eddy got to the corner of Scarth Street and 11th Avenue, he pulled out his smokes and lit up another one. He took a deep drag and looked back at Julean who was still watching him. He gave her the thumbs up sign and then disappeared down Scarth Street.

On Saturday afternoon Henry and Julean arrived at St. Mary's church around two-thirty in the afternoon and found at least thirty parishioners lined up ahead of them, waiting to go to confession. They were leaving for Saskatoon on Monday and Henry wanted to stop in on Father Engelmann and go to confession before school started.

"Julean, do you want to go up front and pray while you wait for me?" Henry whispered. "I want to light a candle for us to the Blessed Virgin Mary. I'll be right back; I'm sure the line for confession will move quickly."

Julean did not tell Henry that she too was thinking about going to confession that afternoon. She just silently walked down the long aisle to the front of the church, genuflected, then entered the very first pew and knelt down.

During her conversation with Eddy on Wednesday, he had suggested that Father Engelmann would know more about Jenny. Hank's parents would know of her as well, but she dare not ask them of their son's former sweetheart. But Father Engelmann may be the very one to ask. He would know most of Hank's past, his life as a teenager. And the way Hank talked of the times they shared on the grey crates behind the store, Hank would have shared everything with him, even the most intimate details of his life. If anyone could help her learn more of Jenny and her whereabouts it would be Father Engelmann.

Yes. It all made perfect sense! I will go to confession and ask Father, and best of all, he is sworn to secrecy and he will tell me what I want to know.

After a while, Julean lifted her head off of her hands and looked over her shoulder to the back of the church. There were only two people now standing in line to confess. Then Julean glanced over to where Henry was still kneeling in front of the Virgin Mary. He seemed deep in prayer. When the last person exited the confessional, Julean got up and made her way to the back of the church. She quickly entered, pulled the curtain shut behind her and knelt down. The partition slid open.

"Bless me Father for I have sinned."

HENRY WAS IN a daze when he finally lifted his head and looked up at the Holy Mother. He glanced around and noticed the line of people was gone and then he saw Father Connelly go into the sacristy. *What time is it?* He looked at his watch.

"Geez, it's almost four o'clock." Henry realized he must have fallen asleep while praying.

He turned to the front pew where he last saw Julean, but she was no longer there. Henry figured she didn't want to disturb him in prayer and must have decided to go outside for a walk. He hurried over to the confessional booth. One booth was occupied, the other one was free. There was still time for him to go to confession with Father Engelmann; he shouldn't be long. Henry approached the available booth, moved the curtain to the side, entered the dark cubicle and knelt down to wait for Father Engelmann to slide open the partition. As his eyes adjusted to the darkness, he could just begin to make out the wooden grill. He noticed the partition behind it was slightly ajar. He faintly heard the sound of whispers…

My God, that sounds like Julean!

FATHER ENGELMANN RECOGNIZED Julean's voice immediately; he had come to love her as a daughter over the years. After reciting the usual short list of minor digressions weighing on her heart, Julean paused for a long while before continuing.

"Father?"

"Yes, my child?"

"I… I have to ask you something in complete confidence."

"Whatever you say in here is between the Lord and me. You can share whatever is troubling you in your heart. The Lord understands and forgives all transgressions."

"For the longest time Father, even before Hank and I got married, I had the feeling that he was still in love with another woman. Ever since our wedding night, this intuition of mine has been confirmed…"

"Surely Henry has not been unfaithful to you? He is an honourable young man…" Father hesitated, realizing he must be careful not to divulge the life of another, even to his wife.

"No, he's not been unfaithful directly or intentionally, as far as I know. It… it is his dreams, Father, that reveal the secrets of his heart."

Father Engelmann was well aware of Henry's continuing struggle over his first love. For years, the young man had shared how his feelings for Jenny followed him all the days of his life and Father was quite certain Henry was still unable to shake himself free from his love for her. Now, Father's heart was going out to Julean. He could hear the pain in her voice and he wanted to help her, but this was not the place to discuss the lives of another. *Mien guter Gott, hilf mir…* Father weighed his next words carefully.

"Perhaps it is just an old friend that you sense, Julean."

"Was the name of his friend Jenny?" Julean asked, pointedly.

Oh my guter Gott, I am losing control of the confession.

Julean interpreted Father's silence as 'yes' to her question and followed it up with another.

"Do you know where in Ottawa she lives? I would like to meet her."

"Julean, I am so sorry but I cannot continue to discuss this further without breaking my vow. It is best, my child, to talk to Henry about what is in your heart."

"Oh Father, I have asked him indirectly many times. I don't want him to feel that I don't trust him or that I am being jealous or suspicious… He gets so upset when I question his love."

"In a marriage, it is always best to bring everything out into the open, my child… to keep the air clear. It is not good to live under the umbrella of suspicion or uncertainty, especially in a marriage.

Trust is first and foremost. We must be open and honest and truthful in all we say and do lest our minds conjure up what might be tainted by our fears, emotions and insecurities."

"Father, I know that Hank loves me above all else, but I also know what my heart tells me. And if honesty and openness is so important, then why doesn't Henry trust me enough to openly tell me about Jenny? I know he is still in love with her and if we could talk about it, I think we could resolve it together. Perhaps it is a part of my roots or my heritage, I don't know, but there is a part of me that is willing to share Hank with the woman he still so loves. My only desire and deepest wish is to make my husband the happiest he can be."

"Julean, my dear child, such a wish is out of the question! No matter how good your intention, it is morally wrong. The Lord is clear on the matter; 'In the beginning, God created only one man and one woman, thus uniting them in marriage.' St. Mark also reminds us in chapter 10 that a man shall leave his father and mother, and cleave to his wife, and the two shall become one flesh.

"Julean, you and Henry are but one flesh and what God has joined together, let no man put asunder. Even your former faith, the Mormon Church, has acknowledged this and that is why polygamy is banned from the Mormon religion today."

"I understand Father, but my heart aches when I hear Hank cry out to his beloved, I don't know what else to do. I am willing to go against the wishes of my former church, Father. If I must, I will go against the doctrines and teachings of the Catholic Church, as well. If I must, I will go against the Lord's commandment... My love for Hank runs so deep, Father.

"*Do you understand now why I need to meet this woman?*"

Father was stunned, absolutely speechless. Julean spoke plainly and with all her senses, yet what she desired was morally not permissible. For all of his life at the store and now in the church it had always been his aim to encourage his brothers and sisters to love greatly, to not shy away from love. Julean's intention for the happiness of her husband was sincere and so great, but unfortunately... *misguided.*

"Julean, this is a matter between you and Henry. You must

bring this out into the open. If you both wish, I would be more than willing to help the two of you to find some resolution to this matter. I shall pray for you both that the Lord gives you the grace and strength to accept what is, to work it out in the best way possible and move on with your lives."

Julean began to cry. "Oh Father, I know what you are saying is true… and yet confusion runs through my veins and thoughts. Yes, please pray for me… for Hank and me…"

After Father gave Julean absolution and she left the confessional, he sat for a moment wondering as to how he could have further counselled her. There was only one other circumstance where he felt at such a loss as to how to assist someone with their troubles and that was the ongoing issue Henry had with Jenny! Even as recently as his last confession a few months ago, Henry had divulged that he still thought of Jenny, dreamed of her, and even loved her. And now, here was Henry's new wife bringing Father the same issue and again he felt somehow incompetent to console.

Mein gutter Gott, was there no end to the entanglements of life?

Father was feeling weary; he almost hoped that no one would be in the other cubicle. Turning his attention to the partition on his right, Father noticed it had been left slightly ajar. Realizing that another parishioner might very well have overheard their entire conversation while waiting to confess, Father gasped slightly and shook his head at his oversight. He shifted on his seat, took a deep breath and slid the partition door aside…

"Hi Father, it's me, Henry."

"*Oh mein gutter Gott*, Henry!" Father exclaimed, as his heart almost stopped beating.

"Geez Father, lower your voice, the entire church is going to know I'm in here with you." Henry softly chuckled.

"I apologize Henry; I was so shocked to see you there. I just thought the confessional would be empty."

"I think I am the last one. Boy, you and Julean sure talked for a long time. And the sliding door wasn't closed all the way, Father …"

"Did you hear what we discussed …?"

"No, I covered my ears with my hands for all that time!"

"That was wise and considerate and thanks for telling me that. I shall be more careful in the future to keep the door closed all the way."

My, my, Father reflected, *wouldn't that have been something if Henry had heard all of what Julean had said... And yet, that is exactly what must happen. Maybe the doors to both sides should have been completely open!*

"So, tell me what I don't already know that is in your heart, Henry."

"Yeah, there is probably nothing, that's for sure, but anyway ..."

Henry fell silent for a moment and then made the sign of the cross and began, "Bless me Father for I have sinned, it's been three months since my last confession and these are my sins: Father, I was and still am upset with God for allowing our son to die ... but I am working on it. I also am angry at Julean's father for not accepting me into their family, I was judgmental of one of the guys at work, I was untruthful to Eddy and to Julean, and that's pretty much it except for ..."

"Yes, go on."

"Well, I'm sure you don't want to hear this anymore, but even after all this time, Jenny is still on my mind. As much as I love Julean, I just can't seem to shake Jenny from my life. I know I have been dreaming quite a bit lately of her too and I feel so guilty about it ...

"How is it possible Father that one can look into someone's eyes and be so smitten? Two months, just two months is all the time we had together and yet it seems to have formed a lifelong attachment. You know Father, I'd be a perfect candidate for an old style Mormon colony. Sometimes I feel like I have two wives. I know it's silly, but that's the way it seems; I love both women. I try and try to get Jenny out of my mind but I just can't. It's like she is a part of me..."

It seemed as if Father completely ignored Henry's last remarks when he said, "First, in regards to your father-in-law and the man at work, ask Jesus to help you to accept others, to forgive others. If unkindness is shown towards you, return kindness. Try always to advance the kingdom of God. The world needs love and people of strong character who are warriors for Christ and are bent on making peace within themselves and with others.

"In the end Henry it is always love that heals and prevails.

"I understand how tragic it was for you and Julean to lose Benjamin. Let God come into your heart and comfort you for the early passing of your son. He understands your pain all too well. He, too, lost His son. When you leave the confessional go to the front of the church and kneel before the altar and look at the crucified Christ. Offer your pain and sorrow up to Him. And keep in mind, death is a door we must all go through in order to receive eternal life. Some meet their Maker early in life and some later but, it is a door we must all pass through.

"Henry, it's clear to me that you and Julean must discuss your concerns over Jenny together. I would be more than willing to act as a counsellor or third party to hear this out. I understand this is a complicated situation to which I do not have an answer or easy solution. But this I know: it is always best to be open and honest and share what lies deep in your heart especially if it affects your relationship and trust."

"I don't know Father; we just lost our son and now to tell her on top of that, that I am still in love with Jenny... I just can't bring myself to do that at this time, Father. It would cause too much pain in my wife's heart."

"But you cannot be certain of that Henry, you may be very surprised. Julean may be more understanding than you think."

Father was silent, he was almost ready to share what Julean had confessed to him earlier as a way to convince Henry, but caught himself.

Father gave Henry a penance to say and administered absolution. Henry thanked Father and left.

Once again Father marveled at how both seemed to think that two wives sharing a man could be a possible solution to their dilemma.

My, my...

CHAPTER TWELVE

M ARY WIPED HER hands on her apron and rushed to answer the phone, "Hello!"

"Hi, is this the residence of Henry Pederson?"

"Yes, well… it was. He doesn't live here any more. Who is calling?"

"My name is Tammy, a friend from high school. I was trying to find out where Henry and his wife lived."

Tammy thought she would throw that out there and see what the response would be; it would tell her a lot.

"Yes, Henry and Julean are living in Saskatoon right now. They just returned last week for their final year of university, but they're planning to move back to Regina next year. I can give you their address if you wish."

"Okay, that would be great."

Mary put down the phone for a few minutes and then returned and gave the address to Tammy.

"So, when did they get married, Mrs. Pederson?"

"They just celebrated their first anniversary on September 9th. They had a baby boy earlier this past summer but unfortunately he died shortly after birth. But I suspect she might already be pregnant again."

"Oh, that is good to hear. And I'm certain everything will turn out just fine this time."

"Well, she hasn't told me yet for sure so if you speak with them please don't mention what I said. I am just going on my intuition. It's a mother thing, you know." Mary laughed nervously. Perhaps she was saying too much.

"Oh, I understand perfectly, Mrs. Pederson, I have a little girl myself and I know all about motherly intuition. Well, I won't take up any more of your time… Oh, by the way, what is Henry taking at university?"

"He's taking Education. He will make such a fine teacher."

"Oh, I'm sure he will… Thank you for informing me about Henry and his wife."

"You are more than welcome… What did you say your name was? Tammy? Is that correct?"

"Yes, it's Tammy." And before Mary had a chance to ask what her last name was, Tammy quickly ended the conversation.

"Thank you again, Mrs. Pederson. Bye."

Oh, poor Jen. This was not what she would want to hear. And he's only been married a year! Had they phoned a year ago, they might have been able to do something about it. But now it was certainly too late. The man of her dreams was betrothed to another.

"Hi Jen, it's Tammy"

"Tammy! I've been waiting on pins and needles to hear back from you. Why didn't you call last week?"

"I'm sorry, Jen, I forgot to tell you Chloe and I had plans to go with Robbie to Florida to watch them play. He sure is a great basketball player, if I do say so myself."

"Yes, yes, Tammy, we all know how wonderful Robbie is! What I want to know is… What did you find out? Did you get through to Henry? Did you talk to him?" Jenny held her breath as her heart began to race uncontrollably.

Tammy hesitated for a moment, not sure how to tell her friend.

"I'm sorry, Jen, it's not what you want to hear. Henry is married. They just had their first year anniversary on September 9th."

There was a long silence. Jenny really wasn't surprised. She had felt for some time now that Henry had found someone else.

Tammy continued, "You know, if we had done this a year or two ago, you might have had a chance, Jen."

Yes, Jenny thought, all it would have taken was a two minute phone call. Why hadn't she pursued it more? What had held her back? Did she allow herself to see too many obstacles? Was it James? And that date... September 9th... Why did that seem to have such significance?

"Are you okay, Jen?"

"Yes, I'm okay, Tammy. I was just thinking of their anniversary date... you said it was September 9th?"

"Yes, Mrs. Pederson said they were married a year ago, September 9th, 1962."

The blood drained from Jenny's face.

"Just hang on for a minute, Tammy." Jenny rushed over to her desk drawer and withdrew her diary. She quickly turned to the back half, where she wrote all her secret stuff and flipped through the pages until she came to the one she was thinking of.

"Oh my gosh Tammy, you're not going to believe this. Last year on September 9th I wrote in my diary that I had an eerie feeling that something was happening to Henry. Ever since then, I haven't been able to feel his love like I used to when I gaze at the star of the east."

"My God Jen, that's the second time you've mentioned feeling some kind of spiritual connection between you two."

"And there's something else that just came to mind, Tammy. I remember my mother had the strangest nightmare earlier that morning. She was screaming at the top of her lungs to *stop the wedding*. I wonder... could she have possibly been dreaming of Henry's wedding? And later that day, she was so concerned about my happiness. It's all very strange, Tammy...And then... oh my gosh, there was a telephone number my Mom had written down that I'm sure was Henry's, the same one I gave you to call... Oh, I better not get into that..."

Jenny's voice trailed off. She began to wonder if her mother was keeping something from her. *But what?*

"Jen, are you still there?"

"Yes... yes. I was just thinking..."

"Sounds like a lot is bouncing around in that pretty little head of yours. It's all too puzzling for me, Jen, but one thing is settled for sure, it looks like you're going to have to follow through and marry James or else start playing the field. I really think you need to let Henry go, Jen… That ship has sailed."

"Yes, I know, Tammy… you're absolutely right. Thanks for making the call, at least now I know."

But then again, Jenny wasn't so sure it really solved anything.

"You know Mom, I still haven't shown the wedding invitation samples to James' mother. I'll give her a call and arrange to meet with her on Saturday if she is free. I know James and his dad will be working over the weekend."

"Another take over?" Edith asked.

"Yes, something like that. They're always into some kind of merger or acquisition or God only knows. James hasn't even had time to look at the invitations, either. I'll leave them with Mrs. Hamilton when I see her and then James and his father can view them when they get a moment."

"Yes, that is a good idea, Jenny."

Jenny followed her mother into the kitchen.

"Would you like a coffee or tea, Jenny? I might if you do, but I'm feeling tired. Perhaps I'll just take a little nap."

"No I'm fine Mom. But, there is something I would like to ask you."

Edith placed the kettle on the stove, ignited the burner, then turned to her daughter. "What is it, Jenny? More questions about the wedding?"

"Well, sort of. I was going through my diary the other day and I read what I wrote back on September 9th, 1962, just over a year ago. Do you remember having that awful nightmare? I rushed into your bedroom, you were screaming so wildly, and had to stop you from banging your slipper on the headboard of your bed."

Edith's legs suddenly felt weak. Her face paled. She pulled out a chair from the kitchen table and sat down.

"I do recall a bad dream. I have no idea if it was on that particular day, Jenny. But that's long forgotten… Why is it important to you?"

"Well, Mom, it's what you were shouting when I woke you up. You kept saying over and over, 'stop the wedding!' Whose wedding were you trying to stop?"

Edith paled further, her skin almost white. She got up and opened the cupboard door, trying to escape the intense scrutiny of her daughter's gaze. Removing a cup and saucer and making her way back to the table, Edith deflected the question.

"Oh, gosh Jenny, that was over a year ago! I can't remember a thing about that dream."

"Well, how about the date? September 9th, 1962? Does that mean anything to you?"

Edith set the cup and saucer on the table and looked up at her daughter. She was speechless. Her eyes grew wide and her mouth opened slightly but nothing came out. Jenny didn't back down; like a detective trying to solve a mystery, she fired two more questions at her mother, one after the other.

"And do you recall that phone number you wrote on the kitchen pad just a day or so before that date? Remember? I asked you specifically about it. And then there was that mysterious brown bag on the kitchen table... what was in it, Mom?"

Edith had to sit down again. "What on earth are you talking about? Good God, Jenny, I can't remember what I did over a year ago. Why didn't you ask me at the time?"

"I did! You never showed me what was in the bag and when I asked you about the number on the phone pad you said you were doodling while talking to your friend and that it was nothing!"

"Jenny!" Edith suddenly exploded, "I don't understand what you are getting at and why these things are suddenly so important to you! And what does your wedding have to do with September the 9th, 1962, for God's sake?"

Jenny pulled out a chair from the kitchen table opposite her mother and sat down. Her gaze didn't leave her mother for even a split second. "I just learned yesterday, Mom, that September 9th, 1962 was the day Henry Pederson back in Regina got married."

Right at that moment the kettle on the stove began to whistle. Edith, feeling cornered and defensive, walked over to the counter and snuffed out the flame on the stove. The high pitched whistle immediately subsided. Edith quickly turned on her daughter.

"I don't know what you are making of all this or if you are suggesting that I had something to do with this boy's wedding. If that is what you are implying, that is the most ridiculous thing I have ever heard!"

Jenny stood up, not backing down, "That is exactly what I am implying, Mom! I don't understand how this all comes together, but I think you and Daddy were somehow involved in keeping me and Henry apart... and... I just want to understand it all."

At that, Jenny sank back down onto her chair. Tears surfaced and spilled over onto her cheeks. "Mom, please tell me what happened. Please."

Edith knew it was now or never. Should she tell Jenny the whole, ugly truth? What good would come of that? Wouldn't the truth just upset everything? Jenny was engaged... Henry was married... There was simply no point in opening that old can of worms.

"Jenny, I don't know what to say. Somehow all these things that happened are just coincidences. I don't know what you want me to say..."

Edith, playing innocent, shrugged and shook her head from side to side with an overall look that indicated she didn't have a clue what her daughter was ranting about. Walking back to her daughter at the table, Edith sat down next to her and gently placed her hand on top of Jenny's.

"Jenny, my dear child, I'm as puzzled as you are about this. I am happy you found out Henry is married. That should give you some kind of closure..."

"But it's not the kind of closure that I want, Mom. I still love him and I hoped above all hope that he would be unattached. Everything could be different! If only I would have known a year or so ago.

"I'm just so confused about everything, Mom... I love James, but it's not the same." Jenny looked up at her mother and gazed directly into her eyes. "Please Mom, is there anything I should know? Were you somehow involved in Henry's wedding?"

Edith began to pale again; the sorrow in her daughter's pleading eyes finally broke through her hard exterior. She squeezed Jenny's cold, trembling hands and said, "Sweetheart, I'm so sorry I can't be of more help to you. Somehow you are trying to blame your father and me for things not turning out to your liking, for Henry choosing to marry someone else. Jenny, the boy had years to write or phone you, but did he? Are we now responsible for that, too?"

Jenny looked at her mother through tear-filled eyes and then fell into her mom's arms. "I just love Henry so much. I don't know why I can't get over him."

As she stroked her daughters shoulder, a look of relief filled Edith's eyes and a soothing calm washed over her.

CHAPTER THIRTEEN

MIXED EMOTIONS RAN through Julean's body as she lay in bed next to her husband. On the one hand she was excited that she was pregnant again and on the other hand she was terrified that something bad might happen again. She knew she wouldn't be able to handle it and it would certainly devastate their marriage. Although she hadn't yet told Hank, Julean had known for many weeks that she was with child. Missing her period in September was the first sign, the visit to the doctor two weeks later confirmed it, and now the growing bulge in her tummy was the visible proof that the Pedersons would soon bring into the world another little human being.

With tears in her eyes, Julean prayed:

Oh heavenly Father in Your divine plan You manifested unlimited power within me to bring forth from nothingness another human soul and giving it to the care of Hank and me. Oh thank you Father for this joy and privilege to share in your creative might. I offer the care of this child to Your heavenly guardian angel that already is here to watch over and protect our little infant's life.

And little Benjamin, I know you are here in spirit as well, helping your mommy bring into the world your brother or sister. You already know who is growing in my tummy, don't you? I can see you rejoicing already and how, in spirit, you will both be playing together. Keep ever watchful of your Mom and Dad, we need your protection and love. Together through God's gift of creation we brought you into the world. I only knew you briefly, but in those few hours that I nursed you and held you in my arms, my dear sweet Benjamin, I loved you for a life time. You will never leave my heart.

Julean tugged at her rosary. Henry had rolled over part of it and he moaned as she freed the beads from underneath his body. The crystal beads felt warm. She hoped her husband would not dream this night. This was their night, the night she had decided to tell him that soon he would be a father once more. Tonight, Julean was not willing to share him with Jenny.

Dearest Mary, as an expectant mother, I seek your maternal love not only for help and guidance but also in my other trials with Hank. You know the doubts and anxieties that entangle and besiege me. You know of my sufferings. But I pray that like you, Mary, I may turn all these sorrows into joy! You overcame anxiety by trusting in God and accepting His will. Please speak to Jesus now on our behalf that we may bear the trials of our marriage in joy and happiness.

"I know you are not asleep honey," Henry softly whispered into the dark. Julean turned her head sharply towards Henry, startled out of her wits.

"Hank! I thought you were asleep. You must have read my mind because I was just about to wake you with my feminine wiles and tell you something."

Henry turned over and gazed at his wife in the dim light of the moon entering the room. The gleam of her white teeth bared her smile but it was the sheen that the moonlight caught on her wet cheeks that revealed she had been crying.

"Honey, I know what you're going to tell me. I've known it for a couple of weeks already. Don't you know how much I love you and notice even the slightest change in that sexy body of yours?"

Henry took hold of Julean's hand and moved it over the little bulge of her tummy that she had rubbed only minutes ago, then leaned in closer until their warm lips touched. The kiss was tender, soft and filled with love and joy. They made love and fell asleep in each other's arms.

"It's too bad we changed the nursery room back to what it was before," said Henry as he gazed into their study room the next morning.

"Yes, in retrospect, it is too bad. But it was so considerate of you and Helen to remove everything, Hank. Besides, we won't be in the suite much longer after the baby is born as we will be heading back to Regina."

"Yeah, that's right. You said sometime in May, didn't you?"

"Yes, the doctor thinks the end of May or perhaps early June. My gosh, that will just be around exam time."

"Julean, you're so smart, you could pass without even studying. I'm the one that has to slave away for every mark I get."

Julean poked Henry on the shoulder. "That's not true at all, Hank! You're at the top of your class."

"Living with you is contagious; some of your smarts just rubbed off, you know."

"Seriously though, I'm glad the baby will be born when we are here in Saskatoon. I really like our doctor and I definitely don't want to change doctors like last time. I sometimes think that might have been the problem."

"Well, it might have, but we'll never know. Father has always told me there is a purpose in everything and perhaps some day we will understand it all. In the meantime, I am going to guard you with my life."

Henry turned to Julean and embraced her. He looked into her sparkling eyes and said exactly what she wanted to hear. "I love you with all my heart, sweetheart, and don't let that pretty little head worry one bit. We are going to have a beautiful, healthy baby that will keep us awake at all hours and drive us nuts!"

During the Christmas recess, everyone back in Regina was so happy to see the young couple come home. When they told their families that Julean was expecting again, Henry's parents were thrilled while Dr. Carter thought it would have been better to wait at least another year.

Julean and Henry stayed at her parents' place. Although it was uncomfortable for Henry, they made the best of it. Henry tried to follow his mentor's advice and accept the old boy as he was and simply ignore some of the snide comments he made on occasion. Most times it was easier said than done. Henry knew a showdown was eminent but didn't want to start something at this time.

Any of the discomfort they experienced at the Carter's home was quickly dispelled at the Pederson residence. Mary cooked an amazing Christmas dinner and as everyone tried to squeeze around the table in the small kitchen for the meal, chairs butted together and slid in and out until all were seated comfortably. Right after Father said grace, he proceeded to share a blessing derived from the crowded kitchen.

"Mary, your kitchen always brings people together in such a close and loving way. I sometimes feel our church is too large and only encourages separation. I visualize a smaller church that huddles us closer together like a herd of lambs and me as the shepherd nudging them with my cane to get closer yet."

"Hold on, David, you better start eating before the food gets too cold or the rest of us eat it all up!" Bill was too hungry to sit through any more of Father Engelmann's pontificating!

"Yes, yes, of course. Pass the potatoes please, and make sure our Julean has a little extra. She has another mouth to feed."

The dinner lasted for over an hour. Each had something to share and the conversation flowed as easily as the wine that was served with dinner. Mary brought up that a woman named Tammy had called, asking if Henry was married and how to reach Henry and Julean. The kitchen fell momentarily silent as they tried to think of who that might have been and hoped that she would contact them in Saskatoon.

Mary had baked an apple pie, a lemon meringue pie and also some Christmas cake. None of them were ready to have desert but agreed that later in the evening they might be able to manage a very small slice. Slowly, after the table had been cleared, everyone retired to the living room.

In the corner sat Father Engelmann in Bill's leather arm chair. Bill always insisted that after Father was ordained as a priest he should have the chair usually reserved for the head of the house. Father knew it didn't do any good to argue with Bill's kind hospitality and took it without making a fuss. Everyone else naturally surrounded Father almost as if he were about to give one of his teachings. Mary and Bill took the loveseat and Henry sat on the other arm chair with Julean comfortably seated on the soft floor rug, resting against his legs. There was a warm glow from the Christmas tree in front of the living room window and a peaceful silence descended as everyone relaxed with full bellies and hearts.

After some time, Julean softly broke the silence with a question directed to Father that surprised all of them.

"Father, how do I come to trust in Jesus with all of my heart?"

Everyone, including Henry, looked at Julean. The direct and personal way his wife posed the question immediately touched Henry's heart. Henry admired her boldness. He rested his hand on her shoulder and almost imperceptibly squeezed it. Everyone's eyes now focused to Father for an answer.

Remembering all too well their conversation in the confessional booth three months ago, Father leaned toward Julean and spoke directly to her just as softly, as if they were the only two people in the room.

"My child, not everyone has the understanding and insight to see that the question you ask is the key to inner peace and fullness of life. You show great courage to come forth and personally ask how to trust in the Lord. Jesus will place a special blessing in your heart for such a question makes Him very happy!"

Leaning back in the comfortable chair, Father continued in a louder voice, addressing everyone in the room, just as he would in a sermon. As usual, he had everyone's undivided attention.

"Yes, how do we trust in Jesus? It would be easy for me to say that you must simply and firmly believe in Him. But just *defining trust* doesn't give you a full understanding or appreciation of what it really means *to trust.*

"For instance, seeing how God actually works in our lives through His divine providence is a tremendous faith and trust builder. Once we become aware of His mighty workings, we often stand in awe of it all. Even the very question you have raised, Julean, and us talking about it is God's sovereignty at work. He is drawing us to come to Him and to trust Him with our lives."

Father shifted again in his chair, this time pulling himself forward so he was perched on the edge of his seat with his elbows resting on the armrests as if he was about to address a classroom of school children.

Henry dared not shift in his chair lest he jeopardize losing the warmth of Julean's body against his feet and knees. He was looking forward to seeing how Father was going to weave a lesson on trusting the Lord into a story that would take everyone by surprise.

"When I was in Gravelbourg studying at the seminary," Father began, "I would go for long walks early in the morning. One morning, as I strolled down the dirt road on the outskirts of the small town, watching the sun rise, a truck approached and stopped at my side. A young man in his forties introduced himself as Tom Harris. He was a pilot who did crop spraying for many of the local farmers in the area. During our conversation I could feel the love this man had for flying. When I told him that I had never flown in an airplane he invited me to go up with him that very morning.

"I decided to skip my breakfast and take him up on his offer. Now Julean, the moment I did so, I felt fear. Perhaps it was the fear of the unknown, or the potential physical danger of leaving the solid ground to fly like a bird, or perhaps it was the uncertainty of the stranger beside me. I don't know; maybe it was all of these things.

"As we drove to the hanger where his plane was, my fear intensified. I could no longer hear his talking or even participate in conversation, my mind was so preoccupied with the impending flight I was about to take. Tom was a young man, but surely he was experienced enough that I would be safe in his hands. I could see him smiling as he chattered. His ease and friendly face gave me a feeling of confidence in the man. I was beginning to trust in him and I had to, because up there I was going to be completely dependent upon his skill and know-how to fly that plane. I became fully aware that when I got into that plane, I was putting my life in this man's hands.

"When we got to the hanger and I saw the small plane with one propeller, fear once again gripped me and concern settled into my heart. 'Is there only one engine on that plane?' I asked him.

"'Yes,' he replied. And then sensing my concern he quickly added, 'Oh, if the engine conks out I can still land this thing anywhere. Happened to me before. But everything is all checked out Father.' And then he said the words that instilled my faith, '*trust me Father,* I will look after you!'

"My heart instantly settled down. I yielded to the man's skill and self confidence. When we boarded the two seater plane his photo and license on the dash board further reassured me.

"You see Julean, each time I got to know this man a little more, I trusted in him more. We were establishing a relationship that over a short amount of time settled my fears.

"But this is not the end of the story, the real example of trust that I want to share with you is yet to come."

"Well, that's a pretty good example so far, Father," said Henry

"Yeah, you made it pretty clear to me," echoed Bill.

Julean stirred and got up. "My legs are starting to fall asleep."

Henry opened his arms and said, "Come."

Julean sat on his lap, put one arm around his neck and settled her back against Henry's chest. Henry noticed tears sitting just on the edge of her eyelids. If she blinked everyone would know she was crying. Father was touching her heart like he was all of theirs.

Seeing everyone was settled, Father began again. "When Tom fired up the engine, exhilaration spread through me. My heart nearly jumped into my mouth. I patted his knee and reminded him to be careful. He just laughed and once again he said those faith building words, '*Trust me,* Father, and enjoy the ride!'

"He hit the throttle and the engine roared louder while the plane started to move forward. I could no longer get out. I wanted to tell him to stop and that I would come back another day but we were already speeding down the rough, grassy runway. We bounced and the plane shook so hard I thought surely it would fall apart and I would land somewhere near Regina!

"And then, just like that, he moved his controls ever so slightly and like a bird taking flight, so too did the plane! I swallowed my heart lest it leave my chest altogether! My stomach was halfway between the ground and the plane. The earth fell away at my side and so quickly everything below grew smaller.

"Up she went, even higher! I remember him faintly asking how I felt but I could not respond. The adrenalin shot through my veins like lightning and an excitement the likes of which I had never experienced before overtook me. I was flying! I felt like one of the hawks I saw every day soaring in the prairie sky. How wonderful it felt to have wings and to feel free in the heavens!

"All at once I realized that my excitement was pure and no longer tinged with fear. I was relaxing in the hands of the man next to me and enjoying the moment. *I was trusting him because we had established a relationship.* But then, what happened next I shall never forget.

"He pointed to the instruments on the dash and said, 'that's the heart of the plane, Father. I have to put all of my trust into those gauges at all times. Without them Father, I would be lost. Oh, I can get along without them for awhile when the sun is shining and everything is going fine, but when I hit the clouds or nightfall comes or a storm comes my way, without these instruments as my guide, my life would surely end in a fatal crash.'

"And that's the way it is with us, Julean. In the same way Tom had to put his trust in the instruments to guide him when he cannot see, we too must trust in the Lord. Not just when things are going well, clear skies ahead, but in all kinds of stormy weather. *Especially* when we are blinded by the dark clouds that can quickly surround us in life.

"Mr. Harris made a point of knowing everything about how those instruments worked, not just haphazardly by skimming an instructional pamphlet. No! He made a thorough and complete study of them because he knew his life depended upon them. He placed his trust in those instruments to get him safely to his destination.

"And so it is with us. To trust Jesus with all our hearts, Julean, we must get to know Him through reading the Bible faithfully and consistently every day. By meditating on His word, saying grace before each meal, going to church, receiving Him in Holy Communion and having discussions like this. The more we know Him, the more He becomes a part of our character and the more we trust in Him and rely on Him.

"In the same way I put my trust in Tom to keep me safe in the sky and the same way Tom put his trust in his instruments, we must put our trust in God. Little by little as I learned more about Tom and his skills, I trusted him more. So too it will be with the Lord. Little by little as we come to learn more of Jesus, we will be willing to put Him into the cockpit and be the Pilot of our lives. He will direct it, He will keep us safe, He will take us safely to our eternal destination. There will be days when He fills your heart to such overflowing you will feel the same exhilaration as I did when the plane lifted into the air and flew like a bird!

"As you see how God's divine providence works, your trust will increase. You will see the futility of trying to fly the plane without Him; the foolishness in not accepting an all-knowing, powerful God that brings love and healing into every circumstance, no matter how bad or impossible it may be, and turns it into good!

"Julean, you have a good heart. Your desire to trust Jesus warms my heart as it does the good Lords. Go to Him, get to know Him inside and out and He will give you the strength and grace to trust Him, to obey and follow His teachings and commandments. Soon your thoughts, words and deeds will become more and more like His as you rely on him to fly your plane. You will only soar higher and higher in a cloudless sky.

"All too often, many of us put God only into our Sunday schedule, if at all. It is impossible to know God this way and to establish a trusting relationship with Him. I cannot stress enough the importance of beginning each day by praying, reading the Bible and meditating on one's life. If we want happiness, inner peace, joy and purpose in life then God, the Father, Son and the Holy Spirit must be ever present in our hearts. We must allow Him to be at the controls; have faith in Him to be the Pilots of our lives just like Tom said to me Julean, 'trust me Father and enjoy the ride!'"

As Father concluded with Proverbs, 3:5-6, Henry and the others joined in and together they recited:

"Trust in the Lord with all thine heart, and lean not unto thine own understanding. In all your ways acknowledge Him and He will make straight your paths."

They all looked at each other with love and laughed.

CHAPTER FOURTEEN

D URING THE BREAK between Christmas and New Years, Jenny and her mother went to Toronto to check out wedding gowns just as Edith had promised. After much traipsing through fancy bridal boutiques and trying on of elaborate, expensive gowns, they both agreed that the Ottawa shops were nicer and the gown they had put on hold there was the one for Jenny. But, mother and daughter did have fun together. Probably the most fun they'd had in years.

On New Year's Eve after a late dinner in their hotel restaurant, Edith wasted no time opening the champagne once they returned to their room. By the time the magic hour rolled around to welcome in the New Year, Edith was more than tipsy.

"Happy New Year, Jenny!" Edith exclaimed several times as she twirled her daughter around and around the spacious suite. And if that weren't enough, Edith climbed onto one of the beds and began jumping up and down like an excited six year old.

"I am so happy for my daughter! Soon she will be married and I shall be the proud grandma of a grandchild!"

"Mom, be careful! You're going to hurt yourself!" Jenny shrieked as her mother jumped from one bed to the other. On her last hop, her mom leveled out on the way down and bounced several times on the soft bed until she came to a stop.

"Oh, Jenny," her mother puffed, "I haven't done that for over forty years!"

Overcome with laughter, Jenny collapsed on the other ruffled twin bed. "You know Mom, after all these years it seems like I really don't know you. I wish we could have done this more often. Why don't we do a vacation together during the Spring semester break?" Jenny turned over towards her mother, but Edith was already fast asleep.

Jenny got up and got a blanket from the closet and covered her mother with it. She gazed down at her mom and softly whispered, "There's a side of you Mom, that I wish I knew." Jenny bent over and kissed her mother tenderly on the cheek. "Happy New Year, Mom… I love you."

When they returned to Ottawa, her mother started making arrangements for the future couple's honeymoon. Jenny and James had decided to leave the day after their wedding for a week in Hawaii. Planning her daughter's honeymoon was not exactly what Edith had in mind when she took over planning the wedding, but with Jenny so busy at university and James with the business, Edith happily obliged. So far she had done almost all of the phoning and planning in consultation with James' mother who seemed very busy and happy to let Edith take care of most of it. From the catering, cars, photographer, head table, speeches, horse-drawn carriage from the church to the hotel… it would be a fairy tale wedding indeed.

Even though the wedding was in the spring of 1965, well over a year away, Edith liked to make certain everything was well attended to. The sooner the better! She couldn't believe the couple still hadn't picked out invitations. Back in September Jenny had tried to arrange a meeting with James' mother to go over the samples, but Mrs. Hamilton had been unable to fit it into her schedule until the new year. Edith would feel so much better once the invitations were finalized and sent out.

On Saturday, January 4, a car came to pick Jenny up and transport her to Mr. and Mrs. Hamilton's estate.

"Good afternoon Miss Sarsky, please do come in. Mrs. Hamilton is expecting you."

"Hi Andrew. My, that's a beautiful drive through the grounds."

"The landscaping is well attended to, Ma'am."

In breezed James' mother who swept across the large foyer and placed a kiss on Jenny's cheek. "Good afternoon Marjorie, it's so nice to see you again."

"Hello, Mrs. Hamilton. Thank you for making the time to see me."

"May I take your package, Miss Sarsky?"

"No, that's fine Andrew. These are wedding invitations I wish to show Mrs. Hamilton."

"Very well. Shall I prepare refreshments, Mrs. Hamilton?"

"Not at the moment Andrew, thank you. You may go now."

"Very well, Ma'am."

Mrs. Hamilton led Jenny into the living room. "Well, come sit beside me and let's look at what you have. I must say, your mother is a real organizer."

Jenny opened the package and took out three samples of invitation cards and handed them to Mrs. Hamilton.

"Oh my, they all look lovely Marjorie; I think any of them would do." Placing the three invitations side by side on the coffee table, Mrs. Hamilton kindly inquired, "Is there one in particular that you and your mother like?"

"Well, I do like the one that describes how James and I met. This one, with the white embossed horse and carriage image," Jenny pointed it out. "It sort of tells a story…"

"Yes, I read how you met in the cafeteria at Springview High and how you were taken by this flamboyant Italian-looking young man."

Jenny laughed. "Even in high school James looked like he was out of some fashion magazine. Not your typical high school student, that's for certain."

"Well, Marjorie, you're a vision of loveliness, yourself. We're certainly pleased that James found a good match in you. Tell me, Marjorie, has James told you much of his background?"

"Not really, Mrs. Hamilton. James doesn't talk much about

himself, although he loves to go on and on about whatever business coup he's working on. Perhaps you can tell me a little about the man I intend to marry."

"As a matter of fact, Marjorie, I had the same thing in mind. I think it would be helpful for you to understand our family history. You have a loving heart, Marjorie, something which we are not used to. I suspect you may be the best thing that has ever happened to James."

Jenny gazed at Mrs. Hamilton with a puzzled look. *What a strange thing to say. They're not used to a loving heart? What does she mean?*

"Yes… yes, I would love to know more about the family, please tell me." Jenny had been trying to find a good moment to tell her soon-to-be mother-in-law that she preferred the name Jenny to Marjorie, but suddenly, that didn't seem very important. This was the first time Jenny had been alone with James' mother and she was anxious to bond with her and learn more about her future husband.

"Excuse me for a moment Marjorie, I think our meeting is going to take longer than I had predicted. Perhaps I will tell Andrew to prepare some refreshments for us. Would you like juice or tea, or is there something else you desire?"

"Tea would be lovely, Mrs. Hamilton."

When Mrs. Hamilton returned, she sat on the couch opposite the coffee table. Looking Jenny directly in the eyes, she took a deep breath and then began.

"Some of what I have to tell you may be shocking, Marjorie, and I hope it doesn't scare you off from marrying our son. I think it is important for you to know these things about James so you may have a deeper understanding of some of his… idiosyncrasies, shall we say."

Andrew appeared at the entrance to the living room, "May I serve the tea now, Ma'am?"

"Yes, that will be fine. Thank you, Andrew."

Andrew placed the silver tray on the coffee table. On it rested two exquisite cups and saucers, sterling silver sugar and cream containers, a platter of assorted dainties and two petite, silver spoons with the family crest at the end of each. The pot of tea in the centre of the tray was hidden behind a floral-embroidered tea pot warmer. Andrew placed a teaspoon on each saucer and then placed one cup and saucer on one side of the table for Jenny and a set on the other side for Mrs. Hamilton. He removed the cloth warmer and poured tea in each cup. He was about to ask if either wanted cream when Mrs. Hamilton impatiently interrupted his service.

"Thank you, that will be all Andrew. We shall look after ourselves now. You needn't return."

"Very well, Ma'am."

As Andrew quietly exited the room, Mrs. Hamilton reached for her teacup and saucer and invited Marjorie to do the same.

"Help yourself to cream and sugar, and a dainty, if you wish."

Mrs. Hamilton stirred her cup of tea after adding cream to it and then continued to sit on the edge of the sofa, holding the cup and saucer in her lap. She took a sip of tea and then said, "I am not James' mother."

Jenny was about to take a sip of tea, but stopped just before it reached her lips. "You're not?"

"No. James' mother died just before his fifth birthday. She crashed her car into a tree just a mile or so from here. When they did the autopsy, they discovered that she had been highly inebriated and never should have been driving in the first place. In fact, James' mother was an alcoholic and her license should have been suspended two years prior when she had had a minor accident with the boys in the car. In any case, both James and his brother were shielded from…"

Jenny gasped, spilling some of the tea from her cup into the saucer. "Did you say James' *brother*?"

"So, James didn't tell you about his twin brother, either? I should have known he wouldn't."

Jenny was stunned. "His twin brother…?"

"I see this may take the rest of the afternoon." Mrs. Hamilton took another sip of tea and then set it back on the table before making herself more comfortable on the couch, resting her hands on her lap.

Jenny just sat there wide-eyed and flabbergasted. She still hadn't taken a sip of her tea. Realizing she was still holding the cup and saucer in her hands, just under her chin, she set the tea on the table and remained on the edge of the sofa waiting for Mrs. Hamilton to disclose the rest of her amazing story.

"Yes, James and Anthony were twins, fraternal, not identical. James was the much more aggressive of the two. The unfortunate circumstances of their mother's death was never properly explained to the boys; it was covered over with a blanket of secrecy. Both boys felt completely abandoned by her and I suspect James, in particular, must have felt that she had never loved him at all. Leena was intoxicated most of the time and constantly shooed those boys away from her. For most of their young lives, they were either by themselves or tended to by the working staff.

"To make matters worse, the boys were further neglected by their father, who of course is now my husband. Unfortunately, there isn't an ounce of affection in the man. Don't get me wrong, Mr. Hamilton is a fine man, Marjorie. He is simply incapable of showing love or affection because it is alien to him for reasons that I am not going to get into today. Suffice it to say, those two young boys grew up believing they were unlovable because their parents were incapable of loving. Mr. Hamilton was never home, all he knew was business and that is all he still knows today."

Mrs. Hamilton reached forward, picked up the cup and took another sip of tea, then returned it to the saucer. "You haven't touched your tea Marjorie, shall I ask Andrew to get you a fresh cup? It must be cold by now."

"No, no, that's fine, Mrs. Hamilton. I am so enthralled by what you are telling me. Please continue."

"Well, as I said, James was the more aggressive of the two boys and the only way he could get his father's attention was to take an interest in his father's business. While Anthony remained in his room reading, James would go to the office with his father. By the time James was eight years old, he and his father would have conversations like two adult business men. James soon learned that he could have his father's undivided attention, if not his unconditional love, if he excelled in business. This was James' way of overcoming his insecurity and to this day, he continually tries to prove himself.

"Both James and Anthony were very brilliant and gifted boys. They were also intensely competitive, but James won out at every turn, especially when it came to vying for their father's attention; James was possessive of his father. As a result Anthony became more and more reclusive, always the odd man out, while James and Mr. Hamilton forged a stronger and stronger bond. Unfortunately, shortly after his fourteenth birthday, Anthony took his own life."

Jenny gasped and put her hand to her mouth. She was speechless and just shook her head from side to side in disbelief.

Mrs. Hamilton watched Jenny's reaction, curious to see what she would say next.

"How did Anthony die?" Jenny wanted to know.

"He took Mr. Hamilton's hand gun from the night table in his bedroom and went outside to the highly wooded area in the far corner of the estate. Unbeknownst to any of the family, even James, Anthony had built a shelter of sorts between four trees. He must have found some refuge there, I suppose. Anyway, he was finally discovered by police dogs after he had been missing for some time. He had shot himself through the side of his head. The coroner suspected that he didn't die instantly, but bled to death, poor thing. Several books lay beside him. He had left a note, but the rain had completely washed the ink away by the time they found him."

Mrs. Hamilton stopped and studied Jenny.

"Are you okay with this Marjorie? I can stop and continue another day."

Jenny was rather horrified by the story and filled with profound empathy for James and Anthony, but she couldn't stop now.

"No, no, please go on. This is so sad and revealing... But what I know of James already makes much more sense, especially why he is so business focused but what about his—?"

"His proneness to cleanliness?" Mrs. Hamilton perceptively cut in.

Jenny nodded; it was one of the things she had always wondered about. His near compulsive obsession with hygiene concerned her.

"Yes, James likes everything very clean and new and you may have noticed he washes his hands excessively. I don't profess to be a psychiatrist, but I believe it has to do with his mother and brother Anthony. I'm sure James believes he is responsible for his mother's abandonment of him and Anthony and for his brother's suicide. On both accounts, James is plagued by unresolved guilt. I think his idiosyncrasies are an attempt to cleanse himself, to be clean and free of the matter in some way; to absolve himself."

Everything Mrs. Hamilton was saying revealed so much to Jenny about the man she was going to marry: *his competitiveness, possessiveness and jealousy... and to lose his mother and his twin brother... Poor James! He must be burdened with such pain and guilt over it all.*

"It is very good of you to share this with me, Mrs. Hamilton. Like I said earlier, it explains so much about James..."

Jenny paused for only a moment and then asked, "Tell me, Mrs. Hamilton, how did you come into the picture? When did you become part of the family?"

"Well, I was married to a man named Leonard who was one of Mr. Hamilton's business associates. They had known each other for years and Leonard was the closest thing to a friend that Mr. Hamilton knew. A few months after Anthony died, my Leonard passed away as well from a heart attack. Jim – Mr. Hamilton – remained a loyal friend and looked out for me. After a while, we began to have dinner together occasionally or go as a couple to social events. About eight years ago, we decided to marry.

"Our relationship is more of a businesslike arrangement than a marriage but I must say, we are very good friends and keep each other good company. I also think it's helped James to relate to a mother figure and I genuinely give my love to both men at every turn."

Mrs. Hamilton paused and studied Jenny intently as if to make certain she should say what she was about to further disclose. She nodded and then continued.

"Ever since James met you, Marjorie, I have noticed a change for the better in him. If you can see past some of his ways, he is a fine man like his father. Unfortunately, both men believe the void in their lives can be filled with wealth and mergers and takeovers. They shun the very thing they need, Marjorie; the power and healing of love would sweep through them like a breath of fresh air if they would allow it."

Mrs. Hamilton sat back in the couch and took a deep breath.

"Well, my dear, that's about the size of it. Welcome to the Hamilton family."

CHAPTER FIFTEEN

THE MINUTE JENNY arrived back home she called Tammy.

"Oh, I'm glad you called, Jenny! Robbie and I just finished making solid arrangements with my mom to come to Ottawa this spring! We felt so bad we had to cancel our plans to visit last summer, we decided to book well in advance this time and nothing will prevent us from coming."

"Oh, Tammy! That's wonderful news. You must have been reading my mind. Just the other day I was thinking how nice it would be if Chloe could spend some time with me on the estate early in June so she could see the Monarch butterflies return. It is so exciting, Tammy, and she could see the wonder of how a butterfly reproduces itself. It would be so interesting and educational for her. And since it will be the last summer I spend at the estate before I get married I would just love to see a little angel in the garden chasing the butterflies!"

Tammy knew that part of Jenny's motivation was to picture her own little Camilla running after the Monarchs, as well.

"Our booking is for the first week in June, so it just might work out perfectly."

"Yes, it sounds perfect!"

"So, what else is new, Jen? Let me guess. You and James decided to elope and you're finally a married woman at last."

"He does keep suggesting that, Tammy, but it's all talk. He could never find the time to squeeze it in. I consider myself fortunate that I get to see him even once a month."

"Hmm, I don't know Jen… I certainly couldn't devote myself to some guy who's never around. There's still time to think this over, you know. It's too bad your prairie sweetheart is taken. Are you getting over that?"

"I think I have accepted it, Tammy. I knew even before you phoned Henry's mom that he had found another…"

"Yeah, the star of the east told you!"

"Oh Tammy, there is nothing that you don't know of me."

"That's what true friends are Jenny, so close their hearts at times beat as one."

"Just you saying that reminds me of one of the notes I had given to Henry via the gate post on my front yard… 'If you were a heart, I'd want mine to beat inside yours.'"

"My God, Jen. You two really had it in for each other. What was the gate post thing all about?" Tammy wanted to know.

"When we couldn't see each other during the week, we would write little notes to one another and place them behind our fence gate post and secure them there with an elastic. I used to read them all the time until one day Dad caught me and suggested I put them away in a sealed envelope. I followed his advice and I still have them in my room."

Tammy was silent; she saw that her friend's love for Henry still ran so deep. "It's too bad you didn't see a shooting star and make a wish for the return of your first love. That sure worked for me!"

"I know, and I did! Do you remember the night James and I came over with the dollhouse for Chloe? Well that very same night, when James took me home, I walked out into the back yard and saw a shooting star streak across the sky!"

"Did you make your wish, Jenny?"

"Instantly, I wished for the kiss that he never gave to me the night I departed from Regina. Remember? I told you, just as Henry was about to place his lips on mine, my mother tore me loose from his embrace. Oh Tammy, I can still feel the warmth of his breath and the taste of his lips…"

"Wow …"

"I thought for sure my wish would come true."

"Well, sometimes it takes a long time for a wish to come true, Jen. And here's the thing, remember when I wished to the shooting star for Robbie to come back and ask me to marry him? Well, as the months went on I had forgotten all about that wish. Then, the very night he called to ask me to be his wife, I was out sitting on the patio when the sky filled with a bunch of shooting stars. It was such a festive, spectacular array of dazzling colour. It immediately reminded me of the wish I had made. The very next thing, my mom calls me and says that Robbie is on the phone, very anxious to talk to me."

"That's wonderful Tammy, but…"

"What I am saying Jen, is that you have to keep hoping and if you ever see a kaleidoscope of shooting stars in the sky, be prepared for your wish to come true!"

"But Tammy, it's all too late for that; Henry has married another and besides… I have decided to marry James for certain. In fact, I just had the most revealing conversation with his stepmother today which I couldn't wait to share with you. She told me all about his childhood and… oh, Tammy, it gave me such insight into why James is the way he is. It explained so much. I think I finally understand all of it. I think that was just what I needed to hear for my heart to really open to him."

"Really? And it doesn't give you any second thoughts?'

"On one hand, perhaps. But on the other hand, I see so clearly how James needs me. His stepmother actually told me she thinks James needs 'true love' and that if I were up to the challenge, then I was the woman who could break through the iron curtain surrounding his heart and ignite that spark of love."

"Wow, Jenny. That's a pretty daunting challenge…"

"Tammy, besides Henry, James is the only other man I've known that appeals to me. I know the love that Henry and I shared together is different than what I have with James, but I guess that's the way it should be."

"Well, I'll keep you in my prayers, Jenny. Just make sure you keep asking your guardian angel for help and wisdom to do what is best."

"I know you're concerned, Tammy, but knowing now what I do of James, the feelings of abandonment that would attack his heart if I were to leave him would be devastating. I love him enough to help him find his true self... the real James I already love."

IN MARCH, JAMES invited Jenny to his parent's home for Sunday dinner. His dad wanted to discuss a very important business matter with her.

"What kind of a business matter?"

"Oh, it has to do with some kind of an agreement he wants you to sign. He discussed it with me briefly at the office, last week. Some kind of an inter-spousal agreement. He said our lawyers urged him to discuss this with you. It's nothing to worry about and I'd sooner have him explain it to you."

"Well, I'll be depending on you to clarify anything if needed. I'm not good at understanding legal and financial matters."

"Don't worry, Marjorie, I'll look after you."

Jenny cringed inwardly at the use of her first name.

JENNY KNEW MR. James Hamilton senior was in his late sixties but she found him to look much older. For several years he had been struggling with prostrate cancer while running the business at full tilt. The doctors had not been able to bring the cancer fully under control, so he was to retire in the fall, much against his own will. That's when James would take over for his father entirely, but in the meantime, Mr. Hamilton had started to turn more of the business over to James.

From what she had learned of Mr. Hamilton's non-affectionate nature, Jenny found him to be surprisingly warm and friendly.

"It's good to see you, Marjorie," said Mr. Hamilton when the couple arrived in the drawing room. Jenny had asked James' parents numerous times to use her middle name, to no avail.

"Yes, we were so glad you could come," added Mrs. Hamilton. "I've had so many nice chats with your mother the past several weeks. She is quite an organizer. I'm so fortunate to have her assistance. Normally, I would have turned the wedding planning over to our staff to arrange, but your mother gets such joy out of doing it."

"Yes, Mom loves to organize and plan and she is so excited about the wedding. It's nice to see you both, too, Mr. and Mrs. Hamilton."

"Come now, Marjorie, let's cut that formality. Life's too short. Why not call us Nancy and Jim? It will make us feel young again and besides, soon you will be our daughter-in-law. So, how about it?"

"All right."

"Come in and have a seat," Nancy said. "Andrew will be in momentarily to take your order for a drink."

No sooner had they all taken their seats than Andrew, dressed in a tuxedo, entered and took Jenny's request for a martini. Before Andrew left the room, he stoked the fire and placed another log in the fireplace.

All through dinner, Jenny waited on tenterhooks for the topic of the legal agreement to come up, but then realized that it probably wasn't proper etiquette to discuss business over a meal. After dinner, they returned to the drawing room for a liqueur. Once settled, Jim finally brought it up.

"Marjorie, there is a very important matter our legal department asked me to discuss with you. First, you must understand that James is part owner of the corporation and will inherit all of the shares when I pass on. Since you and James will marry next spring, as his wife you will assume half ownership."

Gesturing to James and Nancy, he continued, "We don't have a problem with that, Jenny, rather it's our lawyers and shareholders that do. Of course we expect you and James will have marital success. However, should you two come to a disagreement that cannot be resolved, leading to the demise of your marriage, then it could have serious and far reaching consequences for the company."

"What do you mean Mr.—er—Jim? I'm sure James and I will be happy forever. And, I'm not sure how could I possibly affect your company?" Jenny glanced at James and they exchanged smiles.

"As I mentioned, Marjorie, the consummation of your marriage to our son entitles you to part ownership. Let's suppose, hypothetically, that you and James should come to hate each other. The worst case scenario that could come out of this would be for you, Jenny, to take your half of the company."

"But, I would never do that—"

"That may be, but our lawyers and shareholders say we can't take that chance. You could take half the company and sell it. That would ruin the organization we have so carefully constructed over the years. Or, hypothetically, you might take your share of the company and try to run it yourself, and if not run efficiently, it could quickly go bankrupt. Many possible devastating outcomes could arise. Do you understand what we are getting at here?"

"Yes, I think so. What is it you want me to do?"

"Our lawyers have drawn up an agreement that they would like you to sign. In doing so, you will relinquish any and all rights to the company. In other words, Marjorie, anything to do with the company is completely out of the domain of your marriage between you and our son, James. This excludes anything you and James own apart from the company. Those assets will be shared completely."

"I see," said Jenny, her forehead crinkling.

"The company is just trying to protect itself, Jennifer," James interjected. "We don't want you to take this personally."

"Yes," Jim concurred. "It is just a precautionary measure that most, if not all big businesses or companies require. Now, my lawyers made a duplicate copy of the Inter-Spousal Agreement for you. You can take it home and read it, or take it to your lawyer if you wish."

Jim handed Jenny the contract. She read the first few paragraphs, but soon found the legal language confusing. It gave her a headache and the words quickly blurred in front of her eyes.

"I must admit I really don't understand all this legal terminology. I did, however, understand what you said, Jim. And I do agree with the necessity for our marriage to be separate from your business. So, if this is what all this means…" Jenny said, waving the agreement toward Mr. Hamilton, "well then, I'm prepared to sign this right now."

"I'm very happy you understand and feel that way, Marjorie. However, I would like you to think on it overnight. James will bring you into the office tomorrow and we can have it properly signed and witnessed by one of our legal advisors. And, should you have any more queries, they will be happy to answer them for you at that time."

The next day Jenny signed away all ownership and interest to James and his father's company.

Chapter Sixteen

When they returned to Saskatoon after the Christmas break for their final semester of university, Julean began following the advice of Father Engelmann as to how to trust more in Jesus. She would rise at five in the morning, say her rosary, read the Bible, silently pray and then meditate. All in all, Julean spent about thirty five minutes preparing for the day.

Following his wife's lead, Henry started to get up early as well. Sometimes they would pray together in the living room and at other times, they chose to be by themselves. One of them would go into the study room and close the door while the other stayed in the living room. The prayer that was first and foremost of both their minds was for a normal delivery and a healthy baby.

One morning while Henry was alone during his prayer time he discovered a way to keep his mind off Jenny. He soon noticed it seemed to be working during his waking hours as well as when he slept. His dreams were no longer filled with scenes of his first love, and overall Henry felt more relaxed, less guilty, and less anxious. In the days that followed Julean noticed the change in her husband.

"You seem so cheerful lately, Hank. Is it just the anticipation of our new little baby coming or is there something else I should know?"

"Just living with you, Julean, gives me great happiness and joy!"

Touched by his sincerity, Julean approached Henry and, as had been the case with their first child, they both pushed out their buttocks slightly in order that their warm eager lips could meet each other.

Without disclosing his real motive, Henry said, "Well, you know how much I hate taking medicine. So, I figured out during my prayer time how to lessen the feeling of anxiety I have by memorizing Bible passages."

"Oh, what do you mean?"

"About a month ago I read the scriptural passage in Father Engelmann's Bible that he had underlined, John 15:7: 'If you abide in me, and my words abide in you, you shall ask what you will, and it shall be done unto you.' And then I recalled what Mr. Engelmann used to tell me, that no two thoughts can occupy your mind at the same time. He also said that what you feed into your mind usually comes out, that essentially you *are* what you *think*. So if I put thoughts of worry about the baby, about you, or your dad or school into my mind all day, then I will get those same worrisome thoughts out of my mind and be overflowing with anxiety. It's so obvious and yet in the quiet of the morning, this revelation hit me like a lightning bolt: that if His words abide in me, then I should feel more relaxed. Once I started, I found it did."

"So how do you think differently to keep fear or worrisome thoughts out of your mind?"

"Great question, my dear," Henry said, smiling a little smugly. "And John 15:7 gives the answer; He tells exactly what to do. If I abide in Jesus and His words abide in me, I can ask him what I want and he will do it for me. Every morning, I memorize a passage from the Bible and repeat it in my mind throughout the day, especially if a troublesome thought jumps into my head.

"Now that I'm aware of this and actively living it, I'm noticing how many powerful passages there are that confirm it. Listen to this one that Father also had underlined: 'Thou wilt keep him in perfect peace, whose mind is stayed on thee.' Or listen to what Psalm 34:4 has to say, 'I sought the Lord, and He heard me, and delivered me from all my fears.'

"The one I memorized this morning I find very soothing: 'My

peace I leave with you, my peace I give unto you: not as the world giveth, give I unto you. Let not your heart be troubled, neither let it be afraid.' Or, 'Be anxious for nothing, but in everything by prayer and supplication, with thanksgiving, let your requests be made known to God; and the peace of God, which surpasses all understanding, will guard your hearts and minds through Christ Jesus.'"

In sharing his excitement over his discovery, Henry stood in the middle of their small living room, reciting the Biblical passages as if he were a priest addressing his congregation. Julean laughed and clapped her hands delightedly at Henry's joyful display.

"That's wonderful, Hank! I'm so glad you've found a way to feel more peace in your heart and mind."

Henry plopped down on the couch next to Julean and put his arm around her. Julean continued, "I must admit that since praying in the morning, I feel more at peace as well. I especially love saying the rosary and talking to Mary. As the mother of Jesus who understands all the concerns that surround a pregnancy and giving birth, she's giving me so much comfort and peace of mind."

"I'm so happy to hear that, honey. I just know that this time around, everything is going to be fine," Henry hugged Julean reassuringly.

"Oh, that reminds me, Helen was down yesterday afternoon when you were at class. She wanted to know if I needed any of the baby stuff for the nursery again. I told her not this time as we would be going back to Regina as soon as the baby was born. She said if we wanted them, we could take her baby carriage and crib with us as they no longer need them."

"We're so blessed to have such a generous landlady!"

"I know. I told her I would really appreciate the items but that we would pay her for them. Of course, she refused and insisted we accept them as her gift."

"That's great, honey."

"Helen is so nice to talk to; I'm going to miss her when we leave. She told me yesterday she had two miscarriages, one of which happened in her fifth month of pregnancy. It's good to talk to someone who has been through what we went through. And of course, they went on to have four healthy children with no complications. Let's just hope for the same!"

"Yeah, I'm sure everything will be just perfect, and the doctor said at your last checkup the baby's head is down, so everything is looking good, honey." Henry patted her tummy, then spoke directly to the baby inside, "Now you stay in that position, and that's an order!"

Julean smiled, "Well, we better get ready and have breakfast or I'll be late for class."

FINAL EXAMS STARTED during the last week of April, and by Friday, May 8, Henry and Julean were officially finished with their studies. Exhausted from an intense few weeks of studying until all hours of the night, they slept in until almost noon, when they were awakened by the dog upstairs that usually barked when the mail was delivered. Henry, who had been expecting his placement letter, jumped out of bed and ran to check the mailbox. Sure enough, they had cause to celebrate!

Although Henry had been given a glowing report of his teaching abilities from a Superintendent from the Regina Public School Board who had observed him during his teaching practicum earlier in the new year, today's letter was what Henry really wanted to receive. He would be teaching science and physics at Campbell Collegiate in the south end of Regina. It was a new school that had opened just two years ago with an enrollment of around 400 students.

Henry and Julean were elated. With the guarantee of a steady job backing them, they now hoped that the bank would give them a loan to buy their first home. The south end of Regina was developing quickly and they thought it would be a great area to live and raise their family, so close to Henry's work.

By the middle of May there was still no sign of the baby coming and Julean's stretch marks were getting larger by the day. Henry still couldn't get over how it was possible for skin to stretch that much. He was very protective of his dear wife and pretty much took over the household duties and made all the meals. With exams over, Henry enjoyed keeping busy around the house, giving his wife time to rest and relax before the big day.

While Henry paced the floor, polished the baby carriage, and stopped occasionally to look outside the basement window, Julean either read or prayed. With each passing day and still no sign of labour, however, she began to fear that maybe the doctor had made a mistake in his calculations.

Could he have been off by a month?

The one thing she dreaded most was for the baby to be born on July 6, the day that Henry had his most vivid dreams of Jenny. Julean didn't want there to be any confusion for Henry, while awake or asleep, that it was she and she alone that gave this child to him.

As the days ticked on, Henry started to get more nervous as well. The forces of worry over the impending birth and another possible tragic delivery hung heavy in the air. To his dismay, the nausea he had experienced during Julean's last pregnancy and back in 1957 when he thought Jenny might be pregnant, returned. Just as troublesome, his dreams of Jenny began to increase again despite the scriptural passages that Henry ran repeatedly in his mind. However, if it had not been for this ongoing practice, Henry thought he surely would have exploded with anxiety.

By May 22, two weeks after they had written their last exam, the tension in the small suite had built up like a keg of dynamite on a very short fuse ready to detonate. Julean was nearing exhaustion and Henry's nerves were at the breaking point. He just had to go out go for a walk and get some fresh air or do anything other than stay inside a second longer. He knew it wasn't good for either of them to be immersed in their anticipatory anxiety any longer.

"Okay, honey, come on, let's take a drive."

"You go ahead Hank, I think I'll fix a pot of tea and take a nice warm bath. I'm so sweaty and exhausted. I think that will revive me a bit."

Henry came to Julean, kissed her cheeks and said, "Okay, I'll see you in a bit sweetheart. I love you."

When Henry came home, Julean was still in the bath. He went in, carrying the pot of tea, and refilled her cup that was resting on the ledge of the tub. She was submerged in warm water with bubble bath up to her neck. The sweet perfumed suds carried a soothing aroma. With her eyes closed, Henry smiled at how peaceful Julean looked and marveled at how the dome of her belly stuck up out of the water surrounded by bubbling suds as if to crown the treasure hidden below.

"I bought some Chinese food. I'll set it out on the table."

Julean just nodded, then whispered, "Thanks Honey, be out in a bit."

When Julean entered the kitchen she was delighted by the romantic setting. Any of the lingering tension she had felt that day was instantly released.

There, on the small kitchen table, Henry had draped two checkered patterned tea towels to hide most of the Arborite surface. A candle stuck to a saucer was burning in the centre and next to it, one long stemmed red rose stood in a water glass, threatening to fall out. Several boxes filled with Chinese food were crowded together on either side of the candle, each with a stainless steel spoon sticking out, picking up dull hints of light from the flickering candle.

At that moment, not even the finest restaurant in the world with all its fine linen, fancy bone china dishes and sterling silver cutlery could compare to the setting Henry had laid out before her.

"Oh, Hank, this is beautiful and just what I needed."

"Me, too, honey. I'm sorry I've been a bit of a nervous wreck this past week."

Tears filled both their eyes as they approached each other and tenderly kissed as best they could. Henry turned Julean around and cuddled against her back bringing his hands to the front of her tummy. She rested her hands on top of his and together they rubbed their little angel. Gently they swayed to the music in an atmosphere laden with peace and heavenly bliss.

After a romantic dinner, the young coupled retired and had a peaceful nights sleep.

Perhaps it was this message of love streaming through their bodies that woke the child in Julean's womb. Saturday morning, just as Henry was opening his eyes, Julean turned to him, her face as radiant as the sun steaming in their window, and exclaimed, "I'm feeling contractions, Hank! I think this is it."

"Really, Julean!? 'Oh, this is the day the Lord hath made! I shall be glad and rejoice in it!'" Henry bounded out of the bed and nearly fell over in his hurry to pull on his pants.

Julean laughed while Henry hopped around on one leg. "The pain is beautiful, Hank! I offer it up to dear Mary... Oh, Hank, I think you're right, today we shall rejoice!"

Taking no chances, Henry took Julean to the University Hospital early Saturday afternoon even though the contractions were still far apart. He didn't want to leave anything to chance. They sat in the waiting room for close to two hours before an orderly came with a wheelchair and took Julean away. Another couple of hours went by before a nurse got Henry and brought him to Julean's room where she was labouring slowly but steadily.

Around ten that evening, Dr. McCall showed up. He checked in on his patient to find her husband at her side, her hand in his. The doctor told them it might still be a little while but not to worry, everything looked fine and well. Henry stayed right by Julean while the contractions began coming with more frequency and intensity. As the clock struck midnight, Julean was finally scooted into the delivery room.

Henry was mixed with joy and anxiety. "Please, dear Jesus," he whispered, "keep my Julean safe and let her deliver a healthy baby. Oh, guardian angel, protect them... please."

An orderly led Henry to a vinyl covered chair in the waiting room, but instead of sitting in it, he turned to face it and unabashedly knelt down on the linoleum floor, his elbows resting on the edge of the cushioned seat and continued to pray.

Just minutes later, at precisely twelve-ten on the Sabbath, a blessed day, May 24, 1964 Jeremiah Pederson was born.

CHAPTER SEVENTEEN

A S SHE DID every year on May 24, Jenny baked her daughter a small cake, sang Happy Birthday and then blew out the candles while making a wish for Camilla's happiness and safety. This year, unbelievably, there were seven candles on the cake.

Jenny was amazed at how quickly the years had passed. She wasn't sure why, but this year, as May 24th approached, Jenny felt there was an added significance to the day. And she was sure it had something to do with Henry…

But what?

Jenny shook her head and cut herself a piece of cake. This was her private celebration with her daughter and she didn't want to entertain any more distracting thoughts of her long-lost first love.

"Jenny?" Edith called from upstairs. "Can you put the kettle on for tea, honey? I'll be down in five minutes." Jenny quickly cleared the kitchen of any hint of a birthday party as she knew it would upset her mom, filled the tea kettle with water and placed it on the stove.

"Kettle's on, mom!" She shouted upstairs, then she fixed herself an iced tea, tucked her diary under her arm and headed out to her gazebo.

Looking around the grounds at all the flower buds just waiting to burst open, Jenny was filled with excitement and anticipation.

As they had promised, Tammy, Robbie and Chloe were heading up to Ottawa next month and Jenny would have two whole days to herself with her little angel! How Jenny wished it were Camilla that she would watch chasing after butterflies in the garden, but Chloe was certainly the next best thing.

IT WAS THE first week in June and the timing for Chloe's visit to Ottawa and Jenny's home couldn't have been more perfect. The Monarchs had been returning from their winter hibernation in Mexico for several weeks now. Eggs were already laid on the leaves of the milkweed plants, many had progressed to the caterpillar stage, and just that morning Jenny had seen several chrysalis hanging from twigs. The shell of one was so clear she was able to see the Monarch inside; it could hatch at any time.

It was a beautiful morning in Jenny's garden. The loveliness and aroma of the flowers and herbs was intoxicating. Jenny couldn't have been happier. She was surrounded by all the things she loved. Just for a moment she allowed herself to dwell on the fantasy that the little girl skipping and hopping in front of her down the paving stone path was her Camilla. *Someday*, she whispered, *someday we will be together.*

Just watching Chloe so full of life, so carefree and loved, filled Jenny's eyes with tears. How close Tammy had come to aborting this beautiful, precious girl... *Oh, thank you dear guardian angel, for protecting Tammy and for giving her the strength and wisdom to do the right thing.*

"Chloe, come quick I want to show you something!"

Chloe ran to Jenny and took her outstretched hand. "Come, Angel, I want to show you how butterflies are born."

Jenny led Chloe to the milkweed plant she had been studying earlier. When they got to the plant in question, Jenny went down on her knees and invited Chloe to come closer and crouch down as well.

"See Chloe? See the tiny white egg on the underside of the leaf?" Jenny pointed right to it with her finger. "That egg was laid by one of the female butterflies in the garden and look there..."

Jenny pointed again to a caterpillar eating the leaf it was born on.

"That worm, Chloe, is called a caterpillar and it came from the tiny egg. It eats all the time and grows very quickly." Chloe's eyes grew wide as she reached out to touch the caterpillar with her forefinger. As it squirmed, she quickly withdrew her hand and giggled.

"Robins eat worms, Auntie Jen. This one better hide!"

"Yes, that's right Chloe. Birds eat worms but they won't eat this one because the milkweed plant it is eating contains poison that will make the bird sick. Birds soon learn to stay away from this caterpillar. That's the way they protect themselves, otherwise there would hardly be any butterflies."

Jenny was amazed at how transfixed Chloe was with what she was saying, seemingly following every word.

"But come over here Chloe, I want to show you what the caterpillar does next and how it becomes the beautiful Monarch butterfly."

Jenny took Chloe's hand and led her to a small shrub and they both crouched down again.

"Look Chloe, the caterpillar stuck its behind on that twig and then grew a cocoon around itself. That's called a pupa."

"That sounds like a poop, Auntie Jen." Chloe giggled.

Jenny chuckled too, "Yes, it does sound like a poop-a."

"Does the caterpillar die, Auntie Jen?" Chloe wanted to know. Jenny was surprised by the question the four year old child asked.

"It looks like it has Chloe, but something very amazing is happening inside. That big long caterpillar inside that cocoon is transforming into a butterfly with wings." Jenny pointed to another twig that also held a pupa that was ready to hatch. "See this pupa Chloe? This one is ready to hatch. You can almost see inside... See the wings of the butterfly!? That is what the caterpillar turns into. Pretty soon, maybe even later today, we can see the shell open and the butterfly come out. Isn't that amazing, Chloe, how the caterpillar turns into a beautiful Monarch butterfly?"

"It's like a little miracle. Mommy talks about miracles happening every day."

Once again Jenny was shocked by Chloe's understanding. She picked up the little girl and gave her a big hug. "Yes, Chloe, it is a miracle!"

Just then, Carlos came walking down the path.

"Good morning *Señorita* Jenny. I see you have a little visitor today."

"Hi Carlos. I bet you don't recognize her, but this is the little baby you saw here three summers ago with her mom, Tammy."

Carlos bent down and poked his finger into Chloe's chest, "Oh my! So you are the beautiful *niña pequeña* that I saw? How you have grown into such a beautiful young lady! And what is your name?"

"Chloe! We were just looking at baby butterflies in their poop-a. It's a miracle how caterpillars turn into a butterfly."

Carlos looked at Jenny, surprised as well by the insightful statement of such a small child.

"*Si*, yes, it is a miracle indeed, my little one."

Chloe took Carlos' hand and led him to a twig where she had seen the dangling chrysalis.

"Ah yes, *la crisalida*," Carlos said in Spanish.

"No, that's the poop-a!" Chloe looked at Jenny for confirmation.

"Yes, Chloe, that is the pupa but it can also be called a chrysalis, like Carlos said. But show him the butterfly inside."

"Look Carlos," Chloe pointed with her finger just like Jenny had shown her. "See the wings! Auntie Jen said it may even hatch today."

"*Si*, any time it will come. Keep checking, little one, and you will see the miracle, as you say!"

Just then, at that very moment, the transparent shell began to crack open.

"Ah, look at that! It's beginning to hatch, Chloe."

Both Jenny and Chloe crouched down again and looked closer as the crack widened. Chloe's eyes were open wide and filled with wonder. They all remained entranced while the butterfly inside moved and twisted as it laboured to free itself.

"Well, I must get back to work. It was a pleasure meeting you, *Señorita* Chloe." Carlos extended his hand and Chloe's soft tiny hand was quickly lost inside of his.

"I was wondering Carlos, would Teresa be able to come over tomorrow and spend the night? Chloe is going to be here tomorrow as well and I would like her to meet your granddaughter.

Perhaps the girls could have a pajama party?"

"Unfortunately, Miss Jenny, Teresa has gone to spend two weeks with her grandmother. Upon her return she would be delighted to visit with you."

"Okay, that would be lovely, Carlos. We will do it another time."

"Keep watching the butterfly, Chloe, it soon will be out of its cocoon. The wings will be damp so it won't fly right away but as soon as they dry, it will flap its wings and like an angel, it will fly into the sky."

Carlos waved as he left. The girls waved back.

The next day, after much arm twisting, Jenny got James to agree to join her and Chloe for lunch. The girls were going shopping downtown, not too far from where James' company's office building was situated. Jenny was so happy that her fiancé was able to join them.

James rushed in ten minutes late. The girls had just ordered as Jenny didn't know if James would show up or not.

"Sorry Jen," James said, as he kissed her cheek and sat down. "Hi Chloe, do you remember me? You sure have grown since I saw you last."

"That was a long time ago, Uncle James. You set up the doll house for me."

"Yeah, that's right! You have a good memory, Chloe."

"Have you got a kiss for Uncle James, Chloe?"

Chloe looked at Jenny and then at James and smirked, "I don't know, do you want one, Uncle James?"

"Boy, playing hard to get already…" James bent towards Chloe as she slipped off her chair and went to James and kissed him on the cheek. Jenny was elated at the sight!

"Excuse me sir, I noticed you joined the party of two, would you care to see a menu?"

"Ah, what is your special of the day?"

The waiter rattled off three items that all sounded good.

"The half sandwich with soup will be fine," James ordered. Then without missing a beat, he turned to Jenny. "So did you buy out the stores yet?"

"We were in Fanny's but didn't see that special outfit just yet. We'll look some more after lunch. So, busy at work today?"

"Yeah, Dad and I are just closing a major order from Hong Kong…"

"We saw butterflies hatching from their poop-a, Uncle James."

"Did you now? What kind was it, do you know?"

"Yes, it's a Monarch butterfly with big black and orange wings."

"Well, isn't that something…" James was at a loss as to what else to say. Chloe filled the silence.

"Do you know how to tell a boy butterfly from a girl butterfly, Uncle James?"

"No, I can't say I do, Chloe. Do you know?"

"Yes, it's easy. Auntie Jen showed me this morning. The boy has two black spots on its back wings!"

Jenny's heart fluttered as she watched James and Chloe talk. It was at moments like this when Jenny felt she could risk telling James of her little girl, Camilla. What a relief it would be to let him know what happened. *Would he understand and accept what happened? Why am I afraid to tell him…?*

Just then their orders came. Jenny had a salmon salad on a bed of butter lettuce and Chloe had a grilled cheese sandwich and a glass of chocolate milk.

"It's so nice to have lunch with you James, we must do this more often," Jenny gushed.

"Yeah, it's just so hard to get away. We need to hire two more executives. The three we have can't seem to handle the business Dad and I are generating."

"You have to find a balance, James. I recall only one day last year when you took a morning off to play tennis."

"Well…" Then trying to change the subject James asked, "How long is Tammy going to be in town for?"

"Just until Saturday and then they're going back to Houston. Tammy and I are going out on Friday and Chloe will spend the day with her grandmother."

"Is everything fine…?" interrupted the waiter.

James looked up at the young man, "Yeah, yeah…" And continued to eat his sandwich in a hurry.

"My gosh, James, slow down, you just got here."

"I promised Dad I would be back by one..." James checked his watch, "It's almost ten to..."

Jenny gazed at the man she would marry in less than a year. His pursuit of wealth and prestige, his desire to climb ever higher, was so strong. *He misses the life that is right in front of him.* There was simply no time for anything else lest he lose his competitive edge over others, including his father. If only James could understand that even if he were stripped of everything he now so ardently strove for, he would still be loved the same, thought Jenny.

But aloud, all she said was, "Oh James, you and that company... I just don't know..."

Chapter Eighteen

ONCE MOMMY AND baby were ready to travel, Henry and Julean packed up their belongings and left Saskatoon for Regina. Everyone welcomed the happy couple home. All were so relieved that the baby boy was healthy and that there had been no complications during the delivery like the last time. Even Julean's father, Dr. Carter, seemed to escape from his sour disposition upon seeing his first grandson. He even co-signed the bank loan for Henry to purchase their very first home in Whitmore Park in the burgeoning south end of Regina. As they had hoped, their new home was within walking distance to the collegiate where Henry would be teaching. Julean and Henry were overjoyed how everything was turning out so well.

What was even more surprising was that the Carters agreed to attend Jeremiah's baptism at the ten o'clock Mass at St. Mary's church on Sunday July 5. Julean had asked Father for another day in June; however Father was completely booked during that month. She was just thankful that the baptism didn't fall on the day that had always troubled her the most, July 6.

FATHER HAD REQUESTED that Henry and his family, as well as Julean and her family, come to the church fifteen minutes before the baptismal ceremony and get settled in before the Mass started.

He made a big fuss when Julean lifted the white crochet blanket for Father Engelmann to peek at Jeremy.

"Oh *mein gutter Gott*, what a beautiful little angel." He blessed the infant with his thumb and did the same on Julean's forehead, as well. Before Julean turned to properly introduce her parents to Father, he broke out with a huge smile and extended both his hands.

"Welcome to our church! I can easily see that you are the parents of our lovely Julean! What a fine, well-raised girl she is. Henry is indeed a very fortunate man." Father extended his hand to Dr. Carter. "Life is too short for formalities, I am David Engelmann. Call me David or Father or whatever you wish."

Dr. Carter took Father's hand, "I'm Dr. — or rather, Jack Carter and this is my wife, Vera."

Father covered Vera's extended hand with both of his. "I am so pleased to meet you. How proud both of you must be to have a new grandson in the family."

Mrs. Carter's eyes sparkled, "Yes, Jack and I are thrilled, Father."

"I must prepare for the Mass, but I would like to personally escort you to the front of the church so you have a good view of the baptismal ceremony." Father extended his elbow towards Mrs. Carter. She slipped her hand through the crook of his bent arm and Father led the entourage down the long aisle of the crowded church.

After a short homily, Father began the ceremony by explaining the meaning and purpose of Baptism and a quote from John 3:5:

"'Unless a man be born again of water and the Spirit, he cannot enter into the kingdom of God.' The sacrament of Baptism was instituted by Christ at His own Baptism by St. John the Baptist in the river Jordan. At His Ascension, He commanded his Apostles: Go therefore make disciples of all nations, baptizing them in the name of the Father, and of the Son, and of the Holy Ghost.'"

It looked as if Father was going to say more but had second thoughts. "This morning, my friends, I would like to incorporate the rest of my homily with the actual baptism. I would ask Henry and Julean to come forth with their new son along with the godparents, Henry's Aunt Darlene and Uncle Ron."

When everyone was situated around the baptismal fountain, Father began the ceremony. Following Father's instructions, Julean uncovered Jeremy's head and placed him over the basin. Darlene and Ron also reached forward and each placed a hand on Jeremy to show their acceptance of the spiritual relationship. Father then proceeded to pour baptismal water three times upon Jeremiah's head in the form of the cross while at the same time pronouncing the words, "Jeremiah, I baptize thee in the name of the Father and of the Son and of the Holy Ghost."

Jeremy naturally cried when he felt the cool water on his forehead. Julean leaned down, and dried the baby's head quickly and gently while Father announced, "Jeremiah is now washed free from original sin and sanctifying grace was imparted into his soul. Jeremiah is now a Christian, a child of God, with a right to the kingdom of heaven."

Father then smudged the crown of Jeremiah's head with chrism to show that he was now anointed of God and Darlene and Ron were given a lit candle to hold on behalf of Jeremiah to denote the light of the Holy Ghost received.

Finally, Father placed a white garment upon the newly baptized infant and said, "This is to show that Jeremiah's soul is now spotless, filled with God's grace and the light of the Holy Ghost!" Then turning to the congregation he introduced the newly anointed Jeremiah Pederson. "Let us welcome our new soldier for Christ." Father began to clap and the parishioners quickly joined in.

After the baptismal party returned to their pews, Father went back to the pulpit and said, "My dear friends, just think, the child that you see before you at this moment is spotless. Isn't that a beautiful word, *spotless*? Imagine being clean of all sin and filled with God's grace and the light of the Holy Spirit, just like Jesus when he walked the earth.

"Imagine, my brothers and sisters in Christ, if we could transport Jeremiah into the future. Imagine if this child were suddenly an adult who had bypassed all the slings and arrows of life that cover over this state of sanctity. My friends, what you would see is a man filled totally with love. He would love as Jesus loves. He would accept others as they are, he would be free of judgment and condemnation of others because he is free of this in his heart! He would love unconditionally just as the Lord loves.

"Imagine what it would be like to be totally and completely at peace, where your heart only knows forgiveness and only sees the oneness of us all in God, the Creator of heaven and earth.

"Just think," and here Father raised his hands and swept his right arm across the parishioners before him, "you and I, yes, all of us, were like this spotless soul when we, too, were baptized. But over the years, we became stained with sin and the ways of the world.

"You can see how important it is for Henry and Julean, the parents of this beautiful child, to do everything they can so that Jeremiah maintains his pure, loving heart as he grows and be prepared for the slings and arrows of this world! I have said this before, children learn by imitation and identification. Monkey see, monkey do. We need godly parents, and grandparents and great grandparents who have placed Jesus at the centre, so they can be examples of loving Christians for their children.

"Remember, we are what our heart is full of. If we see the bad in others, are critical, judgmental and fault finding, that is a reflection of ourselves and we weaken ourselves and the other; we stagnate and lack inner peace. If we see the good in others, and treat and accept them accordingly, then that is what our heart is full of and we both grow. And more so, it makes us feel good and we are proud of who we are! We reap the benefits of a forgiving and accepting heart and are filled with joy!

"How blind and foolish it is when we fail to see and understand this. *It is love and love alone that heals the heart, gives us inner peace and advances the Kingdom of God.*

"We may not have the purity of heart of this infant, but no matter where we are in life we can begin again. Each new moment has the potential for a new lease on life. Our goal should be to become spotless again. The more we love our neighbour, the more we will love ourselves and the more we will be at peace and work with God for a better world."

Father paused and a broad smile grew on his kindly face, "The only persons you want to get even with are those that do something nice to you!"

Father winked and with eyes sparkling he concluded his homily.

"Invite Jesus into your heart now and let Him infuse you with grace and the strength of the Holy Spirit!

"Through Christ all things are possible!"

THE REST OF the year passed by in a blur for the new parents. With help from both their parents who purchased the living room chesterfield set and also the bedroom suite, they quickly settled into their new home. Julean's Aunt Netta and Uncle Jacob had given them an old Singer sewing machine, an antique rocking chair and a dining room set that Henry especially liked. Henry didn't realize how much he loved antique furniture. Perhaps it was the older furniture in Mr. Engelmann's house that first tweaked his interest.

They pulled all their wedding gifts out of storage from his parents' basement, bought a kitchen table and chairs and used Helen's crib in the nursery to round out the furnishings. It was sparse, but a good start.

Henry enjoyed spending the summer with Jeremy and Julean, fixing up the house, doing some landscaping, and taking long walks with Jeremy in the carriage, getting to know the neighbourhood, but by September he was ready to start his new job. Julean was a wonderful mother and absolutely adored Jeremy. She was glad she had decided not to work, to be a stay-at-home-mom. She couldn't imagine any work more important for a woman than raising a child.

Henry quickly got into the routine of teaching and within two weeks knew all of his student's names. His home room was a Grade 9 class of thirty bright kids with whom he quickly established a good rapport. He taught them science, but the real challenge were his Grade 11 and 12 physics classes. More often than not, as Henry strove to impart the lessons to his students in a simple and clear manner, he found himself using methods he had picked up from Mr. Engelmann.

By December, Jeremy was seven months old, but seemed much older. Henry and Julean decided to host Christmas dinner in their new home and everyone was surprised and impressed by the boy's size and coordination; he was clearly well ahead of other children his age. Although Father Engelmann was unable to attend, both Henry and Julean's parents as well as Julean's sister, Joyce, and her husband, Brandon, were all there, so it was a real houseful. Henry was thankful for the antique dining room table that extended to over six feet. All they needed were a few folding chairs which his dad brought over when he and Mary came.

It was Julean's first time cooking such a big meal for so many people, but everything turned out beautifully. Over dinner, Joyce made an announcement that when Brandon finished his internship at the University Hospital in Saskatoon, they were planning to move to Ottawa. Both Henry and Julean immediately stopped eating and looked at each other, as if sharing in each other thoughts: *That's where Jenny lives!* They both quickly looked back down and kept on eating, totally unaware of Brandon's explanation as to why he wanted to move there.

Neither Henry or Julean had thought, worried or dreamed about Jenny in months. It seemed that with Jeremy's birth and healthy development, their new house and Henry's teaching job, everything had fallen perfectly into place. The young couple was happier than ever, but it was clear by the way Joyce's news hit each of them that the issue of Henry's first love was not far below the surface.

A few days later, while Henry was chasing after Jeremy who had crawled behind the Christmas tree, the light glistening off an ornament hanging towards the back of the tree caught his eye. *It was a pewter angel!* It wasn't quite the same shape as the one he had bought Jenny, but it immediately flooded his mind with memories of the pewter angel he had sent as a Christmas present to her in his last letter back in 1956! That was twice now in one week Henry was reminded of Jenny.

What was going on?

That night, Henry asked Julean about the pewter angel.

"Hey honey, I just noticed the pewter angel ornament you hung on the tree. It's so beautiful, where did you get it?"

"Oh, I'm so glad you finally spotted it, Hank! I got it for you as a surprise and I've been dying to tell you the story of how I found it."

"I'm all ears!" Henry's interest was definitely piqued.

"It was the most coincidental thing. I saw it hanging on a tree in the display window of Eaton's just a few weeks ago when I was downtown shopping."

"Really? But I've never seen you window shop, you're always in and out of a store so quickly…"

"I know! I wasn't paying any attention to the window display. I had stopped to drop some change into the Salvation Army Pot and when I looked up at the Santa to wish him a Merry Christmas, my eye was drawn to this ornament on the tree in the window behind him. It almost seemed to be glowing. I stepped over to have a closer look and saw that it was a pewter angel. It was so pretty and reminded me of the guardian angel prayer that you taught me back when we were courting. I just had to go into Eaton's and get it."

"Julean, that's incredible…" Henry was almost at a loss for words. What Julean was describing was nearly identical to what had happened to him when he had spotted the pewter angel for Jenny. But what Julean said next ran goosebumps up and down his spine for it was *exactly* what had happened to him.

"Yes, but when I went into the store, I was told the ornament was only on display and not for sale. Just then, the manager appeared and so I asked him very nicely if I could purchase the pewter angel as a gift for my dear husband and he said yes! Once I paid him for it and left, I wanted to thank the Salvation Army Santa – after all, if it hadn't been for him jingling the bells in front of the Eaton's display window I never would have noticed the angel in the first place – but when I got out to the street, the Santa was gone and nowhere to be seen…"

CHAPTER NINETEEN

O N MAY 1, 1965, twenty nine days before James and Jenny's wedding, James Hamilton Sr. passed away with only his wife at his bedside. In the end, he had deteriorated rapidly and James Jr. quickly stepped in to assume full authority of their company. At the time of his father's death, James was too busy handling the latest acquisition to be by his side.

When James finally returned home at the end of the day, Jenny, who had been waiting for him in the Hamilton's drawing room most of the afternoon, tried to console her fiancé over the loss, thinking he'd be devastated. Instead, James seemed more interested and concerned about the acquisition than his dad's passing. It was clear that James felt he had to prove himself in the moment and it was a big one. If the deal went through, it would increase the corporation's interest in the manufacture of automobile components proven to increase fuel efficiency. The products were in demand by GM, Ford and Chrysler, and could result in a potential annual profit for the company of well over 1.2 billion dollars.

"Jenny, the meetings and talks have completely stalled. We are so close! We get one issue resolved and then one of their board members brings up another problem. And the Japanese custom is for the head of the families to deal directly with one another during the transactions, so with Dad gone the firm will only deal directly with me. What I am leading up to Jenny is that we may have to postpone the wedding or—"

"What!? You can't be serious, James! Everything is set to go. All the arrangements have been made. The cancellation fees would be horrendous."

"If this deal goes through, the costs to cancel the wedding would be a mere drop in the bucket. Hear me out, Marj."

Jenny was on the verge of screaming at him and even backing out of the wedding altogether, but she kept her mouth clamped shut.

"Dad has been working on this deal for over two years. I know he would want me to see this through. It would be a lasting legacy to his life's work and the highest tribute to a man who started with basically nothing and built a company into one of the largest and most successful in the world."

"The man is dead, James. How can he possibly appreciate what you or anyone else does?"

"It's for his honour, Jenny, a tribute to his success. Even Nancy said so this morning when I talked to her."

Jenny was surprised that James' mother had backed him up on this.

"Oh, James, I don't know. I was looking so forward to this wedding and our honeymoon—oh my gosh, what about our honeymoon? I suppose you want to cancel that, too?"

"Jenny, as soon as this deal goes through, I'll take you anywhere in the world. Please do this one thing for me… and Dad?"

Before Jenny could answer, James continued. "I was thinking Jenny, maybe we should elope, next weekend, and spend a day at the family cottage on Lake Michigan. Remember when we went there last summer and how much you enjoyed it? It's not Hawaii, but the view and the setting is so romantic…. You know, you yourself even suggested it when we first started to discuss marriage that we should elope, remember? You didn't think all the fuss, time and expense of a large wedding was worth it."

"Yes, I do remember, James, but it's different now. It's not just us that are involved. So many people are now included in these wedding plans and… it will break Mom's heart. She is looking forward to it so much and I'm sure a lot of other people are, too!"

"They'll all get over it, and maybe in the fall we can hold a huge reception and treat everyone at that time."

"The invitations have been sent, James! How on earth do you change that?"

"Easy, Jennifer. I'll get one of my staff workers to send out another note to all of the people we invited informing them that due to the death of my father the wedding has been postponed. And then, in a week or so, we can elope and get married like I said."

"If you are using the excuse of the death of your father to postpone the wedding, how can you justify eloping? It doesn't seem right and doesn't make sense."

"A lot of things in this world don't make sense. All I'm certain of right now is it's very important to me and to my father's legacy, to close this deal. I know my dad, and I know that he would want me to push on at all costs. I know it's hard for you to understand, but when you have worked so hard and long on something that's going to make you and the company a huge success, it's worth more than anything."

"More than our wedding? Our honeymoon? Our time together? When will this ever end? It's been like this ever since we first started dating..." Tears welled up in Jenny's eyes.

James took Jenny in his arms and stroked her back. "I promise, Jenny, I will never let this happen again. I will make it up to you and more. If you want, I'll go home with you and we can tell your mother together. I'm sure she will understand. She knows how things work in the business world."

"Yes, she knows, all right," Jenny sobbed. "The business world killed my father. Is it all really worth it?"

James shrugged. "We just have to do it. It's our life."

A week and a half later Jenny and James found themselves in the den of a Justice of the Peace. One of James' executives was his best man and Jenny's mother was her maid of honour. Edith had been terribly disappointed, if not furious, over the cancellation of the wedding. All that work, all that preparation, down the drain.

James' mother, Nancy, sat in the background, as uninvolved with the elopement as she had been with the planning. It was not at all what Jenny or her mother had envisioned.

Almost worst of all was that Jenny's best friend, Tammy, was not standing by her side. The two young women had spent countless hours discussing the engagement and the wedding and they had both been so looking forward to the opportunity to spend a few days together. Jenny didn't even have the heart to call Tammy to tell her about the elopement; she would break the news to her friend soon enough.

As Jenny stood in front of the Justice of the Peace she barely heard any of his words until James said, "I do."

"And you, Marjorie Jennifer Sarsky, do you take James Hamilton to be your lawful husband and promise to be true to him in good times and bad, in sickness and in health, for all the days of your life?"

Those words weighed on Jenny more than any other she had heard in all her life. In slow motion she turned to gaze into the eyes of her future husband. In the same way a person's life flashes before them at the moment of death, so too did all the reasons why she shouldn't marry James cloud her vision. Jenny felt her father's presence next to her so strongly, cautioning her as he did when he was alive: James' fetish towards cleanliness, his jealousy and possessive nature, his total preoccupation with the company, her loneliness and her fear of sharing her past with him… All thoughts closed in on Jenny as she stood mute and motionless.

James' eyes burned into hers… pleading with her. All her instincts pressing her to say 'NO!' weakened as her mother nudged her from behind. Nancy rustled in her chair. The concerned Justice of the Peace stepped closer as Jenny swooned. And then, just in the nick of time, James raised his arms and she fell into them.

"I do," she whispered. She nearly choked on the two little words that would seal her fate. Then raising her head to look James in the eye, believing as she had to, that he would change and be different when they got married, Jenny said more audibly, "I do."

James helped Jenny back on her feet and she stood a bit shakily on her own, facing him.

"By the power invested in me by the Government of Ontario, I now pronounce you man and wife." James sighed then took a deep breath and, as perspiration dripped from his forehead, he stepped into Jenny and kissed her. Again, Jenny faltered and almost fainted.

"Quick, Jenny, sit down. Are you okay?" James led Jenny to an empty chair. She looked pale and felt clammy.

"I'm fine… I think I forgot to eat today in all the rush…"

While everyone else enjoyed a glass of champagne, Jenny sipped a cold glass of water. Soon she felt well enough to leave with James on their honeymoon. It wasn't to James' cottage on the lake as he had initially proposed, as he had meetings early Monday morning that needed his immediate attention. The best he could do was two nights in the honeymoon suite at the Chateau Laurier not far from their downtown office suites.

Jenny woke up at six-thirty Monday morning to find James already gone. She rolled over, stared at the bare hotel wall and sobbed. After a hot breakfast delivered to the room and a shower, Jenny checked out of their room and went home. It was clear James wasn't returning to the hotel any time soon.

A week ago they had discussed living in his parent's mansion temporarily once they were married, but in all their haste to elope, they neglected to finalize it. Jenny's mother clearly wasn't expecting her.

"Surely the marriage isn't over already?"

"James was already gone when I woke up. He mentioned yesterday he had a very important meeting first thing this morning. We never got around to discussing where we were going to live. Isn't that silly?"

"Jenny, this is all happening so quickly. James is so involved with this merger or takeover or whatever it is that he is not thinking straight. I'm sure you two will have things sorted out by the end of the day."

The phone in the kitchen jangled.

"I bet that's your man, now."

Her mother picked up the phone. "Hello? Yes, she's here and feels homeless, I might add. About a half hour ago. Yes, just a moment. Jenny, it's James, he wants to speak to you."

"Hello, James…. Well, I didn't know what else to do. I'd sooner be here than at that hotel all day… you never left a note or anything. Yes, I see. Yes. Well that doesn't sound too bad. Is it ready to move into? Well, okay. I'll see you then. Bye."

Jenny plopped herself onto the sofa. Her mother wouldn't look away.

"Well?"

"He said he would pick me up in about two hours. Apparently there's another estate owned by his company that he's arranged for us to live in. James said he was going to surprise me with it later this afternoon. He already called the staff and they are ready and waiting for us."

"Well, that sounds nice, Jenny. See, he did have plans and things are looking better already."

"I think I will go out and break the news to Carlos; he and his wife were so looking forward to the wedding."

"It is the way things happen in life, *Señorita* Jenny. It was meant to be and we have to accept it and that is all there is to it."

"I'm so glad you're not upset."

"Of course not. So where are you and your husband going to be living? It would be a pleasant surprise if you told me here with your mother."

"No, I hate to leave our estate but James is taking me to the Greystone Estate. It's closer to where his work is."

"The Greystone Manor! That is where my friend Thomas is employed. He is the head gardener there, *Señorita*, the best in the city."

"How do you know him?"

"We met several years ago where we pick up the sod in the spring. He has taught me many things, especially about herbs in a garden. He is the most knowledgeable gardener I have ever met and has such an interesting background."

"Oh, tell me about him Carlos." Jenny wanted to know more.

"Thomas is from Jamaica. His father was a gardener who worked for an English Baron. When his employer died he gave the entire estate to Thomas' father. Thomas went to England to study law and became a lawyer but never forgot his roots. He just got tired of the corporate world, the daily competition, and the constant struggle to make more money than the other.

"One day, Thomas realized how much he missed the peace surrounding the garden that he and his father had worked on. His father always stressed how cooperative nature is. The plants, the trees, the shrubs all know they were made by the same Creator and all plants grow side by side in perfect peace, each doing what their Creator expects of them, living out their existence in peace."

"That's so interesting Carlos! So how did he get to Ottawa?"

"He said that one day he and his wife decided to move to Canada. When he arrived, instead of seeking employment with a law firm, he instead answered an ad for a head gardener position. I believe he has worked for the same family for years; perhaps it is your husband's family! Wouldn't that be something?"

"It certainly would be a coincidence, but I'm going to miss you so much, Carlos. You have been such a dear friend and we have shared so many heart filled conversations."

"*Si*, I shall miss you as well, *Señorita* Jenny. But this is not the end; I'm sure we shall see you when you visit…"

"And perhaps you, your wife and Teresa can visit me!"

"That would be our greatest pleasure."

CHAPTER TWENTY

J ENNY AND JAMES rode together to the estate. She was going to take her small Chevrolet and follow, but James told her to leave it behind and that she could pick out one of the five cars in the garage.

"What kind of cars are they, James? I like mine just fine."

"It's no longer suitable for you, Mrs. Hamilton. There are two BMW's. I think you'll like the blue convertible. There are also two Mercedes, and a Porsche."

The entrance to the estate was gated. An ornate metal archway covered the gates and had a silver sign which read:

WELCOME
TO
GREYSTONE MANOR

A man came out of a small structure when they pulled up and opened the steel gates. He nodded as James drove through.

Jenny noted that the pillars to which the gates were attached were made of grey stone. She suspected that the house would be too. As they made their way toward the house, it was like driving through a well manicured forest. It took a full five minutes before the trees gave way to an opening holding a breathtaking view of the mansion.

"My God, James, I thought you said this was smaller than your parents' house!"

Jenny couldn't take in the entire mansion at once. There seemed to be three main parts to the immense building: a two-storey middle portion that was framed with a three-storey structure attached at either end. There was a huge canopy that projected out from the central structure over the tiled steps as well as the paving stone driveway itself. It was supported with eight Gothic style pillars.

Jenny had never seen such wide steps before nor such elegant front doors framed with stained glass windows as they were, leading into the home.

The entire façade was made of grey stone including the huge fireplace chimney on the end wall of the north side and another chimney that was just visible at the back of the middle portion. Dark grey clay shingles covered the steep roofs on all of the structures. Intriguing small dormers with rounded peaks grew out of the sloped roofs almost at random here and there. They appeared like eyes keeping watch over the estate.

"My gosh, James, it will take me days to find my way around this incredible mansion."

James circled the huge fountain in the front yard and came to a stop under the canopy that led up to the front door. A groundskeeper was trimming a pyramidal cedar near the steps on the left side of the front door.

"Hello, Thomas," James greeted, as he stepped out of the car. "This is my new bride, Marjorie Hamilton."

Thomas quickly rose then bowed, "I'm pleased to meet you, Ma'am. Welcome to the Greystone Manor."

Jenny walked over and extended her hand, "Pleased to meet you, too, Thomas. I already know of you. Carlos, our groundskeeper, said that you are the best and most knowledgeable gardener he knows."

"Why thank you, Ma'am. And yes, Carlos and I are very good friends."

"I can't wait to see the garden. Carlos said it was magnificent! And by the way, please feel free to call me Jenny—"

"No, Thomas, it's Marjorie." James interrupted, then turned to Jenny. "It's always best to go by your legal name and I would prefer it from now on. I'll explain later."

Jenny frowned at James. He knew she didn't like being called Marjorie, and now that was the name *he* preferred her to use? They would have to discuss this later.

Upon entering the house, Jenny was shocked to see how modern the furniture inside was. It clearly reflected James' personality. Everything was ultramodern and highly polished with not a fingerprint or speck of dust marring the surfaces. It felt spacious and open, high-tech, and... cold.

Jenny much preferred the furniture at James' parents' home. It was elegant and each piece of furniture had a history. Jenny immediately pictured how the room would look with some warm antique furniture. It certainly would be more complimentary to the traditional stone exterior of the home, but she was certain James would never hear of it.

"So, what do you think?" The proud look on James' face indicated that he clearly loved what he had done with the place.

"Well, it's very contemporary, James. It's okay."

"Just okay? Really, Marjorie, postmodern is the way to go, not that old stuff Nancy and Jim have." Before Jenny could respond, James rambled on, "Wait till you see the back. If you think the grounds on your parents' estate are nice, they're nothing compared to this. I even had them build a gazebo for you."

Jenny perked up for the first time that day. "That sounds wonderful. Thank you, James. I can hardly wait to explore it in the morning. How long have you had this place for, anyway?"

"It's been the property of the company for years. I just had it furnished the way I wanted this past year and was keeping it as a surprise for you."

"Well you certainly did keep this a secret. I would never have imagined living in such an immense home."

"I'll have Matilda show you to your – or rather – *our* room. Dinner will be in an hour, everything has been looked after, my princess."

James wrapped his arms around Jenny and lunging deeply to

the side, dipped his bride across his body and kissed her dramatically. With equal flair, he straightened up and spun Jenny out and away from him. Jenny, stumbling slightly as he released her, gasped and looked at James, totally taken aback but just as delighted by her husband's uncharacteristic display of affection. He was clearly making an effort to impress her and seemed genuinely happy and excited to show her the new house.

Oh, just look at him! Jenny thought. *Maybe he's beginning to open up already. Maybe he just needed to get the wedding out of the way and now he's ready to allow my love into his heart... to allow himself to change.*

"Matilda? Where are you?" James' voice echoed down the spacious corridor.

A short, black lady appeared at the kitchen door, wiping her hands on her white apron.

"Yes, Mr. Hamilton?"

"Matilda, this is my wife, Marjorie."

"Good Lord, you have yo'self a pretty wife. I be peeling potatoes or I'd shake your hand." Matilda had the same tropical accent as Thomas. Jenny wondered if she was also from Jamaica.

"That's fine Matilda. I'm very pleased to meet you. I can see right off we'll be good friends." Jenny stepped forward and extended her hand. Matilda quickly wiped her hands again on her apron and hesitantly received Jenny's warm offering.

"Pleased to make your acquaintance, Ma'am."

"Where's Charles?" bellowed James.

"I believe Mr. Charles be in the toile... I mean, in the washroom, relieving himself." Glancing at the wall clock, Matilda continued. "Hmm, been in there almost his usual thirty minutes; he should be along shortly."

"Really Matilda, you don't have to be so blunt and give us all the details. Simply say 'Charles is indisposed and he will be with you momentarily.'"

"I'm sorry, Mr. Hamilton. I just be giving you a little extra information so to explain why he be in the toilet... I mean, indisposed, so long."

"Enough Matilda!" James immediately lost the rare warmth he

had just shown and looked at Jenny with his eyes as steely as usual. "If she wasn't such a good cook, why I'd..." James shook his head with disgust and then turned back to Matilda. "When you see him, tell Charles to give Mrs. Hamilton a tour of the place and show her to our room. Luggage is in the trunk; make sure it's taken up to the room as well... Marjorie, I have a few phone calls to make. I'll see you at the dinner table in exactly one hour."

James turned and strode away down the hall. And just like that, Jenny's naïve hope of instantaneous change in her husband was dashed. It was clearly going to take a lot of love to reach that man...

Although she was used to James' abruptness, Jenny was embarrassed by his behaviour towards Matilda and decided she was going to have to be extra nice to the employees to make up for her husband's rudeness. As she followed Matilda into the kitchen, she was pleased to see that the back wall overlooking the grounds was mainly glass with a large patio door in the middle. It was similar to her parents' estate and gave Jenny some comfort of familiarity.

"Oh my, Matilda, the grounds look so beautiful."

"Yes, Mrs. Hamilton. Thomas and his assistants keep evry'ting beautiful and well trimmed. Good enough for the Prime Minister to come visit." Matilda winked.

Jenny laughed, releasing the tension. She liked Matilda very much. "Please, Matilda, call me Jenny."

"Good Lord, Mr. Hamilton hear me call you Jenny, I know I be looking for a new job the very next day. But you can call me Matti. That's the name my sister back home uses and l like the sound of it. More warm feelings surrounding the word, if you know what I mean."

"Of course, Matild... I mean Matti. I know exactly what you mean. Even though my first name is Marjorie, my family and friends have referred to me by my middle name, Jenny, for as long as I can remember."

"Well, I do wish I could help you out, but for now, Ma'am or Mrs. Hamilton will have to do."

"I understand, Matti. Perhaps someday it may just happen."

"Yes Ma'am, 'cept it will be in the next lifetime, so don't 'spect no'ting too soon."

Jenny laughed again and was about to leave when a door opened and in walked a man around 60 years of age wearing a black suit and bow tie. His grey hair was sparse and he had a British air about him. As he walked towards them, the top half of his body leaned forward and his head tilted up. Jenny guessed it must be Charles the head butler, and she was right.

"Why, this here be Charles, Ma'am. As you can see, it will take a spell for Charles to take you all in. 'Spect he never seen such a pretty thing as you before. Charles, this is Mr. Hamilton's new bride. Isn't she some'ting else?"

"You will have to forgive Matilda, Ma'am, she is outspoken at times."

"I really do enjoy her remarks and her openness is rather refreshing. I am very pleased to meet you, Charles." After Jenny extended her hand, Charles reciprocated.

"Mr. Hamilton wants you to show the Mistress around and to the room they be sharing. You make sure the luggage from the car gets to their room too, or we be hearing about it quick enough. Don't want to see Mr. Hamilton ranting around with his shorts on, looking for his pants and they still be in the trunk of the car."

"Please Matilda, no need to go on so."

Jenny laughed again.

"I'll go into the foyer and wait until you have the luggage, Charles, and then I'll follow you to our room."

"Yes, Ma'am."

Charles bowed, backed away and withdrew from the kitchen. Jenny fully expected Charles to have a British accent, but was surprised that he sounded quite Canadian. Jenny stood in the middle of the sparse foyer, feeling almost as empty, as she waited for him to return.

LATER THAT EVENING when they retired to their room after what seemed to Jenny like a terribly formal dinner for just the two of them, she brought up the matter of her name.

"James, we've discussed this before. For most of my life, I have been called Jenny. I know Marjorie is my birth name, but I prefer Jenny. Why is it suddenly so imperative that I be called Marjorie?"

James turned sharply to face Jenny, his expression making her take a step back.

"Marjorie sounds more sophisticated, for one thing. It will command more respect from the staff and our friends. And further, you must sign all documents, invoices, and deliveries as Marjorie Hamilton. The accountant will look for your signature for authorization and—"

"Really James, you're over exaggerating this and I don't agree with you at all. If I want to go by—"

"Look, Marjorie, as long as you're in my home, you'll do what I say!" James' face had flushed a deep red, and the artery on the side of his neck bulged as he added, "and by the way, the cook is not your friend, she is your employee. Please do not let your relationships with any of the staff become personal. Is that understood?"

For the first time in her life, Jenny was struck speechless.

THE NEXT MORNING when Jenny awoke, she found herself alone in the massive king-sized bed. She had heard James get up around six, but she pretended to be asleep. She thought he would come to her and kiss her cheek goodbye, but he just silently dressed and left the room.

Jenny slipped on a pair of blue jeans and headed downstairs to find Thomas. Although she knew she owed Tammy a phone call to tell her everything that had happened, she was dying to get a look at the garden and the gazebo.

As soon as Jenny entered the kitchen she was greeted by Matilda wearing a big smile.

"Why, you be like a ray of sunshine in this kitchen, Ma'am. You look good no matter the time of day! Once I know your schedule I be having breakfast ready for you. I thought you be up much later and want everything to be hot and not wilted, know what I'm saying?"

"Yes, of course Matti. That is very thoughtful of you. Do you have orange juice?"

"Yes Ma'am, squeezed it myself not more than fifteen minutes ago. Last thing that man of yours say—that's what you like and I better have it ready or I sure will be hearing about it when he gets home."

Jenny laughed, and made her way to the fridge to get the juice.

"You have a chair right here Ma'am. I be getting the juice for you. Good Lord, that's what I be paid for."

"Oh Matti, I'll be spoiled in no time…"

"That's my job, Mrs. Hamilton, I get paid to spoil you, ain't that some'ting?"

Matilda filled a tall clear glass with juice and brought it to Jenny.

"Thanks Matti." Jenny walked to the patio door and opened it. "Oh my, what a beautiful morning… I didn't realize the grounds were this large. I see some of the perennials have flowered, will the gardeners be planting more?"

"You ain't seen no'ting, in a couple of weeks they be bringing truck loads of flowers. It be so bright and dazzling, you got to wear sunglasses just to take it all in."

"Oh Matti, you make it sound so beautiful!"

"I 'spect Thomas be giving you a tour when he sees you. This minute, you be the most colourful thing in the whole garden, he'll spot you first thing."

Jenny chuckled, "Oh, I see him and I think he sees me." Jenny waved.

"Didn't I just say he would, he be attracted to the light all the time. Has a nose that can smell beauty. You be finding him a spiritual, God fearing man, Mrs. Hamilton."

Jenny wandered out onto the back patio, ready to greet Thomas who was walking towards the house.

"Well, good morning, Mrs. Hamilton. How did you find your first evening on the estate?"

"Just fine, Thomas. Matti was just telling me more flowers will soon be coming."

"Yes, Ma'am, soon as there is no more danger of frost, we'll begin planting."

"I was wondering, Thomas, if you would show me through the garden? James said he had a gazebo built. I am so anxious to see it."

"Yes, it's a fine structure. I can take you to it now if it's convenient."

"That would be wonderful."

As Thomas led Jenny to the gazebo, she couldn't get over how huge the grounds really were. From the kitchen window over three quarters of the grounds were hidden by trees and shrubs. Suddenly, as they rounded a curve in the path, the gazebo came into view. It was similar to hers, perhaps a bit larger, painted white and surrounded by shrubs and a wide green lawn. It had a swing and rafters above to let the sunshine through.

"Thomas, this is beautiful. Would it be possible to remove the lawn in front of the gazebo and put earth there so I could plant wildflowers?"

"Yes, we could. However, I must tell you we did have wildflowers near the back of the grounds but Mr. Hamilton asked us to remove them as they reminded him of weeds. He likes things very ordered and structured. When we plant the annuals, you will see what I mean."

"I see. Perhaps I will speak to James about that and see if we can't convince him to give up at least part of this immense garden to wildflowers. I just love them, they are so natural and free and bountiful. When I plant a handful, I can't wait to see what's going to come up!"

"Yes, I understand exactly what you mean."

"I also didn't notice any milkweed plants on the grounds. If we don't have any, the Monarchs won't come."

"I understand Ma'am, but once again we removed all the milkweeds at the request of Mr. Hamilton as he considers them a noxious weed."

"Oh fiddlesticks! James has no clue that the milkweed poison protects caterpillars from the birds."

"Exactly, Ma'am."

"Well, I see I'll have to be very convincing, won't I?"

"Yes, Ma'am."

"Have you seen our garden, the one Carlos looks after?"

"No, can't say that I have."

"Next time you meet up with him perhaps he can take you there and show you how it's laid out to give you some idea of what I like."

"Yes, Ma'am, I can certainly do that. But if you get the okay from Mr. Hamilton, I assure you, my co-workers and I can create a very beautiful garden for you."

"And will you plant lilacs and herbs that give off that incredible aroma?"

"Yes, Ma'am, as you wish. We already have an abundance of herbs but we can plant more."

"And the kind in the walkway that yield its fragrance when you crush it as you walk?"

"We already have thyme planted in between the paving stone. You have already stepped on some but it's too early in the season."

"And milkweed plants, Thomas, we need lots and lots of milkweed!"

"We can plant them strategically throughout the garden and an abundance of them around the gazebo so that wherever you look you will see colour and life. The butterflies will abound and it will seem as if you are surrounded by angels."

"Oh Thomas, I see you like butterflies! …And angels too?"

"Oh yes, Mrs. Hamilton. I believe we all have a guardian. I've said a prayer to mine every day since I was a child."

"Me too! What is your prayer, Thomas?"

Thomas appeared reticent to pray before her. Instead, Jenny began:

> *Angel of God, my guardian dear,*
> *to whom God's love commits me here*
> *ever this day Be at my side,*
> *to light and guard, to rule and guide.*
> *Amen.*

"Is that the prayer you say, Thomas?"

The gardener's eyes before her had reddened. At first he nodded and then in a low voice he said, "Yes Ma'am, it's the very same."

Jenny was elated. Perhaps she would like it here after all. She loved Matilda, Charles had charm, and Thomas… now he was something else. Despite James' order to maintain a professional distance with the staff, Jenny knew she wouldn't be able to abide by that; she was already hooked.

AFTER A HEATED argument and much pleading from Jenny, James finally agreed to let her change the grounds. He may not have given in, however, if he knew that she was actually planning to do a lot of the work herself. Once they got the go-ahead, Jenny was up daily at the crack of dawn and out with the gardeners, helping to plant flowers and assisting Thomas with the design of the wild-flower garden.

Just as Carlos had raved, Thomas was as much an artist as a landscaper. He sloped the garden upwards as it receded from the gazebo so more flowers would be visible to Jenny as she swung from the gazebo swing. He incorporated stones and a little running brook that she could hear more than see as it ran in and out between the rocks and flowers. The sound filled Jenny with an unsurpassed peace.

Thomas was able to secure milkweed plants in the country near where Carlos lived. He planted them just in time, before the arrival of the Monarchs. When they came, there weren't as many as on Jenny's parents' estate, but by next summer she was certain there would be even more.

The last thing she and Thomas worked on together was the flower garden by the patio. This was the garden that James would see if he chose to have his morning coffee outside. They planted Marigolds and neat rows of Petunias in alternating colours. The border nearest the patio was lined with Dusty Miller while the far edge backing against a row of green shrubs contained Tiger Lilies, Bleeding Hearts and pink and white Irises. These perennials grew more or less at random but Thomas and Jenny concluded that they were far enough away from the patio for James to notice that they were not planted in some precise manner. Otherwise, everything else had been planted in such an exact manner it was almost as if they had measured the distance between each plant with a ruler.

Although it wasn't Jenny's taste, she appreciated that James had different preferences to her and she respected that. And when they were done and enjoying a glass of juice while seated at the patio table, Jenny and Thomas both agreed that the surrounding garden, as structured as it was, was very beautiful.

"There is just no way one can plant flowers and not see how beautiful they are. It's the Lord's gift to mankind!" Thomas concluded.

By the end of August, Jenny was ready to start her new career as assistant librarian at a high school near the estate. She had never felt more refreshed than she did after working in the garden all summer. A golden tan covered her face and arms. Her blonde hair had bleached more white in the summer sun. When she got dressed in her favourite yellow outfit, ready for the first day of school, she looked stunning. James knew the beauty he had married.

His concern was how to protect his prize from everyone else.

CHAPTER TWENTY-ONE

WHEN SPRING ARRIVED in Regina, Henry and Julean got straight to work landscaping their front and back yards. Not surprisingly, Jeremy had begun walking well before his first birthday and they knew they had to create enough space for him to play and roam outdoors during the summer months. Once completed, it turned out pretty much the way they had planned it.

Petunias filled the planter to the left of the front door while a pyramidal cedar stood sentinel to the right along with different species of Junipers, a dogwood and finally, at his wife's request, a large lilac bush that unbeknownst to Julean, reminded Henry of Jenny; it was her favourite flower, too. From there to the street a new lawn was laid. Since two city trees were already in the front yard they decided not to plant anymore there.

Henry built a sandbox that was put in the far corner of one side of the backyard and a small rock garden with a wishing well Henry's dad helped him build was in the other corner. Except for two more lilac trees and a few shrubs the rest of the yard was lawn area for Jeremy to run and play. The only thing they were not able to get done that summer was to build a deck. That would have to be next summer's project.

Henry loved working outdoors and was well tanned the day he got dressed in his suit to begin the first day of school for his second year of teaching. Things would be a little easier this year as he had a lot of his lessons prepared from last year and he had a much better command and understanding of the subjects he was teaching.

The principal had also asked Henry if he would be interested in two periods of guidance and counselling each day as the regular part time counsellor was going on maternity leave. Henry readily agreed to that offer and his teaching load was reduced accordingly to make time for the position.

He was also assigned Student Advisor for the Student Representative Council and had agreed to coach the girl's junior baseball team which would prove to be a lot of fun. Later in the school year, Henry would also be assistant coach for the junior basketball team when it started. All in all Henry had a busy year ahead of him.

ON NOVEMBER 13, the Saturday following Remembrance Day, Julean planned to prepare another big dinner for the family. Both her and Henry's parents and Father Engelmann were invited. In part, it was to show their appreciation for all their parents had done for them, but also to make a special announcement.

Julean spent most of the day preparing for the big turkey meal. It wasn't easy with little Jeremy playing underfoot. Whenever Julean was in the kitchen, she would give her little sous chef some pots and pans to bang, otherwise he'd be endlessly opening and closing cupboard doors or trying to touch the stove. Besides turkey and stuffing, Julean was roasting potatoes and vegetables. Mary offered to bring over two pies for desert while Vera made her famous Jello salad.

Henry was delighted with the antique dining table Julean's Aunt and Uncle had given them. They hadn't used the table leafs to extend it to its full six feet since Christmas, but it sure came in handy when they had a full house. A table cloth just covered the dark, rich mahogany finish of the table. After Henry set the table with the fine china and silverware they had received as wedding gifts, they were all set.

"That looks great, honey!" exclaimed Julean when she entered the dining room."

"Yeah, we just need three folding chairs and I asked Dad to bring them over when they come. So, how are you doing? All set? I can smell the turkey roasting."

"Yes, everything seems to be fine, but I must admit I am feeling a bit nervous."

"Everything will be perfect, honey." Henry kissed Julean and then went into the living room and knelt down on the floor to play with Jeremiah and his Tinker Toys.

"Look at my tractor, Daddy." Jeremy said, as he pushed the vehicle he had made out of wheels and sticks along the carpet.

"That's great Jeremy! And I see you're starting to make a garage for it."

"You can help me if you want."

"Yeah, sure, pass me two of those spokes…"

It was a little tense when everybody showed up, but Father Engelmann in his usual friendly style soon had everyone relaxed. He had even brought over a bottle of Manischewitz concord wine and Julean's parents brought a bottle of white zinfandel. When everyone was seated, Father said the grace. This was followed by a toast to the young couple, their home, and their careers and…

"To our next baby!" Julean announced. "Hank and I are expecting another addition to our family!"

Amidst the excitement and congratulatory words they all settled into their meal and conversation.

"So when are you due, Julean?" asked Mary.

"It should be sometime in May again. I hope it doesn't fall on Jeremy's birthday, May 24. Wouldn't that be something if it did?"

"Well congratulations, you already have one more than Mary and me. You're off to good start for a family."

"Maybe they will make up for both of us, Bill. Anna could not bear children, but we were blessed by having Henry come into our lives. And I thank you, Bill and Mary, for letting Anna and I share in his upbringing."

Father then turned to Mrs. Carter and continued, "So Vera, I understand you have another daughter?"

"Yes, her name is Joyce and she's a year older than Julean. She's an elementary school teacher in Saskatoon. She teaches Grades 1 and 2."

"That is such an important grade to teach. We need our best teachers forming the minds of our young children. And I understand she is married to a doctor?"

"He specializes in internal medicine, David," Jack said. "He is a resident intern at the University Hospital. He'll be a fine doctor."

"My, my, both your children and Bill and Mary's boy all doing the Lord's work. It makes my heart happy."

"That's a mighty fine dinner you prepared, Julean," said Bill.

"It's absolutely delicious," echoed Mary. "You must have helped your mother a lot to learn how to prepare such a large meal."

"I have to admit, Mom is a great cook and teacher… Oh, is that Jeremy?"

"Let's leave him for a few minutes and finish our dinner," suggested Henry.

"We can try, but once he wakes, he sure seems to be hungry. I was hoping to include him for dinner but he played all afternoon and just fell asleep before you folks came. "

"A growing man needs a lot to eat."

"You can say that again," said Henry.

"So how is your teaching job going?" asked Dr. Carter.

Henry looked at him, kind of shocked. This was one of those rare times Julean's father had shown an interest in Henry.

"It's going great, Jack. I enjoy the Grade 9 and 10 science classes, but must admit I like the challenge of the Grade 11 and 12 physics classes."

"What do you mean by more of a challenge, Hank?"

"I simply memorized a lot of the physics I learned when I was in high school and university. It got me through my exams, but now that I am teaching the subject, it's a different matter; I find that I am really grasping it for the first time. And now that I have a much deeper understanding of all the things I found hard to make sense of in high school, I'm more aware of what my students may find difficult. I'm able to explain it to them in different ways so that they might get it on a deeper level, too. Do you know what I'm saying?"

"I understand perfectly Henry," said Father. "When one has to work through something and comes to understand it first hand, that person – in most cases I would suspect – is probably a better teacher than one who has no trouble understanding a concept in the first place. Such a teacher may fail to understand the difficulty students might have."

"That's it exactly, Father!"

Just then Jeremiah appeared on the scene, rubbing his eyes and carrying his blanket.

"Well, look who we have here," said Father. "Come give grandpa a kiss."

Jeremy just stood there and slowly shook his head, still in a daze and unsure of what to make of all the people sitting at the table.

"Perhaps change him, Hank, and I'll warm up his dinner." Julean got up from the table and went into the kitchen while Henry scooped Jeremy up and took him to the nursery to change him.

When Hank returned with Jeremy he put him in his high chair and set it beside Father Engelmann. All those present tried to get his attention but he would have none of it. Julean brought him a cracker to chew on until his dinner was ready. Jeremy picked up the cracker and took a bite and then just stared at everyone around the table.

"*Mein gutter Gott*, it's hard to believe that this is the same infant I baptized last year. How old is he now?"

"Yes, he's almost a year and a half."

"And soon he will have a brother or sister! My, how the time flies."

"I told Mommy I would like a brother so we can play together," said Jeremy, as he looked at Father Engelmann.

Everyone was shocked by his words. Not only was he an early walker, but had begun to speak in full sentences just after his first birthday.

"Yes, well your mommy might have a baby sister, only time will tell."

"See, the baby is in Mommy's tummy."

"That's right, Jeremy! Julean spends a lot of time talking and explaining things to Jeremy," said Henry. "It's amazing what little children can learn."

Julean brought in a dish of mixed peas and some cut-up turkey and set it before Jeremy. "You better move him away from Father a bit more or his black suit will get covered with food."

"Yeah, that's for sure. Here, give me the bib and I'll tie it on him. Don't know if it will do much good the way he throws everything around."

"I'd appreciate if you would keep an eye on him, Hank; I'll get the dessert ready and heat up the water for coffee and tea."

Mary got up and started to clear the table and Vera followed suit and then said, "Why don't you men sit in the living room while we get things organized and do the dishes in the kitchen?"

"Sounds like a good idea. Come on Jack, David, let's move and let the women do their thing."

As everyone left the dining room, Henry sat beside his son watching him eat his meal. Henry couldn't help but look and listen to the three men chatting away in the living room, so comfortable with each other.

If he were sitting on the couch with them he would be on edge and worried about how his father-in-law was relating to him. He would analyze each and every move Jack made. Henry shook his head at the folly of it all. He could see so clearly how he created his own reality and the internal hell that resulted.

Henry shook his head again and muttered under his breath as if speaking to Jeremy. "Unbelievable how I keep getting caught up in thoughts that colour my life and relationships negatively."

And then offering some advice to his son he said, "There once lived a man named William Shakespeare who said, 'nothing is, unless our thinking makes it so.'"

"Did I just hear you quoting Shakespeare to our son?" Julean put her hand on Henry's shoulder and rubbed it.

"Yeah, you can't get them started too early, you know."

"Here, let me finish with him and you can go chat with the men in the living room."

When Bill saw his son enter the living room he asked, "Can you turn on the TV for a minute? I'd like to know who's winning between the Blue Bombers and the Stampeders."

"Yeah, sure Dad. I forgot all about the game. It might be over…"

Henry turned the dial to CTV. Johnny Esaw was doing the play-by-play commentary of the semi-final game.

"Hey, just in time; only another minute and a half to go in the final quarter."

"I see the score, Stamps: 29, Winnipeg: 9. That's good. I hope Winnipeg loses and good. I'm still peeved over our loss to them. The way Lancaster and that new fellow George Reed play, we should be the ones playing the Stampeders."

Turning to Father, Dr. Carter asked, "So David, do you watch football at all or follow the sport?"

"If you would have asked me that a few years ago I would have said no. But since living with Father Connelly I have developed an avid interest in the Roughriders. I can still hear Father Connelly's Irish temper ringing through the rectory the day the Winnipeg Blue Bombers won over the Riders a couple of weeks ago. And that Mr. Esaw gets so excited when he does the play-by-play action. You could just tell in his voice that he was sorry to see the Roughriders lose out."

"Well, like I said, I'm still pretty upset, too. There's a strong rivalry between those two teams that goes back a long way," said Bill.

"That George Reed was sure a good acquisition this year," observed Jack. "He's like a locomotive when he hits that line."

"Yeah," Henry chimed in just as he turned off the TV and sat down. "I think he will get an award for best player of the year."

"I think Hugh Campbell will too. He's Lancaster's favourite receiver," said Jack. "Sometimes I think the Little General doesn't see anyone else. But you have to admit they're some combination."

"Too bad we didn't make it to the finals this year. We have the makings of a Grey Cup team for sure," Henry said.

"I agree son. And our defense with Alan Ford, McQuarters, Baker and Ted Provost are something else." Bill shook his head and muttered, "I still think they should have beat Winnipeg."

"Now tell me boys, who do the Stampeders play next?" Father wanted to know.

"We're just into the finals, Father. Winnipeg can still be the winner for Western Canada if they beat the Stampeders in the next two games. It's a two game win out of three series."

"I sure hope they don't," said Bill.

"Geez Dad, you sure have it in for the Blue Bombers." And then Henry turned back to Father.

"So Father, tomorrow the Hamilton Tiger Cats play the Ottawa Rough Riders. Theirs is a total point, two game series. Everyone thinks the Tiger Cats are going to win the Eastern finals. They have an awesome team this year."

"So there is still a lot of football to be played?"

"Yup! But we should know by the end of next weekend who the final East and West teams will be that'll meet in Toronto for the Grey Cup! I can hardly wait."

"It's getting late in the season, hope it's not too cold or blizzardy for the players."

"Well, we will have to ask the Lord for more sunshine till then."

"Next year the Grey Cup is at Empire Stadium in British Columbia. It's usually warmer on the west coast. I think I may get tickets and take Mary. She still hasn't been up in a plane and I've always wanted to attend a Grey Cup."

"That would be great Dad! You can hire me to carry your suitcases."

"And mine too," chuckled Father.

"Wouldn't that be something if the Riders went to the Grey Cup next year? I think Saskatchewan would go berserk! Well anyway, how about we make a small bet on who will be in the Grey Cup at the end of the month?"

Looking at his dad and then Jack, Henry made his wager.

"I'll bet both of you five bucks that after next week's games it will be the Hamilton Tiger Cats against the Winnipeg Blue Bombers. Any other combination, you guys win."

"You sound pretty confident son. But I'll bet against those Blue Bombers every time. You're on."

"Count me in too, Hank," said Jack.

Father at first pretended that he didn't hear the gamblers. But then he surprised everyone by saying, "Okay Henry, if you can afford to lose another five dollars, I'll take you on as well... Those Stampeders sure walloped the Blue Bombers today. I don't think they will be able to make a comeback and win the next two games."

"You never know Father, the Blue Bombers are a pretty good team this year."

"That will be the day!" said Bill

"You seemed more relaxed tonight Hank, did you enjoy the evening?"

"Yeah, I did honey. I thought I'd just lighten up a little and not take your dad so seriously, or myself. It's funny, when I let my guard down and take responsibility for my own life and happiness, it's like a big weight lifts off my shoulders... Yeah," Henry repeated, "that was fun tonight."

"That's wonderful, honey."

"I think saying the scriptural passages are starting to sink in as well. You know: 'Be ye transformed by the renewal of your mind.'"

"That's good Hank, but... can I say one thing about that?"

"Sure, what's that?"

"Well, it's just that I question the reason you are doing it. It seems to me, honey, that you are saying these passages to keep your mind off your problems and to be more at peace. It's like you're using the scripture more as a defense strategy to ward off negative thinking and the accompanying anxiety. It takes a lot of energy to keep fighting your thoughts like that."

Henry nodded, as if in agreement.

"Well, what if your purpose was to say these passages to praise Jesus and claim His promises to help you love and forgive more and be more accepting of yourself and others? Then your aim is to be more Christ-like in your thoughts. You're still accomplishing the same thing but with a purpose that is more relaxing and in tune with sound Christian thinking."

"Geez Julean, sometimes I wonder who knows more about human nature and living in peace, you or Father Engelmann? Yeah, the way you described it, the focus is more on the positive than the negative, for sure!"

Julean smiled, but her eyes didn't totally conceal the struggle that she too was still dealing with but had more or less accepted: Henry was still having dreams about Jenny. Perhaps memorizing scriptural passages was preoccupying more of his thoughts during the day, but whether he was aware of it or not, Jenny still entered her husband's mind while he slept.

CHAPTER TWENTY-TWO

I AM SO HAPPY that you and the family are coming home for Christmas, Tammy. I miss you so much and I can hardly wait to see Chloe. I hope you can stay longer than you did last year! You'll have to come see the house and we should go for lunch one day. Maybe we can take Chloe shopping…"

"Whoa, slow down, Jen! We'll get to do all of that and more. We are all so anxious to get home, too. It's too bad you and James decided to elope, or we would have been there last spring, remember? We had our flights booked and everything."

"Oh Tammy, I am so thankful you weren't mad at me."

"I'm just teasing you, Jen. How could anyone be mad at you? But Chloe was disappointed that she couldn't be your flower girl."

"Yes, I know. I'll make it up to her somehow."

"Oh, she has long forgotten about it. Anyway, how's married life treating you?"

"Well, I hardly ever see James, but when we do spend time together he seems very intent on trying to produce an heir."

"Any luck yet?"

"Not yet, but we've only been married six months. James is getting a bit concerned, but I'm not. We both want a child so badly, I know it will happen sooner or later. In the meantime, I'll just have to give all my love to my little Chloe!"

"All she talks about is coming home and seeing you and the butterflies. I have to keep explaining to her the butterflies aren't there in the winter, that they only come in the spring. You made quite an impression on her with the life cycle of the Monarch butterfly, Jen. She still talks about the miracle of the worm turning into a butterfly."

"She is such an adorable child, Tammy. Both Carlos and I were so impressed at her comprehension of it all."

"Actually, since Chloe was bringing it up so much, I got the idea to talk about it with the girls at the health clinic where I volunteer."

"What do you mean? What do Monarch butterflies have to do with pregnancy or abortion?"

"Well, by explaining the life cycle and miraculous transformation of a caterpillar into a butterfly, it helps the girls see the miracle of their own pregnancy. So many young girls who feel desperately hopeless in their situation often just need someone to show them the beauty and miracle of life. I can't tell you how many girls I've seen change their mind about ending their pregnancy after we talk about butterflies!"

"Tammy, that is so brilliant. I'm so glad you're enjoying that work and making such a difference."

"The pro-life demonstrations are really exciting, too, Jen. There was one last weekend that I so wish you could have been at with me!"

"I would have loved to have been there, Tammy; too bad we didn't arrange it in advance! James was in Toronto last weekend at the Grey Cup game. It would have been the perfect time for me to steal away and visit y'all down in Texas." Jenny ended with a bit of a drawl.

"Oh, darn! That would have been perfect. So, who won the Grey Cup, anyway? Mom said the Tiger Cats were playing the Winnipeg Blue Bombers."

"The Tiger Cats won by a touchdown, I think. I'm not that interested in football but James is mad for it."

"Football is a big thing in the states too. The NFL Championship game is in January. It's similar to the Grey Cup, but on a much bigger scale. Robbie has really taken an interest in American football, so maybe I'll try to get him tickets to the big game as a Christmas present."

"Oh, speaking of Christmas presents, I got Chloe a Barbie doll. Do you think she'll like it?"

"She'll love it – that's all she's been asking for. But don't go overboard on her, Jen."

"I'd treat her as if she were Camilla."

"That's what I'm afraid of. It would be Christmas everyday!"

THOUGHTS OF JENNY immediately flooded Julean's mind when the radio announcer mentioned that the only other city in Canada as cold as Regina that day was Ottawa, It triggered that deep desire to someday meet the woman who was still a part of Henry's heart. If only she knew Jenny's last name and where she lived in Ottawa, Julean would have figured out some way to contact her rival. Maybe when her sister and husband moved there next year she could visit them and try to track down Jenny at that time.

But how?

As Julean was thinking on these things the phone rang…

"Hi Auntie Netta, what a pleasant surprise!"

"We were just thinking of you, Julean, we heard there's an awful freeze in Regina right now."

"Yes, Auntie, it's terrible. Hank was just saying this morning he hasn't seen a cold snap like this since '57."

"There always seems to be one final storm before spring, no?"

"You're right! What's that old saying? March comes in like a lion and goes out like a lamb? Well, here it is, March 1st and it's minus 68 degrees with the wind chill. Our car wouldn't start this morning and poor Hank had to walk to work. Luckily it's not too far, but still, in weather like this, two miles is a long way."

"Well, there's nothing wrong with going out into the cold so long as he's dressed for it."

"Yes, he was well bundled up, Auntie."

"How is Henry, Julean? Is he enjoying his work?"

"He really likes teaching but he would prefer to move into guidance and counselling. He connects well with the students. They often come to him with their concerns and he likes talking to them and helping them. He asked the principal already if he could do part time counselling next year to try it out. He will know before the end of the school year if that will be possible."

"And how are you feeling, Julean? How's the pregnancy coming along?"

"I am feeling fine, Auntie. I've had no morning sickness so far, but I also didn't have it with my previous pregnancies, so I guess I'm lucky that way."

"And when do you expect your little bundle of joy to arrive?"

"In May sometime, close to Jeremy's birthday. We're hoping the new baby chooses his or her own birth date, though, so they don't have to share one!"

"Did you save Jeremiah's crib and nursery items? Those will come in handy."

"Yes, we've held onto everything we were given. By the way, Hank wanted me to tell you how much he loves the dining room set you and Uncle Jacob gave to us. When it's fully extended it's able to seat everyone at the table. I think it could even seat another two, if you and Uncle ever care to join us!"

"Aren't you sweet, Julean. Well, do you have enough dining chairs for it yet?"

"No, Hank's father brought over some folding chairs, but we should probably buy three or four ourselves. Hank's discovered a real love of antique furniture."

"Well, I'm glad to hear you're getting some good use out of that table. Oh, I see Jacob walking up the path from the barn, I should get going here. But... before I say goodbye, Julean, I hope you don't mind me asking: how're things between you and Hank? Are you still worried about..." Netta's words trailed off as she wasn't sure how to phrase the question.

"No, that's fine, you can ask, Auntie. I know you are concerned. Henry and I are doing really well and I feel closer to him than ever, but...Yes, Henry still dreams of that woman. I don't notice it as much during the winter months, but in the summer, particularly in July, his dreams are so vivid and real."

"Are you still finding it difficult, my child?"

"Actually, no, Auntie, it doesn't upset me as much. I think I am accepting it as a part of our marriage. Maybe it's meant to be and I am learning to share Hank with her if it means so much to him…"

"… Or maybe Satan is at work and you must not allow it to sabotage your marriage," Netta added, pointedly.

"Well, maybe, but Hank is a very loyal and dedicated husband and father. His heart is true to me in his waking hours. I know he is faithful and so I'll allow him his freedom if it is only in his dreams. I really see no harm in it so long as during the day his present thoughts are of me and our family. I am prepared to share him this way for now, and if Jenny and I are meant to meet someday, the good Lord will bring it about."

"Do you mean…?" Netta did not have to finish her question; Julean knew exactly what she was referring to.

"Yes, Auntie. I am prepared to do whatever is necessary, even if it means living like the women in the Bountiful Colony back in BC. I love Hank very much, Auntie."

Netta didn't speak for a long time and then she said, "Well, dear Julean, it sounds like you have found some peace and acceptance surrounding this. I hope one day you can discuss it all with Hank and in the meantime, we will keep you in our prayers."

"Thank you Auntie, I need your prayers and guidance and the Lord's strength. I hear Jeremiah getting up so I better go tend to him. Thanks for phoning, Auntie. Please give my love to Uncle Jacob."

"Of course, Julean. And our love to you and your family, as well."

"Hɪ Jᴇɴ. To what do I owe this weekday phone call? Let me guess: you're pregnant!"

"Oh Tammy, I wish. Both James and I are so frustrated and exhausted that the doctors have been unable to find anything after weeks of testing. We've been married over a year now and… nothing! James is really starting to lose it."

"Oh, Jen, sometimes these things take time. You've got to just keep trying; you know, practice makes perfect!"

"Don't tease, Tammy! It's getting almost unbearable around here. James insisted I go through every conceivable test to find out what's wrong with me."

"How does he know it's you that's the problem?"

"Well, that's just it. They've checked me for abnormal hormonal conditions, ovulatory disorders and tubal abnormalities and God only knows what else, and they can't find a thing wrong with me. James simply can't fathom that my infertility has anything to do with his virility."

"But that's good news that you're A-okay, Jen!"

"I know. But James is livid now that he's under the microscope. He was so rude to the doctor when he had to answer the routine questions. You know how particular James is about cleanliness? Well, he vehemently denied having any diseases or infections. He's so proud of his impeccable hygiene and later told me he thought the doctor was highly offensive for asking him those questions!

"In any case, today was the third time James was examined and checked for hormonal imbalance. He is so insistent that there's nothing wrong with him, but the doctor explained over and over that a precise balance of some hormone in a man's body called testosterone can determine the success of fertility. James so desperately wants a male heir, he's resigned to do what it takes to figure out what's wrong. I feel bad about it all, but poor James feels even worse, I think."

"Well Jen, if it doesn't happen naturally, you could always adopt."

"I suggested that, myself. James won't hear of it. He was disgusted by the idea. He said the only baby he wanted was one that came out of my womb and that he had fathered. Tammy, he even said one of the reasons he had married me was because I was a virgin."

"Oh, Jen..."

"I know! I can't imagine what he would do or say if he knew about what happened to me. I've always been so worried about sharing that with him and now I know why. I just don't think he could ever accept it. The terrible thing is, I... I think all of this has to do with the fact that I gave Camilla away. I don't think my daughter will ever forgive me for doing that. Maybe I am being punished and will never conceive again!"

"Oh Jenny, please don't think that. You became pregnant under very difficult circumstances. A lot of girls would have aborted the child, Jenny. You were only in Grade 9; you did the best thing for your child at that time."

"I just wish so often that I had kept her like you kept Chloe!"

"It was different with me. I was in my last year of high school and more mature and ready to take care of a baby. You did more than most girls would have done in your place. Please don't punish yourself Jenny, you have a heart of gold and I know the Lord loves you and stands fully and completely behind your decision."

"Sometimes I wish so badly that I'd gotten pregnant with Henry's baby, that he was her father. None of this would be happening..."

Jenny became too emotional to continue. Tammy heard her friend sobbing and went on...

"Jenny, I have told you this many times before but what really helped me decide to keep my baby was when you started to talk to me about guardian angels. You told me that we all have our own guardian angel, even the little baby growing within me. That the moment my little baby was conceived, God sent an angel to its side. I clearly remember you telling me that angels are there to guide and protect us and comfort us and bring us closer to God.

"You've always been like an angel to me, Jen. You've always been there for me, so supportive, so loving. It was through your example that I saw my own celestial being. My guardian angel became so real and alive to me when I was at your place that summer. It was as if I was being led by an unseen hand that had taken hold of mine. What I felt in a spiritual way I saw in a worldly way. You were there at all times for me, helping me, leading me, my hand in yours. Oh Jenny, you showed me the ways of the angels; it was because of you that I came to believe that both my baby and I had an angel, too! Your belief in me and your belief in angels saved both Chloe and me."

"Oh Tammy, you're such a good friend, a true gift that I thank God for everyday."

"Turn to your angel, Jenny and ask her to fill you with joy and peace over your decision. How many times have you told me that you know you will see your daughter again? That there is some plan yet to unfold that will bring her back to you? I think all of these things are connected."

"I…I know what you are saying is true, it's just that I don't want to disappoint James and I so desperately want to have a child… I miss Camilla so much, too…" Then barely audibly, she added, "She's nine years old today." Jenny started to cry again.

"Oh, Jenny, how could I have forgotten? Of course! May 24th; it's Camilla's birthday today. No wonder you called me, and here I totally forgot. I'm sorry, Jen…"

"Tammy, I love you so much. You're the only other person I share her birthday with…"

"Listen to me, Jen: you will have another baby, trust me. You are the most precious person I know and I know how much you love your garden. Try to reconnect with your angel there. I'm certain your protector will come to your aid and is not punishing you for giving your daughter away. There is a reason for everything Jen. There is a reason you gave birth to Camilla; besides the joy you gave to her adoptive parents, someday it will all come back to you."

"Yes Tammy, I know in my heart there is a reason. And yes, summer is just around the corner. I can't wait for it to come and to spend my days in the garden. Thomas, the gardener, has everything arranged so beautifully now. I can't wait for you and Chloe to visit and spend some time with me."

"Before we hang up let's say the angel prayer together. I've always found it so consoling, ever since you taught it to me, Jen."

Tammy started and then Jenny quickly joined in:

Oh Angel of God, my guardian dear,
to whom God's love commits me here,
ever this day be at my side
to light and guard, to rule and guide…

At the end of the prayer, Tammy was surprised as her friend continued almost subconsciously…

my life… and James'… and Camilla's…
and Henry's… forever and ever.
Amen.

Oh Jenny, thought Tammy, *perhaps it's all because it's Henry's child you wish to bear…*

CHAPTER TWENTY-THREE

━━━━◆◉◆◇━━━━

S HORTLY AFTER SCHOOL started in the fall of 1966, Henry sat at the kitchen table with his two children while Julean pre-pared dinner. As usual, Jeremiah was helping his mom, only now instead of banging pots and pans, he was spooning pablum into his little sister's mouth. Allison Pederson had arrived on May 12 and quickly caught the hearts of her brother and daddy. She was quite the little flirt.

Julean put the casserole into the oven and set the timer.

"Thank you, Jeremy, good job," she praised the boy then added, "Mommy can take over from here."

Jeremy ran into the living room to play with his train set and Julean took a seat opposite Henry who had been holding little Allison in his lap while she fed.

"What's bothering you, Hank?" Julean didn't beat around the bush. She knew her husband well enough to recognize when some-thing was on his mind.

For a moment, Henry heard Father Engelmann's voice. He smiled and ducked his head as he realized he could never hide his feelings from Julean either. "I've been thinking about how much I like teaching but I have to admit that I sure love working with the students in the guidance department."

"The students trust and love you, too. They gravitate to you,

Hank. And I'm sure they appreciate all the time you spend with them after school. But it's tricky around here when our dinnertime is being pushed back all the time."

"Yeah, I know, I'm really sorry about that. With all my extra-curricular activities in addition to the teaching and counselling, I feel I need more time than what is allotted to me."

Julean reached across the table, picked Allison up from Henry's lap and began patting her back to produce a burp. "Perhaps you should become a full time guidance counsellor, Hank. You're good at it and you love doing it. I'm amazed sometimes how quickly you pick up what is really bothering someone when I don't see it at all."

"If I went into guidance full time, though, I would have to go back to university and get my Masters in Guidance and Counselling. I'm sure the Board will give me a year off but it would be without pay."

Julean finished burping Allison and winked as she got up. "I'm sure we'll figure out a way to make ends meet." She placed Allison in the play pen that was set up in the corner of the kitchen. Allison lay happily on her back, kicking and squealing as she reached for the mobile above her head.

Henry smiled as he sensed that his wife had anticipated this decision for some time. He rose and followed her to the fridge. He held it shut as she was about to open the door. She turned in his outstretched arms and wrapped her arms around him.

"I love you, honey. You're always so supportive. And perceptive, I might add. Maybe it should be you who takes up counselling."

"One shrink in the family is enough. Besides, I am quite content looking after you and the kids."

"So, you don't miss fulfilling your nursing career—"

Julean shook her head. "I'll get to that one day. Right now this is much more important and fulfilling."

Henry gazed lovingly into Julean's eyes and then kissed her long and tenderly while Allison gurgled and cooed.

The very next week Henry approached the School Board and applied for sabbatical leave to begin his graduate studies in counselling. He also applied for a fellowship at the University of Regina with the hope that he could teach psychology that year while completing the required classes and working on his thesis. Julean was prepared to return to work if that didn't work out.

HENRY HAD NEVER seen his dad more excited. After the idea struck him the year before while watching the Western semifinals at Henry and Julean's house, Bill had gone ahead and purchased tickets for the 1966 Grey Cup game in Vancouver right at the beginning of the season. Although it would have been nice to travel to Vancouver by train through the mountains, they decided to fly. Mary was almost as excited for her first airplane ride as her husband was to be at the big game.

Bill constantly asked Father Engelmann to pray that the Saskatchewan Roughriders would be in the Grey Cup that year and by October it looked like after fifty-six years the team might have their chance to play for the silver trophy. No matter where one went, stores, malls, in homes and workplaces the topic was the same. This was the year for the Riders to finally have their shot. They had secured their spot in the finals by winning the most games of all other Western Canada teams. It all came down to a best out of three playoff between the Riders and their most dreaded opponent and the favourite to win: the Winnipeg Blue Bombers.

Saskatchewan blew its top after the Riders won their first game against the Bombers on November 13, but when they beat their rivals again three days later to become the Western champions, the fans went crazy. Henry's dad kept boasting how smart he was to have purchased the Grey Cup tickets at the beginning of the season because now tickets were as scarce as hen's teeth and worth a good dollar. Henry was surprised that even his mother, who never really showed much of an interest in football, seemed to catch the bug. She had *Rider Fever* like everyone else! Bill sure had chosen the right year to go to the Grey Cup!

On Saturday, November 26, everyone on the prairies was on pins and needles until game time. The Saskatchewan Roughriders were playing the Ottawa Rough Riders for the Grey Cup! Ottawa had tasted champagne from the Cup before, but since the inception of the Saskatchewan Roughriders in 1910, this would be the

Riders very first victory, should they win. Everyone wanted it so bad they could taste it!

Henry had two of the neighbours and their wives over for the game. Eddy declined to come as he was playing pool at the Royal and the pool hall had set up three televisions for the occasion. Julean had tons of snacks prepared and brought them out as the food kept disappearing. Jeremy, wearing a little Riders jersey, was on the floor holding his small rubber football and Allison was in her room, sleeping. With all the commotion and yelling and screaming in the house she would probably be up soon enough!

As 'O Canada' was sung, everyone in the living room was silent. But as soon as it was over, everyone screamed along with the fans at Empire Stadium.

"Geez, it's sure great to see the game in technicolour!"

"The replays will still be in black and white though, Hank," said Dan.

"Keep a watch out for Mom and Dad when the camera scans the bleachers," Henry reminded Julean, as she emerged from the kitchen and sat on the arm of his chair.

"Wouldn't that be something if we saw them there? That would make your dad so thrilled, Hank."

"Yeah, that's for sure. He must be going out of his mind by now." Henry turned to Dan and Kirk. "When they called us last night they had just watched the parade from their hotel windows. They stayed in for the entire evening, just too much hooting and hollering for them. But they sure were enjoying themselves and my mom loved the plane trip!"

"I wish we were there right now! Can you imagine?"

"I know, my dad really lucked out; the Rider's first Grey Cup in 56 years and he's there…" Noticing Dan's empty bottle, he asked, "How's your beer, Dan?"

"I'm ready for another one."

"How about you, Kirk?"

"No, I'm good."

"Would you mind getting Dan a beer, honey, and check with the girls to see what they want?"

"Sorry Hank, I hear Allison crying, you'll have to do it." Julean made her way down the hallway toward the nursery.

"Yeah, okay," Henry got up reluctantly and went to the kitchen. While he was there, everyone in the living room starting yelling, "Oh no!"

On their fifth play, the Ottawa Rider's quarterback, Russ Jackson threw a pass to Whit Tucker and went for a 61 yard scoring play. Henry ran into the living room just to see Tucker run into the end zone, surrounded by several Ottawa teammates. Henry waited for the field goal attempt but it was wide. Ottawa hit the score board, 6-0.

That put a damper on things but not for long. Everyone jumped to their feet when West picked off a pass by Jackson on the 50 yard line and ran it back all the way to the 9 yard line.

"Yeah!" Saskatchewan was knocking on the door.

"Give it to Reed," yelled Dan.

Instead, Ron Lancaster, on a play action pass, connected with Jim Worden for a 9 yard touchdown!

"Yeah! Yeah!" The living room suddenly drowned out Allison's screaming. In fact it startled the infant so much she suddenly stopped crying to see who was making a bigger fuss than she. Jack Abendschan made the convert, and the Roughriders took the lead 7 to 6!

Every now and then the cameras scanned the bleachers. It seemed like half of Saskatchewan was there with their green and white pompoms waving. Henry kept a keen eye out for his parents but figured it would be next to impossible to pick them out of the crowd. He knew they had seats on the 30 yard line, 20 rows up. His dad went all out and paid the big bucks. "You only do this once in a life time, son."

The possibility that Jenny might be at the game had also crossed Henry's mind. While he searched for his parents in the crowd, if the truth were known, Henry was also keeping a watchful eye out for Jenny. When he had first heard the news that Saskatchewan was playing Ottawa for the Cup, thoughts of Jenny had immediately filled his head.

Julean enjoyed seeing Henry so excited over the football game. She had never seen him so feverishly elated about anything before.

As she kept busy with serving food, chatting with her girlfriends and minding Jeremy and Allison, she also wondered if thoughts of his Jenny were crossing Henry's mind while he watched the game. Hank's interest in the game was so strong she doubted it would be possible for him to dwell on his teenage sweetheart, but Jenny was from Ottawa…

Did the name of the city remind him of her?

In the second quarter the entire block must have heard Henry and his friends when Rider Al Ford caught an unbelievable touchdown pass through the outstretched hands of Ottawa's Bob O'Billovich and went all the way! The convert was good and Saskatchewan was leading 14-6.

"Man that Reed has power… Look how he plows through the line. It takes four guys to stop him," observed Kirk

"Yeah, he has tremendous power in his legs. I hear he lifts weights from his legs and feet every day at the YMCA. We sure lucked out to get him last year," said Henry.

"Looks like we might win this one!" exclaimed Sally, Kirk's wife. But no sooner had she spoken those words when Whit Tucker got past West again and went all the way for an 85 yard touchdown. The field goal following brought the game to 14-13. Then, just before half time, Ottawa's Bill Cline booted a 51 yard punt into the end zone to tie the score 14-14. The game was far from over!

Jenny sat alone on the immense couch in front of the TV watching the Grey Cup game between the Saskatchewan Roughriders and Ottawa. Just as he had last year, James attended the big game without her. Not that she minded; Jenny wasn't terribly interested in football. She had brought up the possibility of traveling down to Texas to visit Tammy and Chloe while James was out of town, but James didn't like the idea of his wife gallivanting around without him.

Jenny caught herself rooting for Saskatchewan even though she knew her allegiance should be for Ottawa. She was certain Henry would be watching the game, or maybe he was even at the game! If so, the chance of Henry and James actually meeting amidst 35,000 people was very slim. Still, the thought made her shudder and every time the camera swept over the crowd, it was Henry Jenny's eyes sought, not James.

When Ottawa tied the game just before half time, Jenny's heart sank. Although James would be bitterly disappointed if Ottawa lost the game and would likely take it out on her when he returned, her heart was in Saskatchewan. When the half time show began – a salute to Canada's centennial – Jenny pulled a blanket over herself and curled up on the couch as a hundred people dressed up as candles took the field.

"HEY, THAT'S KINDA cool. Look Jeremy! Look at all the people dressed as candles. They're featuring a salute to Canada's 100th Birthday which is coming up next year." Jeremy climbed onto Henry's lap to watch the half time show.

"Geez I've gotta go, could hardly wait for half time," said Dan as he ducked into the washroom.

"It's sure good to see the game in colour," Kirk repeated Henry's earlier sentiment.

"Yeah for sure. Hey Dan, hurry up, check out the commercial for Pontiac!"

"Wow, would I like to own that Parisienne Sportcoupe," said Dan, as he came back into the living room.

"Maybe I'll trade in my '58 Ford. What do you think, honey?"

"Dream on, that will be the day!"

While Julean brought out slices of fresh rye bread and different cheeses, meats, and pickles, the guys stacked their sandwiches and replayed every play with each other, Julean and the girls talked about the children. Both Sally and June commented on how big Jeremy had grown and how well he played with their children who were a bit older.

"Okay gang, third quarter is starting. Come on, Riders!"

Just then, the camera scanned the Saskatchewan Roughriders getting set on the sidelines. Coach Eagle Keys was talking to Ron Lancaster along with assistant coaches, Jack Gotta and Jim Duncan. From there, the camera tilted up to the stands and suddenly, there was Bill standing and waving a Rider pompom. It was Jeremy who noticed him first!

"There's Grandpa!" Jeremy shouted. Everyone yelled and began to clap and cheer as if someone had just scored a touchdown! Bill was clearly having the time of his life, yelling or singing and waving his pompom frantically, while Mary was sitting quietly beside him with her hands resting on her lap holding a green and white pompom, as well.

"Isn't that great? What are the chances of seeing your folks at the Grey Cup? Wow!" Henry felt so proud to see his parents there; his dad all decked out in his suit and dress hat and mom in her new coat.

"Boy they'll remember this for the rest of their lives. Dad bought a new Kodak camera, I hope they take lots of pictures," said Henry as he sat down with a bottle of beer.

"Now that's what I like watching even more than the game," joked Dan as the TV camera focused on the cheerleaders wearing tight sweaters and skirts while performing high leg kicks. Dan's wife, June, playfully slapped her husband's shoulder scoldingly. "Oh Dan, you cut that out!" Everyone laughed.

Although there was no scoring in the third quarter, the Saskatchewan defense was very impressive in limiting Ottawa to just one first down. Ottawa, however, did have a potential turning point when Mike Blum intercepted a Lancaster pass but it was all for naught when the play was overturned due to pass interference, to everyone's delight.

It was in the final quarter that everything broke loose and brought everyone to their feet. Ronny threw a line drive at Hugh Cambell from the Ottawa five yard line breaking the dead lock.

"Yeah!" yelled the guys as they jumped to the ceiling! Suddenly, time seemed to stand still as the ball came out of Campbell's hands in the end zone. The dead silence lasted only a split second after the head referee, Al Dryburgh, ruled it a touchdown as Hugh had held onto the ball long enough to take the team ahead.

"That's why they call him Gluey Hughie!" exclaimed Hank at the top of his lungs. Everybody laughed!

From that moment on, nobody could sit down, they were so excited. Julean bounced Allison up and down in her arms as she stood behind Henry. Kirk's wife did the same with her toddler.

Dan had to go again from drinking too much beer, but he said his back teeth would have to start floating before he left this game.

"The Riders just have to hang in there. Just another ten minutes of play left!" said Kirk.

"Yeah we've waited 56 years for this one. Look! The RCMP are carrying out the Cup!"

Henry smelled victory. "They have to do it for Dad," he muttered under his breath and then louder, "Come on Riders!"

The defense was playing amazingly well. The Riders continued to hold down Ottawa to just two first downs. Ron Lancaster, surprisingly, was calling mainly a running game so far. Even still, Saskatchewan was leading in all the statistics. George Reed was already rushing close to 100 yards!

There was still a chance Ottawa could come back, there was enough time for anything to happen. But just then, history was made...

Lancaster handed the ball off with an explosive play to George Reed. It's a wonder all the windows and glasses in the Pederson home didn't break into smithereens when Henry and all those present went hysterical as they watched Reed bust 31 yards straight up the middle of the field to the Ottawa end zone!

No one could contain themselves. The hugging, hollering and screaming was so intense it frightened the children to tears, including Jeremy. The poor children failed to comprehend what had just happened and had never seen their parents so stupendously, insanely, incredulously happy!

AROUND TWO IN the morning Julean found herself feeding Allison while rocking in the antique rocking chair that her Auntie and Uncle had given to them. She found the warmth of the little child against her body comforting and reassuring that she was totally loved.

Hank was so excited that day over the football game. The name Ottawa was repeated so many times. She wondered if the name of the city reminded him of Jenny? *It did her.* Throughout the game the girl that her husband dreams of never left her mind. Surely it was impossible for Hank to dwell on his teenage sweetheart; his interest in the game was so strong.

But she was wrong! No sooner had they gone to sleep than Hank's dreams revealed his heart once more.

Julean was happy that her daughter got her up. She could no longer listen to the yearning of her husband.

Allison stirred, "Oh my little one, I love you so deeply."

Julean inserted the bottle's nipple into the infant's mouth and began to rock as her thoughts drifted once again to Jenny. Perhaps other women from the colony who had sat in this age old rocker had been faced with the same question...

Was she really prepared to share her husband with another as so many before her had done?

"Mrs. Hamilton! Mrs. Hamilton, you be okay now. Evry'ting is just fine now. You at home, Mrs. Hamilton."

Matti was standing over Jenny and her face loomed into view when Jenny opened her eyes. She quickly sat up and looked around.

Matti continued, "Why you be sleeping on the couch the whole night through, Mrs. Hamilton? I be wondering to myself '*who be in the living room?*' I know Mr. Hamilton be away in Vancouver, leaving you here all by yourself, but you be talking in here till all hours."

"Oh Matti, I must have fallen asleep during the football game last night. I hope the TV blaring all night didn't disturb you too much."

"Don't you be troubling your pretty little head none. I take one of those tranquilizers the doctor give me and a train could go right through here and I wouldn't be waking none."

"Well that's good. I'm glad it's Sunday morning and I don't have to go to work; I feel like I hardly slept a wink."

"Yes Ma'am. I heard you dreaming when I come in. You be a'calling 'Henry! Henry!' over and over. At first, I thought he be in the room here, it sounded so real-like, but then I see you talking and thrashing about while you be sleeping. Hope you don't mind me waking you like that."

"I was talking about Henry in my sleep, Matti?"

"Yes, Mrs. Hamilton, same as you be talking to me this very minute."

I wonder if James ever hears me talking about Henry in my sleep?

Jenny got up off the couch and passed by Matti on the way to the kitchen. "Is there any orange juice in the fridge, Matti?"

"That's the first thing I do is squeeze fresh orange juice. I know you be wanting some first thing. But here now, Mrs. Hamilton, you know I have to get it for you, or I might as well just stay in bed. You have to let me earn my keep."

"Yes, of course Matti. Could I please have some toast then, as well? Just bring it into the den."

Jenny returned to the couch in the den. She realized that thinking about Henry all night while watching the game had triggered her imagination and brought him back to her in her dreams. But for the life of her, she couldn't remember her dream. Dreams can be so real when asleep and yet the memory of them can disappear as quickly as a mist in the morning sun when one wakes up.

She wondered about Henry's wife and the fact that they had lost their first child. In a way it was like what happened to her. She had lost Camilla too, even though there was still the hope she would see her daughter one day. Had Henry and his wife had another child yet, Jenny wondered?

Closing her eyes, Jenny tried to picture what Henry's wife looked like. Although when she slept, it was Jenny who was married to Henry and bore his children, in her waking hours she hoped and believed that Henry was happily married to the woman he chose instead of her.

The name Julean was so beautiful, so distinct, as if belonging to a different heritage. Jenny thought it would be so nice if she were ever to meet Julean one day.

Just as Matti was about to enter the room with her toast and orange juice, Jenny suddenly remembered what she had been dreaming about: Henry was about to fulfill the wish she had made to the shooting star. If Matti had not awoken her, *his lips would have surely met mine.*

CHAPTER TWENTY-FOUR

B Y THE FOLLOWING spring Henry had been granted sabbatical leave but he still hadn't heard from the university about his fellowship. It looked as though Julean would have to go back to work and they would have to hire a babysitter, which neither of them liked. Henry began to doubt his decision.

"Oh, honey, things will work out," Julean said. "Besides, it may be good for the kids to have someone else look after them. Hopefully they will appreciate me all the more."

"I doubt that. I mean, of course they will appreciate you more. I just meant that it's not good for some—"

Julean approached Henry and stood on her tiptoes. "Ssh, I know what you meant. Don't worry, Hank, things will work out."

SURE ENOUGH, WHEN Henry arrived home from school the next day, Julean greeted him wearing an ear-to-ear grin, and her hands behind her back.

"What…?"

"Guess which hand?"

"That one!" Henry pointed to the left.

Julean shook her head.

"Well, it's got to be the other one, then."

Again, Julean shook her head.

Henry lunged at her, but she darted into the kitchen. When she turned, Henry noticed the letter in her hands.

"Come on, honey, I see it's a letter." It suddenly dawned on Henry that it might be the one he was so anxiously waiting for. "Is it from the university?" His expression changed from annoyance to excitement.

She ran to the other side of the table and smiled. As he worked his way around the table Julean shuffled away.

"You devil, you." Henry lunged across the table toppling two chairs on the other side, but managed to grab her arm. Jeremy appeared in the doorway.

"Here, Jeremy, let's keep this away from Daddy." Julean waved the letter at her son.

"Quickly Jeremy, take the letter!"

Just as Jeremy took the letter and ran out of the kitchen Allison came in. It stopped Jeremy's escape for a moment giving Henry just enough time to catch up to him and snatch the letter out of Jeremy's hand.

Henry wiped the perspiration from his brow as he devoured the letter. "Oh, Julean, this is great. It doesn't pay as much as I would make if working, but I think we can manage and you won't have to go back to work."

"See, it's amazing when one puts their mind to something and steps out in faith how everything seems to work out!" Julean gave Henry a big hug and kiss.

"Yeah I've noticed that over the years as well," concurred Henry.

"Oh, I almost forgot. You also got a letter from Gary today." She pulled a thick, worn letter from her apron pocket and handed it to Henry.

Noticing the date stamped on the envelope as he sat down at the table, Henry remarked, "Geez, it took over five weeks to make it here from India."

As he began reading the letter in silence, Allison came back into the kitchen.

"When is supper ready, Mommy? I'm hungry."

"It won't be for a while Allison. Let me get you a glass of milk and a carrot to munch on. You can be like Bugs Bunny!"

Julean set Allison up at the table with her pre-dinner snack then continued preparing the meal.

"So how are Gary and Jane doing? They're in India now?"

"Yeah, they're working with Mother Teresa in Calcutta! Can you imagine? Gary wrote that she really reminds him of Anna Engelmann. I really wish you had met her, Julean, she was such a saint. You would have just loved her."

"From everything I've heard about her, I know I would."

"Anyway, Gary just goes on and on about the terrible conditions over there. From what he writes, the sickness and poverty is unbelievable. People are dying in the gutter every day. Whole families live on the street, going day to day with nothing, with no one to help them, begging for scraps to live another day. It sounds so sad and heart wrenching."

"Oh, I just don't know how Gary and Jane do it…"

"Apparently Mother Teresa is tough as nails and has to constantly remind the workers not to lose their way in the sight of it all and the magnitude of it all."

"I can imagine."

"Gary mentions that they sometimes feel overwhelmed by it all and that sometimes their work seems insignificant as there are so many in need."

"To do that work, one has to trust and have a deep faith in Jesus. Without Him at the centre of their lives it would be impossible for them to work there."

"He mentions that, Julean! In fact, I want to show this letter to Father Engelmann because Gary is sounding more and more like him every time he writes. Listen to this, Julean:

"'Each day I rise at five for morning prayers and mass. After I receive the love and power of Jesus in my heart, I go and serve for another day. We live from day to day serving each and every moment. If there is a future goal, it is that we can love and heal and comfort and bring Jesus to as many souls as we can. At dusk, we meet again in the prayer room and give adoration and praise to God.'

"'People often ask how we can do this kind of work and both Jane and I tell them that we receive so much more than we give.

The gratitude in the eyes of a man or woman dying in my arms with the love of Christ right there in the centre of it, touches all who come here. We are here as children and people of God, humbly serving, and that's it. We are one human helping another, plain and simple, touching each others hearts as Jesus wants us to do.'"

"Oh, that is so moving," Julean wiped her hands on her apron and crossed over to the table to pay closer attention to Gary's words. When she sat down, Henry continued reading.

"'God is calling us to be our brother's keeper. The Western world must realize their responsibility to help. Love heals, love comforts, love gives in so many forms: in helping, in volunteering, in giving money, in visiting the lonely and shut ins, the sick, the elderly... the needs are everywhere.

"'It's loneliness, Henry. Mother Teresa is right when she says the disease of the world is loneliness, and it's not only here in Calcutta amongst the poorest of the poor, but all over the world. I have seen it at home, in Peru, in the Philippines and now here. The only solution to it all is love.'"

Allison, who had been sitting quietly at the table while her father read a story to her mother, was happy when her parents rose from the table and gave each other a big hug and kiss.

THE NEXT EVENING, Julean's parents offered to baby sit so Henry and Julean could go out to dinner and celebrate the good news of his fellowship. Jeremy answered the door.

"Hi Grandma, hi Grandpa! Yummy, pizza!"

"Hi kiddo! Yep, it's your favourite: Hawaiian." Jack Carter knelt down and Jeremy ran into his arms. Henry couldn't help think how much the old man had softened in the last few years. He just loved his grandkids. "You two have fun now, and don't worry a bit about us," Jack made his way into the kitchen and set the pizza box on the counter.

"Thanks, Dad." Julean, holding Allison, gave her father a kiss on the cheek then passed her daughter over to Jack. "You kids be good, now. Don't give Grandma and Grandpa a hard time."

"Go on, now. Enjoy your evening." Jack and Vera shooed them out of the house.

"You look beautiful, honey," Henry whispered as he gazed into her eyes across the table at the L'Habitant restaurant. Julean had swept her hair up at the back and held it in place with a clip. She called it a "chic ponytail" and was just her quick way to make her hair presentable. Yet, in Henry's eyes, it was sophisticated and captured the elegance and charm of his dear wife.

"You look so handsome," Julean responded dreamily, the flickering candle gleaming in her eyes.

"It is a pleasure to see my favourite couple back so soon," the head waiter announced, interrupting the romantic interlude. "This is the second time this month. A welcome deviation from your usual monthly visit."

"Yes, Claude. We got good news yesterday and so thought we would celebrate."

"Ah, yes, it is important to recognize and acknowledge our blessings." Claude smiled broadly. "Will it be your usual merlot or might I take the liberty to suggest a white wine this evening? An Australian sauvignon, perhaps? A very fine import, it is chilled at the precise temperature. I guarantee you will not be disappointed."

Henry looked at Julean. "Yes, the white will be fine. And, what is the catch of the day?"

"Earlier this afternoon, we received three large fillets of wild salmon from the west coast. The wine sauce our chef has prepared is delicious, an exquisite compliment to the entrée."

"How can one resist such a tempting description?" Once again checking with Julean, Henry ordered the entrée.

After a very fine dinner of salmon, wild rice and steamed vegetables, followed by to-die-for cheesecake, Henry and Julean left the café.

Julean scooted closer to Henry as they sped away towards home. Henry raised his arm and Julean snuggled into his chest and closed her eyes, until she felt the car swerve unexpectedly.

"Aren't we going home?"

"I thought we might do something we haven't done in a long time—"

"Uh oh. And what might that be?" Julean pointed her finger into his chest.

Henry shrugged. "You'll see."

"Where on earth are you going?" Julean asked as they passed the city limits sign.

Two miles later, Henry turned into the Star Light Drive-In theatre.

"We saw that movie years ago and it wasn't very good, honey."

"Well, I have something else in mind."

Julean looked at Henry. "Oooooh, Henry."

Henry parked their Ford station wagon in an isolated spot in the back, and rolled his eyes toward the back area of the wagon. The seats were still down from their previous trip when the kids played cards back there.

"Oh, Henry," Julean whispered again. "I should have known from the way you looked at me during dinner that this was coming."

"Honey, you know me all too well."

CHAPTER TWENTY-FIVE

A LL SUMMER HENRY struggled to find a topic he could write his thesis on when he started his graduate program in the fall. He had met with his professorial advisor who would be assisting him on his thesis and they tossed a few ideas around, but none had really grabbed Henry's interest. It wasn't until the last Sunday in August during Mass that Henry was struck with the perfect idea for his paper.

Since the children had come along, Henry had to admit he found it tricky to really concentrate on Father Engelmann's sermons. It was difficult for the little ones to sit still through a whole service and inevitably Jeremy and Allison were fussing, fighting or having to use the bathroom during Father's homily. On that particular Sunday, however, Jeremy was ill and Allison was very cranky after a poor nights sleep, so Julean decided to keep both children home from church and Henry had the rare occasion to attend Mass on his own.

Perhaps it had simply been too long since Henry had really tuned into one of Father's sermons, but the one he delivered that day just blew Henry away. Father's homily was based upon the Gospel of Matthew, 6:34:

'So do not worry about tomorrow; it will have enough

worries of its own. There is no need to add to the troubles each day brings.'

It was so poignant and seemed to summarize so much of what he had learned from Father back when he owned the grocery store on Victoria Avenue. Henry was so tuned into every word Father said, he could almost repeat verbatim the closing remarks of his homily.

"Every moment of needless worry is a precious moment of our present life wasted. A moment in which we could have experienced joy, peace, happiness and the beauty of the world around us. Just think of how many moments, hours, days, months and even years that our minds are filled with hate, anger, hurt and resentment!

"And for what end? To be right! To be justified! To get even! Over and over the tape re-plays in our minds so frantically we don't even realize the self destructive state we are in. '*Be still and know that I am God,*' says the Lord. Only then can we make a better choice!

"My dear, dear friends in Christ, in every moment is it not wiser to choose peace, to choose forgiveness, to choose love? Isn't that the stuff that heals wounds and creates inner peace? Isn't that better?

"How can we be aware of the moment, the only reality we have and its potential for joy, healing, happiness and for peace, if we drag the worries of yesterday or the fears and concerns of tomorrow into our precious present moments of our life which is fleeting away moment by moment of every day? It does very little good, if any at all.

"Remember, every moment quickly adds up to a day and then a week and soon a year. It seems so insignificant yet when put together, becomes our life! Just like a tiny seed that one can hardly see becomes a mighty oak, so it is with precious wasted moments! So it is when we fret about the little things day in and day out: when added up, these moments become a huge part of our lives that are wasted! Jesus' words in today's gospel clearly reminds of us of that!

"*Meine lieben Freunde!* There is only one way to stop this self defeating pattern of living. I have said it before and I will say it again and again. We must begin our day in prayer, in quiet peaceful mediation. Empty the mind and then fill it with God's Word. If you want to live in the moment free of worry and anxiety, this is the only ticket that will get you there. The scriptural readings are endless:

"'Thou will keep him in perfect peace whose mind is stayed on thee.' Isaiah 26:3

"'Be ye transformed by the renewing of your minds'...Romans 12:2

"'Trust in the Lord with all your heart and lean not on your own understanding. Acknowledge Him and He will make straight your paths.' Proverbs 3:5

"'Peace I leave with you, my peace I give unto you; not as the world giveth, give I unto you. Let not your heart be troubled, neither let it be afraid.' John 14:27

"'The things which are impossible with men are possible with God.' Luke 18:27

"'He that handleth a matter wisely shall find good; and who so trusteth in the Lord, happy is he'...Proverbs 16:20

"'I have learned, in whatsoever state I am, therewith to be content.' Philippians 4:11

"'God is our refuge and strength; a very present help in trouble'... Psalm 46:1

"'Come and invite Me and my Father and We will make a home in your life.'

"What more guidance do we need or want?

"Is it not wise to accept an all knowing powerful God who knows what is best for us in every circumstance? That brings love and healing into every situation and turns any situation no matter how bad or impossible into good? Why would you trust yourself to run your life when there is this loving God ready and waiting to take control and give you joy, peace and happiness?

"Go to Him this minute, this moment, and invite Him into your heart and life. Go to Him each and every day and in the quietness of the moment. He will whisper to you how to take responsibility for your life and stop blaming others for your unhappiness.

He will bring new meaning to help you to let go of that hurt, that resentment and how to solve this or that problem. He will give you the grace and strength to overcome any obstacle. He will help you to free yourself from the things that hold your mind in prison.

"*Through Christ all things are possible.*

"When you fill your mind with the Lord's words, it softens your heart and reshapes it and if you allow me to repeat myself again, soon you will bring peace, love, forgiveness and love into every activity of your life.

"This is how we free ourselves from the endless activity of our mind that wants to focus on me, me, me and my problems.

"It's all so simple my friends: Jesus clearly tells us, 'I am the way, the truth and the life.' Has he also not said? 'I am come in order that you might have life and have it abundantly.' And the truth is clear in 11 Corinthians 5:17: 'If any man be in Christ, he is a new creature: old things are passed away; behold all things become new!'

"*Meine leiber freunde*, this is the path to the fullness of life! Come, let us see Jesus coming into our lives now, feel His presence and visualize how the old self falls away as the wisdom and love of the Lord grows in your heart. Daily you will see your new self becoming ever more alive and *fully engaged in the moment and the world around you so that you will do great things for God and your fellow man!*"

Henry could hardly contain himself as he listened to his teacher. There was his thesis!

A week later, after talking it over with his professor, Henry went to Father to thank him for the inspiration for his thesis.

"Time orientation and one's anxiety level is the subject I have selected to do my masters thesis on! My faculty advisor agreed that it would be an interesting topic and that very little, if any, research had been done on individual thinking patterns."

"Yes, yes. I have often thought how much time of our lives we waste thinking about the past or worrying about the future and the anxiety it creates." Father Engelmann responded with a nod.

"That's what made me think of this topic, Father. How many times have you encouraged me to live more in the present, the here and now of life? And that along with the worrying and fretting comes a lot of anxiety? Your sermon last Sunday was incredible. I knew right there and then that that would be my topic!"

"That is very true, Henry. We do inflict considerable pain upon ourselves mulling over a past hurt or grievance to the point we become ill or even in extreme cases have a nervous breakdown. That's why it's so important to meditate daily, slow down our thoughts and return to the present. This is the only way we become aware of our negative habits and our behaviour patterns."

"It's when I started to take your advice and meditate that I became aware of my busy thoughts and how much I repeated them daily, getting nowhere fast and causing a lot of discomfort."

"So, what is your premise, then?"

"That's the same question my advisor asked me. Well, it's like you just said. Individuals can feel considerable pain or anxiety as they relive the past or fret over the future. Many times you alerted me of this pattern in myself. Remember how plagued I was with thoughts of Jenny?"

Henry caught himself and pushed that thought from his mind. Henry flushed as he realized that Jenny still entered his thoughts more often than he cared to admit. He lowered his head for a brief moment, then raised his chin until his eyes met Father's once more.

"Essentially, what I plan to do is to divide an individual's thinking into two parts: present-time oriented, living fully in the here and now without much thought to the past or future, and non-present-time orientated, that is, thinking mostly about the past or future. What I plan to show is that the person whose thoughts are primarily present-oriented will experience less anxiety than a person whose thoughts are more non-present-time oriented.

"While it may seem like an obvious conclusion, it has to be proven that this is in fact the case. If my hypothesis is proven correct, then a case can be made for people to want to become more present-oriented in their thinking for their own well-being and fulfillment of life. And, one of the solutions would be what you are such a strong advocate of: daily meditation, prayer and reading the Bible."

"That is a very worthy and challenging project, Henry. The results proven scientifically could lead to books on the subject and change people's lives."

"The only problem is, Father, while there are many instruments and tests to measure one's anxiety level, there are none to measure one's time orientation. Well, I shouldn't say none completely as there is an instrument, a personality inventory that Carl Rogers created, and part of it does measure one's time orientation."

"Ah, yes, I remember Mr. Rogers well. He was a proponent of unconditional acceptance of his clients. His aim was to promote an atmosphere of safety and acceptance, allowing his patients to freely explore and discuss their concerns."

"Yes, that's right, Father. But like I said, only a small part of Mr. Roger's personality inventory measures time orientation. My faculty advisor thinks that I would have to develop a more significant or reliable instrument or test."

"That is a major project. It would require a control group and broad testing."

"It would become more of doctoral thesis and probably take more time than I really have."

"I see. So, what do you plan to do?"

"Well, the advisor is going to discuss it with the Dean and some of his colleagues to see if they will accept Carl Rogers' inventory even though it measures time orientation in a limited way. At least it will give some indication and encourage other students to follow up on the idea or consider it as a doctoral thesis."

"Well, hopefully the faculty will agree upon that solution. You have your hands full already trying to complete your classes, instructing psychology to first-year students and still being a father to those two active children of yours."

Henry smiled and shook his head.

By the end of the university year, Henry had completed all of his classes to acquire a diploma in Guidance and Counselling, but fell short of completing his thesis which would have secured him his Masters degree. While the idea had been embraced by the Dean and others, Father was right in that he simply couldn't find the time he needed to complete the thesis. Henry didn't want to just abandon the research, however, and thought he would continue to work on it in the evenings over the following year once he returned to his high school position.

Although he was looking forward to embarking on his new career as a full-time high school guidance counsellor, little did Henry know that God had a different plan laid out for him. Soon Henry would rediscover a yearning that had been planted in his heart so many years ago that would change the direction of his life yet again.

Chapter Twenty-Six

J AMES PACED BACK and forth in his office like a caged lion. Every now and then he caught his reflection in the wall of glass that allowed him a magnificent cityscape view of Ottawa. Business was booming. Under James' leadership, the company his dad had built from the ground up was more successful than ever. To anyone looking in from the outside, he had it all. The only thorn in his side was the impossibility of Jenny's infertility and it drove him mad. They had been married almost three years and she still had not been able to give him an heir.

He wanted so much to have a successor to his empire. Someone, be it a boy or girl, that he could groom to take over in the same way he had for his father. They had gone to several doctors and taken all the medical tests and examinations possible. In the end they were told that there was no physical reason why Jenny was not conceiving. The record simply recorded that the cause of infertility could not be determined and remained unexplained. For James, that explanation was unacceptable.

James had always gotten exactly what he wanted. He prided himself on his acquisitions and success. The fact that he had been unable to impregnate Jenny was his first and only failure and it gnawed away at him. He stayed up nights trying to figure it out; he knew it had to be Jenny's fault. There must be something that could offer a clue to why they remained childless. Something she wasn't telling him. He had always suspected that and one night, he finally confronted her.

"Marj, ever since we started dating there has been something you seem to be hiding from me. I need to know this, Marjorie, and you have to be honest with me."

Jenny looked at her husband, a puzzled look growing on her face. Out of fear, there was only one thing she had kept back from James and that was the birth of her daughter, Camilla. Had he found out …?

"Of course, James. What is it?" Jenny replied in a very uneasy voice.

James turned and gazed straight into Jenny's eyes. "Did you ever have sexual relations with that farm boy back in Regina? His name was Pederson… Yeah, Henry Pederson."

The question left Jenny absolutely speechless. She was stunned, first of all, that James remembered Henry's name and secondly, that he would have entertained the suspicion.

Jenny's silence made James even more agitated.

"For Pete's sake, Marjorie, you didn't, did you!?"

"Of course not, James. I am just so shocked that you could even think that!"

The look of disgust coated with revulsion faded from her husband's face. James settled back and began to relax.

"It's just that I always wondered about that, Marj. I never figured you had. Since you always refused every advance I made, I always assumed you would have treated him the same. But I had to know, Marjorie. I'm sorry if I upset you."

Jenny was touched by her husband's vulnerability, so rarely displayed.

"Oh James, that was so long ago…"

"I know, Marj, but I just can't figure out why I can't get you pregnant! I just thought maybe it had something to do with that old boyfriend of yours."

Little did James know he was closer to the truth than he realized. There was one thing that no one had thought of, something more psychological in nature that could be affecting the couple's inability to conceive. Just as over the years Jenny was plagued with guilt for believing she had abandoned Camilla, in much the same way James felt guilt, albeit unacknowledged, for believing himself to be the cause of his mother's abandonment and his twin brother's suicide. Both James and Jenny suffered from guilt and perhaps that was the root reason for their troubles.

Or was it?

ONE EVENING WHEN James arrived home late as usual. Jenny had already gone to bed but left a note for him on the kitchen table.

Hi James,

Please wake me up when you get home. I have something to tell you that you're going to remember for the rest of your life.

Love, Marj.

James wondered if she might have bought another piece of antique furniture and wished for the umpteenth time that he'd never agreed to allow her to take over the house that way. First it was the garden and then the house and now what?

James fixed himself a drink and recalled how it all happened.

The first year after they were married one of the teachers at the school where Jenny worked came in one day inquiring if any of the staff was interested in antique furniture. His grandmother had passed away and all the furnishings were going to be sold in an estate sale. The teacher told the staff they could have first pick before the sale if anyone was interested. Jenny could not resist and followed her colleague home after school that very day. She couldn't believe the fine furniture that was there and the excellent condition it was all in! Jenny was elated over the find.

When she came home that day, James had never seen his wife so ecstatic over anything before.

"Oh James! You should see this furniture! It's so beautiful, so unique, so full of character. We simply must purchase some of it."

"Absolutely not! Are you out of your mind, Marjorie? Under no uncertain terms will I allow that old, dirty furniture in my house!"

"James, you're being completely unreasonable. Just look at your own parents' house – it's filled with beautiful antiques. Obviously your father loved those rare pieces of furniture; we would be honouring his memory to have a similar décor."

"That's the most ridiculous thing I've ever heard, Marjorie!"

"Well, surely you can agree that antiques would be better suited to the exterior of our home, with its fine traditional Grey stone. It's calling out for something rich, warm and of heirloom quality." Before James could balk at that argument, Jenny continued. "Besides, no matter what you say, I spend far more time in the home than you do and nothing would make me happier than to have it furnished in a way I like, that reflects my personality. Ever since we moved in here, I've felt like a visitor in my own home. I need to contribute to the aesthetic in here, James."

"Marjorie, you know that I prefer the modern, clean-looking furniture that is already here. It is perfectly good – what do you suggest? That we just throw it all away?"

"James, we could furnish the guest houses with all this stuff! Those homes are just sitting empty. The modern look in this house is too sterile looking and cold and every chair is stiff and uncomfortable. But you probably don't even realize that because you're never here long enough to sit down!"

"Marjorie, that's enough! That old furniture is repulsive. It gives me the creeps just looking at it and imagining all the people who have been all over it. My answer is no and that's final."

"James, I don't accept that." Jenny held her ground. "I have already fallen in love with several of the pieces I saw and either you allow me to bring them into our home or I'm not going to stay here anymore."

James stared at Jenny in disbelief. He could see in her eyes that she wasn't just bluffing.

"The only way I'll let any of that stuff in here is if the finish on every, single piece is completely stripped and refinished beforehand."

"James, that's a huge job! These pieces are in immaculate condition. A good furniture polish will suffice."

"No! That's my final offer. Refinish it all or nothing."

"Fine."

And that was the start of Jenny's many purchases of rare antiques that most collectors would die for.

Jenny had a good eye. She checked the paper every week for estate sales and habitually visited antique shops at least once a month. Over the three years of their marriage Jenny made some exquisite and phenomenal purchases. She would have loved to have put an antique bedroom suite in their bedroom, but James would not allow it no matter how times it was refinished.

James crumpled the note in his hand as he walked up the stairs and decided that he would not wake her up. Whatever she had bought could wait until the morning. How could a piece of furniture change his life anyway?

He snuck into their bedroom, flipped on the bathroom light and left the door partially ajar to give just enough light to undress and get into bed. When James turned off the bathroom light and tiptoed to the bed, Jenny snapped on the night table light.

"James!"

He stood next to the bed in his under shorts crouched over and frozen, as if he had been caught stealing something.

"You're not going to believe this, James!"

"Come on, Marj, no games tonight. I'm tired. What is it? Not another piece of that old furniture?"

"Better, James. *Much better!*" Jenny jumped out of bed and rushed over to him. "Feel my tummy, James. Come on, go ahead."

James stared at her then at her tummy. "You're not...?"

Jenny nodded. "Yup!"

"No way?" said James. "Don't kid me about this, Marj."

"I'm not kidding." Jenny's eyes brightened. "James, I'm pregnant. We're going to have a baby!"

James' jaw dropped to his chest. He threw up his hands and jumped around the bedroom like a kindergartner.

Jenny had not seen him like this before and she loved it. Jenny ran to him and grabbed his hands and jumped with him. For the first time in the three years of their marriage, Jenny felt happy.

Really happy!

JENNY COULDN'T DECIDE who to call first, Tammy or her mother? Without waiting for an answer she was already calling her friend's number.

When Tammy answered the phone Jenny could tell she was still in bed. "Hi Tammy, wake up! I want you wide awake for what I'm about to tell you!"

"Jenny, it's not even eight o'clock and Chloe is sleeping in, too. It's Saturday morning, you know."

"Of course I know, but this can't wait…"

"If you're going to tell me you bought another antique I'm going to hang up." Tammy yawned. "I'll give you two more minutes and then I'll call you back at eleven…"

"Tammy, I'm going to be a momeeee!" Jenny squealed so loud Tammy had to take the phone away from her ear.

"You're what!"

"Tammy, I'm pregnant! The doctor confirmed it yesterday afternoon!"

"Jenny! That's wonderful! I knew that hard-nosed husband of yours had a few good sperm in him!"

"I've never seen James so excited Tammy. He went bananas!"

"Oh Jenny, I'm so happy for you! Chloe will be ecstatic, too. She keeps asking when Auntie Jen is going to give her a cousin. Somehow she thinks we're related."

"We might as well be, we may be best friends but to me you're like the dear sweet sister I never had!"

"And you are to me, too! So how far along are you, Jen?"

"Just around nine weeks. It's still early, so we have to be careful. I would hate more than anything to have a miscarriage; that would just be too devastating."

"Oh Jen, don't think like that. This pregnancy was made in heaven! It's a miracle. Here you thought you would never have another child, and poof! Just like that, the Lord plants a little soul in your womb."

Jenny started to cry at it all. "You're so right, Tammy! This is such a miracle. I simply cannot understand how some women take their pregnancies so for granted they feel no qualms about simply aborting their babies. I feel so blessed…"

"I know Jen, I feel the same way. It's terrible, Mom told me the other day a doctor opened an abortion clinic in Montreal. I can't believe a doctor doing that, Jen. Doctors are supposed to protect life, and more and more are signing on to end innocent baby's lives before they're even given a chance to be loved."

"It's so sad..."

"I thank God everyday for putting me in the line of fire against it. Counselling girls is so fulfilling, but the rallies and demonstrations I attend are really important, too."

"You have to be careful at those demonstrations, Tammy. I've seen on the news they can get pretty out of hand."

"Yes, they can be scary and sometimes even violent. Good thing police are there to keep watch. Anyway Jen, I don't want to put a damper on your news. I am elated for you!"

"Thanks Tammy. I can't wait to phone Mom with my news. Tell Chloe first thing when she gets up and tell her she can call me and reverse the charges."

"This one will be on me Jen. Give my best to James as well."

"Hi, Mom! Glad you're up."

"Oh, Jenny, I get up with the sun these days. I guess you need less sleep when you get on in age."

"Oh, Mom, you're still young. Besides, getting up early you get to enjoy the best time of the day. Anyway, I have some news."

Jenny heard her mother's sharp intake of breath.

"Are you sitting down?"

"Jenny, please tell me, I can't take the suspense."

"Mom, I'm pregnant! We're going to have a baby!" When her mother didn't respond, Jenny wondered if instead of dying of suspense, she'd died of shock.

"Mom, are you there?"

"Yes, yes, Jenny, I'm here. I'm just so thrilled that I'm speechless. I'm going to be a grandmother?" Jenny didn't want to remind her mom that, technically, she was already a grandmother. She knew what her mom meant.

"Yes, you are! And you can take the baby for walks and help feed it and buy sweet little outfits for it and—"

"Oh, Jenny, I'm so excited I can hardly wait. When is the due date?"

"I'm about two months along. The doctor thought around the beginning of next January."

"So you will be able to work up to Christmas?"

"Yes, I'm hoping to. I'll let my principal know on Monday and apply for maternity leave. Oh I'm so excited Mom, I still can't believe it. Why don't we go out for lunch today?"

"Of course! This calls for a celebration! Will you pick me up or should I take a cab and meet you somewhere?"

"No, I'll come and get you; I'd like to tell Carlos. He's working today isn't he?"

"Yes, he works on Saturday until all the planting is done."

"Good, I'll be there shortly after eleven. And that reminds me, I want to share my news with my diary and Matti and the rest of the staff so I better go. I'll see you later, Mom!"

"I can't wait to see you, honey. Bye for now."

After hanging up, Jenny hopped down the stairs and went directly into the living room where she kept her diary. There were too many personal things in there for James to see, so she hid it from him in the most perfect place. She'd purchased a round end table about three months ago. Its three curved legs flared out at the bottom, came together in the middle and then flared out again to support the top.

Besides being a very elegant piece of furniture, it had two special features: each leg was fitted with a beautiful brass crow foot, and it had a secret compartment behind the side drawer of the thick table top. She opened the side drawer, reached in and put her finger into a steel ring. As soon as she pulled it, the back end of the drawer fell forward, revealing the diary compartment behind. With her diary in hand, she headed out to the backyard grounds via the kitchen.

"Good morning, Matilda, I have some good news to tell you!" Jenny practically sang.

"Oh, Mrs. Hamilton, you be purchasing another lovely antique? I can hardly wait to see it. Best thing Mr. Hamilton ever done is let you take over some around the house. Feels more like a home every day, so warm and inviting. Why just the other day Charles and I be talking and I tell him I feel like taking off my sweater and evry'ting when I be going into the living room, when before I felt like putting on my coat!"

Jenny chuckled, "I know what you mean, Matti, the other furniture made me feel cold too. And no, I haven't bought another antique, but I am looking to purchase an old tea wagon I saw an ad for."

"Oh, I can hardly wait to see it! I ain't served tea on one of them buggies for as long as I can remember."

"I can't wait to see it either. But, Mattie, I have other news."

Matilda put the knife and potato she was peeling down and stared at her mistress.

"Matti…" Jenny's eyes brightened and she braced herself as if getting ready to jump out of her skin. "I'm pregnant! James and I are going to have a baby!"

Matilda took hold of Jenny's hands, "Oh, Mrs. Hamilton, that's music to my ears, I be so happy for you! Just what the house needs. I 'spect it will really be a home, then."

"I'm so excited. I just have to share it with my diary. James and I have been waiting for this so long and it's finally happened. I'd love to go downtown and buy some outfits for the baby, but I don't know what it's going to be! Oh, I can hardly wait!"

"That truly is wonderful news, Mrs. Hamilton."

"You know Matti, you can call me Jenny when Mr. Hamilton isn't here." Jenny winked. "I consider you my friend."

"Oh, I would sure like to, but we best leave what is, Mrs. Hamilton."

"Really Matti, it's really okay."

Matilda looked a little concerned and tightened her lips.

Jenny suspected there was something else. "Did James have anything to do with this? You can tell me. It will remain between us."

"Yes, Mrs. Hamilton. He told me I best address you this way and I don't mind one little bit."

Jenny didn't want to press the issue should it put Matilda in an awkward position. "Well, that's fine then, Matti, but if you ever wish to call me Jenny, please feel free to do so."

"Thank you, Mrs... Would you care for a glass of iced tea to take outside with you?"

"That would be lovely." Jenny hugged Matilda.

"Good morning, Thomas!" Jenny called as she virtually danced down the stone path towards the gazebo, the ice cubes chilling her iced tea jingling against the inside of the glass. "We're going to have a baby!"

Thomas stood up from trimming the rose bushes and waved. "Oh, that's wonderful, Mrs. Hamilton!"

"Soon you'll have someone messing up your beautiful flower gardens."

"That won't be any trouble at all. It will be a joy to have a little one around."

"I see more and more Monarchs every year in the garden, they are such a delight to watch and flit about."

"They remind me of angels," said Thomas "I often wonder what it would be like if we had a glimpse of what goes on before us in the unseen."

"I have often thought about that too! Angels flying here and there and soon our baby will bring yet another one to the Greystone Manor!"

Thomas chuckled, "The wildflower garden is looking so beautiful, more flowers popping up everyday."

"Yes, I noticed and the fragrance is wonderful. Oh, by the way, Thomas, speaking of angels, that little angel figurine holding a jug amongst the shrubbery in the front entryway. Could you please move it out into the open a little more?"

"Of course, Mrs. Hamilton. You do know it has a broken wing?"

"Yes, I noted that. But, I just love angels so much that I don't mind its condition. And besides, it's a reminder that none of us is perfect."

Jenny entered the gazebo and sat on the sun dappled hanging bench. She set her iced tea on the ledge and opened her diary.

"If James saw what was in here, I would never hear the end of it," said Jenny under her breath. She felt confident, though, he would never find her hiding place. For one thing, he would never bring himself to touch the furniture and if he did, he would never think to look for a secret hiding place in the drawer.

She re-read a few of the entries she had made back when she met Henry and instantly, warm, wonderful memories swept through her. How often she thought of him and prayed that he was happy. She wondered if he and his wife Julean had another baby. She would love to see him and tell him she was going to have a baby. Jenny just knew he would be so happy for her. *Wouldn't it be something if Henry and his wife were friends with James and me?* Jenny smiled at such a silly thought.

She took a pen out of her pocket and started her entry:

Saturday, May 25, 1968

> *Yesterday was one of the happiest days of my life. I learned for certain that I am going to have a baby. Camilla is going to have a brother or sister! And I found out on her eleventh birthday! What a wonderful gift! I wish I could share it with her... I wish with all my heart that someday we will be together as a family.*

Jenny placed the pen in between the pages and closed the diary. She sipped her iced tea and spoke to her angel. "I wonder how James would take it if he knew that I had another child. Would he understand? Would he think differently of me? Now that I am carrying his child maybe it would be okay to tell him."

He seemed so happy, last night.

Images flashed through her mind of what would happen if he wasn't okay with it. *Hmmm. The risk was too great. It's best to leave sleeping dogs lie.*

Jenny set down the glass and continued writing.

> *We'll have to think of a name if it's a girl because Camilla is already spoken for, but if it's a boy, I would like to call him Henry.*

Jenny couldn't believe she had just written that. It would be a constant reminder of her first love. And James would never allow the name Henry. Ever since she had told him about Henry Pederson his jealousy flared up in seconds just at the mention of the name Henry.

No, perhaps it would be best for James to come up with a name if it's a boy.

As Jenny set to write more she glanced at her watch and gasped when she realized it was nine-thirty. She had to get ready for the luncheon date with her mom.

She jumped off the seat and dashed inside to get ready to go. She could hardly wait to tell everyone at school the news. Maybe that would curb the many advances she kept getting from other male staff members and the high school boys who just couldn't help themselves when around her, even though they all knew she was taken.

CHAPTER TWENTY-SEVEN

I n June, Henry and Julean decided to go on a camping trip to Jasper, Alberta. They rented a trailer, packed up the kids in the station wagon, and hit the road. For years they had heard how beautiful the drive was between Banff and Jasper, so after an exhausting year at university it was just what Henry needed. Julean also looked forward to the holiday after the long extended winter, and the kids were so excited they could hardly contain themselves.

After the first hundred miles or so the children finally settled down and fell asleep in the back of the station wagon. Their plan was to try and make it to Medicine Hat and camp there overnight. The next day they would be on the road early enough to get through Calgary before the morning traffic and be at Banff by the end of the day or sooner.

"It would be nice if we could take a small detour and visit Aunt Netta and Uncle Jacob at Cardston. You might find it interesting to visit a Mormon colony." Julean said as they drove along.

"Yeah, I never thought of that. It would be interesting to visit them and see where your roots originated. I remember them from the wedding. Jacob was such a friendly man."

"They are my favourite relatives and I enjoy talking to Auntie Netta. She's a good listener and always has something wise to say. She's similar to Father Engelmann in that way."

"When we get to the campsite tonight I'll study the Alberta map and see how we can visit them on our way home. The kids are so excited to see the mountains, and I must admit so am I. So if it's ok with you, let's head there first and see if we can't swing by Cardston on the way home."

"That would be wonderful, Hank. It will be good for me to see what the colony is like now. We moved to Regina when I was six years old so I'm sure a lot has changed there since then. Dad was never interested in going back, so the only memory I have of the colony is that of a very young child. Mom went back a few times, but she never brought me with her, and I don't think she's gone at all in the last few years. Some of her closest friends moved on to BC in the late forties and early fifties. Dad was adamant that we don't go there as they are the group that still practices polygamy which he is strongly against."

"Wasn't that the reason why he and Vera left the colony?"

"That was part of the reason, but dad also wanted to finish his degree in medicine. We moved to Calgary and four years later a doctor retiring in Regina advertised for a general practitioner to take over his practice. Dad accepted and that's how we got here."

"Yes, I remember you telling me that story... There was something else I recall, something interesting about your dad's name...?"

"Yes, his name is actually Jacob. There were so many men on the colony by that name so he started to go by Jack. He liked it, so it stuck."

"So why do some Mormons still want to have several wives?" Henry wanted to know.

"As I understand it, the founder began the practice, but by the late 1800s the church as well as the United States government banned polygamy. The people who wanted to continue the practice went to different places; some came to Canada and settled in a community near the present day town of Cardston. I think they came around 1905; I'm not sure about that.

"Anyway, the Canadian government started to ban the practice as well and declared polygamy a criminal offence and in time the life style began to disappear.

"Auntie Netta told me that there was a lot of dissention in the community at that time. Those that wanted to continue to practice polygamy moved to BC and founded the Bountiful Colony in a remote valley near the town of Creston."

Henry turned on the windshield wipers. "Oh no, it's starting to rain. I thought it might, with the sky being overcast all morning. Hopefully it will be nice by tomorrow."

Julean gazed at Hank and then turned on the radio. Henry gave his wife a furtive glance back. He wasn't sure if he should continue the conversation about the Mormon history but he was curious.

"So Julean, how many wives do some of the men have?"

"Auntie told me that some men have had up to thirty wives and have fathered up to eighty children."

"Good Lord, how do they tell who each belongs to? Why so many?"

"They believe that the more children a man produces, the better chances of entering the celestial kingdom of God, finding salvation and possibly becoming a God himself."

"I think that's getting way out of control... How can they possibly get to know each other...?" Henry shook his head and muttered, "It's unbelievable."

"Well, there's quite a history to how the Mormon religion started but like I said Hank, the Mormon church of the Latter Day Saints banned the practice of polygamy before the 1900s."

The swishing sound of the wipers grew louder as they tried to keep up with the pelting rain. Julean turned up the volume of the radio just a tad and casually asked, "So, what do you think of a husband sharing two wives...?"

But before Henry could answer, a song that began to play immediately caught his attention. He reached forward and turned up the volume a bit more. Some female vocalist was singing *True Love. That was their song!* It conjured up memories of the time he and Jenny went to see the movie and how they sang the song as they walked home that night, hand in hand. He had never heard this version before as he usually listened to Bing Crosby and Grace Kelly sing it. However, Henry really liked her singing; she sounded like an angel.

Henry could sense Julean stirring in her seat and yet he was so drawn by the words of the song he was compelled to sing along:

While I give to you and you give to me

true love, true love.

so on and on it will always be

true love, true love,

For you and I have a guardian angel

on high, with nothing to do

but to give to you and to give to me

love forever true.

"Geez Dad, would you please turn the radio down and stop singing? You woke me up."

"Sorry Jeremy, try to rest some more, we will be stopping in Swift Current for lunch."

Henry turned down the radio. Actually, he welcomed Jeremy's interruption as it helped to conceal some of the thoughts he was entertaining while humming and singing along with the song. He hoped his sensitive wife didn't pick up on it. However when he turned to Julean to ask if she was getting hungry, Henry knew his wife had already read his thoughts.

Silent tears were sliding down her cheeks.

WHEN THEY GOT to the campsite at Medicine Hat it was still pouring rain. Henry had brought a jacket but not a hat and by the time he got the trailer set up and ran to the office for some supplies, he was soaking wet, through and through. Julean made soup and sandwiches for dinner inside the trailer and then read and played with the kids before they all retired at eight o'clock.

It rained all the way to Banff the next day. The only consolation was the view of the beautiful mountains through the blurriness of the heavy rain. Fortunately, the rain turned into a light drizzle and they decided to have a wiener roast under a sheltered area where they could light a fire.

Henry had cut off some twigs from a nearby tree and sharpened the ends to hold the hot dogs as they huddled around the roaring fire. Things were looking up and they were starting to get a taste of outdoor living and nature.

No sooner had that thought crossed Henry's mind when Allison pointed her hand to the back of the shelter and said, "Look Daddy, a bear!"

"No way…" Henry turned, and there stood a huge bear with his front paws resting on the railing surrounding the shelter. Julean let out a scream and picked up Allison. Henry grabbed Jeremy and they all hightailed it back to the trailer with the bear in hot pursuit.

"Quick, I hear the bear behind us!"

Henry dashed ahead of Julean at the last moment and opened the trailer door. Jeremy, Julean and Allison quickly scrambled in ahead of Henry. The bear was only ten feet behind as Henry clamored inside after them and closed and locked the door. They heard the bear's paws thumping and pawing at the door. Allison began to cry while Jeremy stood by his dad's side not sure what to make of it all.

After things quieted down, Henry peeked out the small window in the door and saw the bear had made his way back to the shelter and was already devouring three of the hot dogs that were left behind on the ground.

They dared not exit the trailer for the rest of the day. Julean made soup and sandwiches for the second time and once again the exhausted Pederson's went to bed early.

The third day of their trip made up for the first two days. They awoke to a bright sunny day. The sky was clear, not a cloud was in sight as they pulled out of their camping spot and made their way to Jasper. Henry found himself driving slower and slower as he was overtaken by the beauty and majesty of the Rocky Mountains. As the winding mountain road did not allow for a divided highway, there was a long line of cars, trucks and trailers behind Henry as he took his sweet time.

Every five to ten miles Henry would pull over and take in another breathtaking vista at which point dozens of vehicles would bypass them. Henry couldn't understand why everyone seemed to be in such a rush! The streams, the tall pines, the wildflowers and the snowcapped mountains overwhelmed him. Wherever he looked, he was surrounded by God's creation and it made him want to stand still in reverence. But it was what he kept repeating that touched Julean's heart.

"Honey, you have no idea how much I would love to paint the scenes before me on a canvas!"

"Yes, Hank, the view is truly spectacular, especially in your eyes!"

By nightfall they hadn't even made it halfway to Jasper. The weather held and so for the first time Henry was able to build an open fire by the campsite. Once again they tried to roast hot dogs and then marshmallows. The family in the campsite just down from them were singing familiar folk songs to the accompaniment of someone who was still learning to play the guitar, by the sounds of it. All in all it was the first enjoyable outing since the start of their trip.

In the morning a forest ranger touring the site suggested they walk upstream for a quarter of a mile to a clearing that held a view they might enjoy. He gave them a bell on an iron ring to take with them and told them to keep ringing it to scare off bears. After discussing it with each other, they decided to take a chance. After all, they came for an adventure and knew they were not going to get one sitting in their trailer.

So, off they went. Jeremy, following the well-traveled trail and ringing the bell, led the way. Julean and Allison followed hand-in-hand, and Henry trailed behind, keeping careful watch. The trail ran parallel to a turbulent stream that was rushing and crashing against rocks as it sped down the mountain. At times the roaring sound was so loud that Henry couldn't hear the ringing of the bell up front. He wondered if that was the case for bears, too. What good was a ringing bell if a wild animal couldn't hear it? He was having second thoughts. They had walked for over ten minutes but Henry decided if they didn't come to the clearing in the next few minutes, they would head back. He didn't want to risk anything happening to his wife and children.

Julean was having second thoughts as well as she turned and gave Henry a look that said, *should we continue?* And just as Henry was about to turn his family around to head back to the campsite, he saw the light of the sun brighten up an opening just ahead. The light drew him and he said, "Keep going Jeremy, we'll follow."

Henry was the last to enter the open meadow that was ablaze with wildflowers. It was as if he had just stepped into paradise. Two majestic mountains were reflected into a perfectly still lake that fed the turbulent rapids they had just walked along. The utter beauty of all that surrounded him and his family was indescribable. He was glad he had brought his camera as he quickly snapped several photos and again seeped in the beauty before him.

He pictured himself standing there with an easel, paints laid out on his palette, brush in hand, capturing this incredible sight on a canvas.

Julean turned to her husband and saw what he was feeling. Softly she whispered, "Oh, oh, here we go again."

If it wasn't for those two, glorious, unforgettable days they really wouldn't have had much of a holiday. Everyday thereafter it rained. Henry contracted a severe cold so they decided to head straight home and not visit Cardston after all. It was a good thing they did, as a trip to the doctor two days later sent Henry home with a prescription for antibiotics to combat what turned out to be pneumonia.

For the rest of the summer Henry lay in bed convalescing. He was so weak, he could barely walk to the bathroom. By mid-August, however, he was feeling better and began to play with the kids. He and Jeremy loved to play checkers and Henry was surprised how many times his son beat him, even when he was trying his hardest not to lose. Henry told Julean to buy a chess game, as it might be more challenging for his son.

A week before returning to school, Henry was resting in bed when his wife came into the bedroom after a day of shopping. She was holding a large bag in one hand and a small gift wrapped package that looked like an oversized greeting card in the other. She handed Henry the large bag first.

He opened the bag and looked inside and saw three books. His heart almost stopped when he took them out and slowly studied each one.

"*Painting Landscapes in Oil*," read Henry aloud, "*Drawing and Sketching*" he read again as he surveyed the second book and by this time, tears were surfacing. He could hardly make out the third book. It was a journal in which he could make notes and draw sketches.

Henry was overwhelmed by his wife's gesture.

"Oh Julean, this is fantastic." For the moment he forgot how debilitating the disease had weakened him. He reached up and grabbed Julean's hand and said, "Thank you, honey, this means so much to me."

"I know, dear."

"I love you so much."

"I love you, too," said Julean as she handed him the second small package.

Henry first read the attached note and then he opened the gift.

Hank, I know how much this touches your heart...Please let me be a part of it and share this with you.
With all my love,

Julean.

Henry gazed at Julean and studied her for a moment as her eyes began to glisten with tears. Henry carefully unwrapped the package, trying to appreciate the loving care in which it was wrapped. He unfolded the blue patterned paper and inside was a single play forty-five record. He picked it up, but tears were already blurring his vision and he couldn't read the label. But then, he didn't have to; he knew the title of the song the moment he saw the record...

True Love.

CHAPTER TWENTY-EIGHT

IT WAS LIKE one of those days when something so unexpected, so tragic, happens it hits you to the core of your being and never leaves you. Like when John Kennedy or Mahatma Gandhi were assassinated or the previous spring when Martin Luther King was shot. It's a moment in time that you never forget; the impact drives so hard and so deep inside, it remains a part of you until the day you die.

It was Saturday, September 21, 1968 just three weeks after Jenny had returned to work at her school. She was heading into the kitchen when the phone rang. Jenny rushed to get it but Matti answered before she did.

"Good morning… I mean good afternoon, this be the Hamilton residence. Yes, Mrs. Hamilton is here; if you'd be so kind as to hold on I'll go get her…"

Matti turned to Jenny and said, "There be a man on the phone for you Mrs. Hamilton. He don't sound too good, I 'spect some'ting not just right…"

Jenny walked to Matti with a puzzled look on her face and took the phone from Matti's outstretched hand.

"Hello…"

"Hi Jenny, it's Robbie…" was all he could say before he started crying.

"What's wrong Robbie…?"

"It's…Tammy, Jen… She's been shot… She's dead Jen…"

Jenny heard what Robbie said through his tears but it just didn't register. She couldn't possibly have heard that her friend Tammy was shot! *Tammy was dead? I must be hearing things…*

She turned and looked at Matti for orientation… Yes, she was in the kitchen with Matti… but there must be some mistake.

"I'm sorry Robbie, but what did you say…?"

Robbie took a deep breath and continued. "Tammy and Chloe were at a protest rally at one of the abortion clinics yesterday and some crazy guy started to shoot into the crowd. Three people were wounded but…Tammy didn't make it. She died instantly. The shot went through her heart…"

"Oh Robbie, I can't believe this… How is Chloe?"

"Tammy was holding her hand when she went down. Chloe didn't get hurt… She is just so confused and overwhelmed by it all. I don't think it's hit her yet as to what all happened."

Jenny was speechless. She was in such a state of shock she couldn't cry, she couldn't think, everything seemed to be going numb as if all the life was being squeezed out of her. She turned to Matti and pointed to a chair and motioned with her free hand to bring it to her.

Jenny collapsed into the chair. Matti looked so alarmed, her face clearly reflecting the sorrow of her beloved Mistress. Matti, too, for once did not know what to say.

"Are you still there, Jenny?"

"Oh Robbie… not Tammy…" was all that Jenny could utter before the death of her dear friend hit her like a freight car. She gasped for air as a deep gut wrenching cry of pain surfaced. The tears erupted along with the anguish and Jenny lost control.

Matti rushed to her side and put her arm around Jenny. She began to stroke Jenny and rock her at the same time. Matti heard the man's voice on the line asking for Jenny but she could not speak. Tears like a continuous waterfall flowed and streamed down Jenny's cheeks. Her stomach heaved convulsively and shook her entire body.

Matti took the phone from Jenny's hand and spoke into it.

"This here be Matilda. I don't think Mrs. Hamilton can talk no more. You best call back later, goodbye."

Matti hung up the phone and came back to Jenny. "Come, sweet Jesus, He be looking out for you. Let's go, I praying for you dear child."

Matti helped Jenny get up and led her to the living room. She lay Jenny on the couch and covered her with a blanket. Jenny was still sobbing so hard she had trouble catching her breath. Matti sat down on the edge of couch and began stroking Jenny's shoulder.

"There, there Mrs. Hamilton, you just cry for as long as you need to. Good Lord made tears just for times like this. I be here for you…"

Matti began to hum soft, sweet and low… It soothed Jenny and her crying subsided. "There now, you just rest my sweet little thing…"

Matti hummed some more and before she knew it her Mistress was soothed into a blankness.

"There, there Mrs. Hamilton, you now be resting in the Lord. Yes sweet Jesus, You fill this child with Your peace."

Matti got up slowly and made her way back into the kitchen. She looked up the phone number for Mr. Hamilton. Usually Charles would make a call to James' office but he was gone for the day so she picked up the phone and dialed.

"Yes, this be Matilda. I work for Mr. Hamilton and I need to tell him his Missus ain't doing so good and he best be coming home real quick and…"

"Just one moment please, Matilda. Mr. Hamilton is in a meeting but if this is an emergency, I can get him for you."

"Yes Ma'am. I wouldn't be calling if this wasn't an emergency. You best call him or I get more scolding, if you know what I'm saying."

"Yes, just a moment please…"

"Is this Matilda?"

"Yes, Mr.Hamilton."

"What in the hell do you want…?"

"Sorry I be troubling you but Mrs. Hamilton, she not doing so good. Some'ting terrible happen to her friend and Mrs. Hamilton taking it awful hard. She crying so hard I 'spect it do no good to the baby growing in her belly, you know what I'm saying?"

"What are you talking about, Matilda? Let me speak to Marjorie."

"She be sleeping now, Mr. Hamilton. Best thing she stay that way for a spell. Best you come home quick and bring a doctor with you... I don't know what else to say..."

Matti heard a click on the phone and the line went dead.

Two hours later James came home. Jenny was still sleeping and Matilda tried to explain what happened. Since she really didn't hear the telephone conversation that Jenny had with Robbie, she frustrated James all the more trying to explain it all. All she knew was that whatever the man named Robbie told her was very upsetting to the Mistress.

Around eight o'clock Jenny woke and through much crying she told James what had happened to Tammy. James, however, was less concerned with Tammy or Jenny and more about the baby. He was worried the stress Jenny was undergoing may cause a miscarriage. He called the doctor who agreed to make a house call.

Upon examination of Jenny his diagnosis was that she was fine physically but very distraught emotionally and gave her a prescription for mild tranquilizers. He suggested that Jenny stay in bed for a day or two.

James filled the prescription and gave Jenny two pills around eleven o'clock which put her back to sleep within minutes.

When James awoke next morning he was surprised that Jenny was up before he was. He got dressed and went looking for her.

When the first light of the sun found its way into their bedroom Jenny got up, put on a heavy sweater and jeans and went downstairs. She tiptoed through the kitchen, not wanting to wake Matti whose bedroom was just off to the side. She quietly slid open the patio doors, stepped outside, and just as quietly closed the doors behind her.

She was glad she put on a heavy sweater as the fall air was chilled. She smelled as she did each year the death of another season, when nature begins to shed its summer clothing and prepares to go for a long sleep. The odour this fall was especially hard for Jenny to inhale. It carried with it the death of her most cherished possession, the best friend she had ever known.

Tears flowed nonstop as Jenny wound through her garden. The tall trees hid the warmth of the rising sun. It would take another hour before the rays would peek through the Maples on the east side of the grounds. She should have brought a blanket. She wrapped her arms around herself and shivered. She considered going back inside until it warmed up a little more, but decided against it. As chilled as she was on the outside, it was nothing compared to the cold pain in her heart.

As she rounded a bend in the path, a beautiful Monarch butterfly flitted just above her head. Most of the butterflies had left for their long journey back to Mexico two to three weeks ago and it was unusual for a butterfly to be flying about so early in the morning. This would be one of the fourth generation butterflies for the summer season and belonged to the migratory group of Monarchs that had a life span of eight to nine months.

Why is this Monarch still here?

The chill that had previously enveloped her dissipated as she grew more conscious of the little orange and black creature. She extended her hand upward to invite the butterfly. It accepted Jenny's invitation and came to rest on her palm. Its touch warmed her further. Tammy and Chloe loved the Monarchs as much as Jenny did. Were they messengers of love, angels in disguise, or spirits who want to let us know that all is okay?

As she made her way to the gazebo, Jenny was amazed that the butterfly made no attempt to flit away. The fragrance of the flowers and herbs soothed her further. She entered her haven, sat down and began to swing. She marveled at the butterfly and the life cycle it underwent. Just like all of nature, the butterflies came and gave fully of themselves, living day in and day out, never worrying or fretting, accepting death as easily and willingly as life. They are always at one with their purpose and their source.

It is only us humans who have the mind to know that we are born to die. Those who have lost touch with the source of their lives are the ones who fear the inevitable the most. Tammy loved life and gave her life to save lives... Lives that were denied to become fully realized.

The butterfly in Jenny's hands fluttered its wings slowly. It was more a gesture than an attempt to fly. It felt so comforting and its soft slow movements seemed an attempt to communicate. If Carlos were here, she knew what he would say, 'The butterfly is a sign from your friend that she is okay. She is sending you her love just like my mother does each year. There is so much, *Señorita* Jenny that we don't understand. So much we must take on faith. God speaks through nature constantly. Listen and see...'

Just then she heard footsteps and her name being called. *It must be James; he is the only one who calls me Marjorie.*

"Geez Marjorie, I was looking all over for you. What the hell are you doing out here so early... What is that on your hand?"

"It's a Monarch butterfly that hasn't left yet..."

"That's an insect, shake it off for Pete's sake."

"Oh James, it's a beautiful butterfly."

"Make sure you wash your hands when you come in."

They looked at each other for a brief moment and then, in a rare moment of compassion, James asked, "How are you feeling...?"

"I don't know James, I feel so empty. I can't believe Tammy is gone. I... I don't know what I will do without her."

"Robbie called..."

"So early?"

"He forgot that we are two hours behind. He said they are sending Tammy's body back to Ottawa today and that he and Chloe are flying in tonight. He wants to know if you can watch Chloe for a couple of days, Tammy's mom is too upset."

"Oh yes, of course I will watch Chloe. Should I phone him back?"

"No, he said he would call you tonight or first thing tomorrow morning... Geez Marj, get that thing off your hand."

Jenny gazed at the little butterfly still gently moving its wings. "You best better start flying, little angel, you have a long way to make it home." She lifted her hand and softly blew the butterfly away.

Jenny picked up Chloe from Tammy's mother's place first thing the next morning. She didn't stay long as everyone was so emotionally upset and drained. Even small talk was difficult and strenuous. When they arrived back home, Matti made pancakes and bacon, but neither Chloe or Jenny could eat.

"Is my cooking getting so bad you can't eat just one mouthful?"

"No Matilda, I'm just not hungry."

"I understand child. You just tell me when that tummy starts rumbling. You come to me and I be cooking you something special real quick."

Matti stroked Chloe's hair, "How old you be, Chloe?"

"I turned eight this past April."

"I 'spect you be in grade six, then…?"

"Just starting grade five, Matilda."

Jenny listened and watched as Matti and Chloe conversed. Chloe was so mature and yet still so fragile. She was trying to be brave but Jenny knew she was hurting. Her eyes looked so sore and puffy from crying.

"I saw a butterfly in the garden yesterday morning, Chloe. I expect it started its long trek back to Mexico, but we can take a walk in the garden if you want and see if it's still here."

"Yes, I would like that Auntie Jen."

"Okay, honey, let's go then."

"Just remember I'm here to cook for you…"

"Thanks Matti, perhaps later." Jenny opened the patio door and the two girls stepped out. Jenny took Chloe's hand and they slowly began strolling down the path. Thomas and Ramon were raking leaves and cutting away the dead parts of the perennials. Thomas waved and put his head down, pretending to be busy. He knew Jenny wasn't interested in chatting today.

"How long did you know my Mom, Auntie Jen?" Chloe wanted to know.

"We met in Grade 9, when I moved to Ottawa from Regina, Saskatchewan. She was the first person to come up to me after class and welcomed me to the school. Your mom was like a ray of sunshine spreading her light and love all around me. We hit it off right away and we became best friends."

Jenny let go of Chloe's hand and put her arm around the young girl's shoulder and drew her in as they strolled along.

"True friends are rare Chloe; when you find one, cherish her with all your heart. I loved your mom so much. We were totally and completely ourselves with each other, we could see into each others hearts.

"Your mom was there for me in good times and in bad. She sheltered and guided me just like my guardian angel does. She knew me better than I know myself. Tammy would not only listen to what I was saying but listen in between my words. She would sense when something was troubling me and always made sure we talked it out before we left each other. I was an open book sharing myself completely to a friend that I trusted even more then my own self and thoughts. Our conversations were never from the head, but from the heart; true and honest.

"That's what friends are, Chloe… A shared unconditional love for one another."

"Mom said you were her best friend, too. She would say all the time that you have the heart of an angel and that your friendship was one of the miracles in her life."

"I consider your mom to be like an angel as well. When either one of us were down and had trouble remembering how to fly, the other would lift us to our feet again. It was as if she held my hand in hers all the time."

They circled a pond enlivened with water lilies and bordered with boulders, blue juniper and what appeared to Azaleas and Vinca; a very beautiful combination in the summer especially when everything was flowering.

"Oh Chloe, we had so many laughs and shed so many tears together. I don't know what I will do without her. You will have to help me Chloe. When you go back home with your dad, I would love it if we could phone each other Sunday nights like your mom and I used to."

"Yes, I would like that too…"

Just up ahead was the gazebo.

"Let's sit on the swing for a while and rest."

When the girls sat and started the swing in motion, Chloe

asked, "Why do people hurt each other, Auntie? Both Mom and I saw that man coming towards us. Mom knew he was up to no good and pushed me behind her. Next thing I heard were all these loud bangs. It's the first time I heard gun shots for real. Mom fell down and the man looked at me for a moment, I thought he was going to shoot me and then he pointed the gun at other ladies beside us. He fired three more shots before the police wrestled him to the ground. When I looked down blood was coming from Mom's chest. I didn't know what to do, Auntie. I wanted to hug her and help her but I didn't know if it would hurt her so I just stood there." Chloe started to cry, but bravely continued.

"I wish now I had knelt down and hugged her to let her know I was there. I was so scared and confused… Next thing I heard was a lady say she was a nurse and bent down to examine Mom and then a doctor came and said the same thing. Together they looked at her. They felt her pulse and looked into her eyes. When the doctor shook his head I knew Mom was dead… There was nothing that any of us could do anymore.

"There was so much noise and yelling and crying and the sirens were blaring. Next thing I knew the ambulance men were there putting Mom on a stretcher. They didn't know I was her daughter. I ran after them screaming and finally they realized who I was and took me with them. It was all so awful, Auntie Jen…"

Chloe started to sob uncontrollably. Jenny already had her arm around Chloe but now drew her in tightly as both girls wept deep tears of sorrow.

What images and memories of terror and sorrow will cloud Chloe's mind of her mother's death? Oh dear guardian angel, erase those images, heal this little child's heart and soul.

"Oh Chloe, your mom was the most beautiful person I knew. Let's remember all the moments of love we shared. Let go of all the rest. It is only our love of each other that is important."

Chloe heard the words of her Auntie but needed to talk more to try to understand…

"It's going to be so lonely and different without Mom around, so hard for daddy and me. I'm frightened by it all. How are we going to live?"

"I know what you mean Chloe; I feel the same way. But we have to take each day at a time and support one another and always remember that your mom is with us in spirit."

"That's what Daddy said. That she is now a spirit in heaven... What does that mean?"

Just then, the same Monarch butterfly that Jenny saw the morning before started flitting about. Jenny felt sure it was the same one. She stretched her hand out but the butterfly just circled the girls.

"It is difficult to understand how your Mom is a spirit because we can't see it Chloe, but it is similar to what happens in the life of a butterfly.

"You remember how we watched the butterfly lay an egg on the underside of the milkweed plant, right? And you remember how it hatched in a few days and a tiny worm emerged? How it immediately ate its own egg and the milkweed leaves and grew very quickly, shedding its skin at least four times? Do you remember when the caterpillar was around two inches long it attached its hind end to a twig by spinning some silk and hanging there?"

Chloe looked at Jen and nodded.

"When it hangs there it sheds its skin for the last time, but this time the new skin dries and hardens into a pupa or chrysalis. Remember? You used to call this a poop-a."

Chloe smiled through her tears and Jenny went on.

"But what happens next Chloe is what you called a miracle for the longest time. Your mom and I used to get such joy out of you saying that because that's exactly what it is. When the chrysalis hangs there and dries and hardens it appears as if the caterpillar died. But something amazing is going on inside the cocoon. It is going through a complete transformation, a metamorphosis, and it comes out as a butterfly that quickly flies away, giving its beauty to the world.

"Well Chloe, in a similar way, that is what has happened to your mom and will happen to all of us. She too was born of an egg that started in her mother's womb and then she was born. She lived her life over many years, growing in body and spirit. And then she came to the end of her life. The moment she died on the outside, a miracle happened on the inside. The spirit that was in her body while she was alive, left her body and emerged as a beautiful, free spirit like an angel in God's kingdom called heaven.

"So Chloe, in the same way that the caterpillar becomes a beautiful butterfly that we can see is so happy and free to flit about in the sky, your mommy has undergone a new life from earthly wings to spiritual ones. We can't see her spirit but we know she is here and will be for the rest of our lives to help, guide and protect us. At times you will sense her presence so strongly that you will become overwhelmed with joy. We will all have another angel at our side!"

It almost seemed as if the Monarch flitting about was listening to Jenny's explanation. This time Chloe extended her arm and the Monarch came to rest on the palm of her hand.

"That's the very same Monarch that came to me yesterday and did the same thing Chloe."

They watched the butterfly resting on Chloe's hand for a moment in silence, before Jenny spoke again, "Do you remember Carlos, the gardener?"

Chloe nodded.

"He believes as I do that God uses nature to send us messages of healing and love. I wonder if your mommy isn't doing that now?"

The girls gazed at the butterfly as it slowly moved its wings on Chloe's palm, its beautiful colour glowing in the afternoon light.

"Mom loved butterflies, Auntie Jen, especially Monarchs. When she was pregnant with me she said that the butterfly reminded her of when she was a child and would chase them. She said the Monarch butterfly made her love me all the more and she couldn't wait till I was born. And now it's reminding me of her..." Chloe couldn't finish and burst into a deep sob.

Jenny loved Chloe as her own. She pulled the trembling girl in as they both stared at the butterfly. Jenny recalled the words of Carlos.

"Perhaps Chloe, the butterfly is a message of love from your mother. She saw the joy the butterfly gives you and wanted all children to be born to chase butterflies. See the butterfly as a message of love Chloe. It's a sign of life for you from your mom; that she is in heaven with her guardian angel. They both now watch over you and love you."

Jen tightened her hold of Chloe.

As they swung softly together in the warm fall day, with the Monarch resting on her hand, Chloe heard Jenny's voice begin the same prayer her mother had said with her every night of her life...

Angel of God, my guardian dear,
to whom His love commits me here,
ever this day be at our side
sweet Tammy and Mommy
to light and guard, to rule and guide...

THE GIRLS STROLLED the gardens and healed and comforted each other in the two days which followed, as they talked about Tammy and her life, their friendship and what a great mom she was. And each day the Monarch followed them wherever they went lifting their spirits.

The funeral was on the third day. Jenny held Chloe's hand on one side while Mrs. Anderson held her granddaughter's hand on the other side. Hundreds of mourners were present including many who never knew Tammy but believed in her cause.

Before they parted, Mrs. Anderson took Jenny aside and apologized to her for the way she treated her when Tammy was pregnant. She thanked Jenny profusely for helping Tammy and guiding her to do the right thing. To think that at one point they had considered terminating the life of Chloe. "You were my daughter's best and dearest friend. Of all the things in her life, Jenny, you were one of her greatest joys and treasures."

Jenny stayed home for another week before she returned to school. Her heart ached as Sunday evening approached. There were moments when she forgot and couldn't wait until dinner was over to phone her friend. Perhaps it was a wish that Tammy was still here and this was all just a bad dream. Jenny stared at the phone waiting for it to ring at the usual time they called one another but this time it was silent except for the tears of sorrow that came from deep inside and echoed softly off the walls.

She was going to phone Chloe but decided to wait until the

next day. She didn't want to transmit the heaviness of her heart to the young child and didn't think she could speak more than a word before crying.

Jenny put on a sweater and went out onto the patio and began to stroll down the moonlit stone pathway. The star of the east was out and shone brightly in the cloudless sky. Neither the rays of the star nor the full moon could console her; they only revealed the sheen of the sorrowful tears sliding down Jenny's cheeks.

Her life would never be the same again. Such a wonderful part of her life that gave her so much joy was snatched away in the blink of an eye. Ones we love are here today and can be gone tomorrow.

Jenny wished she had phoned her beloved friend more often. She had a similar wish when Camilla was abruptly taken out of her life or when she and Henry departed, or the death of her father. She wished for more moments of togetherness then; for more time to create more moments of memory to draw from.

"Never, take each other for granted." Jenny whispered into the cool evening. "Always take the time to tell others how much we care and love them. We never know what tomorrow brings... for it just might be too late."

Jenny turned and headed back to the house thinking of the little spaces of emptiness that were filling her heart with the departure of all her loved ones... spaces that no one else could fill.

Only memories, precious memories that help to heal a broken heart. Jenny stopped and gazed up into the star studded sky...

"Thank you dear heavenly Father for the gift of memories... Where would we be without them?

"And Tammy, besides the memories I have of you and our friendship which I will cherish for always, I know you are here in spirit as another angel at my side..."

CHAPTER TWENTY-NINE

E VER SINCE JAMES learned that his beautiful wife was pregnant, he changed for the better, or so Jenny thought. Initially he was annoyed with Jenny for telling the kitchen staff and groundskeepers that she was expecting. He didn't think it was any of their business, for one thing, and further he didn't like being congratulated by them and having to shake their hands. But once everyone got used to the idea and things settled back to normal, he began to show undo care and consideration for his wife.

"Don't lift that. Are you getting enough vitamins? Are you sure you should eat that? Don't exercise too hard."

He was becoming a real fuss pot, even coming home earlier most nights to keep an eye on her. He wanted to make certain she was cared for and protected; after all, she was carrying his heir. If only he knew what sex the baby was… A boy would make him ecstatic, but a female CEO would be great, too. James felt certain he could train any child of his to be just like him, if not better, *if that was even possible.*

After every doctor's visit James demanded a detailed account of the examination and the doctor's findings. Fortunately, both Jenny and the baby were in consistently good health.

"Good Lord, Mrs. Hamilton, that man of yours he sure be carrying on some. A nervous breakdown coming his way if he don't be settling down! I 'spect he be the one going to give birth to that baby."

Jenny laughed. "Actually Matti, his excessive fastidiousness is a pleasing annoyance."

"I don't quite understand what you jus said, but I 'spect you like the way he be carrying on."

"Yes, Matti, I like the way he fusses. It's unusual for him to show so much care and I must admit I like the attention."

Jenny loved being pregnant. She exuded a radiance that made people stop and stare. The sparkle in her blue eyes was back, revealing her spontaneity and zest for life that her father had loved so much. There were days Jenny even believed that perhaps her new little baby would compensate for the loss of her only true loves.

As the months progressed, many fond memories of being pregnant with Camilla flowed back into her mind. But this time it was different. This was her baby to keep. Daily she cradled her tummy in her hands as if holding the infant already born. She sang and talked to the child and soothed it with gentle strokes of her warm hand against her tummy. After all these years of waiting it was finally happening. The joy and anticipation of her baby's arrival and holding it in her arms overwhelmed her.

Unfortunately, it wasn't long before James' excessive attention and care for her began to take its toll. Just like his cleanliness and hand-washing, it was becoming an obsession with him. Initially, she had welcomed his mindfulness, but now it unnerved her and many days she would stay in her room or take long baths just to keep him away. His interest was so excessive and abnormal she began to wonder if the concern was not so much for her as his offspring. Of course Jenny wanted the baby to be healthy as well, but James seemed to be building up his expectations too much.

Jenny tried to discount that thought, but it gnawed at her. What if the child should die or be defective or stillborn? How would that affect their relationship? James was so focused on having an heir to his throne that Jenny felt the pressure of not letting him down.

If she did, it could prove devastating.

Feeding into that possibility was the irrational feeling of guilt

Jenny had that if anything did happen to the baby, it would be punishment for giving her daughter away. It was the same foolish thought Jenny had when she and James had been unable to conceive. For years, she had harboured the fear that she was being punished. Tammy had always been the one to quell Jenny's fears and quiet her foolish thoughts but now, without her friend to confide in, Jenny could not control the worry and anxiety she felt about it.

The combined pressure of the guilt over Camilla and James' excessive concern over the baby were beginning to take their toll on her and James noticed it.

"What is troubling you, Marjorie? You seem so nervous. Unless you get a hold of yourself, it could have an adverse effect on the baby."

"I'm trying my best James; I guess I'm just anxious about giving birth to my first child. I'm sure most women who are about to give birth are nervous, especially the first time around," Jenny lied.

Despite Jenny's protests, James called the doctor out to the residence.

"Really, I'm fine," she reassured the doctor.

"I'm going to prescribe a mild sedative for you. You may also wish to take a daily walk or two on the grounds. Walking helps relieve stress and you have such a beautiful estate here."

"I already do that, doctor. Perhaps I'm just getting a little jittery about the delivery and all. It would be helpful if you could convince James he needn't be so concerned."

Jenny was not being entirely truthful with either the doctor or James.

She knew how her husband thought and his fetish about cleanliness. If he knew that she had been touched by another... And not just anybody, but a drunken slob who raped her... Jenny shivered at the thought of James finding out.

If only Tammy were alive, she would be able to help me cope with all this.

ONE SUNDAY IN mid-December, just weeks from Jenny's due date, her mother came over for dinner. As they enjoyed their meal the topic of Jenny's anxiety came up.

"Oh James, I remember when I was pregnant with Jenny I was nervous, too. By the time I went in for the delivery I was a wreck."

"But there seems to be more to it, Edith," James persisted.

"Well, if you had lived through what Jenny has, you would be more than nervous yourself—"

"And, what was that?" inquired James.

Jenny brought her hand to her mouth and before she could caution her mother, the words Jenny had held secret from her husband all those years, tumbled out of her mother's unthinking mouth.

"Well, I'm sure Jenny has shared with you her rape and her birth to a baby girl, hasn't she?"

THE MOMENT EDITH said it; she wished she could have stuffed those words back into her mouth. The shock on Jenny's face and the look of horror on James' face instantly told her she had taken the evening, Jenny's pregnancy, James and Jenny's relationship, and their very future to an entirely different level.

For a moment there was dead silence; the calm before the storm. It was almost as if a bomb had dropped miles away and the sound of the explosion was making its way quickly towards them. It was just a matter of time before the entire impact would be upon them, ready to consume and destroy.

"What!?" James slammed his hands down on the table and simultaneously stood. His eyes were ablaze.

Matilda and Charles peeked into the room from the kitchen, then quickly hid.

Jenny was still holding her breath, frozen, unable to speak.

Edith flushed, her gaze alternating between her daughter and her enraged husband. What she had thought was an astute analysis of her daughter's state of mind turned on her. She'd made a serious error in judgment and one which would haunt her forever.

"What is this, Marjorie!?" James demanded, his black eyes flashing.

Edith was going to speak in defense of her daughter, but thought better of it. She had already said too much.

THE SHOCKWAVES OF a reality Jenny had dreaded for years were now upon her, surrounding her, overwhelming her, shaking her. She tried to get up and run away, but her legs wouldn't move, all sense of being was lost. The room swirled, the chandelier above the table was falling, coming down, crushing her and then there was darkness. Jenny collapsed, her head went forward, crashing into the food on her plate and before she slid off the chair, James caught her, instinctively trying to protect his heir.

Jenny's mother rushed to James' aid. James hollered for the butler, and between the three of them, they managed to get Jenny to the couch.

Edith began to fan her napkin over Jenny's face. Her mind was churning, what could she say to heal the wound she'd opened? James was a different kind of person than she usually encountered. In the end she decided silence would be best, at least until she talked to her daughter and came up with some defense.

Although James stared silently at his wife, hate spilled from his eyes. His twisting mouth, contorting and seething, and his convulsing body, clearly revealed that within James' speechless exterior a raging bull was crashing into every crevice of his being. The thought that he had made love with a woman who had not only been raped but had already given birth to a illegitimate child was so repulsive, he shuddered uncontrollably. He wanted to eliminate her from his life, get her out of his sight...

But she's carrying my child!

Words, like low growls, unintelligible, spewed forth. "How dare she do this to me? All along I thought she was a virgin. How could she have been so untruthful? Over and over she told me that this was her first child."

Edith dared lean closer, trying to make out what James was saying. Words she failed to comprehend, however, were spoken clearly by James' body language. Edith could see and feel his revulsion. She stepped back, fearing what he might do and anticipating his vomit at any second. An odour emanating from James began to overwhelm her so that she, too, began feeling nauseated.

He slowly moved closer to Jenny who was still unconscious on the couch, and leaning over with his face hovering just inches above hers, roared, "You... LIAR!" Edith gasped and was about to put an end to James' vitriol when Jenny began moaning. She was coming to. As she opened her eyes, the vision of James' face before her was too overbearing.

"Oh, James," was all she uttered as she passed into oblivion once again.

"James!" Edith cried. "We must call the doctor at once and calm her down. She may lose the baby."

Those words snapped James back to the reality of the situation. He shook his head and stood up. "Charles, call the doctor and get Marjorie's sedatives. They are in the medicine cabinet."

"James, I would like to spend the night here. Jenny needs me."

At least my presence may ward off an ensuing argument, give them both some time to stand back and come to their senses.

For the first time since the truth came out, James looked at Edith. And for the first time since her daughter had married him, Edith felt his fierce wrath. After a moment of calculation, James was finally able to spit forth an answer: "Fine."

He turned and strode from the room, brushing Charles as he was coming in. "Give the damn medicine to her mother. She can give it to Marjorie when she wakes."

*Oh my God, poor Jenny...*thought Edith as she watched him go. *I had no idea...*

The doctor arrived an hour later. By that time, Jenny had revived and was talking softly with her mother. The doctor checked her over, took her blood pressure and temperature. Both her pulse and blood pressure were excessively high. He looked at the medicine Edith handed to him. "Yes, two of these will be fine."

He looked at Jenny. "You need to rest and stay calm. It might be a good idea to get you up to bed. Do you think you can make it if we hold and support you?"

"Yes, I think I can. Thank you for coming over at this late hour."

"I was just at the hospital finishing my rounds, so it wasn't too much out of my way. Besides, we want to make sure you stay healthy. The birth is just around the corner."

After they got Jenny up to bed, Edith wanted to stay and talk to Jenny, but the doctor said it would be best to let her sleep. They turned out the lights and closed the door.

"What got her so excited that she would faint?" the doctor asked.

"Oh, just some family concern," Edith replied loosely.

"Well, she really shouldn't get so riled. It's a good thing she didn't fall when she fainted otherwise it could have been more serious."

"Yes, we certainly will try to keep our conversations on less disruptive topics."

After Edith saw the doctor to the front door she returned to the living room. Ever since James stormed out of the living room earlier, she had not seen hide nor hair of him.

"Have you seen Mr. Hamilton, Charles?"

"I believe he is in one of the guest houses, Ma'am."

"I see. And, where might I retire for the evening?" Edith asked.

"There is a guest room just down the hall from where your daughter is sleeping that would be appropriate and to your liking."

"Yes, Charles, the closer I can be to her the better."

"I'll prepare the room and draw the covers on the bed for you, straight away."

"Thank you, Charles."

That night James did not go to his room to sleep with his wife. Neither did he the second night nor the third after Edith went home. In fact, James never slept with Jenny ever again.

A week after the dinner incident, Jenny was surprised by James' outward change of appearance. After not speaking for days, James approached her and calmly brought up the subject of her rape. While he wouldn't console her physically with a kiss or hug, there was an acceptance of sorts in his tone and in his words.

"It is unfortunate that happened to you, Marjorie. I wish you would have told me at the start and yet, I understand why you didn't. That was an awful, horrible thing that occurred and perhaps I should appreciate that you wanted to protect me from hearing of it."

"Oh, James, I wanted to tell you so many times, but was afraid to. I so hope you won't hold it against me or the baby."

"No, Jenny. I want the baby even more than you do. I don't want you to worry that I would ever abandon this child you're carrying."

Jenny was so relieved that it was now out in the open and she wouldn't have to hide it from him anymore. Her anxiety abated and once again she was full of light and joyful anticipation. When her mother visited the next weekend, she saw the change in Jenny for herself.

"That was very wise of you to reveal what had happened to Marjorie." James said when he saw Edith. "I always suspected she was holding something back from me. At least now we can deal with it openly and reduce Marjorie's anxiety. Nervousness and stress can have a detrimental affect on a developing fetus. Hopefully now, any damage or harm has been minimized."

While Jenny was glad James wasn't raving mad or holding it against her, she was suspicious of his motives. He hardly touched her anymore and no longer kissed her.

Just a week before the baby was due, a new uneasiness began to take a foothold within Jenny. Once again, she was no longer sure of her husband.

Did he really love her or was it the child that she would give him that kept their marriage together? What would happen after the baby was born? *Oh dear guardian angel help me... Tammy, help me...*

CHAPTER THIRTY

TWO WEEKS AFTER the due date, Jenny's doctor decided to break the sac and bring on labour. Jenny was hospitalized and put into a private room that looked more like some extravagant bachelor suite. Jenny was shocked that there was such a spacious room with so many amenities in a hospital. It could easily have accommodated four other patients. She felt guilty having it all to herself.

James popped in twice during the day. He continued to be a fuss pot and an annoyance to the nurses. If she didn't have this uneasy feeling as to his motives, she would have actually enjoyed his attention and care.

Perhaps I am not being fair to him, thinking that he doesn't care about me.

She knew before they married he was a clean freak and had this fetish about wanting things new and untouched, so it was unfair of her to expect him to be different or change quirks he'd had most of his life. She began to relax and be more accepting of him.

At one-thirty in the morning, Jenny's labour began. James was dozing on the sofa when he heard Jenny moan. He jumped up and came to her side.

"What's wrong, Marj? Did you have a pain?"

"Yes. It's like someone stabbed a knife in my back. Let's time it.

It's one-thirty two. Let's see how long until the next contraction."

"I'm not taking any chances, I'll get the nurse and doctor. Don't go away. I mean stay right there."

Jenny chuckled. "Really, James. Of course I'll be right here! Just hang on a bit, though, this could take a long time. I remember when I had Camilla it took—"

"I don't want to hear about that ever again, Marj, and I don't want you to even think about it. Just think about this baby. This is different."

Jenny stared at her husband as his egotistical nature surfaced for a brief moment. The pain that stabbed her heart at his comment was far greater than the labour pain she'd had moments ago.

By five-thirty eight the contractions were less than two minutes apart, so Jenny was transferred onto a gurney and wheeled into the delivery room. James followed. A nurse gave James a white cap and gown to wear then directed him to the chair that she'd placed beside Jenny.

"But I want to see the birth," James objected.

"You may get in the way or even faint. We've had that happen several times before. I suggest you stay where you are."

Jenny's pain had been so excruciating earlier that they had given her an epidural injection into her spine to numb the lower half of her body. Jenny didn't want to do it, but James insisted, claiming he wanted nothing to interfere with the birth.

James could only stay put for a minute, his legs were so jumpy that he couldn't stop them or his hands from shaking. Jenny wished that they had given him the spinal injection. James got up and paced back and forth. One of the nurses suggested that he would be more comfortable in the waiting room.

"Not on your life!"

The doctor checked the dilation.

"It's starting nicely," he called out to Jenny. "Won't be long now."

Jenny thought of her previous birth. She could feel it then because she'd refused pain killers and laughing gas. She'd been fully aware of what was going on. Now she couldn't feel a thing.

"What's happening?"

"I can see the head," relayed the nurse.

James paced to the other side of the room behind the doctor. He stood on his tiptoes. He saw his baby! A rush swept through him. He thought he would float. He bit his lips together and wrenched his hands.

"Come on, we're just about there," he whispered. He felt his bowels push. He would have it out already, if he were doing it. The excrement suddenly sticking to his under shorts was evidence of that.

"Jenny, try to push if you can," directed the doctor. "The head is coming."

"Push, Marjorie!" James cried, no longer able to contain himself. "Push, Marjorie, push!"

He ignored the glares of the two nurses. "Come on, Marjorie!"

Jenny hated it when he called her Marjorie. In protest against James, she pushed hard.

"That's it, Mrs. Hamilton, another minute or two and we'll see what you've got."

James moved closer. He saw the head and then the shoulders. He squeezed between two of the nurses who already expressed their exasperation of him. The heavy-set one stood her ground and pushed him back. But he stood on his tiptoes and raised himself as high as he could until he lost balance and fell in between the nurses again.

"Really, Mr. Hamilton, restrain yourself."

Jenny raised herself on her elbows trying to see what she couldn't feel. "Please! Move the cover. I want to see my baby."

"It's out!" yelled the doctor and James almost in unison releasing some of the tension.

The doctor held the baby and stood up. James shoved the heavy-set nurse out of the way so he could see his baby. All James saw was its tiny red bum.

"For God's sakes, turn the baby around!" James cried.

The doctor slowly and carefully turned the baby. A rush hit James that almost took over his sanity. "It has a penis! I have my son!"

The doctor turned, shocked by James' outburst.

James rushed over to his son. "That's James Junior! Meet my

son, James Junior!"

"That's a nice name," said one of the nurses.

Jenny, however, was shocked. They hadn't even talked about what name to give the child. He'd named the baby without ever asking her. Jenny couldn't believe this was happening.

James twirled and jumped around much like he had when she told him she was pregnant. Jenny watched him more than she did the baby the doctor was still holding. She was frightened and didn't know why. James paid no attention to her whatsoever. He couldn't keep his eyes off his boy.

They cut the cord and cleaned the baby. Once the mucous was drained out of his tiny nose and he was wrapped in a soft white blanket, the nurse picked up the baby and brought him over to Jenny.

"Here, let me have him," ordered James as he literally grabbed the infant out of her hands and began to walk out the delivery room.

Jenny's mind flashed back to when they took Camilla. *Oh, please, not again.*

"James! What are you doing?! Bring him to me," Jenny pleaded, tears streaming down her cheeks.

James turned, looked at Jenny and then at the baby. He paused for the longest time.

"Here, let me have the child." A nurse took the baby and brought him to her. Jenny had waited so long for this moment. How many times had she dreamed of holding Camilla and looking into her eyes and counting her fingers and toes? She would no longer have to do it in her dreams.

Jenny took the baby from the nurse and laid him beside her. She unraveled the blanket and counted his fingers and toes. She picked him up and gently hugged him against her breasts for the longest moment. She put the baby back down onto the open blanket and stared at him through her blurred vision. He had lots of dark black hair. His eyes were closed, but she guessed they were dark and black, too, just like his daddy's. Jenny counted his fingers and toes again. He was perfect.

"Here, Marjorie, let me hold him," James reached out to grab him.

"Please, James, just for another minute."

James pulled at the blanket and the baby started to cry. The nurse thrust the weight of her hip against James and wedged in front of him. She wrapped the baby, again, and walked out. James followed without another word to his wife. Jenny watched as they left the room. Tears filled her eyes; she was emotionally and physically exhausted. She had lost her little girl and now…

"Please, James," Jenny cried. "Please, don't take my son away from me.

At James Jr. two-week check-up, the doctor found the baby wasn't gaining enough weight, so he suggested that Jenny supplement breastfeeding with a bottle. That evening, after a thorough interrogation of what had transpired at the doctor's office, James found the excuse he needed to wean his son away from his wife.

"Jenny, I will hire a nanny tomorrow to begin feeding J.J.. I can't take a chance that he is not getting enough food."

"Oh, James, that's ridiculous. The more I breastfeed the more milk I should produce. I'm sure the next check up will verify that."

"'Should produce' is no guarantee. Why take a chance? It could have serious effects on the boy's health and growth."

"The doctor said I should only supplement the breastfeeding, not eliminate it and besides, breastfeeding creates a strong bond between mother and child and gives him a sense of security."

"Millions of women bottle feed their babies, Marjorie. It does the same thing. Perhaps you should go back to work and let the nanny look after J.J. during the day. You can still see him in the evening."

"Never, James. I took this year off so that I could be with the baby. I've waited so long for this."

"Well, in my opinion you're just wasting time and could be more productive at work."

Three days later, a rather stern looking, middle-aged nanny, dressed in full nanny-attire, appeared on the doorstep. Charles brought her to Jenny in the den.

"Good afternoon, Mrs. Hamilton. I am Ingrid Hardstone. Your husband hired me to tend to his son, James Junior."

His son? Jenny paled as she gazed in disbelief at the woman who was about to take the care of her son away from her.

"I told James that it was totally unnecessary to get someone to help me. Perhaps you can assist with the cleaning—"

"Mr. Hamilton gave me strict orders to feed J.J. at the following times." Ingrid thrust a paper out towards Jenny, which laid out a daily schedule of feeding, play and nap times.

Jenny felt sick to her stomach. She was about to sit down when J.J. cried. With Ingrid following, Jenny went into the next room, picked him up out of the crib and cradled him.

"The timing couldn't be more precise," commented Ingrid as she looked at her wristwatch. "If you would show me to the kitchen I shall warm up his bottle."

Reluctantly, Jenny called Charles to take Ms. Hardstone to the kitchen. While they were gone Jenny quickly began to nurse her son.

It so disheartened Jenny to see her son held by a stranger. This pained her more than anything James had done so far. She tried everything she possibly could to steal as much time with J.J. as possible. As soon as James left for work and at times throughout the day when she thought the nanny wasn't around, Jenny would take J.J. to her bedroom and breastfeed him.

Ms. Hardstone, however, was fully aware of Jenny's actions and reported it to James, who in turn severely reprimanded Jenny. To make certain his orders were obeyed, he began phoning home twice a day and would pop in unexpectedly several times a week.

It was when James started to get up in the middle of the night to give his son a bottle that Jenny lost all control. She pleaded with James, to no avail.

"Jenny, the doctor said you were to bottle feed J.J.. And the doctor was right. It is obvious J.J. is gaining weight. And besides, it's good for a baby to bond with his father, too."

Jenny knew there was something wrong with this picture and regretted ever telling James what the doctor suggested. What could she do, report him? He and his lawyer friends would have an iron shut case in a matter of hours. All they would need to do is get her doctor to verify that the baby had not been getting enough milk and there would go her defense.

Since J.J. was no longer breastfeeding, her breasts were not being emptied and began to ache. It seemed they ached even more than when she gave up Camilla. She was losing her son and she didn't know what to do. *If only Tammy were alive she could help me.* When she tried to talk to her mother, she just made excuses.

"Oh, he's just so excited to be a father."

"But, Mom, there is much more to it—"

"Don't let your imagination get the best of you. When you were a baby I only breastfed you for a week, too. You were losing weight as well, and I didn't want the worry of making sure you were getting enough to eat. James will soon tire of this added responsibility and he'll gladly turn the child over to you to look after. Just you wait and see."

"Oh, Mom, James will never change. You don't know him like I do. Hell will freeze over before that happens."

Little did Jenny know that ever since that night when the truth came out about her past, Edith was quite well aware of the monster her daughter had married, she had just swept it under the rug with all the other secrets and lies...

Matilda, on the other hand, not only saw what was happening, but was deeply moved and motivated by it. It hurt Matilda to see the anguish in her Mistress' eyes as she sat on the sofa and watched her newborn child being bottle fed by a cold-hearted, uncaring nanny. The daily sight of this so bothered Matilda that she devised a plan.

Shortly after lunch, while Ms. Hardstone was sitting on the sofa waiting for James Junior to wake up for his feeding, Matilda brought her a cup of tea. Matilda watched very closely from her spot in the kitchen until Ms. Hardstone appeared to have difficulty keeping her eyes open.

"You be okay, Ms. Hardstone?" Matilda fussed. "You be working so hard this morning, Ma'am, I 'spect you be needing some well deserving rest. Don't let it worry you none. Why I take a nap every afternoon. Here, I be taking your shoes off, Ma'am. You just lie on the sofa for just a minute. I let you know as soon as little James wakes up."

Ingrid was quite reluctant to do so, however she felt so groggy she couldn't resist the cook's kind offer. "Yes, perhaps just for a few moments."

No sooner had she rested her head on the cushion than Ms. Hardstone fell fast asleep.

"Hmm, those sleeping pills be working much better for the nanny than me. Perhaps I be needing stronger medication to get my brain to rest," whispered Matilda.

"Mrs. Hamilton! Mrs. Hamilton," Matilda called from the kitchen patio door.

Jenny looked up from her seat in the gazebo where she was writing in her diary.

"Yes, what is it, Matilda?" Jenny answered, as Matilda rushed down the path toward her.

"There be a problem Mrs. Hamilton. That child of yours, he be awake and is hungrier than all get out… I 'spect he needs to be fed and in a hurry. Can you help out some?"

"Isn't Ingrid feeding J.J.?"

"She be one tired nanny, Mrs. Hamilton. She say she lie down for a minute and in no time she be fast asleep. I tried to wake her, but she tell me to go away. Can you imagine now she be telling me to go away when that child is in desperate need of food! I 'spect you be doing that child of yours a huge favour if you could feed him."

"Yes. Oh, yes. Thank you for calling me, Matilda."

Jenny tiptoed past Ingrid who was fast asleep on the couch then hurried to the nursery where J.J. slept during the afternoon, but he was asleep too. Jenny couldn't resist waking him. She took him to a rocking chair in the corner of the room and began breast feeding him. She knew her breasts were not producing as much milk as before, but she just had to try.

Ingrid slept the entire afternoon.

"She be so tired, poor lady. She said so first thing when she walked through the door today. 'I be so tired Matilda' she said. I feel so sorry for the lady, and I being a Godly woman and all, I just helped her get settled on the couch for a spell. She be so 'preciative I 'spect it warmed her heart some. It sure did mine. And I knew you wouldn't object none to helping her out, now ain't that the truth?"

"Oh, yes, Matilda. I can help out anytime. This was the most enjoyable afternoon I have had with J.J. in such a long time."

The next day the same thing happened. Matilda told Jenny that Ms. Hardstone "be needing so much rest, I 'spect the poor lady be working day and night to make ends meet."

After several days of this pattern, Jenny suspected that Matilda was perhaps more involved than she claimed.

"Do you think we should report her sleeping on the job to James? Maybe he'll fire her—"

"I wouldn't do no such thing, Mrs. Hamilton. No sooner he gets rid of that Hardstone lady, he be finding another just meaner and more miserable than the first."

"But she has been doing this for over a week, Matilda. Don't you think perhaps something is amiss?"

"Well, she be getting on in age and no more spring chicken. Good Lord knows I be needing more rest with every birthday coming along. It's a natural thing, Mrs. Hamilton, as you get on some. Only thing one can do, be taking a nap. Heaven knows, I do all the time."

Matilda made a face expressing weariness and then, trying to conceal a twinkle in her eyes, added, "And besides, Mrs. Hamilton, the poor lady she be getting accustomed to her nap much like your son. Heaven forbid that we be disrupting her schedule."

Jenny smiled at Matilda. "Yes, we certainly wouldn't want to do that, would we?"

Matilda turned her eyes to the floor and lowered her head, trying her best to conceal her devious deviltry. "Oh no, Ma'am, we most certainly wouldn't want to do that. You be doing her a favour, Mrs. Hamilton. You can see how miserable she be when she awake. Why, we just helping the poor woman get away from herself for a spell, you know what I'm saying?"

Jenny tried to hide a smile and hold back a chuckle and then Matti added, "I can say only one more thing, Mrs. Hamilton: you just tend to that child of yours and I be looking after that poor, tired lady."

For almost a month and a half Jenny was able to have most of the afternoons with her son. Her breasts responded quickly to the regular feedings and became full and productive once more.

It was only a matter of time before James popped in one afternoon unexpectedly and found his hired enforcer fast asleep. Ms. Hardstone was severely reprimanded and after that, James made a point of coming home more regularly. Matilda thought it best to discontinue spiking Ingrid's tea. For a while, anyway.

CHAPTER THIRTY-ONE

WHEN HENRY RETURNED to work last fall after his year of graduate study, the School Board transferred him to Balfour Collegiate as a full-time guidance counsellor. On his first day, Henry had been surprised to see so many of the teachers he had as a student still working there! He decided to start his new position by visiting all the classrooms so he could introduce himself to the students and explain how he could help them.

In a short period of time, Henry was inundated with requests from students. Before long, his schedule could not accommodate the demand. This led to the development of group counselling programs to deal with students' personal and career concerns. Henry invited university professors as well as other professional people in the workplace to visit the school and talk about their careers. In turn, these seminars led to work experience programs for students not wishing to go on to higher studies. Henry found his work very rewarding, challenging, and yet at times draining.

He knew he needed a better balance between work and play in his life. Outings and having fun with his family helped, but ever since the trip to Jasper that stirred the arousal of his deep and forgotten passion to paint, he had felt an irrepressible urge to explore that as-of-yet undiscovered part of himself. The art books Julean had given him upon their return only fueled his curiosity. His innate love of art had been covered over by years of study, work, and raising a family but now it surfaced regularly and he knew he had to pursue it further.

It was a visit to his old high school art class that gave him the direction he needed. One day, as Henry was walking down the school corridor toward his office, he passed by the art studio. Stopping to peer in the small window of the door, Henry saw a bunch of twelfth grade students intently studying a bowl of fruit sitting on a small table at the front of the class. Henry's old art teacher, Robert Victor, was leaning over the shoulder of one student, passionately commenting on the painting the boy was working on. Clearly, the art teacher was still just as encouraging as Henry had found him to be when he'd attended his art classes as a student.

When the bell rang, the students poured out of the door and Henry entered the room.

"Hey Rob, looks like you've got a real promising group there."

"Henry! I'm glad you stopped by. I hear you're making quite the strides here in the counselling department. Glad to hear it."

"Yes. It's good to be back at Balfour. I see you're still trying to produce a future Rembrandt."

"Actually, I always thought you were going to fulfill that role, Henry. I'm surprised that you didn't take any art classes at university; you had a lot of talent."

"I wanted to, more than anything, but my faculty advisor directed me into the sciences. He said there was a shortage of physics and chemistry teachers and that the School Board was looking for teachers in that area. I definitely wanted to get on at a high school in Regina, so that's what I did: I majored in the sciences."

After a bit of reflection, Henry added, "you know, Rob, your art class was my favourite. Some days I just couldn't wait to get in here."

"Did you ever do a painting of that sketch you showed me? The one where an old man was holding his wife's hand who had just died? That was sure something."

"I still have the drawing, but no, I never did do a painting of it.

Hopefully, someday I will."

"Have you ever considered taking art classes at the community college? Professional artists are hired to give classes. I took one last winter and found it very good."

"I never thought of that. I've been taking university classes for so long now, a change like that may be just what I need. My wife Julean bought me a book on oil painting just before school started. I was going to buy a set of paints and get started on my own but I think taking art classes would be a better way to go."

"It just so happens a class is starting next Monday night. There still might be an opening."

Henry's eyes brightened and excitement ran through his veins. "I just might check that out, Rob, thanks."

After discussing it with Julean, Henry enrolled in an evening art class through the university extension department. During his very first class, while sketching a still-life scene, Henry's skill was immediately evident.

"Have you taken art before?" the teacher asked, looking over Henry's shoulder at his work.

"Just in high school, a long time ago."

"Your drawing ability and perspective is very good. And the way you caught the light reflecting in the shadow side of the vase takes a very keen and sensitive eye. Very good."

At break time the students mingled about viewing each others' drawings. Pretty soon, several of the students had gathered around Henry's sketch; it was easy to see he had a natural artistic talent. While many of his classmates began to lavish him with praise, Henry certainly didn't seek it, or go out of his way to receive it. He had always made a concerted effort to convince himself that he didn't need the approval of others. His worth came from doing a job as well as he could and comparing himself only to himself. For as Father Engelmann always said, "Live for God's approval and you will always be on track."

In the weeks that followed, charcoal sketching led to oil and acrylic full-colour painting. Once again, Henry's composition, perspective, colour harmony and the light he captured in a prairie landscape painting was remarkable. The artistic abilities that had been put on hold since high school were suddenly released, like hounds on a racetrack, with a passion he had not experienced before. His instructor was impressed at his painting skills and encouraged him to take a winter session oil painting class at the community college.

"I can't tell you how much I enjoy painting," he told Julean one evening as he worked on a landscape propped up on the dining room table.

"Yes, as do the kids. It's a constant struggle to keep them away from the paintings you're working on. Can you set up a little studio in the basement?"

"Yeah, I was thinking about that. It's just that I like to be around you and the kids."

"Well, why don't you do your painting after the children go to bed?"

Henry nodded. "I know I should, but most days I can hardly wait to get home and start painting."

And then Julean sat down on Henry's lap and told him about something else that he was good at creating...

Henry gazed into his wives eyes, "Are you pregn—"

Julean nodded with a twinkle in her eye, "Yup! Number three will be along just before Christmas."

"Wow, that will be some Christmas present! That's wonderful news, Julean."

"Just think, Hank, if you ever decide to put children into your landscape paintings you will soon have three models to choose from!"

"That's amazing that you should think that. I've already been drawing Jeremy in the sketch book you gave me. I knew there was a reason I started doing that. In fact, I will have him walking down the dirt road to the small town in the painting I am working on. Yeah, he'll be carrying books as if he was going to school..."

"Oh Hank, that mind of yours is going all the time!"

Julean ran her fingers through Henry's hair and kissed him tenderly.

The next week, Henry followed up on Julean's suggestion and cordoned off an area next to the furnace room in the basement. At least now he could leave his paints and working materials out and yet out of the reach of eager little hands. However, the lighting was poor in the basement and Henry longed for a studio with natural light. He considered buying a larger home, but they simply could not afford it.

By the end of the school year, Henry was dying to spend his days painting. He was finally achieving a better balance in his life. Not only did Henry love the technical craft of creating a work of art, he found painting to be extremely helpful with reducing his anxiety. When he painted, his mind was completely focused on the task at hand; he was present in the moment! Along with his ongoing habit of reciting scriptural passages, the painting also helped Henry keep his mind off of Jenny. July 6, their anniversary, had even come and gone without him dreaming of her. Or so he thought...

One evening in the second week of July, Henry had returned to his basement studio to work after they had got the kids to bed. A few minutes later, Henry heard his wife call to him excitedly from the head of basement door.

"Come quick Henry, I want you to watch something!"

Henry had just put the finishing touches on the landscape he was working on. He sprayed water over his watercolour pigments then covered the palette with a porcelain lid to trap the moisture inside and keep the paints soft. He had planned to start painting Anna's death scene next, but turned his mind to what Julean wanted.

"What's up?" Henry asked as he walked into the living room.

"They're showing a documentary on the fundamentalist groups within the Mormon Latter Day Saints. Remember I was telling you about them last summer when we went on holidays?"

Henry remembered all too well, including the question she had asked him at the time about whether he would like to be married to two women. He had never answered that question and he didn't want to get into it now.

"Yeah I remember, but I'm not really interested in that, dear. I'd sooner go back downstairs and paint."

"Well, watch just some of the program; it will explain a little bit more of my past. Remember my great-grandfather was a strong fundamentalist and had three wives? Anyway some of the women from the Bountiful Colony in BC were allowed to be interviewed for this documentary and they're sharing their thoughts and feelings about each other and how they spend their days. It might even show some of my relatives."

"I thought your father and his brothers denounced the practice and stayed in Alberta?"

"You're right. All except for Uncle Isaac. He went to the colony in British Columbia."

"How many wives does he have?"

"At last count, four."

"Busy man." Curious and more interested, Henry sat on the couch next to Julean. "Perhaps, having two or three wives may not be such a bad idea," Henry said jokingly.

"I remember talking to one of my surviving grandmothers about it just before we moved to Calgary and she said it had its ups and downs."

"I bet, having to keep up with three or four wives and all the children?"

"Oh, Hank, I didn't mean that. Responsibilities are shared, you always have someone to talk to, share you're most intimate feelings with and you can become very close friends—"

"Or enemies."

"Well, that can definitely happen, but Grandma told me wives are encouraged to get along and that problems are quickly worked out."

After the documentary ended, a silence fell over the room, save the faint ticking of the clock in the kitchen. With every tick, lingering thoughts of Jenny knocked gently at Henry's heart. If he had stayed downstairs and started that painting of Anna like he had planned to, he wouldn't be thinking of her, that was for sure. But it was almost as if Julean was purposely trying to plant the idea of sharing herself with Jenny in his mind.

The movie was hypnotic in the sense that it gave him permission to entertain those same thoughts in the presence of his wife. *What would it be like to have Jenny as a second wife?* The very thought sent shivers up and down his spine, yet the idea appealed to him. And he knew the guilt of that thought would follow him for days and days after.

Julean turned to him. "Are you happy, Hank?"

The question sliced the uneasy silence like a knife.

"Of course. Why do you ask such a silly question?"

As if having just read his thoughts, Julean probed further, "Would you be happier if you had two wives?"

"Wh-why, I don't know. No! Of course not."

Julean gazed directly into his eyes and Henry knew he'd been caught in a lie.

"Julean. What is this? You're not getting carried away with this documentary, are you? Of course I am happy with you." Henry's voice rose slightly for emphasis, trying to be more resolute, more emphatic.

Julean didn't waver. Her gaze on him remained steady and even.

"Would you be happier? Think on it for a moment."

Henry suddenly felt trapped. How had he gotten himself into this? It all started with that silly documentary. Or, had it? He looked down, no longer able to keep his gaze fixed on his wife lest she read his mind like she had so many times in the past. He thought about how he might safely answer. The truth was that he had often entertained that very idea. Concern swept through his body as he cast a furtive glance back into his wife's eyes.

Does she know?

Slowly Henry looked back into Julean's misty eyes, guilt swarming all about him. Was God punishing him for entertaining such thoughts in the past? Often he thought one's sins should be marked on their forehead for all to see then one would think twice before they acted or thought or spoke. He wanted to be truthful and yet not hurt his wife. Father Engelmann was the only one with whom Henry had confided about Jenny and he had always encouraged Henry to be honest with his wife and tell her the truth. If there was ever a time to do it, now was the time.

Which would be more painful, holding back or the naked truth?

He sought a middle road. "Well, now that you mention it,

maybe a second wife might work. Geez, Julean, I don't know." Henry laughed nervously and then tried to put the pressure back on her. "Why is this so important to you, anyway?"

"Sometimes I think that's what you wish for… That you would be happier with another love in your life in addition to me."

"Julean, why on earth would you think such a thought?"

Julean stared at him, tears perched on the edge of her eyelids. She, too, grappled with revealing the truth. What would Henry say, what would he do, if she told him about his dreams? If she told him how passionately he had dreamt of Jenny just this past July 6? She remained silent.

"Honey, it's just this documentary making you think this way. It's part of your past. Maybe we should go to bed. We'll both feel better in the morning."

Henry could not have been happier to hear Allison start to cry but neither of them made any effort to move. Henry could tell his wife wanted him to talk more, to share more. Yet, how could he tell her there was someone in his past that he still had feelings for? That he still thought of her, dreamed of her… missed her.

Perhaps he didn't need to tell her. A growing feeling deep in the pit of his stomach kept telling him that she already knew.

It was Saturday afternoon and Father had just finished hearing confessions. As Henry and Father made their way to the rectory study they passed Father's bedroom. Curious, Henry stopped and peeked inside.

"So this is your room, Father?"

"Yes, Father Connelly's is down the hall on the other side of the study. It still isn't far enough away as his snoring keeps me awake at night."

They laughed and Henry admitted that Julean had that same problem with Henry. Father's room was comfortable. Not too large but it did have a desk, chair and a reading chair beside the window. The bed was single sized and neatly made up. The same crucifix that hung over his and Anna's bed was now above his. On the small table beside his reading chair was a new Bible. It seemed out of character for Father not to have his original Bible but he had given it to Henry.

Just before Henry withdrew from the room, his eyes caught Father's tan coloured suit hanging in the open closet.

"I see you still have the suit you got married in. I recall you saying that is the suit you want to wear at your funeral just like Anna wore her wedding gown at her funeral. Now that you're a priest are you still thinking of doing that?"

"Yes, that's right, I did say that and that's what I plan to have done, Henry. Both Anna and I thought it fitting to wear our wedding attire to celebrate our passing from this life to a new life with Jesus in much the same way we celebrated when God joined us together in marriage."

As Father spoke, Henry's mind wandered to the dream he had had as a fifteen year old in which a man wearing that same tan coloured suit had made an appearance. It was the day he had first met Jenny; he had fallen asleep while waiting to take Jenny to Balfour Collegiate for registration. The dream was so vivid and real and it still haunted him, and seeing Father's suit brought it back in full force.

In the dream, Henry, as Prince Charming, came upon Jenny, who was sleeping on a bed of white daisies in a field of wildflowers. As he approached her, anticipating her lips on his, she suddenly disappeared and in her place was an older man wearing a tan coloured suit with a yellow flower in his lapel. Once again, Henry now wondered if it had been Mr. Engelmann in his dream. He had barely known Mr. Engelmann back then...

Suddenly, unbidden, the rest of the dream came rushing back: a faceless figure wearing a black cloak had held him back from getting to Jenny and the man in the tan suit... the thought sent quivering coldness down his spine now in Father's room, as it did back then.

"Well we better get to the den Henry, it's getting close to our dinner time and the cook gets upset when we are late."

"Yes, of course Father." Henry gazed hard at the tan suit, shook his head and left the room.

No sooner had the two men sat down when Henry wasted no time in getting to the reason he wished to talk to his mentor.

"I've never seen Julean this way before. Out of the blue she asks me if I'm happy. If I would be happier if I had two wives."

Although he didn't approve, Father wasn't surprised to hear that Julean was still harbouring those thoughts. When she had confided in him during confession that time, she seemed alarmingly committed to the idea.

"So, what did you tell her?"

"Well, in the end nothing was really discussed. Allison started to cry. Normally Julean would go right to her, but she just sat there staring at me, waiting for an answer. Allison gave me an excuse to leave. After I had Allison settled down and returned to the living room Julean had gone to bed. In the morning she seemed fine."

"I see."

"Perhaps it was the documentary about polygamy that brought it all on. You know she belonged to the Latter Day Saints faith before she converted."

"Yes, she shared all that with me when she took the pre-marital classes. I distinctly recall her telling me that her immediate family and grandparents broke away from the fundamentalist group that still practices multiple wives in a marriage. Perhaps part of her roots surfaced during the movie and she was trying to deal with it through your relationship with her."

"That may be, Father, but all through our discussion and just the way she stared at me, I feel she knows about Jenny. She may not know her name, but she knows there's someone else. It was like she wanted to know if I would be happier if she were part of our marriage. Like she was trying to say it would be okay if I felt that way."

Father remained silent, nodding his head ever so slightly, not wanting to disrupt the flow of Henry's thoughts. Again, he recalled the time both Henry and Julean had gone to confession with him about this very matter. He had hoped they would come to him together to work this whole situation out, but time and again they seemed to avoid the issue with each other even though it continued to surface.

"She wanted the truth from me, Father. She was adamant that I share myself completely with her. It was the most unusual discussion I have ever had with her."

"Well, perhaps it may be best to tell her about Jenny—"

"But I don't want to hurt her, Father."

"Is your silence on the matter not already causing her pain?"

"But how does she know, Father? I've never told her and I know you and my parents haven't, either. How could she possibly know?"

"A woman has a way of knowing these things. Perhaps it's intuition. I know my Anna knew most of my thoughts before I spoke them. Most of the time she was polite and would let me speak before answering."

"Tell me, Father, I love Julean so much. Why on earth would I still think about Jenny? Why do I still miss her?" Henry lowered his head in shame. "Why would I still love what is just a memory?"

Father sat back in the leather arm chair and crossed his legs. "I'm not certain I know the answer. Perhaps, Henry, you may just have to live with that mystery and ask for God's grace to release its hold on you and its power over you."

"I have done nothing but pray for that for years, Father! I honestly don't think it's ever going to go away. But what should I do? Should I tell Julean?"

"That is up to you. From what I know of life it is always best to bring everything to light and talk it out. I know this is a delicate matter and you don't wish to hurt Julean, but when the moment is right, let her know your heart."

Henry tightened his lips and nodded.

Father uncrossed his legs and leaned forward to lay his hands on Henry's.

"Let us pray. Lord, this is a difficult problem Henry has. It has been a part of him for far too long and we ask that you deliver him from the past that binds him so. We ask you Lord to bless their marriage; that You will be at the centre, guiding them with your light. Give Henry the courage and wisdom to be open and truthful with his partner and help Julean to be open and accepting of this truth. We pray that the truth deepens their relationship, draws them closer together and brings everlasting healing to their marriage. For this we pray in Your name, Amen."

Following up on his art instructor's suggestion, Henry enrolled in another oil painting class when he returned to school that fall.

The teacher was Scott Freeman, a professional artist in his own right. He and Henry immediately hit it off and Scott took his promising new student under his wing. In many ways, Henry considered Scott to be another Mr. Engelmann, a mentor who would instill in him a love for painting, especially outdoors.

Scott was a *plein air* painter. He loved the challenge of capturing a landscape before him. Even in the dead of winter Scott took Henry out to walk around the park, to show him how to study and sketch trees. He would point out buildings reflected on the frozen lake or the different weeds and cattails sticking through the ice.

"Nature is your best teacher and makes you feel what you want your viewer to feel when they look at your work, Henry. If you follow nature's lead, your work will become authentic and convincing."

By spring, Henry had made incredible strides as an artist. Some of his paintings ran parallel in quality to those of his mentor. But it was when Scott started to take Henry outdoors to paint that the apprentice surpassed the master.

It was early in the morning of the first Saturday in May that Henry and his instructor found themselves on the edge of the lake at the break of dawn. Snow still covered the ground and the runoff and melting ice created a mirror-like surface on the lake. Both had their easels set up and their paints out, ready to capture the light. They worked quickly, trying to burn the image before them in their mind's eye and secure it on the canvas. When the early light was gone, they relaxed and continued to paint from memory to finish their paintings. When Scott looked over at Henry's work, he held his breath.

"Most students see the sky and water as blue, but you have captured the quality of the early light. Look how the snow and lake reflect the golden sky, and how you painted the shadows of the trees on the snow with the compliment of yellow. That wonderful purple colour you used is perfect." Scott patted Henry's shoulder.

"You know, Scott, I hadn't even realized what I did until you analyzed it. I was just creating what I saw."

"It comes naturally to you. The Lord has blessed you with a gift."

A month later, Henry and Scott were once again out at the park. It was a humid morning and a foggy haze rose off the lake, partially obscuring the landscape before them. That time Scott didn't paint, he stood behind his student and watched as Henry caught the softness of the edges enveloped by the mist.

"Gosh, Henry, you really captured the moment on canvas; I can feel the atmosphere around the trees and the Legislative buildings."

Later, as the fog burned off by the heat of the sun, Henry noted a winding path leading down to the water's edge.

It brought back a memory that stirred him deep inside.

"Scott, I want to check something out, I'll be back in about ten minutes or so."

"Take your time. You inspired me to do a quick study of this tree over here. It will take me at least a half hour to finish."

Henry walked down the path, certain that this was the one down which he and Jenny had raced their bikes back in ninth grade. He recalled the sailboats and the legislative buildings reflecting in the water that day. As he neared the water's edge, he saw what he was looking for.

Henry approached the tree, and the heart he had carved into the bark so long ago came into view. The edges had crusted over and the pale yellow bark had weathered and browned, but the inscription was still intact – *H loves J*. And he could still make out the tiny angels under each curve of the heart.

Wonderful memories crossed his mind as he stood mesmerized by the carving before him. A smile crossed his face as he recalled his attempt to make love to Jenny that day. How she told him she loved him and how they embraced in front of that very tree. He faintly heard the sound of Jenny calling his name. Then realized the voice was not Jenny's, but Scott's.

"Hey, Henry, you better come and pack up, it looks like rain."

Henry looked up. The sun was hidden behind low dark clouds that were scurrying quickly towards him.

"Holy cow, where did those clouds come from?"

He hurried back to his easel, memories wending their way back into Henry's mind of how Jenny and he got caught in the storm walking back from Balfour Collegiate. How they'd ran over the lawns in their bare feet after the rain and walked hand in hand, talking about their aspirations. Jenny had been impressed by the way he described the trees, their shapes and colour, then she had said, "*Some day you will be a great artist.*"

Henry remembered it as if she were standing right in front of him. He felt her hand in his...

Chapter Thirty-Two

J ENNY WAS RIGHT; James never did tire of looking after James
Junior, as Edith had predicted he would. In fact, James' possessiveness of his son became even more overbearing. If it wasn't for
the time she had with J.J. when James was at work, she would have
felt like an alien in her own home.

James no longer slept in the same bed with her, kissed her or
made love to her. While Jenny was still able to stay centered as a
person through all this, she knew she no longer had a place as a
wife or mother.

When J.J. was two years old Jenny returned to her librarian
position. She would have loved to have been a stay-at-home mom,
but J.J. was looked after most of the time by either the nanny or
James, according to a strict regimen of tasks, activities, and games
that James prescribed. It was not so much for J.J.'s stimulation as it
was to keep contact and bonding between Jenny and her son to a
minimum. Anytime Jenny tried to get private time with her son,
or take him for a walk, Ingrid would report it to James who would
then add an activity to the schedule to fill in the gap.

When Ingrid left at the end of each day, James would take over,
interfering anytime Jenny tried to interact with her son. The child
wanted to love his mother, but James would distract him by engag-
ing him in other activities.

Jenny tried to talk to James about his possessiveness, but he would hear none of it. It became very evident in those precious few moments when she was able to talk to J.J. that he was bonding to James as both a mother and father.

James Junior grew to adore his father and identified completely with him. Everything his father did, he imitated. His gestures, his stance, the way he walked, talked, how his eyes flashed when he received a new toy. James was cloning his son to be a replica of himself.

As Jenny saw it, not only was J.J. a replica of his father, but his relationship with James was identical to the one James had to his own father. This was all James knew. From what Nancy had revealed to Jenny, when he was young his mother was always away on a drinking binge. The only security and love James had received was from his father, who himself was extremely limited in his affection. James was now doing the same to his son.

Unlike James' mother, however, Jenny was completely and utterly emotionally available and wanted nothing more than to lavish her time and love on her son. James simply found it impossible to get over his disgust of Jenny's rape and the fact that she had given birth to an illegitimate child. His wife was tainted, as far as he was concerned, and he did not want her contaminating his son. But not only that, it was the irrational fear of abandonment that motivated James. He could not tolerate the idea of Jenny taking his son away from him. At all costs, the boy was to relate to him only. He could not risk being abandoned again.

While this disturbed Jenny, she couldn't help but marvel at her son's brilliance.

"...ninety-seven, ninety-eight, ninety-nine, one hundred."

"That's very good, J.J.. Let's put your piggy bank away now and I'll read you a story."

"No. Daddy wants me to learn how to count to one hundred with nickels and dimes and quarters, too. Let me show you." J.J. ran to his room and brought out a little bag filled with coins. The first thing Jenny noted was that just like the 100 pennies, the silver coins were freshly minted. Not a one had ever been touched or used before. J.J. was picking up his father's habits for cleanliness.

Jenny watched with awe as her son sorted out the nickels and each time he identified one of them he would count, "Five, ten, fifteen..." And when all the nickels were gone he did the same with the dimes and finally the quarters.

"That's wonderful, J.J.. Did Daddy show you that?"

"Yes, when we go to the office I sit at a desk and the lady who works for Daddy helps me count over and over. She's a nice lady."

Two weeks later, James Junior brought home a leather pouch filled with one hundred one-dollar bills and proceeded to count them out as he did with the coins. He looked like a miniature accountant or bank teller as he stood next to Jenny and counted out the brand spanking new bills on her footstool. While Jenny was very impressed by his developing financial skills, she was worried that her son was focusing too much on money and not on play things or games more suitable for the average two-year-old.

Shortly after his third birthday, James Junior arrived home with his father, toting a Monopoly game under his arm. Jenny suspected he had been playing with it at the office by the comments he made to his dad about Boardwalk, mortgages and donations when speaking with him.

"Can we play Monopoly after dinner, Mom?"

"Yes, I think I can still remember how to play. Do you want me to show you how the game goes?"

"Oh no, I know how to play. Daddy and Susan play with me at the office."

"I see... Well then, why don't we start now and finish after dinner?"

Her little boy trounced her good. Within an hour J.J. owned Boardwalk and all the hotels. James beamed as he watched his son build his empire and beat his mother.

Although Jenny could tolerate far more than most normal people could for the welfare of her son, at times she felt a pervasive fear that James might do something which she simply could not deal with or be able to handle. That he would find some way to crack into the protective world which she controlled and into which she had cocooned herself. Dark clouds always loomed on the horizon, threatening her, ready to move in and consume or oppress her. She always had to be vigilant to James' remarks, his cunning, and his relentless goal to get rid of her.

Jenny drew strength and solace from anything she could. She visited her wildflower patch daily, sometimes twice daily for spiritual sustenance. She could always rely on nature to liberate her from sneaking threats of oppression – her wildflowers, digging and weeding, transplanting, moving from inactivity to activity, introspection to extroversion – anything to ward off self-pity.

Her real strength, however, came from her inner spirit and innate natural ability to accept others unconditionally. This is what kept Jenny centered and able to cope with the abusive conditions that would have caused others to flee in an instant. Jenny would not take James' criticism, fault finding and demoralizing remarks personally as she knew they were unfounded. She understood James had problems and simply would not allow herself to be controlled by his neurosis.

Truth be told, it was her ongoing loneliness that pained her most. She wished she had someone to talk to. *Oh, if only Tammy were still here.* She missed her friend deeply. She was happy to have Matti and Thomas to talk to, but it was not the same as with Tammy. Tammy had been her earthly guardian angel who knew everything about her and provided the other wing Jenny needed to fly.

Even though her mother visited often, they didn't talk much about James and what was happening with J.J.. Actually, her mother discussed the exact opposite.

"Oh, Jenny, you are so fortunate to be surrounded by such a fine estate and looked after so royally."

"Well, it's not all roses, I assure you, Mom." Jenny stopped at the rose bush and plucked off a dying flower as they neared the gazebo.

"These are such beautiful grounds, much larger than mine and better tended, too, I must admit."

"Really? I always thought Carlos did a wonderful job. But, yes, Thomas and Ramon do a beautiful job here. They put in long hours every day. More groundskeepers should be hired, but James doesn't want to spend the money."

Her mother looked at her as she sat on a bench inside the

gazebo, and Jenny knew her mother had no inkling about the depth of emptiness lying beneath the surface of her relationship with James. Jenny had always found it difficult to talk to her mother at a heart to heart level. She could have with her father, but her mother was so different: disciplined and undemonstrative. She rarely gave Jenny a hug and never would in public. Emotional scenes and affection to her mother were considered violations of the social code of conduct. In fact, her mother had taught her directly and indirectly not to express anger, frustration, or hostility and she certainly wouldn't openly invite a heart-to-heart discussion of a personal nature.

Well, at the end of the day, thought Jenny, *would talking with her mother really help all that much?* Since her main goal was to remain at peace and bring peace to the home, talking about James negatively, or complaining and being bitter and angry would only lead to self-pity and self-centeredness. Such thinking could easily spiral her down into a neurosis even more severe than that of her estranged husband.

"Would you care for some juice or iced tea, Mom? I can get Matti to make some for us."

"Yes, iced tea would be nice… Where's my little J.J., by the way? I haven't seen him yet."

"I think he's in the play room with Ingrid learning his multiplication tables. James doesn't want me to interrupt them during his studies."

"His studies? Why? He is only three and already going to school?"

"I'll explain later, let me get some tea for us."

"Hi Matti," said Jenny as she entered the kitchen.

"Hello Mrs. Hamilton. That child of yours be with the nanny all morning and part of the afternoon. And now Mr. Hamilton called to say his secretary be coming to pick J.J. up to go for dinner. He didn't say you'd be going, though…"

"That's fine Matti, I'm visiting with Mom and we would like iced tea if you could make some and I'll take it out."

"Mrs. Hamilton, how many times do I have to tell you: I be here to serve you. Now you go on and visit with your mama and

I'll bring you both a tall glass of iced tea and some fresh baked cookies. I be fixing some right now for Thomas and Ramon."

"I love your cookies, Matti. Yes, please bring some for us too, if there are enough."

"There be more than enough, Mrs. Hamilton. Now, you best be going and have a nice visit. I'll bring J.J. to you before he goes out to dinner."

"Yes, please do, Matti."

As Jenny exited the kitchen, Matti shook her head after her. Matti simply couldn't get over the heart of that girl. Living with so much loneliness, deprived of her son, treated so poorly by her husband, and yet still so loving, so generous, so... free.

CHAPTER THIRTY-THREE

"WELL HENRY, YOU have made great strides in your art over the past six years," commented Father Engelmann as he pushed himself back from a late lunch Julean had made.

"I still can't get over the fact that your last three exhibitions sold out." Julean added.

"I really like counselling, but painting has taken such a hold on me. It's all I want to do."

For years, Henry had maintained his high school counselling position even while his career as an artist had started to take hold.

"You can say that again, Hank. Honestly, Father, once he's in his studio, he paints until all hours. Then it's so difficult for him to get up to go to school."

"Well, we are starting to make extra money with the sale of the art, I think I will approach the Board and ask if I could just work part-time. I could do counselling in the morning and be off in the afternoon to paint. That way I would have a better balance."

"You may want to do that, Henry," Father agreed.

At that moment, five year old Lauren burst through the back door. The arrival of their third child had delighted Julean and Henry and only enhanced their family life all the more. Julean thanked God everyday for bringing them three healthy, beautiful children after the tragedy of Benjamin's death. Many marriages wouldn't have been strong enough to withstand that kind of loss, but their faith in the Lord and their subsequent children only strengthened their bond. Julean still thought of Benjamin every-day, though, and imagined him growing alongside her other chil-dren, ever the older brother, keeping his eye out on his younger siblings, keeping them safe.

"When are we going to Grandma's?"

"Pretty soon, sweetie," said Julean. "Call your brother and sister to come in now, too, and get ready. Grandma is making a big New Year's turkey dinner and she likes to visit before eating."

Henry's eyes brightened. "Yeah, why not come too, Father. Mom would love to have you. She always makes enough food for ten extra people."

"I love Mary's cooking, but I have a benediction service tonight and I still have to think about what I want to say."

"All you need to do is speak, Father, and the words of the Holy Spirit seem to flow out of you."

"That may be so, but I always have to fill up with His Word, first."

Father rose and hugged Julean and Henry. Allison and Jeremy came in just in time to say good-bye.

"Okay, kids, go wash and get cleaned up. We're going soon," said Julean. "Allison, why don't you wear that new dress I bought you? Grandma wants to see it on you."

"Well, Henry, I will pray for you and the decision you have to make. It's a big risk to leave a very secure job and go into the art business. If the Lord wants you to be an artist I'm sure he will paint the way for you." Father winked and left.

TWO WEEKS AFTER Father's visit to their home, the curator of the McKenzie Art Gallery approached Henry and asked if he would be interested in having an exhibition there in the spring of 1977. He would have two years to prepare and it would allow him to keep up with paintings for galleries already exhibiting his work. Henry was thrilled and readily accepted. It was such an excellent example of God's divine providence at work in his life, and just the confir-mation he needed to approach the School Board and ask to lessen his hours as a counsellor to part-time. The Board, reluctantly, consented to Henry's request.

Henry went to work on his show, painting well into most evenings. His makeshift studio in the basement, however, was getting him down. The atmosphere and lighting were poor, and he felt so separated from his family. The only way he saw to fix it was to add another floor onto the bungalow.

"Springtime is not the best time to be taking the roof off your house," Julean lamented. "What if it rains, it will ruin all our furniture. And what on earth will happen to the rest of the house?"

"Yeah, I'm a little concerned, too," said Henry. "But the carpenters promised they would work every day except Sunday, of course. They figure they can build the second storey and have a new roof on in less than ten days."

"I hope you are right. Better call Father and ask him to say several high masses for us."

It was a big decision, but a very necessary one. Henry could no longer work in the basement of his home. If he was going to make this his life's work he needed a studio with natural light. What better place to work and paint then to raise the roof and be on the top floor?

Henry drafted a plan for the second floor himself. It would consist of three bedrooms, a bathroom, and a large studio with a fireplace and sitting area. That way the family could come in at any time to visit and chat. Each child would have their own room and it would also give the house a fresh new look.

The roof on the front would be steep and have three dormers growing out of it, Cape Cod style. It reminded him of the ones he and Jenny looked at when they had walked through his old neighbourhood.

That was so many years ago, why on earth would I think about that?

Henry could hardly wait to see the project get started and finished. Soon he would be painting in the light from a northern sky!

"The principal from St. Mathews School called today about Jeremiah. He and the staff had a meeting and would like to place

Jeremy in Grade 8 this fall."

"Isn't that pushing it? This would be the second time in his elementary years that he was advanced a grade. He's already a year younger than his classmates."

"Yes, but remember how well Jeremy adjusted when he skipped Grade 1? We were worried about him then, too, but he fit right in with those second graders so well, we were glad we made the decision."

"That's true…"

"In any case, I discussed that with the principal, but he and staff feel that Jeremy can handle it. In fact, some of the teachers think he should be at the Grade 9 level. He acts, thinks, reads and learns at a level beyond his years. He is already associating with eighth grade students. His home room teacher says that Jeremy is taller than most of them and just as mature, if not more so. The students just naturally gravitate towards him."

"I had a Grade 10 student like that in my science class. She looked bored to death in my class. Other teachers felt the same way and so we moved her ahead as well. Holding them back impedes their desire to grow and learn."

"That's what the principal said. Until the School Board provides more funding and creates classes for students of different levels, accelerating students seems to be the only option open to them at the present time."

"Well, let's meet with the teachers. Maybe it is best for our son, but I certainly wouldn't want to do it again. He sure is a mature kid, though, always has been… If we go for it, we'll have to closely monitor it."

CHAPTER THIRTY-FOUR

J ENNY BEGAN TO fantasize about leaving James. His mother was right; the things she had revealed to Jenny about James and his past were relentlessly playing out. He obviously didn't love her anymore, if he ever really had, and he was making it almost unbearable for Jenny to live in the same house as him. It was obvious he wanted to get rid of her.

However, Jenny also knew that if she left she would lose her son. James would accuse her of abandoning J.J. and she wouldn't put it past him to argue that her previous child was not the result of rape, but of promiscuity. That was all the ammunition he would need to get rid of her completely. At most, she might get visiting rights or be allowed to have James Junior for the weekends. James' power, influence and legal artillery were no match for her and she knew it.

No! James Junior was her son, too, and she would not lose him. She was strong and clear minded enough to realize that her strength was in her staying. Her presence still had some influence in the upbringing of her son and that was good enough for her. Through her unconditional love and kind interactions with everyone in the home, she could at least provide an example to J.J. that would hopefully have a lasting impression upon him.

While most women would fight tooth and nail with James to

get him to change, Jenny had learned long ago that the opposite approach was the way to go; she never demanded he change as that would only have led to anger, resentment, and frustration. It would have given James all the more cause to attack her and become even more righteous and rigid. Rather, Jenny accepted the fact that he would likely never change.

Perhaps most important of all, Jenny realized that no matter what James said or did, he was not the cause of her unhappiness. She did not have to feel like a victim. She had chosen to enter this relationship and she would have to deal with it and accept responsibility for her happiness and life. Since she was going to stay, she would accept James the way he was and do her best to turn the home into a loving one.

Incredibly, rather than have a home filled with tension, fear, hate, anger, and destruction, Jenny's attitude filled it with cheerfulness, love, compassion and happiness. She was a peacemaker and no matter what James said, she responded with words that didn't disturb the peace or harmony in the home. The staff marveled at how calmly and patiently Jenny could ward off abusive remarks or reprimands from her husband.

"I'm sorry, James, I'll try not to make that mistake, again. Thank you for making me aware of it." Or, "Really, James, I just don't see it that way." Or, at those times when she felt a little bolder, "Oh, James, that's silly and completely unnecessary, but if that's what you want..." Or, "Thank you for pointing that out, but it would be nice of you to communicate your dissatisfaction in a less blaming manner." Jenny was always careful never to give James any ammunition he could use to attack back. Most times James just stood there defenseless, looking rather silly.

In this way, Jenny was able to deal with an almost intolerable environment and show her growing and developing son examples of a good attitude, respect for people and proper ways of speaking. The support of the staff, the beautiful grounds, her work at the school, her wildflower patch and the precious moments when she had J.J. to herself had all helped her settle into an acceptable lifestyle.

"Hi Chloe, it's Aunt Jen."

"Hi Auntie, thank you so much for calling."

"I've been thinking about you all week. How are you and your dad doing?"

"Okay, I guess. We both miss Mom so much. Dad keeps saying how much he would like to visit her in the cemetery and wishes now that she were buried here instead of up there."

"Ah, maybe you two will just have to come home more often. I know your grandma would love to see you both, as would I."

"I was speaking with Grandma yesterday and she and Grandpa might come here for a visit next month."

"That would be great, Chloe. The more we can see one another and give each other support, the better. Are you getting ready to go back to school? You're graduating this year, right?"

"Yes, but I'm not looking forward to going back to school. I'd sooner work at the counselling centre. I miss not going there with my Mom. There are so many girls coming for help in making decisions. It seems like so much more important work than sitting in a classroom. But Dad says I have to graduate."

Jenny was amazed at the young girl's maturity and ambition to help others. "I think it's best, too, Chloe. Finish your schooling and when you graduate you may want to pursue a degree in psychology or something related to counselling. They need trained professional people in that field now more than ever. And please don't attend any more protest rallies. It's just too dangerous."

"Yes, I know... So how is J.J. doing?"

"He is growing up so fast and in constant competition with his father. He claims he already knows as much about business as his dad, too! He can be quite a handful. He has Matilda, the nanny and me going around in circles when he's home. I don't recall your mother ever telling me it was that hectic to watch over you."

"That's because I was always a perfect angel, Auntie Jen!"

"Now that you mention it, I can recall a few times that Tammy offered to give you to me. She said you had inherited her same stubborn streak!"

"No, that comes from Dad. When he says no, there is just no way of changing his mind."

Jenny chuckled, "Well then, you got it from both ends!"

"So have the new Monarch butterflies emerged from their poop-a's yet?"

Jenny laughed at their shared joke. "Yes, Chloe, the garden is filled with the glorious creatures! How I wish I could share the joy of them with J.J., but speaking of inherited qualities, I think he's got his father's dislike of insects."

"Well, keep trying, Auntie! I'm sure if J.J. could experience the grace of a Monarch perched on his hand, he'd be hooked. I will never forget that day after Mom's death when that butterfly stayed with us, just hanging out, passing from my hand to yours… it was incredible!"

"I know, Chloe, I feel the same way and that is a great idea! I'll try that with J.J. when the time is right. Listen sweetie, is your dad there? I would like to speak to him for a few minutes."

"He's talking to someone on the other phone. I'll get him to call you when he's through."

"Okay, I'll give you a call again next Monday. Have a great week, sweetheart. If you need anything or want to call, please do anytime. I love to hear from you. I love you, Chloe!"

"Love you too, Auntie!"

JAMES JUNIOR WATCHED his mother trying to entice one of the Monarchs to land on her hand. Fall was fast approaching and the Monarchs would soon be leaving for their impossibly long migration down to Mexico. Jenny still loved to be with them as much as possible before they left for the winter. Finally, a Monarch landed on his mother's hand and she turned to him to allow him a closer look at the beautiful creature.

"Look, J.J.? Isn't it lovely? Do you know what is it J.J.? A male or female?"

"It's a male of course; it has two dots on its back wings. But why do you let that thing on your hand? It's a disgusting insect!"

"Well, I see it as a very beautiful one. Here, put out your hand, see if he'll come to you."

James Jr. stepped back. "No way, it might be carrying a disease or something."

"Oh J.J., that's nonsense."

"Well, that's what Dad says—"

Just then, Matti called.

"Oh darn, it's time to go already, J.J.!"

Jenny cherished the two hours she had with J.J. in the mornings between the time when James left for work and the chauffeur arrived to take her eight year old son to his private school. Jenny hugged and smothered her boy with kisses as they worked their way back to the house. She walked James Jr. to the front door to see him off, then retrieving her diary from her hiding spot and pouring herself an iced tea, Jenny returned to her beloved gazebo.

As Jenny rested on the swing, admiring the wildflowers, she began to focus on one of the white daisies. Her attention was so intense that the flower seemed to glow. Its whiteness becoming ever brighter before her eyes. As would so often happen in her garden, Jenny was filled with a calm inner peace that restored her wellbeing. Accompanying the serenity that morning, however, was an awareness that it was not so much the beauty of the flower that drew her, but rather its Creator. The outer beauty was but a manifestation of God, the Creator of all things in the universe.

Suddenly, everything in the garden took on a new meaning. Jenny instantly realized in a way she never had before that the flowers, the trees, the sky, the birds and all of nature were not only intended to nourish our senses, but to give us spiritual sustenance and draw us to Him. Jenny eyes filled with tears as she realized why it was that she loved her garden and angel so much. They are all of God!

She had always had a sense of it because her spirit had always been open to what *is,* especially when she was a child. She had loved to play with butterflies, her angels. She loved the sun, the rain and the moon. Over the years as she grew, the ways of the world tried to snuff this fire of life out of her, but Jenny, unlike so many people, had a spirit for life and its beauty that was too strong to be extinguished.

Jenny now understood why she came back time and again to her beloved garden. It was not only the peace and beauty of it, but the still and quiet of the moment when her mind calmed and became open to hear the whispers of God through her guardian angel and receive His healing grace. This was why she really came here. The beauty of the garden was the gateway to all and lasting peace.

After a few minutes of contemplating the meaning of her discovery, Jenny's thoughts once again turned to James. *Perhaps this is why I am able to accept James: at his very core, he is no different than that daisy.* That was it! Jenny realized. At his very core was the stamp of the Creator who, out of love and for love, created James and all of mankind and everything in the universe.

When she looked at James, it was not his words and actions that she responded to, but the love that she knew was at the core of his being. Someday, what had happened to Jenny that morning would happen to her husband and he would realize that it was not the money, the wealth, the power that he was after, but the peace and joy that God had planted at his core. The treasure that he sought had been within him, accessible, all along.

It was all so clear to Jenny in the moment that focusing on the outer layers of people, their toughened exteriors, and getting caught up in the distractions of the world around us divert and separate us from the oneness we all share. She felt light and free at the revelation she had always sensed and now she knew. She felt as if she could fly like an angel, sing like a bird, soar like an eagle, and ride on the back of the wind in adoration of it all!

Unbeknownst to Jenny, Thomas was pruning the bushes nearby. Every now and then, his gaze was attracted upon her, such a beautiful creation of God, so filled with light. He could swear that at times *the sunshine poured from her face.*

CHAPTER THIRTY-FIVE

A GROWING CROWD GATHERED around the Pederson residence throughout the day as the workers began tearing down the roof to their bungalow. At first, onlookers assumed the Pedersons were getting their roof re-shingled, but by early afternoon they realized something more serious was happening.

When Henry came home from school, he was shocked to see how exposed his house was to the elements. He looked to the sky for any signs of impending rain but there were none, just one big beautiful dome of blue.

Despite their evening under clear skies, the next morning Henry awoke with Julean's common sense having worked on him and he realized that he might be wise to take out some insurance. He looked outside; the sky was pretty much still blue except for a few clouds to the east. Still, Julean was right, you never could tell on the prairies when the clouds were going to roll in and open up the heavens.

Henry called his insurance agent and asked if he could take out renovation insurance for ten days. That would be long enough for a roof to once again cover his house. Henry was given a quote and decided to pay the reasonable fee as much for his own peace of mind as for the unlikelihood that he would actually need it.

On the second day the roof was completely off and the two

carpenters began placing new floor joists beside the existing ceiling joists and by mid afternoon the plywood flooring was being laid. The next day the second floor sheeting was done and the carpenters started to frame the walls over top of the new floor. Just one more day and the walls would be up and then the roof would begin.

Henry was starting to regret the decision to take out the insurance. The prairie sky was still blue, the clouds he had seen that morning were gone. It appeared as though the rain that usually came with spring was going to hold off long enough for the new roof to be erected.

Just as they were drifting off to sleep that night, Julean mentioned what she had heard on the evening news.

"I forgot to ask you, did you hear the forecast, Hank? They're calling for rain tomorrow."

Henry got up out of bed and looked up at the moonlit sky. Stars twinkled everywhere, absolutely no clouds were in sight.

"Nine times out of ten weather forecasts are wrong, Julean. Just look outside; not a whiff of rain."

Henry crawled back into bed muttering, "What do they know, even the carpenters said they were in good shape."

"Don't be so sure, you know how quickly the weather can change on the prairies."

The next morning they awoke not to the pitter patter of rain, but to the roar of pouring rain. It made a deafening sound as it pelted against the new second floor. Henry leaped out of bed and his heart nearly stopped as he looked outside. The rain was so thick that he could not see the fence in the back yard. "Oh my God, this is unbelievable!"

Henry got dressed while Julean ran to the kids' rooms to get them up and helping with the mess. As Henry stepped outside his hair was instantly soaked and he could feel rain seeping under the collar of his raincoat. He had a hard time even keeping his eyes open as the wind pelted the rain against his face.

He made it to one of the ladders and climbed up to inspect the second floor. To his horror, the two by six framed walls that were lying on the floor ready to be erected, were filling up with water. It looked like a series of one hundred bathtubs side by side. The water was trapped between all studs and not running off. Eventually it would leak through into the first floor ceiling. And the weight of all that water! Could it possibly all come crashing down?

Why hadn't they put tarps over the floor?

At this point neither a tarp nor a pump to start draining the water between all the studs would do any good. The rain was coming down so hard the framed walls would just keep filling up with water as fast as it could possibly be removed by a pump. Henry felt completely helpless against the elements and slowly made his way back down the ladder and inside.

As soon as he entered the house, Julean pointed to water beginning to drip from the ceiling fixture in the kitchen.

"Oh my God, Julean, we are in trouble. Quickly get a pail!"

They decided to keep the children home from school and Henry called his school to see if he could get the day off, as well. The principal couldn't stop laughing when Henry explained the circumstance to him. He told Henry he could borrow his canoe if he wanted.

There's always a wise guy!

As the day progressed, the rain escalated and by evening, water was finding its way in everywhere: ceiling fixtures, under the baseboards, through electrical outlets and window frames.

Henry and Julean and the kids all worked tirelessly strategically placing, emptying, then replacing every pot, bucket, bowl and Tupperware container they had to try and catch as much water as they could. By seven-thirty that evening, the Pedersons were exhausted.

"Okay everybody, let's go downstairs and go to sleep. It's still dry down there."

Henry turned off the main power switch and collapsed in one of the spare rooms in the basement and went to sleep. The kids crashed in the rumpus room and soon were also asleep. Julean found her way in the dark back to Henry and slipped into bed beside him.

JULEAN SCREAMED WHEN she saw her home the next morning. Henry dashed upstairs and was taken aback as well by the unbelievable mess. The rain had stopped, but the leaking and dripping hadn't. The carpet squished under their bare feet as they surveyed the house.

"Watch out for the drywall on the ceiling, it's sagging and looks like it's ready to fall. Some in the bedroom already has."

"We can't let the kids up here, it's too dangerous. I'll phone Madge next door and see if the kids can go over there until we get things cleaned up."

"Yeah, that's a good idea. But where do we start?"

The carpenters arrived and set to work. They bailed out the water remaining between the studs and by noon many of the framed walls were standing. By the end of the day all the walls were up and the carpenters were starting to frame the roof.

Henry reported the unfortunate mishap to the insurance company. Fortunately all the damage was covered by the construction policy he had taken out just three days earlier. The insurance company reluctantly agreed to pay for the repairs but immediately cancelled the policy. But by that point, the roof was well on its way to completion and Henry did not foresee another mishap.

Henry called in a crew and by the end of the day most of the damaged drywall from the ceiling was removed and the mess cleaned up. Over the next two days roofers finished the job and sealed it with tar paper and cedar shakes. By July, 1976, the project was finished. Everyone had their own room and Henry had his much-needed studio.

"I feel like I'm in heaven," Henry commented as he came down the stairs for dinner and plunked himself at the kitchen table. "I just love the light in the studio; the afternoon sun coming in through the south window is so peaceful. Now I know why Father Engelmann and Anna enjoyed reading by the window in their living quarters above the store."

"Yes, I noticed you reading the Bible there the other afternoon. I didn't want to disturb you so—"

"Oh, honey, please come in anytime. I just love it when you and the kids come in."

"So, what's next, Henry? Leaving your job altogether and painting full-time?"

"Would you be concerned if I did take the plunge? Your parents would probably have a fit. My dad still can't get over the move I made to only work part-time in a job that I spent so many years training for."

"Well, you have to admit it is risky to rely totally on the sale of your paintings."

"Yeah, it is risky. But how would you feel if I went for it?"

Julean made her way over to him, sat on his knees and gazed lovingly into his eyes. "I have complete and total confidence in you, dear. I'm happy when you are."

"HI HANK, IT's Eddy."

"Hey, how you doing? Haven't seen you all summer."

"Yeah, been making a few trips to Jamaica and going back tomorrow morning again for a week or so."

"Is it just the scenery or have you found some nice Jamaican girl there?"

"You must be reading my mind ol' buddy. Matter of fact, I do have a lady friend down there. She's a head taller than me, which suits me just fine, if you know what I mean."

Henry chuckled as his vivid imagination conjured up the image of Eddy's nose bumping into a protruding bust line.

"Yeah, Hank, she's one beautiful babe, smart and sassy as a whip, and a great cook all in one. Never met a girl like her. So what have you been up to, Hank?"

"I've been busy all spring as well. We raised the roof to our bungalow and had a second floor built. I now have a studio and the kids each have their own room."

"Hey, that's great, man. I'd love to check it out when I get back."

"That would be great, Eddy. So what's up?"

"I was wondering if you could drive me to the airport tomorrow morning. I fly out around eleven and would need to be there at least an hour before. I don't want to leave my Caddy in the parking lot; last time some kids slashed the top."

"For sure Eddy, I'd be happy to drive you. I'll see you around nine-thirty."

"Thanks buddy."

WHEN HENRY WENT to Eddy's place the next morning to pick him up he immediately noticed that Eddy had put on weight; his body seemed out of proportion to his long, thin, narrow face.

Henry cautiously asked Eddy if something was wrong when he got into the car, "Geez Eddy, you seem to have put on weight or something."

Eddy winked and a big smile grew on his face. "It's that obvious, is it?"

"Well, your face looks the same but look at the size of your paunch! Looks like you've been drinking too many beers, ol' pal."

Eddy unbuttoned the front of his shirt and Henry's chin almost hit his lap. At least four money belts were strapped around Eddy's middle from his hips to just under his chest. Henry's eyes bulged even further when he noticed packs of 50, 100, and even 1000 dollar bills sticking out of the pouches!

"Geez Eddy, what are you doing with all that money and where...?"

"Just taking a little spending money with me to Jamaica."

"A little money? It looks like you have thousands of dollars, Eddy! What did you do, rob a bank?"

"Nah, this is just a little gift money from my clients. When I make good trades for them, they slip me a few bucks here and there."

"Don't you have to declare it?"

"It's a gift Hank, no different than a buck or two tip we give to a waiter."

"That's more than a few dollars. And isn't it dangerous to carry so much money? Why not put it into the bank and make a transfer to Jamaica?"

"I don't like to leave a paper trail."

Somehow it didn't seem right to Henry, "Geez Eddy, I hope you won't get into trouble."

"Nah, I'm sure it'll be cool." Eddy began to button up his shirt as Henry started the car and made his way to the airport.

"So you like Jamaica?"

"Beautiful place, Hank. I think I just might settle down there. I'm looking at a home to buy with an ocean view. I've already bought a sailboat and Coreena knows how to sail better than I do. Cost of living is cheap..."

"Wow, that's great Eddy! Sounds like you're getting pretty sweet on that girl. Coreena is it?"

"Yeah, I just might pop the question one of these days."

"That serious is it?"

"When an island love-bug bites, the sting is pretty powerful, Hank. Worse than Malaria."

"So what do her folks think of this city slicker coming to the island and sweeping their daughter off her feet?"

"Her folks are dead. A hurricane that swept the island a few years back killed them along with over four hundred others. The only family she has is a sister that moved to Ottawa around twelve years ago. They haven't seen each other in all these years. I was thinking of maybe flying Coreena to Ottawa to see her sister Matilda as a surprise present."

At the mention of Ottawa, Henry's pulse began to quicken.

"That would be a wonderful present to give her. That's something, not being able to see her only family in all those years. So why did Coreena stay in Jamaica if the only family she has is in Ottawa?"

"Coreena helped her parents run their restaurant. When they were killed by the hurricane, she thought of joining her sister in Ottawa, but decided to stay and keep the restaurant going in her parents' memory. It's one of the best restaurants on the island. That's how we met, actually. I was dining there, eating the best lobster of my life, and she came over to my table to ask if I was enjoying the meal. The rest is history."

"What does Matilda do in Ottawa?"

"Apparently, she's quite the chef and works for some big wig by the name of Hamilton on a large estate."

The name Hamilton sounded familiar to Henry. *Oh yeah, that was the name of that guy that answered the phone that day I called for Jenny. Yeah, James Hamilton was his name. He was some crazy guy.* And then, even though it was a long shot, Henry had to ask, "Do you know if the name of that guy Matilda works for is James Hamilton?"

Eddy stared at Henry in surprise, "Geez man, you some kind of psychic or something? Yeah, you're absolutely right. Coreena said the name of the man her sister works for is Mr. James Hamilton! That's crazy, man. The only reason I remember that, is Coreena was telling me that Matilda can't stand the guy! Says he's a real beast and treats her like crap, so Coreena has been trying to convince her sister to move back to Jamaica and cook at the restaurant. The thing is, this Hamilton character is also the CEO of one of the largest companies in Canada and I've made a fortune trading his company's stock! It's a small world, Hank, a very small world."

Henry returned a blank stare to his friend.

As they made their way to the airport Henry thought how Eddy seemed to be indirectly connected to all things relating to Jenny! Henry wondered if it was just coincidental or if there was more to it. *Had Jenny married that Hamilton guy? If so, did he treat her like crap, too?* The thought of it made Henry's blood pressure rise.

"Hey Hank, mind if I smoke?" Eddy asked, interrupting Henry's thoughts. He already had his smokes out before Henry could respond.

"Yeah, sure, go ahead. Maybe just turn down the window a bit."

Trying to connect the dots, Henry continued to probe. "So Eddy, did you hear anymore from Pete?"

"No, not lately. He called me shortly after we spoke that night at the pool hall and wanted to know if I had gotten Jenny's phone number from you. When I told him you didn't have it, he was real disappointed. Kept going on and on about how sorry he was for what had happened that night and still thinks he knocked her up. He's trying to figure out a way to get in touch with her to apologize and ask her if she gave birth to a daughter like he dreamt she did."

Henry still couldn't believe how Pete's version of the story seemed to confirm the premonitions he himself had back then about Jenny being pregnant and giving birth. Cool shivers ran up and down his spine.

"What about that other guy who was there that night? John something or other. What ever happened to him? Did you ever talk to him about what happened that night?"

"Oh yeah, my buddy John McBryne?"

"Yeah," Henry wondered how Eddy considered him a buddy and yet that's how Eddy was: took people as they were.

"He's in bad shape, Hank."

"Oh? How so?"

"He's a pretty hard-core drug addict, Hank. I think he actually shoots up. Probably drinks, too. Anyway, I hardly recognized him when I saw him last week. Lost a lot of weight, long hair all scraggly. Reminds me of a pencil, tall and thin. I could tell he's still into dope."

"Yeah, that's too bad. Funny how Pete seemed to go straight and narrow and John headed in such a different direction."

"Well, I've gotta tell you Hank, if it wasn't for you I just might be keeping John company."

Henry made an almost imperceptible appreciative nod as the two drove on in silence.

Chapter Thirty-Six

Matilda, carrying a tray of coffee and cookies, walked briskly toward the shed. Her footsteps were louder than usual that morning as she practically stomped her way along the paving stones of the walkway. Thomas and his helper, Ramon, were already seated in the shed.

"Morning Matti. Heard you coming soon as you stepped out of the patio door. I suspect something is bothering you this fine morning."

"You be too perceptive for your own good, Thomas. It be the man of the house that has me all fired up again. Ooo, it makes me so mad! He be worse than a swarm of biting mosquitoes to that sweet little missus of his. His words be so unkindly and she just returns kindness! Good Lord, I'd have swatted him from kingdom come by now. I 'spect my blood be boiling soon."

"Now, hold on Matti, the steam rising from your face is fogging your perception of the situation."

"What you be talking about now, Thomas? It be Mr. Hamilton's perception that needs clearing. Why, he has the prettiest, most gracious little darling in his vision and he be too blind to see it. A good whack of my frying pan to the side of his head, be what he needs! I either knock some sense into that man or I be giving him one big concussion."

"Matti, take a load off and sit a spell." Thomas turned over a five gallon pail, set it beside Matti and brushed the top off with his hand. Carefully, she sat down, making sure the weight of her behind didn't pull her centre of gravity too far back and topple the makeshift chair.

"Tell me Matti, who do you think is more at peace about the matter of Mr. Hamilton, you or Miss Jenny?"

"That ain't the point, Thomas. She been abused by his impatience and mean words for too long now. She ain't thinking straight no more!"

"How would you have her react, Matti?"

"She should be madder than a hound dog at that man! Tell him a thing or two. Stand up for herself!"

"And how do you suppose he would react if she did that?"

"Why he'd get all riled up, that for sure. That'd be one big fight…"

"And to what end, Matti? Seems to me Miss Jenny is trying to maintain peace in the family and herself and be an example of how people should communicate…"

"Communicate! Hummmph!"

"Now just listen a moment, Matti. Not only is she bringing peace and civility into the home, she is loving that man unconditionally. Now *that's* power, Matilda. Someday that man is going to hit bottom so hard and then the seed of what that wonderful woman has planted will begin to grow. Just you wait and see, Matti, someday she'll make a new man out of Mr. Hamilton."

"I be long gone into the blue yonder before that be happening."

Matilda got up and poured the men a second cup of coffee and then carefully sat down again.

"Hear me out, Matti," Thomas said. "Every situation that we encounter is neutral, it has no meaning until we react to it, until we give it meaning."

"What in God's name are you talking about, Thomas? You make no sense!"

"Listen, Mattie. Take your reaction to Mr. Hamilton. You see how mean and inconsiderate he is which makes you feel upset. You automatically assume that Miss Jenny would have the same thoughts and feelings as you, but this is not so, Matti. Like I said, we create our own reality and give meaning to everything we encounter based on our own perspective of the situation."

Mattie shook her head. "What you be talking about…? Get to the point now, Thomas."

"Well, in Miss Jenny's case, she sees what her husband is doing like you do, but she chooses not to react to his inconsiderate actions by getting upset. She chooses not to be controlled by him and his weakness, but rather *she chooses peace and love.* She knows that deep in the core of Mr. Hamilton is his true self that was created by God. And *that* is what Miss Jenny reacts to.

"When he is unkind, she returns kindness. If she returned anger with anger, unkindness with unkindness, then she be no better than him! No, she chooses peace. This is how Miss Jenny loves and accepts others unconditionally. You see Matti, Miss Jenny brings love and peace and healing into the situation."

"You trying to tell me it's my own thinking that makes me be so upset and not that miserable man of hers?"

"No one can make you upset unless you choose to be, Matti. On some level, you are choosing. That is not to say that we should condone abuse and violence, but to see and understand that we have power within ourselves. You can see Miss Jenny chose differently than you even though her husband's remarks are aimed directly at her. This is why it is so important to choose our thoughts carefully. Our thoughts snare us quickly and entrap us into a whirlwind of misery. Can you imagine how troubled that sweet lady would be if she allowed herself to entertain thoughts like you and I do over the deviltry in that man of hers?"

"Okay, what you be saying is starting to make sense. It's like she be wrapped by some invisible shield around herself that only allows thoughts of love and kindness in and out. When Mr. Hamilton shoots unkindness at her it boomerangs back to him all wrapped up in sugar. He be standing there confused by her sweetness. He don't know how to react!"

"That's exactly it, Matti! Every time she returns love instead of the usual reaction he expects, she is planting the seed of redeeming love in his heart. Eventually it will begin to overpower him. She is giving the man a chance to look at himself as he is instead of getting entangled in a quarrel which gets everyone defensive. She gives the man no reason to further attack her or defend his position. Someday, hopefully, he will see in himself what she sees in him: the real Mr. Hamilton. And the truth shall set him free. That will be some day!"

Thomas shook his head and added, "The irony of it all is that she may look weak, but who really is the stronger one? Who is more at peace?"

"I got to hand it to you, Thomas, you'd make one fine pastor. And you Ramon, you sitting there like a dead log of wood, nothing to say."

"I like listening for the most part, Matti. But I agree, there's a lot of truth in what brother Thomas says. You see Matti, the trouble with most of us is that we have been living so long reacting this way, it's hard to see like Miss Jenny does that there is another way that brings love into the situation and not anger and hate. One way improves the world, and the other perpetuates the hate and darkness. That is why the good Lord gave us nature: so we stop and smell the flowers and calm our busy minds so we can see the error of our ways. Why in my book, she's acting like Jesus would want us to act. She is a fine example to all of us."

"Amen brother," said Thomas as he and Ramon slapped hands in mid air.

"Now I've heard it all! Seems like I be in church or something over here instead of behind an old shed. I have to think if this be Sunday, both of you'd make fine preachers. Now I best be back to work and I 'spect it's time you worked off them fine cookies I baked, too."

"Oh Matti, you make the best coffee and cookies there is."

Matti went over to the dusty wooden table. She made a move to pick up the tray with the coffee pot and empty cookie plate but instead turned and went first to Thomas. She stood in front of him and gazed into his sparkling, dark eyes.

"When I be around the Mistress, I feel as comfortable if I be wrapped in a warm blanket. With my sister, my only family, back in Jamaica, Miss Jenny be more like my sister than I her maid around here."

"I have the same feeling around her as well, Matti. It's as if we are all family and isn't that the way relationships should be? Are we not all created from the Lord? We strive so hard to be separate from each other, to compete with each other. This just perpetuates the troubles on the earth. What Miss Jenny does is accepts what *is* and allows the Lord to deal with the situation. There's enormous power and peace in that approach because it's all filled with love."

"Thomas, you be a Godly man, I consider you my brother."

Thomas got up and hugged Matilda. Ramon was already up and waiting for his hug, too.

"Just remember the scripture Matti: 'The blind cannot lead the blind or else both will fall in the ditch!" said Thomas, as she made her way to the door.

"Oh my good Lord, I be carrying you in my pocket for the next month to keep reminding me of what the good Book be saying. Maybe then I can keep the fry pan in the cupboard and not on that man's head!"

They all laughed as the shed brightened with the love and mutual respect that had filled the air.

As Matti left she added, "You two sure done filled me full of good feelings this fine morning. 'Spect I'll be singing all the ways back to the kitchen!"

CHAPTER THIRTY-SEVEN

W HEN HENRY CAME up from the basement, Julean was sitting at the kitchen table staring off into space.

"Thanks for putting the clothes into the dryer for me. Want a coffee, honey?"

"Maybe later. I started a watercolour 15 minutes ago and I would like to apply the second coat while I can still picture the colour I want it to be. Oh, how did the doctor appointment go? Everything okay?"

Henry was unable to read Julean's expression.

"Yes, everything is fine. I'll tell you later. Better get back at your painting."

"Oh, it can wait." Henry stopped and gazed at Julean, "So, what did Dr. Crossly have to say?"

Julean got up and drew near to Henry. "Go finish what you want to do with the watercolour. I will come up to your studio once I've changed."

"Is everything okay, Julean? You're acting a bit strange..."

"Everything is fine," she shooed him with her hands, "I'll be up in a few minutes."

Julean kissed Henry's cheek, picked up a large bag resting on the floor by the front foyer and walked down the hall to their bedroom.

"What did you get from Antoine's?"

"You'll see."

Henry's eyes followed her for a moment.

"Come up right away. It will only take me a few minutes to put another wash on the sky."

About 15 minutes later, Henry heard a soft tap on his studio door. *The door is open, why doesn't she just come in?* He turned then stared, speechless, at his wife. Every now and then she did something totally out of character and this was one of those times. Cradling a frosted bottle of wine in one arm and holding two crystal glasses in her other hand, there was his wife, dressed from head to toe in Parisian apparel, leaning seductively against the door frame.

Henry had never seen Julean quite like this. It was the extra thick soles of her stiletto heels, along with the black fishnet stockings that led up to a very tight, shiny, black leather mini skirt that made her shapely legs look as long and slender as a fashion model's. Heat sizzled through his body as he gazed at her red angora sweater clinging to her voluptuous breasts. A black beret tilted to the side and resting in her auburn hair completed the Parisian look.

It was the makeup, however, that perfectly transformed her from a conservative housewife to a come-hither lady of the night. Julean had applied bright red lipstick well beyond the outline of her sensuous lips and excessive rouge covered her cheeks. She had even gone to the extent of attaching long black eyelashes that drew Henry swiftly into her lurid, seductive world. The heat radiating from his body accelerated the drying time of the watercolour wash on the worktable beside him so rapidly it left a jagged watermark across the sky.

"*Monsieur*, have we time to celebrate. *Non*?" Julean smiled and fluttered her long eyelashes.

Falling right into the role of the scene, Henry rolled his eyes and casually returned her smile.

"*Oui, oui* Madame! I shall drop everything for you!"

Henry couldn't hide his ear-to-ear grin as he walked over to his shapely, provocative wife. He had no idea what had prompted this display, and at that moment, he didn't really care.

Julean pushed herself away from the door and swayed her hips as she met her overcharged husband halfway into the studio. She opened her arms and Henry immediately fell into them. After a long sensuous kiss they parted.

"If this is the result of your doctor appointment you can see him weekly from now on." Henry winked and then continued. "What aphrodisiac did he prescribe?"

"You are so sexy, *Monsieur*, none is required." Julean couldn't hold back any longer and burst out laughing. "Honey, you look more made up than I do!"

Henry's lips and cheeks were smeared with lipstick and rouge. "I look like a clown, do I?"

"A loveable one." Julean leaned into him again and kissed him.

"So, what brings all this on?" and then Henry added hopefully, "not that we need something to celebrate like this every day."

Julean set the glasses down on the table next to the watercolour Henry was working on and filled them with the chilled wine. She picked up the glasses and handed one to her curious husband.

"Well, I wanted you to see a more spontaneous side of me. I sometimes gather from your dreams that you would appreciate that of me."

Henry gazed into his wife's eyes and an unwanted memory surfaced; he had to admit that this was something that Jenny would have been more apt to do. He quickly counterbalanced that thought, not wanting to invite thoughts of Jenny into this extraordinary encounter with Julean.

"Honey, I love your quiet, unassuming nature."

"Well, there is another, much more important, reason I thought we would celebrate your wife's sexy figure because before too long..." Julean's eyes sparkled as her body shimmied and shook. "Honey, you are not going to believe this after all these years.... Your dear wife is once again with child!"

By this time Henry was so weakened by his luscious, enticing wife, the news threatened to keel him over. "No way! How far along are you?"

"The doctor estimates that the baby may be well into its fifth month."

"What!? But you don't look pregnant—"

"That's what had me confused. I skipped a period, but then the next month I had some spotting, and I'm not feeling pregnant like I did with the other kids. Most of all, I'm not showing in the least! It must be a small baby so far. Apparently this happens to lots of women."

Henry set his glass down on the table and fell to his knees. He pushed up Julean's sweater, exposing her tummy. He gently felt it and then tenderly kissed her belly button. "I love you so much, honey," Henry pressed the side of his face against her belly button and hugged her midsection. He got up and took his wife's hand and led her to the sofa. Within minutes they were lying side-by-side making love.

They were still in a daze, lying in each others arms, when they were startled by the slamming door downstairs followed by Lauren's voice.

"Mommy!"

"Oh my goodness, is school out already?"

Lauren's footsteps padded up the stairs. Henry and Julean looked at one another and jumped off the chesterfield. They were both half undressed and their faces looked on fire. Henry quickly pulled up his trousers while Julean hid behind the sofa. Lauren met her panting father at the studio door.

"Daddy, you look so funny. What did you do to your face?"

"I-I splashed watercolour all over. I had an accident."

"You look like a clown." Lauren laughed. "Where's Mommy?"

Henry side-stepped, blocking his daughter from being able to see into the studio. "She is down in the basement putting wash into the dryer. She told me to tell you to go down there when you got home. I think she has something for you."

Lauren turned and hopped down the stairs. Julean came out from hiding, giggling like a naughty teenager. Her sweater was twisted and skirt still unzipped. Henry laughed at the sight of her. Her lipstick was smeared, her eyeliner ran from the few tears of joy and one of the false eyelashes dangled from her left eye. She looked like a lady that had had a long hard night's work.

"Quickly, get down to our bedroom and change. Lauren will be up from the basement as soon as she discovers you're not there."

Julean tiptoed past her husband and tossed him a sexy kiss before disappearing out the door.

Just as she made it to the bottom of the stairs, Allison and Jeremy came in the front door. Julean, totally embarrassed, tried to cover her face with her beret and ran off to the bedroom.

"Was that Mom?" Allison asked her older brother.

"Yeah, it looked like her"

Lauren came up from the basement. "Did you see Mom, Allison?"

"Yes, she just ran into the bedroom.

"Mom? Mommy!" Lauren hollered as she ran down the hall and burst into her parents' bedroom,

Julean had jumped into the shower and Lauren peeked behind the plastic curtain. "I'll be right out honey, go watch TV."

"Dad said you got something for me, what is it?"

"You'll see."

At dinner, Julean shared her news with the children. The kids were very excited. Lauren wanted to know if it was a boy or girl.

"I don't know, yet. I am going for a an ultrasound next week, though, and—"

"What's that?"

"It is a new type of machine that can see the baby in my tummy and the doctor can tell if it's a boy or girl."

"How can a machine see through your skin?"

"Remember when you sprained your arm and the doctor took X-rays to see if the bones were broken? Remember he showed you a picture of the bones under your skin?"

"Yes, I remember."

"Well, this machine can do that, too. It's pretty exciting. They didn't really use ultrasound back when I was pregnant with you kids, so we had to wait until you were born to find out if you were boys or girls."

"I hope it's a girl, I would love to have a younger sister," Lauren said.

"No way," Jeremy groaned. "Two girls in the family are enough.

It's gotta be a boy."

"Well, whatever it is, it will be a welcome addition to our family," said Julean.

THE FOLLOWING WEEK, Henry and Julean went for the ultrasound. They held each other's hand as they walked into the office. Julean was taken in first and prepared for the test and then Henry was called in. The attendant squirted a gel from a tube onto Julean's tummy.

"I am so excited. I just can't wait to know what we're having."

Henry sat down beside his wife and held her hand.

The technician began moving the scanner over Julean's stomach. "It all depends if the baby is in the right position for us to see the genitals. Oh! Yes, there it is. Do you want to know?"

"Yes!" said Julean and Henry.

"It's a boy!"

"Jeremy will be happy to know he has a brother. Isn't that something? Two boys and two girls. How much more perfect can you plan a family?"

Julean's eyes filled with tears. "This is such an unexpected baby. I thought our family was complete a long time ago. Well, now it's perfectly complete!"

CHAPTER THIRTY-EIGHT

"I WANT YOU TO paint a picture on my bedroom wall, too, Daddy."
Lauren looked at him with pleading eyes. Henry had just finished painting the scene of *The Little Engine That Could*, puffing its way up the mountain as the clown, children and animals cheered on. In the upper part of the sky next to the sun, Henry had written, "I think I can...I think I can" in each puff of steam.

"What would you like me to paint, Lauren?"

She thought for a moment. "I don't know. You'll have to help me."

"Well, honey," Julean chimed in, "how about Cinderella or Snow White—?"

"Yes, yes, Snow White! And, can you paint the seven dwarfs, too, Dad?"

"Oh, I think I can handle that. I'll do a sketch tonight and if you like it, I'll paint it on your wall this weekend when you're home from school. Maybe as I paint, you can think of things to add and help me paint, too!"

Lauren jumped up and down. "Let's start tonight."

"The weekend is only two days away, Lauren, and Daddy has to do a sketch, first. Now go play for a minute, I want to talk to Daddy."

Henry chuckled as Lauren pranced off to her room, no doubt planning the exact place on her wall for each of the dwarfs. Julean came to Henry's side and put her arm around his waist.

"The nursery looks so nice and colourful, Henry. The chest of drawers and change table you made match perfectly. Since they're both the same height I can have everything I need on the chest in easy reach."

"Your wish is my command, sweetheart."

"I thought you were going to paint a monkey scene with Curious George going into the forest on the nursery wall?"

"At the last minute I changed my mind. Earlier this morning, I came across the story about the *Little Engine that Could*. It was a favourite of mine as a kid and thought it might give our little boy inspiration when faced with difficulties."

"What a great thought, Henry. It really is a positive story and it even helped my own self-confidence every time I read it to the children."

Henry smiled. He turned and patted Julean's tummy which had grown immensely over the past two months. "Well, our little boy can come along any day now."

"The doctor estimates at least another three weeks, but if it's anything like the last three children, he'll be here sooner than later."

"That's what I mean. They were all so eager to see their mommy and daddy." Henry winked at his wife who looked even more radiant when expecting.

"Are you sure you don't want to be present during the delivery? Dr. Crossly says it's fine with him and that you could be a big support to me."

Henry gazed at Julean. Deliveries were always an anxious time for him. It started with his suspicion and worry over Jenny being pregnant and surfaced again just prior to Benjamin's birth. The death of his first son only reinforced his concern about deliveries. Rather than see the birth of his children as joyous times to celebrate, they were frightening events until he knew for certain that Julean and the babies were healthy and well.

"I'd like to be in the delivery room with you, but I think you and the doctor would find me more of a hindrance than a help. I'd be just too nervous, honey."

"You did come to the prenatal class with me and you were so encouraging and helpful with my breathing."

"Well, that's a lot different from being in an actual delivery room and besides, at least I will be able to help you until it comes time to deliver."

Julean shifted her tummy sideways and kissed his cheek.

"Think about it, dear. You're more capable than you realize. Perhaps it's just in your mind."

THREE DAYS LATER, around 2:00 a.m., Henry felt a persistent nudge in his back. He groaned, shifted his body and settled back to sleep.

"Honey, it's time to go. Come on, get up…pleeeeease."

"What did you say?" Henry moaned.

"My labour has started. I've been timing the contractions for the past hour. They're less than five minutes apart. We have to go to the hospital."

It suddenly dawned on him that his wife was about to have the baby. He jumped out of bed.

"Where is it!?"

Julean chuckled. "It's not here, yet. You have to take me to the hospital. Oooh, there's another one."

Julean looked at the clock. "That was only four and half minutes after the last one."

Henry flipped on the light and rushed to his wife's side. "Take it easy honey, everything is going to be fine. Where are your clothes, I'll get you dressed?"

"I can dress myself, Hank. You better get dressed and wake Jeremy. Let him know he has to keep an eye on the girls until you get home."

"Yes, of course." Henry ran up the stairs to Jeremy's room.

Julean was already dressed when Henry returned and standing at the front door holding her small suitcase.

"My God, you're ready, already!"

"Well, I have done this before, dear," Julean said calmly before another contraction overtook her and she had to sit down on the foyer bench. Henry ran into the bedroom and quickly dressed. He put on his shoes and ran back to the front door. "How are you doing honey? Everything okay?"

Henry felt her tummy. The contraction had passed. "Now, you stay in there for another half hour, do you hear?"

Julean smiled. "He'll be fine, Hank. Get the keys and let's calmly go. I already phoned the hospital and asked them to call Dr. Crossly. Hopefully he'll be there by the time we arrive."

Just as they got to the car, Julean had another labour pain. "Ooooh, my gosh this is a strong contraction. Better...ooooh... get going, honey." Julean climbed into the back seat while Henry jumped behind the wheel.

Henry struggled to keep the butterflies down. Despite having been through this himself four times, he was as nervous as he had been the first time around. After several attempts he jabbed the key into the ignition and fired up the car. He backed out of the driveway, threw the gear into drive and screeched off down the deserted street.

His eyes frantically bouncing back and forth between the road and his wife in the rear view mirror, Henry remembered the instructions he received at the prenatal class.

"Breathe deeply, Julean. Take a deep breath and then let it out slowly. Come on now, do it." Henry took in a deep breath to demonstrate.

"Well, let's wait until the next contraction, shall we?"

Henry couldn't believe how calm Julean was. He sped down Wascana Drive and turned onto Broad street. A mile or so away from the hospital, the car started sputtering. Henry looked over his shoulder at Julean in alarm.

"Come on, keep going," he coaxed the car, but it sputtered and coughed, then finally jerked to a halt in the middle of the road. He turned the key. The car threatened to start, then died. "What's wrong with this damn car?" He turned the key again. The motor turned over and over but didn't start.

"Oh, my gosh, Henry, the baby's coming! Oooh...did you forget to fill up the gas tank again?"

Henry banged his head on the steering wheel, realizing she was right.

"What are we going to do?"

Henry checked the rear view mirror, not a car in sight, but there was a car coming in the other direction.

"I'll try to flag down that car. Wait here."

"I'm not going anywhere, honey."

Henry switched on his blinkers then ran across the street, waving his hands manically above his head. The car slowed down, but drove around Henry and sped off.

"I'm not going to hurt you. I need help!" Henry yelled after it.

Panic swept through Henry as he ran back to the car. He could run to the hospital, but it was really too far and he didn't want to leave Julean alone. If only there was a house nearby, a door he could knock on... But there wasn't a single residence within a three block radius; only businesses closed for the night and a dark apartment block lined the street. How was he going to get help?

He heard Julean screaming, but could no longer see her in the back seat.

"Julean, where are you?"

"I'm lying down. Come and help me, I can feel the baby coming."

Henry's heart threatened to jump out of his chest. "What can I do Julean?"

"It's okay, honey. You can do this. I'll help you. I assisted many deliveries in my nursing internship and I've been through this four times before."

"Julean! I could never deliver this baby. Never!"

"You can, Henry. Take a deep breath and let it out slowly. Do what you told me to do."

Henry was so nervous he didn't know if he was breathing in or out. His body shook as he leaned into the backseat.

"That's it, calm down, honey. Oooooh!" Julean screamed. "It's coming, Henry. Julean pulled her knees up higher. Her skirt was hiked up around her hips and she had apparently taken off her underwear when he went to flag down the car. Henry could see the baby's head in the dim light.

"My God," muttered Henry.

A siren approached, growing louder and louder. For a minute, Henry couldn't tell if the ringing in his ears was really a siren or

Julean screaming again. A car pulled up beside them and a police officer rushed to Henry's side.

"Do you need help, sir? A man phoned in a few minutes ago that someone was trying to flag him down."

"That was me! My wife is having a baby. Do you know how to deliver babies?"

"Yes, I've delivered three, but I'll call for an ambulance first."

"Honey, I want you to do this," pleaded Julean. "Please. I know you can do this. Do it for me and for your son. Think of the scene you painted in his nursery."

A flood of adrenalin swept through Henry as an unknown strength surfaced. With every breath he recalled the words of the *Little Engine That Could*, "I think I can, I think I can." Each time Henry repeated the phrase it propelled him forward until he realized why the Lord had urged him to paint that scene in his son's nursery. It wasn't so much for his son as it was to prepare him for the task at hand! Another surge of confidence swept through Henry. "Yes, Lord, I can do this!"

Julean was almost in constant pain, as her contractions were just seconds apart.

"Breathe deeply, honey, and let it out slowly. That's it. Just relax, dear."

Henry reached up and turned on the interior overhead light.

"I see more of the head, Julean. Can you push with the next contraction?" Henry said with the tone of a seasoned doctor.

Julean's hair was matted to her head with sweat, and her clothes were soaked. Henry realized he was sweating profusely as well and raised a hand to brush the sweat from his brow.

"Oh, Henry, it's coming. It's coming, honey." She screamed. "Guide the head out, Henry."

Henry reached forward and felt the baby's head, ready to hold it. "This is a miracle honey! I can't believe it. Push, dear, it's coming."

The officer crouched behind him watching carefully. "You're doing fine."

Julean shrieked as the head came out along with a gush of fluid. And then, in one fell swoop, the baby slithered out, pouring fluid all over Henry's knees. His eyes widened so much they threatened to pop out of their sockets as he found the baby resting in his open hands. "I've got it honey! I've got it!"

Tears streamed down his cheeks as he looked at the newborn infant. "My God, I've delivered my son!" The baby was covered in blood and fluid, but Henry instinctively pulled him close to his chest. The baby started to cry.

"Oh honey, I'm so proud of you." Julean tried to keep her head up, but was so exhausted she fell back crying joyously that it was all over.

"What's that thing dangling at the end of the cord?"

Julean raised her head. "That's the placenta. It's okay." She unbuttoned her blouse. "Here, give the baby to me, I'll start to nurse him. That will make everything calm down."

Henry reached forward and gently laid the wet, blood streaked newborn on Julean's chest. She guided the baby's mouth to her breast while Henry took off his sweater and tucked it around the baby.

"He's so beautiful, honey. I love you both so much." Henry kissed Julean on the forehead and stood up next to the officer. Both men had tears glistening on their cheeks. A memory flashed into Henry's mind.

"Shouldn't the umbilical cord be cut?"

Henry turned to the officer who just raised his shoulders and shook his head indicating that he didn't know.

"What shoes are you wearing, honey?"

Why on earth is she asking me that? Henry looked to his feet to appease his dear wife and was surprised to see that in his haste he had put a loafer on his left foot and an Oxford on his right. "You're not going to believe this, but I put on two different shoes." He chuckled.

"Does one have shoelaces?"

Henry looked down again. "Yes, the Oxford does."

"Good. Remove the lace and tie it around the cord. The baby no longer needs the blood or oxygen from the placenta and this will prevent bleeding."

As Henry tied a tight knot around the cord another siren

approached from the distance. Moments later, an ambulance pulled up and two paramedics jumped out.

"Where is the expectant mother?" asked one of the attendants.

"She's in the back." Henry pointed into the car and smiled. "The baby is already born. I delivered it!"

Henry stepped back to let them examine Julean and the baby before transferring them to the ambulance. Henry followed along and told Julean he would tend to the car and come to the hospital straight away.

Before the two paramedics went into the ambulance one turned to Henry and said, "Good job! Your first delivery?"

"Yeah…"

"The next one will be easy."

And the other driver winked and added, "You may be able to do the next one at home… no need for the hospital!"

Henry laughed, relieving some of the lingering nervous excitement. "No way!"

Henry raised his shoulders and then let them slowly fall along with a long sigh of relief. The siren came to life as the ambulance sped away announcing the birth of Justin Pederson.

Luckily, the police officer had a three-quarter full gas can in his squad car and offered to help Henry start his vehicle.

"You did a good job, Mr. Pederson."

"Yeah, I never thought I could ever do that. It's amazing what you can do when you have to. It's a good thing you pulled up, too."

The officer nodded and congratulated the happy father. In turn, Henry thanked him for coming and for his support then got into his car with the hope of catching the ambulance.

By the time Henry parked the car and went through the rigmarole of finding out where Julean was, she was already cleaned up and resting in a nice warm bed. Dr. Crossly was in the room with Julean when Henry walked in.

The doctor looked at Henry and struggled to hold back a belly laugh. Henry's pants were soaking wet, his hair matted and dishevelled, his shirt smeared with blood and his eyes red and puffy.

"Congratulations, Henry. For someone nervous about deliveries, you did a very fine job."

Henry looked from his smiling, proud wife to the doctor, then back again to Julean. A broad grin crossed his face. "It was a piece of cake, doc."

Three days later, the kids could hardly wait to see little Justin when he arrived home. Henry had difficulty controlling the children. They all wanted to touch him and hold him.

"Oh, they're fine, honey. Let them welcome him."

As the oldest, Jeremy got to hold Justin first, amidst Allison and Lauren's protests.

"Oh, please let me hold him. He is so cute and I love him. Please, Mommy. I waited so long for him to come home."

Henry sat Lauren on the sofa next to Julean and carefully lifted Justin onto her waiting arms. She snuggled her head into the baby's head and rubbed it until the baby screamed.

"I know you love him so much," said Julean, "just be gentle."

Julean shifted closer to Lauren and together they fondled the tiny infant.

In the days that followed, Jeremy and Allison lost a little interest in the new arrival to their home, but Lauren didn't for a minute. As soon as Justin woke for his feeding, Lauren was right there accompanying her mother. Justin was her Barbie and she loved every inch of him.

With each passing month the novelty of a new baby in the family gradually wore off. Justin was considered as a normal part of the Pederson family and assumed his hierarchy amongst the children as last in line. To Julean, however, Justin was a surprise package from heaven that completed her motherhood.

It was during the late night or early morning feedings when she was all alone with her son that she would thank the good Lord for sending this special little angel into their lives.

CHAPTER THIRTY-NINE

THE SUN WAS bright and hot and shone directly into Matti's eyes as she hurried to the tool shed. Beads of sweat covered her forehead as she entered the cool hut.

"I could hardly wait to get here, the sun be like fire today outside and it be no better inside, neither."

"Why Matti, it's nice and refreshing in here, the smell of potting soil is in the air—"

"I don't mean in here, Thomas, I be referring to the main house. Feels hotter then Hades, like Satan and his helper taking up permanent residence."

"I'm sure your boiling temper is only adding to the heat in there. What's got you riled up today?"

"Thomas, I understand what you saying to love your brother but that man ain't no brother of mine. Why, he be the devil himself and I ain't loving no devil, that's for sure! Why, he be stealing that poor woman's own child from her. And that nanny be doing the very same as if she be cloned from the devil herself. Good Lord, what's the world coming to?"

"I know it's hard to understand Matti, but in this situation the alternate is too upsetting and would create untold turmoil. If you think that Mr. Hamilton is the devil well let me tell you that right now the home has a piece of heaven in it with Miss Jenny being the way she is. But if Miss Jenny sets on a different course of action then what you are saying now about the home will become a living hell."

"I know you be right, Thomas, but what that man be doing is worse than a low, mean, sly coyote. I never seen such a thing as a husband taking a child away from his mother. Just when she be wanting to take the boy out he be snatching the little one away and starting another one of his stupid activities!"

"We must support Miss Jenny at all costs; help her to make her life here as pleasant as possible. Her example is so admirable. Most people in her situation would be on their knees each day pleading with the Lord to deliver them from her hell, whereas Miss Jenny is thanking the Lord for her blessings."

"What blessings, Thomas? I be blind or something?"

"She gets peace from the garden, joy from her son and don't forget, she doesn't see Mr. Hamilton the way you or I see him. She looks beyond the man's exterior to his real heart. And I say this again, Matti: the seed she plants there daily is ever so small now, but someday it's going to be a mighty oak, full of such power the man won't be able to do anything else but get on his knees and beg for forgiveness!"

"I sure hope you be right. Maybe we can stand that man under the sprinkler every day and make the seed grow faster!"

Thomas and Ramon chuckled.

"Well, we can pray about that, Matti," continued Thomas, "but I saw something the other day that would please Miss Jenny and give her great joy. The instant I saw it I said to myself, 'now that captures the thankful spirit of Miss Jenny—'"

"What did you see, Thomas?"

"You've got my interest now too, Thomas," chimed in Ramon.

"Well, it all started last week when my friend, Frank, the caretaker at the Memorial Gardens cemetery called and asked if I would do him a favour and drop off some sod for him. As soon as I drove my half ton through the gate to the cemetery, I slammed the brakes so hard the pile of sod on the back of the truck shot forward and hit the back of the cab with a powerful thud. What I saw took my breath away. It not only reminded me of Miss Jenny but also an old legend I once heard."

"Oh, oh, I 'spect you be stretching this story out some. I'm gonna get another cup of coffee, how about you, Ramon?" Ramon nodded his head. "And you, Thomas? 'Spect you be needing some if you be milking this story a spell longer."

"Yes, fill her up, Matti."

"Well, you got Ramon and me on pins and needles now, so what's this thing you see and what this legend be about?"

While Matti poured Thomas and Ramon another cup of coffee, Thomas shared his story with his co workers and even pulled out a photo of what he had seen for a visual aid. Matti and Ramon agreed with Thomas that it was absolutely beautiful and totally captured Miss Jenny's heart.

"You can see why I was so excited. It will make Miss Jenny's garden perfectly complete and fill her with such joy!"

"Yeah, it would make a heavenly gift for sure, but how much is it? Seems way out of our price range," said Ramon.

"Here is the reason why I believe in God's divine providence. I was meant to deliver sod to my friend that morning! As you know from how busy we were last week, Frank's request couldn't have been at a worse time. But that's the way God works. He sets everything up and there is no way we are going to get out of it. He knows our minds and hearts and every move we will make."

"Good Lord, Thomas, get on with it. I need to be getting back to the house. Listening to your story, I drank too much coffee and I need to use the toilet real quick. Only concern be that Charles may be indisposed and I have to be holding on for thirty minutes. I may need to hide behind one them rose bushes."

Ramon and Thomas laughed. "Best you watch out for the thorns!" They all laughed again.

"Okay, Matti, I'll be quick. When I asked Frank about it, he said that this here statue was up for sale. Apparently, it had been commissioned by a business man years ago but he never picked it up from the sculptor. It was paid for and sat on the grounds for years. The sculptor felt the statue was spooked and wanted to get rid of it. He found out the man had died—which is why he had never bothered to pick it up—and was buried at the cemetery. So to follow through on the sale, the sculptor decided to have it delivered to the cemetery to get it off his hands and property.

"Now, here's where God's sovereignty is something else."

"You best be hurrying, Thomas or you have no need to water the plants in this here shed!"

"I'll hurry Matti, Frank told me the marble statue is valued at thousands of dollars, but the cemetery management wanted it removed from the entrance to the property."

"Did Frank tell you what they wanted for the statue, Thomas?" Ramon asked again with a note of impatience in his voice.

"The delivery charge they would have to pay to get rid of it… and that's all! Can you believe that? Right then and there I thought perhaps the statue was commissioned for us by way of all these circumstances! I said a prayer to St. Joseph and stepped out in faith. I thought if we were meant to give this to Miss Jenny, I was prepared to give everything in my wallet. I checked and counted $324.30. Normally I don't carry that much cash but two hundred of that was intended to pay for our home utilities. Anyway, Frank took me to the office and the secretary at the counter gave me the freight invoice that I had to pay. Now you're not going to believe this—"

"Good Lord, why you be carrying on so? Please just tell us, Thomas!" Matti's legs where bouncing up and down and her hands couldn't sit still either.

Thomas reached into his back pocket and pulled out the invoice. "Now look at that, the freight charge was exactly $324.30. I darned near fell over. Now if that wasn't divine providence in full action then nothing is. It's as if that statue was commissioned especially for Miss Jenny, no two ways about it!"

Matti had a quick look at the invoice, "I have to pee so bad I be tasting it soon."

She jumped up and headed for the door. "I be contributing for that gift for the Mistress, that's for sure. Thomas, you be bringing the coffee pot to the kitchen… Good Lord, I sure hope Charles ain't indisposed… This be the usual time of day he be working on his plumbing…"

CHAPTER FORTY

H ENRY'S EXHIBITION AT the McKenzie Art Gallery turned into two years of tours at other public galleries in Saskatchewan. While most of the paintings sold, Henry was very pleased that one of the purchasers was the Mendel Art Gallery in Saskatoon. The final three unsold paintings were already picked up by a commercial art gallery in Vancouver.

After this success, Henry decided to pursue a new avenue in his art. Open Studio in Toronto offered courses in how to use several methods to make prints. He hoped to reach more customers who couldn't afford an original painting, but would gladly purchase an original print. After receiving a grant from the Arts Board and arranging an eight week leave of absence from the School Board, he was set to go.

He and Father Engelmann discussed all the ins and outs during one of Father's visits.

"So, you're off to Toronto."

"Yeah. It's the best place in the country to learn how to make prints."

"What kind of prints will you be making?"

"Open Studio in Toronto teaches several methods. The ones I am familiar with are silk screens and ones where the artist etches the image on a metal plate. I suppose after I've learned the different ways to produce prints I'll select the one I like the most and try to do it here."

"Hi, Father," said Julean as she came through the door carrying Justin. Lauren trailed close behind.

"Grandpa!" yelled Lauren as she dashed over to Father, leaping onto his lap and flinging her arms around him.

"My, my, Lauren, every time I see you, you've grown an inch."

"Guess what my mom bought me at the store?"

"Tell me quick, I can hardly wait."

Lauren pulled out a long, slender plastic object that dispensed square candies one at a time. "Hold out your hand, Grandpa."

Lauren popped out a candy on Father's palm, which he popped into his mouth.

His lips puckered and his eyes scrunched. "Oh my, that's sour."

Lauren laughed. "I knew you would do that." She hopped off Father's lap and headed for the living room.

When Julean let Justin down he trotted over to the men.

"And, how is the young man of the family?" asked Father, as he tickled Justin's tummy. "Soon you will catch up to Lauren. My, my, how quickly the children grow."

"You've got that right, Father," said Henry as he picked up his two-year-old son and tossed him in the air. "Now that he's walking, he's into everything, including my studio. I think he will be another artist. Isn't that right?" Henry nuzzled his head against Justin's.

"Let me down, Daddy! Lauren, I want a candy!"

"Okay, little guy, off you go. Your sister's in the living room."

"So, did Henry tell you the news about his grant to go to Toronto?" Julean asked, as Justin toddled after his sister.

"Yes, we were just discussing it, Julean."

"Did he tell you what else he's been thinking?"

Father looked at Henry. "There's more?"

"Well, this may be too soon to mention, but we are starting to make quite a bit of money with the sale of my art and I was thinking of leaving my job and going full-time into painting."

"Now that's a big decision, Henry. Don't you like counselling anymore?"

"Yes, I love it, Father, but I think I want to paint even more.

Even when I am at work listening to students, my mind wanders to the painting I am working on. It makes me feel guilty that I am not doing my job."

"I see."

"I talked to Mom and Dad about it. Mom thinks it's okay, but Dad thinks it's too risky to try and make a living that way, especially with four children and all. Julean's parents definitely advise to stay in counselling, but Julean and I anticipated that reaction."

"And what do you think?" Father Engelmann turned to Julean.

"Well, Henry can do so many things and once he sets his mind to something it just seems to turn out so well. And I suppose if we run out of money, I could always go back to work."

"Well, there you are, Henry. If the boss has confidence in you, what more support do you need?"

Henry smiled and took Julean's hand.

THE NIGHT BEFORE Henry was to leave, a common early-spring blizzard blasted through, causing the cancellation of some flights and delays of many others. Henry's flight, which had been scheduled to leave at eight o'clock in the morning, was rescheduled to depart that afternoon at one-fifteen.

While Henry waited for the taxi to arrive to take him to the airport, he gazed at his fifteen year old son and saw not a boy but a man. His demeanor, his eyes, his towering stature gave Henry confidence that he would look after things in his absence. Henry couldn't believe that his son would be going into his twelfth grade next fall. Jeremiah had grown up so quickly, beyond his age.

The taxi honked, snapping Henry out of his thoughts. "Well, this is it, I'm off to Toronto! Now, I want you all to help your mother and listen to what she says. Jeremy, you're the oldest, I'm expecting you to help out with looking after everyone."

"Yeah sure, Dad. Don't worry. Everything will be okay."

Henry kissed the kids good-bye then held his teary-eyed wife in his arms. "I'll phone you as soon as I get there. I love you very much."

"I love you, too. Have you got everything?"

"Dad, the taxi honked again!" shouted Allison.

"Go wave to him. Let him know I'm coming."

Henry was excited and nervous. He gave each child another hug and kiss then turned to head out to the taxi when Justin started to fuss and grabbed Henry's leg.

Henry bent down to his son and hugged him.

"It's okay, son. Daddy's just going away for a little while and he will phone and talk to you when he gets to Toronto."

Julean picked Justin up and he snuggled into her neck.

Henry kissed Julean's cheek, grabbed his suitcase then hurried out to the cab.

Once seated, Henry rolled down the frosted window and waved to his family. He stuck his head out the window as the cab skidded away. The snow crystals hanging in the air quickly blurred their image and then there was just white.

The master printer giving the course was a well-established artist, known all over the world for his printmaking. It didn't take him long to realize Henry showed great promise and was pleased he had an apprentice who would appreciate his skills and knowledge in the fine art of printmaking.

Of all the methods Henry studied, silk screening was his favourite. He liked the physical work involved in pressing ink through a fine mesh. After two weeks of study, Henry decided to do a limited edition of two hundred silk screen prints. It would be a seventeen colour serigraph of a boy holding a hockey stick and skates over his back on his way to the rink.

Henry would have to do seventeen different drawings, each representing a different colour. Each colour would have to be pulled through the screen, and eventually all the colours would come together to produce the image. The instructor didn't think Henry would have enough time to draw all the images necessary and do the actual printing itself in the six weeks remaining.

At the end of the fifth week, however, Henry had printed 14 of the 17 colours. It was amazing how the image was coming together. Henry hardly slept many nights so he could keep up with the drawings necessary for the next colour. At the rate he was going, there was no doubt that Henry would be able to complete his project before the two-months wrapped up.

When a fellow artist wanted to use the silkscreen press, Henry gave up his slotted time since he had managed to pull ahead of schedule. He used the afternoon to rest at his apartment. After lunch, Henry plunked himself down on the sofa to watch TV, just in time to get the weather report of another four inches of snow in Ottawa. This was the second heavy snowfall there in the past week and the residents still hadn't shoveled their way out of the last storm.

As pictures of Ottawa flashed on the screen, so did thoughts of Jenny in Henry's mind. This was only the second time he had allowed himself to entertain such thoughts of his first love since he said goodbye to his family. During the flight to Toronto he remembered that he had planned to make this trip after his Grade 12 graduation all in a bid to try and locate Jenny. He'd had his tickets and hotel room booked… he even had the phone number to call her that to this day he kept on a piece of paper in his wallet. And then, he had met Julean and his whole life changed.

As images of the snow-covered streets of Ottawa panned across the television screen, Henry considered how easy it would be to fly there from Toronto. *What did Jenny look like, now? Would I recognize her?* It would really be something to see Jenny after twenty four years… She would probably be married and have a family, much like him. He wondered again if she had married that jerk, James Hamilton…

It would be nice to know how life was going for her. He was sure she would want to know what had happened to him, too. They were both adults and would surely be able to see each other again without harm. It would all be innocent enough – just two friends coming together after years of being separated to catch up on each other's lives.

Feelings of longing mixed with a twinge of loneliness stirred within Henry. He reached into his back pocket and pulled out his wallet. He found a slip of paper he had put there many years ago. He took it out, unfolded it and gazed at it for the longest time. He went to the phone and dialed a long-distance number. As the phone rang, Henry looked at the number on the slip of paper and then crumbled it up and tossed it into the garbage can.

"Hello?" said a soft voice. "Hello, is someone there?"

"Hi, honey, it's me. I miss you so much, I just had to phone."

"Oh, hi, Hank. I'm so glad you called. I miss you, too, and so do the kids. Your mom was going to call you tomorrow morning, but I might as well let you know... Your dad was admitted to the hospital today."

"What happened? Is he okay?"

"When I talked to your mom this morning, she said he had been feeling dizzy and had shortness of breath... and... oh, yes, his feet were so swollen he couldn't put on his shoes."

"I know his heart has been giving him trouble. The doctor put him on high blood pressure medication over a year ago. I hope everything is fine."

"Your mom called about an hour ago and said he was much better when she left the hospital. I'm sure everything will be fine. So, how are you doing there? Have you finished the silkscreen print you told me about last week?"

"Yeah, just three more colours left. I should have it done by the end of this week. And since I will finish early, I was thinking that maybe you could fly here for the last weekend. We could go out on the town and celebrate, see the big city."

"That sounds wonderful. Do you think we can afford it?"

"I already have the suite, so it's just the plane ticket. I'm sure we will manage. Maybe phone mom or your parents to see if they can watch the kids for three days."

"Okay, I'll do it right away. I would love to come to Toronto to see you and I know the kids will be okay for a few days without me. Jeremy's been a big help. I think you will notice a change in him. He is so mature for his age and just keeps growing. I'm sure since you've gone, he has grown another inch."

"Well, let me know as soon as you can if you can make it here. Phone Air Canada, first thing, and arrange your return flight so it's the same as mine. Hopefully, we can sit together on the way home."

"Just a minute, Justin keeps pulling on the phone, he wants to talk to you and so do the rest of the kids. Think I'll say good-bye now. I love you, honey."

"I love you, too, dear. More than you'll ever know."

"Oh, and by the way... Ottawa isn't too far from Toronto, is it?"

Henry hesitated for a brief moment, "No, not really, why do you ask?"

"Oh... I was just interested..."

HENRY WAS EXHAUSTED after having completed two more colours on his print and was glad to be back at his apartment. He'd finished dinner and was about to sit down and relax with a steaming cup of coffee when his mother called. His father was doing fine. His congestive heart failure was about the same. He did, however, have a little more fluid in his lungs. The doctor had increased his medication to remove the water from his system and the hope was that his father would be home in a day or two once they regulated his medications.

Not long after Henry hung up from his mother, Julean called and told him she had managed to get a flight during his last weekend in Toronto! Her parents had agreed to watch the kids.

Henry was counting the days for Julean to come and now knew how his dad must have felt when he had wanted Mary to visit him in Toronto when he was there on a training program for Coca-Cola. It still bothered Henry that his mom hadn't gone. Henry imagined they could have had so much fun.

Two days later, while Henry was silk screening the last colour of his print, the Open Studio secretary called him to the office to take a call from his wife.

"Hello?"

"Hi, dear. I have some sad news to tell you. Your dad passed away an hour ago."

Henry felt like he'd been hit by a car. He'd been anticipating this call, but not this soon. His dad was only in his early seventies. Henry took a deep breath. "Did he have a heart attack?"

"Yes, I guess it was a massive one. They tried everything to revive him. I'm sorry, honey."

"How is Mom?"

"She just called from the hospital. She said she will be home around supper time."

"I'll finish off what I'm doing here and pack. Should be home by tomorrow night. I'm sure I can get a flight. I'll call and let you know when my flight arrives in Regina. Tell Mom I will call her this evening. Give her my love. "

HENRY'S TRIP HOME was a sentimental recollection of the past. He was sorry he did not see his dad before he died. He knew if he were at home now, he would be busy making arrangements, helping mom, consoling the kids, immersed in the funeral plans. He thought of the last time he had made funeral arrangements, so many years ago… He would probably have to jump right in and take over when he arrived home, but for now, flying high above the clouds, he felt at peace, as if time and the busyness of his life were standing still.

Memories crossed his mind in no particular order. They just gradually faded from one into the next: when his dad had given him his first nickel to spend, how nervous and afraid he'd been when his dad came home from Vancouver… He pictured his dad running alongside the tricycle he had bought him when he was three.

For a moment, the clouds opened up and he saw the fields below, houses and a town. He saw people and cars, like tiny ants, moving around on the ground so far down. *How insignificant we appear to be, how short our lives on earth. We come and in a blink of an eye we are gone. And yet the love within us, that created us, can be so powerful and lasting.* Henry felt a deep love for his dad. He would just be a memory now. Henry would never again see him face-to-face.

Of all the memories, the one Henry liked the most was the one he had of his dad at the cemetery the day of Anna's burial. That day, his dad had chosen to be free of his past and seek forgiveness. After that day, they had grown closer and closer and became a family again, even stronger than they had been before he had left. At that point, Henry felt his father's presence and the loving energy of God that connects everything, and realized that through God's divine providence, love does heal and turn everything for the good.

TWO DAYS AFTER Henry arrived home, his father was buried. Two days after that, his mother asked Henry to take her back to the cemetery. His father's grave was filled with dirt and leveled off. Flowers from the church and those that were atop the coffin were now nicely arranged around the site but showed signs of dying off, too. The tombstone would not be placed until the summer. His mother stared for what seemed like an eternity at the ground where his father lay.

"Was there a particular reason you wanted to come out here, today, Mom?"

"Yes. I wanted you to show me something the day of the funeral, but too many people were around."

"What was that?"

"Do you remember the day Anna was buried and you told me later that Bill asked you to forgive him after seeing somebody's tombstone?"

"Yeah."

"Well, I would like to see that tombstone."

A puzzled expression formed on Henry's face, as he gazed at his mom. She had tears in her eyes.

Henry led his mom to Anna's grave and then tried to remember where his father had taken him that day. Henry finally found the tombstone.

JACOB STEVENS

1873 - 1946

ETERNALLY I ASK FOR FORGIVENESS

Henry and his mom stood side-by-side and stared at the granite stone for a long time. The sun was shining bright and warm. It soothed their spirits. Henry waited for his mom to speak, as Mr. Engelmann's words so often came back to him: *You can't share your heart in a hurry.*

"You know, Henry, a few days after Bill asked for your forgiveness, he asked for mine. Oh, he had before, but not like that day. He told me about this tombstone and how deeply it made him realize his sins and need for forgiveness. He was so sorry. I can see his eyes even now, pleading out to me. I so wanted to forgive, but I couldn't. Every day I tried.

"The twin beds deeply hurt him. Not so much that we no longer slept together, but it was a reminder of what he did. I punished him day in and day out. I even pushed the beds closer together inch-by-inch and yet it was like a canyon that separated us. In the darkness I would reach out my hand, but always stopped short of touching him. It was when I would awaken and hear him sobbing, I knew the depths of my unforgiving heart and the pain it caused."

She took a Kleenex from her purse and patted the tip of her nose.

"Bill was a good man. He made a mistake like we all do… I was too hard on him. I focused too much on my hurt and his faults and weaknesses…"

Mary shook her head. "Oh the needless pain and suffering… my, my. Then, during your high school valedictorian speech, you of all people touched my heart when you spoke of unforgiveness and how it keeps a family in bondage. I saw the pleading in your eyes, too, to forgive Bill. How I was holding our family back kept us from moving forward as a family.

"Thank God He used you to finally break my foolish pride. For two years we could have loved and prevented so much sorrow." Mary started to sob. "It is at times like this that we realize how short our lives really are and… oh, how we squander our precious moments."

His mom walked over to the tombstone and touched it. "Thank you Mr. Jacobs for your public example. It touched Bill's heart and finally mine. My heart may have remained like this stone."

Henry gazed at his mother and realized that one never really knew what went on in the inner worlds people live in. As close as they were, Henry never suspected his mother of harbouring such feelings. He walked over and put his arms around her.

"But, you did forgive, Mom. You may regret those two years, but how much greater would be your sorrow and regret, had you not forgiven at all?"

His mother looked into his eyes and nodded. "Yes, I might have ended up eternally regretting my unforgiveness, like Mr. Jacobs, here. Thankfully, your words touched me and I forgave Bill. I could see in your eyes how happy you were when I ordered that king-size bed for our room. You knew then I had forgiven your dad. It was the only way I knew how to really let you know… to free you.

"And now, in front of this tombstone – to let Mr. Jacobs know he didn't die this way in vain – I ask for your forgiveness, too, Henry, for keeping you in bondage during that time."

And before his mother could say another word, Henry squeezed her tight like his father did to him that day in that very same spot.

"There was never anything to forgive, Mom. All I see and ever will remember is the loving person you are… I love you with all my heart."

CHAPTER FORTY-ONE

EARLY ONE MID-SUMMER morning Jenny headed out toward her beloved gazebo. The sprinklers had been running since dawn and together with the high humidity, a mist had settled over the cool grounds, creating an ethereal atmosphere. It was as though Jenny were walking amongst the clouds. The softness of the trees and shrubs and their silhouettes in the distance added a feeling of space, mystery, and peace. It was quiet, still and calm save the distant sound of a robin or chickadee. She sat on her chair in the gazebo and swung gently to and fro, as if floating in the air. As the sun began to burn off the thousands and thousands of moisture diamonds glistening in the air, her gaze first fell on the wildflowers just outside her haven.

Gradually, more of the beautiful flowers with their array of dazzling colours appeared and intensified as the mist receded. As the sight grew more laden with beauty and fragrance, Jenny slowly brought the chair to a stop. She touched her toes to the floor of the gazebo, making certain she was still on earth and not in heaven. Emerging from the mist to the side of the wildflower patch was a glowing white angel holding a basket filled with a bouquet of flowers, poised as if walking through the garden toward her. Her eyes brightened and opened wide. Her heart began to race and a rush of overwhelming awe and excitement swept through her!

Is that my guardian angel coming to me?

Jenny rubbed her eyes to make sure she wasn't dreaming or seeing things.

But the angel seemed stationary, frozen in time.

Is it real or an apparition? The flowers in the basket look so natural like they were just picked from the garden!

Slowly, Jenny got up and walked over to the white angel now shimmering in the rays of the sun. As she neared, she began to realize the angel was a tall, almost life-like statue made of marble. She touched one of the outstretched hands of the angel and a warm sensation tingled through her body.

"You are so beautiful and graceful. Where on earth—or heaven—did you come from?" Jenny asked her.

Jenny noted a card attached to the exquisitely glorious bouquet of flowers in the basket held by the angel's other hand. Almost in a daze, she reached for the note, unable to even begin to imagine who would have given something so utterly beautiful to her. She opened the note and began to read it through blurry tear-filled eyes:

Dear Miss Jenny

There is a legend of two angels who come from heaven every morning, each carrying an empty basket. One angel picks up prayers that are requested by God's children while the other gathers the prayers of thanksgiving. The basket belonging to the Angel of Requests is soon overflowing while at days end only a few prayers of gratitude have been collected in the Angel of Thanksgiving's basket.

Miss Jenny, you have been a shining example of one who gives so bountifully each day in thanks and praise! How happy your angel must be!

Knowing how much you love angels we have in an indirect way commissioned a sculptor to create a special statue. Two weeks ago, the 'Angel of Thanksgiving' arrived and is

*our gift to you. In her basket she carries our thanks in the
form of flowers for the joy you give to us each day. Your
cheerful acceptance and love of God's creations are truly
inspiring and angelic.*

*With much appreciation, admiration and love, we remain
your faithful servants and friends.*

Matilda, Charles, Thomas, Ramon, Carlos

"Thank you, thank you, thank you," whispered Jenny, as tears of
joy and gratitude coursed down her cheeks. A much needed peace
swept over and filled her heart to overflowing. She looked up to
the sky and stretched her arms and hands upward in praise and
thanks! "Oh thank you, dear Jesus! Oh thank you, dear guardian
angel, Oh thank you, dear God!"

This is what heaven must be like!

That morning and in the days that followed, Jenny was just a
step on this side of heaven. The glow that surrounded her was as if
she were walking in a constant stream of sunshine.

Each day was a day of thanksgiving for her friends, her mother,
J.J. and James... and her lost loves: Tammy and Henry. Jenny
would cut a flower in honour of each of them and place it in the
basket of the Angel of Thanksgiving. She became so attuned to her
Creator, more than ever before, that she was filled with a love and
peace that surpassed all understanding.

Jenny knew the key to life and happiness, despite the circumstances she found herself in. Nobody could take that away from
her! She accepted life as it was and brought peace into every situation, moment by moment. Her heart was like that of the angel
before her.

Two weeks later, when her mother arrived for a visit, Jenny
could hardly wait to show her the statue.

"Oh my, Jenny, that is so beautiful. Her pose is so elegant and
graceful. It's almost life-like, as if walking through the garden!"

"Yes, isn't it amazing how the sculptor caught the angel in
such an action pose? When I come out into the garden at night,

it appears like the angel is floating through the garden, collecting the thanks and praises people have offered for the blessings they have received."

"What a beautiful gesture, Jenny. And that was so thoughtful of your staff…"

Edith's words trailed off as she studied the angel closer. Her face began to pale and reflect a look mixed with puzzlement and amazement.

"Is something wrong, Mom?"

"There's something about that statue that looks so familiar…"

Edith shook her head and almost in a whisper said, "A year or so before your father passed away he had commissioned a sculptor to create a statue of an angel carrying a basket. He often saw you collecting wildflowers in the garden. You were always his angel and towards the end he wanted to do something special for you to make you happy. He wanted to see the sparkle in your eyes that he so loved."

·"Oh Mom, that is so beautiful!" Tears filled Jenny's eyes.

"You know, I think I still have the sketch that the sculptor drew and your father approved. I came across it when I was going through your father's things after he passed away. I know he paid a lot of money for it but in all the commotion in that last year before he died I simply forgot all about it."

"Mom! This is unbelievable! When Thomas told me the amazing way that he had come across the statue, you'll never believe what he said: 'Miss Jenny, the Angel of Thanksgiving must have been commissioned especially for you! It's wonderful to witness how the good Lord makes sure it gets to its rightful owner!'"

Mother and daughter looked in awe at the angel and then at each other. Tears filled their eyes. Jenny gently shook her head, "Could it be possible that this is the very statue that Dad…?"

A wonderful, eerie feeling swept through the ladies on that warm summer day. But they knew that the warmth that spread to their hearts had more to do with the presence of Ted's spirit standing between them. There was no doubt in either of their minds the miracle that had just unfolded before them.

"You know Mom, at this point in my life, Daddy couldn't have made me happier!"

Edith reached out her hand and took Jenny's in hers and smiled. "This is all so wonderful; I don't know what to say. Look how fresh and beautiful the flowers are in the basket the angel is carrying. They look so radiant in the sun; did you pick them this morning?"

"This is all so amazing, Mom. The strangest thing, or perhaps the most wonderful thing about all this is that I cut the flowers in the basket ten days ago! No one has watered them, and as you say, they look so fresh as if they were just cut from their stem."

"Well, how can this be?" asked Edith, a puzzled look growing on her face once more.

"We can't explain it! Perhaps they are sustained by the love and gratitude that is within all of us, especially Daddy."

CHAPTER FORTY-TWO

HENRY WAS SEATED in his arm chair reading the Bible when Julean walked into his studio.

"Hi, honey. What a peaceful image you make with the sun streaming in and striking you like that. I love the way the light outlines your profile and bounces off the page of the Bible, making it so brilliantly white."

"Uh, oh, another emerging artist," Henry chuckled, as his wife kissed his cheek then settled into the sofa across from him.

"Yeah, I just love this time of day. It's sure good to be back home and in my studio. And I must say, I really appreciate the fresh air here as compared to Toronto. Not only was the air pollution from all the traffic unbearable, but also the terrible air quality in Open Studio. I don't know how the staff can put up with the odour of the paints and cleaners day after day."

"Don't they have an exhaust system?"

"They do, but the turpentine they use to clean the screens is so strong it's virtually impossible to get it out of the air. Well, anyway, I am very grateful for the experience, but it's good to be back. By the way, I made reservations at L'Habitant for Saturday night. You more than I need a night out. I really appreciate you looking after things here."

"It was difficult at times, but Jeremy was sure a help. It wasn't really all that much, honey."

"Oh, I know better. I know how demanding the kids can be."

Henry closed the Bible and set it aside, then switched from his chair to the sofa. "I love you so much, honey."

"I love you, too," Julean said as she worked her way under his arm and laid her head on his chest.

"Maybe we should plan a trip and take a holiday, just the two of us. Get away for the weekend. I'm sure mom wouldn't mind staying with the kids now that she is alone."

"Where would we go?"

"We could just go to the Hotel Saskatchewan again, where we started our honeymoon, or maybe go back to Minot."

"Perhaps Minot would be better, I'm sure they must still remember you at the Hotel Saskatchewan."

Julean chuckled and so did Henry as they both recalled that unbelievable episode with the fire hydrant and him standing there soaking wet.

"Yeah, let's do it, honey. It'll be fun and we both need a break."

Julean worked her arm around Henry's back and snuggled in closer. Henry relaxed and just let himself revel in his wonderful wife's arms. He thought of that documentary on polygamy they had watched and how Julean had questioned his happiness with only one wife. She had never brought up that issue again, but Henry thought for certain Julean knew of Jenny and tried at times to be like her.

Henry thought it was amusing how they just seemed to have settled into a sort of acceptance of the situation without ever really talking it out. Henry knew it was probably best to do so; even Father Engelmann advised it and prayed about it. Perhaps if it worked out and they got away that weekend to Minot, just the two of them, he would tell his wife everything. Hopefully, it would all be for the better.

"What are you thinking of honey?"

"Now that the kids are back in school and I'm home every afternoon, I could give up reading the Bible and we could be doing other things," Henry whispered in Julean's ear as he kissed the side of her forehead.

"Oh, no, you don't." Julean squirmed in his arms and jabbed her finger into his side. "Come on, get up and get back to work." Julean tried to pull herself away from Henry, but he gripped her all the tighter.

"Come on, honey, just this once?"

"Nooo! Jan from next door is coming over for a coffee in a short while and I promised the kids I would bake some brownies for them this afternoon."

"Well, you will have to make up for it, tonight, and doubly if we get to Minot."

Henry relented and Julean pulled herself away.

"Come on, let's get back to work. I want to see a masterpiece on that canvas by dinner or no dessert for you later, if you know what I mean."

Julean winked and extended her hands to Henry and pulled him up. She put her arms around his neck and drew him in.

"I love you, honey. It's so good to have you back."

They kissed tenderly and Julean exited the studio. At the door, she turned and lifted her skirt teasingly until the white of her panties showed. She fluttered her eyes and then dashed away with Henry in hot pursuit.

THE NEXT DAY, Henry stopped in to see his mother on his way home from his morning at the school.

"Hi, Mom," Henry said, as he walked through the front door, expecting to see his mother standing at the doorway to the kitchen. Perhaps she hadn't heard him. He headed towards the kitchen. "Mom? Mom, I'm home."

But she wasn't in the kitchen at all. For as far back as he could remember, whenever he'd entered the house, he had always found his mother in the kitchen. Henry went to the back door and looked out into the back yard, thinking she might be working in the garden now that the snow had melted. But she was not there, either. Concern began crawling up his spine.

In near panic, he walked down the hallway towards his parents' bedroom. The door was open and light from the bedroom spilled into the hall. Henry stopped at the doorway and peeked into the room. His mother sat weeping on the foot of the bed, holding what he assumed was his dad's death certificate.

"Hello, Mom."

His mother turned her head and looked up at him with red and swollen eyes. Henry shook his head and entered the room. His eyes misted as he sat beside her and wrapped his arm around her.

"Oh, Mom, I'm sorry I didn't come over sooner." Henry gently pulled her close, her chest heaving in between sobs.

"I miss him, too, Mom. I am sorry I was away when he passed on. I'm glad I saw him the Sunday before I left for Toronto. I can still see him on the edge of his chair rooting for the Montreal Canadians. He sure loved his hockey. When I was in Toronto, the Leafs played Montreal. I thought about going and then phoning to tease him and tell him what a great game it was and that it was too bad he wasn't there. Boy, would he ever have loved to see a live NHL game. Remember when you two went to the Grey Cup game in Vancouver?"

His mom squeezed his hand. "Bill loved that. He was also glad you were such a sports fan. He so enjoyed the rivalry between you two when you would watch the games together."

"Yeah, I know he did. I think I enjoyed that part even more than the game itself."

"I know he did, too, son."

Henry tightened his grip on his mother's hand and he looked around the familiar room. Henry's gaze fell on the dresser where his mother's treasure chest sat open.

"Going through treasures of the heart, Mom?"

FOR THE FIRST time that day, Mary snapped out of her grieving. The chest not only held keepsakes, but secrets as well. It had taken all her courage that morning to get the chest from the upper shelf of the closet. Ever since she'd hid the letter from Jenny to her son in there, she had felt a presence and light in the closet that she never could understand or explain. Most days she kept the closet closed because the light reminded her of her deed and the lingering feeling that she should undo that action.

"Are you okay, Mom?"

"Yes. I got the chest down so I could put Bill's death certificate in it. I decided to go through a few of the items. I couldn't remember what I had stored in there."

Henry slid his arm off her and stood. Mary's heart sped up. Henry looked down on the dresser and saw the letter he had written to her when he decided to abort his plan to find Jenny. It was beginning to yellow around the edges. She knew he noticed a few of her trademarks on the page. She had read it earlier and several tears caused the ink to run on the second paragraph. Henry picked up the letter to make out what he had written around the smudge.

"You must be hungry. Let's go to the kitchen and I will make you something to eat."

Henry didn't hear her. He had entered another world.

Mary got up from the bed and Henry began to lay the letter back on the dresser when he picked up a pink envelope from inside the box. Mary's heart stopped completely.

"You still have a sealed letter, here, Mom. It smells of lilac." Henry brought it up to his nose. "Who is it from? Why haven't you op—"

"Oh, it's nothing, just from an old friend." Mary grabbed the letter just as Henry turned it over to see who it was from. The pewter angel flew the length of the envelope and the tip of the angel's wing pierced the end of the paper. Mary caught her breath as the ceiling light glistened off the protruding metal.

"My gosh, does that letter ever feel warm. You must be storing the chest near a heat register or something."

Mary began to panic, heat rose in her face. She thrust the letter into the chest and slammed the lid shut.

"Come. Let me prepare lunch for you." Mary looked at her son and motioned him on. When he didn't move right away, she pushed him out the door. "Come, let's go. A little lunch would perhaps do me some good, as well."

Henry studied his mother for a moment. He wondered about the sealed letter; its weight and lilac scent had triggered a far off memory. When they came into the kitchen Henry sat down while his mom began making soup and sandwiches. His mind was still on the fragrance of the letter when his mother asked, "How is

Julean, Henry? She must be happy you're back home."

"Yes, we both are, Mom. I lucked out when I married her."

Perhaps it was the perfume and the memory of Jenny it triggered that encouraged Henry to bring up a subject with his mother he hadn't since before he and Julean married.

"I don't want to upset you, Mom, but you know, after all these years I still haven't completely gotten over Jenny."

Mary's face flushed instantly. "Oh Henry, you are not still thinking of your teenage friend, are you?"

"I know it's strange, Mom, but she is still in the recesses of my mind and I know Julean senses it. Father says I should talk it over with her and get it out into the open. It's going to be so hard to tell her that after all these many years I still have feelings for my first girlfriend. I know it's foolish Mom, but I just don't understand how these feelings have hung on. In a way, Julean and I have silently learned to cope with it and to live with it."

Mary's knees were so weak she pulled back a chair from the table and sat down. "My, my, son. I don't know how to advise you… Do you think it's wise to tell her after all these years?"

"I thought it would be best when we go away on a holiday together without the children around. I don't know how Julean is going to react. At times I just shudder at the thought of telling her something that might hurt her so deeply, and then at other times I sense she already knows all about it."

"What do you mean, son?"

"Well, the thing is Mom, Julean indirectly told me she thinks it's okay for me to have another woman in my heart and that she would be willing to share me with another woman if it came down to that. I know she's talking about Jenny when she says that. It sounds so ridiculous, but she grew up in a faith that for years accepted and encouraged men to have more than one wife. Even though polygamy is no longer practiced in the Mormon community, Julean is the kind of woman that would sacrifice herself to share me with another."

"I have never heard of such a thing. She loves you so much Henry, you must get over this thing with Jenny… It's in the past and over and done with."

"Geez Mom, I've tried! I've prayed about it for decades but for some reason it's a part of me and Julean seems to understand that. Sometimes I sense that Julean is trying to be like Jenny so as to indirectly satisfy my heart's craving. What I'm saying Mom, is that I think Julean is trying to be both herself and Jenny to me!"

"Oh Henry, that's impossible!"

"Mom, I know it sounds weird, but Julean is doing just that! She tries to be more spontaneous like Jenny was... I even found a blond wig in a bag at the back of our closet the other day. She hasn't worn it around me yet, but one of these days, I'm sure she will."

Mary just kept shaking her head in disbelief. "But how would Julean know the colour of Jenny's hair?"

"I don't know Mom, but somehow she knows. And something else, Julean gave me a forty-five recording of that Bing Crosby song, "True Love," and that was my and Jenny's song! And with it she wrote a note asking if she could share in my heart's attachment to that song."

Mary reclined in her chair, almost out of breath, it seemed like the air in the room had been sucked away. Her decision to keep Jenny's letter away from her son that day in 1962 was coming back to haunt her... Deep down she knew at the time it was wrong. Our sins always come back to us eventually, whether it be in this lifetime or the next...

The letter in the pink envelope in my treasure chest!

Mary had held that letter in her hands right before Henry had entered the room.

It should be in Henry's hand along with my confession.

But how can I possibly tell him now what I did?

The pain and regret and turmoil that would pierce my son's heart at this point would be so great. God knows what would happen? And with Julean willing to make such a sacrifice for Henry... Oh my, I can't bear to think of the consequences of such a revelation now!

Please do not judge me too harshly Oh Lord; I am trapped in my wrong doing. I love my son too much to inflict this upon him now and his wife and family...

Oh Jesus, forgive me... Have mercy on my soul!

CHAPTER FORTY-THREE

As EDITH DROVE home one summer afternoon after visiting her daughter, several things coursed through her mind. For one thing, she knew Jenny was lonely, but she didn't know what to do about it. James had proven to be quite a hard man to live with and by the conversations she had with Jenny, he kept her from spending any time with her son. Perhaps if she lived closer to them, she could spend more time with her daughter and help ease some of her loneliness.

In any event, it was time for Edith to move off the estate. The company wasn't pressuring her to leave, but her health was deteriorating; her arthritis was slowly crippling her and her liver was failing. She thought moving into a smaller apartment and hiring a housekeeper or caregiver would prolong the eventuality of moving into a dreaded care home.

By the time Edith turned onto her beautiful estate she had made up her mind to move. She would miss the grounds. She loved them almost as much as Jenny, but time was moving on and spending more time with Jenny and her grandson had to assume greater importance.

A move to an apartment would mean downsizing. Major downsizing! She would have to give away furniture and items that filled a seven thousand square foot home, retaining enough to fit into perhaps a fifteen hundred square foot apartment. Clearly decisive action was needed. There would be no room for nostalgia; ruthless decisions would have to be made.

The next morning, Edith called a realtor and laid out her wishes. That done, she visualized what the space in a new apartment might look like, then took a sticky pad and inventoried all her furniture, putting a yellow Post-it on the ones she would keep. The rest would be donated to charity. She had enjoyed years of pleasure from these items and now it was time to give them to someone else. She knew James would not be interested in any of it even if her daughter were to be. It might just be another source of contention between them. No, out they must go.

Having gone through the entire house, an exhausted Edith trudged up the winding staircase to the second floor and down the long hallway to her bedroom. Memories of Ted and a young Jenny flashed through her mind. It struck her how quickly time had gone and how all those precious moments had faded into the past. By the time she reached her bedroom, tears had filled her eyes.

What an old softy she was becoming. Sentimental. Not the hardnosed woman she was when Jenny bounded through these halls. Lately, she cried when watching sad movies; something she had often criticized her much more sensitive husband for doing. She wept at night over her daughter's unhappiness and felt deep regret for the pain she had inflicted uncaringly upon her family.

Oh, if I could just turn back the clock, I'd do it all differently... Beside the huge walk-in closet, there was a smaller eight-foot one designed so that when the doors were opened, two spot lights turned on, illuminating the clothes inside. For the first time in thirteen years, the moment Edith opened the doors, both bulbs burnt out at exactly the same instant.

The flash startled and blinded Edith for a brief moment and then the gentle darkness soothed her. Only the light from the lamp on the end table by her bed lit the floor behind her. As Edith looked up at where her clothes hung, a soft aura of light formed a halo around her mother's treasure chest. At first, Edith thought she was seeing things, or that the spirit of her mother was returning to retrieve her chest. But slowly it began to dawn on Edith what was generating the awesome luminescence. It was the last letter to Jenny from that boy in Regina.

Edith stepped back and her heart jumped into her throat, as she recalled the fear Ted had exhibited so many times when he had dreamt of the letters.

It's been in here for all these years and no harm has befallen me. Not yet…

When she had learned of Henry's wedding and realized how much her daughter still yearned for him, she had to admit that perhaps she and Mrs. Pederson had made an error in denying those letters to their children. But as time progressed and Jenny grew closer to James, she had convinced herself that perhaps they had done the right thing.

Deep in her heart, Edith now knew she had made an error and felt compelled to undo the action she had caused. But how could she? Both Henry and Jenny were married, what good would it do now?

The thought to grab the chest and toss it into the fireplace crossed her mind. But that would mean destroying the other items in the box. Perhaps she could open the chest and remove the letter and just throw it away; out of sight out of mind.

Edith summoned her courage and moved into the closet. As she reached for the chest, the light grew brighter and the air warmer. Clearly she was agitating some supernatural force. She decided right then and there to just leave well enough alone. For all these years nothing had happened and she wasn't about to upset the apple cart now. She would simply ask the movers to pack the chest along with all of the rest of the things she would take to her new apartment.

Having made her decision to let things be, a *peace* Edith had not experienced before *swept through her.*

WITHIN TWO WEEKS, Edith had found the apartment she wanted. It was only fifteen minutes away from the Hamilton estate and near a shopping mall that the rich and famous often patronized. Edith was excited and could hardly wait to share the news with her daughter.

"Are you sitting down, Jenny? Do I have news for you!"

"What is it, Mom? Did you win the lottery?"

"Better! I'm moving off the estate and I found an apartment near you. Less than fifteen minutes away!"

"Are you serious? You were just here two weeks ago and you didn't mention a thing."

"I know. It was on the way home that day when I made the decision to finally let go of paradise. It's getting harder for me to manage such a large place and besides, I want to be closer to you and J.J.."

"Oh, Mom, that's wonderful. When are you going to move?"

"At the end of the month. The apartment is on the eighteenth floor and has just been completed."

"Oh, Mom, that's wonderful. I'm so happy for you."

"Well, Jenny, I've already picked out the furniture I'm taking with me and the rest I will be giving away unless there is something you want."

Jenny thought for a bit. "Are you taking the grandfather clock Dad liked so much?"

"I was going to, but you can have it if you want. I was having trouble fitting it into the living room arrangement."

"I'll have to sneak it in. You know how James doesn't like anything that's old or antique-y."

"But it's a family heirloom and such a beautiful piece."

"There's no point arguing with James, Mom. But I'll find a way to bring that beautiful clock in here without him noticing. Maybe I could come over this Saturday and see if there's anything else there I might like to remember you and the estate by? I would also like to see it one last time and say goodbye to Carlos. Does that work for you?"

"Of course, Jenny, Saturday will be fine."

Jenny slowly hung up the phone. *It will be nice for Mom to be closer. Soon she will see that I am as alone in this estate as she was in hers.*

ON SATURDAY MORNING Jenny drove back to the Sarsky estate for what would be the last time. She remembered the first time she and father drove up this very same drive; the beauty of the estate had momentarily helped assuage her aching heart for the first time since she had left Regina. Remembering back, Jenny relived her heart break… Why hadn't Henry ever written her? Especially after she sent the last letter with the pewter angel? They both had so loved their guardian angels; it was what bonded them with an everlasting love. The little prayer that they had discovered they both knew and then recited together was beyond coincidence.

Angel of God, my guardian dear,
To whom Gods love…

Jenny couldn't finish… Tears filled her eyes.

Edith was standing at the front door when Jenny drove up. They waved to each other. When Jenny got out of the car her mother came down to greet her.

"I've been standing here for over fifteen minutes waiting for you. I didn't want to miss seeing you drive up to your home one last time."

Edith hugged her daughter. Jenny felt her mother's love and the depth of her touch. Her mother was changing, mellowing, becoming warmer.

She liked that… She liked that a lot.

"I was just thinking the same thing as I drove up."

"I see it brought tears to your eyes, as well."

"Yes," Jenny agreed. She didn't want to tell her mom she had really been thinking about her first love.

"Is Carlos here today? I would like to see him and thank him for contributing to that beautiful Angel of Thanksgiving statue. It would be so nice if he could come work on our estate now with Thomas and Ramon."

"No, he is off today and yes, it would be so nice for him to have employment there. I don't know what will happen to the staff when I leave. The president of the company still prefers his condo."

"Well, I can run it by James, although he vetos everything I suggest."

Edith gazed at her daughter but decided not to go there. "Come, let's go inside and break the rules. I'm going to have a morning glass of wine with some orange juice in it. I hope you will join me."

"I think that would be wonderful, Mom."

Jenny slipped her arm under Edith's and together they made their way inside. The grandfather clock was too beautiful and nostalgic to pass up. She would sneak it into the estate somehow and keep it in her room. James never went in there anymore, so he would never know.

When they went upstairs and walked down the hall toward Edith's room, Jenny suddenly stopped. "Mom, if you don't mind, I think I would like to visit my room one last time. Please go ahead, I will be along in a minute."

When Jenny entered her room, she saw that nothing had changed since she left. In fact, it looked untouched, just as she had left it when she got married. Jenny looked at her desk and the chair just in front of the dormer window. It was here that she had written so many letters to Henry. Letters filled with so much love and longing. Those feelings surfaced yet again now and overwhelmed her.

Oh, how you torture yourself!

Jenny shook her head. Although she could accept James and detach herself in her present moments from his hurtful words and actions, she simply could not detach from or forget Henry. It was a secret choice that gave her solace. It was the consolation she allowed into her present moments even though she knew it was far from reality.

So much has happened in this room, thought Jenny as she looked around. Yes, there were the letters to Henry, but then there were the talks that she and Tammy had shared. Oh, how she missed her friend, her other half, her earthly angel. They were closer than sisters. There was nothing they could not share.

Even when Jenny tried to hold back, Tammy saw into the crevices, the little dark secret corners. Her instincts and insights were like searchlights lighting up the shadows, bringing everything out into the loving care of acceptance. Suddenly, Jenny felt Tammy's spirit next to her as if she were standing there in person.

And there in the corner was the cedar chest that was filled to overflowing with toys and outfits she had bought for Camilla over the years when she celebrated her little girl's birthday on the 24th of

May each year. Jenny opened it and gazed inside. On one side were stacks of clothes and on the other, rattles, dolls, books, ballerinas, music boxes… each with a special memory.

She lifted out the white jumper with an embroidered butterfly beside three yellow daisies on the front and she recalled the day she had bought it. How she had visualized her daughter chasing butterflies amongst the wildflowers. Jenny had always thought of Camilla as a growing wildflower budding into such a beautiful free little angel. Through tear filled eyes Jenny picked up the pale yellow short sleeved sweater that Camilla could have worn underneath the jumper. Jenny smiled as she remembered the strange looks she would get from the store clerks when, pretending Camilla was with her, she would ask her daughter how she would like this or that outfit.

Jenny had stopped buying outfits for Camilla after eight years and began buying clothes for Chloe instead. Chloe was real to her and Jenny could visualize how her own little Camilla would react and look in the outfit. Jenny considered the two little girls as sisters, in much the same way Jenny considered Tammy as her sister, as well.

Even though Jenny may have stopped buying clothes for Camilla, the monthly and yearly celebrations never ceased. She had celebrated twenty three birthdays. Oh, how the time had flown by. Jenny would give anything to see her daughter again…

Just as Jenny was about to close the chest, she noticed a small box in the corner and then she remembered what it was. It was a gift she had bought for Camilla on her Grade 12 graduation. Jenny opened the box which contained a sterling silver heart shaped locket. It had a tiny angel embossed on top of the heart. Inside the locket Jenny had a photo of herself. She always thought that when Camilla returned to her, she would replace that photo with one of them both cheek to cheek. Jenny turned the locket over and tears surfaced as she read what she had inscribed on the back:

'You will always be my little angel.'

Jenny sat at her desk and almost absently opened the bottom drawer. She gasped when she saw the big brown envelope she had left there containing the secret notes that Henry had written to her and hid behind the fence gate post. She knew she should have torn them all up years ago, but she could never bring herself to do it.

Carefully she slid her little finger under the sealed flap and gently re-opened the envelope. Her heart fluttered as she pulled out the notes and started to read them one by one...

Jenny,

If you were a chocolate bar, you'd be the sweetest ever made!

Oh Henry

Dear Sugar and Spice,

Thanks for letting me know. I'll count the minutes until tomorrow night when I can see you again. And if you were a watch, I'd keep you in my breast pocket next to my heart so I could feel you tick all night long.

Henry

Tears silently slid down her cheeks; the notes brought back so many fond memories... It also reminded her of the day her father had come into her room and caught her doing exactly what she was doing now. Jenny recalled seeing the pain in his eyes that her yearning for Henry was causing him and her mom. But there was something else... Jenny had always felt that her mom and dad knew more about the letters she had sent to Henry than they let on. Her dad was so nervous that morning and also seemed to know about the angel gift she had sent to Henry. It was he who had suggested she put the gate post notes in a sealed envelope and try to let go. And then there was the confrontation she had had with her mom just before she married James. Edith had flatly denied any involvement, but just like with her dad, Jenny had the feeling that there was more they were hiding from her... *much more.*

Jenny returned the notes back into the envelope, then sealing it again with tape, she wrote on the outside of the envelope:

Love notes from my first love.

She decided to take them with her. She remembered her mother saying that she kept a love letter from her first boyfriend in her hope chest as well. It was just a memory thing... Wasn't it?

Jenny got up, crossed to the window and, pushing the curtains aside, looked out at the grounds below. She would never forget the day her dad encouraged her to get up and go outside. *I was so depressed after giving up Camilla for adoption I thought I would never have joy again.* But it was the scene before her now of the grounds that had brought her back to life. And it was still nature, the beauty of God's creation, that did the same.

"Jenny, are you still in your room?" There was a gently tap on the door.

"Yes, come in Mom. I forgot about time, somehow. There were so many memories that kept flooding back to me."

"I know what you mean, honey; memories and tears seem to occupy my days. Are you looking at the grounds outside?"

Edith joined her daughter by the window. Her eyes were drawn to the envelope on the desk and what was written there:

Love notes from my first love.

Edith put her arm around her daughter as they gazed upon the beautiful grounds below, but that view was quickly covered over by the vision of burning letters: letters her daughter had written filled with love and longing. Letters written by Henry, pleading to be delivered. Letters that tore at Ted's heart both day and night. Letters filled with hope and promise for a future together... *all destroyed.*

Edith's legs felt weak as the deep sorrow of what she and Ted had done pierced her heart. But even more so, Edith could feel the aching love her daughter still felt for her teenage sweetheart. She realized that after all these years and after all the wicked deeds she and Ted had done to cast Henry out of their daughter's heart, Jenny's love for him had only deepened.

Would it ever fade and go away?

CHAPTER FORTY-FOUR

"H ELLO?"

"Hi, honey, what are you up to?"

"Well, the washing machine backed up and I spent nearly a half-hour mopping up. I had trouble getting Justin to go to school and less than ten minutes after I get home from dropping him off, his teacher phoned to report that he got into another fight with Bobby Getz. Sears called and the dress I ordered for Lauren's first communion won't be in on time... Should I go on?" Julean was just about in tears.

"Oh, honey, sounds like you are having a bad day. But it's all about to change. At precisely eleven o'clock, my mom is coming over in a cab and will make lunch for the kids and see that they get back to school for the afternoon. I've hired someone to pick you up at noon and take you to a very special and fancy place for lunch. Then after—"

"Henry! You remembered!"

"Well, of course I remembered."

"Now, dear, think back to the last three years. But forget that, I'm thrilled that you remembered number eighteen!"

"And that's not all; right about now, you should receive..." He heard the doorbell peal over the phone, then Julean rushed to the door.

"For me?!"

"Yes, Ma'am, and I'm also instructed to wish you a very happy eighteenth wedding anniversary."

"Thank you! What a lovely surprise."

Julean rushed back to the phone. "Henry, thank you for the roses. They're beautiful!"

"Not as beautiful as you are, honey. Look, it's almost ten-thirty, which gives you a little over an hour and a half to get ready. Drop everything. Don't do another stitch of work. I have a student knocking at my door. See you later, honey."

No sooner had Julean unwrapped the roses and set them into a vase when the doorbell rang again.

"More flowers?"

"Yes, Ma'am, and all of us at Regina Florists wish you a happy eighteenth anniversary."

Julean was flabbergasted. Her eyes misted as she walked back into the kitchen and searched for another vase. This time the bouquet consisted of a mixed batch of flowers in fall colours. Julean looked in awe at the beautiful gifts her husband had sent her, the morning's frustration already overshadowed by effervescent joy.

Once the second bouquet was taken care of, Julean dashed into the bedroom and turned on the shower to give the water a chance to warm up while she undressed. She caught a reflection of herself in the dresser mirror and had to take a second glance. Smeared on the mirror with soap, Henry had written, 'Happy 18 Honey!' and underneath, 'I love you.'

"Oh, Hank, you're wonderful."

When she got into the shower and picked up a new bar of soap from the tray she discovered that Henry had carved "I love you" in the soap.

After drying off, Julean rushed to the closet, debating what she should wear. She recalled Henry had said a fancy place. She was thrown backwards when the closet doors didn't open to her tug.

"Oh darn, the door is sticking again." Julean yanked at the door and was startled by a loud bang. "What on earth was that!" As she yanked again, the door burst open and out poured well over a dozen different coloured balloons that read, 'happy anniversary.'

Julean was beside herself. The doorbell rang again. She quickly put on her robe and rushed to the door.

Mary opened the door partially and called in, "Julean, it's me Mary."

"Oh, hi, Mom, come in. What a morning this has been. Hank called and said you were coming over. Make yourself a coffee. I have to dry my hair and get dressed before noon—"

"Yes, run along, I know what's going on."

Julean kissed Mary's cheek and dashed back to the bedroom. As she dried her hair in front of the mirror she opened the drawer of her dresser to retrieve her make-up kit. Sitting on top was a bowl of cashews, her favourites. In the centre was a note: 'Happy anniversary, Honey... I'm nuts over you!'

Julean burst out laughing. "Oh, this is so wonderful! He's certainly making up for the past three years."

Julean popped a cashew into her mouth and as she gazed at her reflection beyond the soap-written note on her mirror, she saw a very happy woman.

Just as Julean declared herself ready for whatever her husband had planned, Justin crashed through the back door. His squeals of excitement over seeing Grandma bounced off the walls and reverberated into the bedroom. Julean barely heard the doorbell over the blaring Flintstones episode Justin had turned on in the living room. Mary just beat her to the front door.

"Mrs. Pederson?" a tuxedoed chauffeur inquired.

"No... I mean, yes, I am Mrs. Pederson, but the wrong one."

Julean stepped forward and the man's eyes brightened. "I think I am the one you are looking for."

"Yes, Ma'am, your limo is waiting."

"Oh my," Mary said, bringing her hand to her mouth.

"Thank you. I will be there momentarily."

"I shall wait at the car for you, Mrs. Pederson."

Julean turned and gawked at her mother-in-law. "Did you see that?"

Mary shook her head and smiled. Both giggled.

"How do I look, Mom?"

"You look even lovelier than you did on the day you married my son."

"I feel so nervous, like I am going on my first date. Here I go!"

Mary watched Julean walk down to the limo. It was precious moments like this one that confirmed her decision to keep Jenny's letter to Henry a secret. Julean was such a wonderful girl. No other woman could have been more perfect for her son. And yet, incredibly after all those years Henry tells her he still has feelings for Jenny and that Julean is trying to be both for him.

"I was so sure I had made the right decision. And now... Oh, good Lord please help... I don't know what to do."

Just as Julean got into the limo and the driver closed the door behind her, the older children came running, crashing into the chauffeur.

"Where are you going?" asked Jeremy.

"I want to come," shrieked Lauren, banging on the window.

Feeling totally embarrassed by her children, Julean pressed the button to open the window.

"I'm going to meet Daddy for a special lunch. It's our eighteenth anniversary. Grandma has lunch waiting for you. I'll tell you all about it later."

"Can we go just around the block in the car, Mom?'

"No, Allison, I'm late already. Jeremy please take the girls and go into the house."

"Awww," cried Lauren.

"Come on, let's go," summoned Jeremy, grabbing Lauren's arm and pulling her away from the window.

"Thank you, sorry about that. We can go now," Julean said to the driver who beamed from ear to ear.

Julean blew kisses out the back window as her waving children disappeared into the distance.

When the limo pulled up to the front door of the Hotel Saskatchewan, the doorman opened the car door. A distinguished gentleman dressed in a charcoal suit greeted Julean as she stepped out.

"Good afternoon, Mrs. Pederson, I'm Pierre, the hotel assistant manager. Your husband is waiting in the dining room. May I please escort you?"

Julean stared at him then calmly said, "Yes, of course."

She slipped her hand through Pierre's bent elbow and climbed the stairs to the front door which was already held open by another doorman.

At the entry to the dining area, Julean was transferred from the assistant manager's good care to that of the host.

"Right this way, Ma'am."

HENRY'S EYES BRIGHTENED as he saw Julean enter.

She gets more beautiful with each passing year.

As she followed the host to the table, not only was Henry mesmerized by his wife's elegance and beauty, but many of the lunching business men turned their heads as she walked by.

For a woman who had had four children to have still such a youthful figure was amazing. The outline of her body was further enhanced by the black taffeta, off-the-shoulder sheath dress she wore. Her hair was swirled up at the back and clipped, the way Henry liked it, and soft red lipstick with a tinge of complimentary rouge set off her luminous skin. One would never have known or remotely suspected that Julean had spent much of the morning in the basement of her home mopping up water from a backed up washer.

As Henry rose, aware of the envy of onlookers as they realized he was the lucky guy, his legs wobbled beneath him. He circled the table and kissed his wife's cheek.

"You look stunning, honey."

Julean blushed. "You look very handsome, yourself."

The host pushed the chair under Julean as she sat down while Henry returned to his seat.

They were approached by a waiter.

"Good afternoon, my name is Jonah. I will be your waiter for lunch today and will make every effort to make your experience as enjoyable as possible. Would you care for some wine before ordering?"

"Yes. What is your house wine?"

"We have a shiraz from Argentina that is very nice and a French sauvignon that is not quite as dry."

"The sauvignon would be my preference, Hank."

"The sauvignon it is, then."

When the waiter left, Julean leaned towards Henry.

"Hank, I'm thrilled by what you did. I couldn't believe the flowers, the carved soap and the nuts in the drawer with that cute comment. I just loved it all so much, honey."

"Well, the day isn't over." Henry winked.

Julean's dark brown eyes brightened and sparkled. "There's more?"

Following a leisurely two-hour lunch, Henry and Julean headed out to the lobby. Fully expecting they were on their way out, Julean was surprised when Henry pulled her toward the elevators.

"You didn't, Henry?"

"Oh, yes, I did. There are no free lunches, honey."

"Is it just for the afternoon?"

"You'll have to put up with me 'til morning."

"But, honey, I didn't bring any overnight things."

"What for? You won't need anything, will you?" Henry winked as they got off the elevator at the third floor and strolled hand-in-hand to their suite.

"This looks familiar… Is it the same room we spent our first night in?"

"The very same." Henry picked up his wife and carried her over the threshold as he had eighteen wonderful years ago.

The scent of flowers and sweet perfume filled the air. The drapes were drawn and lighted candles flickered on the hutch. The air conditioning was on, but so was a fire in the fireplace.

Julean kissed him, long and tender. "I love you so much, Hank. Thank you for doing this. I would never have believed this morn—"

Henry kissed her again and gently set her down. He turned and pressed the button on the record changer beside him. An LP fell and Nat King Cole crooned "It Had to be You" through the speakers. That was all either of them remembered as Henry laid her on the bed with another deep kiss.

WHEN JULEAN EMERGED from the bathroom in a white robe after her shower, she found Henry on the phone.

"Yes, we will be down at four-fifteen."

"What was that about?" asked Julean, drying her hair with a towel.

"You'll see." Henry checked his watch. "Oh, it stopped again." He looked at the clock on the night table. It read three thirty-five. "Oh darn, I was hoping we might have time…" He winked at Julean.

Julean smiled coyly. "If we have to be someplace in a half hour you better take that shower and get dressed!"

WHEN THEY RETURNED to the lobby Julean heard a laid back female jazz singer's voice drifting seductively out of the lounge. "Oh, wouldn't it be nice to go in there for a drink, Hank?"

"I've got a better idea."

The doorman held the door open wide as the anniversary couple made their way down the front steps of the hotel. It was a gorgeous fall afternoon. And just before they entered the back of the limousine, the sun struck their faces catching the joy, the happiness and love in their eyes.

Soft, romantic music filled the spacious interior of the car. A tinted privacy window separated the back seat area from the driver. A bottle of champagne nested in an ice-filled, sterling silver bucket with a white, crisply folded linen cloth draped over its neck.

"This is just unbelievable, Hank. You must have planned this for a long time. Can we afford all this?"

"We may have to watch our budget for the next year," Henry jested. "Let's not worry about that now, just enjoy every moment."

"So, where are we off to now?" Julean asked, her eyes filled with an I-can-hardly-wait look.

"The tour has all been pre-arranged, my darling Julean. Would you care for a glass of champagne, Ma'am?"

"That would be lovely, kind sir."

After a brief trip down 11th Avenue, giving the citizens of Regina a chance to wonder which celebrities were honouring their fair city, the limo pulled up in front of St. Mary's Church.

"What are we doing here?" Julean inquired.

"Well, my dear, may I remind you this is where the most important and happiest event of my life occurred and I have never been happier since that day."

"Oh, honey." Julean set her glass in the holder and thrust her arms around Henry, kissing him tenderly.

After a long embrace Henry nodded and the chauffeur stepped out of the car, scooted around to Julean's side and opened the door.

"Are we going into the church?" a puzzled look covered Julean's luminous face.

"Yes, let's just check out this old place."

They followed the driver who had led the way and was holding the church door open for them.

They walked through the lobby then entered the door to the main church. Despite the length of the church it was obvious that Father Engelmann was standing in front of the altar. The first few rows were filled with parishioners, but it was impossible to tell who they were from that distance.

Henry took Julean's hand and led her down the aisle, as a piano started to play, accompanied seconds later by the unmistakable voice of Margaret Tearhorst who had sung the very same song on the same day in 1962. Tears welled up in both their eyes as they slowly walked down the aisle, reliving the wonderful day of their wedding.

"Let go, I want to see Mommy," shouted Justin. "Let go, Grandma."

Justin stepped over a few other people in the pew then ran up the aisle toward his parents.

"Mommy, Daddy!" he shouted, as he jumped gleefully into their waiting arms.

Henry held him tightly as they proceeded to the altar.

Father Engelmann beamed as they approached him. Family and friends from both Henry's and Julean's sides of the family clapped and cheered. After a shortened version of the wedding ceremony, the happy couple renewed their wedding vows. Henry was still holding Justin who said "I do" along with his dad while Lauren, by this time, stood by her mommy as if she were a supporting bridesmaid.

Following the Mass and wedding ceremony, everyone, including the chauffeur, went to the church hall for a delicious pot luck supper. When it was time for the wedding couple to go, Justin and Lauren fought hard to go along. Jeremy and Grandma struggled to hold Justin back as the happy couple sped off for their evening honeymoon.

The sun was just setting to another day as Julean and Henry stepped out of the limo and strolled along the winding path at Wascana park. By the time they returned, the moon was high in the sky and reflecting off the placid lake. The sky was cloudless, allowing millions of stars to sparkle and twinkle in the meadow of the heavens. Julean squeezed Henry's hands before they entered the car and returned to the hotel.

After making love and watching the candles dance on the ceiling of their honeymoon suite they quietly talked of their wonderful day. After a while a silence fell in the room and both were just content to be lulled asleep by the romantic LP still crooning away in the background. Just as Henry was about to turn and kiss his loving wife good night, he felt a dampness on his chest below her head. She had been crying. *Must be tears of joy*, thought Henry.

Just then, she spoke as soft as a cloud floating through a windless prairie sky. "I am so happy, Hank. Thank you for a wonderful day. Thank you for a wonderful life… I hope you're as happy as I am…"

Henry just moaned quietly and gave his wife a gentle squeeze. After another moment of silence, Julean whispered, "Would you be happier if you had a second wife? If it is your wish, I would share you with another."

Henry was suddenly jolted awake. This was the first time in ages Julean had brought up having a second wife. It was almost as if she were reading Henry's thoughts about Jenny. Henry had fought sleep earlier because he didn't want to dream of making love to Jenny as he did the night he had married Julean. It was in this same room, exactly eighteen years ago, probably close to this exact same hour that he had been with Jenny in his dreams.

Henry felt his dear wife sob quietly next to him and his heart ached. He knew her suggestion came out of her love for him. He knew she had some idea of the love he carried in his heart for Jenny, although he didn't know how! *This must be her way of trying to show me how much she loves me... But won't the truth devastate her?*

He just couldn't bring up the subject of his first love now. Not now. Not tonight, not after such an incredible day. Henry pretended he was asleep and didn't answer her. Finally, Julean's gentle heaving subsided and she drifted into what Henry prayed would be a restful sleep.

The music had stopped long ago, along with the last crackle of the fireplace. The one pillar candle that burned far beyond its expected life fought to keep its light going longer, but it, too, flickered one last time and like the others, drowned in its own melted wax.

AT FOUR IN the morning, Henry was still wide awake, struggling to ward off haunting memories... and dreams of the past.

CHAPTER FORTY-FIVE

PERHAPS IT WAS when James started to take J.J. to the office for the entire weekend that Jenny began to break down.

"James, Saturday and Sunday are the only days I have off to be with Jimmy during the day. Can't you please leave at least one of those days for us?"

"After working all Saturday it's too long of a drive to come back here. J.J. is hungry and tired and it's much easier for the both of us to go to my condo near the office. The chef has dinner for us and shortly thereafter J.J. retires for the evening, ready to go again on Sunday."

"That's too much for a young boy. He needs other interests and other children to play with. And I need to spend some time—"

"Marjorie, you might as well get this straight. J.J. is almost eleven and destined to take over this corporation. I was several years younger when I started to go to work at the office with my father. He needs to know at the outset his role in this family. Besides, you still see him in the evenings during the week."

"But that's only for an hour or so. By the time I drive home from school it's after six which doesn't leave much time for—'"

"I'm not going to waste my time discussing this with you, Marjorie. This is the way it's going to be. If you're unhappy with this arrangement you are free to leave."

Jenny stared hard at the man she no longer wanted to call her husband. This was what it was really all about: he was trying to break her down. To find ways to start fissures in her protective shield… Wear her down and, sooner or later, she would have to go. But Jenny was determined to stay and fight for her child, even if it came down to sharing only a minute of the day with him. No, she wouldn't play into James' hand and be accused of abandoning her child. She did it once and she wouldn't do it twice.

Jenny stood and walked over to James and looked him straight in the eye.

"Very well, James, so be it." She smiled, kissed his cheek and walked away. As she neared the doorway she saw James' reflection in the mirror hanging over the antique buffet. He was frantically rubbing away the kiss she left on his cheek with his handkerchief, completely oblivious that once again, Jenny triumphed through her seeming defenselessness.

In the weeks and months that followed, they continued their estranged relationship. Jenny made every effort to remain a mother to J.J. in the time allotted to her despite James' relentless attempts to do otherwise. Some weeks, that amounted to maybe two or three hours. James always had some excuse to take J.J. into his study, usually under the guise of teaching him some new game or discussing business matters.

Her heart shattered when she learned that Susan, James' secretary, took J.J. to a men's clothing store and had him measured for a custom-made suit. Jenny confronted James that he may be hurrying J.J.'s growth too quickly, but he wouldn't hear of it. He reminded his wife of the apparel he had worn at school against the accepted mode of dress at the time. He had ignored the ridicule of his peers and he challenged them to look at him now and the position he held.

"No, Marjorie, the boy must learn to dress in the clothes that reflect his future position."

"Well, at least let me take him shopping rather than some office worker."

"No, Susan is much more familiar with the dress code of our

company than you."

Jenny couldn't possibly fathom that James could find any other way to hurt her or completely snuff out her spirit. But he did.

The weekend of J.J.'s eleventh birthday, James kept J.J. engaged out of the house the entire weekend. Jenny had been looking forward to having dinner together and celebrating. Matilda had baked a double layer chocolate cake, and eleven candles in the shape of a football stood on the top, ready to be lit. J.J. was a staunch supporter of the Ottawa Rough Riders.

James had said he would be home by four, but that time came and went. By six, Jenny started to worry. She phoned James' condo and office, but there was no answer. Matilda covered the food and placed some in the oven to keep warm.

Shortly after seven, a car drove up.

"It's Mr. Hamilton and Jimmy!" shouted Matilda.

Jenny knew Matilda was trying to cheer her in the only way she knew. She got up from the table, choking back tears and anger. At least she would get a happy-to-see-you-hug from her boy. Jenny walked to the foyer as James and J.J. entered.

Something was wrong and Jenny sensed it instantly. There was a change in J.J, almost as if he had completely lost his childhood. He was quiet and looked much older than his eleven years. Rather than run excitedly toward his mother, he walked stiffly over to her. Jenny opened her arms ready to receive her usual hug, but instead, J.J. stuck out his hand.

"No hug for Mom today, Jimmy?"

He clearly wanted to, but he looked at his dad then turned back to her and said. "I'm to call you Marjorie from now on and shake your hand."

"Oh no, Jimmy. Call me Mom, and hugging is—"

"It's best he calls us by our first names. It's more manly and assertive in front of our staff when I take him to the office. And from now on, I want you to call him J.J.. 'Jimmy' is too babyish"

"Aren't you rushing things a little?" Jenny challenged.

He cast a stern look at her and walked away.

Jenny looked at her young son, still holding out his hand. She felt sorry for her son for the amount of pressure James was putting on him to act grown up. For turning him against his own mother, stealing his youth, and brainwashing his mind to develop the characteristics and traits of a man who would never be at peace with himself or others.

But what could she do?

Jenny looked down at her son. Holding back tears she said, "Very well, then," and slowly put out her hand. They shook for a brief minute.

"Can we play Monopoly, Marjorie?"

"Yes, we can, J.J.."

Later that evening when J.J. was asleep in his room, Jenny snuck in and gazed down at her son. He looked so sweet, so young and innocent lying there, gently breathing through his open mouth. She bent over and kissed his forehead then bent a little closer to give him, and herself, a much-needed hug.

J.J. sleepily opened his eyes, gazed at his mother and whispered, "Good night, Mom."

"Good night, Jimmy"

About two weeks later something happened at school which lifted Jenny's heart. A new teacher who had arrived in the fall from Saskatchewan was raving about a painting he had just received for Christmas. Apparently, before he and his wife had left Regina, he had commissioned an artist there to do a landscape painting that would remind them of the prairies. At his mention of an artist in Regina, Jenny put down the book she was reading.

"It's a beautiful sunset scene. The last rays of sunlight are sweeping across the landscape just glistening off the standing wheat and rows of swaths lying on the rolling hills. Lights are coming on in the town and homesteads in the distance. The artist even wrote a personal note to us on the back."

Call it feminine intuition, a sixth sense or whatever, but Jenny suddenly had goosebumps. She sat up and leaned towards her colleague.

"Spencer, the artist of that painting wouldn't by chance be Henry Pederson… Would it?"

Spencer paled as he gazed, surprised, at Jenny. "Why, yes it is.

How on earth did you know?"

Jenny's eyes brightened. "I knew him years ago in high school before we moved to Ottawa. I just knew then that he would be a great artist someday." And after a bit of cautious reflection she asked, "did he ever go into teaching?"

"Yes, he did. He was a teacher of physics and science for about six years and then went into counselling. I remember him telling me he was the guidance counsellor at Balfour Collegiate before he left to pursue his art."

"I attended Balfour for two weeks before my dad was transferred here to Ottawa. Isn't that interesting? I understand he is married, would you know how many children he has?" Jenny flushed. The other teachers looked at her.

"Yes, he is married and I think they have four children."

Jenny wanted to pepper him with dozens more questions, but was too self-conscious to ask. She was already afraid she had revealed too much of her heart. "That's great." Was all she said. "I always wondered what had happened to him."

In the days and weeks that followed, Jenny did not allow the knowledge of Henry being married with four children to deter her from still thinking of him and deriving some solace from it. She would have loved to see the painting Spencer had purchased and starting thinking about how she could buy one of her own.

RATHER THAN WORK in the garden, Jenny carried her diary towards the gazebo. It was a beautiful Saturday spring morning and James and J.J. were away for the day, unlikely to return until Sunday evening. James never gave Jenny a firm time when he would return.

Jenny had woken with the sun and had sneaked downstairs to the kitchen so as not to wake Matilda. Jenny no longer made a full cake from scratch on her daughter's birthday, but on the way home from work the day before, she had picked up a cupcake with a frosted daisy on top. Putting a birthday candle in the cupcake and lighting it, Jenny sang a silent song of happiness to her Camilla. Afterwards, she sat at the table for a long time thinking about her daughter and how she might be celebrating her birthday, imagining all kinds of various scenarios. Finally, Jenny got her diary from the table in the living room and decided to go out to her haven.

"Good morning, Mrs. Hamilton. It's a fine day to be up early."

"Yes, Thomas. That it is. Everything is so fresh and I just love the natural aroma of the flowers in the morning air."

"Not everyone can smell the perfume of nature unless their nose is directly in front of a flower."

"Well, I must have the nose of a dog," Jenny chuckled, "I find it almost intoxicating."

"It's your fine sensitivity and appreciation of nature, Mrs. Hamilton."

"Thank you, Thomas. I must admit the sun and flowers are my closest friends. Which reminds me, I wanted to place a flower in the angel's basket for them. You have a nice day."

"And a fine day to you, Ma'am."

Jenny sat down and gently swung back and forth on the suspended chair. She gazed at the Angel of Thanksgiving and gave thanks and praise for the beautiful day, closed her eyes and tried to visualize the sunset painting Spencer described. Spencer was so emotional about it. It must have been some painting to move him so strongly. *I knew he would be a teacher and an artist, someday. Perhaps I will ask Spencer if I can drop by his place next week and have a look at the painting. I would love to see it… to touch it… to feel his brush strokes.*

Opening her diary, Jenny began:

May 24, 1980

It was this day, twenty-three years ago that my sweet little daughter Camilla was born. I so hoped that by now she would have contacted me. She is a young woman now, perhaps married and may even have children.

Jenny smiled at the thought of being a grandmother and not even knowing it. How strange things can be in the world. Five years ago, when Camilla would have been eighteen, Jenny had tried to track her down. She had phoned her social worker, praying that her adoptive parents had revealed to Camilla that she was adopted and that she had begun the search for her mother.

But as the days, then months and years slipped by, there was no news of anyone trying to contact her. Jenny sent a letter notifying the agency that if her daughter should ever try to find her that she would be more than willing to meet with her.

Jenny continued writing:

Oh, guardian angel, my guardian dear, hear my prayer, a mother's prayer, that one day I will see my daughter again.

Jenny closed the book and her eyes, and began swinging again, dreaming of her two loves... Wishing that the warmth of the morning sun on her skin were the soft touch of Henry and Camilla's hands.

CHAPTER FORTY-SIX

AT THE END of July, just one month before school started, Henry submitted his resignation to the School Board to pursue his art career. It was risky leaving a secure position and a handsome salary. Working only part-time as a counsellor had been a blessing, but even that had lost its appeal. Henry yearned to paint and with his wife's support, Henry forged ahead into a profession often described as one in which either feast or famine prevailed. As Father Engelmann noted, however, "Anyone who takes the roof off his house in the rainy season of springtime isn't afraid of risk."

During the first week of September, Henry received two major painting commissions that would net him more than twice his normal teaching salary. Following the example of one of his colleagues, Henry used the extra money he made to buy revenue properties. The first home he purchased required very little down payment, was in a good area and, after just minor improvements, he was able to rent it out very quickly. The rent covered the mortgage, the insurance and upkeep and netted him just over two thousand dollars. Encouraged, he purchased other homes.

When looking at one home close to his in the south end of Regina, he asked the owner why they were selling.

"We just bought an acreage in the Lumsden valley."

"You know, I've had a dream of doing that for as long as I can remember."

"There is another acreage for sale about a mile away from the one we bought. It's considerably larger than ours and has a really spectacular view."

Henry got the directions and without telling anyone, went out to view the property the next day. It was a cedar log home situated on the side of a hill, overlooking the most beautiful view of a valley Henry had ever seen. No matter where he looked, to the north, south or east the view was incredible.

"To have a studio and paint on a spot like this would be heaven," Henry told the owners.

Although the price was high, and the two-bedroom log cabin was too small for his family, Henry felt it was worth every penny. In a leap of faith, Henry said, "I'd like to purchase the property on the condition that I get financing."

Later that day, he met with the listing agent and put in a formal purchase agreement offer.

His mind whirled as he drove home. How would he tell Julean, and would the kids want to live in the country? It was only sixteen kilometers from the city, but would need an immediate addition to accommodate the family. The water supply was good, but a new well would need to be added, and the road leading up to the house would be better around the hill than over the top. It certainly had its challenges, but it didn't dissuade Henry for a moment. The view and country living eliminated all anticipated problems. As far as Henry was concerned, a dream had come true.

The next day, Henry took Julean and the kids to view the property. It was early fall and the leaves in the valley were just changing into their spectacular array of colour.

"The view is beautiful, Hank, but the cabin is way too small. It would require an addition even larger than the one we made to our house in the city."

"Well, we did it then, Julean, and we can do it again. We have some experience and I can just visualize the two-storey overlooking the valley."

"Are you certain you want to move? Our home is so beautiful

and comfortable. We worked so hard to get it done. We would have to start all over."

"But I love building, and just look at that view. Sure our home in the city is nice, but when you go out the back door what do you see? Rows and rows of houses. People would die for a view like this."

Julean's silence and expression told him she still wasn't convinced.

"It sure is a nice view, Dad, and it is so close to the city," offered Jeremy in support.

"I just love it here," blurted Allison. "I'm going to take Lauren and Justin for a walk in the valley. Do we have time?"

"Sure, go ahead." Lauren and Justin were playing with the owner's dog and were already halfway down the hill heading toward the stream that snaked along the valley bottom. "It won't take them long to adjust to the country."

Turning to Julean he continued. "Well, honey, what we could do is rent out the acreage until next spring and figure out whatever plans we would need to make. I'm sure we could easily sell the property again, should we decide not to go for it."

"Yes, that might be good idea." Julean relaxed. The tension and concern written over her face left, for the moment anyway.

The next hurdle to surmount was the financing. The value of their home had gone up considerably over the years, especially with the addition of the second storey. The home they had paid $15,000 for in 1964 was now appraised at $105,000. Some of that equity had been used to buy other revenue property, but there was a sufficient amount left to make the down payment on the valley property. Also, with Julean working part-time as a nurse, the bank approved the financing on the very last day, removing the condition on Henry's offer to purchase. It was none too soon as three other buyers were now interested in purchasing the property, too.

Henry was easily able to rent out the cedar log cabin until spring. This would give the family time to think this all over and also time to draw up plans for the dream home and studio in the uninhabited hills and streams of the Lumsden valley. As the year progressed, Julean began to see the possibilities of a larger home and its close proximity to the city. Her initial reluctance to move showed signs of dissolving. She still worried over the lack of amenities and the isolation, though. The kids, on the other hand, warmed up to the move more quickly, especially after Henry added a horse and an all-terrain vehicle to the deal.

In early December of 1980, a family meeting was called to order.

"I just hired a construction crew to begin the renovation to the log cabin in early spring. Mom and I thought of putting our house up for sale first thing in the New Year and hope to have it sold before we move. Jeremy is graduating next spring and so he can help out at the farm with the construction and you..." he looked at Allison, "...can commute back and forth to finish your last year of high school in the city. Is that okay?"

"Sure, I would sooner do that then start at Lumsden and I don't mind driving on the highway. What about Lauren and Justin?"

Lauren was doodling on a sheet of paper and Justin was shoving her arm to bug her. Neither of them were listening.

Answering for them, Julean said, "They will attend elementary school in Lumsden. Lauren can then start high school there, as well." Suddenly aware that they were being discussed, Lauren blurted out, "I can hardly wait to ride on the bus to school."

"Yes, that's one problem eliminated, not having to drive you and Justin, but I'm sure there will be other problems," said Henry and quickly added, "but we can handle them."

"I just hope the addition to the cabin is finished before we move in. I dread the thought of all of us having to live in a two room house."

"I'm sure they will be finished and we will love our new home." Henry said excitedly.

Julean rolled her eyes, obviously reserving her opinion until the time came.

WHEN YOU WANT to slow time down, it just seems to move all the faster. Spring started earlier that year on the prairies. By the end of March, most of the snow had melted and the streets were drying up.

"Oh, we have so much to do before we move. And, how are we going to fit all of our furniture and things into that small cabin if the addition isn't finished?" Julean fretted.

"There's a tack shack beside the barn we can put a lot of stuff into," replied Henry. "I suppose we could even put some furniture into the barn and cover it. There's only the one horse and we can keep her out until winter. Hopefully by then we'll be finished the renovation… if not before."

"I'm just so nervous about it all. I find it hard to visualize how six of us will fit into that little house."

"It won't be for long. The carpenters are starting in May. That gives them a good three months."

"I'm glad you got the new owners of our house to give us until the end of July to move."

Henry rose then put his arms around her. "It will all work out, honey. I know you won't have all the stores and services we have in the city, but we'll adjust. Lumsden is only a five minute drive away. It will be a real exciting adventure, just wait and see."

CHAPTER FORTY-SEVEN

J UNE 1981 WAS the wettest summer in the history of the province. Fields everywhere were flooded to the point that for most
farmers, it simply wasn't worth putting a crop in.

The rain kept the construction workers off the work site. The
promises that their renovation would be completed by July never
came to pass. And so, rather than moving into a finished new log
home in the valley, Henry and his family moved into a partially
framed home in which only one bedroom was available for the
entire family to sleep in. The first week in the valley proved to be
a disaster compared to the wonderful vision Henry and his family
had envisioned.

Henry tried to say comforting words whenever he could.

"The roof is over the second floor, now, it won't be long until
the bedrooms are framed out and everyone will have their own
room."

Julean was in tears as she sat in the middle of the future kitchen,
still filled with dirt and dust. Henry's reassuring words passed over
her head as quickly as clouds chased by a one-hundred-mile-an-
hour wind.

Henry and Jeremy worked day and night to speed things
up, but still, progress was slow. Finally, Henry decided to let the
present city contractor go and hired another crew from a nearby

town. The following Monday, four carpenters set foot on the property, accompanied by trucks, trailers of supplies, toolboxes and an attitude that said, "Let's get the job done." They all wore suspenders and heavy artillery hung around their waists. Huge hammers, squares, and deep pockets housed nails of all different sizes.

Within a week the bedrooms were framed out, and within another week the renovation was ready for dry walling. Henry was ecstatic and Julean wonderfully relieved. By the end of September, everyone had their own quarters.

Henry was in heaven. The huge studio that overlooked what glaciers had carved out billions of years ago was truly inspirational. And when the sun sank into the west, the view and shadows cast across the valley was nothing short of spectacular.

Henry was also happy his family was adjusting so well and had accepted the move from the city to country living. He decided he would never go into the city again unless he had to for supplies or to visit with family and friends.

Destiny, however, would soon take him down another completely different path once again!

During the first week of October when Henry drove into Regina to visit his mother, he missed the turn from Albert Street onto Victoria Avenue. Wondering how he could have made such an error, he carried on towards the corner of 14th Avenue and Smith Street where he had to stop for several cars to pass. As he waited, he studied the two-and-half-storey house on the corner that was for sale.

The thought occurred to him that the old house would make a nice gallery. The location was perfect. It was on the corner and the one-way street and Avenue he was on both led directly to it from downtown. There also was another gallery only a block away. With renovations already in his blood, a seed of excitement to renovate the old dilapidated home into an art gallery was planted.

"You know, Mom, I've always wanted to own a gallery and display not only my work, but other artists' as well. There are so many talented artisans and painters in the province. The thought of exhibiting shows that would display two- and three-dimensional work together would be fantastic."

"What do you mean?" asked Mary.

"My paintings are two-dimensional. Pottery and sculptures, for example, are three-dimensional. I would like to hang my two-dimensional paintings on the walls and display three-dimensional work on stands or the floor for larger pieces. I think the exhibitions would be more interesting and draw more people to come to the shows."

"But you just finished your home in the valley and are just settling in. Are you certain you want to start another project like this so soon?"

Henry smiled. "Yeah. Julean will probably say the same thing. She'll wonder why we moved out to the valley only to turn around and work back in the city again."

"Perhaps you may be able to find someone else to run the gallery."

"Perhaps."

The next week when Henry drove into Regina, he purposely went a block further just to turn onto 14th Avenue and pass the old house again. His heart almost stopped as he saw a real estate agent removing the "For Sale" sign. He pulled over and talked to the realtor who, to Henry's relief, informed him that it had been for sale for over a year and the decision was made to demolish the house and turn the property into a parking lot.

He took Henry through the abandoned house. It had been badly vandalized; paper coffee cups, torn magazines, empty wine bottles, broken glass and caked mud were scattered all over. Cobwebs inhabited every corner, and the windows—which were surprisingly not broken—were so dirty they barely let the light in.

Mice scurried into the shadows as the realtor's flashlight found them out in the dirt-filled basement. The wiring was outdated and the plumbing and sewer would have to be replaced as well. What probably discouraged all previous potential buyers, Henry simply ignored. He looked past all the debris and what needed to be done and visualized what each room would look like finished and displaying wonderful prairie art.

After inspecting the old dilapidated house, he crossed the street and stood on the sidewalk, surveying it from the short distance. He liked the layout. The basement was good, the structure sound, but would need a new concrete floor. The old porch would have to be torn down and replaced with a beautiful entryway that would connect all three floors. And perhaps the small window on the third level could be replaced by two garden doors that opened to a terrace on top of the new addition. It would be a wonderful view of the lake and park.

Excitement swept through him as he no longer saw an old building but his new gallery! It took all of two further seconds to affirm a decision he knew he would make from the moment he saw the house the week before. Henry accompanied the realtor to his office where he signed an offer to purchase the property.

The next challenge was to figure out how to tell Julean. As soon as the kids retired for the evening Henry sat on the sofa next to his wife who was reading a novel.

"Honey, I did something today that I have to tell you."

Julean set her book down and turned toward him. Henry knew that posture and that look. He had to say it in just the right way....

"Now, don't get excited. Let me tell you what I did, why I did it and why I think it will be such a great thing."

"What on earth did you do now?" Julean's eyes widened in barely restrained panic.

"I bought another property near downtown. It was up for sale for an entire year and the owner was planning to demolish the house and turn the property into a parking lot."

Julean didn't think that sounded too alarming. Henry owned three other properties in the city and they all seemed to be working out quite well for them.

"Well, is it in a good area?" Julean asked, her shoulders relaxing.

"It's in an excellent area."

"Is it a property we can afford?"

"If we take the equity out of the other properties we own and if the offer I put in today is accepted we would be able to afford the property, but..."

"But, what?"

Henry could see Julean's tension return. He pressed his mind to find the right words.

"Honey, you've got to see this place and the location. It's a two and a half storey home right on the corner and… It would make a wonderful art gallery!"

Julean gazed at Henry for a long time and shook her head.

"You're unbelievable. You just get one thing done and you're off to the races with another project."

Henry smiled and raised his shoulders, conveying the expression that he just couldn't help himself.

"So, this would be another major renovation?"

"Yes, it would. I know we can't afford to hire a contractor so I thought I would do much of the work myself."

"And, how long will it take to turn this house into a gallery?"

"Oh, just a few months…"

Julean rolled her eyes and shook her head again. "Well, I know once you get something in your mind there is no stopping you."

"Oh, honey, this is going to work out so well. Can't you just see our gallery? My work along with many other artists' displayed throughout?"

"You're unbelievably incredible," said Julean, as she leaned into her husband and rested her head on his chest.

CHAPTER FORTY-EIGHT

B Y THE TIME J.J. was going into Grade 8, he was spending more and more time at James' office and James was spending virtually every night at his condo. It broke Jenny's heart that on those rare occasions when they were home, it was obvious that James had successfully turned her son against her. His aloofness was so much like his father's.

During the second week of Jenny's summer break from school, James met with her in regards to the staff still employed at the estate. Over a month ago, Charles had been reassigned to carry out his duties at James' condo. Also James had fired the chef at the condo and he needed another cook.

"J.J. and I decided the best cook to have at the condo would be Matilda. She knows our tastes and is used to our schedule. So as soon as you go back to school in September, Matilda will begin work at our condo."

Jenny just gazed at James. Slowly he was removing everything that gave her some joy.

"That's fine, James. I was wondering, have you asked Matilda how she feels about that?"

James hadn't even given it a moment's thought.

"What difference does it make what Matilda thinks? She works for me and she'll do as I say."

Jenny just stared at James, trying to figure out her next move. Finally, as per usual, she acquiesced.

"Okay James. But, would it be okay with you, since the guest houses are never used, if Matti might enjoy one for the rest of the summer? Her small room is so confined and it would be our appreciation gift to her for her years of service here."

"I can't believe how you think, Marjorie. You get way too close with the staff. There is no way that I would ever allow that. She can consider herself fortunate that we supply a room for her."

"Really James. You don't consider yourself better than her do you?"

"Of course we are better—"

"Oh James, don't you see how your relationships with others could be so much richer and fruitful. Think of people as beautiful flowers, we all turn out so differently, yet we all come from the same source. We are all created by God. Do you think for one minute He made one flower, one person, better than the other?"

James studied his wife for a moment and said, "You've been out in the sun and that garden of yours too long. Matilda's last day at Greystone Manor will be August 30, perhaps sooner if we can't find a temporary chef." James stormed out of the house.

When Jenny told Matilda that she was going to be moved into the condo, Matti's heart almost broke.

"Oh, Mrs. Hamilton, I don't want to leave you. We are family, you closer to me than my own sister. I be looking for other employment before I work in that condo for Mr. Hamilton."

"Matilda, it won't be so bad. You still have Jimmy there and besides, your presence will have a positive effect on Jimmy and make it more of a home."

"I don't think I can work for Mr. Hamilton any longer..."

Jenny couldn't blame Matilda one bit for feeling that way. But with Matilda in the condo with J.J., Jenny would certainly hear more about him and know that she was keeping an eye out for her son.

"Please give it a try Matti... For Jimmy's sake and as a favour to me. If it doesn't work out, then look for something else."

"Well, my heart sure ain't in it, Mrs. Hamilton—"

"And that's another thing, Mr. Hamilton is no longer around, it would make me so happy if you called me Jenny. We are such good friends and being called Mrs. Hamilton puts a barrier between our relationship. Please call me Jenny."

Matti looked at Jenny so sorrowfully, "I be doing this for so long, I don't know if my lips can say that. My heart has be saying it for some time, but my head gets in the way."

"Well, why don't you try calling me Miss Jenny? That would be a start…"

Once again Matti gazed at her kind, benevolent Mistress who was more a friend to her than an employer. She knew Thomas called the mistress Miss Jenny… Perhaps she could too.

"I'll try for you, Miss Je…Jenny…"

"There, that wasn't so hard. And it sounds so nice coming from you."

Jenny approached Matti and gave her a big hug. "You are such a dear friend Matti, you have made my stay here so enjoyable."

"And you be the best thing that has happened to this house in all the years I be here, Miss …Jenny. Good Lord, I say it a second time… It sure sounds good to hear my lips say Miss Jenny… It tastes like honey on my lips."

Jenny smiled lovingly at Matti who unfortunately had lived too long under an umbrella of fear, intimidation and inferiority. Jenny was so happy to see her dear friend begin to break the shell of that horrible prison of prejudice and separation.

Matti's eyes widened and brightened as she turned and made her way to the kitchen. "I'll squeeze some fresh orange juice for you, Miss Jenny. Yes Ma'am, I do so right quick, Miss Jenny… It be the best orange juice you ever tasted, Miss Jenny."

Tears welled up in Jenny's eyes as she saw Matti go into the kitchen repeating her name over and over.

Now, what am I going to do? Jenny thought as she strolled the garden in the early evening. Perhaps in the fall she might move as well. In any case, she was firm on enjoying the summer in her lovely garden.

Jenny was so grateful for the staff at the estate but it was time she develop other friendships. There had always been Tammy there for her...

Her mother lived closer now so they saw more of each other, but Jenny needed companionship. Someone she could talk to about her interests and wishes and dreams. Someone who understood them and, perhaps, shared them.

For most of her early life, Jenny dreamed of a happy marriage, jetting off on exotic holidays with a man who would sweep her off her feet each night when he returned home. But all those dreams had disappeared in the vastness and loneliness of the Hamilton estate and her empty marriage to James.

WHILE HER MAJOR solace remained her garden, Jenny did start to enjoy her monthly visits to the bookshop at a nearby mall. She tried to convince herself that she only went there for the books, but she couldn't deny that the proprietor, Patrick, had a little something to do with her visits, as well. In fact, she thought she might go there that afternoon as there was a book she was interested in. The thought brought a flutter to her heart.

"Hi Jenny, it's so good to see you. You look very nice today."

"Hi Patrick, it's nice to see you, too."

She tried to ignore his extra comment, but couldn't stop the rush of red to her cheeks. For the first time in ages her heart fluttered as if it had wings.

"I was watching a talk show the other night and the guest spoke of a book. I wrote down the name, I hope I got it right," Jenny glanced at the note in her hand.

Patrick took the slip of paper, "I haven't heard of any book by that title, at least not lately, but I'm sure I can track it down."

"That would be wonderful. It sounded like an inspirational book that helps one deal with different aspects of life using insights of psychology and religion."

"I like those kinds of books, as well. Have you ever read any of Erich Fromm's books? There are two that are outstanding. Come, I will take you to that area."

Jenny followed him through the maze of shelves. Along the way, Jenny glanced over to the cash counter and caught a middle-aged lady behind the cash register glancing her way. She smiled at Jenny then put her head down to run the cost of a book into the cash register for the customer she was serving.

"This section has a lot of books you might find interesting." Patrick thumbed through several rows, "Ah, here is one by Mr. Fromm, *Escape From Freedom*. I've read this one, Jenny. It's a classic and probably one of his most important works. He talks about how people lock themselves into prisons of their own making and how they can free themselves."

Jenny took the book from Patrick, turned it over and read the blurb.

"I think I will take this one, Patrick. It sounds like a fascinating subject."

Jenny gazed into Patrick's eyes and she sensed that he knew why she was interested in the book. She wondered if Patrick was married or not. He didn't wear any rings. Of course, she was technically married, but did their relationship really constitute a marriage? She hadn't seen James for almost two months, they hadn't had sex in over eleven years. She finally reasoned that there was no reason a married woman couldn't have female *and* male friends.

"Here is another book by Erich Fromm, *The Art of Loving*." He picked the book off the shelf and held it out to her. "This is an excellent book, Jen. I've read it over three times and each time I get more out of it."

Jenny liked the way he called her Jen. Tammy used to call her that.

"You know, Patrick, I'm not even going to review it. I'll take your word; I'll take that one, too."

He smiled. He was going to point out another book and then hesitated, "I think you have enough reading material for a day or two. These books require a little slower reading, especially *Escape From Freedom*. Erich uses insights of psychoanalysis as probing agents and… Well, I won't spoil it for you. You'll see what I mean soon enough."

Just as Jenny was about to turn and look at some of the other books on that shelf, Patrick said, "Jenny, I'm going for my coffee break next door… Care to join me?"

"I don't have to be anywhere for a while. Sure, perhaps you can tell me more of Mr. Fromm's insights."

A FEW DAYS later, Patrick called her at home.

"Hi, Jenny. I got a hold of that book you asked me to search out for you. It's been out of print for years, but I found one at a second-hand bookstore. It still looks to be in good condition."

"Oh, thank you, Patrick. I'll be over later today to pick it up and pay for it."

"Actually, Jenny, it cost less than five dollars, I'd like to give it to you."

"Well, that's very nice of you, Patrick, thank you."

"Why don't you meet me at the coffee shop, you can pick it up there."

Jenny thought for a moment. She didn't want to start anything or give him the wrong idea, but it was so nice to talk to someone who liked the same things she did.

"Okay, Patrick, I'll meet you there around three o'clock. Does that work for you?"

"That's perfect, Jen. Three, it is."

He called her Jen again. She hadn't felt so exhilarated in years. She loved their chat in the coffee shop the other day. He was so well-read and interesting. And they seemed to have so much in common. She could hardly wait for coffee time.

When Jenny walked into the café and Patrick saw her, he stood and walked toward her, waving the book. Jenny beamed.

"Here's the book, Jen." Patrick handed her the book and at the same time reached forward and kissed her cheek.

Jenny was startled and her face reddened.

"Oh, I'm sorry, I didn't mean to—"

"That's fine, Patrick. I just wasn't expecting.... Oh, it's fine, thank you so much for your trouble and getting this book for me."

"It's all my pleasure, Jenny. I felt like a detective for two days, following lead after lead across all of North America until bingo, there it was in a second-hand shop just across town."

"Which only goes to prove that mysteries are many times solved in one's own back yard."

"An astute observation. Come on, I'll let you buy me a coffee for my efforts."

"You've got a deal, Patrick."

And so it went for the rest of the summer; they would either meet at the coffee shop or stroll along the Canal or find a quiet spot in a nearby park. Jenny loved the stimulating discussions they had about books they were reading at the time. He was so easy to talk to; she began to look forward to their visits more and more. She was beginning to feel like a woman again.

"My gosh, Patrick, it's almost four-thirty. We've been chatting for over two hours. You have to get back to work."

"I'm the owner, remember? And I have very capable staff."

"This has been such an enjoyable summer. I'm not looking forward to going back to school like I usually do. It starts next week."

"Yes, I will miss our occasional afternoon get together. How about dinner this Saturday, Jenny. You've turned me down three times. Let's celebrate the summer and your return to school."

Jenny gazed into Patrick's congenial eyes. He was a handsome man, a few years older than she and very intelligent. Streaks of grey running through dark brown hair gave him an air of sophistication. And his lean body all done up in his casual outfit was... very appealing. But despite the admirable qualities Patrick displayed, she was still a married woman and Patrick knew that. She also knew the attraction she felt to her first love could never be replaced by any suitor. Either consciously or unconsciously there was always some form of resistance which surfaced.

"Let me think on it, Patrick. There's a cookbook I want to pick up for my mother at your shop. I'll see you sometime Friday and let you know."

Patrick looked disappointed. He extended his hand, "Okay, that's a deal." He shook Jenny's hand and held it for a brief moment longer than he should have then bent towards her. She anticipated his kiss and backed away.

"I really must run, Patrick. I promised Mom I'd be over for dinner to view her new apartment and I still have to change." Jenny turned and ran off. "I'll see you tomorrow."

CHAPTER FORTY-NINE

IT WAS THE last week in August and Jenny had asked Matti to bake one of her best double layered chocolate cakes for Ramon's surprise birthday party. When Matti entered the tool shed with the cake, she nearly dropped it when everyone clapped and cheered and yelled, "Surprise, Matti!

Jenny took the cake from her and set it on the potting plant table and then rushed back to hug her dear friend. Thomas, Ramon, and Charles followed in turn.

"I don't know what to say! Is this all for me?"

"The cake is only part of it," said Jenny with a twinkle in her eye. "Come, we have everything set up by the gazebo."

Jenny took Matti's hand and the rest followed. Charles brought up the rear carrying the chocolate cake. When they turned the corner around a group of flowering trees, Matti was shocked to see the tables set up with food, streamers, and balloons. Thomas ran ahead to turn on his battery operated tape machine with some lively music.

"Next week you're moving into the city to James' condo so we thought we would have a party for you, Matti!"

Tears were sliding down Matti's cheeks, she was so touched by the scene and the thoughtfulness of her friends.

"I don't know what to say. I made a special cake for Ramon and here I be baking for myself. Good Lord, I just don't know what to say..."

"Never thought I'd see the day to see you'd be tongue tied, Matti!" Everyone laughed, agreeing with Thomas.

"And we just don't know who we're going to get, that can bake such fine cookies and banana muffins and make such good coffee," said Ramon.

"Why, we've been interviewing and sampling cookies and muffins all summer and none have come close to yours!" said Thomas.

"And we asked you to bake the cake because we knew there wasn't anyone else in all of Ottawa that could make one as good as you. And we all know how much you love chocolate cake. So to make sure you were happy with it, we knew you would have to make it yourself!" said Jenny.

"We certainly are most fortunate that you're coming to the condo Matilda," said Charles. "The cooking there has been rather unpalatable. Unfortunately our gain is Mrs. Hamilton's loss."

"Yes, I will miss Matti so much. Her food is one thing for sure, but the food she fed us all daily with her pleasant smile and cheerful manner is what we will miss so much."

Just then the Harry Belafonte song, "Matilda" began to play on the tape machine. It couldn't have been more perfect!

After the first line or too, everyone stood and formed a circle around Matti and began singing along with Harry...

Hey! Matilda, Matilda, Matilda, she take me money and run Venezuela.
Once again now!
Matilda, Matilda, Matilda, she take me money and run Venezuela...
> *Five hundred dollars, friends I lost:*
> *Woman even sell me cat and horse!*
Heya! Matilda, she take me money and run Venezuela.
> *Everybody!*
(Matilda,) Sing out the chorus,
(Matilda,) Sing a little louder,

Matilda, she take me money and run Venezuela.
   Once again now!
   (Matilda,) Going 'round the corner...

Between the clapping, hooting and hollering the song went on for almost fifteen minutes, even longer than the record time of twelve minutes when Harry Belafonte performed the song at Carnegie Hall.

After a short stop for refreshments and a slice of Matti's chocolate cake, the music started up again. This time it was "Waltzing Matilda!"

No sooner had the lyric began than Thomas jumped up and took Matti in his arms and began waltzing away. As the two of them danced everyone sang the chorus...

Waltzing Matilda, Waltzing Matilda
You'll come a-Waltzing Matilda, with me
And he sang as he watched and waited till his billy boiled,
You'll come a-Waltzing Matilda, with me.

It was such a beautiful sight for all. Dancing and singing among the flowers, the aroma of the herbs, and the warm friendship of love in the air—it couldn't have been a more perfect party!

But everyone had to agree that Charles took the cake when he came up to Matilda, swung his arm with an air of grandiosity to his chest, bowed deeply and asked as if he were speaking to the queen, "It would indeed give me great pleasure, Matilda, if you would do me the honour to have the next dance?"

Matti took hold of her white work dress on each side of her round hips, pulled on them as far as the cloth was able to give, and ever so daintily, curtsied and replied, "It'd be a pleasure to dance with you, Charles."

The sight of a highly dignified, sophisticated and refined Charles with his head tilted slightly up with a gesture of holding a most beloved treasure in his arms, and a down-to-earth island girl with black sparkling eyes gazing tender-heartedly into her partner's eyes, couldn't have blended more beautifully. And if that vision couldn't split the most hard-hearted heart there ever was, then nothing ever would.

In the days to follow, Jenny got several calls from neighbours as far as a mile and a half away inquiring about the Calypso music and how wonderful it sounded!

"That was sure one great party, Miss Jenny. I ain't had such a good time since I left the island. And I be in for another big party soon enough. My sister Coreena is coming for a visit this Christmas! I ain't seen her for over sixteen years."

"Oh, that sounds wonderful, Matti."

"The man she be marrying wanted to give her that gift for years but she refused to accept it until she decided she be marrying him. Just ain't right taking a man's money unless he be's her man."

"So did she find someone in Jamaica—?"

"Good Lord, she be marrying a man from Regina, Saskatchewan, of all places!"

"Really, Matti?"

"Yes, she be seeing him for over eight years. She tells me he's a rich man."

Jenny was curious, she wondered who from Regina that might be, not that she knew anyone there besides Henry. "What is the man's name, do you know, Matti?"

"A fella called a Eddy Zeigler, says she be a good head taller than a high wave in his hair."

Jenny's jaw almost dropped to the floor. She wondered if it could possibly be the same Eddy Zeigler she knew who attacked her and Henry that night after the show?

"You okay, Miss Jenny? You looking awfully pale all of a sudden."

Jenny gazed at her dear friend and shrugged her shoulders. Of all the people in the world, she would never have expected to hear that name... Eddy Ziegler. Surely there couldn't be more than one in Regina... He was short and had a big pompadour. Henry sure didn't like that boy and neither did Jenny after what he and his friends did to her that night.

As images from that night surfaced, Jenny suddenly thought

back to earlier in the evening, when she and Henry had gone to that show... *True Love*. That was it! *That was our song...*

Jenny turned and began walking out of the kitchen, one memory after the other tumbling over and over in her mind. But it wasn't the thoughts of what the boys did to her that night that she allowed to preoccupy her mind, rather it was mainly the words of their song that touched her heart...

As she wandered away singing, Matti shook her head, just watching her go.

While I give to you and you give to me
true love, true love
so on and on it will always be
true love, true love.

For you and I have a guardian angel
on high, with nothing to do
but to give to you and to give to me
love forever true

CHAPTER FIFTY

"MOM! THE APARTMENT is great and the view of the city is spectacular. My goodness, it's lovely." The bay window of the apartment faced the downtown core. Being up so high, it was easy to follow the Ottawa River up behind the Parliament Buildings with the flag on the Peace Tower being whipped around by the wind. The hills of Gatineau followed along the other side of the river. Jenny had seen the Gatineaus in their full, fall colours from the ground; it was heavenly to see them from her mother's window.

"I love it, too. I never thought I would get over the estate, but I must say this is very nice."

"I recognize some of the furniture from home, but these are new." Jenny flopped into one of the armchairs she was referring to.

"Yes, I had to buy some new pieces because of size restrictions. Our living room on the estate was at least three times the size of this one. The furniture didn't appear large there, but it certainly overwhelmed this small space. Well, why don't you relax, I'll get you a glass of wine while I make dinner. I'd invite you into the kitchen, but it's a little crowded."

Jenny surveyed the apartment again and pictured herself moving off of James' estate. *Perhaps soon it will be my turn to make this decision...*

She pushed herself off the couch and began to wander the apartment. She couldn't get over the close proximity of the rooms to one another as compared to what she was used to at both her parent's and James' estates.

Wandering into the bedroom, Jenny noted it was small, but eloquently decorated. Her mother always did have a knack for interior decorating.

Jenny was drawn to the closet and opened the door. The aura of light emanating inside filled Jenny with a strange peace and inexplicable longing.

"Oh, here you are," said her mother from the doorway, carrying two glasses of wine.

"Mom, what is this strange light in the closet? It feels so warm and alluring."

Her mother stood there without saying a word.

"The light seems to be coming from your hope chest, Mom. Isn't that strange? I remember as a little girl watching you put different treasures inside the chest. I would just love to go through it with you. It must contain important documents and letters and perhaps..." She turned toward her mother, "...a secret or two?"

Was her mother blushing? Secrets, indeed, apparently.

"Perhaps we can some other time, but dinner is ready. Come, let's sit down and here..." her mother extended her arm, "...enjoy your wine."

Jenny reluctantly closed the door, stood before it for the longest moment and then followed her mother to the dining room and took a seat at the table her mother had prepared. The dining area was so much smaller than they both were used to, but cozy and, once again, the view over the Ottawa River and the Gatineaus from the eighteenth floor was magnificent.

After Jenny offered the blessing they helped themselves to salmon and wild rice.

"By the way, J.J. was looking for you, today. He wants to borrow your convertible for the weekend. A friend of his is old enough to drive and apparently James approved it. I told him to check at the bookshop you often frequent."

Jenny shook her head, "I think he is too young for the car and to give it to one of his friends. Jimmy is growing up much too fast and hanging out with older teenage friends is asking for trouble."

"If James approves of it there is not much you can do."

Jenny shrugged her shoulders and cut another piece of the tender fish with her fork. "Actually I must have just missed Jimmy. I was at the bookshop for a short while and then Patrick, the owner, and I went for a stroll in the park."

Jenny stopped eating and looked at her mother whose fork had leveled off in mid-air.

"Oh, Mom, it's not what you think. He's just a good friend and besides, there's nothing wrong with having male friends… Is there?"

Edith knew her daughter was lonely and by herself much of the time in that huge estate, yet she didn't want to see her get into a situation that could become… dangerous. Edith was well aware of James' jealousy and fierce temper.

As she gazed at her lovely daughter, Edith couldn't help but thank the Lord for Jenny's grace, charm, forbearance and centeredness in a marriage that could have sent anyone spiraling into despondency. Edith knew from experience that it could be difficult living with a top executive, but her daughter's life with James was unbearable. But then, Jenny was so filled with love and acceptance that she couldn't help herself but to be loving, even in such a dire circumstance.

"My dear sweet child," started Edith, gently reaching across the table and putting her hand on Jenny's. "From the day you were born you were like a bird that had to fly, like a song that had to be sung, like… like the sun that has to shine." Edith smiled at the thought and Jenny's eyes filled with tears.

"That's what Daddy always used to say…"

"Yes, he always felt that the sunshine was trapped within his little girl's spirit."

Edith wondered if her daughter's love and maturity had pressed upon James in any way to change. Would Jenny's kindness, tenderness and love she continuously displayed ever have any effect on her husband's uncaring, cold heart?

Surely, even a hard nosed man like James must feel something stir at the core of his being to be accepted in a loving way by one who knows all of his sins, weakness and faults and is subjected to the stress of all of them?

What would her daughter's life have been like had they not interfered with Jenny's relationship with that boy in Regina and she had married Henry?

"It's a miracle you still shine forth, darling, even though many in your shoes would have long ago turned dull and bitter. I know how lonely you are, Jenny, just please be careful. I don't ever want to see anything bad happen to you..."

Edith guessed that had Jenny married Henry instead of James she probably wouldn't be able to recognize her own daughter through the light of radiant happiness. Edith struggled to suppress such thoughts and the pangs of guilt that accompanied them. Ted was dead right in what they should have done with those letters and she was dead wrong.

AROUND TWO O'CLOCK the next day, Jenny parked her convertible three blocks away from Patrick's bookstore and decided to walk. She had a lot on her mind. Maybe she should do what her mother had done and find a smaller apartment. She had remained on the estate for one reason only and that was to keep some contact with her son and now he was rarely there. She loved the beauty of the grounds, the Angel of Thanksgiving, the flowers, and the gazebo and of course her daily visits with Matti and Thomas, but now with Matti gone...

She was lonely and locked into a beautiful estate with invisible bars around it. It was as if she were dying of thirst and the odd sprinkle of water she received when J.J. showed up was no longer sufficient to quench the arid desert within. Perhaps if she and James separated she might feel freer and less guilty about accepting invitations from other men. The thought sent a chill through her, cooling the hot rays of the fall sun.

When Jenny entered the bookstore she noted the cashier no longer smiled or appeared as friendly as before. As she walked over to the cookbooks, her intuition told her that something was wrong. She was all prepared to accept Patrick's invitation to dinner Saturday evening, but now wasn't sure if that was such a wise decision.

No sooner had she found the book she wanted to buy for her mom, when Patrick barreled over to her side, almost floating at the sight of her.

"Hi, Jenny, it's so good to see you."

Jenny looked at Patrick and then cast a furtive glance over to the cash register. The lady at the counter was staring at Jenny with a look that was the complete antithesis of Patrick's beaming countenance. Embarrassment and guilt rushed through Jenny, how could she have been so silly not to ask or check it out?

"Patrick, are you married?"

Patrick looked at Jenny, a puzzled look growing on his face. "Yes, I thought you knew."

"But, you don't wear a wedding band that would—"

"I'm allergic to metals; I can't wear rings or watches."

Jenny flushed, completely overwhelmed by the revelation. She cast a glance towards the counter again. The lady had tears in her eyes. Grief, guilt and remorse spread through Jenny like a tornado.

"Patrick, is that your wife at the counter?"

He wanted to look, but couldn't. He was trapped in a mire of deceits; Jenny could sense him slipping into the muddy mess he created for himself… and her. Patrick's look gave her the answer.

"Patrick, we can no longer see each other." She turned toward the counter to pay for her book but then realized she didn't want to face his wife. She thrust the book into Patrick's chest then turned to go.

Patrick took hold of Jenny's arms. "But, Jen, I love you, I thought you felt—"

"No, Patrick, I'm sorry if I misled you. You're just a friend to me."

"Please, Jenny, don't let this be the end," he whispered, trying to confine their conversation to themselves.

Jenny shook her head, "This will not work any longer." Jenny stepped back, trying to free herself from Patrick's hold as well as the awful thought of what his wife must be thinking. He tightened his grip on her and he tried to pull her to him so he could kiss her.

As his lips descended, Jenny turned her head so his lips landed on her cheek.

At that very moment, J.J. walked into the bookstore looking for her. He saw Patrick holding his mom and kissing her cheek. His reaction was the same as his father's would have been. His eyes flared red, his face twisted and turned. To Jenny, it was as if she were seeing the mirror image of James, an expression that pierced her heart.

But it was what J.J. said next that horrified her. Jenny couldn't hear his words, but could clearly read his lips. Every word was distinctly formed with exaggerated movements and sent with such hurtful conviction that the message she received exploded in her mind and would reverberate forever in her heart.

"You're a cheat, a whore!"

CHAPTER FIFTY-ONE

A s was the case with the log cabin, the renovation to convert the old house into a gallery took much longer than the few months Henry had anticipated. In fact, it took a year to the day to complete. The headline on the third page of the November 5, 1982, Leader Post read: "Artist Also Handy With a Hammer." Henry had hired a young carpenter just out of trade school and together with the help of an architect friend; Henry transformed the old dilapidated house into a major work of art, reflecting the heritage style of the neighbourhood.

When they opened the gallery for business, it was an immediate success. The philosophy of the gallery was "Art is for All." Paintings, pottery and sculptures to suit all tastes and budgets were on display by nearly seventy artists in the province. Both the astute collector and the beginning collector felt equally at home in the Pederson Art Gallery.

In the New Year, after a very busy fall and Christmas season, Henry and Julean were celebrating the success of the gallery at their favourite café when the topic of a much needed holiday once again came up.

"It's been over two years since you promised to take me to Minot for a little mini getaway," Julean reminded him, as she gazed into his dreamy eyes.

"Yes, I know we both need a break. Do you think just a weekend across the border is enough or should we plan a major holiday in Costa Rica or some island in the Caribbean?"

"Oooh, that sounds exciting."

"Why don't we look into it? Check how much it would cost to take the kids along. They deserve a break, as well, and maybe this is the start of a major family trip every year."

Seizing the moment Julean quickly said, "I'll call the travel agency tomorrow, but we should also consider taking a weekend off, just the two of us. You've been working hard on so many things, the renovation, opening a new business, and painting for your shows. Why don't we sneak away to Minot like we planned several years ago?"

"That's a good idea. Let's see if we can get into the same motel we stayed in on our honeymoon." Henry winked at his wife as pleasurable memories of that evening crossed his mind.

MARY AGREED TO watch the kids while Henry and Julean finalized their trip across the border into the United States. Henry was excited as he drove his mom out to the acreage.

"Well, this has been a long time in coming, Mom. It will be good for Julean and I to get away. I wish we could take the kids but perhaps next time."

"Yes, you both have been working very hard. I hope everything goes well for you and Julean while you are there."

Henry turned and looked at his mom not sure what she meant by that remark. "Why would you say that, Mom? Of course everything is going to go well…"

"Well, I don't want to start something, but the last time we talked, you had shared concerns about Julean being aware of Jenny and that you were going to discuss it with her when you went away. I've prayed so much about it and that everything turns out okay. Julean is such a lovely girl, I would hate to see her hurt by all this."

"Oh that! Well, I know it's still a concern with me and every now and then I sense Julean is bothered by it, too. But for some reason we both have just accepted it and sort of live with it. I know it would be best to bring it all out in the open. Father Engelmann suggested that a long time ago. But I always chicken out at the last moment. It's like you just said, Julean is such a sweetheart and I love her so much. I don't want to hurt her either, but who knows? Maybe living this way with uncertainty and the thought that there is another woman may be even more painful to her. Yeah, maybe I will. If I feel the time is right, I'm going to finally do it."

Henry reached over and placed his hand over his mom's. "Thanks for your prayers and please don't worry, everything will turn out okay."

I hope!

After a three-day romantic trip to Minot interspersed with lots of shopping for the kids, Henry hesitatingly drove into a heavy snowfall as they left the outskirts of the American city for home. Visibility was poor and the forecast was for strong winds. Henry knew the trip would be slow and treacherous.

Surprisingly, the weather held for most of the way until they passed Weyburn. It was then that the prairies revealed how a February blizzard could rage. Just a few miles out of the small city, Henry suggested they turn back and spend the night in Weyburn. It was only sixty miles to Regina, however, and they had made it safely thus far so they decided to go for it.

Very quickly, the tension Henry had left behind during the mini-vacation was back full force as he drove carefully along, the headlights dancing off the ice-spotted highway. Gusting winds meant zero visibility at times and the constant swooshing of the wiper blades added to the distraction.

A car behind him grew larger in his rearview mirror. *My God, I hope he sees me, he's coming up pretty fast.* At the last possible moment the speeding car pulled out to pass. Henry shook his head in disbelief as the passing car swirled snow in their direction, reducing the visibility again to almost nil. Henry slowed further, hoping he was not heading into the ditch as snow replaced any semblance of road or sky ahead of him.

"I don't know why drivers have to be in such a hurry in these wintry conditions."

"Yes, that person isn't using common sense, that's for sure," echoed Julean in a nervous tone of voice.

Henry kept his car steady, going from memory and hoping the direction he was pointing the car would keep them on the highway. He slowed even further, trying to escape the lingering twirling snow. Gradually, visibility improved and they both sighed in relief. He found himself more in the centre of the highway than he would have liked. Luckily no one was heading their way from the other side.

"I just hate winter driving. You can't see a thing in this storm. Why people drive so fast and have the need to pass in a storm like this is beyond me."

"Yes, the few minutes they gain isn't worth it."

Julean turned on the radio and searched for relaxing music.

"That one seems nice, Julean, leave it there for a minute."

As Henry's eyes returned to the road, his foot reached for the brake pedal and coasted the vehicle to a stop on what he hoped was the shoulder. Lying in the middle of the highway was a deer. It had just been hit. Its head was thrusting up and down and its legs splayed into the blowing snow. It was trying to get up, but its legs were rigid, unable to move.

"Looks like it's paralyzed," Henry surmised, as he pulled up beside the frantic animal. "It'll have to be put down and moved off the highway before someone else hits it."

"Look there!" shouted Julean. A vehicle was overturned in the ditch with one headlight buried in the snow bank. The flashing taillight had caught her attention.

"It's probably the car that passed us earlier. They'll need help."

Julean's nursing instincts kicked in. She snatched her coat from the backseat.

"I'll go check on whoever is in the car."

"You have to put your boots—"

"I'll be fine." Julean twisted in the front seat and slipped her coat on.

"I'll be there in a few minutes once I figure out how to get that deer off the road."

Henry stepped out of the station wagon and opened the tailgate. After shuffling suitcases he dug out the tire wrench from underneath the carpet where a spare tire was stored. When he returned to the deer, it had stopped trying to get up. It was barely alive. Its underside was split open and its spinal column severed. Blood oozed out and froze as it ran into the white snow, turning it red and steamy. Henry raised his hands, took aim then closed his eyes as he crashed the metal wrench into the deer's head. The sound of the skull shattering sent eerie shivers up Henry's spine along with the shivers from freezing cold.

"Julean, how are you doing over there?" Henry shouted into the howling wind. He couldn't hear her reply. He decided to check on her and then come back and remove the animal.

Julean was trying to get in the car, but it was locked. She had checked all the doors.

"I see a man inside," she shouted. "We have to get to him."

"Move over, let me see." Henry peered into the car, the light from the dashboard illuminated the interior just enough so he could make out the position of the man. He appeared to be alone.

"Stand back." Henry ordered as he forcibly rapped on the window with the blood-stained tire wrench. Suddenly, the window shattered, allowing him to reach in and unlock the door. The driver's side of the car was tilted up so Henry had no trouble opening the door.

"Here, let me examine him. I hope we can safely move him." The man was crouched down on the interior ceiling of the car. His head seemed bent the wrong way. As Julean checked for injuries and to verify a pulse, her hands became coated in the man's blood from cuts on his arm and forehead.

"His pulse is weak. Let's try to get him into our car. We have to get him to the hospital."

"Move for a minute," requested Henry. He reached inside and grabbed the man and pulled him partially into view.

"He's heavy," Henry grunted.

"He looks young," Julean said, as his face turned toward her. She grabbed hold of the man's jacket and helped Henry get him fully out of the car. For a moment Henry lost his grip and the man collapsed into the snow, staining the pure whiteness with stark red blood. He was completely unconscious and absolutely huge;

almost seven feet tall. Julean immediately felt for a pulse. It was there, but weak.

They each grabbed a shoulder and dragged him up the ditch and to their car. They were surprised they could even move him, but in addition to being extremely lanky, the man was rail-thin; a fact initially concealed by his bulky winter coat.

By the time they got him to their car, both were exhausted from the struggle and soaked wet with perspiration. Julean opened the back door and battled with the man until he was propped up against the running board. Henry climbed into the back, knelt on the seat and took hold of the man's shoulders. With short heaves, inch-by-inch, Henry finally pulled the man into the back seat. Henry couldn't get over how tall the man was. His knees had to be bent all the way just to close the car door.

Julean ran back to the man's car making certain no one else was there. The car was still running. She reached in for the keys and scraped her hand against broken glass. As she withdrew her hand, she noticed several syringes where the man had been lying. She wondered if he was a diabetic.

By the time Julean got back to the car, Henry had tied their camping rope onto the deer's leg. It was too heavy for him to pull by himself so he tied it to the back bumper of the station wagon and left as much slack in the rope as he could.

Julean hopped into the front seat, rubbing her hands together to try to stimulate blood flow to them again. Her feet were frozen. She moved them closer to the heater and turned the fan up as high as it would go, stomping them on the floor. Henry jumped back into the car and slowly drove forward until the rope became taut. The back tires slipped and skidded as it tried to overcome the inertia of the huge buck. Finally, it gave way from the road and Henry sped off.

"You're not going to drag that deer all the way to the city are you?"

"No, I want to work it off the highway as much as possible."

As the car picked up speed, Henry began to swerve sharply from side to side, causing the heavy weight of the animal to swing in the opposing direction to the car. Right when Henry thought the deer had swung far over to the shoulder, he hit the brakes. He got out to check on the deer's position and was satisfied the animal was far enough out of traffic's way. He undid the rope at the bumper and left it lying on the road.

They were both relieved to see city lights up ahead. Julean turned and knelt on the seat to check their passenger. She turned on the overhead light, reached for his wrist and felt for a pulse. There was none.

"Henry, there's no pulse." Julean climbed over the front seat. "He's not breathing." She began CPR. After a few tense moments, the man started breathing on his own. Julean remained kneeling on the floor board beside the man and tried to comfort him as he groaned. "We will be at the hospital soon. Just relax."

Henry sped down Albert Street going through two red lights after quickly noting no one else was around. On 14th Avenue he turned right, passed his gallery on Smith Street and rushed to the emergency at the General Hospital.

The next five minutes seemed like organized chaos as the man was wheeled through the doors. After both Henry and Julean were examined and treated for cuts and bruises they relayed to the police what had happened and the approximate location of the man's car and the deer. One of the officers used the desk phone to contact the RCMP.

"Did the man die?" asked Allison, when Henry and Julean told the kids their story.

"He was alive when we got him to the hospital," answered Julean.

"But he had stopped breathing on the way," reminded Henry, "Mom got into the back seat and revived him."

"You actually brought him back from the dead, Mom?" probed Jeremy skeptically.

"Yes, I gave him mouth to mouth resuscitation. It's something I want all of you to learn how to do in case of an emergency."

The phone rang and Allison got it. "It's some doctor for you or Mom."

"You better take it, if it has to do with medical stuff, you know more than I do."

Julean rushed to the phone. "Hello, this is Julean Pederson. Thank you for calling, doctor... Oh, that's good, so he doesn't have AIDS?... Good, that makes me feel better... Yes, it was a concern, thank you for checking and letting me know. How is the man doing?... Oh, that's good. Yes, just tell him we were happy to be there at the time. Yes, okay, goodbye."

JULEAN LOOKED AT Henry and shook her head. When the doctors had examined Julean's cuts, they expressed concern about her having possibly contracted from the man she had helped some new disease called AIDS. She had never heard of it, but apparently it was quite deadly, extremely contagious and contractible through exposure to contaminated blood. Henry wiped his forehead in relief that Julean hadn't gotten herself in trouble by saving someone's life.

The next day when Henry got home from the gallery, Julean was complaining of a headache and stiff neck.

"You must have caught a cold or a touch of flu from being out in the storm the other night. Why not take a Tylenol and go to bed?"

"I think I will, honey. I've started dinner. It's nothing fancy; just hot dogs and corn on the cob I took out of the freezer."

"And onions, too. I smelled them as soon as I came in. Are all the kids home?"

"Except for Jeremy. They're all in the family room watching TV. Jeremy is eating at his friend Tom's place and will be home by ten o'clock. Gosh, I'm feeling so tired, I just have to lie down for awhile."

Julean kissed Henry's cheek. Henry studied his wife for a moment as she turned and traipsed off to bed.

LATER THAT EVENING, after visiting with Jeremy for awhile, Henry decided to turn in for the night. He flipped on the ceiling light as he entered the bedroom. Julean immediately stirred.

"Oh, please turn off the light. Please turn it off." Julean's voice rose, sounding frightened. Henry turned off the light and sat next to his wife on the bed.

"What's wrong, honey? How are you feeling?"

"I'm so cold. She pushed her hand out from under the cover and touched Henry's. "Just feel how cold I am. Please get another blanket from the closet."

"How's your headache and neck, any better?"

"No, it still feels stiff and sore. Would you please get me another two Tylenol and some water?"

"Sure, honey." Henry got up, his face covered with concern. When he returned with the pills, Julean had trouble swallowing them and then quickly dove under the covers.

"Are you sure you're okay? Should I call the doctor?"

"No… it's just the flu. You know how you feel achy all over and tired? Just come to bed and snuggle up to me. My backside feels so chilled."

Around three in the morning Henry was perspiring profusely. His wife was burning with a fever and with the added blanket he was almost suffocating under the covers. Just as he got up to go to the bedroom, Julean began to vomit in her sleep, gagging herself. Henry flipped on the light, ran over and immediately shook her shoulder. "Julean, Julean, wake up."

She opened her eyes and threw up again. "Turn the lights off. This is no circus." Julean appeared confused and frightened.

Henry got up turned the light off, but left the one on in the bathroom. He rushed back to his wife's side.

"Julean, are you okay? I'm very worried about you."

"I'm…" Julean gagged, threatening to vomit again.

Henry picked up the bedside phone and called the emergency call number. He explained to the nurse on duty his wife's symptoms and she agreed with Julean's earlier diagnosis that it was probably the flu. Just as Henry was about to hang up he mentioned one other symptom. "She seems frightened when I turn on the light. I guess that has to do with her headache, right?"

"What did you say your wife's symptoms are again?"

"Headache and stiff neck were her first complaints and later she felt very chilled and wanted to go to bed. She was so tired. She now has a raging fever and has vomited several times. And as I said, she seemed afraid of the bedroom light."

Silence passed through the phone line. "Did anyone in the family have meningitis?"

"No, I really don't know what that is, but I would if one of us had it."

"Was your wife in contact with anyone or in a crowded place recently?"

"No, but come to think of it, she did give CPR to a critically ill man a couple of days ago when we were retuning from a holiday in the States."

Silence sizzled through the line, again, but this time for only a split second. "You better bring your wife in for examination, sir."

"In the morning?"

"No. Right now!"

CHAPTER FIFTY-TWO

JENNY GAZED OUT of the patio door onto the snow covered grounds of her estate. Winter had come early the previous fall and had not let up right through the first month of the New Year. And if the pattern were to follow, February didn't promise to be much better. Jenny couldn't wait for spring to take her daily strolls along the winding paths to her gazebo among the flowers.

She had tried calling Jimmy earlier, but there had been no answer. Since the day he saw Patrick kiss her at the bookstore he had refused to speak to her, hadn't returned any of her previous calls, and otherwise had vanished from her life. Jenny wanted to explain what had happened and it bothered her immensely that her son may be thinking ill of her. His total lack of communication confirmed that was the case, but Jenny hoped over time he would at least give her a chance to explain.

After thinking about it for some time, Jenny had made the decision to move into an apartment, but after the incident with Patrick she thought she better stay on the estate. If she moved her son might think she did so to be with Patrick. It would possibly reinforce that awful image of her he carried around in his mind. At least until she explained her side and felt that her son clearly understood the situation, it was best for all concerned to stay put.

The one consolation was Jenny was quite sure her son had not shared the kissing incident with James. Had he done so, James would surely have confronted her about it by now. God only knew what that man might have done. At the very least, he would finally have the reason he had been looking for to get rid of her.

Jenny thought that might not be such a bad thing. She was basically alone and now with Jimmy pretty much out of her life as well, perhaps a separation might be a first step. That way she could consider going out with other men and not feel guilty about it. Almost every other week someone asked for a date and there were men on staff whose company she thought she would actually enjoy.

Besides fretting over Jimmy and her estranged relationship with James, Jenny was also concerned over her mother. As soon as winter set in, her mother's arthritis flared up. During dinner the previous Sunday, her mother could barely carry her plate to the table. It would be sad if she had to give up her lovely apartment and move into a care home. Jenny wondered if she should move in with her mother and help care for her. She never really felt that close to her mother, perhaps this would be a way to improve their relationship. But then again, it just might drive them further apart or would only complicate her life further.

Jenny felt confused, emotionally drained and lonely. Her life had been on hold for so many years, spinning but going nowhere. It was not often that Jenny allowed herself to be depressed but at that moment, gazing out onto the grounds, both her beacons—the wildflowers and the sun—were concealed under the cold bleakness of winter, unable to come to her aid. Without Charles and Matti in the home, she was as cold as the tree skeletons without their summer blanket of leaves. And Thomas only came around in the winter to clear the snow. She was glad it was snowing. He would be by tomorrow.

During the summer when she felt this way usually a stroll through the grounds quickly lifted her spirits. And the Angel of Thanksgiving was such a Godsend. Over and over it brought such healing to her heart and memories of her father. *Oh Dad, if only you were here to talk to.* She wanted to share so much with him and she always had the feeling that he wanted to share something important with her, as well. Just as her eyes misted and the heaviness of the moment overwhelmed her, she got the urge to get dressed and take a walk through the snow-covered grounds to the gazebo.

In all the years she had lived on the estate she had never thought to venture out to her gazebo in the dead of winter. Suddenly filled with a growing spirit of adventure, Jenny put on her coat and boots, pulled a red woolen toque over her ears and tucked several strands of hair beneath the matching long scarf she wrapped around her neck. She put on her mittens and opened the patio doors. Snow leaning against the glass fell inside onto the tiled kitchen floor and spread further in by a gust of wind.

Jenny ventured out and closed the doors behind her. The brisk wind seemed to freshen her spirits. She tried to locate the walkway but the snow was too deep and spread evenly over the entire grounds, completely obscuring the landscape below. She looked through the swirling snow for orientation, but was unable to see the gazebo. She knew it was off to her right some two hundred feet and began plunking her boots in and out of the deep snow as she made her way to her beloved haven.

Halfway there she got concerned she may have gone in the wrong direction, but within another minute, she was relieved to see the outline of the gazebo. By the time she got there she was exhausted from trudging through the snow. The gazebo was filled with snow and her swinging chair was submerged in a high snow bank. She had intended to sit there and relax, but with that option closed Jenny simply allowed herself to collapse on her back into the soft snow.

As she gazed into the white sky filled with swirling, heavy snow-flakes, a smile hidden by her scarf crossed her face. A memory of long ago revealed why she was prompted to go outside. In her last letter to Henry, the one with the pewter angel, she had written how wonderful it would be to hold his hand in the winter time and to make angels in the snow so close together their wings would intertwine.

She pushed the snow away with her arms like two windshield wipers arching from the side of her body to almost the top of her head, carving a pair of wings in the snow. In the same fashion she spread her legs creating the bottom of the angel's robe. She pictured herself as if on a cloud and looking down on the image. It comforted her troubled soul.

Softly she whispered the Guardian Angel prayer, the one that Henry said, too. Jenny got up as carefully as she could not to disturb the sculpture she had created in the snow. She gently raised one leg and then the other, moving over just a bit and then plunking herself down again in the snow. She repeated her actions, creating another angel beside the first one. She got up and gazed at her creation. The wing of Henry's angel intertwined with hers. "Oh Henry, if only you were here."

She snapped off a twig from a nearby shrub and using it as a pencil, she drew a heart with an arrow going through it in the space between the angels. Into one of the wings she carefully carved a J and into the wing of the other angel she inscribed an H. A tear dropped onto her mitten and froze in the knitted wool. She believed so strongly in her angel and yet at times it seemed so distant.

"Is it childish to think that Henry still loves me?" she whispered into the howling wind. "And even if he did, what could our angels do...?"

Within minutes the sculptures she had so carefully created in the snow were filling in with the swirling snow. Soon the heartfelt image before her that gave her a moment of solace would be gone and just a memory like all the rest.

Jenny turned to see if the Angel of Thanksgiving was visible. It was buried in two feet of snow and its basket was filled with a huge puff of snow piled high. Along with a sudden gust of wind a stream of what looked like flaming red snow swished by Jenny's head and began to circle above the Angel of Thanksgiving.

As the colourful stream began slow and hover above the snow covered angel's basket, Jenny was shocked to see that the swirl was really butterflies. They were the same colourful butterflies that she saw as a child flitting above her as she lay in bed before she drifted off to sleep. She recalled the night her father saw them too and told her that the butterflies were angels, dancing and singing to her. Jenny felt the presence of her father now as she did then, and warmth spread through her.

She gazed at the Angel of Thanksgiving, standing frozen in the snow yet seemingly aglow by the light of the colourful butterflies. The image before her was all so amazing and unbelievable, and yet it was exactly as it should be. Jenny knew she was witnessing a miracle. Her father's presence strengthened as she watched in awe. Drawn to the image before her, Jenny began to move closer to the statue.

Suddenly, the dazzling swarm of butterflies slowed still further and entered the snow above the basket. As the snow melted, the flowers she placed there last fall began to come to life as if blooming for the first time before her eyes. First it was the red poppies, followed by the yellow daisies and then the candytuft, the bellflower and finally the geraniums.

She trudged over to the angel and was astonished to see the bouquet she had placed there last fall, looking as fresh and vibrant as the day she put it there. Tears ran down her cheeks and began to freeze. Her eyelids began to stick together as she struggled to see the miracle before her. The sight made her spirits soar. A surge of pure exhilaration filled her being.

Once inside the kitchen, she made herself some hot chocolate and got a vase to put the flowers in. She set it on the wide window ledge beside the patio doors. She loved the way the soft winter light caught the peaceful nature of flowers. If only she could freeze the image before her. A camera could do it, but Jenny thought it needed the skill and eye of a painter to catch the inherent beauty of flowers. She thought of Henry once more.

Yes, he could capture the essence she was feeling. He would know how to paint nature and transmit it to others. Look how he captured the prairies and the light of the sunset in the painting he did for Spencer and his wife. They were both so moved by what Henry had painted; she must see that landscape.

Jenny sat down and sipped her hot chocolate, enthralled by the miracle bouquet before her. The depression she had been slipping into earlier had passed. How could anyone not be filled with joy over such a beautiful sight? A soft echo of thanks to her angel and to the spirit of her father bounced softly off the kitchen walls as Jenny was once again filled with the hope and wonder of what the future might bring.

CHAPTER FIFTY-THREE

HOLDING HIS EMOTIONS in check was not one of Henry's strong points. Panic swept through his body as if his guts were being attacked by a swarm of wasps. He ran down the hall and woke Jeremy and then Allison.

"Mom's awfully sick. I have to take her to emergency."

"What's wrong?" asked Jeremy, groggily rubbing his eyes.

Allison was more alert. She ran into the bedroom to see her mom. The two men heard her cry, "Mom, are you okay?"

"Jeremy, we may have to carry mom to the car. I could call the ambulance, but we'll make better time if we take her in. When I leave you're in charge. You'll have to wake up on time and get Lauren and Justin ready for school if I'm not back. I'll make certain Allison gives you a hand."

Henry led Jeremy to the bed and gently rolled the covers down except for the top sheet, which he wrapped around Julean.

"Come on, sweetheart, can you sit up? Jeremy and I will help you to the car."

"What's wrong with Mom, Dad?" Allison squealed.

"She'll be fine. Come. Hold the sheet up behind her so she doesn't trip."

Henry and his son slowly lifted Julean to her feet. It took forever to get her down the stairs and into the garage. Allison ran ahead and opened the doors.

"Open the tailgate, Allison."

Jeremy and Henry sat Julean in the back and gently laid her down. Next, Henry crawled into the back and pulled on the sheet as Jeremy raised her legs.

"Allison, run upstairs and bring down another blanket."

"Ooooh, it's so cold," groaned Julean, her jaws chattering and body quaking.

"Allison's getting you another blanket, honey."

Henry suddenly realized he still had on his pajamas and sent Jeremy inside for his trousers and sweater from beside the bed. Allison returned with a blanket with Jeremy close behind with his clothes. Henry laid the extra blanket over Julean then slipped his pants and sweater over his pajamas, positioned himself in the driver's seat and backed out of the garage.

"I'll call you from the hospital. Get the kids ready for school in the morning." Henry waved his hand out the open window and sped off.

An ambulance was loading a stretcher as Henry pulled up in front of the emergency entrance at the Pasqua Hospital. He would have liked to have taken her to the General, but this one was closer.

Henry rolled down the window and called out to the ambulance attendants for help.

As soon as Julean was transferred to the stretcher, Henry pushed it through the front doors. The waiting room was packed. The attendants followed Henry to the front desk where he addressed the nurse.

"Excuse me, my wife is awfully sick, could a doctor please have a look at her?"

"May I see your Group Medical card?"

"Yes, could you please admit her and I will give you all that information after."

The nurse studied Henry for a moment. Father Engelmann and Julean had always said that he wore his emotions on his sleeve. He hoped that was the case this time and that the nurse would notice. She slipped out from behind the counter and looked at Julean. She had her hand over her eyes shielding them from the light and was groaning.

"She has a high fever, headache and she seems frightened by light. The lady at the emergency call centre asked if anyone in the family had had meningitis when I described my wife's symptoms."

Just then Julean rolled over and threatened to vomit, but she gagged instead and had difficulty breathing.

The nurse looked at the attendants. "Bring her in through that door and follow me. You better stay here. I'll need some information from you about your wife when I return."

Henry bent over and kissed Julean's cheek, tears sitting on the edge of his eyelashes, beginning to spill. "It will be okay, honey, I love you."

Henry walked behind the attendants, rubbing Julean's shoulder until they reached the double doors. His last vision of Julean before the doors swished shut was of her shuddering body being wheeled further and further away from him.

AFTER WAITING NEARLY three hours in the emergency waiting room, a nurse informed Henry that his wife was in the intensive care unit. Several nurses bustled about the nurse's station when he approached the counter.

"Can you tell me what room Mrs. Pederson is in?" Henry asked wearily.

"Are you Mr. Pederson?" asked a doctor at the other end of the counter.

"Yes, I am."

"I'm Doctor Filmore." He came over and shook Henry's hand. The doctor looked down on his charts and then at Henry. "Your wife is seriously ill. We believe she has meningitis, but we're not sure which kind. We're certain it's bacterial in nature judging from the symptoms and its rapid onset. We did a CT scan and spinal tap, we're just waiting for the results. That will confirm the presence of meningitis and also the type. We took X-rays, and there was no sign of pneumonia or fluid in her lungs which is encouraging. We've started her on antibiotics just in case."

Henry gazed intently at the doctor. The information he was

hearing overwhelmed him. His Julean was sick with some sort of disease. It wasn't just a severe case of the flu. His legs began to buckle.

"Are you okay, Mr. Pederson?" The doctor took hold of his arm. "Nurse, bring that chair here, please."

Henry collapsed in the chair seconds after it arrived behind him. The doctor studied him for a moment and then asked, "Do you have children, Mr. Pederson?"

Henry nodded. "Four."

"They will have to come in immediately and get vaccinated, so will you."

A daze settled over Henry. This couldn't be happening. Just days ago they were on a second honeymoon in Minot, so happy and everything so wonderful...

"I... I don't understand, doctor. What is meningitis?"

"Meningitis is an inflammation of the meninges, the layer of tissue that surrounds the brain and the spinal cord. It's the result of an infection occurring in the cerebrospinal fluid surrounding these membranes."

Henry stared at the doctor...

"I'm sorry. Basically, the fluid that surrounds the brain is infected by a bacteria—"

"How... how serious is it? Can she die?"

Dr. Filmore nodded. "I don't wish to alarm you, Mr. Pederson, but the disease can cause death. Bacterial meningitis is fatal for one in ten people who get it. Even with treatment, up to one in five survivors will be left with severe handicaps such as deafness or brain injury."

The doctor's words hit Henry like a truck. His world closed in and began to crush him, just like when Jenny had left.

"But she can get well, right? There is a chance, isn't there?"

Once again the doctor studied him. "Yes, she can get well. Later this morning we will know for certain that it is meningitis and whether it's bacterial rather than viral. If it is bacterial and we know the type we can administer the appropriate treatment. And as I mentioned, we have already started antibiotics to reduce the risk of other complications."

Rushes of worry, anxiety, what to tell the children... his wife... their life... Henry placed a hand on the nurse's desk to steady himself.

"Are you okay, Mr. Pederson?"

"Can the children see their mother?"

"Yes, they will need a shot and be required to wear a mask and gown. Do any of your children show signs of fever or—"

Henry shook his head. "So far none show any symptoms."

"That's good. You will need to bring them in for vaccination as soon as possible. Are you or any of the children allergic to penicillin?"

"No. I've already told that to the nurse at admissions, as well."

"I will instruct the nurse to give you a shot straight away."

HENRY CALLED THE children and informed them that their mother had an infectious disease and would be in the hospital for a while. The possible fatal part of the illness he kept to himself. He also said they would have to be vaccinated as soon as possible so they didn't catch what their mother had. Henry instructed Jeremy to keep the two younger children at home until they had a chance to be examined and have their vaccination.

Henry was given a shot and instructed not to kiss his wife and to make certain he washed his hands when his visit was over. The lights were dim when Henry walked into the quiet hospital room. He was not prepared for what he saw. An endless spiderweb of tubes and wires were attached to his wife, feeding her fluids, administering antibiotics, monitoring her blood pressure, temperature, and pulse – all signs that his wife was in serious trouble.

Julean's eyes were closed as he approached the bed. She appeared peaceful. He didn't want to wake her, but he just had to hear her voice, look into her eyes.

"Honey, are you awake?"

Julean stirred, the peaceful repose turned into an expression of discomfort.

"It's okay. Rest if you must. I'll wait. I'm here."

Julean stirred again, and opened her eyes, squinting. She searched the room, orienting herself. Finally, her eyes rested on him.

"Hi, honey," she whispered.

He wanted to hold and kiss her so much.

"How are you doing, Julean?" His eyes misted, his voice caught and he couldn't say any more.

"I feel so tired… and that headache, I wish it would go away."

Henry wondered if she knew of her disease. Should he ask? Should he tell her?

"They took so many tests," Julean said almost inaudibly. "I heard them say I may have meningitis. I hope it's just the virus."

Julean was a nurse and would understand the implications of a bacterial infection. Henry didn't really understand the difference between a viral or bacterial infection. The doctor had told him they suspected bacterial, but Henry didn't want to upset her, so he kept that to himself.

"Yeah, they told me, too. I think they're hopeful it's not bacterial."

Julean's face however didn't reflect that optimism.

Henry hesitated and then took Julean's hand, he bent over and kissed her forehead through the mask. He reached up, pulled the mask down and tenderly kissed his wife's forehead again.

"I love you honey, everything will be fine."

Julean nodded and tried to smile before her eyelids lowered again.

"I'm so tired. How are the children? Did they get to school today?"

"Yes, Jeremy and Allison got Justin and Lauren ready to go on the bus, but I told them to stay home. I'll pick them up later and bring them to be examined and get vaccinated."

Julean was silent for awhile and then murmured, "That's good."

Julean drifted off. Henry didn't know what to say or do. The love of his life lay there so ill and he felt helpless. He did the only thing he knew how…

"Dear Jesus," he whispered. "Help Julean. Please make her well. Please."

He reached for the chair off to the side, pulled it over and sat down. Exhaustion was at his doorstep, he wasn't sure how long he could go on. He hung his head and wept.

Julean squeezed his hand. "It will be fine, dear. Everything works out to God's plan... and Hank please bring my rosary from home..."

HENRY KNEW HE had to go home, check on the kids and change his clothes. He was torn, not wanting to leave his ailing wife for a moment. He asked the nurse checking on Julean if a cot could be brought into the room so he could stay around the clock. She didn't think that would be a problem.

Julean didn't wake up for the next hour while Henry sat there. His gaze never left her face or her chest. He wanted to see signs of her breathing and trusted her movements more than the monitors. When she didn't respond to his soft calling, Henry decided to go home and return as soon as he could.

At the nurse's desk, he phoned his mother and asked if she would come out to the farm and look after things. That was a given. Henry also asked her to call Father Engelmann to let him know Julean was in the hospital and in need of prayers.

When Henry and his mom walked into the home, one glance relayed that the daily household routines had broken down. Dirty dishes were piled in the sink in addition to the morning cereal bowls, lunch plates and cutlery that were left on the table, and the floors needed vacuuming. Mary immediately went to the sink and started sorting out the dishes. The TV blared in the family room.

Henry didn't know what to tell the kids. He didn't want to create unnecessary alarm and yet if it was life threatening he'd want them to see their mom and know what was happening. Hopefully the antibiotics and good hospital care would do the job and their mother would be home in a few days.

Jeremy was watching TV when Henry walked into the room.

"Oh, hi Dad." He turned the volume down with the remote. "So, how's Mom?"

"Not too good. She was sleeping when I left. Where are the kids?"

Jeremy checked his watch. "They all went over to Bonnie's place. I told Allison I would pick them up at four. I'll get them in a half hour or so."

"Well, Grandma is here to make the meals and so on until mom gets back home. Please help her out as much as possible. I'm going back to the hospital to stay with Mom. Maybe come out to the kitchen and help with the dishes. I have to phone Julean's parents and let them know what's going on."

"Sure, Dad." Jeremy clicked off the TV.

"I'll go with you to pick up the kids. Maybe Justin and Lauren can come with me to the hospital for their shot. You and Allison can follow and then you can bring them all back home in your car."

Just as Henry was about to leave the phone rang. It startled him. He hoped it wasn't the hospital calling with bad news… He went to the phone and hesitatingly picked it up on its third ring…

"Hello."

"Hey Hank old buddy, how ya doing?"

Henry let out a sigh of relief. "Oh, hi Eddy. I'm not doing so hot. Julean is very sick and in the hospital."

"Geez, that's not good. What's wrong with her?"

"Doctors aren't sure yet. They think she's got meningitis… some kind of a disease that attacks the brain."

There was a moment of silence and then Eddy said, "That's tough man, hope things work out okay."

Henry didn't respond and Eddy filled in the growing silence, "Yeah, well, I was calling to see if we could shoot a game of pool on Saturday but I guess we'll just put that on hold."

"Yeah, Eddy… listen I better go, I want to get back to the hospital—"

"Which one is she in?"

"The Pasqua Hospital…"

"That's too bad, I was just going up to the General Hospital, a buddy of mine was in an accident and I'm going up to see him… maybe I'll swing over there to see Julean tomorrow if I can get away. Give my best to the missus."

"Yeah, sure Eddy. See ya."

When Henry walked into Julean's room at eight-fifteen, he noticed two changes: a cot had been brought in, and Julean now had tubes in her nose supplying additional oxygen. Henry glanced at the heart monitor as he drew near to his sleeping wife. He pulled a chair to the bedside and was about to sit down when the nurse walked in.

"Good evening, Mr. Pederson."

"How is she doing?"

"She has been sleeping a lot. Dr. Filmore has changed some of the antibiotics since this morning."

"Do they know the results of the tests? Has Julean got meningitis?"

The nurse gazed at Henry. "Yes, she does."

"Is it that bacterial kind?"

"You will have to speak to the doctor and he is gone for the day, however Dr. Crossly, I believe he is your family doctor..."

Henry nodded.

"...was in and checked on your wife and so did Dr. Carter. I believe that is your wife's father?"

Henry nodded again. He could phone either of them, they probably know everything by now. Exhaustion was creeping in on him so strongly that he didn't want anymore input from anyone. He just wanted to sit quietly with his wife.

Before he sat down Henry retrieved Julean's rosary from his pocket. He reached over to the other side of Julean and slipped the rosary into her right hand positioning her forefinger and thumb around the first bead of the first decade. It was a sight he had seen so many times during their marriage.

Henry straightened, pulled the chair beside him closer and sat down. Reaching over, he covered her left hand with his and curled his fingers underneath. She didn't stir or move. He bowed his head and began to pray.

"Mr. Pederson, perhaps you want to lie down on the cot."

He had fallen asleep. It was eleven-thirty. He looked up at the nurse and nodded.

"Yes, I think I will do that. Did Julean wake up at all?"

"No, she has been sleeping the whole time."

When the nurse left, Henry pushed the cot closer to Julean's bed and lay down. He snuck his hand through and past the tubes and under the sheet until he found her arm. He gently laid his hand on her skin and almost immediately drifted back into a deep sleep. Neither the constant in and out of the nurses nor the commotion around three-thirty in the morning roused him.

"How is Julean doing?" Henry asked groggily, as he gazed at a nurse adjusting Julean's IV.

"She was awake a half hour ago and instructed us to let you sleep. We had a little problem earlier this morning, but the doctor will explain that to you. He wants to speak with you in the conference room. The nurse at the station will direct you to where it is."

Henry was more awake now and walked around the bed and looked down at Julean. She looked so peaceful; he couldn't imagine the bacterial bugs in her system working hard to destroy her.

"Better put your mask on, Mr. Pederson. I'll let the desk know you will be out shortly to see the doctor."

Henry bent over and kissed Julean on the forehead. He wanted so much to kiss her sweet lips. Julean looked at rest.

Surely she will be all right. Surely the doctor will have good news for me. He patted her hand, turned and left.

He waited over an hour and half before Dr. Filmore came into the room. He was sorry he wasted all that time when he could have been with his wife.

"Sorry to keep you waiting. We had another emergency."

Henry immediately made a mental shift which included forgiving the doctor for his tardiness. It dawned on him there were other problems in the world beside his. The doctor sat at the end of the table and took a deep breath. Henry could see the man was tired and the day was just beginning.

"Well," he started out, prolonging the news for as long as he could. "We got the results back and your wife does have meningitis."

Henry couldn't wait. "Is it the bacterial kind?"

The doctor's nod instantly dashed Henry's hope for good news.

"Yes, it is as we suspected. Because of the type we changed the antibiotics yesterday. Since many bacteria have become resistant to penicillin, we've found combinations of different antibiotics to work better. We're also considering steroids to decrease the severity of the disease in lieu of what happened last night."

"What happened?" He had been there the entire time, nothing happened.

"Around three-thirty a.m. your wife had a seizure. We suspect that the blood vessels in her brain are inflamed, preventing enough oxygen from getting to the brain. That is why she is so drowsy, unresponsive and sleeping so much. She could fall into a coma at any time and perhaps she may already be in one."

Henry couldn't believe what he was hearing. It sounded like some movie or soap opera. Did these things actually happen in real life?

"I didn't realize your wife's father was also a doctor. I met with him late yesterday. He wants to have a specialist from Toronto fly in to examine your wife and perhaps prescribe more aggressive treatment."

Henry shook his head not knowing what to say.

"We are concerned how your wife may have contracted the bacteria. Was she in very crowded conditions prior to her being admitted? Her family doctor reports no pneumonia or serious infections."

"We were on holidays in Minot last weekend and on the way home we came across a car accident with an injured man. I had to break the driver's side window to unlock the door and get him out. After we dragged him out of his car, Julean cut her hand on the broken window. We got him into our car to take him to the hospital. On the way, Julean had to perform CPR. A doctor from the hospital called and told her that the man didn't have AIDS so we assumed everything was all right."

"Where is that man now?"

"We took him to the emergency at General Hospital on Sunday evening."

"Do you know his name?"

"No. But he should still be there. We gave a report to the hospital and the police. Do you think that is how Julean might have gotten the disease?"

Dr. Filmore tilted his head to the side and tightened his lips. "It's quite possible. We will check it out immediately."

Henry struggled to pull his mind away from that eventful night. It could have all happened then, but with his wife on the doorstep to death he had to turn his attention to his family and everything else.

"Can the children come in and see their mother? And, heaven forbid, should Father give her the last rites?"

The doctor nodded. "Yes, I would advise you to do all of that. She may take a turn for the better, but right now... I just don't know."

CHAPTER FIFTY-FOUR

PERSPIRATION SOAKED HIS arm pits as he phoned home.

"Hello, Mom? Are the kids still at home?"

"Jeremy is just leaving and the other three went on the bus over an hour ago. Why, what's wrong?" Mary could tell when her son was anxious.

"I just met with the doctor and it doesn't sound good. Julean is awfully ill and could… She could die, Mom!"

"Now, Henry, things have a way of working out. I called Father last night and he said Mass for Julean this morning. He said he would be up later on."

"The doctor says that maybe she should be given last rites."

"I will call Father and let him know. Do you want all of us to come in?"

"Yes. Ask Jeremy to pick up the kids at Lumsden. Perhaps go with him and then bring them to the hospital. I'll pray she is awake when they come so at least they can speak with her."

"Trust in Jesus, Henry, your faith needs to be strong now. We'll be there in about an hour. Is Julean still in the intensive care ward?"

"Yes. I'll tell the nurses at the counter to take all of you to the conference room. They can come and get me. What should I tell the kids, Mom?"

His mother didn't answer. "We'll see you in an hour, son."

Henry rushed back to see Julean. He passed a nurse coming out of her room when he entered. No one else was in there, much to his relief. He quickly made his way to her side and took her hand. His eyes misted as a rush of worry, concern, dread and anxiety swept through him. His hand had tightened on hers so he quickly loosened his grip and gently stroked her hand.

"Honey, the kids are coming up to see you. If you can hear me try to be awake for them. Honey, I love you so much, please get better."

A light rap sounded on the door and Julean's mom and sister entered.

"Hi, Henry. How is Julean doing?"

Henry lowered his head and shook it.

Joyce ran over to Julean and took her hand. "It's me, Julean. I came home to see you. Can you hear me?"

When Julean didn't respond Joyce began to cry. "Mom, she can't hear me. Can't we do anything? Call Dad."

Vera slid her comforting arm off Henry and drew near to her daughter.

"She is very ill, Joyce. The doctors are doing everything they can." She turned to Henry. "Has she been awake this morning?"

"The nurse told me she was for a half hour before I woke up, which would have been around six-thirty, but since then she has been asleep the entire time. I think the medication is making her sleep, as well."

Vera turned back toward her sleeping daughter. Henry stepped off to the side so he could see Julean's face past the two women. He stared intently, watching for an eyelash to twitch, an eyelid to flutter, any sign that his dear sweet wife was reviving, getting better, ready to come home.

A nurse popped her head in the door, "Mr. Pederson, your family is here. They are waiting for you in the conference room."

"Okay, thank you. Well, Vera, I better go and prepare them. I'm glad you were able to come, Joyce. Julean will be so happy to see you when she awakens."

Joyce didn't turn or answer Henry through her sobs.

"We'll only need another fifteen minutes or so. We'll be gone when you bring the children in. Do they know how serious this is?"

Henry shook his head and left.

HENRY FOUND HIS mother and the four children sitting around the large table. Lauren and Justin were poking each other. Jeremy and Allison, being more aware of their mother's illness, stared at their father, waiting for him to speak.

"Did you find a parking space okay, Jeremy?" Henry said, stalling.

"Boy, is it hard finding a space around here. We drove around the block three times. Grandma suggested we park in the public parking lot. She said she is going to pay for it."

Henry looked at his mother. "Thanks, Mom. How are you doing? The kids behaving themselves?"

"Oh yes, they are just fine. Very well behaved and I'm enjoying their company so much. Since Bill passed away it's too quiet at home."

"Well, kids, Mom is very sick. The disease she has affects her brain and she has been sleeping quite a bit. I haven't been able to talk to her all morning and I'm not sure if she will wake up when you come in."

"She's going to come home, isn't she Dad?" asked Allison.

"I'm hoping she will, Allison, but I want you all to know she is very sick. I know your mom wants to come home so much, but she has to get well. And the doctors are doing everything they can."

"What kind of a disease has she got and how did she get it?" asked Jeremy.

"It's called meningitis. We are not sure, it may have been the night we were driving home from Minot and mom gave that man mouth-to-mouth resuscitation. He may have been a carrier of that disease."

"Why did Mom have to do that?"

"Well, Allison, your mom is a nurse and cares for others. She saved his life."

"But she may now lose hers." Jeremy blurted out.

"That's not fair, Dad. God shouldn't punish someone for doing good," Allison continued.

Henry didn't know how to respond. By now, Lauren and Justin had stopped their poking and sat still and quiet. They likely still didn't understand the situation completely, but Henry knew they understood that their mother was sick.

"God isn't punishing your mom, Allison," said Mary. "He loves her as much as we do. Sickness is just part of the world we live in."

"But, He is not going to let her die, is He?"

Lauren's eyes widened. "Is Mommy going to die, Daddy?"

"I'm not sure honey, I sure hope she doesn't. The doctors are doing everything they can."

"When is Mommy coming home?" Justin piped in, concern growing on his face.

Henry got up and walked over to his six-year-old son. He pulled back an empty chair and sat facing both Justin and Lauren. "Remember when Grandpa got sick and he had to go to the hospital? We all wanted him to come home, but his heart just gave out and he went up to Jesus. He is looking down on us right now like an angel."

"I don't want Mom to die like Grandpa!" exclaimed Allison. "God has enough people in heaven. We need Mom at home."

Things were getting out of hand and Henry realized a discussion of death at this point might be premature. "Listen, everyone. I don't know what is going to happen. I'm trying to prepare you for the possibility of Mom getting sicker, but maybe we should deal with that if it comes. For now, let's go in and see Mom and tell her how much we love her."

Henry got up and hugged Lauren and Justin, then Allison. The younger ones looked after, he turned and patted Jeremy's shoulder.

"Okay, let's go."

The nurses helped the kids put on their masks and instructed them not to kiss their mother. "We don't want anyone else to get her sickness, do we?" said the senior nurse with a smile.

"Did Julean wake up while I was gone?"

The nurse shook her head, her expression clearly telling him that she wished Julean had.

When Henry and his family walked into the room, they were surprised to see Father Engelmann there. He was wearing his vestment collar and just finishing giving Julean the last rites.

"What a nice surprise to see you here, Father."

"What are you doing?" asked Allison.

"Oh, I was just giving your mom a special blessing and praying that she gets healed soon."

"Why is it so dark in here?" asked Lauren, as they all surrounded their mother's bed.

"The light bothers her," said Henry.

"Can she hear us?" asked Jeremy

"Yes, I think she can—"

"Why doesn't she answer or wake up then?" Allison cried.

"A part of her brain wants to, but the other part is too weak to do it. We're praying for that part to get well," offered Father.

Justin approached his mom and grabbed her hand.

"Mom," he whispered. "Mom, wake up." He moved her hand. "Come on, Mommy. Wake up."

When she didn't, Justin started to cry and then the entire family did. Everyone looked at her eyes waiting for her to open them. Jeremy discretely touched his mom's foot at the end of the bed and ever so slightly started to move it back and forth. Henry noted his eldest son's lips repeat Justin's words.

"Well, children, your mom is having a nice rest. The best thing we can do for her is to say a prayer to Jesus." Father wiggled his way in between Lauren and Allison and took their hands, then asked everyone else to join hands with them. "Dear Jesus, if it is Your will, we pray that you heal Julean and make her well and whole. The children need and want their mother to come home. Henry needs and wants his wife by his side. They love her, as all of us do. In Your infinite mercy and goodness we ask You to heal our loved one. This we ask in Your name, Amen."

"Will she wake up now, Grandpa?" asked Justin, looking up at Father.

"Well, she just might. Why don't we sing her a song? Come on everyone... His peace is flowing like a river, flowing out of you and me. His peace is flowing like a river, setting all the captives

free... Come on, everyone now. His love is flowing like a river..."
Softly, Mary joined in, then Henry. The children stumbled in here and there.

"His healing is flowing like a river, flowing out of you and me. His healing is flowing like a river, setting all the captives free. What is another verse we can sing?"

This time Henry began, "His joy is flowing like a river, flowing out of you and me. His joy is flowing like a river, setting all the captives free."

Then Allison softly began, "Our hearts are flowing to our mother, flowing out of you and me. Our hearts are flowing to our mom making her as well as she can be."

"Oh, Allison, that was beautiful." Father put his arm around her.

"That was very nice," echoed Mary and Henry.

"Well, kids, maybe we should say good-bye to Mom for today. Why don't you all go to Grandma's place for lunch? I will phone you later. If Mom wakes up I will call you right away. If not, you can go back to the farm and perhaps come in again tomorrow. If you want to kiss Mom on the forehead, go ahead."

One by one they went to Julean's side and kissed her. It pained Henry to see Jeremy holding back his tears, trying to be tough. After his son kissed her goodbye, Henry gave him a big hug. There was no need for words. Allison and Lauren leaned over their mom and whispered that they loved her and wanted her to come home. When it was Justin's turn, he once again shook his mother's hand. "Wake up, Mom. Say good-bye."

Henry picked him up into his arms and leaned Justin forward over his sleeping mother.

"Give Mommy a kiss, son, hopefully tomorrow she will be awake."

CHAPTER FIFTY-FIVE

JENNY DECIDED TO take a cab to her mother's place. On cold mid-February days like this, her convertible wasn't the warmest place to be, even with a highly efficient heater.

"Hi, Mom," Jenny called, as she entered the apartment and removed her winter apparel. "Oh, I can hardly wait for spring to get out into the back yard. Mind you I am discovering the joys of winter out there, too. The other day I went out in a blizzard and made angels in the snow."

"Oh, Jenny, you've always been one to do spontaneous things."

"It was the strangest... or rather the most wonderful thing, Mom. When I looked in the Angel of Thanksgiving's basket, it still carried the bouquet I put in there last fall, as fresh as the day I placed them there!"

Jenny didn't mention the butterflies as her mother didn't believe they were angels like her dad did.

"What? How can that be? It's the dead of winter. Either you have a little wildflower fairy who's placing fresh cut flowers in that basket every morning, or I'd say it's a miracle."

"Well, I think it's a miracle. It has something to do with Daddy. It's his statue and we've both felt his presence there so strongly."

"That's right, I do remember that other time I was at the estate and you told me the fresh looking bouquet that was in the basket hadn't been watered for days... I did feel a strong presence of Ted then..."

"The statue also makes me feel a close connection with my guardian angel... As if she is constantly looking out for me. I hope she answers the prayers I have sent her over all the years."

"And, what prayers are those?"

Jenny didn't know if she should get into the Henry and Camilla thing. "Oh, it's just something special between me and my angel, Mom. Perhaps someday I will share it with you. Daddy knows for sure!"

Edith looked at her daughter, reflecting on what she had just said. Ted had thought angels were involved with Jenny, too, especially regarding those letters that he had pleaded be delivered on his death bed. She still dreamt about those last moments of her husband's life. Perhaps that explained the unusual bright light around the chest in the closet which held Jenny's letter from Henry. Maybe Jenny was right. Maybe her guardian angel was taking special interest in her. Flowers lasting for a long time, surviving bitterly cold winters... Letters emitting a warmth and aura... Ted's angel statue commission showing up after all these years... *What did it all mean?*

"Are you okay, Mom?"

"I'm sorry, honey, I was just thinking of your backyard. It really is something else. See, that was another reason I moved. If ever I miss my estate and the grounds, I can always zip over to yours and get my fix."

Jenny smiled. Today was not a day to bring up the topic of her contemplating moving. She went over and kissed her mom's cheek.

"So, how are you feeling, Mom?"

"If it wasn't for this darn arthritis, I would be on top of the world. It's my left hand and wrist that is just so painful."

"Can't the doctor prescribe something for you?"

"Well, he did mention a new medication that has come out. But, he would like to see the reaction of the drug on two of his other patients first before using me as a guinea pig."

"Well, that's encouraging." Looking out the large living room window, Jenny exclaimed, "What an incredible view. The

snowflakes soften the cityscape. Looks like a fairyland out there."
Jenny sat in a chair across from Edith.

"How are the men in your life doing, honey?"

A rush of heat flooded Jenny's cheeks. Should she share with
her mom how things really were? She didn't want to worry her
mother, and yet their conversations were usually so superficial,
this was a good opportunity to add some depth to their exchanges.

"To be honest, Mom, things could be better. As you know, James
is hardly at home and stays at his condo most days and, as far as
Jimmy is concerned, he hasn't returned my calls since last fall."

"Why on earth not?"

Jenny hesitated and then forged ahead. "It has to do with
Patrick. You remember the store owner of the bookstore I used to
frequent?"

"Oh, yes. You were having casual dates with him."

"Yes, that's right. They weren't really dates… more like little
chats you would have with a friend."

"Did he see it that way?"

"That's the problem, Mom." Jenny was surprised by her mother's instinct. "Once I discovered that Patrick was married, I cut off
the relationship. Of course, he let it be revealed that his feelings for
me were more than platonic. He leaned in to kiss me, but I turned
my cheek and at that precise moment, Jimmy walked into the store
and saw him holding me and kissing my cheek."

"Oh my. So, what happened?" Her mother shuffled in her chair
and sat up.

"Well, I won't repeat what he called me, but since that day he
hasn't come home, called or answered any of my messages."

"That's not very good, Jenny. Is there anything I can do? Would
you like me talk to him?"

"That might be a good idea. I was going to write him and
explain the situation, but if James got a hold of it… Well, there is
no telling what might happen."

"Leave it up to me, Jenny, perhaps I can smooth things over."

THE FOLLOWING MONDAY at school Jenny spoke to Spencer about
the painting he had purchased from Henry.

"You know, Spence, I know it's been a couple of years since you mentioned that painting Henry Pederson did for you, but I would just love to see it. My curiosity has got the best of me."

"Sure, Jen. We are free Wednesday night or anytime Saturday would be fine."

"Let's make it Saturday. I think I know where you live, getting there during the day is better for me. Say shortly after one?"

"Sounds great. We'll have a private viewing for you then!"

The weather announcer issued a warning, advising against travel only if absolutely necessary. The roads were treacherous and visibility poor. If Jenny had not been anxiously awaiting this all week, she would have used her better sense and rescheduled the appointment. However, she was willing to risk anything to see the painting her colleague had purchased from the man of her dreams.

Several times during the week she had wished she had taken Spencer's offer to come on Wednesday. All day Friday and Saturday morning had crawled by until Jenny finally skidded to a stop in front of Spencer's place.

Jenny's heart raced as she rang the doorbell.

"Hi, Jen," said Spencer as he opened the door wide.

"Who's that, Daddy?" a blonde little girl asked as she wrapped her arms around her father's leg.

"This is a friend of mine from school. Jenny this is my daughter, Jessica."

"Oh, what a lovely name. If I ever have another daughter, that name would be at the top of the list." Jenny poked her finger into her tummy. Jessica laughed.

As Jenny stood, Spencer's wife came into the foyer. Spencer introduced Jenny, and then took her on a tour of several paintings they had purchased over the years. Jenny didn't really pay much attention to his descriptions. The only painting she was interested in was Henry's.

"I have to admit, Jenny, Henry Pederson's painting is our favourite. Come, it is in a place of honour over our chesterfield in the living room. I bought a light at his suggestion to place over it. And he was right. It's amazing how that brings out all the colours that would normally be lost in regular, dim light."

Jenny thought her heart would bounce out of her chest it was beating so hard. As soon as she entered the living room, she froze. The warmth and light exuding from the painting struck her heart like lightning. Here was a work of art unlike any she had ever seen, created by the hand of her one and only love. Seeing it carried more impact to her than if she were viewing the world's most famous painting in the Louvre.

Slowly she walked over to the painting. Halfway there she stopped, again noticing more detail. There was a truck leaving the farm yard with its headlights on, illuminating the path, traveling to the distant town. But the sunset... Yes, he so often spoke of his love of the prairie sky and how much he would miss them should he ever move.

"The sunset is spectacular, Spencer." Jenny could no longer hold all that beauty and excitement inside. "And you are right, look how the sun dances off the tips of the field. I can feel the field swaying in the gentle breeze."

Jenny moved still closer and tears gathered on her eyelashes. She struggled to hold them back, but she was just too overcome with emotion. She reached out her hand and gently touched the brush strokes. She could feel Henry's touch, his strength, his creativity... His love.

"Are you okay, Jenny?"

"I'm sorry, what did you say...?"

Spencer walked over and took her arm. "You're so taken by that painting, Jenny. If we didn't love it so much, we'd consider selling it to you."

Jenny chuckled nervously, suddenly becoming aware of the situation. "I would never take that away from you. It would be like trying to take the sunset away." Jenny wiped the tears from her eyes. "Oh, this is embarrassing. I knew Henry when I was just starting Grade 9 and we hung out together for the summer before we moved to Ottawa."

"Well, that must have been one romantic summer," observed Spencer's wife.

Jenny blushed. "Yes, it was nice...very nice. I remember us

walking home together after a rain storm one afternoon and just the way he described the trees, the colour of the grass and the leaves… I just knew he would be a successful artist someday."

"I'm sure you could buy one of his works if you got in contact with him, Jen."

"Yes, I may consider that. Well, I don't want to use up any more of your day off, Spence, so I will be heading back."

"Before you go, Jen, you may want to read the commentary he wrote on the back. It's such a beautiful description of the sunset. In fact your comment was so expressive, it reminded me of what Henry wrote and the emotion he must have felt, too."

"Well, if it's not too much trouble I would love to read it."

Spencer struggled to remove his daughter from his leg, then knelt on the chesterfield and carefully lifted the painting off its hook. He brought it over to Jenny and turned it over. He took out a folded paper from a sleeve which was attached to the back.

"Here is Henry's biography, Jen. If you want, you can take it with you and return it to me on Monday at school. It gives his address and phone number if you want to contact him in regards to purchasing a painting."

"That's wonderful. Spencer, thank you so much." Jenny took the folded paper.

"The note I want you to see is here." Spencer directed Jenny's attention to the writing on the upper right of the painting.

Jenny immediately recognized Henry's handwriting, how long had she waited to see it again. She leaned closer as Spencer held the painting for her. Slowly she read his words. She raised her hand and slowly touched the words as she had the brush strokes of the painting. She ran her finger over them, feeling them, savouring them. She waited so long to see his handwriting again…

'…The last rays of the sun swept across the landscape, glistening off swaths lying neatly on the rolling hills.'

She read the last sentence, but it blurred as her eyes misted again. A tear fell on the back of the painting.

"Oh, I'm so sorry, Spencer, what is wrong with me?" Jenny's mind raced trying to come up with some excuse. "I… I can see why his commentary means so much to you." Jenny quickly rubbed the wetness away, embarrassment covering her blushing face.

"Not a problem, Jen. Now we can boast that not only do we have a painting by Henry Pederson, but also a tear that his girlfriend from long ago shed for him."

They all chuckled somewhat nervously.

"Oh, Spence, this is so silly." She looked at his wife and knew from her expression that Janice saw much more than a summer romance and a prairie landscape painting.

She saw a woman still very much in love.

CHAPTER FIFTY-SIX

F OR THREE DAYS Julean slept. The doctor said she was in a
coma and that her blood vessels were so inflamed and swollen
the oxygen flowing to her brain was severely restricted. Her skin
colour confirmed that assessment; it was developing cyano-
sis, a bluish tinge caused by a lack of oxygen. The medical team
was doing everything they could to reduce the inflammation
and increase the blood pressure in the hopes of supplying more
oxygen. The bacteria teeming through Julean's bloodstream had
been resistant to all the antibiotics they had tried so far.

On the second day, Henry had the telephone company install
a telephone in Julean's room. He made further arrangements to
have his phone, his Aunt Darlene's phone and Father Engelmann's
all connected at eight-thirty each evening for a conference call. His
objective was to start a Novena like the one they had said years ago
for his father's return home. Henry never forgot, on the ninth day
their prayers had been answered and his father came home.

"All glory be to the Father and to the Son and to the Holy
Spirit."

"Amen," they all said at the end of the prayers.

"Well, this is day two of the Novena. I thought I noticed her stir
as we were saying the petition for her healing," said Henry to his
prayer partners.

"If it is His will, she will be healed," said Father Engelmann, his voice hopeful yet cautious.

"Do you want me and Jeremy to bring in the children tomorrow again, Henry?"

"Yes, Mom. I think it's important for them to see her each day. I'm noticing they seem to be more accepting of her illness and are slowly realizing just how ill their mother is. They should be prepared..."

"Well, gang, I better get going," chimed in Darlene. "I have to let out two pairs of Ron's pants by an inch or two. Too much of my good cooking, I'm afraid. Talk to you all tomorrow."

"Goodnight, Darlene," they all responded.

"You better get some sleep, too, Henry. These days are very trying. I have you all in my prayers."

"Thank you, Father, and thank you, Mom, for looking after the kids."

"It's a pleasure, Henry, no problem at all. You have a good rest, son."

After Henry hung up the phone he silently prayed at Julean's bedside. A nurse came in, checked the IV needle and level of the fluid and as she turned to leave, patted Henry's shoulder. It made him think about nurses and the work they do to look after people in need. It was the same calling Julean had to give and serve others even at the risk of endangering her own life. Even if she hadn't been a nurse, she still would have tried to save that man's life. It was just in her nature to help others.

"Angels of mercy, that's what nurses are," Henry muttered. Suddenly, images of Jenny crossing Victoria Avenue and almost being hit by a car flooded his mind. He had prayed for God to surround her with a protective shield as she had crossed the busy street. Miraculously, just before the car struck her, she was lifted out of harm's way. The image was so deeply burned into his mind; he recalled the scene now as if it were yesterday.

It was her guardian angel that saved her.

Henry reached out now, again, to God. He thanked Him for all the nurses in the world and those who were caring for his wife. Just as Jenny's guardian angel had saved her that day, he prayed that God would also send an army of angels to protect his dear wife. That Julean's guardian angel would pull her out of this terrible disease, restore her health and bring her back to him and his family.

A prayer he had not said in a long time tumbled from his lips,

Angel of God, my guardian dear,
to whom God's love commits Julean, here.
Ever this day be at her side,
to light and guard, to rule and guide.
Amen.

LATER THE NEXT day after the children left, Henry's heart ached for them. For days, they had been coming to see their mother, to talk to her, but never received a response. While the older children were able to control their sorrow and frustration, it was just too difficult for Justin. He was determined to wake his mother at all costs. At one point Henry had to restrain him from shaking the IV out of his mother's wrist.

Absently, Henry got up, crossed to the window and looked out onto the inner courtyard of the hospital. Nurses and aides on their break, as well as a few visitors, were gathered there. *How different the world is that we find ourselves in from day to day.* The people below were chatting and laughing and enjoying their drinks, while just a few floors above, others were suffering, families hurting. He contrasted the turmoil in his mind and heart to those sitting there with a sense of omnipotence.

Julean's father had told him the evening before when he came to check on his daughter that the man whose life she had saved was a carrier of meningitis. He had had pneumonia six months ago and was just getting over a severe sinus infection. His addiction to drugs had weakened his immune system to the point that doctors thought he would die several months ago. Henry wished he had. Perhaps none of this might have happened. Why did they have to stop at the accident scene or why did they even leave Weyburn in the midst of that terrible storm? *If only I would have known.*

Henry often wondered how God was able to see the past and the future at the same time. To help himself understand this power,

Henry would picture God sitting on the top corner of a tall building and looking down. From that vantage point God could easily see a car coming down the street on one side of the building and another speeding up the other side. An accident was inevitable. He could see it about to happen. If only he could have seen into the future before he and Julean had decided to take that little holiday to Minot. The past was so clear now. It was the future, and the fateful decisions they had made that came crashing down around them now.

"I'm dying, aren't I?" The words pierced the silence like a sharp knife deepening the wound in his bleeding heart. For a moment he thought he was imagining those words. He slowly turned and could barely believe his eyes. Julean was awake and staring at him with her soft brown eyes. Henry rushed to her side and took hold of her hand.

"Oh, darling, you've come back. You've been sleeping for days. How are you feeling?"

"I feel as if I am going away and I have to ask you something before I leave."

"Oh no, honey. You're back now. This is a good sign that you are getting better. If only we hadn't stopped that night, none of this would have happened. The man whose life you saved gave you this awful disease. I am so angry at him. If only we had known..."

Julean squeezed Henry's hand. "It is upsetting, honey, but that's the nature of the world we live in. Things are not always perfect or the way we would like them to be."

"I wish *he* were dead. It's just not fair that you should be suffering for his addictions and illness."

"Honey, you must forgive. Please don't harbour ill will. You know what the Lord asks of us. If you do not forgive, then He cannot forgive you. Henry, I want the best for you. Please listen to me."

Henry fell into silence. He knew she was right. How many times had Father preached that same message to him over the years?

"I'll get the nurses and the doctors and let them know you're awake."

"Just wait a moment, Henry, there is something I need you to share."

Julean smiled weakly and gazed deeply into her husband's eyes. Henry recognized that look. Julean had something on her mind that was very close to her heart.

"Tell me about Jenny."

"What?" Henry snapped alert, his eyes widened, his breath caught.

"It's okay, honey. I know there has always been another love in your life—"

"But, I've never gone out with another woman; I've always been faithful to you..."

The blood fell from Henry's face. He was sure that his complexion matched that of his critically ill wife.

Julean gazed unwaveringly into her husband's eyes, waiting for an answer. "Tell me about her, Henry, it's okay. I know a little of her. I want to know what is in your heart, though. I've always wanted to meet her; she must have been such a lovely girl for you to be so smitten by her."

Henry still could not believe his ears and yet he had always suspected she knew. For years he had held this secret within himself, harboured so much guilt for carrying the love for another in his heart, all the while married to Julean. It would have been better to share this with her when she was strong and well, but why now? She is sick and perhaps dying... He wished he had brought it up when they went to Minot like he had said he was going to, but they were having such a wonderful time...

Julean squeezed Henry's hand. "There should be no secrets between us, especially now. It's healing to bring everything out into the open, have no regrets later down the road."

She wanted to absolve him of all guilt for holding onto such feelings toward another woman. She wanted to free him. His eyes misted as he shook his head. Julean was right. There never should have been anything held back between them, but he had never been able to bring himself to tell her... until now.

"How... How do you know of Jenny? Who told you?"

"You did—"

Henry's head snapped back. "But I've never shared that with you or anyone all the while we were married."

"I knew on the day we were married and you have told me many times of her since then."

Henry crinkled his brow.

"You shared your love when your defenses were down... Your dreams revealed her to me. The night of our wedding, after we made love, I will never forget what followed. I tried to wake you, but you were making love to Jenny in your dreams."

Henry remembered that night all too well himself and the guilt he'd felt for days after for having such a dream. Henry raised his eyes and looked tenderly at her.

"I am so sorry, honey. I didn't realize you heard. That you knew..."

Julean nodded, tears sliding down her face disappearing into her auburn hair on the pillow. "I know she has blue eyes and blonde hair... and she's bubbly and spontaneous. Tell me about her. I want to know about the woman with whom I've shared my husband for all of these years."

Henry stared at Julean, realizing that keeping the truth from her now would hurt her more than revealing it. She wanted the truth and the truth would set them both free.

"Oh, honey," he whispered as he sat down, took her hand in his, and told his dear sweet wife about his first love. It was painful and yet liberating for Henry to share with Julean those memorable two months when he had met and fallen in love with the girl three doors down. He couldn't explain how knowing a person for such a short period of time could result in a love that was so long lasting. All the while he reassured his wife that it was really she who had swept him off his feet and that he loved so dearly. He just couldn't explain why his heart hung onto a memory so strongly.

"Perhaps it was because you never had closure. To this day you still don't know what happened to her or why she just left, never to write or get into contact with you again."

"Yes, that is part of it for sure." After a long, reflective moment Henry added, "I just can't explain this pain or perhaps it's a yearning inside of me for her, almost as if my heart was pierced by her and it never healed."

"Perhaps the only way it will ever heal is for you to see her again or become a part of your life."

"Oh no, Julean, I would never want to leave you for her or anybody. It's you I love with all my heart."

"Maybe my ancestors' way of having more than one wife is a good way... or, at least in this circumstance I convinced myself it might be."

"Julean, I would never want to share you with anyone. I thought I made that clear that night."

"Even back then I pursued that discussion to encourage you to talk about Jenny and to consider the possibility. Your happiness was always forefront in my heart, Hank but... I realize now I could never have shared you with another."

"Oh Julean, this is all too foolish to continue to talk about. I do feel relieved somewhat in telling you about her, but it has long been over. Why it's still in my thoughts is something that I just can't explain."

With that Henry got up, leaned over his wife, "I love you so much, honey." He slowly lowered his head to hers and kissed her long and tender.

"When I get to heaven I will pray for her or someone else like her to return to you. A man like you should marry again and not be alone."

"Oh, Julean, stop it now."

Julean smiled weakly at her husband. "Tell me Hank, *True Love* was a song you shared with Jenny ...?"

Henry slowly nodded. Unable to speak, tears filled his eyes again.

"Promise me, Hank, when you hear or sing that song you will remember me, too."

Henry could barely get the words out, "Oh Julean, I will love you for always. You will forever be my *true love*."

"And I will love you into eternity ..."

Their lips met once more and their tears of love intermingled.

CHAPTER FIFTY-SEVEN

Y OU'RE LUCKY TO be alive… It's a good thing that couple came along when they did," said the examining doctor.

John McBryne lay still on the bed, his eyes fixed on the ceiling light. This was the second doctor who had expressed his good fortune in the last two days. The previous doctor informed him of his accident and how Henry and Julean had come along and rescued him. Along the way to the hospital his heart had given out and luckily Julean, being a nurse, administered CPR and resuscitated him. The only thing wrong with this picture was that John was informed that morning that he was a carrier of bacterial meningitis and the very one who saved his life had contracted it. Julean was now struggling for her life.

Since arriving at the hospital three days ago, John had been in and out of consciousness and also struggling with detoxification. He had been a drug addict since high school and in trouble with the law for just about as long. The day of the accident he had made a trip to Weyburn to secure some morphine and pot from another junkie to feed his habit for another day. His life was a mess. His wife had left him two years before, his family had disowned him, except for his mother. The only good thing was he didn't have children. He had destroyed enough lives and now it looked like he was going to destroy another; he wasn't worth it.

For the first time in months John had some semblance of reality and consciousness. His body craved drugs and was far from over his addiction, yet a strength enveloped him. He could attribute it to the medication the doctors were giving him to ease the withdrawal, but he knew the effects of medicine and drugs. He had ingested every conceivable kind in the last few years and he knew exactly how each pill or injection made him feel. Clearly, the high or indescribable warm feeling that was suddenly and gently swarming through his sickly body came from a different source. *But what?* In the minutes that followed John was about to find out.

No sooner had the attending doctor left the hospital room than Father Engelmann entered. Since the day Henry shared with Father what had happened the night of the accident, the man whose life Julean had saved was in Father's prayers. After Father learned of his name and that he had spread his disease to Julean, Father knew he was in even more need of desperate help. Along with the masses and prayers he offered up for Julean, Henry and their family, so too was John McBryne offered up to the Lord for healing.

Father made his way over to John's bedside. A lean, tall figure was revealed by the outline of the thin sheet over the lower part of his body. His height astonished Father as his feet extended at least six inches over the edge of the foot of the bed. Brown, matted, long hair hung over part of his left eye while the more visible right eye revealed a somber, blank stare. Father had seen many despondent people in his life time, but the man before him appeared bereft of any hope, totally defeated, crushed of all life.

John's gaze on Father hadn't left him since he saw him in the doorway. He studied Father for a long moment and finally responded to Father's extended hand. It was a lopsided handshake; for the most part it was carried by Father's firm grip.

"Good morning, John, I'm Father Engelmann."

John stared intently at the man before him. The mention of the name "Father" sent revulsion through his being. He wondered if his mother had sent for the priest. For years she had prayed for him and for years he shunned her efforts. The years of abuse by his alcoholic father completely convinced him that there wasn't a

God. How could a creator that claimed to be all loving and kind allow such horrific actions? Unforgettable images of beatings he and his mother received under his father's headship in the home had driven John to atheism long ago.

Finally, stiff, tight lips cracked and his long narrow face gave some semblance of life.

"Did my mother send you?"

"No. I came on my own, John."

"How do you know of me, then, or are you just making the rounds?"

Father studied John, reflecting on his answer. He didn't need to, as only the truth would come out.

"I heard of you from my good friends Henry and Julean Pederson."

John's thick eyebrows quivered, "Is she the lady that saved my life?"

Father nodded. "Yes, it is the same woman."

"How... how is she doing? Has she still got my disease?"

Father thought it best not to reveal how critically ill Julean was, for the moment at least. "Yes, John. They are treating her. We are praying that the good Lord will restore her health."

"You're wasting your time," John snapped. "Hopefully the medicine will do the job. The doctors say I am getting better so... probably she will, too."

Father didn't answer momentarily.

He was about to speak when John blurted out, "If you're here to save my soul, forget it. There is no God as far as I am concerned. Look at the real world, Father, show me where the love is. Nobody gives a damn about anyone. Everyone is for themselves."

Father nodded. "Yes, that may be the case with many, but there is a lot of good. Did not Julean reach out to you?"

John's head jerked back and his eyes widened as he stared at Father. He was speechless. Besides his mother, Julean was perhaps the first person in years to help him. Not only help him from a distance, but willing to sacrifice her own life. John remained silent as his eyes misted. He lowered his head.

"The good in the world far outweighs the bad, John. Perhaps

with effort we can help to make it even better."

John remained silent, motionless.

"Is there anything I can do for you, John? Is there anything you need?"

"No. Just leave me alone. Get the hell out of here. You better go now."

"Yes, of course. I am coming by this way again tomorrow, though, may I drop in for a visit?"

John shook his head negatively and then raised his shoulders almost negating his first response.

"It was good to meet you. Perhaps I will just say hello when I am here to make my rounds."

Father reached forward and touched John's shoulder who jerked away slightly and kept his head down as Father turned to leave.

Father was about to walk out the door when John softly spoke in a low, crackly voice. "Father..."

Father quickly turned. "Yes, what is it John?"

"Tell them, I... I am grateful for what they did." And then barely audibly he muttered, "It would have been better if they had left me to die."

Father gazed at the confused, sorrowful young man for a long moment, then turned and made his way to the door, silent prayers ushering rapidly forth from his lips.

Just as Father was leaving the room he bumped into Eddy Ziegler. "Hey Padre, good to see ya."

"Yes, it is good to see you too Eddy. What brings you here?"

"I'm here to see my ol' buddy, John McBryne."

Father's face paled, *miene gutti Gott dos is enbeleiveable.*

"I'm in kinda of a hurry Padre, I'll see you on Sunday."

"Yes, Eddy I will look forward to seeing you there." Father watched Eddy enter John McBryne's room.

How life can get so entangled!

CHAPTER FIFTY-EIGHT

B Y THE TIME Henry returned from the nurse's station with Dr. Filmore, Julean had slipped back into a coma. He deeply regretted leaving her for those few minutes but had thought maybe his love, his presence, or their sharing would have sustained her. Henry shook her hand just like his son Justin had earlier. Once again, Julean was drawn back into the deep abyss of unconsciousness.

Later that morning when Henry phoned home to ask when the children were coming in, Mary informed him that they would be at least an hour late because the children had something special planned for Julean's birthday.

"My God, Mom, I forgot all about that. It's just been so hec—"

"I understand, son. You've a lot on your mind. The children have asked me to bake a cake and want to bring it in for Julean. Is that okay?"

"Geez, I don't know, Mom. Julean is still in a coma."

"The children have their hearts set on it and… I do believe that people in a coma hear what is going on. I think Julean would love to have us celebrate her birthday."

"Yeah, maybe you're right."

AROUND ELEVEN, MARY peeked into Julean's room. Henry was at

his wife's bedside, holding her hand.

"The children are here. Is it okay if they come in now?"

Henry nodded, got up and slid the chair away so the kids could get next to their mother. His mother went out and whispered something to the children, then she and Father Engelmann led the children in, with Justin and Lauren each carrying a present, and Jeremy carrying a birthday cake with thirty-eight candles lit and glowing. Father started them all singing a happy birthday to their mother…

They were all gathered around Julean's bed with Jeremy right next to Julean's face. They were all expecting their mother to wake up and blow out the candles. An uneasy silence ensued until Justin laid his present on the end of the bed and ran to his mother's side.

"Wake up, Mommy. Blow out the candles." Justin shook her arm and pleaded again for her to wake up.

Father bent down and picked up the distraught boy. "Mommy is asleep, Justin. I know she would like for you to help blow out the candles for her. Come now, let's blow real hard."

Father and Justin opened their mouths and took a deep breath. Father feigned to blow, while Justin leaned toward the cake, his eyes sparkling in the light and blew with all his might. A few candles went out and the light in the room dimmed. He blew again and again, his little chest taking in all the air it could and expelling it as best he could for his mom. With each huff and puff the brightness lessened until the light in the room was as before. It helped to conceal the glistening tears flowing from everyone's eyes.

Lauren stepped forward with her present. It was beautifully wrapped with shiny gold paper and a purple ribbon and bow. She placed it near Julean's hand with the hope her mom would pick it up and open it.

Allison stepped forward. "I think Mom wants us to open it for her, Lauren. Can I help you?"

A tear fell from Lauren's eyes as she began to unwrap the gift she'd so carefully wrapped earlier. She slid the ribbon off the side and with Allison's help they unfolded the gold paper. The box contained a bottle of perfume from her Barbie doll make-up set.

"Mommy likes to smell nice for Daddy." Lauren took the bottle and pressed the atomizer until a jet of perfume sprayed Julean's arm.

"Can Mom hear us and smell the perfume?" Lauren asked as she looked at her dad.

Henry didn't answer directly. "I love that smell, Lauren. I know Mom loves it, too."

"Let me down, Grandpa. I want to give Mom my present, too."

Justin ran to the end of the bed and returned to Julean's side nudging and wiggling in between Allison and Lauren.

"Here is my present, Mom."

It looked like it was wrapped with old issues of the Leader Post's newsprint. Instead of a fancy bow, the gift was held together with a string from his Tonka truck, clumps of mud stuck to it.

"Come on, Mommy, open up your present."

"Here, let me help Mom open it up, son." Henry knelt down on one knee and untied the bow that Julean had taught him to do only a few weeks before.

"Come on, son. Let's open it together." Henry tried to muster the same enthusiasm written all over his son's face. Together, they quickly unraveled the creased paper and tossed it on the blanket. To everyone's surprise, under the layer of newsprint were several layers of toilet paper. Henry realized that Justin thought the bathroom paper was the same as the white tissue he had seen his mother wrap gifts in. Justin pulled excitedly at the paper with both hands, as he smiled and glanced intermittently at his mom.

"Can you guess what it is, Mommy?"

Finally, under several layers of torn and shredded paper were the treasures he had brought: a soft miniature teddy bear he had received the previous Christmas and a shinny silver plastic ring with a diamond on the top from a Cracker Jack box.

Justin looked at his dad. "Mommy likes to cuddle with my teddy bear. She can have it till she comes home."

He tucked the bear between his mother's arm and chest then picked up the ring and eagerly tried to put it on her finger. "Put it on, Mommy!"

He tried to force it on her ring finger, but the plastic ring was a little too small.

"Here, son, let's try her little finger." Henry guided his son's hand and the sparkling diamond ring slipped on.

"Do you like it, Mommy?" he asked enthusiastically, looking at her for a response.

Henry's eyes misted as he looked at the golden wedding ring with its dazzling diamond he had given Julean at their wedding. It paled in comparison to the plastic ring his son had just slipped on the next finger.

"Mommy loves the ring, Justin." Henry picked up Justin and leaned him forward to Julean's forehead. "Mommy wants a kiss, son."

"Well, let's have a piece of birthday cake," said Mary as she reached in a bag and pulled out paper plates and plastic forks.

"Yes, yes," Father chimed in, trying to continue the spirit of the party.

Just then the day nurse and Dr. Filmore walked in.

"Celebrating someone's birthday, I see," said the doctor.

"It's Mommy's birthday today!" Justin announced, eyes beaming.

"Well, happy birthday, Mom. And… I see she got a teddy bear."

"That's my present to Mommy," Justin replied.

"Perhaps we should go to the conference room and have our cake there," Henry suggested.

"Yes, it may be a little easier to have the cake there," Mary concurred.

"Our examination will take about ten minutes, Mr. Pederson. We're also changing the combination of antibiotics. I'll discuss it with you later."

"Okay, let's go, kids." Henry turned and as he kissed Julean's forehead, he noticed a tear had streaked from her eye. "You know gang, I think Mom heard everything we said to her and loved her birthday presents. We better come back when the doctor is finished and continue the party."

For the next two days, Henry and his team continued the Novena, but it seemed too mechanical for Henry's liking. Something was missing. Perhaps they didn't really believe God was going to perform a miracle. Kind of like when he and his mother had said the Novena for Jenny. The expectancy of faith seemed to be overshadowed by worry, concern… doubt.

The children visited each day, their sadness deepening as their mother continued sleeping, unable to speak with them, touch them, or comfort them. The heart of their home was ailing with devastating effects on everyone. The joy and happiness that typically flowed in the Pederson family was at a very low ebb.

The doctors had tried everything, including some of the new treatments initiated by the doctor from Toronto, but Julean didn't seem to respond to any of them and remained in her coma. Her blood pressure steadily decreased, her pulse weakened. Another spinal tap showed the stronger presence of bacteria in the cerebrospinal fluid. Blood tests indicated an increase in her white cell count. Neither the corticosteroid drugs to reduce swelling and inflammation nor the antibiotics were working as they hoped. So far the only treatment that was working was anticonvulsant medication as Julean hadn't experienced any more seizures. However, they feared the infection was spreading and that septicemia (blood poisoning) was setting in.

The doctors began to question whether Henry had really spoken to his wife at all, and wondered if it had just been a figment of his imagination, a desire so strong that he experienced a waking dream. When Dr. Filmore questioned him on it, Henry became upset.

"Of course I spoke with her. She… she knew she was dying. Out of the blue, she said so. I was standing by the window when she woke up. We talked for at least twenty to thirty minutes before I went to the nurse's station."

"It's just that her oxygen supply from day one has been so restricted by the disease and the blood tests, urine samples and cerebral fluid all indicate the infection hasn't abated. It seems odd that she would come out of it, even for a brief time, and be able to have a lucid conversation with you."

Henry studied the doctor. *Perhaps that was the miracle they had been praying for.*

LATER THAT EVENING after saying the Novena prayers, Henry asked Father to stay on the line.

"She knew about Jenny, Father. She knew it from the dreams I had. Since the day we married, she said, I revealed it to her in my sleep and she lived with that for all these years. Several times after our discussion at church, I wanted to tell Julean, but the opportunity never presented itself. After all these years of keeping this secret, Julean tells me she's known all along.

"She told me she felt like she was dying, Father, and wanted to set me free. She knows how sensitive my conscience is, that guilt would be in my heart. She woke and pressed me into talking about it at this critical time... to set me free."

Henry heard Father sigh through the phone.

"How life can be filled with such incredible happenings. Love between people can bring on miracles that defy medical explanation. My Anna knew me through and through as well, Henry. There were no secrets between us and that is how it should be. Your precious wife recognized that, too, and has given you a rare gift. Rather than react hurtfully or resentfully, she has responded in love, understanding and concern for your welfare. Accept that gift she gave you and honour her for it."

"As you know, Father, she even told me at one time she would be willing to share me with another woman. Would that have to do with her past, her roots?"

"Perhaps she would be more amenable than another might to such an idea having seen it within her own family. But, I believe it is out of her love and concern for your future happiness that she is trying to rid you of any guilt from the past and to let you know that if anything should happen, she would want you to go on and be free to wed another."

Henry couldn't speak. He was frozen in time. After several minutes of silence, Father learned what thoughts had been keeping Henry captive when he suddenly cried out, "If only we hadn't stopped for that drug addict, Father, none of this would have happened. I wish he had died in the accident and then Julean would never have administered to him. With every passing day I want to go over and tell him what he did and... hurt him. I know I shouldn't be vengeful, but Julean could die over this. I wonder if he is still in the hospital?"

Father remained silent, weighing every word his dear anguished son had said. He anticipated that the words he was about to say would inflict perhaps more anger, more pain but the truth had to be spoken and he knew sooner than later, it would set Henry free.

Calmly, gently, softly, Father said, "Yes, Henry, John McBryne is still in the hospital."

John McBryne!? The name immediately burned in Henry's mind. It was the name of one of the three guys that had taken Jenny to the park and raped her. He recalled Eddy telling him that John was heavy into drugs.

Oh, God... please no! It couldn't be one of the guys that raped Jenny! It couldn't be the same John McBryne, could it?

"Father!" Henry blurted. "That's the name of one of the guys that took Jenny to the park that night! You remember—the night Jenny and I went to the show just before we started at high school? We were jumped and they dragged Jenny off... I wonder if it could possible be the same guy? He was one of Eddy Zeigler's friends, do you remember?"

Father was silent but for only a moment. "Yes, Henry, John McBryne is Eddy's friend—"

ONLY A SPLIT second of silence was allowed on the telephone line before it sizzled with Henry's next outburst.

"Oh Father, you haven't been seeing him, have you?"

"Yes, Henry, a few days ago I included in my rounds at the General Hospital a visit with the young man. I went back yesterday and this morning but he refused to see me. He deeply regrets what has happened, Henry."

Henry couldn't believe his ears. For the first time in all the years he had known Father, he was upset with him. Not only angry with him, but he felt betrayed by his closest and deepest friend.

"How could you see that man, Father. He has been the cause of Julean's grave illness and possible death. This is the second time he's come into my life and tried to destroy a person I love so much.

Father, he's a terrible, terrible man... He should die... I wish he would."

Father's silence only drove Henry on. "Shouldn't your prayers and visits be to Julean?"

"Yes, Henry, but there are other needs as well, and... Is he not a child of God, too, who has gone astray?"

"But, Father, why now...?"

"Henry, what kind of Father would I be if I taught you only to love the loveable or those that did only good. Did not Christ come to save the sinners?"

Henry remained silent. All reason and understanding were overshadowed by his grief and hurt and anger. He knew Father was right and Julean had encouraged him to forgive, too, but right now it didn't seem right.

"I regret that this news has upset you, but if you don't soon come to terms with this, you will suffer all the more."

Henry knew all about the bondage of unforgiveness. He had seen it in his home, with Eddy, with Jenny's parents. In his heart he also knew Father was trying to help him deal with it, but the pain was too deep, the anguish so overwhelming that to even consider forgiveness was too far removed. He was not capable now. Father had pushed him to his limit and forgiveness at this time was impossible. He hated the man too much.

Once again, Father broke the tense silence with words intended to heal. "Henry, perhaps my words are not sufficient now. Let us turn this matter over to the Lord. Matthew 5:44 and Romans 12:17-21 speaks about this."

Tears had already filled Henry's eyes. He could speak no more. God was already at work. As soon as Father gave him the first scripture he turned to it while still on the phone. He grasped at anything which might ease the horrific pain in his gut.

"'But now I tell you: love your enemies, and pray for those who mistreat you, so that you will become the sons of your Father in heaven. For he makes his sun to shine on bad and good people alike, and gives rain to those who do right and those who wrong. Why should you expect God to reward you, if you love only people who love you?'"

Henry could read no more, he turned to the second scripture hoping it would be less convincing… it was all the more.

"'If someone does evil to you, do not pay back with evil. Try to do what all men consider to be good. Do everything possible, on your part, to live at peace with all men. Never take revenge, my friends….'"

Henry could no longer go on.

Father heard his son weeping; his heart was filled with sorrow, with love and compassion for Henry. His arms begged to go through the phone and hold his hurting son.

"'Come unto me ye that labour and are heavily laden and I will give ye rest.'

"'My peace I give to you, my peace I leave unto you. Not as the world gives but as I give unto you. Let not your heart be troubled nor let it be afraid.'"

Having said his piece and after a little while longer, Father hung up.

LATER THAT EVENING, Julean's father came into the room to check on his daughter before going home. He was moved by the scene before him. Henry was leaning over on the bed, his head resting on his right arm next to Julean's tummy. The Bible lay open before him and his left fingers were entwined in his wife's pale hand.

Dr. Carter could see the love his son-in-law had for his daughter. Guilt washed over him and he was compelled to place his hand over Henry's shoulder and stir him. It took several gentle shakes before Henry opened his red tear-filled eyes. He leaned up and back and turned to see Dr. Carter standing behind him.

"You need rest, Hank. Better you go lay on the cot and sleep properly."

Henry could see tears had welled up in his father-in-law's eyes. Just as Henry was about to get up and make his way over to the bed, Dr. Carter spoke softly.

"I am ashamed to say Hank, that it would take my daughter's illness to open my eyes and make me aware of the fine, devoted young man she married. I am very sorry for not welcoming you into our home and family properly. Please forgive me."

Henry slowly rose and faced Julean's dad. Both men had tears in their eyes and neither could utter another word. The air in the room was laden with sorrow and then... All at once, a spirit of reconciliation drove out the heaviness. The love that is always at the core of our being welled up in the men's hearts with such tenderness that they were helpless but to stride into each others arms and warmly embrace.

HENRY AWOKE THE next morning to a new sound in the hospital room. The nurses had attached a respirator to assist Julean's breathing.

Dr. Filmore arrived later that morning and met with Henry. The doctor's news only compounded the pain and agony over Julean's illness and the lingering hurt over Father's visits to his arch-enemy. Only last evening he had experienced the power of forgiveness and yet now he was tested again. Could he do what Julean's father did to him only hours ago? The words that followed from the doctor quickly shut the door to that option.

"I'm afraid there is nothing else we can do. Hopefully the antibiotics will kick in and attack the bacteria that have such a strong hold on her."

Henry could not believe that in this day and age, with all the advances in science and technology and medicine, that the doctors could not arrest the disease inflaming his wife's brain and blood vessels.

"Are there doctors in Europe perhaps or different types of treatment in China or whatever that we could try?"

"I assure you, we have tried all avenues open to us and more. Even though this is my area of specialty, your father-in-law has sought out things to try beyond even what I had thought of doing. It's just that meningitis can come on so quickly and strongly and within a short time can have fatal consequences."

Henry tried to listen to the doctor's medical explanations through the emotional darkness enveloping him. Although the doctors had told him that his wife was seriously ill and could possible die, he had never really believed it or that it could happen to them... until now. Such a dreadful plausibility was knocking at his doorstep and the accompanying fear was too horrific to contemplate. He couldn't imagine what life would be like without Julean, not having her stabilizing and loving presence in the home. The kids without their mother, dealing with their one and a million questions and concerns... Being there for the children's school events, graduations and... Weddings. My God, what would the future hold?

At the risk of being impolite, Henry shook his head, turned and walked away. He wasn't heading for Julean's room. He wasn't heading anywhere, in particular. He was beside himself; a hopeless sinking feeling was sucking him down into a dark spinning vortex. Life was beginning to lose its meaning, its hope, and the inward stresses were too violent to bear. He experienced these feelings at only one other time in his life: when Jenny left. He never thought he would ever feel such devastation again. For Julean to die would be the complete end of life for him.

He tried to pray, but God seemed hidden... So far away.

"Her angel," he whispered, as he grasped for a miracle from anywhere in the supernatural. "Yes, Jenny's angel would help. Her angel saved her from being struck by a car. It was a miracle. I know it was and so did Father Engelmann. Oh, guardian angel, save Julean now, too. Pull her away from this terrible disease as you did Jenny from the car that day. Shield my Julean from harm."

"Doctor, come quick!" shrilled a voice from Julean's room. It reminded Henry of the time he was coming to visit Julean just after the birth of their first son, when he had heard Julean's anguished cry at the news of the death of their son. The shout now carried the same blood curdling sound. Shivers of pure terror raced down Henry's spine. He was at the far end of the corridor and at once, turned and ran for Julean's room.

Just before Henry went into the intensive care unit at the far end of the hall, the elevator doors opened and his mother and the children stepped out.

"There's Daddy," shouted Justin and ran towards him.

Henry saw his son, but the urgency of what might be going on with Julean drew him there. Three nurses and Dr. Filmore were working on his wife when he burst into the room. Julean had vomited and was breathing very rapidly; it appeared she was having a seizure.

"Doctor," said one of the nurses, "her blood pressure is falling. Her pulse is slowing."

"She's going into septic shock. Quickly, increase the IV fluid. Inject another 2cc's of dopamine," the doctor ordered.

"The pressure is still going down. We've lost her pulse... cardiac arrest."

"For God's sake, do something!" Henry muttered, his fists clenched.

A nurse handed the readied paddles to the doctor.

"Stand back!"

Julean's body thrust upwards, her eyes rolled. Henry was frozen with fear and dread as he looked upon something he should never have witnessed. After several more charges to revive her heart the monitor remained in a straight steady line.

Justin crashed into the room and went to Henry's side. "Is Mommy awake today, Daddy?"

Henry didn't feel his son tugging on his sleeve, waiting for an answer. He was numb, paralyzed.

The doctor put the paddles down and told the nurse to record the time of death.

Henry tore away from Justin's clasp and charged the staff. "You can't stop now. Try something else. Insert a needle in her heart, press it up and down. Sometimes people can come back." He'd seen it done many times on TV. Henry grabbed the doctor's hands and pushed them to Julean's heart. "Press down. Please. Please. Bring her back."

A nurse came to Henry and put her arms around him. "She's gone, Mr. Pederson. There is nothing more we can do. We are so sorry."

Lauren entered the room followed by her brother and sister and Mary. A tense heaviness filled the air. Confusion and the slow realization that the most dreadful thing in the world possible had happened took hold.

"What has happened to Mom?" Allison's voice rising into hysteria with each word.

Henry couldn't answer; he just stared as the nurses tidied the area around his wife as much as they could. The doctor removed the tube from Julean's mouth and motioned the nurses to leave. Within moments, Henry and his family were left alone to say good-bye.

Justin ran to the bedside as the rest of the family closed in around their mother, crying and wailing.

"Mommy, wake up," he pleaded. Julean's lifeless arm rolled back and forth as he shook it harder and harder.

Realizing Henry was too overwrought to come to his son's aid, Mary went to Justin and picked him up.

"Why doesn't Mommy wake up, Grandma?" The sadness and sorrow of the moment nudged its way into his understanding that something was very wrong.

Silent tears streamed down Mary's cheeks as she whispered to her grandson, "She has gone to heaven, Justin."

CHAPTER FIFTY-NINE

As soon as Jenny arrived back at the estate, she took the biography Spencer had given her to the kitchen where she picked up a chair and placed it in front of the patio doors. She shivered at the sound of the wind hissing its way through the worn weather stripping of the sliding door. Even though the grounds were laden with snow and the sky covered with silver clouds, the promise of spring and the flowers underneath winter's blanket gave her hope. The filtered rays of the sun entering the room assured her, as well, that just behind winter's storm and the dreary cloud cover, the sun still shone in all its glory.

The bouquet of flowers that she had retrieved from the Angel of Thanksgiving's basket in the vase on the window ledge next to her was certain proof of what she had reflected on. The flowers hadn't deteriorated one bit, in fact with each passing day they exuded more radiance and beauty and the aroma of their sweet scent that filled the air, ever more pungent. It was as if spring had already arrived and come indoors. A gift of love was given to her. Her yearning for summer flowers was granted as a winter miracle, already filling her with hope. Again, she felt the presence of her father.

Jenny sat down and unfolded the stiff grey paper. She read about the acreage Henry and his family lived on and imagined the panorama of uninhabited hills, trees, streams and the constantly changing face of nature. She recalled the many times over that summer with Henry how he had described the trees, the colour of the leaves and the grass as the summer had progressed. She thought about how much Henry must adore living where he did.

The paragraph relating Henry's philosophy towards his work intrigued her. *"His art hinges on his inner response to what he perceives and lives through in the present moment."* She, too, valued the now and it was in the present moment of nature where she received her healing and sustained her spirit.

It is in the present when we are most aware of nature, of life, our Creator.

The painting Spencer had purchased from Henry drifted into her mind's eye. Jenny could feel the moment when Henry had captured that beautiful sunset on canvas. He often said that if ever he moved away from the prairies it would be the sky and its ever-changing colour and moods that he would deeply miss. Warmth swept through her as she imagined Henry painting the last lingering rays of light sweeping across the prairie landscape and glistening off the neatly harvested swaths of grain.

A strong gust of wind struck and rattled the patio door. The hiss of the wind stealing by the weather stripping turned into an eerie whistle. Jenny raised her chin and gazed at the raging storm. She shuddered and wriggled her body trying to nestle deeper into the cushioned chair like a hen into its nest.

If Henry were there, he could bring warmth out of that blustery scene before her. She pictured him in the kitchen, standing there at his easel painting the landscape she was witnessing. He would combine subtle colours of yellow, crimson and the warmest blue on his palette so masterfully that the cold white snow would be transformed into warm shimmering sunlight. She framed the picture in her mind so vividly that it was as if he had just completed the painting and she could smell the odour of the fresh pigments lingering in the air. She thought she would melt right then and there at the sight of the winter landscape exuding such glowing inner luminosity.

Jenny lowered her head, unaware that a tear had fallen on the edge of the pamphlet. She was surprised by the number of exhibitions he'd had and the long list of corporations which collected his work. He must love painting so much to be that prolific.

Her eyes brightened when she read that he had received an arts grant to study print making at Open Studio in Toronto just a few years ago. A flutter sang through her heart at the thought of possibly running into him on one of her and her mother's shopping trips. Would she have recognized him? Of course. She would never forget his green eyes, his dark brown hair and ruddy handsome face... *Never.*

The last paragraph of the biography revealed Henry's wife's name, *Julean,* and sent her spirit zinging. Jenny remembered that her name was Julean; Tammy had found that out years ago. But to see it in print beside Henry's impacted Jenny so much more.

"Julean," she said out loud, its sound ringing merrily in the quiet kitchen, echoing softly off the walls. "What a beautiful name."

Jenny wondered what she looked like. What was the colour of her hair, her eyes, her complexion? If only the pamphlet displayed a photo of Henry and his wife. She would give anything to see them together. What a lovely couple they must make and their marriage, she imagined, filled with joy and love.

A seed of envy was planted within Jenny as she visualized Henry and Julean holding hands like she and Henry had done, staring into each others eyes over a romantic dinner, going on vacations during the summer with the kids... Doing all the things that a happy family would do. Jenny smiled as she saw Henry tossing the children into the air and playing with them in her mind's eye. She heard the sound of joy and playing children ringing throughout their home. A beautiful family filled with love...

A long weary sigh slowly expelled from Jenny's trembling lips as the kitchen suddenly fell dead silent. The hissing and whistling of the wind coming through the cracks stood still and the tick of the nearby clock grew distant as if it was hushing itself. The air grew heavy and darkened. A storm was building not on the outside but within Jenny. It was like an anxious wave agitating in the pit of her stomach, surging forward and upward at great speed bringing into Jenny's full awareness the state of her marriage and her life as compared to that of Henry and Julean.

All the things she had just imagined about Henry's marriage and family life is what she had always desired with all her being. She was filled with so much love that screamed to have expression, but at every turn it was blocked in her stifling marriage. She wanted to be loved, to be held, to be kissed, to make love... An explosion of denied emotion filled the silent room, vibrating the air that surrounded her. If it hadn't been for the memories of Camilla or that of her first love to sustain her in those moments of desperation...

"But they are just memories, dreams of hope...without the warm touch of someone's hand or tender embrace."

She had always known that her marriage lacked love and happiness, but the utter emptiness that consumed her now as she compared it to what could have been overwhelmed her. One scene after another whizzed through Jenny's mind as the turbulent wave tossed her up and down in the sea of her life. What could she have done differently? How did she fall into such a lonely, despairing life? The thought almost drowned her. Each time she bobbed up for air and tried to defend her decisions another greater reason that she should have left pushed her down again.

How James stole their son from her which eventually led to Jimmy's rejection as well, was unbearable torture. Jenny could still feel the pain in her breasts for not being allowed to nurse her own child. The sight of her newborn being bottle fed by a nanny, while her throbbing breasts, aching to yield its nectar to her offspring, dried and shriveled unfulfilled as nature didn't intend. James' abandonment of her, his disrespect for her feelings... Even her name had not been good enough for him. Jenny gasped for air as the avalanche of tears now threatened to drown her.

She felt irreversibly trapped in the pains and sorrows of the past, trying uselessly to struggle free like a fly caught in a spider's web. It was not in Jenny's nature to wallow in regret or self pity. She had been caught off guard by the life she had envisioned her beloved Henry and his family were enjoying. Her heart had soared at the very thought of such happiness, but then plunged like a stone thrown over a cliff into the sea of thoughts of her own family. She wanted so much to have a good, happy marriage...

"Like Henry and Julea…" she started to say and then her words trailed off.

It would have been so wonderful to have a family like that, but it was always one sided in hers, it was never reciprocated. James never returned even a drop or scrap of love. She was like a plant that wanted to flower, but she never received any water. Rather, she lived in a desert for years and years, going around and round in circles, being denied one of life's most joyous and basic needs – a wholesome, loving relationship.

Jenny felt depleted and silently ached like a wounded bird yearning to fly. She raised her shoulders as if they were wings and slowly let them fall along with a long sigh. Love can be so wonderful and yet so painful, concluded Jenny.

The sobbing subsided as the storm within her calmed. Jenny wiped her eyes with the back of her hands and then her fingertips. The bouquet on the window sill from the Angel of Thanksgiving were the first things Jenny saw as she raised her head and opened her eyes. The flowers in the vase had turned from the light outside and leaned towards her as if to draw nearer. The gesture comforted her and brought a gentle smile to Jenny's face. The pillow on which she sat grew softer. The tick of the clock returned, its sound carrying the beat of a march towards better times ahead. The wind hissed soothingly, the air brightened and the walls reflected more light. The entire room anticipated the whisper of words that were more in keeping with Jenny's spirit.

"Yes… I could have left." Jenny slowly began. "Yes… I could have gone out with other men. God knows there were enough at my doorstep. Yes, I could have fought back and hated and resented James. Yes, I could have fought for Jimmy in the arena of the courts against formidable odds. Yes… but, but… I chose to stay, to try to raise my child, to stay committed to my word, to love and honour in good times and in bad. *Love is a decision and not a feeling.* And having made that decision to stay, what good would it have done to become the victim, to revel in anger, self pity and unforgiveness? It would have only added to the potential life-stifling arrows that James projected daily. It would have created a house filled with conflict, sorrow and misery. What kind of an atmosphere would that have been to raise a child or for any of us, for that matter?"

No, she thought silently, her actions at least gave some semblance of what a home should be like to her developing and growing son even though he was turned to be against her. And at least her spirit was never broken and she had not turned inward on herself, as so easily could have happened.

Jenny knew in her heart that all that is not given is lost. Each moment we live, whatever we withhold is lost and never to come again. If she withheld love from James, what has she or James gained?

Nothing.

At least by offering acceptance and love she was instilling in James the seed that may someday grow and flourish.

Yes, she chose to stay and made the best of it. She loved those times she was with her son, watching him grow, albeit they were short and far between. She loved those times with Matilda and the secrets and laughter they shared. And the precious little chats with Thomas were like gold that she treasured and recalled when she needed the comfort of kindness and a soothing voice. And the garden, the wildflowers and the Angel of Thanksgiving that brightened her life so much...

"Yes... there is much to be thankful for and... perhaps as our Lord says, good can come out of the most devastating situations. Perhaps... perhaps, some day..."

Jenny gazed at the pamphlet and rubbed away at the tears that had fallen there. She pictured Henry and his family on their beautiful acreage once more. A look of longing and a touch of envy still lingering in her heart settled on Jenny's pretty face as she raised her head and gazed outside. The wind had carved and sculpted sharp banks of snow on the grounds before her. With each gust, a trail of snow wisped from atop the banks and followed the wind. It reminded Jenny of star dust trails behind a fairy godmother's magic wand. Jenny found herself immersed in a rare moment of time in which she allowed an unchecked thought to surface. If she were granted a wish, she would wish that just for a day, she could walk in Julean's footsteps.

Chapter Sixty

F ATHER HAD RETURNED from visiting with a family in the parish
and was about to continue his preparation for Julean's funeral
the following morning when the phone rang. A Dr. Kennedy from
the General Hospital was on phone. Father recalled meeting him
when he was visiting a patient there over a month ago.

"My reason for calling Father is that the staff has informed me
that you visited John McBryne recently."

"Yes, I saw him once. Since that time however, he has refused
to see me."

"Well, since he was informed two days ago of Mrs. Pederson's
death he has become very despondent. He refuses to eat or take
medication. Surprisingly, we have managed to detoxify him in a
short time, but we are afraid in his state he may quickly revert to
drugs again. There is no telling what he might do. Fortunately, just
over an hour ago he requested to see you. Would you have time
to see him?"

"Yes, yes, of course. I shall be there later this afternoon."

"Thank you, Father, I sure hope you can help him."

SHORTLY AFTER THREE-THIRTY, Father entered John's room. He
was curled up into a ball, lying on his side and staring at the wall
away from Father. His position concealed his height, but not his

501

frailty. He appeared even thinner than the day they first met.

Father slowly made his way to John's bedside and softly spoke, "It is me, Father Engelmann."

When he was next to John he reached out and touched his shoulder. Not knowing what to say, he kept his hand on the troubled man and began to pray for John and God's guidance.

After what seemed like a long time, John spoke, his voice dry and cracking.

"I killed her, Father... I deserve to die. I've done many wrong things in my life but this tops it all. The family must be..."

John struggled to hold back tears, but no sooner had Father said he felt his pain and sorrow that the damn broke loose and John wept with agonizing, gasping, gut-wrenching sobs.

Father sat on the edge of the bed and slid his arm under the frail figure, turned him over and drew him near to his heart and held him as if cradling a child.

"Why do you keep coming, Father? You know about me, the terrible things I have done... I am not worth it. I have made so many mistakes, have led such an awful life. Look what it has come down to... and yet you still come."

Father slid his half-asleep arm away from under John and sat on the chair next to the bed so he could look into the troubled young man's eyes.

"John, you are not the mistake. Yes, your involvement with drugs has had the affect of hurting someone and yourself, but beneath the layers of mistakes you are a beautiful child of God and He makes only good things. You have a good heart, my son, with the potential for so much good and service to others. The seeds of greatness are within you. All of us, John, are entreated to walk in a manner worthy of the calling with which you are now called. You must now live in a manner that reflects that calling and glorifies the Lord. "

"But my mistakes have resulted in the death of another, such pain to a family, how can I ever live with that, or correct it? How can I ever look at myself again for what I have caused?"

"Right now it seems insurmountable. No, we cannot bring back Julean. Mistakes you have made have led up to this, but as I said before, we are not our mistakes. We cannot go back and undo the wrong, but from this day forward, this moment you can choose more wisely for the betterment of others and for yourself. Yes, it is tragic, but you can choose a new way, a way filled with life, hope, peace, love. We are all servants for the Lord, His ambassadors to make the world a better place."

John sneered, his eyes flashing with anguish. "But how, Father? I am a failure in everything. What hope is there for me?"

Father shifted in his chair and leaned closer to John. "You are at a crossroads, John. During a person's life, God brings us to such a point, time and again, giving us the opportunity to choose life or death, to be for Him and others or ourselves. You can weep, blame and hate yourself and continue along in your old ways, or you can accept the mistake or mistakes you have made and say *yes* to a new way of life. Perhaps you are now called to help others who have drug problems to see the error of their ways before their mistakes lead to situations like you are in. Remember, God causes all things to work together for good to those who love Him and who are called according to His purpose.

"No matter what you have done, if you seek forgiveness, the Lord forgives and is ever ready to help and guide you to live a wholesome life that he has wished for you from the beginning. You have a free choice to live your own life, but choose to live it for the Lord. Become his helper to make the world a better place. This is the crossroad, choose wisely for this opportunity may not pass this way again."

John raised his chin until his forlorn eyes met Fathers. So much suffering was in that gaze that Father reached forward and clasped John's hand lying limply at his side.

"You are not alone in this. We are all sinners and have made many mistakes, many I know much bigger than yours. But in the end we are all in this together. God made us social creatures, interdependent on one another. We do not travel down the road of life alone. You have gone down the empty road alone for far too long and where that has led? No man is an island. We need each other, like the air we breath."

A curious look grew on John's face. He tilted and turned his head aiming his left ear slightly more directly to Father's words.

"You are of great value, John, not only to others, but God needs you, too, don't you see?"

John's expression once again changed from curiosity to skepticism and then a glint grew in his eyes that revealed possibility.

"Next to bread, John, we all hunger to love and be loved. As we bear witness to one another, we help each other grow in self-love and other-love. It is a law of life just as real as the law of gravity. My coming today helps you to see the good that was always within you. You see it reflected in my eyes. And as you *show* your love and appreciation of me I in turn *feel* your love and gratitude. This is how we grow as children of God and help the good Lord improve the world!"

Once again, John's expression changed. This time a glint in his eye and a curl at the corners of his lips almost suggested, heaven forbid, a smile.

"It is the latter that most people do not realize... That God needs us."

"Yes, Father, I still do not fully understand. If God is so almighty and powerful, why would He need help from the likes of us, especially me."

"Once you completely understand this you will begin to fully realize your importance as a child of God and how much power you have in the evolution for a better world. You see, John, when the good Lord made a world in which he gave us free will to choose the path we follow, He had limited Himself. He needs us to help Him keep the world on track, to improve it. If He interferes, He takes away our free choice. So, for the most part, except perhaps when a miracle occurs, the world goes on and follows this law just as other laws that govern the universe.

"Do you see now how important you are in this picture and how much God relies on the choices you make? He needs you to cooperate with Him, become His partner, a collaborator if you will. Every choice you make either helps or hinders Him."

"Yeah, I suppose I've been quite a hindrance."

"But now that you know how important you are, you can choose to make it all different. Right now I venture to say God is very happy with our discussion and is wearing a broad smile. Let us help Him to keep smiling."

Father could see John settle more deeply into the pillow behind his back, accompanied by a peace that Father could also feel.

After a long silence, Father continued, "As I said before, you are at a crossroads. The question you have to ask yourself right now, John, is how you want to live out the rest of your life from this moment on. You regret the way it has been going, so now is the moment of choice. If you choose to live for God, you become a vessel He can use to improve the world; you become a co-Creator for a better earth and a wonderful new life for yourself."

"Father, can that really be possible even after what I have done?"

"Yes, John, it is as real and possible as you and I are here now, this very moment contemplating a new future. Right now, you're in limbo, John, with no purpose, no sense of belonging. Your self-esteem is low and at times like this you have a tendency only to look at the bad within you. But with new choices you will see the good and eventually, just as the good in the world outweighs the bad so, too, the good in ourselves outweighs the not-so-good. As we then grow and make better choices, the bad will stay more in the shadows and will no longer wrongly claim the light.

"We can be our most severe, worst enemies, or we can become our best friends. As you choose His way John, you will receive unlimited strength and joy and know the true meaning of love. As I said, God turns everything into good if we trust and love Him. I see good coming out of this tragedy. Julean has given her life so that you might live. Let it not be in vain."

John hung his head and nodded. "What a beautiful lady she must have been. I wanted so much to visit her and thank her and tell her how sorry I was. And now with her death, I feel such sorrow. How is the family doing, Father?"

"As well as can be expected. They are suffering over her loss just as you are. Your prayers for them are greatly needed."

"Yes, I shall try." After a long silence John went on. "You know, Father, what you just said about the Lord needing our help and giving meaning to our lives fits in with what I saw on TV the other night. It was about children and people living in India and Africa that were suffering with sickness and starvation. Their lives are so ruined, even more so than mine. It's such an epidemic, the sorrow in the children's eyes so terrible. For perhaps the first time in days, months and years I forgot myself… My heart went out to them."

"See, John? See how the Lord is making you aware of others and the needs in the world? See how good and compassionate your heart is? See how sorrowful and regrettable it is over Julean's death? You are a good person that momentarily went astray and made many mistakes as do we all. But this is all about to change. You are a beautiful child of God who will come to be a soldier for the Lord, to spread His message and make a better world. Don't you see how important you are, John? Perhaps missionary work is what the Lord is asking?"

A glimmer of understanding joined with a seed of possibility and crept its way intermittently into John's awareness. With each new insight, as he continued to speak, a glow pulsated upon his face like a dying ember flickering back to life.

"The next day after watching that show, Father, I asked the day nurse for a Bible. Within the hour she brought me one. But all I read was empty words, gibberish and the next time the nurse entered the room she caught me throwing the Bible into the corner. She looked at me in horror, Father. She picked up the Bible and kissed it and held it close to her chest for moments longer than I care to remember. She straightened out the pages and gave me a sorrowful look before making her way to the door."

John's face glowed more brightly, evenly.

"Rather than leave, she turned and came back toward me. I fully expected a scolding, but instead, she softly smiled and gently laid the Bible on the end table, turned and left. If she had just left in the first place, like I was expecting her to, Father, I do believe that would have been the end of this, but her actions of kindness and acceptance of my behaviour and her willingness to trust me again, touched me."

Father's eyes widened, threatening to jump from their sockets. "Do you see how important we are to each other, John? The tremendous power we have to influence lives!?"

"Yes, I see and… I see it in you, as well. In such a short time, how I wish I were like you and be filled with such peace. You are the first glimpse of a loving father I have ever had. It gives me hope."

"Yes, yes, see how the Lord is touching you, John. He wants you to see that you can do the same. This is how the Lord uses us to create a better, kinder world. He relies on us to help Him. That is His Plan! Using our free will, we make wise choices and collaborate with Him. Just as that kindly nurse influenced you by her actions, you can do the same. Don't you see the power and influence you can have? Yes, we so need each other and God's strength to carry out His will. Don't you see what an important instrument you are for His peace and goodness to spread throughout the world?! We are all called to be like Saint Francis!"

Father was so excited; he almost pounced on the bed next to John like a child eager to wake his parents. He struggled to restrain himself from taking hold of John's shoulders and shaking him.

Father half stood up and blurted out again. "Don't you see how the Lord wants to use you? He is touching your heart and awakening the love that has always been within you from the very beginning!"

John's eyes brightened, filled with hope. "You know, Father, after the nurse gave me back the Bible, a page was still bent after I hurled it away. When I opened the Bible to straighten the page a scripture was underlined there which touched me after I read it. I know I would never have understood it before that day, and I still don't know if I do, but it seems to say that despite my sins, God forgives."

"Of course He forgives! If we come to Him with a sincere, repentant heart, He will never turn us down—which scripture was it, John?

Josh reached for the Bible and opened it to the page which was still bent. Father took the Bible and looked it over.

It was Acts 26:18. Father knew of the passage and immediately the words touched his heart, as well. Wiping the blurriness from his eyes, a tear fell on the page as Father read the passage out loud: "'To open their eyes, and to turn them from darkness to light, and from the power of Satan unto God, that they may receive forgiveness of sins, and inheritance among them which are sanctified by faith that is in me.'"

"You see Father, even though I have been in the gutters of hell, I can receive forgiveness and start anew… And what you have been saying all along confirms it. Isn't that so?"

Father found it difficult to speak at first, amazed at how the Lord was at work in this troubled young man.

"Yes, yes, John. No matter what we have done, no matter how impure, immoral and unholy, we can receive freedom, forgiveness and full life through faith in Christ!"

John stared intensely into the holy priest's tear-filled eyes. Receiving acceptance, approval and love from this almost total stranger, despite his failings, touched John deeply. It was even more compounded by Julean's giving of herself that he might have life. Emerging from the depths of gratitude and sorrow was a glimpse of the seeds of hope and new life that Father spoke of earlier. His life from this moment on would no longer be squandered, nor Julean's life gone in vain. A peace began to sweep through John, gently pushing out his old self.

At first it was just a simple "Yes" that John uttered and this was followed by a nod. But Father knew what was going on. He felt the Holy Spirit present and was about to witness His power. A radiant splendor began to lick John's features. A transformation was taking place; his face glistened like a rain-washed stone. The red veil over his eyes dissolved along with the steely vacant look, leaving in its wake warm, crystal clear eyes with sparkle, depth and beauty. It was clear to Father that God and God alone dwelled in that man's heart now. In the next instant it was revealed what Father expected to hear in all its glory. When John spoke it was as if his lips were coated with honey sweetening his every word.

"I see it Father… I see my purpose!"

NIGHT HAD FALLEN when Father left the hospital. He immediately put on his beaver hat and lowered the flaps over his ears as the cold wind pushed him back against the door he just came out of. He hailed a cab and sat in the back rather the front as he usually did.

The winter storm had worsened and driving was difficult enough without distracting the driver with idle talk. Furthermore, he just wanted to sit back, relax and praise the Lord for so deeply coming to John's rescue and filling him with His spirit.

The sound of horns, flashing lights, and mild curses spewing from the driver and the swooshing of windshield wipers grew distant as Father prayed that the Lord would touch Henry's heart as it had John's. Their pain was the same only driven by a different motivation. John's was self-hatred and Henry's was hatred of John over what he had done to his wife.

Hate and love, reflected Father, opposite sides of the same coin. So close, almost touching, yet miles apart when one's heart is filled with darkness. And yet, Father marveled at how quickly John had responded so completely to God's calling while Henry, who had a lifetime of exposure to the truth still struggled with it all. *Perhaps it was because when one is closer to the utter bottom of darkness and despair, it is easier and quicker to see the truth and the light.*

CHAPTER SIXTY-ONE

F OR THE FIRST time since his wife's death, the fierce winter blizzard came close to matching Henry's raging inner storm. He
stood stone-faced, huddled with his children as gusts of swirling
snow obliterated their view of Father Engelmann, standing only
feet away at the edge of Julean's grave. Father was shouting out the
prayers yet they couldn't hear a sound, as each word rode the tail
of the wailing, tempestuous wind.

Only a few braved to come to the internment. Julean's parents
and sister stood next to Henry's family, surrounded by a few supporting relatives. Mary had one arm around Justin and the other
interlocked in Jeremy's, bracing herself against the wind. Others
remained cocooned in their cars; better they had stayed at the hall
since all they could see was swirling snow.

Father pulled down the flaps of his beaver hat and reined in
the stole around his neck as it fluttered deliriously in the wind.
It was useless to put the ashes on the coffin and so he proceeded
to give the final blessing. In one blink the onlookers saw him
raise his arm and in the next he vanished into the blustery churning snow. He emerged like a ghost and drew near Henry and his
family.

"Come, let us go back to the hall and have lunch and get
warmed up."

Henry didn't budge. "Take the children, Father, I will be along shortly."

Father could see frost bite forming on Henry's cheeks. His eyebrows and lashes were caked with snow. "You need to get inside."

"I'm fine, Father, please take the children."

Father pulled his scarf out of his overcoat and hung it around Henry's neck.

"Put it over your head, keep your ears warm and don't stay too long, the children need you."

It was Father's last words that instilled some recognition of responsibility back into his life. He recalled driving home, faced with the task of explaining to his children how such a tragedy in life, the death of their mother, could possibly happen. The doctors had failed, God had failed. Life had failed. His world crashed in on him just like it did when Jenny left, but even more so now. He grasped for help from the past, tried to recall words of hope Father Engelmann had offered him, but everything seemed so distant and futile. Even God seemed concealed, hidden somewhere in the cold winter of death and utter despair. Henry was submerged in unbearable emotional and mental agony, and nothing could console his devastating loss.

Henry stood motionless like a frozen statue staring at the coffin which every now and then materialized in the snow. It was as though not even his heart were beating. He ignored the stinging numbness of his feet. Only the funeral director remained, standing like a sentinel at the head of grave where Father had stood waiting for the workers to come and bury the coffin.

The workmen seemed to come out of nowhere, appearing like apparitions on the scene, and removed the tarp that covered the soil. They shook the snow and folded it, revealing its green, sod colour. The director pushed a lever and lowered the coffin until it disappeared from Henry's view. She was really gone.

The two cemetery attendants removed the brass frame and straps around the grave and carried them away into the twirling snow. Henry expected them to return but instead a backhoe emerged like a giant monster coming out of a mist. It struck out its large paw and easily cut into the frozen pile of dirt. For a brief moment Henry heard the sound of the machine groan as it lifted its bucket and moved above the hole. Its sound faded in and out like a radio signal. Slowly it descended into the grave, gently releasing its load over the coffin below. The powerful machine worked rhythmically without feeling the task it was engaged in. The falling soil was like a curtain going down on her role in the stage of life.

Within five minutes the grave was filled and in another minute the black sod was painted white by the blizzard, leaving no trace of Henry's loving wife below. Emptiness swept over Henry and consumed him. Julean had vanished from the earth, vanished from his life. He would never see her again or feel the touch of her warm hand. Nothing would ever be the same.

With burial complete, the director made his way over to Henry. He put his arm around Henry and gently tugged him on. Moments ago Henry would have resisted, but his strength was all but totally depleted. Life had defeated him. The director shook the snow off the scarf Father had left and placed it over Henry's head, covering his ears and tying it under his chin like an adult helping a child get dressed. Henry simply stared straight ahead, oblivious to what was going on around him.

The director locked onto Henry's arm and they walked toward the car. Off to Henry's left, an image of a person emerged like a shadow behind white translucent glass. Henry wondered who would care enough to be out in this storm. He felt drawn to the tall figure and pulled the director in that direction. As they drew near, the profile of a man emerged. His collar was up, his back hunched and his hands buried deep in his coat pockets. His long hair fluttered like a flag in the storm.

The wind escalated and the man was momentarily lost in the churning snow. Henry and his escort stopped and searched the white out. He leaned more and more into the wind, which was blowing gusts of snow into his face. Henry hesitated… and leaned even more and more intently forward into the heavy snow because he knew something terrible was at hand.

They moved slowly ahead and just as they thought the man must have moved on, the wind abated and he stood there before them. Henry looked up and immediately recognized him. It was the man he had dragged out of the overturned car. It was the man whose life Julean had saved... John McBryne. The man who had killed his wife.

Hatred fuelled by bitterness, regret, and pent up anguish soared like the raging wind through Henry's spirit. He wanted to attack, to hurt him, to make him pay, and as his strength waned, instinct possessed him. His innards, exploding with agony, combined forces and overpowered his sense of decency and care for others. Nothing could stop the storm in his heart. He struck out and pounded his fists on the man's shoulders. The man made no effort to move, to dodge or restrict Henry's release. Tears ushered forth from Henry's eyes and froze on his cheeks even before he collapsed into the snow. The man and the director took hold of Henry's shoulders and dragged him to the car.

CHAPTER SIXTY-TWO

HENRY NEVER DID remember what happened that day at his wife's funeral. He recalled seeing the man whose life Julean had saved and after that his mind went blank. He was told that the funeral director brought him to the hospital emergency for treatment for frost bite, that he was given a sedative and that Jeremy had picked him up and taken him home.

The winter storm continued to rage across the prairies that week and, like Henry's sorrow, showed no end in sight. His mother stayed at the farm to help out with the children while Henry tried in vain to pick up the threads and weave his and his family's life back together again.

Out of concern for her son's state of mind, Mary called Father for help.

"I've tried everything, Father, but Henry continues to withdraw into his studio. He misses Julean so terribly. The house seems to have turned into a funeral home. Perhaps you can help. He looks up to you so much."

THE NEXT MORNING, Father showed up at the door after Mass. Henry was surprised to see him.

"How did you come, you have no car?"

"Oh the Lord always has an angel on duty to get me from here

514

to there." Father winked.

"That's very nice of you, Father, to take the time to come, and especially in this blizzard."

"The Lord was sitting on Saint Christopher's shoulders, leading us all the way. So, how are you doing, Henry?" Father asked as they made their way up to Henry's studio.

There was a long silence after they were seated. Father could feel that the house was filled with sadness. Dark circles framed Henry's swollen eyes that were filled with an ocean of grief. His cheeks were drawn and colourless like white chalk. The spirit of Henry's oppression surrounded him. The only glimmer of hope was the rosary Henry held in his hand. It was Julean's; Father recalled how happy she was when he blessed it for her.

After a long while, Henry struggled to speak. The blood rose to his head and with a burning look in his eyes he said, "I know we have talked about this before, but I just can't seem to understand why God made a world in which there has to be death and sorrow. One minute Julean and I were so happy and in the next, it was snatched away from us in the blink of an eye."

Father, with a calm, peaceful light in his eyes, gazed solemnly at his troubled son, "Yes, especially in our darkest hours it is difficult to understand. We yearn for things to be different and for God to change the laws He has established and restore things to the way they were. At times the Lord does alter things and a miracle happens, but in nearly all situations, life follows its natural course."

"But why, Father?" A wild look flashed in Henry's weary eyes. "We have led a good life. It almost seems as if He is punishing us."

"Oh no, Henry, that is clearly not the case. This is something I am often asked. It's the eternal question."

"I'm just so angry Father. Angry at John McBryne, angry at God, angry at myself, and... and, angry at Julean in a way! I feel so sick to even say that, but it's the truth. I'm angry at her for leaving me... for leaving our family." Henry bent his head down into his hands and sobbed.

Father bent forward, resting his elbows on his knees, drawing nearer to Henry. "I'm not sure what I have to say will help you or is the complete answer, but first let me say the Lord understands your suffering and He is here present with us now, desiring so much to help you. Remember the Lord knows suffering personally. He died on the cross for us, and remember, too, His Father in heaven didn't deliver Him either from the pain of sin and death."

That is true. Henry sat up, hoping that Father might say something would bring him solace. His pain crippled his body, soul, and spirit; he'd lost all hope and all his dreams to emptiness.

"In the Lord's wisdom, He created a world in which man was free to choose to love Him or go against Him. He saw that many would choose the latter and, yet, He decided to let man be free, not like robots where they would have to cater to His every whim. In such a world, Henry, perhaps we could have avoided pain and suffering, but then there would be no individuality, no freedom, no choice. Man would be as a puppet on God's string."

Father sat up and raised his right hand to reinforce the truth of God's plan. "No, in His infinite wisdom, God created man with his own will and freedom to choose. This is the world He created and thus is governed by the accompanying laws of life. When we choose to do wrong we pay the consequences and even when we do good at times we must pay for the consequences of others who made an unwise choice—"

"Like that man who gave Julean the disease she died from."

Father nodded and continued. "Along with freedom of choice comes a world which is inevitably imperfect. Fortunately, the good overshadows the evil as history shows. But there is evil, heartache, and sorrow along with the tremendous good, beauty, and joy. When tragedy strikes, we would like things to be different. We would like God to change His laws and deliver us. As I said, at times He does intervene, but only in very special cases does He alter the course of man, but in most cases life goes on."

Father sat back into his chair and reflected further before he continued. "Water is needed to sustain life and, yet, a person could drown by this same life-giving force. Fire gives warmth and cooks our food and, yet, it can destroy our homes and lives. Man can love, but he can also choose to kill and do evil. This is the world we live in and God asks of us to become his obedient partner, a collaborator to make the world better so more people choose to do good and to love.

"Death is inevitable for all of us, Henry. Sooner or later we all die. Julean's untimely death teaches us how fragile life is and motivates us to make the best of every moment the good Lord has given us. The presence of death makes more meaningful all the values of life. It motivates us to use our time wisely and makes us aware of the fragility of life and our dreams."

Henry shook his head, this was the first time in days such inspiring thoughts entered his head. He suddenly realized how important it was to have caring friends.

"Thank you, God," he whispered.

"We have to accept what life gives us and believe that God will turn everything out for the good. Always remember, God does not abandon us. Through His divine providence He is constantly working to help us and bring us back to Him. So, too, are His angels and the Holy Spirit. As difficult as it may be, Henry, you are asked to accept and transcend your sorrow when you are ready and take up your responsibility to face life head on. Invite Jesus into your heart and God will give you the grace and strength to emerge from the peaks of your grief and begin once more to live in the valley of peace with your children and friends, and most importantly, yourself."

Father's words left Henry hanging in the air, feeling empty. Before this discussion he could attack God and others for his sorrow, but now he was confused and forced to look at himself openly and honestly. Henry could tell Father recognized his dilemma and waited for his wise teacher to deliver him once again from the edge of a breakdown.

"God uses us daily as instruments or channels of His divine message. The way we live determines whether we help or hinder God's purpose for man. Because we are free, God needs us to be His co-workers in the developing evolution of a better world. As I just said, and will say again and again, turn to Jesus and His helpers, keep Them at the centre of your life, yield your will to Them and do the will of the Father. This will bring us peace and bring love and healing into every situation. As we understand this, it should motivate us to relish each and every precious moment, and to choose to live life fully and improve the world while we are here. Julean did in a lifetime what might have taken others twenty, thirty, or forty years longer to do."

Father paused, suddenly realizing he had gone off on a tangent, in a direction that Henry was not yet ready to take. He stared at Henry then led him more in the direction that the moment needed.

"I'm sorry to ramble on so. Your question of why there is evil and sorrow in the world got me into an area that I had not intended for today. Tell me, my son, I know you're hurting deeply. Share with me your feelings of sorrow."

FOR THE NEXT three hours, Henry and Father sat in the studio and chatted. It was one sided; Father listened with his heart and encouraged Henry to talk of his wife. It reminded Henry of the time he did something similar for Mr. Engelmann when Anna died. He had brought a chair from the kitchen and set it beside his grieving teacher where he and Anna sat at the south window and did for him what his teacher was doing for him now.

What touched Father's heart so deeply was when Henry spoke of Julean's example of faith at the doorstep to death.

"You know Father, the day after I brought Julean into the hospital and before she slipped into a coma she asked me to bring her rosary from home. She was in a deep sleep when I returned so I placed the rosary in her hand in the position that I had seen many times whenever I would wake up before she did. She would say the rosary all the time in bed as she drifted off to sleep. She had a close relationship and deep love for the Holy Mother; it was such an example of faith to me.

"The doctor allowed me to keep the rosary in Julean's hand after she slipped into the coma. As the days progressed and she remained in her coma, Father, she continued saying her rosary. Her hand would be on the first decade and then when I would look an hour or two later her hand had moved to the third decade and then the fifth. I thought that maybe the coming and goings of the nurses and doctors had moved it… but no. She was praying. Twice I saw her fingers slip from one bead to the next… "

Henry stopped as his words were caught by surfacing tears. Father was also touched; almost imperceptibly his head moved from side to side as an expression of awe. He brushed away a tear with his hand.

"On the last night of viewing at Speer's funeral home I was the last to leave the room. Julean looked so at peace, Father, without all the tubes and wires attached to her. She looked as if she was asleep, just like I had seen her so many times in our bed. I stared at the pearl beaded rosary that was intertwined in her fingers and I felt so strongly prompted to take it. It was almost as if she wanted to give it to me as a gift. I had every intention to leave it there as we had done for my dad when he died. I still remember the black beaded rosary in his hands, as well.

"But it was the last thing Julean had in her hands before she died. It was what she loved so much and *I wanted to feel that love and her touch through the rosary.*

"I thought it might be difficult to remove the rosary as it was threaded in and out of her fingers. Would I even be able to remove it? But when I touched her hand there was no stiffness or coldness. Her hand was warm and soft and so tender and pliable, Father, like she were alive. Her fingers opened so easily, it was as if she were handing it to me… *it was her last gift to me… her gift of love and faith.*"

Henry stopped and could no longer speak… His fingers tightened around Julean's rosary in his hand and brought it to his lips…

Neither spoke for a long while after that. Henry and his beloved teacher sat silently savouring the miracle of life and death and the mystery of faith and love.

And so it continued: Henry would share more of his heart and then there was rest, followed by more sharing…

By two o'clock, Henry had talked himself out and a peaceful silence fell over the studio. The quietness was no longer laden with despair, but transfused with uplifting hope. Shortly before Father left he prayed over Henry and his family.

In the four days that followed, Father's visits continued in the same pattern: Henry was led to express as much grief as he could actually feel. Henry thought Father was encouraging him to grieve more and indulge in self-pity, but he slowly began to realize that his mentor was gently leading him to face his emotions and grief honestly and openly so he could get on with his life.

Henry also realized Father was helping him to remove himself from the deep physical and emotional ties of living together with his loved one over the years. Henry knew his life was, in essence, built around Julean, her love and support. He had come to expect it and relied on it. It was important for him to talk about that loss and the magnitude of her absence and how he now faced life alone. She had always brought out the best in him through her encouragement and loyalty.

"What will I do without her support and love, Father? Sometimes I panic and fear that I can't go through life without her."

"Henry, you are a gifted and talented man with great strength and abilities. Remember how much confidence Julean had in you to do anything. She readily agreed to all the career choices you've made because she had such faith in you. Death is a part of life and you can go on. The world wounds, but it also heals. As you step out in faith and trust, God will dish out His healing balm in many ways and forms. You must be open to life and its grace and blessings."

Father was right, as usual. He must pick up the threads of life again lest he get caught in the web of sorrow. Father had always taught him how important it was not to remain stuck in the past, and to live fully in the present so as to create a new past, full of life. The words Father spoke next would remain in Henry's heart and mind forever.

"*The melody you heard Julean sing daily in your life will never be sung in the same way again by anyone, yet the song of life goes on and we must be open to its music.*"

For a brief moment, Henry felt something promising, hopeful, and reassuring. The Lord wants his children to be servants of life for as long as they live.

"There is one more thing, Henry," his wisdom-filled friend went on to say, "I would like you to do something that may be very helpful to you and your family. Could you spend some time after I leave or this evening and write a letter to your wife, expressing all your love for her and what she has meant to you. Even share with her your anger if you need to get that out and ask for her forgiveness. And when you have written your love letter, write what she would say to you and what her will or wishes would be for you. Lastly, write what God would will for you and finally what you can begin doing to fulfill the will of your beloved wife and your dear Lord."

Whenever Father came to visit, Henry insisted that he sit in the armchair next to the south window as it reminded Father of the chair he and Anna used to sit in by the south window of their living quarters at the grocery store. It was exceptionally significant, that day, as the winter storm had been pushed out by a Chinook rolling in from Alberta allowing the warm sunshine to stream in, bathing Father with shimmering light.

It reminded Henry of what his holy mentor always maintained, that behind every storm the sun was ready to cast its healing rays on any burden. And that's exactly what Father's presence always did. Whereas Henry would look at the cruelties of life pulling him down, *Father seemed to be gazing at some unseen beauty that was constantly nourishing his spirit and then radiating it out to others with warm, healing power.*

In and out he breathed peace.

No wonder Henry felt a sudden coolness when Father left for the day.

"You know, Father, that was a wonderful assignment you asked me to do. It helped me to both look into myself and see where I was in this struggle and to get outside of myself; to see where I needed to go and see the tasks waiting to be done. Julean was such a quiet force in my life, I never fully realized or appreciated it until now. The family is hurting so much and there is no one to fill her shoes. I see and hear them crying."

Father rested the notes on his lap and looked up with a hopeful gaze. "God gave us tear ducts to use in our hour of darkness, let the kids weep and don't be ashamed of yourself, either, to let it go; it helps to reconstruct the broken fragments of our lives. The children need to discuss their sorrow with you like you are with me.

It will take time and don't expect immediate results or think it can be swept away. It is unwise to shorten the stages of recuperation into a magic cure. There are many steps on the pathway to healing from sorrow to renewed peace and life.

"*Tears, talking it out and support are very important.*"

Henry stared at his mentor, he could see the pattern Father was following and realized he was trying to instill in him the same method to follow with his children. Henry had to first listen to his children, grieve with them and support them in their grief, then establish new patterns of interaction with his family and others without his partner.

As if reading his mind, Father continued, "Henry, you are a good father and have a good relationship with your children. This will strengthen your ties with them. Be a strong guiding light to your children by taking up the threads of life again."

Father's words, as usual, were like an insightful incision that cut right to Henry's heart. In an atmosphere of unconditional acceptance, Father placed a mirror before him in which he saw his self-inflicted inward flaws and spiritual crevices. And in the same reflection, he guided Henry to hope and promise and the potential for a better day.

"You know, Father, I am beginning to see how my sorrow is infectious. It spreads like a dark stain in the fabric of my children's lives. I've avoided talking to the children about Julean and her death, especially with Lauren and Justin."

Father gazed at his broken protégé compassionately. "The children need to talk about this just as you need to. Even Justin can stand the tragedy and sorrow of his mother's death. Tears and talking openly to them at their age level about it is far better than sugar coating, or evading the issue.

"Sometimes we fall into the belief that children cannot stand grief and sadness and must be coddled and sheltered against the tragedies of life. No, your sons and daughters should be dealt with in a straightforward and honest fashion. They should be allowed to share and participate in the family's hardships as well as the triumphs. Children, even the young, are much stronger than we think."

"I know you are right, Father, it's just that I am having such difficulty dealing with it myself that I am transferring this burden onto my children."

"Perhaps working through it with them will help you understand it on a deeper level, just like when you started teaching physics, you came to understand it on another level through the eyes of your students. Rest assured, Henry, that within you and your children is the strength to withstand the shocks and woes of life. And you are part of that healing, Henry."

"I hope I can emulate the guidance you have shown me. For most of my life you have been such a role model and guiding light. In fact, I was just thinking earlier that you are my hero in life."

"That is kind of you to say, Henry, but right now that is exactly what *you* must be to your family. The children are hurting and they need direction and guidance. You must replace your grief with a life of quiet joy for you and your family. They need a hero to light the way in their darkness. They need the cheerful warmth of your care and love to flow into their lives, leading them to hope and the promise of a bright future."

The front door slammed, startling Father and Henry. Minutes later, Justin's footsteps charged up the stairs. Henry was ready to whisk his son away so as to continue his heavy discussion with Father, but the naked truth of what he should be doing blasted him straight in his face.

"Hi, Grandpa," Justin said with sparkling eyes and then rushed excitedly over to his father's side. He shook his dad's hand which immediately reminded Henry of the time in the hospital when Justin wanted his mom to wake up. If she could have, she would have jumped up at the chance. Henry was waking to his new calling in the family, but was still somewhat asleep. The words that flowed from his son's lips in the next instant, however, brought him wide awake into the reality of life.

"Come, Daddy. Don't be sad anymore. It's so nice out. Let's go outside and play catch."

Without hesitation, Henry rose, took his son's hand and walked with him out of the studio. The passive discussion at hand was no longer required; *it had been activated by a cheerful heart.*

Father gazed out the window and saw Henry and Justin each with a baseball glove, go outside onto the driveway. Wrinkles of amusement and joy gathered at the corners of his eyes as a favourite scripture, John 10:10 came to mind, "I am come that they might have life, and that they might have it more abundantly." Father's eyes misted as he faintly heard Henry shout to his enthusiastic son, "Let's play ball!"

CHAPTER SIXTY-THREE

I T HAD BEEN such a long cold winter Jenny could hardly believe that spring had finally arrived. Her spirits needed a lift in the worst way. J.J. still hadn't returned her calls despite her mother's attempts to bring about some kind of reconciliation. James was home for two weekends during the winter, but only to gather more of his belongings and had kept J.J. away. It was clear that their marriage was over, but Jenny didn't know what course of action to take.

She could move out and into an apartment like her mother, but the estate and grounds gave her so much joy and peace. Despite her loneliness, she enjoyed a sense of freedom there far better than looking at four walls in a cloistered suite. Moving in with her mother did not appeal to her. She knew it was best for her to be on her own and help as she had been doing. At least that way she still had a home to go to and one in which she had no trouble filling her days.

If only James had stepped back and looked at their marriage from a panoramic perspective and saw the joy and happiness that were just a heartbeat away. For a brief second Jenny visualized herself, James and Jimmy really being a loving family. What a wonderful life they could have had together. It was unfortunate he was always so glued and focused on the business, never enjoying the treasures right under his nose, but rather striving day and night for more: more money, more power, another acquisition, always chasing an illusion that would never give him peace or happiness that a loving family relationship would have.

Perhaps that is one of the blessings for me from this marriage, thought Jenny, *to see what is really important in life... Love, relationship, family, enjoying God's creation, using our talents to serve. Perhaps someday James will see...*

"Well, it's easy to be critical and dwell on the 'if only' in our life. At the end of the day, neither blame nor 'what could have been' gets one anywhere." Jenny murmured as she strode into the kitchen.

Rather than dwell on the past negatives, she was buoyed up by the fact that she had learned patience, tolerance, and acceptance in her relationship. She could have very easily gone the other way and become a miserable, vindictive, hateful wretch! Jenny was well aware of how people become affected by their environments and products of those they live with. She could have lost her personhood and succumbed to James' controlling whims and neurotic obsessions.

A smile covered her face over these thoughts and her blue eyes brightened at the sight of the vase of wildflowers soaking up the sun on the window sill. Jenny was thankful for the winter bouquet the Angel of Thanksgiving had given her. It gave her so much spiritual sustenance, hope, and strength over the cold winter days. Amazingly, it was only over a week ago the flowers in the vase began to droop and wither away. It was as if they anticipated spring and that Jenny would soon be surrounded and supported by all the new growth and beauty of the grounds.

It was this knowledge of nature and herself that Jenny decided to do what she had done at countless other times in her life when loneliness and despair were knocking at her door. She dressed in her jeans and an oversized sweatshirt and made her way out onto the grounds. Thomas and Ramon were unloading some of the annuals and Jenny wanted to help.

"Good morning, Miss Jenny. It's that time again to beautify the grounds."

"Yes, I was going to ask if I could help you plant them again. It gives me so much satisfaction to work with the soil and like you say, 'cover it with beauty.'"

"Of course, Miss Jenny, if it gives you joy, by all means."

"Thank you, Thomas. Here, can I take those marigolds and is it okay if we plant them near the patio doors?"

"Yes, Ma'am, I'm sure wherever you plant them the good Lord will make them flourish. Did you see the wildflower patch? I've never seen the flowers come so early. I'm certain I saw a few even peek through the snow."

"Yes, I did notice that the other day when I strolled through the grounds." Jenny was going to tell Thomas of the winter bouquet, but he continued with an uplifting thought.

"I believe it is because you love the wildflowers and they are over-anxious to please you and make you happy."

"Thomas, what a wonderful thing to say. See, I knew I just had to come out here today and work in the garden. Not only will the flowers lift my spirits, but your kindly words have done so, too."

Jenny smiled and leaned forward to peck Thomas' cheek. If his skin had not been dark, his reddening cheeks would have been far more evident. Jenny took two trays from Thomas and skipped off to a section of freshly turned-over dirt near the patio. By noon, the rich black soil was covered with dazzling colour.

"My, my, Miss Jenny, you surely do work quickly. You have a natural knack for gardening."

"It's the one constant in my life that never fails to give me peace. I love nature and the sun has always been my friend. Oh and by the way, Matti called yesterday and said to say hello to you and Ramon. She misses us very much. We are going out for lunch on Saturday. She said she is going to bake some cookies and muffins for you and Ramon and give them to me to bring home for you."

"That would be wonderful, we sure do miss Matilda's cooking, but most of all we miss her and our lively chats in the tool shed. She is quite the lady."

"Yes, she sure is," concurred Jenny. "I miss her terribly as well. And I'm so looking forward to hearing her tell me all about how Jimmy is doing."

Jenny tossed her hands high up into the air and twirled around as if trying to catch the sunshine. She was so happy spring had arrived and that she was out in the garden. Thomas and then Ramon stopped what they were doing and stared with widening eyes as if they were seeing a dancing angel.

After lunch, Jenny, with diary in hand, made her way to the gazebo. Since the day before, even more flowers had emerged in the wildflower patch. The aroma was so uplifting , filling the spring air with an intoxicating fragrance. Jenny sat down on her swinging chair in the gazebo and rested her eyes on the Angel of Thanksgiving.

"My dear, dear angel," whispered Jenny, "Thank you for the spring, the flowers, and all the beauty."

Despite all of Jenny's trials and tribulations, her spirit and trust and faith in life had never wavered. The beauty of God's creation had sustained her. Jenny pushed her foot against the floor of the deck and set the swing in a gentle motion. She realized that her life was not perfect, that she was lonely and would love to have companionship. She was still a married woman and really not free to date other men. She could file for divorce. James would easily give it to her, but then what? She would have to leave this beautiful estate and surely then J.J. would vanish from her life completely and probably blame her for the demise of the marriage.

Jenny often wondered why women stayed in unsatisfying or even abusive marriages. It dawned on her that perhaps it was the unknown, the uncertainty of what might be in store. Down deep Jenny believed in her ability to handle anything.

The swing had stopped before Jenny realized it was no longer swinging. She reached for her diary and jotted down the date:

May 22, 1983.

I am so happy spring is here! The beauty, the fresh smell of the air and the perfume of the flowers is delicious. Soon the lilacs will bloom: my favourite scent. How appropriate that Camilla was born at this time of year; every year her birthday coincides with the bursting of life and colour that surrounds me!

If the truth be known, perhaps the only other thing that has warmed my heart through the cold winter besides my miracle bouquet, are my thoughts of Camilla and Henry. Even though my dear daughter is adopted and could be anywhere and Henry is married and has a beautiful wife and family, I just know that someday we will all meet again.

Jenny hopped off the swing and made her way to the flower patch. Thoughts of Henry's wife, Julean, had been on her mind off and on during the past winter, but even more so the past several days as Camilla's birthday approached. Whenever thoughts such as these came along, she usually sent off a little prayer or best wishes of some kind for them. Jenny snapped off a yellow daisy and placed it into the Angel of Thanksgiving's basket. The sunshine brightened its golden petals.

"*This is for you, Julean, and your happiness with Henry.*"

CHAPTER SIXTY-FOUR

S LOWLY, AS THE winter progressed toward spring, Henry and his family accepted Julean's passing. With Father's help, Henry replaced his grief by emerging as a stronger father and taking on the responsibility of raising his children. And just as Father had helped Henry come to terms with his sorrow and pain, so Henry did the same with all of the children. It was Allison's anger toward God for taking her mother that Henry found the most challenging to deal with. But using Father's insight as to why there is sorrow in the world and explaining it at his daughter's level of understanding, she finally warmed up to God again.

One evening, after the children had gone to their rooms, Henry and his mother found themselves alone in the living room.

"That was so good of you to stay with us for the winter and help out. I know we couldn't have managed without you and the kids love you so much, Mom."

"The children are such a joy, Henry, but I must say looking after four is much different than just having to raise one child like you. I can really appreciate the challenges Julean faced."

Henry could see on his mother's face she wasn't sure if she should have brought up Julean.

"Yeah, Julean was such a good mother, too. Just like you, Mom." Henry smiled.

"Well, it will certainly be a drastic change going into an empty home, but now that spring is here I do look forward to working out in the garden."

"Yeah, that has been a big part of your life. I can hardly wait for fall when you make Borscht soup from all your garden beets."

"I could buy some vegetables and make it sooner, you know."

"It just wouldn't be the same, Mom. There's nothing like vegetables right from the garden and the fresh dill you add is incredible."

His mother's eyes widened as if the mention of dill triggered some memory.

"Well, the children seem to be adjusting much better and it might be good for you and the children to be alone for awhile and…" his mother hesitated then added, "…perhaps you need to go out and meet new friends, as well."

Henry studied his mother. He knew what she was referring to, Father recently alluded to him as well to consider going out with both male and female friends.

"You know, Mom, that afternoon when I was alone with Julean and she came out of her coma for the last time, she suggested that I go out and marry, again. I never told you, but Julean also brought up Jenny."

Again, his mother's eyes betrayed her surprise.

"Do you recall that day shortly after dad died I told you that I thought Julean knew of Jenny. Well, I was right. Even though I had never told her about Jenny, Julean knew of her and my feelings towards her."

"But, how would she have known if you had never told her?"

"Through my dreams. Incredible, isn't it, that after all these years I would still dream about my teenage girlfriend and reveal it to my wife as I slept."

His mother smiled, but it didn't quite reach her eyes.

"And, what's even more incredible and what I also suspected, was that Julean said she would have shared Jenny with me in our marriage."

"Oh my, I don't think that would have been a good idea. The Lord made marriage for a man and a wife."

"Yeah, I know. I think that it's just because of Julean's

background in the Mormon faith and her wish to… Well, it's too silly to contemplate. I guess what I was trying to say was that Julean, too, did suggest I seek other female companions, but right now I don't think anyone will ever replace Julean. Not even someone like Jenny. I loved her so much and I always will."

"Well, perhaps it's best not to rush things. Everything has its own time."

MARY LOOKED AT her son and how the sorrow over his wife's passing still weighed so heavily on his heart. Her face mirrored that same loss. It reminded her of the time Jenny left Regina to go to Ottawa. How he had anguished and was lost and forlorn for so many years. Finally Julean came along and restored his life and now, once again the poor man was thrust back into the throes of a similar but even more painful situation. Mary sat back into her chair as if to appear to be relaxing, but far from it.

She wondered about the letter in her treasure chest and the almost supernatural force it seemed to be exerting on her to give it to her son. It just seemed to have a destiny of its own. But, what if Jenny were married and had a family which, in all likelihood she had, what good would it do? It just might create even more problems.

CHAPTER SIXTY-FIVE

IT WAS THE first of June and one of those days on the prairies when there was no wind and the sun overhead shone with all its radiance. It had been busy at the gallery over the noon hour and then had quieted down. For the past several days it had been on Henry's mind to visit his wife's gravesite. The funeral director had mentioned several months ago that they would be placing the bronze tombstone there first thing in the spring.

Henry parked his car just inside the cemetery gate and decided to walk the rest of the way to Julean's gravesite. Not a cloud in the sky impeded the warm rays of the sun. It had been a long, arduous winter for prairie folk to bear and Henry more than welcomed sunny days like this.

As he strolled peacefully along under the shade of the elm trees lining the road he thought how his life had changed so drastically since his wife's untimely death.

Unwanted feelings of anger stirred as he thought about the circumstances of how it all happened. How tragedy had come out of an act of selflessness and care for the life of another. Henry wished he had never heard the name John McBryne.

"Oh Lord," he whispered, "Forgiveness is such an important part of life and freedom for us all." He recalled the day after his valedictorian speech when he and Eddy had fully reconciled and the deep joy and freedom he had felt. Later that day he had shared this with Mr. Engelmann. The words his teacher said came back to him now: "Remember this moment; sear it into your heart so when others hurt you in your life journey you will remember the freedom and joy of forgiveness and do so quickly."

Oh please help me Lord.

Henry stopped and gazed at the sea of tombstones before him to get his bearings. He was certain the gravesite was about a block east from where he stood. He got off the road and decided to take a shortcut by weaving in and out of the tombstones. In the hope of distracting his mind from the clutches of unforgiveness, Henry began reading the names of those who had died and the range of years they had lived. He was surprised at how many had passed on in a life span even less than that granted to his wife. In a sense it made him feel better that he was not alone, but the thought "misery loves company" wasn't really that consoling.

When passing the tombstone of a young girl who had barely lived twelve years, he bumped hard into a large granite stone. He immediately recognized the huge marker.

JACOB STEVENS

1873 - 1946

ETERNALLY I ASK FOR FORGIVENESS

"The Lord simply doesn't want me to forget his command," Henry muttered. A smile covered his face as he stared at the words chiseled in stone and how this huge marker had affected both his parents' lives to forgive.

"Perhaps it is I who needs the lesson, now."

Henry patted the grey granite almost as lovingly as an old friend would pat his buddy and went on his way.

Forgiveness once again weighed heavily on his heart. Henry struggled to push down the tears. Although his discussions with Father Engelmann helped, he wasn't ready to completely forgive and thought he never would be.

As Henry drew near the site where the body of his dear wife was laid, he suddenly stopped and understood what the Lord was preparing him for. A beautiful bouquet of spring flowers was draped over the slight mound and at the foot of the grave knelt Henry's most loathed enemy slouched over in prayer.

Hard, cold anger chilled Henry's warm, rising tears. He had hated this man since the night he and his friends raped Jenny. And now the love of his life had been taken away from him and his children because of his actions. One of the scriptures Father Engelmann gave to him the other night blared in his enraged mind's eye:

"But now I tell you: love your enemies, and pray for those who mistreat you, so that you will become the sons of your Father in heaven. For He makes his sun to shine on bad and good people alike, and gives rain to those who do right and those who wrong—"

"No!" Henry's mind screamed, then aloud he whispered, "Lord I can't...."

Tears poured from his eyes, blurring his vision. He stumbled and his hand caught a tombstone for support.

Father's passages returned but they came in the form of questions:

"Did God not create all people out of His love for them? Can you separate the man God created from his deed? Is retaliation, hate and condemnation the answer Henry? To what end...?"

"No, no more..." Henry wiped his eyes and shook his head to rid himself of such thoughts; he did not want to be swayed from his mission ...

Revenge is what his heart cried out for.

He shook his head once more and as he made his way to the next tombstone and then the next, clinging for support, Father Engelmann's words and teachings gripped his mind with even more conviction. With each step, the struggle between war and peace raged on.

"It's all about choice Henry. What do you choose to focus on, the hate and your desire for retaliation or on the good that God created and how you can help to restore this child of God?"

But he killed my wife and the mother to our children—

"Henry, do you want to be right and justified in your anger or do you want peace and freedom and to make the world a better place?

"What would Jesus do… ?

"What would He want you to do… ?

"What actions of yours would give witness to Jesus' love and foster healing and growth…?

"Think carefully now, the choice you make reveals your heart and where you will continue to dwell".

At that moment Henry hated Father's wisdom, it always cut through his thinking and its truth overwhelmed him. Father should be on *his* side and support *him*… Couldn't Father see the terrible thing this man had done?

Henry's mind remained focused steadfastly on the injury and his desire for retribution. His heart tried to melt; to turn from its icy coldness into a warm, soft, pliable putty to be remolded by Father' words, but Henry remained unrelenting. The tears of pain, sorrow and anger erupting from deep within would not allow appeals for compassion and mercy.

It was when Henry was just a few feet from striking blindly at the man that an image of Julean's spirit appeared beside the man and instantly the words she told him the last time they spoke in the hospital rushed back.

"Honey, you must forgive. Please don't harbour ill will. You know what the Lord asks of us. If you do not forgive, then He cannot forgive you. Henry, I want the best for you. Please listen to me."

As Julean's spirit faded as suddenly as she had appeared, Henry lunged towards her, grasping, and stumbled directly behind the kneeling man. With tears streaming down his cheeks, his heart raging, Henry raised a clenched fist high, ready to crash down with a mighty blow… And then, the Lord confirmed both Father's and Julean's words, revealing to Henry the only road to *peace*:

"Whoever loves Me will keep My word, and My Father will love him, and We will come to him and make Our dwelling with him…"

The Words enveloped Henry's hardened fist like a soft cloud and unraveled it. His open hand gently floated down and rested upon the man's shoulder as softly as a feather.

Without looking up, the man reached back and placed his hand on Henry's and pleaded, "*Mr. Pederson, please forgive what I did to you and your family.*"

The image of Julean's spirit was no longer there, but had now united with Henry's. For the first time since his wife's death, real tears filled with healing and love like a natural spring bubbled up from the depth of his innermost being and ushered forth like a gusher. And through his sobs, Henry whispered…

"*I forgive you, John McBryne.*"

Chapter Sixty-Six

THE REFLECTION THAT Mary looked at in the mirror did not please her. It was filled with guilt and deceit and a desire to make everything right. She shifted and moved away from it, but her image followed, mimicking her every move. After almost an hour of pacing the floor between the kitchen and the bedroom, Mary summoned up the courage to get her treasure chest from the closet shelf. She wanted to store Julean's funeral remembrance card in the box along with other memorabilia.

Although her son's marriage to Julean had turned out to be wonderful, Mary could never rid herself of the memory of that pivotal day, less than two weeks prior to their wedding day, when she had decided not to give Jenny's letter to him. Try as she might to justify her decision, down deep she knew it wasn't hers to make. Mary honestly believed that the aura of light surrounding her chest was a constant reminder of a love never resolved and the fateful part she played in it.

Just thirty-eight years old. Mary stared at Julean's card in her hand. So young to have had life snatched away. A mother and wife in the prime years of her life. Mary felt such a deep compassion for her son to once again have to undergo the painful separation from another woman he so deeply loved. Had Henry married Jenny, would the same destiny have occurred?

"Oh stop it, right now," Mary muttered. "Here you go again, trying to play God."

Tears welled in Mary's eyes as she read the poem on the card Henry and the family had written of Julean:

We understand why you were here...

...the sun will never shine so brightly again...

Mary couldn't read the poem again. It was filled with all the beautiful things that described Julean's life as a wife and mother. How death had awakened the deep love they shared and had taken for granted. Each child had written a reflection and the last two verses expressed Henry's love for her.

Mary kissed the photo of her lovely daughter-in-law and opened the lid of her treasure chest. Jenny's letter was at the very top. She recalled throwing it in there after taking it from Henry's hand shortly after Bill's passing.

How close Henry had been to knowing the truth about it all. But, what good would that have done? Julean was still alive.

The glint of a tiny silver metal protruding from the envelope caught Mary's attention. She remembered seeing it that same day when she snatched the letter and the object broke the seal. She was certain Henry had seen it sticking out, as well. Mary always wondered what that heavy object was inside the envelope. Curiosity getting the better of her, she grasped the metal between her thumb and forefinger and slowly pulled the metal from its paper chamber.

"It's a pewter angel and... it feels so warm."

Mary ran her fingers around the outline of the angel's wings. No wonder it seemed to fly in the envelope. She could almost imagine the tall silver wings fluttering, trying to deliver the letter to its loved one. The thought was eerie yet soothing; supernatural, yet real.

"An angelic letter," muttered Mary. A letter with a power to seemingly create its own destiny.

"Watch over my Beloved," whispered Mary as she read the inscription at the foot of the angel. *What a beautiful thought. If only Henry could read this, how soothing and healing it might be to him.*

Mary carefully slipped the angel back into the slit of the

envelope. She took a bobby pin from a jar on her dresser and slipped it over the opening, hoping that would seal it and prevent the angel from flying out. Was the bright aura of light in the closet due to the angelic nature of the letter? A look of wonderment and awe covered her face as she laid the letter back into her chest and covered it with Julean's memorial remembrance card.

"My, my," Mary whispered. The two women in her son's life now side by side, buried in her treasure chest. "*What on earth will come of all this?*"

"THANK YOU so much for taking me to the doctor, Jenny." Edith was perspiring by the time she made it to the chesterfield chair in her living room suite.

"Now that school is out for the summer, I'll be able to visit and help out more, too."

"The doctor recommends I either get a nurse to live in or move to a care home. Oh, Jenny, I love my apartment so much. I'd hate to move again so soon, but I know I need help. Some days my arthritis is so bad I can't get a plate from the cupboard."

Jenny gazed at her mother compassionately. She could have her mother move in with her at the estate, but her mother needed more help than she could give and the doctor was also concerned with her heart.

"I know this isn't what you want to hear, Mom, but there are some very good care homes that offer different levels of care. You could still have your own suite and yet your meals could be pre-pared for you. And more importantly, many of the homes have nurses on staff and doctors that visit."

"I suppose you're right, Jenny. I do worry, especially at night, if something should happen. I know you're available, but as you say having access to medical help and assistance when needed is prob-ably what I now need as much as I hate to admit it."

"You're welcome to stay with me on the estate. We could try it out for the summer while I'm at home. In the fall when I return to school, however, we would have to hire someone to come in."

"That is so kind of you, Jenny, but I think my days on an estate are over and I really don't want to become an imposition on anyone. Perhaps you could help me find a suitable place this summer."

"Well, I recall one of the teachers at work mentioning new homes on the outskirts of the city that provide individual rooms with lovely views and grounds to stroll through. I'm sure there is something out there to suit your needs and liking. And, as I said, you can come to my home on the weekends, whenever you wish."

"That does sound nice, Jenny. Please look into it for me."

Jenny surveyed the apartment and all the new furniture her mother had bought in the past year.

"Perhaps the care home you move into will accommodate some of the furniture you purchased for this apartment. I'd hate to see you having to sell or give it away."

"Oh, it's just stuff, Jen. The main thing is to be healthy and as happy as you can be in your old age."

"You're not old, mom. You just have a few medical challenges and new medicine is always coming out."

Her mother forced a smile. "Well, as soon as we find a place I can decide on what I need and what I can give away."

Jenny rose, studied the furnishings around the room. "Most of this will most likely be too big and too much for a care home. But some of it I'm certain we will be able to fit in. Come, let's look in the bedroom."

Jenny helped her mom off the chair and hobble into the bedroom.

"Oh, Mom, I'm afraid this lovely bedroom set might be too large. What you may need is a motorized bed that tilts up and down and helps you get out of bed."

Her mother rolled her eyes. "It's coming to that already, is it? Soon I'll need a motorized wheelchair, walker and God knows what."

Like the time when Jenny first viewed her mother's apartment, she was once again drawn to the closet. She opened the door and instantly was spellbound by the aura of light surrounding the chest resting on the top shelf. It seemed brighter than the first time she saw it and in fact, seemed to be shimmering like a signal or warning of some kind.

Edith stood frozen and momentarily forgot all about her painful arthritis.

"What a wonderful light seems to be around your hope chest, Mom. Why don't you rest on the bed and we can go through it together. I would just love to see all the memorabilia in it."

"Jenny, I like your first idea for me to lie down and have some rest. That trip to the doctor took the wind out of my sails. Perhaps another time we can explore the chest and its contents. Right now our first priority is to find a place for me to stay."

Jenny gazed at her mother. She really did look exhausted. She had always been such a strong person in so many ways. Seeing this weakened, fragile side of her mother frightened her.

"Yes, you're right, Mom. You need some rest and there's always another day to go through boxes and things before your move."

AFTER JENNY LEFT, Edith lay down for a nap, but couldn't sleep. She tossed and turned for over an hour until finally she got up and made her way to the closet door.

"It's what is in that chest that is keeping me from sleep," Edith muttered. "Sooner or later, Jenny is going to discover that letter, lest I take it out and destroy it." Almost instantly, apprehension swept through her at the very thought. She recalled Ted and the anxiety he'd felt daily over this letter and the others he had destroyed at her bidding. Edith felt weak and could no longer stand. She left the door open and backed up toward the bed and sat down on the edge.

It was the letters that really started it all. The decision not to show them to Jenny and then this letter that arrived years later after Ted's death. The pact she and Mrs. Pederson had made to destroy them and never to reveal them to their respective children. Edith's mind swirled with regretful memories. She wondered why she had never been able to destroy the letter in her chest. There was such a mystery and supernatural force surrounding it. Edith marveled at the light coming from the closet. She had not seen it so bright before.

Ted's last words came to mind. "Please deliver them... the letters…. The angelic letters... deliver them…" What on earth did he mean by 'angelic letters?' Maybe that was what was eerie and unnatural about all this. *What did Ted see or know that she didn't? Was the light something else, or simply Ted telling her to carry out his final wish?*

CHAPTER SIXTY-SEVEN

B Y LATE FALL of that year, things began to normalize. Perhaps what accelerated the healing, especially for Henry, was one, his forgiveness of John and two, the absence of guilt for having entertained thoughts of Jenny when Julean was alive. In both cases, it was his dear wife who was instrumental in helping to restore his peace. Henry was still astonished how she knew of Jenny through his dreams and the miracle of her coming out of her coma to bring it all out in the open to free him of guilt. He would never forget her apparition beside John that spring day, either. Even in death, she cared for his soul.

Henry made no effort to seek other female friendships as Father encouraged him to do. For now, he firmly felt that there would never be another who could ever possibly replace his wife. Instead, Henry worked on getting closer to his children and immersing himself in his business.

He'd purchased the confectionary building next door to his gallery and turned it into a café and gift shops, all of which he joined to the gallery. It was a huge complex and one that was well received by the city. In his spare time, the little he had, Henry continued to buy revenue property much to Father's chagrin.

"Thrusting yourself into one project after the other is no way to forget the past. Cherish those memories, Henry, as a part of your life and move forward to new relationships," Father would often say in one form or another. Julean had said those words, too, but for now he just wasn't ready and wondered if he ever would be.

On the home front, Henry was pleased with the way things were working out. Allison had attempted to fill her mother's shoes and often took care of Justin. Even though she and Lauren were a few years apart, over the winter and past summer they had grown closer and became very good friends. Jeremy, too, had long grown out of his teenage mindset and was a mature and responsible young man. It was hard to believe that his son was going into his third year of university next fall. The grades he had skipped during his elementary school years had never affected him adversely.

Julean had always thought there was some special reason for their son's giftedness. And like Allison, the care and attention he showed to his siblings was admirable. All in all, the children seemed to rally together and got along well with each other. Henry was very proud of the children and the excellent job his wife had done in raising them. *If only his dear wife was still here.*

One evening, as Henry and his daughter were doing dishes together, Allison brought up a subject that touched upon his son's flourishing attraction to the opposite sex.

"Dad? Have you noticed the change in Jeremy since he started back at university this fall?"

"Well, he is filling out and at least a head taller than me."

"That's not what I mean. Don't you notice that dreamy daze in his eyes?"

"He does seem to have a far off look, and come to think of it, I had to ask him three times to get up and take the garbage out yesterday. Normally he does it without my asking. Is that what you mean?"

"Well, I think it has to do with his new girlfriend. He told me he was sorry he had asked his old girlfriend, Sharon, to the university Thanksgiving dance because two weeks ago he met someone else. I guess they've gone out a couple of times and he seems really taken by her."

"Well, now that you mention it, he does seem to be smitten by something. His appetite has slowed, but that's a good thing. Maybe

I can save a bit on food bills."

"Oh, Dad, this is serious. Last night he asked that since he can't take his new girl to the dance, he was wondering if he could at least bring her to dinner next Sunday. He asked me to ask you."

"It would be interesting to see the girl that is sweeping him off his feet. What would we make for dinner? Should we ask Grandma to come out and help?"

"It would be nice to have Grandma out, but I could bake the chicken casserole Mom used to make. She taught me how and it's not that difficult a recipe to follow."

"Yeah, I would say you do an excellent job with that dish. There wasn't a spoonful left when you made it last time."

"Thanks, Dad."

"Well, maybe we all better check out this young lady. I'll tell Jeremy when he comes home later that it's fine with me."

"That's great, Dad. Lauren and I are reading a teenage romance novel about this guy who falls in love with a girl at first sight. We can't get over how much he reminds us of Jeremy. I can't wait to see this girl."

Love at first sight. "Yeah, it's been known to happen, Allison."

"WHERE ARE THE keys to the car, Dad?" Jeremy asked, hopping from one foot to the other.

"Aren't they on the table by the front door?"

Jeremy wandered from one room to the other. "No, I don't see them."

"I'm certain I saw them there, too," said Allison. She walked out to the foyer. "Yes, here they are." Allison smiled at her anxious brother as she gave him the keys.

Henry gazed at his son. He looked so tall and grown up. His face seemed manlier of late and Henry detected signs of a mustache.

"You look handsome in that burgundy sweater, son. Are you going to bring your lady friend right back or just before dinner?"

"We should be here in about an hour. When is dinner?"

"The same time as usual, five-thirty."

"Oh, Jeremy, I can hardly wait to meet your girlfriend." Allison stepped forward and hugged her brother.

Henry was touched by the exchange and gesture. It reminded him of what Julean would have done. In many ways, Allison was a reflection of her mother.

"Drive careful, son."

Henry and Allison watched Jeremy back out of the driveway.

"Boy, Jeremy was sure jittery all morning," observed Allison.

"So will you be when prince charming comes along," said Henry, with a Father Engelmann wink and twinkle in his eye.

"I can hardly wait to see her. She's all he talks about lately," Lauren piped up from the checkers game she and Justin were playing on the floor.

"Yeah," continued Allison, somewhat mockingly, "She's the most beautiful girl in the world... she goes to university and is soooo smart... and business has increased tenfold since she started working at the Tux Shop..." Breaking out of her silly character, Allison asked her dad, "Did I tell you that's how they met?"

"No, you didn't." Henry laughed. Then trying to muster a straight face, said, "And you shouldn't make fun of your brother that way. So what happened? How'd they meet?"

"Well, when Jeremy went to the Tux Shop to order his suit for the Thanksgiving dance—the one he was taking Sharon to—he was fitted by this new girl! Apparently, they just totally hit it off."

"You don't say? That's quite a coincidence..."

"He did say too, that she was a few years older than him, but that they don't mind."

"I'm looking forward to meeting her too, girls. I guess we'll all know soon enough."

Henry turned, walked around Lauren and Justin, told Lauren to help her sister set the table, then headed up to his studio.

"Allison, they're here!" Justin shouted.

Lauren and Allison rushed to join Justin at the front window to see the car stop in the driveway. Jeremy got out and walked over to the passenger side and opened the door.

"Oh my, what a lovely girl," Allison observed.

Henry was coming down the stairs from his studio when

Jeremy and his sweetheart entered the house. It was her golden, wheat-coloured hair glistening in the light of the foyer that stopped him in his tracks and nearly stopped his heart. His feet seemed to suspend in mid-air.

When he realized his children were all looking up at him, his feet slowly touched down and he made his way down the rest of the steps. The blood drained from his face as he gazed into her cerulean blue eyes. A ghost from his past stood before him, rendering him momentarily speechless.

"Dad, Allison, I'd like you to meet my friend, Camilla."

"It's nice to meet you, Camilla," said Allison.

Henry toppled backwards at the mention of her name. His heart skipped a beat. The blood drained from his face and pooled in his feet.

Camilla? It couldn't be… could it…?

"Is something wrong, Dad? You look so pale," asked Allison.

Henry shook his head, "No, no, I'm okay." And looking at Camilla he continued, "It's just that you remind me so much of someone I once knew. Yes, wel-welcome to our home."

Camilla met the rest of the family and then Henry invited them to sit at the table as dinner was ready.

"So, Jeremy tells us you're going to the University of Regina?" Henry asked as he helped himself to the chicken casserole.

"Actually, I just finished my degree in social work this spring. It took me a long time to get it as I had to work for a few years and save enough money to continue. But it's a good thing it took me so long, otherwise I would have graduated years ago and never would have met Jeremy." Camilla looked over to Jeremy and they shared a secret, knowing smile before Jeremy continued the story.

"And if I hadn't skipped a couple of grades in elementary school we wouldn't have been at university at the same time. It's sure funny how it turned out that we should meet," said Jeremy, with love clearly reflecting in his sparkling, brown eyes.

Turning back to Henry, Camilla continued, "I would like to start my Masters degree next fall, but I'm considering working for another year before I continue. I've been offered a very interesting position but I'm worried that if I put off graduate school too long,

I won't go back."

"Well, you never know, Camilla," replied Henry, trying to act as normal as possible, but overwhelmingly distracted by her resemblance to Jenny. "I went back to get my Masters degree years after I initially got my Bachelor of Education. If you put your mind to it, I'm sure you'll follow through."

"You're older than Jeremy and yet you seem so much younger looking," observed Allison. What is your age difference?" Allison wanted to know.

That's a great question! thought Henry. Camilla looked in her teens. If the girl before him had been Jenny's back in 1957, that would make her almost 26 years of age. *That would be impossible. Jeremy is only 19!* Henry set his fork down and gazed intently at the blonde haired, blue eyed girl in front of him.

"Well, I may look younger but there is quite a big difference in our ages. But what is so amazing is that we have the same birth date. I was born May 24, 1957, exactly seven years before Jeremy!"

Henry could no longer eat. Suddenly, all the dots seemed to be connecting. Was it possible that everything he had suspected for so long was true? In a rush, he recalled Eddy telling him years ago in the pool hall that his friend Pete had dreamt of Jenny giving birth to a little girl with blonde hair and blue eyes... And the date! May 24, 1957 still stuck in his mind so vividly. It must have been that very day when he had had thrown up in class after months of nausea and anxiety... Sweat ran down Henry's armpits as an eerie feeling spread throughout his body.

Could it possibly be that the girl now sitting at his table was Jenny's daughter?

As Camilla talked about the job offer she had received to work in the Tutorial Program at Balfour Collegiate, counselling unwed girls in deciding whether or not to give up their child for adoption, Henry found it difficult to concentrate on her words. She was so full of life, so spontaneous and bubbly. The sparkle in her eyes when she spoke and how they radiated the warmth of the sun, and her oval-shaped face provided such a striking resemblance to Jenny, that for the first time since Julean's passing, a memorable warmth stirred within Henry.

The cool fog that had covered his spirit began to lift and gently burn off as he stared at this lovely creature. And her name, *Camilla*. It was the same name Jenny had said she would give to her daughter. Henry hadn't heard or said that name for years; he had never in all his life ever met someone named Camilla.

It must be her…

A flood of memories almost choked Henry as he dared ask the question burning in his mind.

"Camilla, tell us a little about your parents. What do they do? And… what is your mother's name?"

Henry sat on the edge of his chair waiting for an answer. Camilla stared at him for a moment before answering. Her hesitation was too much for him to bear.

Unable to wait a second longer, Henry blurted out, "Camilla, by any chance, would the name of your mother be… Jenny?"

CHAPTER ONE

WHAT AN AMAZING career you've had, Mr. Pederson. Or, should I say careers? And you seem to be successful at almost anything you do. You're a carpenter, a teacher, a guidance counsellor, an entrepreneur, a curator of an art gallery, a professional artist and a very successful businessman. This may seem like an odd question to ask, but who are you really? Will the real Henry Pederson please stand up?"

Henry leaned forward to rest his elbows on the table, his fingers intertwined. Henry knew how he answered would reflect his character both in terms of the interview and in terms of the feature the Regina Sun planned to print in one of their Sunday magazine issues. Brenda Oakley was right. It did appear to everyone that he was successful at many things – otherwise he likely wouldn't be doing this interview. But did any one of those things truly reflect his heart?

"Well, Brenda, I guess I am all the things you just mentioned. I have never been able to do just one thing. I am always looking for a new challenge and will use all the expertise I have acquired to-date to meet it. And if I am lacking in a certain area then I will learn the skill or knowledge needed for the situation. I may not be one hundred percent successful at the start, but I know within a short time I will have the necessary skills to meet the challenge. That's just the nature of the beast. I am a very hands-on type of person.

"Unfortunately, doing so much does sometimes distract me from doing just my art, or carrying on just my business or spending the time I'd like to with my family and grandson. I do have a tendency to spread myself too thin, at times. But, once I get an idea how to improve something – whether it's a business strategy, a painting or renovation – I'm driven to make it a reality."

"Yes," Brenda replied, "it's difficult to slot you into an easily identifiable, one-dimensional role. It's like trying to put a round peg in a square hole. It just can't be done!"

Henry laughed.

"That's an interesting way of summing up my character, but I guess what I do and the way I operate is what has helped me to become successful. For example, in establishing the art gallery, I blended several skills I had acquired over the years; my carpentry abilities, my pursuit of art and love for dealing with people are all skills needed in business.

"I mentioned to you yesterday about how Mr. Engelmann and I worked together to turn a failing business into a successful one in a very short time. I combined what I had learned from that four years of experience with my other skills and have made our gallery a very successful business that just keeps expanding. We went from being just an art gallery, to include a café, a card shop, a ladies boutique on the second level as well as several other boutiques."

"Whew! Just listening to what you have accomplished makes me tired. How on earth do you manage to get it all done?"

"Well, there is a trick," Henry said, with a smile and tongue in cheek. "You have to be disciplined, committed, and prepared to work hard and long hours. There are no short cuts to being successful. You have to pay your dues."

"Well, you certainly have, Mr. Pederson. It's very impressive what you have created for the city."

Brenda flipped through her notes. Her eyes brightened as she re-read a note she had made earlier.

"So, tell me a little bit more about Mr. Engelmann and how he fits into this picture? You mentioned him several times during our last two meetings and then again, just now."

"The good Lord gives each and every one of us certain aptitudes and abilities. These inherent tendencies, however, must be worked at and developed to realize them."

"Like your skill as an artist."

"Yes, that's right. I love to work with my hands and I love to create, but to paint landscapes and beautiful paintings, I had to work long hours to develop the inherent skills I was gifted with. If I hadn't taken classes and painted hundreds of paintings to come up with really good ones, it would never have happened. The gift the good Lord gave me would simply have laid dormant or died with me, never to be realized."

"What has this all to do with Mr. Engelmann?"

"Well, it is to him I attribute the discovery of many of my aptitudes and skills, such as relating to people, my business skills, my wanting to be a teacher and then a counsellor, and even an artist, as well."

Brenda wrinkled her forehead as she studied him for a long moment. "How can one person trigger so many interests and skills?"

Henry sat back in his chair, sipped his cooled herbal tea and allowed his mind to drift back almost 29 years to July 7, 1956 when he started working for Mr. Engelmann. Henry was about to share that day with Brenda, when his mind somehow drew him into the day before. That memorable, unforgettable day when Jenny, his very first love, moved into the neighbourhood, three doors down from his house. His mind pictured it vividly, as if it were yesterday.

…How she had captivated him as she strolled past his house… how he'd followed her to Engelmann's Grocery Store. Henry had never forgotten the moment he had knocked over all the salmon tins when he first looked into her cerulean blue eyes. It truly was love at first sight, a magical, spiritual moment, there was no other way to explain it.

Without realizing it, Henry had thrust his right hand out towards Brenda as he reacted to the memory of that wonderful phrase Jenny always said as they crossed busy streets, "Quickly, hold my hand." It was as if Jenny were there beside him. An electrifying thrill coursed through him as it had that day when their hands engaged and every time he thought about it since.

Henry's heart warmed as he recalled that summer. How he and Jenny had grown closer together. How they dated and almost made love in the park. And then, just two weeks after high school started, it ended. Jenny and her parents moved to Ottawa and he never heard from her again.

He recalled packaging up over 40 letters and mailing them to her father's business, but she had never responded. It was as if she'd vanished from the face of the earth. Henry's hand landed on his chest as his heart ached.

"Mr. Pederson...? Henry, is everything okay? You drifted so far away."

"Oh, I'm very sorry, Brenda," Henry said, as he shook his head to snap himself back into the present. "As I thought back to how I got started with Mr. Engelmann, I somehow began thinking of a very special person that also came into my life at that very same time—"

"It must have been a girl to put you into such a deep trance so quickly," Brenda interjected with a smile.

Henry looked at Brenda and smiled back.

"Yes, it was a girl, she was my very first lo—" He stopped. It was too private, too personal to share with a reporter he hardly knew.

Henry couldn't get over how quickly and utterly absorbed in the past he still became when he remembered Jenny and how immediately he felt the pain of their parting. It took considerable effort on his part to let go of the momentary grip it had on him. He shook his head again and said, "Oh, I better not go there, Brenda."

Henry sat up trying to shake off the reverie that was still trying to draw him back. Brenda looked a little disappointed that he wasn't going to share where his mind had so strongly drifted to.

"Well, let's get back to your question that I was going to answer which I believe was, how did Mr. Engelmann influence me, my skills and my careers in so many ways?"

Brenda nodded.

"Well, Brenda, he not only touched my life, but the lives of many, many people in the neighbourhood. Let me see now...Mr.

Engelmann…What can I say in a few words that would capture the essence of the man? Perhaps, I'll start by giving you a little background and then share examples of what I meant.

"It was 1956 and I had just finished Grade 8 and was starting my summer holidays when Mr. Engelmann called my parents and asked if it would be okay for me to work for him during the summer. It was okay with my parents, but it was I who wasn't sure if I wanted to work for him. I had always perceived him as sort of a grumpy old man, who usually gave us boys a stern look when we entered his store. Not that he was unjustified in doing so. Our intent most of the time was to snitch a chocolate bar or two.

"Something told me to work for him, anyway, and in a matter of days, I began to respect Mr. Engelmann and soon came to love him like a dad or grandfather. Soon, I began to see him as one of the greatest and wisest persons I ever knew. And, I might add, my opinion of that judgment hasn't changed one iota over all the years, in fact, it has only deepened."

Brenda looked intrigued and nodded for Henry to go on.

"Well, let's see… Mr. Engelmann's business was failing and on the verge of bankruptcy. He owed money to his suppliers and was behind in paying his taxes. His wife, Anna, was very ill and could no longer help her husband with the business. Gradually Mr. Engelmann became overwhelmed by the daily grind of looking after both the store and his wife. They hired me to help out and that's what I did."

"Why someone so young and inexperienced?"

"Well, perhaps it was all they could afford. In fact, I never received an hourly wage. On Saturday night after the store closed, Mr. Engelmann would give me a five or ten dollar bill from the cash register, whatever he could afford. But you know, Brenda, I would have worked for nothing. I derived so much joy and inner satisfaction from helping Mr. Engelmann fix up the store and get it back on track. Also the joy it gave to both he and his wife to see it all happen so quickly, was more than payment enough. Within six months, the store was back on track and making money again. All of his debts were paid within a year and his savings account was growing."

"That's wonderful. So, what exactly did you do?"

"Nothing out of the ordinary. I started by organizing the shelves and the stock. I painted the basement, and then the upstairs store and then the exterior.

"Seeing something so deteriorated and disorganized drew out my characteristics, aptitudes, and potential ability. And then seeing the improvements and the joy the results gave to Mr. and Mrs. Engelmann and to the customers was so satisfying it just motivated me all the more. I kept the shelves well stocked all the time, developed a delivery service, remembered people's birthdays, organized coupons and sales and so on. Mr. Engelmann treated me as if I were an adult, an equal, almost a business partner. Things which we developed back then, I have implemented in my business today."

"That's really something," said Brenda.

"But, Brenda, that is really the least of what I had learned while working for Mr. Engelmann. The biggest and most important part is what I had learned about life."

Henry sat back in his chair again. Brenda followed his lead and sat back in hers and assumed a more relaxed position.

"Shortly after I began to work for him, I developed such a deep respect for him that he became my closest friend, counsellor and mentor. Over the months and years that followed, I shared everything with Mr. Engelmann."

Brenda remained silent. She sat up in her chair, encouraging him to go on.

"Perhaps the main reason why I so readily opened up to him was because he accepted me unconditionally. I never had to be defensive because he never criticized. He always took me exactly where I was at and helped me talk and work through any concern or problem. Out back behind the store, Mr. Engelmann and I would sit on two old grey crates, drink soda pop, and talk. This was Mr. Engelmann's classroom, what he referred to as his 'school of life.' It was there, behind an old grocery store, that he not only helped me meet life's challenges, but also imparted to me very valuable principles of life to live by."

"Hi, Henry," called a customer as he passed by.

"Hi, Nick." Henry turned and waved.

"I need to get another one of your paintings. My secretary is retiring."

"Shelly is in the gallery right now, she can help you out."

"Great. I'd like you to personalize the painting to my secretary, though."

"I will be happy to Nick."

Henry waved Nick off and turned back to Brenda. "Now, where was I?"

"You said Mr. Engelmann taught you the principles of life."

"Ah, that's right. In helping me solve my personal problems and concerns, he also explained important lessons surrounding it all, accepting others and their weaknesses, forgiveness, living with integrity and never to compromise honesty, truthfulness, kindness; to separate the person from their acts, and to live in the present moment."

"Live in the present moment?"

"Yes. Most of us are only half-aware of life and our surroundings in our moment-to-moment functioning. Most of the time, we live in the past, worried about something that happened to us, reliving a regret, angry over someone who hurt us, and anxious about it all. We literally drag into our present moments the concerns and worries of the past which is such a waste of precious time. We are also guilty of worrying about the future; being apprehensive about upcoming events or happenings, worried that this or that might happen. In short, we fill our present moments, the only real reality of life in which we could be fully alive, with a lot of yesterday's garbage or worries about tomorrow."

"Oh yes, I have seen several books on the market about that subject."

"Yes, that's true, but back then it was just coming into discussion and consideration. Anyways, you can see how Mr. Engelmann influenced me to be a teacher and then a guidance counsellor."

Brenda nodded with a smile.

Henry sat up and sipped his tea.

"What developed my character perhaps more than his words and teachings, though, was that I saw him walk the talk daily, without fail. He never missed an opportunity to show kindness or love. He always encouraged me to reach out to others, to give of myself, my time, and act out of kindness. To always do it when the opportunity presented itself as you may never pass that way again. That is what our Lord will judge us on – how we have lived, how we have loved."

Henry looked intently into Brenda's eyes and continued, "What I realized over time, Brenda, was that both he and his wife, Anna, were not so much selling groceries and trying to make a living, as they used the store as an avenue to carry out their mission in life; to reach out and serve their fellow man."

Henry stopped for another moment and sipped his cold tea.

"I so desired to emulate him, but not without a lot of bumps and hard knocks along the way. It wasn't until I followed another one of his precepts that I finally started to make some progress."

Brenda leaned forward and closer to the edge of her seat. Her actions reminded Henry of himself seated on the edge of the old grey crate behind the store waiting for Mr. Engelmann's next tidbit of wisdom.

"What helped me to grow and follow somewhat in Mr. Engelmann's footsteps was when I began to acquire the habit of daily meditation and prayer."

"Do you mean being on your best behaviour at all times so as to be an example to others?"

"Well, that's very important and we so need people to be models in this day and age. But what I was getting at was the importance to continually examine your life and prepare for the day. Perhaps you meditate already, Brenda, and realize this."

Henry studied her for a brief moment, but Brenda didn't respond.

"Unless one examines his or her life continuously, and checks the direction in which one is heading, one can easily get stuck in a rut, get caught up with just trying to live out the day, then go to bed, get up the next morning, only to think basically the same thoughts and perform the same actions and behaviour all over again. Many of us spend our lives this way, as sad as it may be, it is a fact. I know, I was guilty of it and still am many times."

Brenda was about to say something when Henry blurted out, "It all comes down to how one starts each and every day. The heart must be fuelled daily with a restful solitude, meditation, thoughts of gratefulness and faithful prayer. Without this, success is difficult, the road a struggle. We spend day in and day out with the same self-defeating behaviours and thoughts."

They both sat in silence, sort of staring at one another. What was supposed to be an interview to learn about Henry's business and his background had somehow turned into a philosophical and spiritual dissertation.

"Well, Brenda, this is really not getting you any further in your interview about the article you want to write. You can see, however, how all this influenced me and the choices I made throughout my life."

"Yes, I can definitely see that, Mr. Pederson, and it's all very enlightening." And after a further reflective thought, Brenda added, "It is so true how easy it is to get stuck in the process of daily living and not really grow. And it is true that we do have a tendency to think the same thoughts over and over."

"After learning so much about human behaviour and helping others from Mr. Engelmann, I was motivated to become a teacher, and then after four years of that, I went on to become a guidance counsellor. And after that, it was time to pursue my love of art and then business. My four years working with and for Mr. Engelmann very definitely led me to do and realize all these career choices."

"Yes, I am beginning to understand and for sure, I see what you mean. He has been a big influence on your life…." Brenda's voice trailed off, like she didn't know what to ask next.

"You know, Brenda, an article about Mr. Engelmann would indeed be highly interesting."

"Is he still alive?"

"Well, yes, he is. In fact, around 1960, shortly after his wife died, he decided to enter into a new career, a natural for him."

"He became a psychologist?"

"Well, in a way he did, but he became someone even better, at least I think so. He went into the seminary and became a priest."

"Really?! That's fantastic."

"Yes, it certainly is. And would you believe, he is still active as a priest today, at St. Mary's Church. He's in his eighties, looks like he's in his late sixties and acts like he is in his forties. The Archbishop has been trying to get him to retire for years now, now, but he always says, 'next year.' He maintains that his flock still needs him and that he, the shepherd, is still able to walk the hills and valleys."

Henry smiled and quickly added, "But I do think he is beginning to think seriously about retirement of some kind. Last Sunday after Mass when I talked to him, he mentioned that he might want to move into a care home. He sees all too many lonely people in there when he visits them, living day in and day out just waiting to die. 'Perhaps I can help,' he said to me. So, he has something up his sleeve."

"So, what is next on the agenda for you, Henry?" Brenda popped the question with a sparkle in her eyes.

"Well, Brenda, I have always wanted to write a novel, but that is on the back burner for now. At the present time I have a crew that is completing several major renovations to other revenue property I have, including an office building just down the block."

"So, you're a developer, too!"

"Yes, sort of. Like I told you before, I love renovating. I acquire houses, fix them up and either sell them or rent them out as another source of revenue. I love doing that. I derive great satisfaction out of taking something that is run down and turning it into something beautiful. That is what motivates me in my painting and everything I do. Starting with a blank canvas, for example, and turning it into a beautiful prairie landscape, taking an old house and turning it into a work of art, just like we did to the gallery and then the café and so on. I've always been like that.

"In short, Brenda, I like to make the world a better place. I get a lot of satisfaction when people come in to our business and tell me how much they love it here and how good it makes them feel. That's what it's all about."

"It's amazing how you still manage to find time to paint as an artist."

"Yes, I hear that all the time. But it's like I said, it requires commitment, hard work, and long hours. It's like they say, if you want to get something done, give the job to a busy person."

"Hmmm, that's interesting. A busy person doesn't procrastinate and gets on the job right away," Brenda analyzed.

"I certainly don't paint as often as I used to. In most cases I just do it and get at it in a very committed way, so in a way you are correct," Henry replied, "but I must admit I am guilty of procrastination. If I overcame that, I would really get a lot more done."

Brenda's eyes grew wide with a look of disbelief. "As I listen to you, you have really accomplished what most people only dream to do. Most of us fail to act on our dreams and visions."

"That's so true and a very sad state of affairs," Henry said with a nod. "Perhaps one of the biggest factors why people don't do things or act on their ideas is the fear of failure. I have seen it over and over again, not only as a counsellor, but also talking to people who tell me how they envy my success. Perhaps they always dreamed of opening up a café, but for them, all it was, was a dream, they never acted on their vision. When we decided to open a café, over and over business people advised me that a café would never work...."

"Yet, you still went ahead," Brenda interrupted.

"Yes, I believe when you do something, do it to the best of your ability, don't cut corners, do it right the first time and just believe that it will work. Wasn't it William James, the well known psychologist who said our belief at the beginning of a new venture is the one thing that insures the successful outcome of your undertaking?"

"I'm not sure who said that, but it's true. We do tend to attract what we think."

Henry nodded with a smile.

Brenda looked up. "I really must say I am very impressed by your total commitment to life."

"Thank you, Brenda, that's very kind of you to say. But really, if I can do it, so can anyone. I'm just an average Joe. I suppose that what I have learned is that to make it happen you must do one very important thing."

"And...?"

"You have already alluded to part of it earlier when you said one must 'act' on it. To achieve anything in life, to realize your vision or dreams, you must begin to do it and keep at it until it's done. So many of us have great ideas, profound visions, but instead of acting on them, we snuggle into our security blanket of safety and comfortableness, afraid to act. Slowly we watch one dream after the other whither and die or see it realized by another who dared to act."

"You said that's part of it, what is the other part?"

"Dreams. Ideas, visions, have to do with the mind, Brenda. It's the heart, however, which realizes them."

Brenda looked at Henry quizzically for a moment, then her eyes brightened.

"The heart must always follow the idea, push it, be committed to it, desire it with fervor and passion. It is the heart, the inner vision that keeps one focused and motivated until one's dream or goal is accomplished. That is what makes all the difference in a person's life and being successful in achieving their dreams and goals. *Action and passion are the key!"*

It was now Brenda's turn to just nod. After a long moment, she asked, "But, what if your project or venture fails. No matter how hard you try or as you say, how much heart you put into it, it just may not be in the cards to succeed."

"I think I answered that question, earlier. I don't believe in failure."

Brenda looked puzzled, but remained silent.

"We learn from everything we do, Brenda. If something doesn't work it doesn't mean we have failed, it just means we have to try something different, perhaps another approach, a minor adjustment to what we are doing. If what we have done isn't quite working, then I am thankful that I know, so I can shift gears and get going again. Look at the great inventor, Edison, when he invented the light bulb. He had many setbacks before he achieved his goal, but he learned from each setback and then opened another door.

"So often, Brenda, we are at the door to success, so close and we give up. I carry around a little poem in my wallet that I have had for years and years. I came across it when I was a guidance counsellor, it's entitled, 'Don't Quit.' I gave it out to all my students and I follow its lesson to this very day: Stick to your dream or goal until it's done."

Brenda shook her head slightly, raised her eyebrows and smiled broadly. "Well, Mr. Pederson. It's clear that you have followed that creed your entire life. You're the epitome of success."

Instinctively, Henry humbly averted his eyes at the compliment and cast a glance around his busy café. Brenda was clearly impressed by Henry, yet, a feeling of smugness tugged at his bowels. Or was it a twinge of guilt and hypocrisy. He had all the answers and knowledge of how to succeed in the world. His gallery, café, wealth, and all the property he possessed was evidence of that. But was he *really* successful?

Sure, he'd used his skills to bring beauty to the world around him. Sure, he'd used his business to serve others and help those in need. Yes, his accomplishments were many. However, deep within, Henry also recognized that his success indirectly kept him in bondage to worldly distractions. Instead of gaining freedom, inner peace and happiness that he thought would come with wealth; he felt an uneasiness, a void that could only be temporarily filled by accomplishing and accumulating more. Over the years, his skills and aptitudes gained him recognition and status which he had come to enjoy and depend on, but he had also bought into the false belief that the more he had, the greater was his worth in the eyes of others.

Henry recognized that his striving and desire for more outweighed his wisdom. He knew better, and he had been taught better. Henry clearly saw in Father Engelmann what it was that he lacked. Father was free of all attachments. He knew his purpose in life and his place in the scheme of things. He had a single-minded devotion to only one Master and one Master alone and that was his Lord. His Lord was at the centre of his life whereas for Henry his worldly success was at the centre of his. He knew he could not serve two masters.

Somehow over the years, especially after Julean's death, he had become duped into the illusion of believing more in his independence and success and less on his dependence on his Lord and placing Him in the driver's seat. The pursuit of abilities and honours and riches had kept him from coming totally to his Redeemer.

Brenda was staring at him quizzically, again. She was probably wondering if he'd returned to his earlier reverie about his girlfriend.

Henry shifted uncomfortably in his chair. The thoughts he was entertaining were unsettling. The Lord was asking too much. For too long he had felt the comfort and security of wealth. For several years now he had been struggling with this issue. He knew where the treasures of his heart really lay. His integrity – the need to be forthright and honest – weighed on him. He didn't want to leave Brenda with a false impression of where he was really at in his life.

"You know, Brenda, I don't want to mislead you. I may be a success in the eyes of the world, but true success is when one's main goal and ambition in life is to love and serve his fellow man. Father Engelmann is the only person who I know that has achieved that goal. I don't want this to end as a sermon or a spiritual dissertation, but there is a scriptural passage that Father Engelmann talked about several weeks ago in one of his sermons that keeps coming up in my mind. It's the one about a rich man who asked Jesus what he needed to do to gain the kingdom of Heaven. 'Sell everything you own, give it to the poor, and come follow me,' was His answer.

"Now, if we take that literally, how many of us could do that? How strong and deep is our attachment to the world? Could I really place my trust completely in Him and not in my wealth and possessions? Where would the treasure of my heart really be?"

Henry paused. "A little further in that same scripture the Lord goes on to say that it is truly easier for a camel to go through the eye of a needle than it is for a rich man to enter the kingdom of heaven."

Henry knew his thoughts surprised Brenda. She and everyone he knew thought he was on top of the world with his success and, yet, he still struggled in a way he knew many people had never given much thought to.

"We work and strive so hard to be a success in the world and lose sight of the fact that nothing is really ours. We are simply stewards of God's blessings upon us. At the end of the day, of what value is wealth, possessions, talents, and gifts if they are not used for others? That is the kind of life that has lasting value and one that will be truly rewarded. To fully recognize that and be totally free of our attachment to things and the ways of the world – that is to be successful."

Henry winked at Brenda and smiled. "I'm still working on it."

Brenda and Henry fell into a reflective silence. The morning sun streamed through the south windows and flooded the patio just outside their window. It was a beautiful day and customers were taking advantage of outdoor eating, a luxury that prairie folk have for a very limited time during the summer. If it's not the wind, it's the wasps or the coolness in the air. Today was perfect to be outside, and customers were coming early to beat the noon-hour rush to the patio.

"So, one final area I want to be clear on. This is a family business?"

"That is correct. My wife was a graduate nurse, but she never really pursued it after we married. She wanted to stay home and raise the children. She did however help out with the gallery when it first opened, but shortly after she contracted meningitis and passed away. "

"Oh, I'm sorry to hear that," said Brenda.

"Yes, it happened suddenly. I miss her very much. I still haven't gotten used to it. I have four children. My oldest son, Jeremy looks after the café and along with my oldest daughter Allison who runs the gallery, the two pretty much help me run the business. My other daughter Lauren helps out in the boutique shops upstairs and is also a waitress when she isn't in school. And my youngest son, Justin who came into the family much later in our marriage helps out with odd jobs in the kitchen and gallery when he isn't also in school. So, it is as you say Brenda, a family run business.

"Well, I guess that just about does it. I have more than enough material. It's certainly been a pleasure talking to you Mr. Pederson."

"Think nothing of it, Brenda. And please, call me Henry; after all, that's the guy who owns this place."

"Well, this has just been great, Henry. If I have any more questions as I write up this interview, I will call you. In any case, we will get it into print and out in a month or so. Thank you, again, for your time, I appreciate it very much."

"You're welcome, Brenda. And, as a special treat, I would like to offer you our house specialty 'Henry's Oh So Creamy Cheesecake.' It is, without question, the best cheesecake you will ever have."

Brenda's eyes opened wide in anticipation. "I can hardly wait to taste it."

Henry signaled a tall, handsome young man in his twenties who just finished seating some customers.

"Jeremy, I would like you to meet Brenda Oakley, the reporter from the Sunday Sun…"

"Hi, nice to meet you Brenda." Jeremy extended his hand and gave her a warm smile. Brenda could see the family resemblance.

"Yes, it's a pleasure meeting you, too. Your dad tells me you run this place."

"It's a joint affair, actually. Most days Henry is in the trenches right along next to us…" and turning to his dad, he continued. "Tamara phoned in sick at the last minute which is why I'm seating people until Zack gets in. I want to check how the kitchen is doing, I think with the weather being so nice we're going to get slammed today. Oh, and I'm expecting Camilla and Joshua any minute; tell her to go into the gallery…"

"Actually, Jeremy, here they come now," announced Henry, who was seated facing the front door to the café.

Brenda turned to see a beautiful, blond haired woman and a small boy enter the busy room. The woman took a look around, spotted Jeremy and Henry, and with a smile that was brighter than the hot June-day sun, gave a small wave.

"Oh my," said Brenda under her breath and then more audibly, "Isn't she just as lovely as an angel…"

"You'll have to excuse me, Brenda," Jeremy said, "it was nice meeting you."

"Yes, that goes for me too, Jeremy."

As his son was leaving the table, Henry remembered why he had called him over in the first place.

"And Jeremy, send over a slice of our house special dessert for Brenda."

"You got it, Dad!"

Jeremy made his way to the door to meet his wife. The young boy freed himself from his mother's hand and ran to Henry yelling, "Hi Grandpa!"

"Hi Joshua, how's my boy?"

Henry stood just in time to scoop up the two year old, then turned to Brenda. "Well, I better start helping out, Brenda, but… if I can just add one more thought for the record before I leave…"

"I'm all ears, Henry."

First turning to Jeremy who was just giving his wife a peck on the cheek and then back to Brenda, Henry said, "Given everything I've said over the course of this interview, this is the most important: Never take life for granted. *Never.* Never in a million years would I have expected that blond haired, blue eyed young lady to enter into our lives and become… my daughter. *Never!*"

About the Author

HENRY RIPPLINGER IS the bestselling author of *Pewter Angels* and *Another Angel of Love*, the first two books in the six-book series "The Angelic Letters." The overwhelming response by readers to Henry's novels gives testimony to Henry's gifts as an author to write books that touch human hearts and offer direction to their lives.

Henry's empathetic abilities, combined with his lifelong experience and eclectic career as a high school teacher, guidance counselor, professional artist and businessman, prepared him to craft this inspirational christian romance series and indirectly realize his aspirations of writing a self-development book.

Henry is also one of Canada's foremost prairie artists. His work is on display at private and corporate collections across Canada, most notably in Saskatchewan, his home province, and can be seen in the critically acclaimed book, If You're Not from the Prairie.

He resides with his wife in the panoramic valley setting of Lumsden, Saskatchewan, Canada.

Please e-mail Henry at: **henry@henryripplinger.com** or visit **www.henryripplinger.com** for more information about Henry's work and art. He would love to hear from you!

ALSO BY HENRY RIPPLINGER

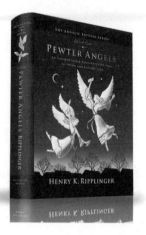

PEWTER ANGELS
BOOK ONE OF THE ANGELIC LETTERS SERIES

*"He hath given his angels charge over thee; to keep thee
in all thy ways...In their hands they shall bear thee up:
lest thou dash thy foot against a stone."*

PSALM 91:11-12

...Suddenly, she turned to Henry as if to speak, catching him off guard. He didn't have time to pretend he wasn't staring at her. He'd been caught. Their eyes met now for a second time and although he felt his face warming again with a blush, this time he couldn't turn away. Her gaze locked with his and his with hers. They rose from their knees simultaneously, as if lifted, and were at once standing, facing each other.

Nothing existed except this moment and this place.

A charged, earthly attraction united their hearts while a spiritual energy traveled the length of the gaze they shared, drawing their souls from their bodies and joining them at the halfway point. The aura around them brightened...enclosing both in the surrounding glow of their celestial connection.

Time stood still...

Pewter Angels will grab your heart, squeeze it
and hold it to the very last page.

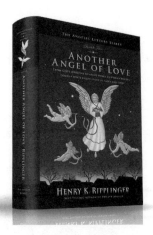

ANOTHER ANGEL OF LOVE
BOOK TWO OF THE ANGELIC LETTERS SERIES

"God causes all things to work together for good to those who love God, to those who are called according to His purpose"

ROMANS 8:28

It was as if Jenny had vanished from the face of the earth. Two years after she and her family moved out of Henry's life, Henry still longs for her, their whirlwind romance gone from his life but not his heart. He was certain she would respond to his last letter, a pewter angel tucked inside —but there have been no letters, no phone calls. Nothing. A country apart, Henry and Jenny are unaware Jenny's parents have burned all the letters but the last... it is protected, it seems, by an angelic power.

Henry continues to rely on the love, support and powerful insights of his mentor Mr. Engelmann, and his secret plan to seek Jenny out sustains the hope that one day his love will return—until he meets Julean Carter.

But, is their new-found love deep enough and strong enough to overcome the heavenly touch that entwined Henry and Jenny's spirits when they first gazed into each others eyes?

Another Angel of Love...glows with moments of tenderness... deeply inspirational....will captivate the heart of every reader!

If You're Not from the Prairie, written by David Bouchard and
illustrated by Henry Ripplinger, is a poetic and visual journey
depicting the prairies and the people who have made this
diverse land their own...a treasure for the mind and soul.

To contact the author and for further information about these
books as well as other artwork, limited edition prints and other
products, please visit:

www.henryripplinger.com